PRAISE FOR
AS SEEN ON GOODREADS AND BOOKSTAGRAM

NECTAR OF WAR — THE SONG OF VERITY AND SERENITY

"This story has all the trappings of a much-needed new classic filled with the depth and diversity necessary for contemporary storytelling."
—*Alyce*, @eveningedits_

"The prose is magical . . . sucks you in within a few sentences."
—*Peyton*, @lifeasliza__

"Strong world-building, strong women, sexy, sensitive . . . supernatural creatures and prose that's like poetry."
—*Becky*, @books.becky.read

"Set in a rich and intricate fantasy world, where Greek Mythology meets faeries, werewolves and magical characters . . ."
—*Daniela*, @bookroadpath

"Diversity that, unlike most, is not pretentious . . ."
—*Bec*, @mother.bec

"Leilani Helen Aki's writing is incredible. It is the perfect combination of substantial and lyrical . . ."
—*Gabrielle*, @literahua

"I started reading it in the morning, and had completed it before I went to bed . . . It drew me in and kept me there . . ."
—*Avery*, @averyofgreengables

"Badass female characters, mythical creatures and much needed diversity are some of the things that'll make you fall in love with this story."
—*Gabriella*, @gabbireads

MORE BOOKS TO COME . . .

A second series of LEILANI HELEN AKI'S is in the making.
An Adult High-Fantasy Romance series with its first novel as a
RAPUNZEL RETELLING.

And the succeeding novel in
THE NECTAR OF WAR SERIES.

Nectar of War
THE SONG OF VERITY AND SERENITY

LEILANI HELEN AKI

NECTAR OF WAR: THE SONG OF VERITY AND SERENITY is a debut Arcane High-Fantasy Romance written by LEILANI HELEN AKI. With enthralling magical elements and poetical style to its gore and kakistocracy—Leilani created THE SONG OF VERITY AND SERENITY with the people in mind who get erased when it comes to not only the genres of Romance but High-Fantasy as well.

We, Leilani and all who have worked tirelessly on NECTAR OF WAR, look forward to the readers that will show reverence for this expansive universe and the readers who will not comprehend such a world.

COPYRIGHT © LEILANI HELEN AKI PUBLISHING

All rights reserved. No part of this publication may be reproduced or transmitted in any form or by any means, electronic or mechanical, including photocopying, recording, or any information storage or retrieval system, without prior permission in writing from the publisher or the author.

ISBN: PB: 979-8-218-02831-2

A NOTE FROM THE AUTHOR

The fictional world of *Nectar of War: The Song of Verity and Serenity* are inspired by events and legends from various parts of the world. None is intended as a faithful representation of any one country or culture at any point in history.

TRIGGER WARNINGS

Alcohol Usage, Blood, Death, Emotional Abuse, Enslavement, Eugenics, False Imprisonment, Gore, Graphic Language, Malnutrition, Manipulation, Mental Illness, Mentions of Incest, Mentions of Suicide, Parental Abuse, Parental Manipulation, Possessive Parenting, Poverty, Prostitution, Weight Gain, Weight Loss, Sexual Assault, Sexual Scenes, Starvation, Strong Use of Language, Verbal Abuse, Violence

For Grace

Contents

Chapter   *Page*

Exordium 1

PART I
VOSCHANTAI UNIVERSE

ONE
   Years Ago 8

TWO
   Outlanders 26

THREE
   Live Bait 37

FOUR
   A Weeks Time 43

FIVE
   Once a Lady 48

SIX
   Hanging by a Thread 55

SEVEN
   Old Promises 65

EIGHT
   The Dragon 73

NINE
   Strong Souled 79

TEN
   Passing Through 90

ELEVEN
Aiding the Oppressor 98

TWELVE
Tree of Gods 105

THIRTEEN
What of Respect 116

FOURTEEN
The Nuisance 131

FIFTEEN
Soul of Terror 139

PART II
PORTAL OF DERELICTION

SIXTEEN
Six of Spring 146

SEVENTEEN
Lavender Oil 153

EIGHTEEN
Cures & Fears 166

NINETEEN
Her 176

TWENTY
Mountains 180

TWENTY-ONE
Western Seas 185

TWENTY-TWO
Ending Solace 194

TWENTY-THREE
Peculiar 201

TWENTY-FOUR
Now She Rests 207

TWENTY-FIVE
The Porvienia 211

TWENTY-SIX
The Sunset Province 218

TWENTY-SEVEN
Beacon of Life 225

TWENTY-EIGHT
War & Women 229

TWENTY-NINE
At Her Expediency 242

THIRTY
Sate of Dilapidation 252

PART III
CARVING A KING

THIRTY-ONE
Return of Spring 263

THIRTY-TWO
A Fae King 268

THIRTY-THREE
Out of the Woods 280

THIRTY-FOUR
A Mother's Adornment 287

THIRTY-FIVE
Welcome Home 296

THIRTY-SIX
Ancient Blood 300

THIRTY-SEVEN
The Lake 305

THIRTY-EIGHT
Reveries Are Heard 311

THIRTY-NINE
At Her Expediency 318

FORTY
Summer Solstice 327

FORTY-ONE
Visions of Ruin 334

FORTY-TWO
The Caves 341

FORTY-THREE
Purpose & Worth 355

FORTY-FOUR
Prince of Rancor 362

FORTY-FIVE
The High King is Home 370

FORTY-SIX
The Way I Did Before 376

FORTY-SEVEN
Birth of Twins 382

FORTY-EIGHT
Falling Stone 393

FORTY-NINE
Dirt of the Dead 401

FIFTY
Crystal Cleanse 409

PART IV
VERITY

FIFTY-ONE
Two Nations 417

FIFTY-TWO
Wings of Summer 429

FIFTY-THREE
A Bond Grows 442

FIFTY-FOUR
White Roses 448

FIFTY-FIVE
Discovering the Opponent 458

FIFTY-SIX
Moonlight in Provas 470

FIFTY-SEVEN
Call Bluff 477

FIFTY-EIGHT
Suitors 482

FIFTY-NINE
The Past 488

SIXTY
Vehemence 494

SIXTY-ONE
Nadrexi Nights 506

SIXTY-TWO
Trusted Circle 519

SIXTY-THREE
Never a Damsel Again 525

SIXTY-FOUR
Angel Upon Water 534

SIXTY-FIVE
Vylorda Vanox 541

SIXTY-SIX
Vague Proposals 547

SIXTY-SEVEN
Be as One 556

SIXTY-EIGHT
Misery of Verity 566

PART V
NEVER SURRENDER

SIXTY-NINE
Coronation Day 572

SEVENTY
Time & Healing 582

SEVENTY-ONE
Everything at Once 586

SEVENTY-TWO
You & Me 591

SEVENTY-THREE
Mourn Your Dead 596

SEVENTY-FOUR
Mortal Lands 602

SEVENTY-FIVE
The Strangest Dream 607

SEVENTY-SIX
Mean Boys Die Early 617

SEVENTY-SEVEN
Old Kings & Queens 627

SEVENTY-EIGHT
This Over Everything 643

SEVENTY-NINE
The War Has Begun 650

Acknowledgments 657

A Sneak Peek of:

RANCOR OF FATE
THE RING OF REIGN AND RUIN

Book Two in The Nectar of War Series

Bonus Chapter 660

THE CITADELS

Vaigon Citadel 669

Quamfasi Citadel 670

THE HOUSES

House Arvenaldi 673
House Valendexi 676
House Provanseva 679

NECTAR OF WAR
THE SONG OF VERITY AND SERENITY

EXORDIUM

STRAVAN PROVANSEVA
PROVAS CITADEL — REALM OF THE FAE

Savarina paces the floor of my study as I levitate a silver orb—her silver eyes glower at it. "No, I will not allow this."

Our youngest brother Sloan laughs. His head falls forward as it shakes from side to side; he, too, finds it comical that Sava assumes she can tell me what I may and may not do, especially regarding this situation.

Both of them are lucky I am sharing this information with them and not just going to other realms on my own.

"Sava," I close my hand into a fist—the orb that was once floating above my palm turns to dust, falling like a gentle snow onto my bureau. "I was not enquiring for your assent."

"Do you ever? *High King*."

Derision.

"No," I smile, "because I need acquiescence from no one." Then, leaning back in my chair, I realign the white gold rings on my fingers before witnessing her glowering shift to me.

"What would Dyena say if she heard you speak like this? What would she do if she saw the obtuse way you have been acting?"

And just as the words leave her mouth, all rational thought begins to fade as she thinks she is reminding me of why I am behaving the way I have. From the corner, Sloan stands, wary of what may transpire. He urgently glances between Savarina and me, he is prepared to diffuse anything that may arise.

"*All of this* is for Dyena." I remind her.

As I rise to my feet, the ground gradually thunders below us in a deep tremor. I press my hands into the tan stone of my bureau, and Savarina stiffens. "Every *bit* of what I am doing is for her. Do not ever forget it."

A twinge of fear dances in her eyes. "Tame your anger before your magic tears our home to shreds."

The more I sense her distress, the more satisfied I become.

"Strav," Sloan forebodingly calls. I mind him no attention.

"You wish to call me obtuse; I will act as so."

The ground reverberates deeper—the wall to our left forms a small crack, and Savarina grimaces at the destruction.

"How would you react, Sava? How would you retaliate if your mate went missing? You wake up discovering your bed is empty. A trace of nothing." Novels and small statues fall from the shelves as the walls increasingly convulse. I can hear the sound of tearing books, and sculptures around us erupt like stars on Solstice. "Not a single scent of who took them. Everything is in place as it was before you went to bed, but they are gone. How could that possibly be?"

She assesses the mutilation around us and looks back at me pleadingly. "Please, Stravan . . . stop this."

Windows around us begin to shatter—one by one. The echoing burst of glass rattles through the land, igniting the outlying animals to move in a frightful run.

Savarina's head whips toward me, her silver braid swinging with the motion. "Must I beg you?"

Shrugging in response, I sit down in the chair.

The quaking comes to a stop.

The room is repaired as if it was never destroyed.

She begins again. "You cannot–" I cut my eyes at her.

"For fucks sake," Sloan rubs his hands over his eyes to ease the stress I know we both are causing him.

She corrects herself. "You *can* go to other realms, but it is not logical. You ruined the last realm you visited in search of Dyena. Half of the Sorcerer's Realm was left in near ash."

"Savarina," Sloan scoffs. "What would you do?"

His lavender eyes bore into hers. She is at a standstill, choosing not to respond. "If Daevien went missing you would detonate the wrath inside you fiercer than you would ever know. So, do not stand here as if you would be a modest Miss Innocent."

"I would not have destroyed an entire continent. He left Galitan in ruins!"

"As he should have." Daevien smoothly walks into the study, fixing his black leather topcoat. He looks over Savarina before meeting her ice-cold silver eyes. "Do not forget he restored it as well," Daevien approaches her, wiping away a stray tear. "They were withholding information on Dyena; they are lucky he gave them back what he took." Sava leans into him as his hand rubs down the sleeve of her sheer, black dress.

I look away from them, unable to watch a bond thrive before me while remembering my own was taken.

Daevien steps forward. "That was their augury, their promise. Lie again, and the Sorcerer's Realm will be removed from the map without a trace of them ever living." As I glance up, Daevien's head is turned to look at Savarina. "Do not question Stravan's actions, love. I would rip this universe to pieces if you went missing as well."

Sava starts again. "Why have you not asked the Gods for help? Go to them, plead to them."

Finally, I look at the beautiful pair again. "I have not gone to the Gods because I do not trust them, just as I did not trust the Sorcerers."

Sloan speaks before Savarina can say another word. "If we convince the Realm of the Wolves to ally with us, they would possibly offer help. Perhaps propose the assistance from the Gods, *their* Goddess."

Artemis, Mother of the Moon. She is not as bad as her brother. Another untrustworthy bastard.

"They *are* the second largest realm in our world." Sloan adds.

"You alone are stronger than the High Four," Daevien nods in agreement. "Ask for a coalition and use it to your advantage; see if all your intellects are correct in not trusting the Gods. The Wolves' High King is an absolute pain, but he will know not to fuck with you upon arrival."

Savarina unexpectedly ascends from the room, leaving in a purple mist. Now all that leaves is Sloan, Dae, and me.

"I will speak with her." Daevien nods toward the fading purple haze. He huffs and pushes a hand through his blue-black hair before his arms tightly cross over his chest.

The room silences. The only sound there is; is the waterfall outside of the study—repeatedly, I tap my finger on my bureau.

I stop.

"Twenty-four," Daevien counted.

Slowly, I nod at him. The white and silver strands of my hair fall over my eyebrows with each nod.

"It has been twenty-four years—" I fight the tremble moving over my lips.

I push from the chair, walking to leave the study. "I am only giving one more year to find Dyena. If she is not in my hands by the twenty-fifth year, by the time that clock strikes midnight, find me wiping this entire fucking world clean to find her."

"Strav," Sloan calls.

I stop at the doorway, narrowly turning my head to hear what he says.

He grabs my arm, turning me around. His hand grips the back of my head, and it becomes harder to fight the trembling. "What did Ma always tell us?"

We only ask for forgiveness, never permission.

"We will find her." He promises.

Their words will mean nothing until I have back what I want, what I need.

* * *

The melody is the same as it is every night. The piano is quiet, building louder and faster as I move my hands across the black and ivory keys.

I close my eyes, and she is there. She is donned in her favorite white silk dress.

She leans over my shoulder, smiling as I play—play for her, play for us. Yet, something is missing.

Something this song should be giving back to me. As if it is rebuilding the bond play by play, but I am not channeling it deep enough to make it take its course.

Where is it? Where is that dwindling connection?

Where has her soul run off to that I cannot find?

'If I am ever lost, play this song.' I can feel the embrace of her arms wrapping around me, and the melody slows once more, gradually picking up pace again.

Those long, perfect nails gently trail over my skin.

Her scent swarms me, wild citrus and vanilla. It suffocates me until it turns into taunting. And at that moment, wicked mirth bores over me until I can no longer endure it.

The tears I must fight through my days glide, landing under my fingers that now trail salted liquid across the piano.

Strength is all I show to my people for hours upon hours while I am fading bit by bit. The eras in the night are my only chance to shed that harboring weakness so that I am capable of persisting in life.

I have played this song every day.

There were weeks I did nothing but play this every hour until my fingers felt crippling. Hoping there was some magic Dyena laced through the song to compel herself into appearance. But there is nothing.

Nothing. Just an antagonizing melody and reflections of her.

That indignation I know well returns; I yield. I clench my hands into fists so tightly my knuckles turn nearly white. The piano soars across the room, crashing into the stone wall. It sits there . . . broken under the moonlight casting from the ceiling.

The sound of the cracking piano keys spheres through the room and leisurely comes to a stop.

And then, I am sitting under that same moonlight. Wailing and begging, splintered and broken, shattered into pieces. All I can do is scream until my lungs give out, and then my screams become silent cries.

Irreparable pieces.

Only allowing myself a short period of time in this sorrow, I push from the cold floor. Subsequently, I sway a shaking hand to mend the piano and start the song over once more.

PART I
VOSCHANTAI UNIVERSE

1
YEARS AGO

LAVEN HEPHAESTUS ARVENALDI, II
VAIGON CITADEL — REALM OF THE WOLVES

*S*pring has always been the season of evolution, a revival of our land and us as one. It is meant to bring prosperity; it is the time frame of beginnings, never endings—especially not endings for the innocent.

'Where is she?' Roaner shouts as he finds me by the sound of my feet striking into the dirt. He desperately tries to keep up. He pushes himself to remain within a small distance of me. But, even I cannot keep up with myself as I ram into a tree; my body heaves backward by numerous lengths at the strength I hit the bark.

Roaner seizes my shoulders to hold me steady. 'Laven, where is Levora?'

He heard her scream just as I did. Of course he did.

'I–I do not know,' my breathing immeasurably increases as I look about the woods—scouring for a single sound of her possibly being near. 'I do not know,' tears fall down my face as I frantically stand.

'Calm down,' Roaner pleads. I try to run again, but he seizes me once more. 'Laven! I beg of you; please calm down!' Yet when I look at him, he is just as distressed as I am.

'She was just here,' I cry out as I look around once more. 'W–we–we–' Roaner stops me in my stutter and urges me to stall speaking.

'Breathe,' he nods, but all I can do is cry.

'Where is my sister?' I grip my hair, and Roaner stands, glancing roughly *through the trees encircling us.*

He breathes in the air around us, and my eyes broaden as his eyes flood in a fog of grey and orange. Then, he grasps my arm, and we ascend through the woods. We come to an abrupt stop, and his eyes return to normal as he looks down at a small trail of pink flowers messily bestrewn, and at the end of the short path lies the destroyed stem of a flower with scarcely any petals left.

It is a Snapdragon. The flower that is given and only given when a love proposal is accepted. Then, the accepter gives the flower to the proposer.

Snapdragons are captivating yet grotesque when their petals are gone—a perfect symbol of love's most compelling and hideous moments.

We both can sense that this is where she stopped, or worse, was stopped. Her scent goes no farther than this exact placement. Yet, somehow, there is no other scent lying here, only hers.

A strangled cry flees from the depths of Roaner's chest as he kneels next to the flower ravaged in pieces. This . . . this is what one of the symbolisms of these flowers mean—the aghast countenance on his face when love is taken away.

Roaner grips the flower stem, and it deteriorates in his fingers as he stands; the remnants of the flower fall as ash to the ground. He stares at the petals below him as his chin trembles, and the tears he defied now fall down his face.

His eyes cast toward the sky, he is shouting Levora's name with such aggression that the trees splinter and snap around us at the growing powers of a Sorcerer within him.

Neither of us will ever be the same.

"Laven," my companion, Amias, pulls me from my thoughts. His eyes read me with a troubled gaze, but he says nothing of it. "You and I will have training before our run with the Mandem. Will you still be attending?" He asks as I try to finish off my meal.

"I believe I would enjoy amalgamating with today's sparring session." Morano says as he pulls a leather band from his wrist to tie his unruly black hair away from his light brown skin.

Amias raises an eyebrow. "The three of us... dueling at once?"

"No," Morano answers. "Roaner will join me."

A heavy breath is released from Roaner who gives a slight shrug as he tosses a green grape into his mouth. The orange hues in his greyish-blue eyes spark in amusement, he has been waiting weeks now to get revenge on Morano for how their last duel ended.

I lean back in my chair, slouching deeper into the seat as I stretch my arms across the chairs next to me. "Are you two not assigned to be in New Quamfasi this afternoon?" I remind them of the duties I am sending the both of them on in Xenathi.

Morano mischievously smiles. "Oh, believe me, I do remember. Which is why I am stalling, but," he raises a finger. "You could go in my place."

I chuckle at him.

"You know why Laven cannot cross the wall, Morano." Amias's arms fold tightly over his chest.

"We will still get there in due time," Roaner eases into the conversation. "We will spar first. Will we not, Morano?" Roaner's eyes shift across the large table toward Morano, who is smirking as he looks down at the half-cut eggs on his plate.

Amias lays a heavy hand on Morano's shoulder. "I wish you luck, and I cannot wait to watch this duel transpire."

"It never fails for the three of you to be a pain in my ass, does it?" Morano rhetorically asks with a mouth full of eggs.

"This is what you get in return for becoming our brother, hellion behavior at its—"

I stop speaking and lean my head toward the opening dining room doors.

That familiar musky scent of the sweetest citrus and sea salt forces through the room. It is hard not to recognize the smell that has crippled me in my strongest moments.

I grip the chairs my arms are resting on, all it does is gain unwanted attention as the wood begins to quietly crack within my palms.

Morano's eyes shoot in my direction, drawing more attention to me. I urgently remove my hands from the wood and push them through the curls in my hair.

"Oh! I–I did not know you all were still eating; I can come back later." Maivena flushes, quickly backing away. Her long dark curls project over her shoulder as she sharply turns through the doors to leave.

"Ah, no worries over it. We were just finishing up here. We will be on our way." Amias stands, sending the servant a cordial smile. She does not see it; she never does—only because no servant is allowed to look a royal in the eye.

"Is this your obligation to clean the dining hall?" I raise an eyebrow.

Her fidgeting begins.

She will lie.

Maivena never tends to the dining area. It is an elderly servant that cleans this room, Miss Rovelle, to be precise.

"Yes," she answers.

I smirk and stand as Amias, Morano, and Roaner leave the room and I follow.

As I stop at the door, her head keeps down to the wooden floors.

"After this," I begin. "You are done preening the dining hall from now on. I will give the chore to someone else."

"I am capable of cleaning the area."

"No, you are not. Not when you have not consumed enough fare to compensate for your work throughout the day. The chore is not yours. You are to rest and eat when you are done here."

* * *

The piercing sound of Vaigosian silver colliding together electrifies the air, bouncing off the trees and echoing over the river. The shrieking blare startles outlying does and their fawns, causing them to rush by in a burst; birds move through the air, their frantic wings shaking leaves from the trees. Amias strikes from a perfect angle for my thigh, and misses by a hair as I divert to the left.

At each swing of our blades, sweat glides from our skin and hair in a flick of rain. It streams down our bodies as we spar under the beating spring warmth, soaking the hems of our trousers, making the fabric cling to our skin with every movement. We could, and we have gone hours upon hours, challenging the other in an enduring fight to see who will prevail and who will deplete first.

If we have any strong suit other than being born Wolves and given gifts of power, it is our agility with swords. From the day Amias and I were born, our fathers had this silver intricately crafted as presents of our birth; our mothers were frightened by such gifts, and we were never allowed to use them until we came of proper age. Although, we got our hands on them when young and ignorant, we were soon caught after the silver cut through my hand at nine years old. The scar is still deeply embedded into my palm as a memory of the destruction silver can do to a Wolf.

We proliferated into our bodies, filling out into men as young teens, naturally growing wiser and more robust due to our blood being of Werewolf descent. All four of us were swinging these lethal weapons around before our mothers anticipated. Our loving bearers may have wanted to keep us safe at all times and from all beings, but they are the reason we are the men we are today.

My blade whispers through the wind; Amias drifts to the side in an easy lean.

"Did you see the young woman your mother brought with her from Gordanta?" I swiftly sink below the swing of Amias's silver. It strikes the tree next to me—bark flies from the body of the tree in the form of tiny sharp arrows.

"Apolla brought someone with her from Gordanta?" Morano asks as he intently watches our movements. "Who?"

I roll my eyes at the mention of her. "She did, and I have not an inkling of her name nor do I know who she is. She never introduced herself to me before I found her lying naked on my chaise when I returned to my chamber from my run last night." The sex-crazed girl was sent back to the dorm she was staying in with a sheet thrown in her face. She left this morning, putting my unease to rest, gladly knowing there would be no naked surprises from women I do not know.

"Oh?" Amias grabs his sword from the flesh of the wood. "And did you forget your name when her thighs wrapped around your waist?"

"Amias," Roaner warningly calls.

"Fuck you," I lash my sword, and it cuts through his trousers, nicking his skin in a small thin line. His eyes straighten, holding a threatening gaze.

His jeering persists. "Did I press a nerve in virgin Prince Laven?"

"Here we go…" I hear Morano mumble under his breath.

I indignantly whip my sword again; it fiercely shrills through the air; he jumps backward at the unforeseen strike. His movements are sudden after my thrashing—sudden yet expected. Although, if I were a random person against Amias, I would be dead by now going against his unpredicted actions. Nonetheless, this is why I chose him as my Right Hand the day I turned eight and ten. He nearly has as much equal say in what happens within the Four Courts of Vaigon as I do. I decided on him because Amias has been my trusted companion for years; he can control and wield his powers faster than any man or woman I have met. If anything were to happen to me, he would be next in line for High Prince and the Throne.

"You are rather aware that I touch none and bed none other than the woman I will belong to." The tip of my sword just barely touches his neck, and he smiles hellishly.

"If that is so," Amias begins. "Then tell the truth as to why you had a lady's scarf in your chamber last night." I press my forearm firmly against his throat and I block his sword with mine, preventing his from gracing my skin. I will the force field building in my forearm to a stop before I throw him through the woods. "Are you lying about what you did with that woman last night?"

His dark skin is dewy. Locks of his hair dangle over his forehead, and drippings of sweat land on my arm as he diabolically smiles at me.

"Not a chance," I respond.

"Enough," Roaner steps in. "It is now my turn with Morano." He unstraps his waist vest letting it fall to the ground as he unties the laces at the top of his undershirt and pulls it over his head exposing the tattoo we all share along the length of the right side of our body:

a Wolf sigil encompassing our initials layered upon each other.

Roaner's sword draws from his sheath, and he looks down at the shining silver held sharply outward. It is the sword left behind from his father after his death. The very last thing he has of him. "The problem lies within it being normalized that men must always want to have sex just because a beautiful woman is in front of him." Roaner steps forward as Amias and I move, and Morano follows. "Or, somehow, it justifies our worth as a man by the number of women we have laid with. Especially a naked, beautiful woman. For some, that is not the norm."

"Perhaps some men should measure their worth by the number of women they truly satisfied in bed and not by the amount they have laid with." Morano lightens the mood with his wittiness as he too removes his upper clothing. "For me, my worth would stand higher than the Terseian Mountains."

Roaner, Amias, Morano, my brothers. My vilest headache and my utmost treasure. We are bonded; our blood courses through each other's veins by the Blood Bond Ritual. The day I turned eight and ten, I chose them all. The Blood Bond Ritual is often between two people only, but the four of us knew we came into this life to find one another, so I made sure to have it sealed that night.

Roaner lightly moves on his feet, not a sound can be heard, but it is seen—his precise footing echoes nothing.

After Amias as my Right Hand, the third of us is Roaner; he is just as quiet as he is murderous. His bloodline is directly linked with Martana, one of the deadliest Sorcerers known in our history—making Roaner my Assassin, my executioner. He massacres silently with not a trace of you left behind, and he elates in it.

Morano gradually forms position as he draws his sword. The weapon lays across his arm with the point of the silver measured perfectly with the tip of his elbow. Most importantly, he is always steady on his feet.

Morano is four. My Emissary, my seer, and searcher. He finds critical information with the ability to see through your thoughts without you ever knowing he was there. Although he does not barricade through minds often, he has the charm to con anything out of you that he wishes. Or, if there must be an alternative, he can be vile and destructive until he finds what he needs. His appearance can be ever-changing to get what we must descry; he could appear to someone as a woman, man, or child. Any creature he can summon, he can be. But to all of us, he is always in his authentic form.

Roaner and Morano each have a different approach when fighting, making both of them difficult to take down. And they both will fight with whatever strength they have until they die, most importantly, they are harder to take down when it comes to protecting their own.

"Begin," I call out, and their blades begin ringing against one another louder than mine and Amias's were.

The High Priestess performed the Blood Bond Ritual the year we all were between the ages of eight and ten and nine and ten. It is held on the sixth full moon of every year, Summer Solstice, a time in the year considerable enough to be our holiday, lasting for a week until the full moon is gone and the waning gibbous takes its place.

"One!" Amias yells the moment Morano is pinned to the ground under Roaner's sword. Slowly he begins to circle their duel to be sure all that is transpiring is fair.

The Blood Bond Ritual is performed in the manner of a slight indentation to each of our wrists, conjoining our skin at the cut and holding until the bond is complete.

Something different sparked between our bonds. Each of us advanced stronger than we went in. All four of us now bearing a bit of the other's powers. We truly knew we came out different from how we went in when Artemis arrived the moment the ritual was complete. Then, each step she took toward us made the world silent.

Dark, prosperous blue cloaks were placed upon us—looping around the neck, falling right over our left shoulder. Still, to this day, we wear the cloaks. A white gold chain brooch gathers the fabric in perfect drapes. At one end of the breast-pin, an arrow sits in the middle of our shoulder, holding the thick blue linen. The other end of the brooch is Artemis's bow that gathers fabric right below our neck. Four chains loosely hang in heavy gold across the left half of our chests, four chains of rich white gold signifying each of us.

'The world will know you as the High Four, you bear my weapon, and a gift of power now touches you from the Gods of strength and resilience to enhance what you now own as one. Your alliance is like no other; alone, you have the strength to conquer; together, you are lethal. Wear these consistently, especially in war, and you will always walk out the way you went in.' Her words struck unfathomably; it became our constant prayer the day she spoke them into existence. That day, we became the true Leaders of House Arvenaldi.

As swift as an arrow from Artemis's bow, Roaner's feet launch him into the hovering tree above; he has grown to be choreographed to each footing and branch that hides him perfectly.

Silence.

Morano circles below the tree, searching for him, but one particular spot will always keep Roaner hidden from sight. There is only scent that Morano could use to find him.

Smoothly, he jumps from the tree, the silver in his hands held high, the sharp point directed downward.

Roaner purposefully misses him, Morano collapses to the ground beneath Roaner's weight; the leaves from the tree spring up and move with the direction of the wind from their collision. Morano's sword is now in Roaner's hand, and Roaner's is entirely impaled into the earth next to Morano's cheek.

The blade ever-so-lightly kisses Morano's neck as he pants.

"I have a question," Morano says as he lies on the ground.

Roaner stands. "And what might your question be?"

"The young servant girl . . . she would not have anything to do with that scarf Amias found, would she?" He slowly stands. "Maivena, is it?"

The three of them watch me with questioning gazes.

I do not answer him as that twinge of fear arises.

"Your Wolf is pushing forward—one eye beaming brightly blue. I know this look, Laven." Morano's demeanor diverts from playfulness to trepidation. "That is the same stricken expression as every other person when words are spoken of their mate."

Naturally, I begin to pace. "I do not know what you speak of."

"You lie." Amias watches me trace every step back and forth. "How long have you known?"

I do not respond to him.

"*Laven*," Roaner hardens his tone as he calls my name.

"It was seven years ago . . ."

"Seven years ago?" Morano shouts in disbelief.

They all hold a puzzling mien as I take a glance at them.

I continue my persistent path.

"My Gods, Laven," Amias rasps out. "You have known for seven years, and you have not said a thing?"

I laugh, shaking my head. "And what would my uncle say about me being mated to a servant?"

He would have her torn to shreds.

"Forget what Lorsius would think, have you told her?" Roaner points down the path to the Servant Grounds far off through the woods. I helplessly look down the way in the hope of seeing her walking along, even using my vision to its highest capacity; it would be as if seeing her at a glance. And I would take it.

I exhale, anticipating easing the rising tension in my shoulders. "Maivena has yet to come into her Wolf and know of me."

I want her to feel what I felt when I found her; she will know the day she comes into her entire self that I am bound to her in an immutable manner, as she will be bound to me . . . and we shall have one another in all the ways the Gods created.

I just do not understand why she has not shifted into her Wolf yet. How is it taking so long?

"I have her scarf because she left it in the dining hall. The guards were going to burn it, but I knew that smell. I know it belongs to her; she always wears it."

Scarves to their people represent more than just some garnishing clothing piece. I could never allow something with such a profound purpose to be burnt.

"And you still have not told her you two are mated yet; *why?*"

Morano presses further for answers.

"You discern *why*." I stop my consistent stride and sit down, leaning back against the tree, I close my eyes. All the possibilities, all of the horrifying outcomes roam through my mind. If her outcome were anything near what I went through, I would have this entire nation blown to smithereens.

Finally, I open my eyes. The three of them now sit in front of me, and Morano fiddles with a small white flower that fell from the spring tree.

"Lorsius has been stuck in his ways for years." Amias says. "I do not think it is possible to get someone like him to revoke the laws of Royals and servants not having the right to be mated. What I do believe is that if you speak with him, he may–"

"He will not . . ." I swallow to rid the dryness in my throat, remembering the day. "I have already tried once before."

Roaner falters. "You did not tell him it was her, did you?"

"It will be one cold day in the very depths of hell before I tell him it was Maivena and myself that I spoke of." I reach down and grab Amias's sword from the ground and hand it to him. "May you do something for me?"

Amias smiles knowingly and nods. "I will look after her while you are away in Terseius."

"And even after that," Morano states. "We all will when we are home."

Roaner nods in agreement. "You should not have kept this to yourself for so long."

He may be correct, but this was something I was allowed to keep to myself.

I fill with reassurance knowing she will still be under reliable protection while I am away, it may not be as extensive as mine, yet Amias is an onlooker and protector like no other. There are reasons he commands our Mandem, his fighting skills being one of many. Nothing in my mind says he would not be suitable to watch over her while I am gone.

"I do not–I am not partial to leaving her," I speak lowly.

"We understand . . ." Amias nods, not making me say what I fear will happen without my watch over her.

"We are not the Leaders of House Arvenaldi for performance—although we are a sight for a sore eye." Morano lifts an eyebrow with a simper plastered on his face and I chuckle, kicking at his shoulder.

Roaner looks down at the mark branded on his wrist and ours. "I am with you all until death; my vow is just as much over Maivena as it is over you all."

"I do love you, Laven," Morano begins. "But I will never forgive you for assigning me to go to New Quamfasi so unexpectedly."

Amias holds up a hand to stop Morano from carrying on. "I will say, you sending them to New Quamfasi is quite dangerous."

"Yes," Roaner nods. "But we are the only ones the people of Old Quamfasi respect out of us all, we both keep quiet and give them no reason to attack. And if they did attack and we are innocent, that is blood they would not wish to have on their hands."

"Given how desperate we are to find a cure for this rabid fucking disease being spread by rogues, hopefully they will provide us aid. If I provide them enough coin–"

Amias chuckles, and I know what he is about to say next. "The Old Quamfasian people want nothing to do with us, New Vaigon. No matter how many coins we provide. And we cannot blame them for wanting to keep their healing secrets to themselves for so long after what Lorsius did those years ago."

"I am trying to build an alliance," I say through gritted teeth. Bitterness is all I feel hearing of how my uncle treated the Quamfasian people. I listened for years and years to how he took their women, how he slaved the children, and what he did to the men to ensure they could no longer breed Quamfasian children. Even to this day, I still must hear him crow about what he has done.

"And does Lorsius know of this?" Morano asks.

"Lorsius can kiss my ass," I retaliate. "He got us into this mess of a rivalry, and I am trying to get us out of it."

"You need to remember the history before trying to regain an alliance with them. Your uncle fought pettily those years ago, he won that war by cheating, and he knows how the Gods feel about that. He is lucky Artemis did not come and strip him of his powers. Quamfasi was precious to Artemis, yet Lorsius still has many of their people enslaved here," Amias points toward the servant grounds. "Yes, there are servants here from our lands, but you and I know well enough that Maivena is one of those children that Vaigon's guards took."

The three of them sit there as still as statues after Amias speaks.

As I look at them, I project the memory of her arrival from my eyes to theirs.

'She is even more beautiful than Helen of Troy. Who would like her first?' My uncle looks at me from the Throne with a crooked smile as he nods his head toward the naked girl lying nearly lifeless on the shiny floors. Bruises and cuts are all over her skin. Her dark hair is matted with dirt and leaves.

'Uncle Lorsius, I–'

'Either you take her to your chamber and do what you would like with her, or I will let Benjamin here,' he points to the guard standing above the girl with a smirk, he gropes himself, and I turn my head away. 'I could let him take her to the guards' grounds; he can show you how to do it.' I snap my eyes toward Lorsius, and he is not looking at me. Instead, his eyes are devouring the girl lying curled on the ground.

I look toward my mother, and she refuses to glance at me.

'Mother.' My voice cracks through the bond.

'Breathe, my love.' She gently responds. 'Take her to your chamber, have her bathed, fed, and clothed. I will discuss this situation with your father after you are gone. Be careful; she looks hurt.'

I hesitantly step down the stairs from the Throne. When I reach the girl, I gently lift her from the ground, hiding my face from my uncle and the others as the tears threaten to slip from my eyes.

She does not fight; I do not know if she is even breathing as I pick her up.

I ascend from the Throne Room and appear in my bathing chamber before Lorsius can say another wretched word from his brutish mouth.

I pull my cloak off and wrap it around her as she sits still as the night, staring toward the ground. I kneel in front of her trying to catch her gaze, but her head is hung too low.

'I–I am Laven. What is your name?'

There is a tiny breath that escapes her lips, and I ask her again . . . and again.

'Maivena . . .' her voice is dry and soft.

Maivena.

'Did they–did any of those men touch you?' I think I may throw up.

Her head shakes.

'Please, do not feel like you have to lie to me.'

Her head shakes again. 'They only took my clothes . . .' her voice is even quieter than before.

I let the tears fall down my face as I tighten my cloak around her. I pull myself together as I see her own tears staining the purple fabric wrapped around her. One of us must be the stronger one here; I will not force her to be that one.

I can practically feel the hollowness inside her.

How lifeless she appears.

'One day,' I promise, 'I am going to kill them.'

There is a slight shift in her, but she will not look at me. 'Why?'

My jaw tightens. 'Because they touched you, and you will learn fast here, Maivena, that I do not tolerate men touching women outside of their consent.'

Her eyes lift to mine, and I can see how young she is. She looks barely my age, four and ten? If even that.

'Laven,' she mumbles. 'You are kind.' She says with a flat expression.

I find a small smile in this ever-growing hell we are trapped in. 'Let us see if you still find me kind when I deliver their heads to their families.'

Their eyes are still staring intensely into my own. "And you did." Amias remembers the fall of many of our guards who held a hand in bringing her here.

"Yes, attached with a charming note to raise better men." Nailed with a spike to their foreheads. Their orders were not to strip her naked and gawk at a young girl; they chose to do that. And I got my revenge for it.

"You turned eight and ten not long after that . . . when you found out she is your mate."

I still remember the surge of wrath, the blood-thirsty anger I had within. "And I slew them one by one—elation is not strong enough to describe the pleasure I felt when taking their lives. Benjamin specifically." It was a full moon; I had just found my mate, and I was fucking livid. I also had new powers to test after the Blood Bond Ritual.

"I did not know it was for her," Morano says quietly.

I smile. "No one did."

"You should have let me help you." Roaner sharply speaks. "If you let me help you that would not have led Lorsius to imprison you and no one would have known we did—"

"I did not want help." My response is immediate. I did not desire help, nor did I require it. And I do not want to allow my thoughts to go near those hell-filled years in Wyendgrev Tower. "I wanted Maivena to know that I will rend apart any man who comes near her by myself. I savored the feeling of Benjamin's heart beating to a stop in my hands." After I carved bits of his skin from his body, I found delight in his screams and cries for help.

"You are a psychopath," Amias says through our mind link after hearing my thoughts.

"I was slightly ruthless then."

They bellow out a laugh. "Then?" Morano questions. "And did you just say slightly? You still are incredibly ruthless. You are just in a man's body now. Which makes it all the more worse."

As I go to speak, a member of our Mandem is vastly approaching. "There you all are," Alexanti calls. "Hua is summoning all for our afternoon run."

I nod as he rushes off to where the others are waiting.

Amias, Morano, and Roaner stand first, holding their hands out for me to take. I reach upward and their hands grasp my arm to pull me from the ground, the hands that will always pull me up no matter the circumstance, as mine will do the same.

* * *

For the past seven years, I have had to grapple with the pain of having someone so close, yet so far. I have become the servant to despair in all of its ways. There were days when I would ask: why did Artemis pick her for me? Why would my fate be held in the hands of someone I cannot have? And for the most part, someone that cannot have me. But then I see her; I hear her quiet humming as she performs her duties, and every negative thought I once had diminishes. It disintegrates like winter, meeting the spring, and just as the sun rises; ridding the snow into poppies, Maivena beams within the flowers; glistening, waiting, as if I am finding her for the first time again.

I have heard stories as a young boy about the person I would be given—as I grew older, I learned how to treat my person to come. I watched the countless men and women who would bed many women and men, only to find their mate soon and be abandoned in return for their actions. But then, there was a shift in them. Their anger grew untamable, the desperation for connection, the treacherous screaming in the night. The bond was being rejected.

'That is how you will not act.' My father would whisper. He had bred me into being the man Maivena deserves, while she is already everything and more for me. Maivena may not know I see it, yet I am very aware of her soul's tendencies; it is pure, genuine, and whole.

"Laven, are you listening, dear?" I flicker my eyes to my mother as she watches me intently.

Hua, one of our Generals, my mother, and I are discussing my leading of the Mandem in Terseius. The outbreak of rouge Wolves' rabid with infection is what we are currently gaining control of and why I have Morano and Roaner in New Quamfasi asking for help or a cure.

Terseius being the land with the highest grade of injuries and deaths, I am being sent to lead and rid them of the outlanders. This will not be my first time leading a Mandem into battle. At the age of seven and ten, I led Partalos through a war of rebellion with my father; the Quamfasian people that once ruled New Vaigon returned for revenge years after my uncle stole what rightfully belonged to them.

That was no easy battle to fight, mentally nor physically. Those of Old Quamfasi are well known for their unusual magic and unbelievable powers; many of the Quamfasian's have a line of Fae blood and Sorcerers' blood that makes them Hybrid superiors.

We nearly lost that war until my father allowed me to choose to concede or continue. After that, the Quamfasian people did not wish for the land back; now, it was just a horrid memory. They did not covet a Throne. All they wanted was to be left in peace. That is all they have ever asked for.

During that war, there was not a single person I killed; there were only men that I hit hard enough to knock out. I kept in thought that one of those men or women could be a relative of Maivena. I would never forgive myself for such a thing. She would never forgive me.

When word got back to Lorsius of my decision to concede, he had no choice but to comply with conceding as well. His tormenting and taking of their people ended that day. If only that war had happened six seasons sooner, Maivena would still be with her family, and I would find her the right way.

"You set sail at sunrise," my mother says as she brushes a hand over my hair. I open my mouth to speak, but she quickly interrupts. "You will not ascend to Terseius. Ascending with that many people will weaken you and render your powers short. So instead, you will sail and keep your strength before I allow you to ascend back and forth numerous times across the continent."

I smirk and nod.

"Now, remember to stay fed, drink, and watch over yourself."

"Mother."

"I am smothering," her face falls, and guilt arises within me.

"You are not smothering, but I am not a boy anymore." Of course, I no longer need to be reminded of such things, but if it puts her mind at ease to say them, I will allow her to remind me repeatedly.

"How long is Lorsius in Gordanta?" I ask.

"However long the Duke needs him. May it be forever." She happily announces, feeling freed from his presence.

"Well," I nod, "stick with Hua while I am away. I have already asked her to keep you accompanied while I am gone. She mentioned going hunting; you could join her if you would like."

She smiles up at me, placing a gentle hand on my cheek.

"I am proud of the man you have become."

I smile while shaking my head. "Was I given a choice to turn out otherwise?"

The hand that was touching my cheek pushes gently at my shoulder. "Yes, yes you were." She nods.

Like Lorsius.

"You are given knowledge; it is up to you to retain it and give it purpose. You did exactly that. Your father would have been so pleased to see you grow over the years."

* * *

Reaching across my bureau, I toy with the soft fabric of the white and beige scarf, simultaneously writing on a blank notecard. I have written this note ten times throughout the night in fear of frightening her or possibly my words not sounding the way they do in my head as she reads them.

Meet me at the East Lake ten sunsets from today.
I will be awaiting you in the courtyard;
find me in the maple tree.

2
OUTLANDERS

ROANER KORSANA
XENATHI — QUAMFASI CITADEL

THE HORSES CARRY MORANO and me through the city of Xenathi; we are on one of the main paths to get to the palace—where the meeting is being held to discuss the drastic measures going on in our land, drastic measures that will more than likely reach here.

Rouges: infected beings of our kind that have been taken over body and soul by a disease no one seems to know anything about. Or, as I refer to it, mutation. We have been living in hell for six months. Constantly being on our toes wondering when the next attack will happen—afraid it will be a child or someone of the elderly. Nonetheless, anyone dying of this contagion is a tragedy.

It is amusing how one moment a want-to-be-King is pinching land, and now we need help from those he managed to pilfer. But, of course, his ego would be too impaired to disclose his crimes and then beseech for aid.

Xenathi initially belonged to High King Stravan of Provas, that was until he heard the people of Quamfasi who once ruled lost their Throne. Then, Stravan gave all of the land over to King Vallehes and Queen Penelope; he knew he did not require the ground more than the people who were then homeless.

When this land belonged to Stravan, it had only an unused palace sitting upon thousands of acres of land. It is beautiful how New Quamfasi has made this their home from the ground up. Captivatingly cast with stone of diverse colors, the touch of nature takes over with its green ivy and leaves encompassing the structures bit by bit.

They have made this into more of a home than their prior land was. And that is all those could ask for them after the war.

Morano and I are already receiving mysterious glances as we drift by people and small shops in the city. Our black leather armor and dark blue cloaks reveal that he and I are not from here, a clear indication we are those of Vaigon. Two of the four that Artemis picked.

There are other women and men that watch us on our way through. They are clad in their burgundy leather gear—signifying they are Warriors in the Quamfasi Mandem. The slightest wrong movement from either of us could end with a spear through our chests.

We speak when we finally get through the city's depths and reach the wooded trail that takes you to the citadel. But we are sure to be careful with our words; we are both aware that we are being watched and heard, although we are now out of the vast city.

"Do you truly believe they will help us?" Morano asks.

I shrug. "It is valuable to inquire; the only way we will know if they will is to ask."

* * *

Our horses come to a stop at the porticoes, and we are quickly approached by two guards who patrol the entrance gates.

QUAMFASI is engraved in the middle of the iron gate, written in pure white gold, and the immaculate palace view is behind it. In the expanse of the land surrounding the chateau, courtyards sit along either side. From my sight, I witness a father playing with his daughter.

They weave through the pillars, bustling with laughter as they chase one another around the large fountains within the enclosure.

"Thousands," Morano mutters as he observes the father and daughter. "He took that life from thousands of happily free families." He exhales slowly, looking away from them, and then his eyes drift to me. "We will need a fucking godsend for Vallehes and Penelope to help us after what Lorsius has done. If I were them, I would have never arranged this meeting. I would have happily let us struggle and die. But, unfortunately, the destruction we are facing in Vaigon is our karma, and we are serving the consequences of Lorsius's actions."

There are people who speculate the disease over our land was made by Artemis herself. Yet, we all know she would not put so many lives at stake. She values the quantity of us, as well as the quality.

Numerous feet before us stand two guards outstretching their spears, grasping them at a longitudinal angle. The javelins begin to radiate in a golden hue, and the gates gradually open. The protective shield that once maintained the entrance slowly withers away; it is riveting to hear the energy of such power as we observe the white electricity diminish before us.

As Morano and I enter, the threshold closes, and the shield returns—sheathing the iron and fading as if it was never there. Yet, if someone were to try to break through that gate, they would meet the competition of magic.

"Leave your horses," one guard starts with a short tone. "Follow us; King Vallehes and Queen Penelope await in the Consultation Room."

They scarcely make eye contact with us as they speak; this is not out of submission. On the contrary, the lack of eye contact is out of hatred. Little may I know; we could still be holding someone from either of their family's hostage on our citadel.

As we travel down the hallway to the consultation room, I hear the pounding of heels beating into the shiny stone floors at a hard and steady pace. As the woman appears from around the bend of the hallway, two other women quickly follow behind her in a nervous trail. They give short glances at one another after meeting both my and Morano's eyes.

"I do not care what Val nor Pen says. I will not be cordial with Vaigosian scum! They may continue with this meeting if they like. I am the Right Hand of this nation, I do as I please, and I say no when I desire. Even if those people were to free my family, the answer has been and will always be *no*." The woman storming down the hall is clad in a sheer dark blue dress that slightly catches wind at the speed of her pace. Her golden eyes just barely cast over my own as she passes by. Suddenly, her feet stop and then gradually grow closer. "You," she shouts.

When I look over my shoulder, the woman that was passing is urgently approaching again. I do not know if I should defend myself or simply take whatever she may do or say.

Her dark brown skin slowly pours out a mist of a sort, moving directly toward me.

Right Hand, I repeat her words in my head . . . this is Esme. She is the woman who can blind you to life itself. Even your own reflection in a mirror. She has the ability to make you not see or sense anything you once were able to for however long she chooses to. She is also one of the most highly educated people on this continent; Esme is of the few who can say they know nearly everything.

"Since you need a favor from us, I need a favor from you." Smugly, she speaks at me. "Take this message back to Penelope and Vallehes, distort my words however you would like, say it harsher, say it nicer. But you will be very transparent with them that I will not ever say yes to helping you and your bastard nation survive. You could at least have the mere decency to apologize for eradicating the lives of my people before pissing all over our land with your presence. I hope you and your people die in that mutation, eating you all alive limb by limb." And she means every word as her golden eyes bore into my own. "I expect an answer after I speak to you." Her anger is thrumming through these halls, and the blinding fog protruding from her could take my vision or blind me to anything at any given moment, and I will be defenseless.

"I will tell them." I nod stiffly.

Her hard exterior does not shift. "I expected nothing less."

The longer I look at her, the more I begin to recognize her face. And she identifies mine.

There is nothing but the ground-shaking resonance of war barricading the land Lorsius is aiming to take as his own. Unsettling cries and screams from those who have fallen roar through the sky in breathtaking agony. Around me are multitudes of people fighting off others as they surround the body of their loved one in protection until a healer can ascend to the war field and remove the body.

Laven, Amias, Morano, Hua, and I made a pact that we would not kill during this war. There would be no one we would touch. Laven was who proposed this, he did not say why, but I can imagine it is for the purpose of us not having a hand in the death of innocent people. Neither of us agrees with what is transpiring, but there is an abundance of things in life we do not have control over, and this war is one of them.

So, I stand here. I do nothing. I cannot do anything. I will not do anything.

As I take in the perimeter around me once more, my eyes fall upon a woman standing in the distance. Her stance is unwavering; she holds herself as strong as a tree that the storm can never shake. I heighten my hearing and draw my sight in deeper. Every breath she takes, I can hear it above the harrowing sounds of battle.

Before I see it, I hear it. I recognize that soft drag of an arrow sliding from the archery quiver along her back, tucking into its bow, and then the spiraling turn as it whips through the air moving in a perfect direction for the center of my chest.

I raise my hand, casting a small shield in front of the arrow. As it draws through the shield, it desiccates, disappearing before our eyes.

Her chest rises and falls as the rage in her grows.

This time, I am unprepared. Her spear is drawn, igniting in a glow of silver the moment she touches it. And, within one easy motion, it veers across the vast land between us. You can hear the energy of the unwavering magic soaring through the spear and to my shoulder—propelling directly through me. The force of her spear throws me backward by multiple feet.

As I collide with the ground, it pushes the spear farther through me, forcing an excruciating scream to tear from my chest. I can just barely see through the pain, and just as I think it could not get any worse, the spear is ripped from my shoulder at an angle meant to make the wound worse. Stiffly, I lift my head, and the spear soars from my body and back to her hand. She catches it in a firm grasp and places it along her back. She watches me for mere seconds before ascending.

'Roaner!' Hua hollers as she rushes toward me. 'For fucks sake, I leave you for a moment, and you nearly get yourself killed.'

I do not have the strength to respond before she is hovering over me. Hua grabs my chin and yanks my face in her direction. 'Who?'

There are no words for me to speak, I can barely see her due to the agony blurring my vision.

'Who did this to you.' Each word she speaks comes out sharper than the one before.

I weakly shake my head. 'I do not know.'

'Then point!' She screams.

Finally I can focus and I witness the pink specks in her purple eyes glow in anger.

'We promised, Hua.' As I speak, my voice strains at the pain.

She grumbles in response while touching my chest and we ascend to the Healers Tent.

"Pardon my aim," Esme commences. "That spear I lodged through your shoulder on the battlefield was meant to kill you."

"My Lady," one of the meek women at her side speaks. "We must go. You will be late to meet Prince Vorian." She touches Esme's arm to prevent her from ripping me apart any further with her words.

Sharply, she turns on her heels and is down the hall with her maids rushing to keep up behind her.

"That is the woman who nearly killed you during the war?" Morano asks as we both watch her recede farther away.

"Yes."

"I am surprised she missed your heart and only punctured your shoulder," Morano chuckles. "She does not strike me as the person to miss the opportunity of a killing so easily."

"Believe me. I thought I was going to die."

"This way," the guard leading us to the consultation room shouts in a tone that is just borderline of agitation.

Morano and I follow at once. We have already pissed off their Right Hand; we do not need to do any more damage by pissing off the High King and High Queen with a late arrival.

As we approach a set of double doors, there are no knobs or handles to enter. Instead, the guard touches the sleek tan stone with a hand, and the doors leisurely open to Penelope and Vallehes.

Upon entering the room, the entire ceiling is open to reveal the beauty of the sky. The chamber is large, expansive enough to fit a couple of hundreds of people. Surrounding half of the room is a simple stone railing; in the other half, walls stand firm.

Vallehes and Penelope stand at a large circular table encompassed with a map of their land. You can see the beauty they have bred on this land as you glance behind them. From the health of the ground to the birds that fly through the trees, this was once what my home looked like.

Their eyes meet ours, and Morano and I bow before them in virtuous respect. We bow in their technique, not the technique Lorsius has forced upon us. Each continent has its own respective form of bowing; to not follow it is the utmost disrespect.

Neither Penelope nor Vallehes have changed in appearance; their age- less glamour remains intact. There was blather that they chose to no longer phase into their Wolves and gave up immortality, but I never acknowledged it. If I reflect well, the High King and High Queen I knew would never give up so readily on mending their people and continuing to restore a home for them.

Penelope still maintains her long locks. They are always kept perfectly done, falling around her darkened skin. She is attired in her red leather armor, as Vallehes is donned in formal dark attire.

"Roaner, Morano," Penelope says, glimpsing us over.

No matter how well we mean, they will always give us an overlook for detection of any weapons we may be bearing.

"Your Right Hand has quite the colorful personality if I do say so myself," Morano announces as we sit at the circular wooden table.

He is trying to be humorous and amuse them in some manner. I should tell him to shut up before his wit gets us anchored with no help.

"She does, does she not?" Penelope smiles.

Perhaps his comedic charm could conceivably get us somewhere. Vallehes looks at her and then towards us. "What is it that you wished to ask of us?"

Morano stays silent. We both discussed that I would be the one to prepare the deed of what we are looking for aid with.

"Over the course of six months, something strange, dark even, has erupted in Vaigon. A disease—a mutation of some sort has been taking our people. We believe it began with one host, then spread from one to the other. To describe what is happening to them is unearthly. It is as if their soul has been corrupted. After speaking with Laven, he explained that he does not believe this was a disease that just began. This is unnatural. Given that thought, we can only suspect this virus has been made. We do not know the purpose and do not have an inclination to who could have done this, but we do know that our people are dropping at a rate we have never seen."

Penelope's eyebrows furrow together as she hears every word and connects them. "What exactly happens to them after they have been in reach of this?"

"Well," I begin. "It seems to initiate with a bite, a laceration—possibly, but we know it is a wound inflicted upon you to change you. Every individual we executed was bitten and had claw marks someplace on their body.

"Seeing these people in action is like watching a child contain powers; they have no idea what to do with themselves, so they run rampant and inflict harm everywhere they walk and even upon themselves. Their skin can turn, fading to a pale dark grey appearance. Each person mutated all hold the same eye color—an eerie blue nearly the pigment of the whites of their eyes."

"I would say we could help you, but I do not see it possible." Vallehes pushes a hand through his light hair, pondering on the correct words to say before continuing.

"We are not only here to ask for help solely for our benefit," Morano chimes in, so Vallehes needs to think no farther. "We want to forewarn you."

Nodding in agreement, I presume. "There is only a matter of

time before they can navigate their way through the border. That is all you are, a *single* border away. Whatever may happen to us has the grave potential of happening to you. So this is not only our cry for help but our call of prophecy. We do not hope you will lose more people than you already have over the years."

Vallehes smiles. "We thank you for your consideration, but there is no requirement to worry for us, nor our polity. I believe we have everything under proper management here at this point."

"We would never doubt it. We remember the leaders you were to us, and it does not go forgotten." Morano nods his head in admiration. Out of us all, Morano praised the Queen and King more than anyone my brothers and I knew.

Penelope looks toward Vallehes, and I can tell they are communicating with one another through their bond, the mating linkage. She nods, standing from the table. "I must go to our General; she is calling upon one of us. But I know there is more Val may wish to speak with you on that he will fill me in on later. It was lovely to see you two."

Before we can repay our respects to her, she ascends from the room, leaving behind a white hue that glides upward and out through the open ceiling.

"We have our land under control, yes," Vallehes proceeds. "Nevertheless, we will keep our eyes open and our Warriors and people on guard. You are correct that we are only one wall away, and anything happening to you is undoubtedly prone to happen here. Yet, there is nothing I can offer you until I witness what you speak of firsthand. Until then, I thank you for your warning."

"Well, there is one more thing," I inform.

I can see Morano's head turning to me from the corner of my eye. His perplexed glance at me prompts Vallehes to shift his eyes between us.

I turn to Morano. *"Wait outside,"* I privately tell him.

"What are you about to ask him?" He demands to know.

"I will tell you," I falsely promise. *"Leave before he begins to suspect, and you eradicate my plan."*

"There is something I need to ask of you for myself and not as a person of Vaigon."

Vallehes raises a single eyebrow and waits for me to continue.

Morano finally stands and saunters out of the room.

Vallehes still awaits.

"A little over five years ago, Levora Arvenaldi went missing, just before the grace of Spring. We did not know how. One moment she was there; the next, she was gone. Laven and I scoured for months after we uncovered where her scent stopped. We were aware that there had to be another trail of where she was taken to, but there was nothing. Her scent stops directly in one placement and carries no farther than where it is. The only possibility I can surmise is that someone disguised her smell. Yet, I am half Sorcerer, and I have the ability to remove any mask someone may have put over a scent to uncover their trail, but there is nothing. She ends entirely in one place."

Vallehes stands. "And, who is this woman to you?" He questions as he walks across the room to the shelves of books.

"My *vosalis**." The words move effortlessly from my mouth.

It is what she would be right at this moment and what she will be when I bring her home.

"Not your mate?" Vallehes comes to a stop as he glances over at me.

"Deeper than that."

He nods, and his arms cross as his eyes meet mine. "I will help you with this," he sits across from me. "Though, we will bargain."

I nod, knowing there would be something in return that he would seek. There will invariably be a bargain for whatever a person wishes for while simultaneously fulfilling the other's wants and needs.

"I assist you in your discovery of Levora's whereabouts, and you will assist me." His hand makes a small motion, and a contract appears on the table before me. "I need to discover the placement of someone, and then, you will arrange their execution."

---

* *Old Quamfasian: Vosalis   Translation: Wife*

"Who am I to find?" I simply ask.

Vallehes grins and a quill and ink develops in his hand as he walks toward me. "You will be rather fascinated by whom I need you to locate." Before I say another word, I am signing my name.

VAIGON CITADEL

"You called upon me?" Heshy, my Auxiliary, asks as he enters my study.

"I did, come in," I motion for him to enter from the doorway, and he sits in one of the black leather chairs near my bureau. "I have something that needs to be done and it will stay between us and whoever we find to complete what I need done."

Heshy nods. "Name the person and I can find them."

"There is one, his name is Ezra Harst, he is a messenger that knows Voschantai Universe almost as well as us. I believe he can complete the assignment, but I need to meet with him first, question him and be certain of it. This task is no easy task to undertake given who is behind it and what must be done."

Heshy stands and fixes his cloak. "Ezra Harst you say?"

I nod. "Can you find him before the end of a fortnight?"

Heshy smiles. "I can find him before tonights end."

3
LIVE BAIT

LAVEN HEPHAESTUS ARVENALDI, II
TERSEIUS — NORTHERN COURT OF VAIGON

"PRINCE LAVEN IS IN Terseius at last." I advert my gaze to the Duke's daughter. I narrow my eyes at her as she circles me. The longer she trails around, the abundance of her perfume gags me. Her hand reaches out to grace my chest, but I catch her wrist before she can near any closer; she gasps at my grip on her wrist as I stop the unwarranted touch.

"Keep your wandering hands to yourself, Mora." She smirks, taking a single step backward. "Where is your father?"

"His study with the men and women in our Circle, they are speaking about the intrusion of rogues while waiting for your arrival." She speaks as if she has rehearsed this over in her head multiple times.

I nod and turn on my heel. The moment my hand touches the door, she calls out my name; I grimace at the sound of her tone and turn to the girl that stalks toward me.

Her pale skin is drowned in the black dress, the black dress of Quamfasi silks stolen from the people during many raids of their homes and seamstresses' workshops.

"Do you have a mate yet, Laven?"

I lie. "No."

She stands there, her eyebrows raised. Mora tucks her red hair behind her ear, waiting for me to say more. Something she will not get.

"You are not going to ask me if I have a man of my own?"

I sigh. "If you do have a man of your own, I pity him."

Her head throws back as she lets out a horrendous giggle. "Do not fret; there is no man for you to pity . . . I do not believe in such a thing."

"Well, you should." I trim our conversation short. "I must leave now—"

"You can join me in my bed tonight," she interrupts. "Or all of your nights you are here, if you crave to."

I smile while holding my finger out, motioning for her to come closer.

It is almost dreadful how desperate this woman can be.

I near her ear as she closes the space between us.

"You would never measure up to the woman I have running infinitely in my head . . . you want someone like me in your bed chamber because my uncle is the High King, you wish for a throne that will never be yours." As I stand up straight, I see I have proven my point by looking at her face. Her cheeks are paler, her eyes now dark as her promiscuous Wolf falls back.

"Go beg to fuck another Prince; I am not one to take to mistresses nor bed slaves."

Years ago when my uncle first claimed Old Quamfasi, he promised Adir, Mora's father, an arranged marriage of me and her.

Since Lorsius does not have children, it was me who was offered up, and offering me means giving Adir high stature in House Arvenaldi, and he would no longer be only a Duke. He would no longer only rule here in Terseius, but our Realm as a whole. My marriage to Mora would have given him immediate grant in our House. A grant he does not deserve.

The day I was released from Wyendgrev Tower, and I found out what Maivena really was to me, I had the marriage revoked.

Nothing angered my uncle more than that demand. Without me, he cannot reign. There must be an Heir to the Throne if anything happens to him and I threatened him with my leave if he does not agree.

But, not only Lorsius was enraged over my request. Adir was as well.

'You will allow a boy as young as Laven to decide who he will marry?' Adir shouts at uncle Lorsius as he leans across his bureau, nearing so close to his face that flecks of spit flies from his mouth. 'My daughter will always be the most appropriate fit for a high role of this Kingdom. Mora has poise, she has the highest education, she is strong and quick, she learned to wield her powers faster than your average individual. And you wish to deny the marriage you promised me because a child demanded it?'

If only Adir knew my uncle more, he would be well aware that questioning him will make him hate you.

Lorsius slowly rises from his large chair and walks around his bureau to stand in front of Adir. Adir's tan skin flushes.

'Mora, your daughter,' Lorsius pauses and holds up a finger. 'Your illegitimate daughter that you adopted from the orphanage.'

My uncle waits for Adir to say something, anything. He does not and Lorsius continues.

'She is not of your blood—'

Adir immediately interrupts. 'That does not make her any less my child.'

Lorsius smiles in that sadistic way he always does when ruining others with his words. 'Yet, she is not of your blood,' Lorsius continues where he was interrupted. 'That making her barely acceptable for anything. Her legitimate parents could be commoners, poor folk of Old Quamfasi. And the longer I thought about it, the more I figured she is not the most appropriate fit because of her blood not truly being of yours. I will not allow her to ruin House Arvenaldi without knowing where her origins are from.'

I open my mouth attempting to defend Adir, but Lorsius holds his finger up to hush me.

Leaning against the wall again, I allow them to continue, but it does not. Adir slowly turns and ascends from the room going home to Terseius.

Lorsius is callous, and always has been, it is rare that I ever agree with anything he says or does. Especially now. Nevertheless, he is getting me out of this marriage, I have no choice but to stand here, be quiet, and allow him to say whatever he wishes to get me free of this.

He turns his head to me. 'You are welcome.'

I should have ignored that finger he held up to silence me, but I could not. The only thing there was left for me to do was send a written apology to Adir for my silence. The written apology that went unanswered but did not go unnoticed.

Adir may have been wronged by Lorsius, but this does not excuse his hand in what happened to the people of Old Quamfasi. I will no longer allow those who held such a strong hand in the harm of their people in my House. I have worked tirelessly to keep House Arvenaldi strong; no one will ruin this for me, specifically not someone who has caused more destruction than growth.

From that day and on, I made an oath to myself to never be silenced by anyone ever again.

* * *

As I enter the Duke's study, he looks to me in relief.

"Laven," Adir sighs, motioning for me to see the map of the land. The men and women around him bow at my presence. A formal gesture I have always despised.

"How many deaths today?" I ask as my finger traces from one landmark to another. His routes to track the rogues are smart but not intelligent enough. Rogues know that we mean to locate them and disperse them one by one. Therefore, this path must be innovated and diversified by many lengths.

"Not as many as this past week," Adir responds. "How many have lived that were not killed?" Not a word is spoken.

"It is unknown, my Lord." His Emissary Quinlan says lowly, aware of the grave danger this causes.

I exhale heavily. "This infection they spread can injure, kill or turn a man, woman, and child into a pernicious Wolf—as well as in our human form we can become infected. Without certain numbers of those who are still alive—no matter how we go about this—we could be handing ourselves our own death wish."

"What do you suggest?" Adir asks while rolling up the map in front of us.

"We must know their numbers." "And how can we do that?" "Bait," Quinlan mumbles.

I nod. "Yes, and I have just the person."

"We will use a servant," Adir says. "One of the attractive."

My face turns at the idea. "Leave those poor men and women to their duties; they do enough for you all as it is. Either way, the rogues we are dealing with will not want much with a poor servant. Whoever is behind creating such rogues want power."

I look up to Adir, and his defense goes up. "You will not use my mate; that is a limit not to press." He warns.

I smile. "I was not thinking of your wife."

"And I am not too fond of throwing Mora in such danger either . . . but she is fast," he slowly nods. "She can outrun them."

Adir places a new map on the large wood table; I grab the quill and red ink, drawing a large oval around the perimeter of these winter woods.

"I have been studying these lands for the past week; it seems they gather most within the heart of the woods."

"My Lord, if they gather most at the heart of our land, why not attack from the outside in? We could force them all into one area and attack from there."

I do not know the young woman speaking; I look at her and circle my fingers around the inside of the heart.

"If we use our method of bait in their safe space, they all will gather. The goal is to chase them out of their safe interior and into land they are unfamiliar with—"

"We get them to an unfamiliar land; they will panic and we have the upper hand." Adir adds up my calculations as I continue to draw them out.

"Exactly," I nod. "Warn your people, but silently, the last thing we want is for the rogues to know exactly what is coming. Have them prepare arrows, poison them with Lernaean Hydra Blood Oil, coat their spears and swords in it as well. Use a thick cloth when applying it; you do not want to touch an oil like that. The moment the oil enters their bloodstream, they will be executed. I wish we had an alternative option, as of now, death is the only answer."

Adir motions his hand to the young woman who spoke; she nods, rushing out, taking three other men with her to prepare.

Quinlan steps closer to us. "What will we do if this does not see through as we plan?" He lowly asks.

Adir groans; sitting down, he rubs his hands over his face and through his dark red hair. "This needs to follow through."

"Well, if this does not go accordingly, I will send a messenger to the citadel to call upon Hua and Amias. They will be on the first ship with our Mandem; I will have them bring the Warriors; we attack from every angle. If this fails, who knows what your rate of infected-living will go to.

"Although, neither plan should falter. I am planning for failure not to be an option; I would like to go home soon."

4
A WEEKS TIME

LAVEN HEPHAESTUS ARVENALDI, II

WE DODGE THROUGH THE trees, eyes fixated all around us.

The past week we have trained in speed, agility, and strength—all of us unsure of how to properly defend ourselves against the rogues, so, we practiced in all areas necessary.

Mora, at the lead of the chase jumps from the ground and upward to the trees where the beginning of the city starts. I can hear the quiet commotion coming from inside the small homes in the town, I can even hear it through the many feet pounding into the dirt around me.

Just as we thought they would, the rogues, both Wolf and human form begin to panic the moment they reach the entrance to the city.

The Archers are readied as they sit atop the rooves. Their elbows are sharply pointed, with an unwavering focus as the chaos begins to grow and the rouges retaliate against us outlying on the grounds.

A loud scream staggers my sprint, as I look, there is a young man fighting off a rogue, but poorly fighting. He is not wearing our black leathered armor, but night clothing. There is a water pail spilled over next to him and a crying child banging on the window of their home.

My sword rings as I draw it from the sheath around my waist.

I quietly near closer, although all of the havoc wreaking around us should not make a difference, it does. If I have noticed one thing about those of the diseased, their hearing is heightened to a degree even I do not hear.

The moment I am angled close enough with my sword, I cut smoothly through the rogues neck, and a profuse smell immediately erupts.

The rogues body twitches as it falls to the ground and the young boy scurries backward while quickly wiping the blood of the rogue from his face.

"It is all right," I hold my hand out as I step nearer, attempting to calm him after such a traumatic experience.

The child in the window is still crying as they watch us interact.

Where are their parents?

"No, do not come closer!" He shouts.

I look to where his eyes are fixated, and he tugs at his pants leg looking at the deep bite around his ankle.

I slowly exhale, unsure of what to do next.

Mora appears from her ascension and wraps her sheath around the base of his knee. She tightens it so tightly the boy shouts in agony and grips her shoulder.

She fixates her gaze on him. "You can be saved, but half of your leg will be gone."

He does not think twice, he stiffly nods, and I hand him the leather sheath from my dagger to bite down on. I will not be surprised if he completely bites through it.

"Close your eyes." I say, but, instead, he looks to the child in the window still weeping, shouting *Jededyah*' repeatedly.

"Your name is Jededyah?" Mora asks as a distraction as he holds on to her hands.

"Yes," he winces.

I stand from the ground and take Mora's sword; it would be useless to use my own. The infection from the previous rogue would only spread right to him.

Kneeling at a level to make this smoothly pass I hear the quiet conversation between Mora and Jededyah.

"I have to live, if I do not live no one will take care of my sister."

Mora and I slowly make eye contact.

He is clearly very young, too young to be doing this on his own.

"Your sister will never have to worry," Mora tells him. "You are living, Jededyah."

And just as he opens his mouth to speak, I cleanly cut the sword through his leg.

* * *

We continued to move through the impaired city after caring for Jededyah and his little sister Janessa. It seemed whoever the messenger was, they did not perform their job well enough, there were more people like Jededyah to be found outside of their homes. Some could not be amputated, some had to have their lives taken.

All of the infected fell one by one, screaming in agony; some were too stricken with pain to bellow out a single cry. Every vein in their body was protruding, turning from blue to black. Those stuck within their Wolf shriveled, crippling at the flow of Lernaean Hydra Blood Oil moving through them. Their howls called deeply through the woods before their final breath.

We allowed the families to decide if they wished to see their loved ones in such a form, black veins trailing throughout the face, eyes filled with blackness, arms, legs—the entire body coated in black jutting lines. The blood oil was setting within them, putting each individual full of disease into a final rest of sleep. Death was not the only solution I was hoping for. I wished for a cure before coming here, but that seems nearly impossible.

Whether the families wished to see them or not, we held a funeral for each fallen. Finally, we called upon their lovers and family to say an ending prayer before the body is burned into ash.

The vision of the child in my arms appears, a little girl thrashing about, rabid in disease. I held her arms at her side as I watched one single drop of blood oil upon her lip pull her into peace. She was one of the few children who survived and the only child I did not allow to be struck with an arrow to cause more pain than needed. Her mother and father were young, only a year or two older than me. Carolena was her name, their first child. The cries of them both have yet to leave my ears.

I could not look at the little girl for a prolonged time. I watched her face begin to mold into the shape of my sisters when she was that small, and the sight of her was too painful to bear. I did not stay long after Carolena's passing.

"Since you will not allow us to thank you with a celebration, let me give you some of our finest clothing." Adir pulls me from the screaming in my head. "We have jewels and healing herbs you may take along with you." Adir motions his hand, and two men walk into the study bearing gifts.

As I try to respond, I look upon a scarf, which is blue with beautiful stitching of white and tan.

I point. "That one . . . it is all I will take."

Adir nods. "Wrap this for High Prince Laven and bring it back here—wrap it well, he has four days of a journey ahead."

* * *

I sit down on the large rock as the men make final touches to the ship before leaving. There is a familiar wretched scent that forces into my nose. I do not need to acknowledge or turn to know that it is Mora sitting next to me.

"I lied to you," she begins. "I do have a mate . . . but she is no man."

My hands rub over my face. "Why do you speak of her so despondently?"

"She frightens me." Her voice cracks between her words.

"Why?" I look at her as she plays with the white fabric in her dress.

"Because she is the most beautiful thing I have ever seen, more astonishing than flower fields that bloom in the spring . . . I cannot get close to her because the day will come that I lose her to whatever it may be, and I will lose myself as well." The tears she was fighting fall down her ivory cheeks.

Confusion strikes. "Then why did you do that to me the day I arrived? Why say such things to someone when you already have another?"

She forces a laugh. "Foolishness . . . trying to find something—someone to push away the pain.

"We are not exactly the luckiest nor the most loved beings the Gods have created. We are given mates, someone specifically crafted and created only for us. Either we fall in love with everything about them or not—there is always that deep-rooted connection that holds our soul to the earth. When they perish, we do as well; we may still be here, but it feels as if we are dead—a walking, living corpse.

"We have the chance to hold on to immortality and youth if we continue to phase into our Wolves, yet all that means is merely living, being here as just an object. When they die, a part of us dies as well. We can either live with the emptiness or end it all to be with the person destined for us. Those are our options. We carry on cut in half or die to be whole again. There is no living in-between the two after someone so dear to you is ripped away."

5
ONCE A LADY

AMIAS HERACLES TORANDI
TERSEIUS — NORTHERN COURT OF VAIGON

I WALK ALONG THE Training Grounds, watching every designated area. All around me are the echoing sounds of battle; the sharp collisions of swords meeting edge by edge, the hard thud of bodies being struck into the ground, the strong whistle of arrows being sent through the air. Each multiple acre of land is designated to specific aspects of training. Some of the people here are young men and women being trained for the first time in their life—the beginners. Some are seasoned Warriors who must always keep sharp with their agility, there are plenty of men and women who reside on the Training Grounds in the homes just near in the woods.

In the vast distance, arrows dot the sky, as I measure their landing, they are almost close enough to hit those practicing in the Hand to Hand Combat Unit. Not too far off, spears pierce the ground surrounding those practicing in the Swords Unit. But the massive area containing acres of land where the spears came from are where frontline Warriors are made—that is where Hua is, as well as Naius, Maivena's father.

Naius steadily flows backward, drifting beneath the throw of Hua's spear that just barely grazes his nose. Just as he falls back, his sword rotates to his left hand and veers upward, slicing through the center of her spear and breaking through the wood. The slice into her spear is smooth, stopping it right in its movement. He has now ridded Hua of her most prominent weapon.

"General," Apolla, Laven's mother says as she approaches me. She smiles and the sun catches her glowing dark skin.

Her blue eyes shift to where I am looking, and she nods.

"Naius Fondali, former General of Old Quamfasi Mandems . . . all of them."

Then, it slowly comes full circle, Hua is not training with him, she has asked *him* to train *her*.

This all does not make sense the longer I think. Anyone of Old Quamfasi descent was taken—pulled from their homes and taken as a hostage. How does someone of his combativeness be taken?

"Apolla, how in the Gods names did he end up here?" A Warrior a strong as Naius makes it out alive in an ambush. Maybe he will come out of the attack with scratches and possibly a limp, but someone who fights at his stature does not end up here by force.

Apolla's shoulders shrink. "He came here himself."

I raise my eyebrows, and nod for her to continue because this does not make any sense.

"He begged me to be allowed in, at first, I told him no. Then he explained that his daughter was here, and I immediately allowed his entrance. There was another man with him, a family member, he was looking for his mate, so I allowed the entrance of them both."

The brutality of Lorsius was excessive, there has not been anyone of our time to commit to anything he has done to their people and get away with it.

We have one of the greatest Warriors of time on our land because Lorsius took his daughter and they have no choice but to be here.

"Did Laven tell you of her arrival?" Apolla asks.

"The arrival of who?"

She glances at Naius, who is no longer training with Hua, and now someone new. "His daughter. I believe her name is Maivena, she is a stunning young woman." Pity is now all there is on her face as she speaks her name.

I only nod, knowing Apolla is not aware of the bond between her son and Maivena. But, I also do not wish to think too long about what I saw. I have no thought as to how I would have reacted in the situations Laven has been forced into at such a young age.

Never in my life would I have made it out alive in the predicaments Laven has been in.

I turn to Apolla. "I will see you soon," I say while bringing her into an embrace. "I have to get to the Training Headquarters, there are new recruits."

She smiles. "Be nice, Amias Heracles."

I smile back mischievously. "Always."

* * *

When I reach the headquarters, Hua is standing at the doors with the young women and men who have requested enlistment.

Hua excuses herself from the herd of youth and strides across the distance to meet me halfway. Her eyes are glancing over me, examining, just as usual.

"They are all strong in mentality, but we shall see how strong they are physically. I am going to have them begin how we usually do, weighted swimming, long distance running, strengthening. We will take it day by day, they are rather young." She looks over her shoulder at the adolescents who talk amongst each other.

"Well," I say. "If you have this under control I will leave, I have other duties to tend to while you are with them."

Hua looks up at me and I glance away, I cannot bear to look at her longer than I need to.

"Amias," she says my name in a tone she once used to get me to bend at any need she wanted. She reaches out to touch me and I step backward.

Slowly, she creeps into my mind. Searching for something to latch on to that will tell her exactly what I am feeling. I block her out and she flinches at the sudden protection I put around myself . . . even from her.

We are both at a standstill, waiting for the other to talk first.

She begins. "You cannot stay angry with me forever."

"You," I point and step closer.

I close my eyes and inhale deeply, trying to control my emotions from bursting. "You do not get to tell me how to feel about this. And we are not speaking of this around so many people. Have a bit more respect than that, could you?"

Turning away from her I start to leave until she speaks again. "Fine, then we speak of it tonight."

Naturally I shake my head at her need to always have the final word.

Yet, I have no time to think about her any longer as I am called. "General, care to meet with me about an insignificant concern?" Evangeline, the leader of the grounds whenever Hua or I am gone approaches me. "We need to consider expanding each area of the Training Grounds, some of the men in our Mandem are not too pleased with being nicked by spears."

* * *

I give a slight nod to the owner of the market as I pass through in search of the vegetable stand.

The line at the stand is unbearably long, I nearly debate standing here for a short moment and telling my mother the food she sent me for they did not have. Although, if I return to her home without the vegetables she demanded I retrieve for her, I am certain her slipper will make its way off of her foot and towards my head with perfect aim.

"Hi Amias," a set of fair twin women say in unison as they walk by with bright red cheeks and smiles from ear to ear.

I only nod and continue on.

There is a slight chuckle from the woman in front of me after their passing and I tilt my head at her.

"May I know what entertains you?" I ask.

"No, you may not." Her tone is sharp yet soft. She does not turn around; she only speaks with her back toward me.

"And why is that?"

"Because I said you may not. You do not get to pester me as to why I tell you no."

The woman abruptly turns, and her eyes extend promptly, now realizing she is speaking to a royal.

I smile. "You are not as quiet as I thought you to be."

Maivena only stands there, with wide eyes.

I believe Laven may have his hands full with the attitude contained in this small woman.

"Lady Maivena, it does appear that you are next in line." I nod toward the man who patiently waits for her to move upwards.

Maivena places the small basket of vegetables in front of him. By the looks of it, there is not nearly enough food to serve two people in there. She and her father both cannot survive on this.

"Four silver coins," he says.

The small black pouch is pulled from the pocket of her long skirt, and the coins are poured into his palm. Every coin she had left.

Four silver dollars and she is barely capable of feeding herself.

I fathom I never understood the importance of money until I just witnessed it before my eyes. Four silver dollars to myself is nothing, to her it is everything and more.

She says no more to me before quickly walking off after her money is handed over for her fare. I follow right along behind her while digging for the gold coins in my vest.

She is expertly dodging through the small crowds of people to make her way out of the market. I know she is also aiming to run from me.

Trust me, Maivena, my goal is not to harm you. I would rather not wake in the midst of the night with both Laven and Naius holding daggers to my throat.

"Lady Maivena," I call as we escape the crowds.

We now enter the path leading to the woods that take you along the servant grounds. She now has free reign to walk even faster.

"Lady Maivena, a word please."

This time, she stops.

"I am no longer a Lady," her voice comes quietly. "You may call me only Maivena."

She turns around and her eyes meet mine once more.

I almost feel sorry for Laven, I am receiving a moment that should be his.

"Once you are a Lady, you are always a Lady."

Maivena stands there, pondering the thought, but not for long. "What may I help you with?" She questions.

I let go a short breath before looking at the now empty pouch dangling on her wrist. "You need more." She glances down at her wrist and her head slowly shakes.

"No, this is fine. I need nothing more."

"That is a lie you and I both know you are telling. I would like to give you more money, I only have gold dollars with me, but no one should question you of it. If they do, you may come to me or any of my brothers for help. Especially Laven." I believe he will kill the person asking why she has gold coins.

Her eyes broaden as she looks at the multitude of gold in my hand.

But, once again, her head shakes.

"No, I need no coin. I am fine. I will manage all right."

My eyebrows furrow. "You do so need this money—"

"I do not but thank you. I must go, my family is waiting for me."

But, as she walks away, she is turning down a path toward the city. Not her home.

I mind my boundaries and turn back to the market.

IT IS MIDNIGHT BY the time I reach my chamber, and when I arrive, Hua is walking in right behind me.

She stands at the door in her robe as she watches me undress.

"It was not my intention, Amias."

I bend a fake smile. "It may have not been your intention, but you did it." I stand up straighter after tying the laces of my night trousers and she is looking about the room. Looking everywhere but me.

"All our lives, you knew what I wanted. I always spoke of it, I prayed for it, Hua. I did not just pray for it with anyone, I begged to have it with you, and you knew this. Then, the second I have it, you rip it from me—"

"I did not mean to." She speaks so low I can almost not hear her.

"This is not something that can be replaced . . . I can never have another chance with this, all because you withheld the truth for years while letting me sink deeper and deeper. I have every right to stay angry with you for as long as I please. I am glad that you have come into who you are, but where does that leave me?"

Hua continues to quietly stand in the doorway.

I say nothing more.

I stall, conscious that it is coming.

In my mind, I can hear it before she speaks it aloud.

"I love you, Amias."

There is no comfort nor sanctuary in those words, there is only pain.

"Not in the way I need you to."

6
HANGING BY A THREAD

AMIAS HERACLES TORANDI

I seize falling to the floor as a searing pain shoots through my shoulder and down the entire right half of my body. I try to speak, but it feels as if my throat is closing with each breath I take. Then the pain moves, it navigates from the right half of my body and to the left, taking over my entire body. I try to grab something, bang anything, but I cannot. There is no purpose in moving a muscle; no matter how hard I try, the numbing sting will not allow it.

"Amias, Laven! What is happening?" Roaner bellows across the bond.

I cannot respond even if I try my hardest.

The door to my chamber bursts open. "Amias!" Hua shouts. "Amias, wake up!" She holds on to my shoulder, shaking me. Her knee barely grazes my skin, and I hiss in pain at the slight touch.

Hua's hands find my face. "Are you hurt? You must wake up, look at me."

The moment I open my eyes, I am begging for air to enter my chest as I desperately need a deep intake of breath. I look down at my arm as I gain back the strength within the right side of my body, and then the left. The pain is disappearing, and as it leaves, sweat begins to bead down my chest and neck.

"What happened?" Hua panics while looking over me, touching, exploring for a wound.

Sitting up, I look down at my hands—slowly opening and closing them.

"By the Gods, Amias, do not ever do that again." She shakes her head, gripping onto the long strands of my hair. Her forehead presses to my own as I still try to understand what has happened. "Are you hurt?"

"I do not know . . ." I touch my shoulder and leg, grateful to perceive something other than agony.

"What the fuck just happened? Laven! Amias!" Morano is now screaming for answers.

Whatever I felt, they must have felt it too.

"I do not know." I simply respond because that is the only answer I can form.

"Why is Laven not responding?" Roaner stresses.

There are loud drums from afar. Hua and I lift our heads at the sound. It gradually grows in capacity, rumbling through the night, and echoing off the walls. The beat does not signify danger.

I rush to the window seeing the ship from afar; the horns bellow out, moving across the sea and toward land.

"No," I shake my head. "Hua, it is not me that is hurt."

I dress at a speed quicker than I have ever moved.

Hua shadows my frantic path. "Then what was that?"

"That ship," I nod to the windows as I tie my trousers. "That is the ship Laven left on. Something is not right."

She grabs my arm, and I turn to her. "What you felt," she nods.

"Whatever happened to him, I went through it too. So did Roaner and Morano."

Her head shakes as she endeavors to understand. "How?"

"I do not understand yet, come." I nod my head forward for her to follow me. "There is a possibility that it is linked through the bond, but I cannot be too sure yet."

"Amias, if you do not tell me what the fuck is going on, I swear to the Gods I will—"

I quickly interrupt Morano. *"It is Laven. He is hurt; I will let you know what is happening after I see he is fine."*

The bond goes quiet.

We have not felt uneasiness like this since the day Laven was taken from us for prison.

The moment we are outside, I see them lowering a boat to get across the sea quicker.

"My Lord, may I help?" I turn to the servant; it is Maivena's father, Naius.

"Yes," I nod. "Please," I urge him quicker.

He kneels before the sand; his hands glow in a bright misty blue before disappearing beneath. His eyes close as he whispers low words of Old Voschantai tongue that I do not know. This language is much before my time of birth, even before Naius, who is centuries old.

My eyes widen as I watch the water turn to stone. It spreads from the beginning of the sand to the ship, creating a long path sturdy enough for them to cross over. Blue, thin spheres begin to spin beneath his palms before skipping over the water. The further they move, I notice the water still wholly, stopping the ship from swaying as the guards try to recede with Laven strapped to a cot.

The men far out in the sea stare down at the stone path, only frustrating me with their hesitance.

"They will have to rush," Naius calmly announces. "I will not be able to hold this for long. Poseidon is not fond of it when I do this. I do wish for my sleep this evening."

"Come, Alexanti! There is no time to yield!" I yell over the water and above the drums.

"Papa!" I rotate to the distant voice approaching, it is Maivena rushing to her father. Naius is still kneeling, his hands have returned to the sand, holding the path as the men run across. "What are you forcing him do?" She snaps, her glare blazes in my direction.

Something in her eyes flicker as she stares through me, and both Hua and I step away not knowing what she can do.

"It is fine, my girl. I proposed my aid." He tries to calm her.

"Maivena, I would never force your father to do something he did not request to." I speak in an attempt to diffuse the mounting situation. "He is only helping get the men across, and we are done from there, I promise."

Her eyes are still ablaze, and Hua quickly speaks. "It's Laven; he is hurt."

Maivena looks to the men who stop next to me, carrying Laven on the cot he is strapped to. As I look him over, blood has seeped through his thickly bandaged right shoulder. His black and silver-streaked hair is soaked in sweat, and his once brown skin is paling . . . and fast.

"What happened to him?" I walk toward the palace, and the carriers urgently pursue behind me.

"There was a rouge aboard our ship. It was hiding; Laven walked in unaware just hours ago. The rogue clawed him before—"

"Wait," Maivena runs over. "You will not want to keep him strapped to the cot, it—" her words are cut off as a guard swiftly backhands her cheek. As I reach out, her father appears behind her from ascension. He catches Maivena's head before she hits the sharp rock just below. Her gentle, frail body collides with the ground, and blood begins to form on her lip at the contusion.

She gives a weak smile to her father, his anger is rising within; quickly, she shakes her head, not wanting this to transpire any further.

Maivena sits up, hiding her face. I gust over to her, tearing cloth from my undershirt to rid the blood from her face. "I am all right," tears threaten to rain from her eyes as she chokes out her words. Her father wraps his arms around her tightly; that is about the only thing he is allowed to do. He cannot lay a hand upon the guard, not ever. But I will let him it if he tries.

"You do not speak over us." The guard's finger points at Maivena. Her father is shaking, threatening to phase into his Wolf that I know could be lethal after seeing the magic this man possesses.

"So help me God, Amias. If you do not kill him this instant!" The mind link between Laven and I loudly erupts.

Laven begins to yank viciously in the cot holding him down, he may be weak, but I have no second thought that this man will rip through the straps. The men struggle to hold him, and in their endeavor to calm him, they only make the situation worse. "Alexanti," Laven looks up at him, raging. "Touch me once more and I shall kill you the moment I am released from these fucking fastenings."

None of the men touch him again as he continues to thrash about.

One band pops, and I stand here; hoping he escapes to get his hands on this man.

Before Laven can fully tear loose, Hua's hand is already around the guard's neck. He gasps for air as she pushes forth the strength of her Wolf. Her hand tightens, and I wince, hearing a tendon snap in his neck—the sharply pointed length of her claws break through his skin.

"Let me make this very explicit," she wrenches his face, which is turning dark red, down to her own. Her Wolf's dark purple eyes stare deeply into his own. "I will drag your body into the sea and hold you there until you drown, lay your hand upon her again, and I will have your limbs torn off by the Water Dragons!" I jump as she throws him, and his spine collides with a nearby tree.

Her head turns in the direction of the other guards, and they flinch. "That message goes for the rest of you." They nod simultaneously, having no choice but to agree with what she has said.

"No, he does not get the alternative to live. Drown him in that fucking water for all I care."

I try to push out Laven's thoughts and focus on Maivena but he is loud in his demands.

"Maivena, what were you saying?" I ask, wiping the blood from her chin.

"No," her father interjects. "I am sorry, I cannot allow her to help if this is how she is treated when she speaks."

Maivena tries to put in a word, but her father's fear is evident. "No, Maivena. I will not allow it."

I look to Hua for help, and she shakes her head.

"Respect his wishes." Her voice is low as she speaks through our bond.

With a glare, I watch the guard who is still struggling to get up from his crash with the tree.

"You just could not keep your mouth shut and your hands to yourself." He flails beneath my shoe as I press into his neck. "If he dies, you die. And may the Gods help you when he tracks you down."

"Come!" I shout to the men as I storm to the palace. Hua stays back to walk Maivena and her father to the servant grounds.

I reach my hand out to the cot, ascending us from the shore and to Laven's chamber.

* * *

Carefully, we transfer him from the cot and to his bed. He is panting heavily, tugging at the cloth wrapped over his shoulder that is covered in blood. I can smell the healing herbs mixing with the copper scent of his blood; the more he tugs, the stronger the smell becomes.

"Stop before you make it worse!" I grab his hand, and his claws grow. His left arm swings up, attempting to death grip my neck in his forearm.

The men rush over, pinning down his only strong arm as the one that is bitten lays limp.

"Laven!" I grip him by his neck. "I swear, if you try to kill me, it will be the last time you ever try." His eyes begin to fade in and out from heterochrome hazel and blue to silver. "This is not you; it is the disease. We are getting help."

Quickly, I see it. I see his death in my arms and my jaw tightens as I swallow that hard lump growing in my throat.

There is no help.

There is only waiting for the disease to fully overcome him and his soul is taken away by Hermes after his death.

I turn to the door as I hear Hua approaching; Maivena walks in after with a large wooden box in her hands.

"I would like to help. If I am allowed." A bruise has grown on her face, I reach to heal her before Laven can see, but Hua's voice quickly flows through my mind. *"Do not. If you or any man in this room reaches to touch her or interact, I am afraid it will scare her off."*

I nod and move back to where I was previously standing.

"What about your father?" I ask.

Maivena still smiles given her previous encounter. "I will speak with my father; he will be fine."

She looks over Laven's face, and his eyes are already fixated on her. I step forward, knowing he is not exactly in the right mind; his Wolf could become fatal. He could live with himself if he hurt me because I can hold him off, but not this fragile woman. His woman.

"I thought you would never come." I say to Maivena.

There is a gentle shrug she gives as a piece of her response. "Laven is kind to me, the least I could do is try." Maivena looks at the long claw marks in his chest and she drifts to his right shoulder that is deeply bitten.

She opens the wooden box, pulling out a small glass concealed with a cork. There is an oil in the glass that she pours into a tiny bowl; she places droplets of some form of water in the bowl before swirling everything inside it.

"What is that?" A guard asks, and I have the ever-growing urge to smack him.

Maivena's bright green eyes lift, looking directly at him. "Poppy, jasmine, and willow oil."

"And that?" He asks, his eyebrows furrowed at the glowing, blue bits she puts into the mixture. It is spun together until it is dissolved, the oil and water begin to sparkle in the bowl.

"Moss, from the Tree of Gods." She calmly responds.

"What will this do?" Hua asks.

"The poppy, jasmine, and willow will put him to sleep." Maivena answers. "The moss will heal him."

There are legends about that tree, not only legends—many if not all stories have been proven to be accurate that the Tree of Gods has healing capabilities like no other.

It is sacred to Old Quamfasi and guarded by them every moment of the day.

Maivena hovers above Laven; he intakes a sharp breath at her gentle hand lifting his neck.

"I am sorry, I must help you lift your head." Her voice is gentle as she speaks.

Trust me; it is not the pain he is feeling. I stifle my laugh.

Then it occurs to me . . . this is the first time she has ever touched him.

She is holding a petal from a poppy flower above him; her finger probes his mouth open as she places the petal beneath his tongue.

The laugh I am holding almost erupts at how he quietly groans at her touch. Hua smacks my arm, and I clear my throat.

"What is funny about this?" She asks.

Then, I remember, I have not told her what we now know. *"I will explain later."*

"Why is he allowing her near him so simply?" A guard retorts.

Laven's only functioning hand softly grabs Maivena's hand that contains the mixture she is trying to give him. His eyes cut at the man, and he deeply growls at him.

Even in this state, he knows her.

"Shh," Maivena quiets Laven.

She helps him to drink the concoction, and it is only seconds before he is fading away.

The men move from the bed as Laven sleeps, and Maivena begins to clean his wounds. Her shoulders rest when I dismiss the guards, and I question just how much damage they have inflicted on our servants.

I sit down in a chair near the bed. "Would you mind telling me exactly what the Tree of Gods' moss can do?"

"No, I do not mind," she shakes her head as she continues to clean the gash across his chest and shoulder. "What do you want to know?"

"Why not topically put it on his wounds? Why have him drink it?"

Maivena finishes wiping away the excess blood on his skin and around his wounds.

"You can do both; with the extent of his injuries, I made sure to have him consume it and receive it topically. It will move through his bloodstream, cleansing it before the infection can spread any further. A rouge bite deeply affects the mind; the moss will cleanse his soul. After I finish cleaning his wound, I will topically apply it, I would have threaded his lesions, but he is already healing on his own—at a languid pace. The moss will get into the abrasion and discharge the infection. So this wound will need to be cleansed frequently."

Hua steps closer. "Will he be fine tomorrow? He is not going to die, is he?"

Maivena pushes the glowing moss into his lacerations. It is almost as if it is alive; specks of light flicker through the blue moss like stars.

I lean in closer, staring unbelievably at the particles of this sacred tree.

"Watch it," Hua teases, *"it may poke your eye out."*

Smirking, I look back at her as she also stares in amazement.

"No, Laven will live. He will need to rest the next seven days, as much as possible. He will be weak for quite some time, and his connection with his Wolf will need to be strengthened. Someone must watch over him in the nights to come to be sure he is healing and not fussing with the bandaging. Half of his body is completely weakened; that will also take time for strength to rebuild."

Hua smiles. "You seem to be the only one capable out of us three."

Maivena is hesitant to respond. As she looks down at a sleeping Laven again, she nods.

"The connected chamber is for times as this," I begin. "You can stay in the chamber through that door, since it is the closest you can reach him. But, for now, I believe it best we stay here through the night. I will be down the hall in his study, as it seems I will be taking over more for the next week."

Hua stays with Maivena in the large chamber, urging her to sit by the fire and warm her thin frame.

Laven will argue with me over this decision, but it is indeed what is best. Maivena has healed him like no other I have seen, better than our doctors. She will continue to help him, treat him, and care for him as he needs for the next seven days. Either he agrees or not.

She may also be the cure to this disease that we have been looking for.

7
OLD PROMISES

LAVEN HEPHAESTUS ARVENALDI, II

I try to sit up, but whatever the hell she made me drink is impairing my vision and agility. The pain in my shoulder is still there, almost bearable, but there. As I try to move my arm, I hiss, falling back into the bed. The cloth is wet and cold beneath me, and I can feel a new sweat beckoning.

"Be careful," her scent vigorously hits me, stronger than the herbs she made me drink. Yet she is hovering above me with another tea in the small wooden vessel.

I do not know if I am panting because of how close she is or because of a new fever threatening to rip from my skin. The bandages begin to itch, I know I should leave them, yet I cannot help it.

Maivena catches my wrist; she pleads another warning for me to be careful, reminding me not to touch any of the rather slowly healing wounds.

I attempt to sit up again; this time, I have her help. She grips my stronger hand while supporting the other side of my body.

"Here," her voice is but a whisper, I still my vision on her. She is bringing the vessel to my lips, her hand grazing from my shoulder to my neck, shooting a shiver down my spine. I grunt in replacement of the moan that menaces from my chest.

I look down to the steaming liquid questionably and raise an eyebrow. "I would think you are trying to sedate me again." I speak lazily, and I still fight keep my eyes open—to look at her without hazing sight.

I espy the corner of her lips raising at my remark . . . then I see it. The large bruise on her cheek nearly reaching her eye, the split in her lip, and the cut in her chin.

The hazing in my vision is gone. I push away the vessel she holds, and her eyebrows furrow.

I summon every bit of strength I have left, sluggishly, I bring my only hand I can use upward. She looks down, the faint golden glow flickers in my left palm—my healing capabilities are faltering in my current state. I heavily breathe through the weakened parts of me to will every bit of healing power I can.

Maivena grabs my hand and leisurely shakes her head. A smile on her face appears and soon fades.

"I can heal that," I force out the words.

"You should not weaken yourself more; savor your energy. I am fine," she tries to bring the tea to my lips again, and I move my face away.

I attempt once more, pulling forth more pieces of strength I have to heal her.

"It may not work."

"And why would that be?" Annoyance is laced through my tone.

"Your body is trying to use its own healing abilities to cure itself. Please, do not waste the last of your energy you have tonight on–"

"Do not say what I think you are about to." I concentrate again, ignoring her pleas. If it is the last thing I do tonight before blacking out, it will be to heal her face. Fuck that tea in her hands.

"Come closer," I beckon. That salty citrus scent rocks through me, almost knocking me unconscious as she closes in.

I grunt through it again and reach out as Maivena hesitantly sits closer; my palm is steadily glowing in its healing shade of gold.

"You are weakening . . . do not. You–"

"*Hush*, Maivena," I say in a pant.

I lean in closer as my hand gently touches her bruised cheek. "It will tingle," I warn.

She slightly jumps as the bruise slowly fades, taking her purplish skin back to its glorious brown shade. I cannot look her in the eyes; if I do, I will completely lose focus.

The cut in her lip seals over, fading her softly rounded chin back to normal.

The moment I try to look into her eyes, I cannot.

I nearly collapse into the bed, feeling rendered short of all energy and power. But, instead, she catches me by the arm and holds me up.

Maivena coos. "Thank you."

"Do not—do *not* thank me . . . it is my absolute *right* to take care of you."

I can feel her gaze studying my face, even as my eyes are closed now.

I always know when she is watching me. Even when she thinks I do not realize, I feel those green eyes at any given moment.

I begin to sway, but that one hand manages to keep me steady enough to bring that damn vessel to my lips that she has been shoving at me.

"It is a pain-relieving tea; it will help keep you asleep as well." She informs, realizing my avoidance.

Finally, I drink it, tasting the essence of chamomile and jasmine.

Maivena slowly lays me down, keeping my naked body covered with the sheet, anything heavier will make this fever worse than it already is. I do recall fighting with Amias as he removed my clothing, so Maivena did not have to.

She moves to stand, but I call after her.

"Remember that promise I made you?" I ask. "Seven years ago. *That* promise."

My death wishes upon anyone who harms her.

She is slow to respond as she fumbles around with something on the nightstand. "Yes," she mumbles.

"He is next."

"LAVEN, YOU MUST BATHE, you smell like–like *shit*." I weakly open my eyes to Amias hovering above me.

"I will change the bedding," Maivena says. "But if he is too weak to get out of bed, he should rest more."

I lazily smirk. "She says I should rest more."

"You weakling." Amias glowers. *"You are eating this up, are you not? You just love being treated so tenderly by her."*

"Yes, I do. And I will be weak for as long as I can while she gladly heals me."

Maivena clears her throat from across the room, watching Amias still hover above me. Neither of us are speaking aloud. To her, we are only staring at each other with smirks on our faces, our faces that are relatively too close to seem casual.

"I–I can leave if you. I just–if you both are–" her words jumble, and my face beats red.

"She believes I am trying to fuck you." Amias grins.

"Get the fuck out of my face!" I reach up my arm that is still in good health, pushing him far away before Maivena thinks any more than she already has.

"It was the mental bond. We were only talking," Amias smiles and sits in a corner chair.

She refuses to look at us and I shoot a warning glare at Amias, who is suppressing his laughter.

Maivena gathers a food tray as Roaner and Morano ascend into the room with smiles on their faces. I can feel their judgmental words fighting to escape their mouths before they say them.

"You just had to get beaten up by a rogue." Morano chuckles.

Roaner goes to speak, but he stops. He looks toward Maivena, who is standing against the wall, one hand hidden behind her back. Looking down at the table next to her; only the sheath that holds my dagger is sitting there. Her chest is rising and falling rapidly. Her fear lingers like a heavy cloud over the room.

Too many. There are too many men in this room for her to feel comfortable.

Roaner and Morano sense something is off as well.

I watch only her. And the death grip on my dagger behind her back.

Roaner takes a step backward, creating more distance between him and Maivena. Morano follows in his lead, taking a stride backward as well.

"Maivena."

She ignores me.

Her eyes are only fixated on Roaner and Morano, she even glances over Amias.

"They will not—"

"How do you know." She interrupts.

She is not asking questions. She is demanding.

She is only focused on the two new faces that have entered the room.

I force myself to sit up, the pain in my shoulder eats me alive. Then, groaning lowly at the near numbing agony, I push further through it.

"Bonded by blood or not, Maivena, if they ever fucking thought of it—"

"Which we would never," Morano growls.

Roaner's Wolf is dancing in his eyes. I can sense the same anger in him as the day he killed the men who assaulted his mother.

"As I was saying," I continue. "Bonded by blood or not, they would suffer just like the rest did." There is confusion on her face after I speak but she does not look at me.

Did she not believe me when I said I will rid the world of the men who hurt her?

I grip the bedding, stopping myself from screaming at the pain radiating through my body as I move across the, nearing closer to where she is.

"Maivena, look at me." I plead.

She does not respond; she still has that steady grip on the dagger hidden behind her back.

I turn toward Roaner, Morano, and Amias.

They all nod before leaving the room, shutting the door quietly.

"I–" she begins.

I hold my hand out. "Come here," I speak low and tenderly.

Maivena immediately, but stiffly, walks toward the bed, stopping where I am seated.

Her shaking fingers place the dagger in mine; I toss it onto the bed and take both of her hands in my one. The only hand I am capable of using.

"Breathe," I look to the woman whose eyes only stare at our conjoined palms. She finally takes in a sharp breath, her corset slowly rises and falls. "They will never touch you. *Ever*."

"But how do you know?" Her voice cracks before her cheeks flood with tears that fall against our hands.

I tug on her hands that I still hold; my stomach tightens, feeling her fingers gripping mine back. Those generous green orbs finally look up, and the wind is sucked from me. This is the look I have always feared seeing—pure sadness and fright. "I cannot be the one to explain it. What I can do is help you trust them. I could tell you all day that I know they could never bear the thought of harming you or any woman in any form. Nonetheless, in the end, it is you that must develop the trust there. I cannot do it for you, but I can help you."

She nods. "I–I am sorry. I was not going to use the dagger–"

"Do not apologize for this. You have every right to fear any man who just glances at you. You are one devastatingly beautiful creature, Maivena. It is a blessing and a wretched curse to be a woman in this world. And I can protect you from anything and everyone, and when I am not around, they will. Although, that dagger you wielded in mere seconds may convince me that you know how to defend yourself."

I continue to stare upon her. I cannot make out a single emotion in her eyes, yet I know she feels entirely safe right here. Right where she is.

I smile, and I see her lips twitch. "Who taught you to use a dagger?"

"My father." She whispers.

"If you would like," I offer. "I can arrange training for you so your memory is refreshed on wielding all weapons." If she is ever alone, as Amias said she was when leaving him at the market, I need her to know how to defend herself.

He told me of the direction she was going, and it is the exact direction of the brothels in the city.

"I will need to speak with my father, he will want to be present or request to be the one to reteach me. With the restrictions of servants not being allowed to train, unless supervised or permitted, I have not been trained in years."

"Did he teach you to wield any other weapons?"

"A bow and a sword, but I am not great with a sword." She shakes her head.

As I try to question her comfortability with other weapons I can feel Roaner tugging on the bond before speaking. *"May I come in? It is only me."*

"Roaner is outside. Are you fine with him coming in? He will stay by the door."

Maivena glances between the door and me.

"You can say no."

She shakes her head. "I am fine."

"If you frighten her," I warn.

"I would never. Is she all right if I come in?"

"Yes," I answer. *"Move gradually. Let her see every movement you make."*

The door pushes open, and the strings of his untied undershirt are dripping with blood. Maivena steps closer to me and I cut my eyes at him.

"It is done."

"*What* is done?" I snap.

"His name was Curtus." Roaner fixates on Maivena. "The guard who laid his hand upon your face . . . more than once. He admitted to it."

I do not dare to look at her or think of the number of times that fucking man has tried to put his paws all over her.

"How did you do it?" I ask.

Roaner looks down at my hand that still holds Maivena's. Then, as fast as possible, she tugs away and takes multiple steps backward.

And so suddenly, that moment I was cherishing is gone. And I do not know when I could ever get it back.

Roaner holds his hand up that is coated in fresh, dry blood, and I nod.

"I took his throat." He says all too casually. "There are consequences for these acts Maivena, always."

8
THE DRAGON

LAVEN HEPHAESTUS ARVENALDI, II

Maivena has left to help a servant in the kitchen now that my brothers are here to watch over me. It allows Roaner and Morano to inform Amias and me of any further information found on the rogues that are roaming.

"Well?" Morano asks while staring at my shoulder and chest still covered in medical wrapping.

Roaner is near, tying the strings of his newly clean, white linen shirt. "How are you still *you*?" He crosses his arms while looking me over curiously.

Morano adds. "It is rare, Laven. For someone to survive being bitten or even scratched by the disease in those rogues."

"Not rare, impossible," Amias corrects. "The only reason he was saved is because of Maivena. She and her father have access to the Tree of Gods just outside of Xenathi; the moss is what she used to not only help heal the wound but cleanse his soul from being overtaken."

Morano scoffs. "That tree is like the God's blood."

"They did not tell us of it while we were in Xenathi," Roaner announces. "I forgot it still existed."

"There is reason," Amias begins. "That tree is sacred, a gift to Old Quamfasi from Artemis since the beginning of their reign. After Vallehes and Penelope were dethroned they made it seem as if the tree was destroyed so people will forget it—a constructed lie to minimize attacks on them for the tree while at their weakest. But some did not forget.

"Maivena and Hua spoke after she cured Laven; she begged Hua not to tell anyone of the tree and what it did for him. It has already been sought after by other realms, and plenty of her people have died while protecting

it. She wants no more harm brought to them." And most importantly, Lorsius.

"Then we lie," I say.

Morano laughs as he shakes his head. "And say what? Those fucking guards run their traps far and wide. I would not put it past them to have already shouted from the bell tower that Maivena used the Tree of Gods to heal you."

"They will not," Amias holds his hand up to calm Morano. "I had their memory cleaned of what she did last night for that specific reason. They were already asking too many questions for her liking; I could see it in the way her shoulders tensed."

"And what will we say when they ask how he is surviving and is still his normal self?" Morano pushes further for more answers.

"We say it was the Gods, say it was the blessing they put over us on Summer Solstice during the Blood Bond Ritual." I try to bring movement to my right shoulder, but I can feel the pain pulling, and I stop.

Roaner responds with a light shrug, nodding at my plan.

I glance between both Roaner and Morano. "We must discover a way to get to it secretly. This alliance with New Quamfasi must be formed sooner than later."

Roaner pulls a folded paper from his pocket and hands it over to Amias. "The High King of Provas was visiting Xenathi while we were. You know he has always been in close contact with the Quamfasian people."

"Because most Old Quamfasian's have a strong bloodline of Fae in them, practically making them Hybrids, but not enough to form wings." I pick at the dried blood on my arm. "What does that say?" I look at Amias as he rubs the hair on his chin, and he hands me the paper.

"He is coming."

I skim over the letter. "He wants an alliance?"

Stravan is King of the largest realm in Voschantai, what could he be in need of?

"I will show you." Roaner says, reading my thoughts, and he projects their meeting with Stravan to all of us.

The doors to the Consultation Room force open and Morano is taking long strides towards me, he stands at my side and I can sense his unease.

Before he can tell me what is wrong, I see him.

Stravan, High King of the Realm of the Fae.

'He wants to speak with us.' *Morano personally informs me.*

'Of what?'

'I have not a clue,' *he stands taller as Stravan swarms closer.* 'We are about to find out.'

Stravan smiles at both Morano and me before turning to Vallehes. 'Vallehes, may I have the room for a moment, please?'

Vallehes smiles. 'Sure.' *He all too smoothly replies before ascending from the Consultation Room.*

'What may we be of service to you for?' *I immediately ask, breaking the silence before it drags on for too long.*

'Dyena, my wife. She has been missing and I need help finding her. It has been years and I have scoured all lands possible, all but Vaigon and Misonva, the Realm of the Vampires. So, now, I am in need of your help. If you could,' *he holds out a folded letter that is sealed with black wax and Fae wings imprinted into it.* 'Give this to High Prince Laven, I believe it will be better suited in his hands than the High King.'

"Did you know he tore almost half of Galitan to pieces?" The Sorcerer's Realm. That was two years ago, if not more. They fed him false information of where his mate could be, and he reacted.

If I remember one thing from those years, I recall the validation that came over me. I am not the only person in this universe willing to ruin lives for the one they love.

"Considering I do not know how many of them he has, I could not answer that." Roaner remarks.

"He has four," I confirm.

"An angry, lonely father and four children who miss their mother are coming to visit us. How fucking wonderful." Morano sarcastically cheers.

"They are all Fire Dragons," I say. "The largest is Tuduran; Stravan will be riding him." I track back to the names of the others. "There is Nara; she is white and silver, close in size with Tuduran. Next, Calypton, he is a deep red, almost brown. Last is Vion; she is dark green with scales of white on her chest."

"What does Tuduran look like?" Amias asks, visibly disturbed. He begins to itch as he always does in situations that make him uneasy.

"He looks like Stravan's wings. Jet black, scaled in iridescent blues and silver. To see either of them in the night sky would be impossible. But anyone could feel them near."

Morano shakes his head. "Fantastic."

"If we ally with the Fae we have an immediate connection with Quamfasi," Roaner points to the letter. "Whatever it is that Stravan needs of us, we ask for what we need in return."

Amias nods. "We ask him to get moss from the tree."

"We must respond soon," Roaner voices while walking to the whiskey table in the corner of my chamber. "That letter is just his request to come. Respond when you are healthy, we will want him to visit when you are at your strongest."

"Let me have one of those." I nod to Roaner as he finishes pouring into his glass vessel.

"Ah, ah," Amias waves his finger. "Nurse Maivena would not suggest you drink alcohol in your state."

"Speaking of Maivena, I looked her up in our books," Morano admits. "She is precisely the same age as us, five and twenty. Why has she not phased into her Wolf yet?"

"That is a question I have been asking myself for years. Unfortunately, I could not give you an answer," I take the glass from Roaner as he hands it to me.

The dark liquor warms my chest, leaving that satisfying burn in the back of my throat.

It is easy to tell when someone has shifted into their Wolf. There is a deep feeling within us that calls, not just us, but our inner being. It is the grasp of our Wolves knowing each other through profoundly rooted bloodlines while we, as people, exist on our own.

"I can look into it if you'd like." Roaner offers.

Immediately, I shake my head. "None of you will pry into her life and the decisions she makes. She will tell me if she wants to; all I need you three to do is watch over her. She will speak to me when she wishes."

They all nod in unison.

"When does Lorsius return?" Amias dryly asks.

"When he gets the border under control in Gordanta." Which will take who knows how long, the border is out at sea, making it more challenging to fulfill what Misonva is asking for.

Morano smiles, hearing my thoughts. "Ah, Misonva."

"Misonva wants the treaty rewritten." I inform them. "The border along the water is too close to their land; they want it pushed further into Gordanta, so their sea has more acreage."

"It would not be hard to fix," Amias shrugs. "Your uncle makes every task harder than it must be because he is a fucking asshole. The troubles between Gordanta and Misonva should have been left up to me to handle."

"Yes," I nod. "It should have, but I needed you here." I remind him.

"We would not be dealing with this at all if Lorsius was not so stingy with land that is not his to begin with." Roaner grumbles over his glass as he swirls the dark liquor.

The door to the attached chamber creaks as it opens, Roaner's eyes widen, and he moves swiftly across the room. The short glass in my hand is gone, and he shoves it toward Morano.

"You will not get me in trouble." He harshly whispers in response after I curse at him.

The three of them ascend from the room in a quiet fit of laughter just as Maivena enters the chamber with a basket of fresh healing herbs.

9
STRONG SOULED

LAVEN HEPHAESTUS ARVENALDI, II

Maivena peers down at me as I flinch; she cleans and redresses the wounds on my arm and shoulder while explaining that I have a much farther way to go than a week. I mentioned fully walking on my own in a week's time and she quickly protested it.

"Does that hurt?" She asks, gently squeezing my forearm again.

"No," I shake my head. "It feels tight."

"It is your circulation trying to correct itself; it is trying to flow new blood while dispersing the spoiled blood here," she touches the wound on my shoulder. She grabs my hand and turns it over, three of her fingers press against my scarred palm, they glide upward and directly over the tight spot in my forearm.

Maivena repeats the action a few times over.

I look up at her, and she is thoroughly focused on my arm; her hold is firm yet soft—the press of her three fingers dragging directly in that same back and forth path.

"Who taught you to do this? To be a Healer."

"Mrs. Patro, the head of the kitchen."

I nod. "Yes, I know Mrs. Patro. Her cooking is remarkable."

Maivena gives her usual small smile while still focusing on my arm. "It is."

"What are your favorites?"

A complete smile this time, my head tilts, wanting a better view—my own stupid grin matching her own.

"She makes my father and I a fish stew at the end of the week; it is full of different potatoes, carrots, celery, kale, onions, and whatever seasonings and herbs she puts in it." Another drag of her fingers pulls me closer.

"What else?"

There is a shift in her. "Mostly that."

My eyebrows furrow. "Is that all you like?"

"That is mostly what I eat," she speaks lowly. "The stew will last my father and me the week; we get replenished again after the five days."

"What about fruit?" There is ease from the tightness in my arm, but the rest of my body continues to be tense due to this conversation.

"Fruit is a delicacy here; my father and I cannot afford fruit." Her hands pull from my arm, and she walks away from the bed, grabbing a warm cloth from a rather hot bowl of water. She shakes the fabric over the bowl and steam evaporates into the air as it cools down. She then proceeds to clean the blood from my shoulders.

"When was the last time you had fruit?"

"It has been a while." Is all she says.

Since before she arrived here . . .

"Your father, how long has he been here?"

She dips the cloth into the water, ringing it out, and cleans more of the skin on my arm. "He came here looking for me; he offered Lady Apolla a hand in working here as long as he could be with me. She placed my father as a Warrior in the Mandem."

"Do you not have siblings?" I ask as she helps me sit up straighter to clean my back.

"Oh, I do," Maivena nods. "I have a little brother; he is not here—he lives with my grandparents in Provas."

"The guards took you from Provas?"

"No, we lived in Xenathi then; my father moved my brother to Provas when we realized it was no longer safe for him."

It leisurely comes together.

"They brought you here in his place."

She continues to clean off the old blood on my shoulder.

"He deserved a full life; he needed somewhere to grow, mature, and be safe. He did not need to come here."

I turn, looking back at her from the corner of my eye. "And you did not deserve all of that?"

"I am older; it was my place to do it. Would you not?"

My blood runs cold at the littlest thought of remembering how I failed to save my sister's life. I could not imagine the might she holds knowing her brother is safe at home.

"Yes, I would." I respond, unable to deny that datum.

My sister is already gone. If either of my brothers fell into suffering, I would lay my soul down for them without a beg for return of it. Even if there was a way to bring my sister back to life, I would give my soul over so she could live the life she deserved.

Maivena shifts from behind me to rinse the cloth.

"That does not mean you do not deserve those things just because you were older. You were still young, too young to be here." Too young being chased after by these perverted men. "Where was your mother throughout this?"

"Both of my parents were away that day; afterward, my mother left with Ira for Provas."

The water that is being rung from the cloth drips into the water bowl; the sound practically bounces off the walls around us in this silence.

"Ira?" I question.

"My brother."

It is rare that siblings do not have names that begin with the same letter.

I choose not to question it.

I let the silence sit over us this time.

The only sound is our breathing and the dripping of water into the bowl.

The doors to my chamber burst open, and my mother and Axynth, Amias's father, come rushing toward me. Maivena makes haste as she backs away to allow room, her posture changes, and her eyes quickly find the floor.

"My Gods, Laven, I told you to be careful!" My mother gasps as she grabs my face and looks me over.

"I am fine, healing over as well as I can be."

Axynth steps closer, smirking as he pokes my wounded shoulder; I only wince, not giving him the satisfaction of any further reaction. He has a pestering personality just like his child, Amias.

"How did you survive this?" Axynth asks. His face scrunches up as he sees the swelling and redness on my arm. "It is never heard of to come out as yourself after an attack."

Maivena quickly looks upward, she steps forward to speak, but I beat her to it.

"The blessing from the God's." This is not entirely false. "The blessing the day of the Blood Bond Ritual." I make it more transparent.

My mother grabs Axynth's arm. "This was what I was explaining earlier, that the boys would not be affected like others because of the blessings. And given Amias's abilities as a shield, they should not be as harmed as others since part of his blood runs through them after the ritual.

"I am so sorry I could not have been here sooner; the Priestesses need my and Vyn's help. I came back to town as soon as I–" I grab her hand, stopping her long and drawn-out apologies.

"Ma, I am fine. I have been taken care of better than others can say they have been."

She touches my cheek again and turns to Maivena, whose eyes are still cast to the floor. She stands from the bed and stealthily walks across the wooden floors to stand before Maivena. Her hand reaches outward, gently lifting her chin.

"Maivena, it is?" Maivena is given that beautiful smile my mother has always held. Even through her worst days, she smiles.

'I smile because you never know whom you can come across that may need to see it.' So, she always said when I was a child.

She nods. "Yes."

"You are General Fondali's eldest." Axynth says from across the room.

I look from Maivena to Axynth.

General's daughter?

Axynth glances at me and back to Maivena.

"I am," her voice trembles. "My father is the former General of Quamfasi's Mandems."

That would make her father high ranking royalty . . . and herself. That is why she looked so well-nourished when she arrived. But, of course, Lorsius did not have the guards take just any girl; they took the eldest female child of a General.

"Well, Maivena," my mother starts. "You have grown to be a magnificently talented Healer, especially one without education."

"Thank you." She nods.

Maivena looks over my mother's dress. The long purple silk fabric is stitched in gold, just grazing the floor. The sleeves are fitted to her arms and meet at a point, wrapping around her middle finger. Purple has always accented her dark skin, which is why she is seen in the color often. Her light brown hair that was in its coily curls when I last saw her are now in perfect knotless braids.

"We have an academy for Healers—Vuamsati Academy of Healing, in Vuamsati, of course. I would love it if you could visit it with me tomorrow. I can have the boys watch over Laven while I take you."

Maivena gives her a weak smile. "I do wish I could, but my father and I do not have enough pay for a single class."

"I do," Maivena's wide eyes quickly look toward me. She does not need to speak; her facial expression is already speaking loudly for itself.

"It is the least he could do after you brought him nearer to health. And I cannot allow your abilities to go to waste; we have done this before with other servants when we see their strengths."

My mother's hands rest on Maivena's thin shoulders.

"What will I wear?" Maivena asks. "Am I allowed to go in this?"

"I can have that arranged too." The expression I receive from her is softer; for the first time, I think I can see a glimpse of happiness there. It gleams the longer she looks at me.

"I do believe you can thrive there, Maivena."

She smiles at my mother, nodding again, not finding any words to say aloud.

"Oh, Axynth." My mother raises a finger. "We must go; Vyn is waiting for us in my study."

Axynth smiles while shoving a hand through his white hair. "Yes, she is. It was nice meeting you Maivena," he looks towards me. "And you, we will discuss High King Stravan's arrival later; Amias informed me of it just as I arrived back. We will plan when you are in full health."

I nod at him before he and my mother ascend from my chamber.

Looking over at Maivena, she is already watching me.

Her voice is but a whisper. "Thank you; you did not have to do that."

"I told you, it is my right to take care of you, and if that means getting you out of here and far away from this palace." And me. "I will do it . . . you too need somewhere to grow and prosper, Maivena."

I see a quiver in her chin; she hurriedly hides it and replaces it with a smile.

"Not only for that, but hiding the truth about the Tree of Gods as well. It is sacred to my people; they fight every day to protect it." Her fingers fumble around with one another. "Thank you, truly."

"Taking care of you does not mean only taking care of you; it means taking care of everyone else that comes along with you."

"You are different from the rest; I wish my friends at home could see it."

I shake my head. "You seeing it is all I care about, I could not give a damn what anyone else thinks of me."

There is a quiet laugh that escapes her. "My father used to say that to my mother."

I grin like a fool. "Your father is a smart man."

"I should finish wrapping your shoulder." She points.

I begin to wonder how much longer I will need to be bedridden; I am growing sick of having Amias and Morano help me bathe every day.

As I count the days of healing I should have left, I then remember.

Meet me at the East Lake ten sunsets from today. I will be awaiting you in the courtyard; find me in the maple tree.

"Yesterday, did you by chance meet anyone?" The fingers that were quick to work on my shoulder freeze in motion.

"No," she continues wrapping my arm.

"And what about that letter you received?"

She glances down at me. "How do you know about that?"

I grin. "I know of every letter that passes on to my servants. So, why did you not go?"

She studies me and I could wither beneath her stare.

"Because I do not meet with people I do not know."

I smirk. "Good girl."

A sudden, sharp pain shoots through my leg, and I grunt, falling back into the pillows. I have had about enough of this shit.

"Here, drink." She helps me lift my head and raises the steaming tea to my lips. It is the pain-relieving tea, but also that tea she sedates me with, and that is exactly what it does.

* * *

'Twelve men, Laven.' My uncle says as he stands over me. 'A season here in this prison per man if you do not speak about what you did.'

'And counting,' I add.

Lorsius steps nearer. 'What did you just say?'

I aggressively shake the chains gripping my wrists as I stare into his eyes. 'Did you hear that?'

'Yes, I fucking heard that.'

'Good, then you will hear me when I say Benjamin was not the last. There are plenty more bodies you will never find.'

My father who is standing far off in the corner furrows his eyebrows and his eyes shut as he pinches the bridge of his nose. He has tried to seep into my mind but knows he cannot. I am the one person whose mind my father cannot barricade.

His straight white hair falls around his face as his head cascades forward.

'I cannot do this,' *Lorsius says turning to his brother, my father.* 'You deal with him, he is your son.'

My father faces Lorsius. 'If I recall, I never told you to come here in the first place.'

'My Kingdom is finally well, and my nephew and Heir decides to murder twelve men and I am expected to just not speak to him about it? What does that say about me?'

'Because he is your nephew you leave it alone.' *My father is now in Lorsius face. Standing a solid four inches above him.* 'Your blood, Lorsius. Not a prisoner, not a captive, your blood. Our blood.'

'No one is above the law.' *Lorsius says in a hardened tone.*

There is rooted hatred laced in those words.

'Really?' *I question as I stare at the blood slowly dripping down my wrists.* 'Does the law not apply to you?'

'I do not need to listen to a child.'

'I would mind myself if I were you,' *my father retorts.* 'That child has killed men stronger than you.'

Lorsius stands there, waiting for us to say another thing.

We do not and he leaves.

My father walks forward and kneels in front of me as I sit on the wet ground.

His hand steadily hovers over my bruised and bleeding wrists, healing them.

'Why did you do it?' *He asks as the golden hues glowing from his palms reach my hands, ridding them of any pain and injury.*

'You would not understand.' *I mumble a response.*

'I cannot hear you when you mumble.'

I speak louder. 'You would not understand why I did it.'

He is smirking. 'Try me.'

'No,' I pull from the conversation. 'Another day.'

'If you do not speak with me, then who? The boys are only allowed to visit you sparingly, if not ever. You have already refused to allow your sister to see you in here and the both of you are thicker than blood. Your mother and Roaner are comforting Levora at all hours of the day because you are closer to being on death row than being forgiven. 'There is only me Laven. I have a place to know why my son has lost his fucking mind, and I have even more of a place to know if it was rightful what you did or if you need help.'

'Get me out of here alive and I will tell you everything. I promise.'

He grips my black and white streaked hair. 'You are an Arvenaldi, born from the blood of Orviantes. Strong souled. We never die, Laven.'

Before he lets go of my hair, he kisses my forehead and stands. 'I will tell everyone you give them your greetings.'

Hours have passed since my father has been gone, hours since anyone has been in here. With each hour I have watched the sun fall deeper into the sea as I sit on the edge of the open cell at the top of the tower.

I hear the heavy stone door slide open, I crane my head in the direction and two guards walk in. The same two from last night who thought they could torture it out of me, what I did to their friends.

They near closer. One lowers down, his face hovering right over my own. 'We will do this every day until you confess.'

'I hope you have enough stamina for a threat as that.'

He grabs me by my hair and I begin to fight back as much as I can being confined by chains.

My shirt is being torn from me sleeve by sleeve until it is in shreds on the ground.

The sound of cracking whips echoes through the cell and my head is forced to the ground.

'Laven!' My name is shouted from somewhere, but I cannot find where.

'Laven!' The voice is strangled.

'Laven, have you gone mad! Let her go!'

Upon opening my eyes and I see Roaner tugging Maivena from my grasp; coming to, I release her neck from my hand. Immediately, she begins gasping for air, a hoarse cough ripping through her as Roaner falls to the floor holding her.

I stare at what I have done. I stare until I am calling for her over her strangled breathing

"Give her a moment," Roaner serenely speaks to only me. *"I think she is aware you were dreaming; she was trying to wake you. Let her regulate her breathing first."*

"How did you arrive so quickly?"

He is slow to respond. *"The nightmare went down the bond again."*

"Fuck, Roaner, I am sorry."

"Do not ever apologize for that. Those guards are lucky it was your father to kill them and not me."

Roaner touches the back of her neck and I can already see the golden glow in his hand healing her of the damage caused.

I do not dare to look away from her until she finally catches a solid breath of air.

I swallow past the knot growing in my throat. "Maivena?"

Roaner helps her stand, and she fixes the white linen robe that is loose around her shift. I can feel her withdraw as she takes a step away.

She glances upward and our eyes meet.

You know I would never intentionally harm you.

"You were having a nightmare . . . it is fine."

Roaner looks between the both of us. "I will be in the hall; I can come back to check on you both." The moment he is gone, I am trying to stand again, but it is no use. Maivena rushes over as my hand slips on the spilled tea over the nightstand.

Her hands wrap around my arm as she struggles to lift me back onto the bed; I gently grab her arm as she turns to clean the mess of tea I made on the nightstand.

"I am sorry, I would not–"

"I know," she stops me from continuing my apology. "You were having a nightmare. Those reactions are normal."

"I could have killed you . . ." I choke on my own words, and I see her step closer.

Her eyes are forgiving as they look right back into my own. "But you did not."

She could never understand this fright unless she knew the truth.

"Do you wish to speak of it?" Maivena's voice is low as she asks.

And dump my issues all over the woman carrying enough of her own? "No."

There is a gentle knock on the door and Roaner returns. He puts on a short smile. "Strong tea?"

Maivena nods. "Next time, I would rather you punch me than choke me." I can feel the playfulness in her words; they pull a smile to my lips and Roaner fights his smile.

A smile in a moment when I never thought it possible. Her dark sense of humor brings light to this unfortunate night.

"That is not funny." I shake my head, still amused.

"What can we do to avoid such vivid dreams?" Roaner asks.

"No more heavy doses of this tea; it keeps him too far into his sleep." She cleans the small mess of tea before turning to me. "I will adjust the dosage in the morning."

The chamber falls quiet, and I look over to her as she throws the dirty rag into the cloth bin.

"Thank you, Maivena."

"It is the least I could do."

10
PASSING THROUGH

ROANER KORSANA

MAIVENA EMERGES FROM THE chamber connected to Laven's, and I see him visibly light up. His hazel and blue eyes watch her every move as she looks over the dress made to suit her. The dress is white satin; it flows down to the floor, stopping perfectly above her shoes. The fabric is fitted to her chest, with a thin layer of lace covering it. The sleeves are sheer and loose, stitched with tiny flowers. Her long, dark curls are concealed half up in a braid, the rest flows down her back with small strands falling around her cheeks.

Wearing white signifies strength. The quality of your clothing matters; your appearance needs to be strong, which is precisely why Laven had this made for her. He wants her to hold just as much power and strength as he does, if not more.

Putting Maivena in white will help her achieve just that. Her appearance alone makes her differ entirely from the woman she was yesterday. She has the blood of royalty in her veins; she should look and be treated as so.

Maivena is still touching the dress, toying with the fabric, admiring it. I can only imagine how long it has been since she has been in actual clothing other than the usual skirt, corset-vest, and shift.

"Roaner will be showing you around the academy. Are you okay with that? My mother has meetings with the school leaders; Roaner offered his help since he grew up knowing the grounds."

She nods with a faint smile, still mesmerized by the cloth on her skin. "Yes, that is fine with me."

"There are also many markets around the academy you can go to for food," Laven announces; I nod my head in agreement. One of his biggest requests is to make sure she eats an abundance of food; her frail state would be worrisome to most.

"Oh," Maivena holds her hand up. "Excuse me a moment," she rushes off into the connected chamber and quickly returns with a paper. "These are the instructions on how to care for your wounds while I am gone; I made them easy to follow so there are no mishaps." Her eyes rapidly move over the paper before continuing. "Wait, I have to add one more thing." Maivena is quickly heading back to the connected chamber to add whatever it is she forgot.

She made the directions idiot-proof for Morano and Amias because I think she knows something wrong would be bound to happen without her guidance. Yet even though she is applying the instructions, Morano and Amias are still pinioned to fuck this up.

"Have a bit of faith in them, please," Laven says through the bond after hearing my thoughts. *"I am already angry enough that I am not walking yet."*

I smile internally. *"Have you told her?"*

His eyebrows raise. *"About?"*

"About you attempting to walk while she is gone."

"No, do not mention it either." His tone is sharp as he speaks.

I look over his face as he gazes out the window. I can see the tension settling within his eyebrows.

"You do know I will not leave her side all day." I try to soothe him.

Laven looks back at me and nods. *"I know; I sought-after being the one to take her."*

"All right, it is done now." Maivena walks toward Laven with the paper in hand, her smile is nervous. I begin to wonder if she can feel his stress although she has no idea of them being mated. She may have yet to shift into her Wolf, but it is magnificent how a bond grows even when one is unaware.

Laven smiles. "I will make sure they see this."

"We will not be gone long, will we?" Maivena turns to me, and I shake my head no. "Hopefully, I can be back before you need a new dressing on your wounds."

Laven shakes his head. "Take your time. There is no need to rush to be back so soon; these instructions will do just fine." He says as she drapes a new beige cloak over her shoulders. It clips in the front, right at her neck, with a bow, arrow, and four small chains.

She now bears the same symbol from our tunics.

"Go before you are late," Laven says.

"Maivena," I call, holding my hand out. She looks down at it and back to Laven before nodding. "Have you ever ascended before?" I ask.

Her eyes widen. "No," she pulls her hand from mine. "Can we not walk there or take the Pegasi?" Her eyes drift off as she continues to back away.

I smile. "Not unless you would like to arrive within days."

She does not respond; her eyes glance around the room and stare through the window, nibbling on her lip.

She is afraid.

"Maivena?" Laven unobtrusively beckons her. He sits up and moves around easier than he was capable of yesterday. His pale brown skin is slowly returning to its healthy complexion.

She turns to him.

They only look upon one another. Not saying a word.

His eyes relax the worry building in her shoulders.

It takes a moment, but soon enough, she nods and looks back at me.

"Do not let go of my hand." A gentle command. *"Please,"* she roughly adds.

"I promise, I will not."

Grabbing my hand again, her grip is tight enough to break a

bone. If she had the strength of her Wolf, she could.

"Are you ready?" I ask.

She nods once more.

The moment we begin to fade, she gasps, clinging to my arm for dear life.

"Breathe," I try to calm her. "Open your eyes."

"Tell me what it looks like first."

"It is as if seeing the wind, like we are moving through wisps of color."

She grips my arm tighter. I look down and one of her eyes peek open and quickly shut. Soon after, both of her eyes gradually open. She does not fill with fear; she watches the movement of the world around her flow by.

"What are the colors we see?" She wonders.

"The color of everything around us as we move through it."

"It is pretty . . . can people see us?"

"No, not even the Gods can see us." I answer. "Ascending is like moving at a degree so briskly, even the greatest eye could never detect it."

"Like running?" She asks.

"No, ascending is purely from magic, which is why we disintegrate into a form of mist before leaving." It is why not everyone has the ability to ascend.

"Has anyone ever run fast enough to move at the speed of ascending?"

I smile. "Yes."

"Who?"

"Laven."

She falls quiet.

Little moments go by before she speaks again. "Can we walk some of the way?"

I come to a stop at the Western Lake near the academy; she has to catch her balance before taking a step forward.

"May I ask you something?" She says as we walk over the bridge of the lake. Her eyes peer upward as she looks at me.

I nod.

"What happened to him?"

An immediate knot catches in my throat, knowing exactly what it is that she speaks of.

"That is something I believe he should tell you." Even me and my brothers do not know everything Laven went through while imprisoned.

It took months for him to be comfortable to show his skin without a shirt on. I removed many of his scars, but some were too painful to take away. Most specifically the scars on his back that did not properly heal.

His father would visit him daily to heal him . . . that was until his visits stopped.

Maivena shakes her head, her brown cheeks heat in what seems to be the embarrassment of asking. "He will not tell me, yet I am aware people call him the Mad Prince."

We have always despised hearing people refer to Laven as that. We knew he did not go mad and that there was logical reasoning behind him snapping. And during the time when he was declared manic not many knew, only close family know of the seasons of pain he went through after being released from Wyendgrev Tower. Then, it seems the Healers and doctors began to talk, and slowly the citadel knew.

"What makes you so positive he would not tell you?"

"Laven is different from others; he cares. He cares almost too much for others to speak about his burdens."

"You appear to have him thought out already."

"No, I just know very few people like him. They are hard to forget." Maivena looks from me and outward to the lake. The trees speak as the wind moves through them, birds fly around, chirping in unison with nature herself.

"You may not think he will tell you, but he will."

Maivena shrugs a shoulder. "Perhaps, but I am only helping him heal for a period of time. After that, life will fade back to normal."

"Roaner," Laven calls through the bond. *"Where are you and*

Maivena?"

"The Western Lake by the academy, why?"

"Get her to the academy, now. Tell everyone to get inside, leave her with Hua. Morano is on his way, keep your eyes toward the sky and put a shield around the continent."

I hear them before I can ascend, the force of their wings push Maivena unsteady. Morano appears, catching her arm and holding her steady at the might of wind.

"Now, Roaner!" Morano yells before ascending with Maivena.

The loud call of them nears closer.

Quickly I flatten my hands against one another. As I separate my hands a dark sphere rotates between my palms: deep, sacred magic flowing from my fingers into the orb, causing it to spark and expand. I tap into the very magic my mother taught me as a child, searching for the strength held within ancestry power.

The orb nourishes with the magic put into it, I look toward the sky and force my hands upward, channeling the spheroid into the blue. It separates and stretches, hooding over the continent and creating a barrier between them and us.

It takes no time for them to appear.

I immediately recognize the Dragon as he flies overhead.

Tuduran.

He is with his sister Vion; their screams shake the ground as they pass. Tuduran expands over the lands, his wings splaying out as he glides overhead. The iridescence of his blue and black scaled chest reflects off the shield. His jaws open, showing teeth the size of Pegasi. He releases another roar through the acres of land he is covering; it moves far out across the sea in echoes. His blue eyes catch sight of me, and he ignores me like I was never here. They are not here for an attack; at least, that is not what it seems to be so far.

Vion latches on to the shield with her talons, her purple eyes looking down at me as she lands. The white spikes on her chest scrape over the curve of the barrier, and she looks through me. I am convinced she would try to kill me if it were not for this shield. Vion hears another call, and she is back into the sky, following her brother.

The span of half his body and tail still slowly glide by as he fades further out. He darkens the vast area below him, making it as if it is night for a short period of time.

"Why are they here?" I ask Laven.

"This is our warning; respond to Stravan's request soon, or he will come on his own." I can barely hear him over the roaring of Tuduran and Vion.

"He cannot do that. So by treaty, it is not allowed."

"You forget how powerful he is. Stravan is above any treaty and law known to this world. You must remember who ruled over every realm before we were split. He is the law, Roaner."

I watch, waiting for them to finish passing through Vaigon, their wings flap, rattling the shield as they move higher into the sky until they are practical shadows.

"You are not healthy enough to have him visit, and with Lorsius away—"

"I will not sit around and wait for Lorsius to arrive," he interrupts. *"We send word now. Summer Solstice is not far off; we will invite Stravan then. He does not seem to be in a rush to arrive; he only wants a response from us and a set date."*

"Why wait until Solstice?" I finish walking across the bridge, following the shadows of large, spiked bodies and wings in the sky.

"Because I want to be in full strength before he is here, and I want Maivena to know how to defend herself before then. If he attacks us as he did Galitan, I want her prepared. So, she trains this week." The worry for her in his voice is evident. If he could walk, he would indeed be pacing.

"And if she does not wish to?"

"She will." He certainly speaks. *"Her father, Naius, is one of the strongest Generals ever to live. I learned that Chiron himself trained him; he is known to move like Achilles. It is in her blood to fight."*

"Who will train her?"

"All of us, her father included. Although she has yet to shift into her wolf, we should see if she can wield her powers if she has any. I want her to learn every possible way there is to protect herself if we are not around."

"I will help her with it," I offer.

*"That will work; Morano is bringing Maivena home. Axynth has shut the

academy down until there are no more sightings of Tuduran and Vion."

"I will be home later, I told my mother I would visit her today, I must be sure she is safe."

"Bring her to the palace if you must." That was more of a demand than an offer.

"I will."

I look up to the shield. It will hold until I summon it to undo. I do not leave the lake area until I can no longer see or hear Tuduran and Vion in our skies.

11
AIDING THE OPPRESSOR

ROANER KORSANA
XENATHI — QUAMFASI CITADEL

I would think the only reason Vallehes would assign Esme as the person to assist me with finding Levora would be to kill me. I can admit she would be the one person who could manage to bury me in my grave after successfully eradicating me.

I did extensive research on her after we met.

Every Quamfasian Game Esme has participated in, she has won. She has won all but two, she rang in second against a woman named Ivella Fondali, I know this woman is related to Maivena or her father, Naius. Possibly a mother or cousin.

The Quamfasian Games were once known as the Voschantai Games—when all realms were identified as one land and there was no separation. The games were permanently used to identify the strongest amongst us mentally and physically to become the greatest Warriors of all time. The games would last for days dependent upon the courses assigned.

After the war resulted in the split of Voschantai and sent us into individual realms, the games stayed, but everyone developed their own rules. Even death is allowed to win.

Vaigon is currently the only realm to not use the method of the games, but that is why some of our Warriors are weaker than most. We have tried to push Lorsius to instill the games so we are stronger as a continent, but for no reason at all, he will not. One day, we will suffer for it, and I fear that day is soon.

Esme stands before me, suited in Quamfasi red armor. The same sword and spear she used on me during war are crossed behind her back.

"Levora Apolla Arvenaldi, is it?" Esme asks as she walks away from the entrance of the border.

Warriors are sat upon their horses and Pegasi, they intently observe me as I follow her.

"Yes."

"She is one of six. There are five people who went missing the exact same day and time as her. Phyv, Greyce, Levora, Finley, Jeddu, and Helena." She veers off to the right—a long path that takes you through the woods and towards the city. "Phyv was taken from Provas, the Fae Realm. Helena, she is a Sorceress removed from Galitan. Finley, he is a Vampire from Misonva. Jeddu is a Banshee from Vosand. Lastly, Greyce, a Hybrid woman from Ramana."

I finally catch her stride and her eyes are set forward.

"Do you have an indication of where they all have been sent to? There is no chance that this is purely coincidence that they all disappeared at once."

"Of course they are together, or in the same place at least." She speculates. "I have an inkling as to what method was used to confiscate them, but I do not want to speak too far ahead of myself before I know for sure."

"And what method is that?"

Esme stops walking and looks up at me. "Portals."

She grabs my arm, and we ascend from our current placement in the woods to a brothel located in the heart of New Quamfasi.

I raise my eyebrows as I glance at Esme after taking in my surroundings.

"Do not think so highly of yourself." Esme warningly holds up a finger. "Follow me and keep your hands off of our women."

Past me would argue with her about why I would never think of touching a woman here without having signed a contract first to be able to do so. Instead, I leave it and shadow her trail.

Bodies upon bodies. Each table and chair is occupied by a pair gently touching and caressing. The work up—the beginning stage before it leads to private chambers and suites then all you will hear is erratic moaning and headboards sounding as if they are about to break through the wall. But, it seems this brothel has the rooms sealed off to be soundproof, giving everyone their own piece of privacy.

"Esme," a man says from a chair not far from where we are walking.

The young woman in his lap is only clothed in a white sheer shift. She moves from his lap as he nods his head for Esme to come over and she does.

He leans forward and his elbows rest on his knees as he looks up at her with dark orange eyes. "You brought a Vaigon boy here?"

"Not willingly," Esme laughs. "We need the library. He and Val have a deal, I am helping him see it through."

He looks me over before standing and stalking forward, stopping right before me.

"One shout," he says. "One shout is all it will take for me or my brothers to be at her aid and pulling your tongue from your throat. Vallehes may not want any Vaigosian blood on his hands, but I do."

"Ajax," Esme calls his name, and he slowly recedes back to where he was; seated in the chair with the woman hoisted on his lap.

Whenever I am here, this is all I will be. A threat that becomes an open target.

I need to do more than just tread lightly.

Esme is fully capable of defending herself, but I doubt that would stop the men from protecting the Right Hand of their nation.

"Unfortunately, we cannot kill him. He is needed," Esme looks at me over her shoulder with intense golden eyes. "He has a deal to seal."

She walks away from Ajax, and I track behind her.

We move farther into the brothel, weaving through multitudes of couples before finding a double staircase that leads to separate hallways. Each hall is protected by a single guard, we go down the left that has a wall plastered with books.

Esme pulls on the corner of four different books in a specific order and the wall rotates, exposing a hidden library.

"This library contains some of the most ancient books known to our world. But this is the only library that contains the novels on what I believe happened to not only Levora, but everyone else who went missing along with her."

"Portals."

She nods.

"I have not heard of the use of portals since—"

"The first Domestic War." She speaks for me. "When we had to call upon Lorvithinan Universe to aid us, and the only way for them to get to us was through multiple portals from their universe to ours."

The most epic war of our entire world. The war that had to be stopped or we all would end in ruin. Everyone was against everyone to have division so we could exist individually. Realm by realm. Even the Sea People had to participate in the war to protect their Waterland's from one too many borders.

When I step into the library the wall concaves and closes off.

Three sets of candles sit above each shelving, lighting up the titles of the novels below it. The library is not large, but it is great in height. There are three levels above where we stand in the squared off room, and a glass dome ceiling that allows in a form of lighting along with the candles.

I cannot say it is relatively smart for there to be a glass ceiling in such a sacred room.

Esme sharply turns toward me, and I stand, waiting for something to be said.

"Come," she demands before ascending to the second floor.

As I emerge from my ascension, she is reaching for a book from the shelf. There is not a title on it. It appears as just an old, tattered, black leather book concealed with consecrated magic.

"Use your powers to shrink it," she says while placing the book in my hands. "We must take it with us."

"Take it where?" I ask as I place my other hand atop the book, and it decreases in my palm.

"We are going to the woods where Levora was taken."

"Wait," I halt.

Esme turns.

"Why did you decide to be the one to help me?" I remember how she felt, and I remember how that spear felt moving through my body. Hatred such as hers does not change so easily.

For the first time, I see her falter. "Because I know how it feels to suddenly lose people you hold so dearly."

VAIGON CITADEL — SOUTHERN WOODS

I stand in the South Woods with Heshy as we wait for Ezra to arrive. It did not take long for Heshy to locate him; after our first meeting, Ezra was found traveling with a message that Laven needed sent to all the leaders of our Courts. The message contained information about the passing of the Dragons to notify the Courts that we are to be held under observation until further notice and no one will be allowed to pass the shield. Given the severity of this message Heshy advised Ezra to complete the task assigned and that he will find him again to meet us here.

"The sun has set," Heshy observes. "He will be arriving soon."

"You may go, I will find you when we are done here."

Heshy nods before ascending and as he fades I hear a soft brisk wind soar by. I sharply turn toward the direction it came from.

At a young age my mother taught me how to stop someone in ascension.

I rotate my hand in a small circle and a hue of blue appears as I draw a force field, pushing my palm outward, it ricochets the force field through the woods, and it bursts. Just after it erupts, it pushes

Ezra out of ascension, and he falls from mid air and collides to the ground.

He swiftly stands and turns to me with large, dark eyes.

"Seems you found me before I found you." Ezra says as he stands under the moonlight casting over his dark skin.

"I did."

He walks forward and bows. "Ezra Harst." He formally introduces.

"You are known for being a quick messenger and quiet in your path," I say. "Have you ever considered furthering your placement as a messenger?"

"No," he shakes his head. "I have never known how."

"This is how, right now, by this conversation. If you wish to."

He stands taller. "If I gain more coin than I do currently, I will do whatever I must."

"You would have a great increase. Your job would be of an Emissary, my Emissary. You seem to be rather equipped for the role." His eyes draw wide once more. "I need you to find someone, locate them, speak with them, and guide them here. Do it however you must but never disclose that you are being led by me and I will not have to kill you."

"Me?" Ezra questions. "As your Emissary?"

"Yes."

"And the result if I do not perform my job well or fail?"

I shrug. "The result will depend on how you ill performed and failed."

Ezra's arms cross over his black leather vest as he contemplates. "How much coin will I receive for my placement?"

"Twelve Vaigosian Gold coins a day."

"I will do it." He agrees.

I tilt my head observing him due to his sudden urgency after hearing the amounts he will receive daily, amounts that are not for someone of a commoner's life. "This is very in-depth labor, Ezra. The pay matters, yes, but what this will consist of depends greatly on if you can handle it and the person involved that you must locate and bring here."

Ezra steps closer. "I can give you my word that I will not fail at this. If you need it in writing I will provide that as well. And no, I have never in my life done labor as this, but I have dreamed of it, and in those dreams I do it well. Not only will this pay give miracles for myself and my family, I do not take this gently. I will do this job and do it well."

"Good," I hold my hand out to him and he firmly takes it. "Welcome to House Arvenaldi Ezra Harst."

He smiles. "Who am I to find?"

12
TREE OF GODS

LAVEN HEPHAESTUS ARVENALDI, II

Roaner finds us in my study, and his eyes draw wide as he looks me over. I am dressed for the first time in days, back in our black leather fighting gear. It has not been too long since I have last worn armor, yet, I have to loosen the leather collar around my neck as I turn; the edges dig into my skin at every rotation.

Roaner looks toward Maivena; she says nothing, her face still set in stone. Roaner continues to peer around the room. Morano hides his smile as he ties his black hair into a bun, trying to act casual about the situation when we are far from it.

"Yes," I say, breaking the silence. "I am walking. Fine, perfectly fine, actually."

Maivena's head turns to the window, ignoring every look given to her.

Morano precariously stares at Roaner. "What is this scent on you?"

"What scent?"

"The scent of roses and brothels."

He ignores Morano as if he never said anything. Roaner runs a hand through his messy black hair and shrugs off Morano's interrogations.

"How?" Roaner asks, his gaze focusing on me as Morano continues to look him over, sniffing the air.

From the corner of my eye I see Maivena shift.

Morano bursts into laughter. "He ate a rather large helping of moss from the Tree of Gods. Cured his ass in an instant; you should have seen the way he moved when he got up."

"He was not supposed to eat that much." Maivena's voice differs from the look on her face. Her tone may appear to be gentle, but her expression, not so much.

"I panicked," I try to reason with her again, but I may be treading on thin ice with her for some time. "The moment I heard the Dragons approaching, it was my first thought."

She says nothing in return.

"I ate a large sum of the moss, wondering if it would quicken the healing process . . . it did."

"And you could have had complications!" Maivena's gaze blazes in my direction.

I stand up straighter at the luminosity in her eyes.

For the first time, I see it.

Sparks of orange dance in the green of her eyes. Her Wolf is trying to push through.

Almost immediately, mine responds.

Then, briskly, she angles her head away.

"Morano is going on a patrol of the land," I say while draping our dark blue cloak over my shoulders. "Amias and Hua have already gone off to fetch the Warriors in our Mandem; they will be commanding them through the lands to be sure no one passed through on the backs of the Dragons."

"You believe Stravan would do such a thing?" Roaner asks.

I clip the bow and arrow together over the tunic and shake my head at him. "No, that is the issue. I do not think so, but I have been wrong about people before. We must double search, triple even."

"Where will you be?" Morano questions.

"Provas."

Roaner steps forward. "Say that again?" He tilts his head, leaning in an ear.

"You are going . . . alone?" Morano stands, his arms cross his chest as he looks me over.

"Yes, alone. All of us cannot go together; the four of us going into Provas at once will seem like a threat. If I go alone, Stravan will not be threatened. I have already sent our messenger to ask Stravan if I can visit, just him and I."

"And your mother is aware of this?" Morano asks.

"Yes, she is still at the academy guarding the gates if anyone from the Realm of the Fae tries to enter. Having someone like Stravan slip through the cracks is a death sentence, so taking every precautionary measure is crucial."

"No, what *you* are doing is a death sentence." Morano fires his words. "His sister and brother are strong as well, Laven. Stravan, Savarina, and Sloan in one room is death standing at its strongest. You are foolish to believe the three of them will not be waiting for you."

"It will only be Stravan and me, no one else." I know saying this will do nothing. Out of us all, Morano worries the most, but within good reason. This was the reaction I was expecting.

"And you believe that?" He sarcastically asks.

"I do." I nod. "I need his trust if we are going to cure this disease running rapidly through our lands; I–we have to trust him. We need his alliance; you all know we do."

"May I ask something?" Maivena quietly speaks from the corner of the room.

"You do not ask to speak here; you speak freely." I remind her.

Her eyes glance between all of us. "What do you need the Fae's alliance for?"

This is the question I was afraid of.

She waits, hoping for a response from at least one of us.

"The tree . . . I cannot allow us to be aware that there are full healing properties behind the moss and not try to give it to our people who have been bitten."

"No," Maivena shakes her head; the anger she was ready to

throw at me just minutes ago reappears. "You cannot swarm my people again, and you will not take—"

"Maivena," I stop her. "We are not swarming, nor taking. None of us are allowing that; I am giving them the option. If Vallehes and Penelope accept our alliance through the Fae, we will stay on the other side of whatever boundary they have. If they say no, they do not wish to help, then the answer is no, we stop."

"They will ask why we think the moss will heal," Roaner adds.

I nod. "I will do my best to explain."

Maivena is fast to move; her feet carry her straight through the doors of the study, and that bit of fright I recognize settles in.

I aim to follow her, but Roaner appears before me; his hand is held tightly on my shoulder. "Do not," he shakes his head. "You will just agitate her more by following."

"She feels taken advantage of," Morano calmly says. We both look at him as he watches Maivena storm down the hall.

He is in her thoughts.

I push Roaner out of my way. "What is she thinking?" I implore.

"She believes you knew of the healing properties in the moss beforehand, that we knew how to use her to get to the tree." Morano slowly looks back at us.

I stare at him, trying to read his expressions.

"What?" I worry.

His head shakes. "Nothing more."

Then, I hear footsteps; Maivena is returning, making her way up the vast hall, eyes staring directly into my own. She stops at the doors.

"I would like my scarf back, please. I know you have it, it is mine, and it belonged to my mother."

My face heats.

Morano and Roaner cautiously look at me.

"My *scarf*," she snaps. "If you are suddenly unfamiliar with it, it is beige and white with gold trimmings." Her voice roughens with each word.

I walk around my bureau and pull out the drawer containing

the box with her scarf. She steps forward, snatching the box from my hands; she sets it down and opens it. The scarf is removed, and she leaves the box sitting open.

"I will be returning this dress and the cloak by tonight."

"They are yours, Mai–"

"No, they are not." She interrupts. "I did not purchase them with my own money; therefore, they are not mine. I do not take, nor do I keep things that do not belong to me." She closes in. "And if I did not speak plainly enough for you, stay the hell away from the tree and my people. Your family has done enough damage as it is; cunning and falsely caring for others until you get what you want.

"Sacred land, golden coin, white silks, and satin. Taking and never giving a thought to how it would affect those on the other side. Just like your uncle." I flinch.

Maivena tersely shifts on her heel before carrying herself from the room.

Roaner and Morano both continue to focus on me.

"She is angry, Laven. And scared. She has every right to be; whether we like to see it this way or not, we held part in everything that happened to them." I ignore Roaner and turn to Morano.

I open my mouth to speak, but the words catch in my throat.

Tightness seals my jaws shut.

"I will summon the messenger to call off the meeting in Provas." He nods before ascending from the study without question.

"She will come around," Roaner tries to diffuse the war building in my mind before it can begin.

It is too late. I am already there.

I open another drawer in my bureau and pull out another box. "Give this to someone you know, preferably the woman whose smell is lingering all over you."

He opens the box, grabbing the blue scarf I brought back with me from Terseius days ago.

He calls after me the moment I ascend.

Morano looks to me as I find him at the meeting grounds; the messenger he speaks with nods at his words before leaving.

"Are we going on foot or paw?" He jokes.

I ignore him, shifting into my Wolf as his answer. The sound of bones cracking and moving into a new form echoes in my ears like never before.

Unyieldingly, I run through the woods.

Just like your uncle.

I push myself further; I can hear Morano's paws beating into the ground as he runs to catch up. If I wanted to, I could leave him behind, but I do not want any more angry people in my ear.

Lorsius has ruined plenty of things in my life that I wished for.

Now the person I care for most cannot believe my affection is genuine because of his past actions. Lorsius convinced many people in his life to trust him, only to stab them in the back when he got what he wanted. Unfortunately, that is word for word what he did to Penelope and Vallehes.

I have spent years making it known to myself that I am not him; and that I could never be him. I could never participate in such acts that he has. But, no matter how deep I am convinced, I cannot persuade others unless they believe it themselves.

It is almost as if people hold me hostage to this. That I am destined to be that same person my uncle is for the sole reason of his blood coursing throughout my veins.

I remember the man my father was before he was taken from us. I still wish to this day to be merely compared to him. To love like him. To be strong like him.

The wrong man always seems to wear the crown.

"She was speaking out of anger, Laven. Anger we do not apprehend, we could never truly understand what it is that she and all the people of Quamfasi feel unless we go through it ourselves." Morano says.

I do not respond to him.

I am well aware of this.

The sun is almost set, the sky is darkening as I look at it through Roaner's shield still covering the continent.

"Laven?"

"I am fine," I bite out.

I come to a stop and lift my nose to the air, inhaling deeply.

Morano looks at me, his brown Wolf stands in alignment with mine. He says nothing before taking off along another path; his white paws trample along the dirt road until he is out of sight.

Turning down another path, I stop.

I tilt my head to a scent that is not of the Fae. Then, I narrow in on a woman far out. She is covered in burgundy gear; one arm is clothed while the other is left free. Her red hair is in a tight braid, and a spear is concealed against her back from the left shoulder to her right hip.

I can see the brightness of her grey eyes as she smiles. But it is no welcoming smile.

I let go a deep growl as she steps forward. Digging my rear into the ground, I hold my head downward and release a force field that rattles, shaking the trees and earth beneath us. Her spear is drawn swiftly; it ignites in a glow of blue as she holds horizontally. The force field bounces off of her spear, and it retreats; soaring back to me.

Running forward, I bear my head down, shattering through it.

An arrow is shot over my head, and I look backward. Hua is drawing back another hand, running directly behind me.

The first arrow is cracked through as the woman spins the spear in her fingers.

Hua lets another arrow loose; it whistles, ripping sprucely through the air. Then, just as suddenly as I saw the woman, she disappears. She ascends, leaving behind a dark hue of red that leisurely fades.

I slide to a hard stop; peering around the area of the woods, Hua jumps into a tree, climbing upward. Her eyes beam purple as she scans the woods, listening for a single sound.

I shift and my clothing reappears on my skin as each limb forms into place.

"Who was that?" Hua lands gracefully on her feet as she jumps down from the tree.

"I do not know, but I recognize her leathers."

"Who do they belong to?"

I exhale. "Xenathi, Quamfasian Warriors."

She crosses her bow over her chest. "Are they aiming to claim their land back?"

"No, she must have slipped in during the passing of the Dragons, maybe she was already here . . . However, I will call upon my mother and ask if she has seen anyone near."

"Where is Maivena?"

I stiffen.

For the first time, I do not know.

* * *

"Who was she?" Morano asks as we all sit in the study.

Amias and Hua are rolling out the map of Vaigon across the table in the middle of the study. They stand around, and I point to exactly where she was located.

"I do not know who she is, but as I mentioned earlier, I know her armor. We all know the Quamfasian people wear red leather as their gear. Do any of you know if and when she could have entered?"

"She had to of been here before Roaner put a shield over the continent. No one can break through that other than himself," Amias says.

"She will not be able to get out until it is down," I add. "There is only so far she can ascend before hitting the wall of the shield and ending up right back to where she was." I look to Hua. "Lead out the Warriors, have them be on the lookout around the walls of the shield, and send word to all of the courts. Give them her description, every bit of what you remember of her face, her height, her hair, her eyes, every single thing."

Hua looks up to Amias and he nods. "I will walk you out." Together, they leave, putting the room down to only Morano and me.

"When Roaner arrives, I will send him to Xenathi. Try to have him reason—find out why a Warrior was roaming our land."

"You and I both know well enough why they would have Warriors roaming here." Morano crosses his arms as he inspects the map. "The exact same reason they were roaming last year, and the same reason why servants went . . . missing, so to say." His eyes roll dramatically.

I nod, considering it. "Could be, but this does not feel like a mother or father looking for their child. She was looking for something else."

"Did she try to kill you?" Morano asks, looking me over.

"No, but I suspected she was going to. It is as if she wanted to be seen. She was standing under the opening of the trees, right at the end of the pathway. She stared at me with a grin on her face; she was quick in motion, moved at a rate to crack Hua's arrow. It never touched her. And her spear, it sent my own magic back to me, it bounced off of her spear like a ball to a racket." I let the scene continue to play over in my mind.

"The magic they hold is contained in their weapons." My eyebrows knit together at Morano. "When they establish their powers," he begins to explain. "They craft their spears from the wood of the ancient trees. Because they molded their own spear, their power goes into it. No one else can use the weapon other than the person who created it. Even if you got near her to take the spear, it would either kill you or completely vanish from your grasp."

"When did they discover this?"

He shrugs, shaking his head. "I am unsure; it could be recent. Or it could even be ages ago that they learned it. I am not fully aware."

Maivena's father would know . . .

"He would," Morano confirms my thoughts.

"No, we will not ask him that."

I sit down at the table and lean back. Through the floor to ceiling windows, the moon beams in, it ignites the silver ink etched on the map lying on the table.

Soon enough, Roaner arrives. He tosses a large, black linen bag on the table. It slides across the map, landing right in front of me. The fabric is tied off with a thin rope at the top concealing it shut.

I sit up as he motions for me to open it.

"It was the only bag she had that would hide the glow and also the only bag that would fit it all," Roaner says.

My palms press into the wooden table as I stand over the piles of moss in the bag.

"How much does she have left after this?" I watch him from across the room as I re-tie the rope.

"All she had, is what is in that bag. Maivena said it would be enough to stop the spread building in Gordanta."

"And what if she gets bitten?" I ask, anger laces through each word. "What will we do after Gordanta has all of this and we have nothing left to cure her?"

Roaner points to the bag. "If you are smart, you will keep some to yourself for that specific reason."

"No," Morano stands. "If you are smart, you send it back to her, all of it. None of the Dukes and Duchesses in any of our courts deserve this, nor the people that praise them. These bastards are greedy, Laven. The second they find out about this, they will want an endless supply for not only stopping the spread of the rogues but themselves.

"That tree could make someone filthy rich; that is what people want. And everyone here knows that coin is power; these men and women would make Quamfasian people pay for their own fucking worship. Quamfasian's have never used the tree for financial benefit; they strictly use it in healing and worship.

"Give that back to her and let this disease rip those people apart for all I care. Whoever gets the disease deserved to get it; this is karma. That is all this disease is, karma for taking land that never belonged to us in the first place."

"And what of the children? I have seen what this does to the young, Morano. No child deserves that." My eyes taper on him as he shakes his head. "You cannot blame them for their parent's mistakes."

"Then pay attention to your children better." He continues to argue his view.

"Morano," Roaner intervenes. "Accidents happen."

"An accident is a child spilling their water, not leaving your adolescent alone for so long they get fucking bitten by a rogue. Tell these people to be better parents and learn to defend themselves." Rage pours from him, making his skin redden.

Out of the four of us, sometimes I believe Morano hates his people more than I did a few years ago. That was until I became second in line to rule.

Though, much of Morano's hatred for irresponsible parents losing their child is rooted in his past as a child.

I may argue with Morano's irrationality, he is not wrong. Our people are privileged with an abundance of guards and Warriors; they no longer want to learn to fend for themselves when alone.

"I will speak with her," I grab the bag, and Morano holds his hand up.

"At least bathe and change your clothing before you see her; stench clings to these leathers like bees to a flower."

"Yes, father." I satirically respond as I leave.

* * *

The moss was her apology, but I will not take this. None of it. Not after seeing the way it tore her apart to know of the peril Xenathi would be under after handing this out.

Handing over something this sacred to me is an apology that is too large.

But Morano is also correct; everything he spoke was true.

The second any Duke or Duchess sees what this can do, they would go to war over it. Another war none of us need.

As I approach Maivena's cottage, I see her with a lantern, planting a seed in the soil along the side of her home. She stands, and my hand tightens on the bag of moss.

Like a beacon in the night, she is radiating in the blue scarf.

13
WHAT OF RESPECT

LAVEN HEPHAESTUS ARVENALDI, II

Maivena waits to see if I will speak first or if she will have to. She wraps the blue scarf tighter around her robe and shift before standing.

I hold up the bag of moss and she glances over it.

She shakes her head. "Even trade."

"What exactly for?"

I hold the bag tighter to suppress the shaking of my hands. I did not think it would be this striking to see Maivena in the scarf, but it is. Maybe it is because she is happily wearing something that I picked out for her. On the other hand, perhaps the vision I had of her in this hits me better than I imagined. Either way, it is bliss.

"This," she plays with the corners of the fabric wrapped around her.

Fuck.

"You told her," I shoot down the bond to Roaner.

"Yes, I did." He responds. *"Leave me alone; I am busy."*

"Busy with the woman I smelled on you earlier?"

He does not answer.

Maivena picks up the lantern on the ground and walks forward.

Staying at a distance, she looks over my face.

"I am sorry for what I said to you," I can hear her deeply swallow. "I knew it would hurt you, and I regretted the words after I said them."

"You do not have to give me an apology, I–"

"No, I do. I would not like it if I were you and you said it to me. So, I am sorry, I did not mean what I said." She stares far into me as she says every word. The gaze does not falter; it does not move. She is solely focused on only me.

I smile. "Thank you, but I can only accept your apology if you take this back." I walk closer, in desperate need to close this too wide space between us.

"You require it more than I do," she holds her hand up, preventing me from handing it over.

"You think you do not need it until something happens, and you do. Besides, I spoke with Morano. He made sense in the reasons I should be returning this to you." I do not know what I will do if any of what Morano said happens.

I would lose her. I know I would.

Maivena looks down at the bag and back up to me, a smile on her lips. I try not to step any closer, but I do.

"You are a High Prince," she hums. "You were born to know how to lie well. So, lie about where you got this from as well. It is yours now," her finger taps the knuckles of my hand holding the bag. I reach up, an instinct, a need to have back that short moment from days ago.

The moment our skin connects again, she takes in the way her hand slides into my palm.

This she is doing herself.

I am unsure of what to behold the longest; the trails her fingers draw as they move over my palm or the way her long curls fall around her face as she leans in.

Shivers migrate over my skin as she gets to my wrist; her thumb gently rolls over the healed cut from the Blood Bond Ritual.

"You are shivering," she mumbles. "Would you like tea?" Her

voice is smooth.

She is well aware that this tremble is not from the cool spring night; cold does not affect those who have shifted into their Wolf. Consistent heat is what always pours from my skin, especially now.

Before I can answer, her name is called from a distance. I think it is her father that is appearing, but it is not. Instead, it is one of our young Warriors. His walk is solid and leveled, it is the unwavering strength of a seasoned Warrior.

Just like before, that moment of her hand in my own is gone. She takes various steps backward.

He approaches within sight and stands next to Maivena.

A slight nod is given to me before he drifts to the woman next to him.

She looks up to him with a smile, one I have never seen. It is soft yet confident.

Her eyes are daring as he watches her. His scent is unavoidable. *Him.* He is the male I have smelt on her before.

"Are you all right?" He lowly asks Maivena. "Do you want me to stay with you?"

He has the right mind to wish to stay with her. Although, I would like to kindly tell him to fuck off.

"I am fine," she is sure as she tells him it is safe to leave her with me.

"Where were you earlier? Ethel was looking for you." His accent courses through his words.

He is dark in skin and his black hair is closely cut to his scalp. As he talks, I can hear it in his tone, the way his voice deepens as he speaks. It is the same inflection that Maivena's voice has when she says certain words. He is Quamfasian as well.

"I was on my way to the academy." She answers. "Do you want to take tea with you?"

He shakes his head, gently knocking his knuckles against her chin and she smiles harder.

I will break that hand.

"I will come by later after I bathe." He watches me for a moment before mumbling under his breath.

Maivena nods at whatever he said as he leaves.

He does not acknowledge me further before leaving, and walking down a path to a cottage not far from here.

"Well?" Maivena smiles. "Tea?"

"Yes," because I have some fucking questions.

She turns on her heel, walking to the door of her small home. Her slippers are taken off outside the door, and I follow suit, unstrapping my boots before leaving them next to the others.

The only items in the house are a table, a cornered mattress that lays on the floor, a small fireplace, and chairs.

Her mother's scarf is neatly folded and laid on the mattress sheets; next to it is the dress she wore this morning, the cloak, and the bow and arrow brooch.

The wood along the walls is wearing away. I examine the home more; the window is nearly broken, the fireplace is barely big enough for two logs, and the table in the middle of the room has deep cuts in it. I can tell that is where she cuts her food if she ever has the money to purchase any.

Is this truly what they live in?

"How do you get warm in the winter?" I continue to look around the tiny home.

Maivena quietly laughs. "I move the mattress in front of the fire; it is not all that horrible."

An iron rod is used to pull the boiling teapot from the fire; she sets it down on the table before grabbing a pair of mitts to handle the pot. She pours the steaming water into a bowl, but not too much.

I observe everything she does. Her footsteps are quiet and light while moving delicately around the tiny home. She lifts open a large wooden trunk at the other side of the room, and grabs a glass jar containing tea leaves and another that holds honey.

I shift from foot to foot as past, sweet dreams attack my thoughts seeing the honey.

"Who was the man outside?"

"Kaden," she announces.

"And he is your . . ." my words trail off as she looks at me.

Her eyes widen, almost dropping the jar in her hands. "Oh, no! Kaden is not whom you think; he is my cousin through marriage. He came with my father when he was looking for me; Kaden's mate, Ethel, my cousin, was taken just before I was."

"Did he find her?" I hesitantly ask.

She smiles. "Yes, Kaden will always find Ethel." There is a slight giggle in her voice.

Maivena opens the jar filled with tea leaves. Two small scoops of the leaves are put into the steaming water, she allows it to steep while finding a small strainer.

"Can I help with anything?" Although, I have no idea what I would be doing.

"No, you may sit if you would like." She nods to one of the empty chairs at the table.

"I am feeling a tad useless here."

"Have you eaten?" She asks, still staring down at the bowl in front of her as she slowly stirs it.

"Not yet; I will eat when I return to the palace."

I look at the middle of the table where a dish is covered with a cloth.

I cannot eat her food; that is the equivalence of stealing from the poor.

"Where is your father?"

She stops stirring and lifts the bowl, pouring the tea into small stone vessels. "He is on his way to Wanora with other members of the Mandem."

I sit down as she approaches. "You will be alone tonight?"

"Yes," she puts down a vessel in front of me before walking around the table and sitting. "I will be alone for however long he is gone, but not essentially. Kaden watches over me while my father is gone. Occasionally, both him and Ethel will come here, or I go to them."

"And if Kaden were not here as well?"

"If Kaden were not here, I would most likely be dead." I almost choke on the tea. She smiles and brings the tea to her lips, gently blowing on the steam.

I take another sip of the tea. "Dark humor."

"Someone has to have a sense of dark humor in this world." Her finger trails along the rim of the stone as her knees are pulled to her chest. "It is the last resort before complete distress." The smile she had is gone. She seems lost as she looks down at her tea.

"If I stay, we play a game."

She lifts her head. "What game?"

"Questions is all." I lean on the table.

The corner of her lips edge upward. "Can we lie?"

I simper. "No, absolutely not."

"Your game is no fun . . . but I will play."

I chuckle, not daring to renege and give her the option of lying.

"Gentlemen first," she smiles, waiting.

I sit here for a moment; Maivena sips her tea. "Wine or tea?"

"Wine. You?"

"Wine," I nod in agreement. "Wine now?"

She grins. "Yes."

Good, because I need it.

"I have quite the amount. My father makes it from the wild grapes in the fields. It is a bit stronger than your usual wine, but I think it tastes immeasurable compared to others." Maivena stands from the table, heading to the trunk she retrieved the tea and honey from. The bottle is pulled out, and she grabs a wine opener. The pop of the cork leads after like music in my ears.

She opens a drawer in the table, pulling out two more small stone vessels.

"This has been aging for years; it may be strong." She warns while handing me a cup.

It is strong, but not too strong—a smooth dry, just barely sweet, and a slight bite touches the back of my jaw.

Maivena's eyes close as she sips the wine. Her cheeks begin to hint red as we sit here, drinking and saying nothing more.

I sit up. "Your question." I nod for her to go on.

I reach for the dish of food sitting in between us. She hands me a fork, and I dig it into the mashed potatoes topped with tender venison and carrots.

"There is bread too; I made it all. Mrs. Patro allowed me to start a roast very early in the morning after I caught the deer." She reaches in, taking my fork after I have stuffed my mouth.

So you are a skilled hunter.

She begins to eat next. The bread loaf is pulled from the linen, perfectly golden along the edges. It is already precut; she takes a slice, digging it into the potatoes and meat.

Her hand motions for me to try it, and I beam over her pure joy for food.

"What is your favorite food?" She asks.

"I am thinking this," I nod to the addiction of bread with potatoes and deer.

Maivena grins. "I will let you know if I make it again."

If only we can do this again.

I swallow. "My turn."

As she waits for my question she remains eating.

"Why have you not shifted into your Wolf yet?"

I figure this question will stump her, but it does not.

We take more sips of the intoxicating wine; she lets her food digest before answering.

Stilly, she speaks. "I suppress her."

"How? She is you, half of you, if not all of you." How do you suppress who you are?

Her voice goes low. "Contraception."

"Why would you do that?"

This entire time she has been preventing her Wolf from taking form. There is nothing wrong with her; she is doing this herself. I have heard of others doing this, but there are complications when taking contraception such as that.

"What advantages do I have here shifting into my Wolf? I am not a Warrior; I do not need her for strength. But, despite that, I do believe it is possible to have strength without her. There is no nobility here for me, nothing. Transforming into her brings me nothing here."

"What of your mate?"

She tries to hide the sadness in her eyes as she peers upward. "That is not in the cards for me either."

"Do you not care to find him?"

Seeing the expression her face holds makes me afraid of the answer she will give me, almost as if I already know the answer. Yet, I have to hear her say it. I will not torture myself with constant guessing with her. If she is willing to tell me and be honest with me, I will ask her as many questions as possible.

She is slow to respond. She takes another sip of wine and reaches for the fork. "There would be nothing I could do about it," she pauses, her lips parting to speak. "So, no. I would not wish for that since there is no chance of me being allowed to be more than just a bed chambermaid to a King."

I say nothing more, ignorant of how many more questions I can handle the responses to.

"I want to ask something now." Our eyes meet as she speaks. "Is that why you are here?"

"What do you mean?"

"You have riches. You are among the most attractive in Vaigon. Yet, you are never seen publicly with women. Many high people come here in search of a servant to . . . *impress*. A servant to provide things for them such as intimacy of all sorts, and in return they are granted wealth and a form of freedom. Is that why you are here?"

I reach for the bottle of wine and pour more into the vessel, almost right to the brim. Then, I stretch across the table, filling hers as well.

"Is that something you would be intrigued by?"

Almost half of the wine in my vessel is gone within one sip.

"With you?"

"Yes, me. Only me."

If this will be the only way for me to have her in all forms of intimacy, I will do this if she agrees.

She nods. "Yes." The vessel is brought to her lips, and she takes a long drink.

I voraciously gape at her throat, watching as she swallows the wine.

"What would you want?"

"Whatever you would want." Her tone is that of a vibration. "When?" She inquires. I gaze at her lips—a soft pink flushing a deeper red at the kiss of wine.

I lean further in on the table. "Now," I breathe.

"What of conditions?"

"We will devise a contract later."

Maivena gasps at the force of speed I move at. As quick as ascending, I am around the table, standing in front of her chair. She sits up straighter as I get to my knees in front of her and lean back against my heels.

Her breath catches as I trail my hand up her leg. "Am I not supposed to be the one doing this first?"

Her skin is soft under my touch, tender against the calluses on my hands.

"Not with me, you do not."

I reach upward, slipping her robe down her shoulders and it catches in the curve of her arm, falling right over the scarf.

The trim of her night shift is lined in lace; the peak of her nipples tease the white fabric.

A groan pulls from the depths of my chest as I lean in to press my lips to her neck. Her hand reaches out, catching my chin and lifting my head.

"Kiss me," she touches the bow of my lip as I sit up on one knee, our noses just nearly leveled as she sits in front of me.

Grasping the back of her legs and tugging her forward her hand rests on my shoulder as her legs lift to wrap around my waist.

The feeling of her wrapped around me is safe—I am warm and succulently held.

There is a smile pulling onto her face. I can hear the sound of every breath she takes, and let's go. Her scent is welcoming, comforting, and sensual. But most of all, it is familiar, a fragrance explicitly made for me.

Maivena bends further in. Everything within me is begging to be closer, to feel her flesh against mine.

Our lips are grazing. They play, never fully touching, slight caresses.

"Maivena," I beg.

I venture, finding my way under her shift. Her skin heats at the connection of my fingers to her thighs; I unearth the swell of her hip and squeeze.

"Not yet. I want to savor you." With each word, I quiver.

The bit of self-control I have left is crumbling, just nearly gone.

Her quiet breath comes out in a low moan, barely audible as I knead at her hips.

She scoots closer, edging the end of the old chair that creaks with every move.

As the tip of her tongue ever so lightly touches my lips, I grip the edge of the chair, willing away the voice I hear creeping down the bond.

"Laven!" I flinch as Amias shouts, crashing through the barrier I try to build.

Maivena intakes a sharp breath. She looks at me, eyes filled with worry. "I am sorry," she speaks just as Amias and Morano force their words through.

I cannot keep up with them and her at once.

She unravels her legs, and I try to hold them in place while managing the multiple voices.

"Shut up! One at a fucking time!" I yell over them both.

They quiet quickly.

Maivena watches me. "Are you all right?"

"Yes," I answer, realizing the timing of this intrusion. "It is not you. Amias and Morano are trying to speak to me." It takes a moment to register, but she comprehends, nodding. I stand, leaning back against the table. She reaches for the vessel of wine, sipping more of what is leftover.

"We have been trying to get you to answer the past fifteen minutes!" Morano says agitatedly.

"I have been occupied; did you not consider it? What do you want?" I snap.

"All right, you two hotheads, calm down." Amias interjects before it can escalate. *"We have been trying to reach you because the Duke of Gordanta sent out a messenger. There is another Warrior from Xenathi roaming; he was terrorizing the land. Lorsius has moved on from Gordanta to Partalos to handle other matters. Either way, this is a job for us, not your uncle. He would manage it horribly if it were in his hands.*

"The Duke is calling for us immediately, but especially you. You will arrive before us; we will be gathering my father and your mother to come back here and keep the land under control while we are gone."

Maivena stands from the chair, and I reach out, taking her hand in mine. I pull her forward, causing her to collide into me, a smirk tugs onto our faces. I play with the thin strap of her shift and the robe and scarf still hang, gathered in the nook of her arms.

"Is he even listening?" Morano cuts in.

"Doubtful," Amias responds. There is a hint of playfulness behind his tone.

I hold my finger up as Maivena goes to speak.

"Yes, I am listening. I heard every word you said." I say aloud.

Her head tilts as she inquisitively stares at me.

"Why are you speaking out loud?" Amias asks.

"Because," I sharpen my tone. *"You are ruining everything for me right now. I will be there soon to get the rest of the details."* Just as they try to speak again, I block them, putting up a wall none of them have learned how to break.

Maivena continues to stare, and those bosky orbs rake over my face.

"We have somewhere to go," I finally speak to her.

Her eyebrows furrow. "Who?"

"Us, you and me."

"Where?" She instantaneously questions.

"Gordanta, our Western Court. I will be back here soon; Amias and Morano are waiting for me." She flinches as I ascend from the small cottage, leaving the bag of moss at the foot of the chair I sat in.

* * *

I find Amias and Morano in the dining hall; they both are eating at the long table lit in candles and lined with varieties of food.

Morano holds a smirk as I approach, I try to be as stealth and unreadable as Roaner, but sometimes it seems nearly impossible.

"Hello," Amias casually acknowledges me.

"What else is there to know?" I ask.

He smiles. "Well, whoever is roaming Gordanta seems to be playing at a game. Duchess Lorena saw him; the second she chased after him, he ascended and then reappeared. He was playing at this consistently for minutes until finally vanishing. They have not traced him since. Our Warriors were sent out to locate him, but it is nearly impossible. He does not leave a scent, not a trail, nothing.

He is just taking them on unending chases. This is all too close together, Laven. Finding Warriors from Xenathi roaming and terrorizing."

"They are not attacking," Morano adds. "If they are not attacking, it is unclear of what it is they are doing here, how they are crossing or when they crossed through. Roaner said he will not remove the shield until they are found."

"We all go," I nod. "I will go tonight. I am sure Carmen and Lorena will be expecting me to be there soon. You two wait until my mother and Axynth are back to control these grounds, have Alexanti take the place of my mother, and guard Vuamsati Academy." I button the sleeves of my undershirt, thinking of anything else we may need in place before my mother returns.

"And what of Maivena?" Amias asks.

I button my other sleeve. "She is coming with me tonight."

Morano smirks. "Coming with you, how?"

I narrow my eyes at him. "Do not," I warn.

"Wait, how are you arranging this?" Amias probes.

"In my own way," I ascend from the dining hall and to the kitchen, finding Mrs. Patro cleaning off the wooden countertop.

"Ah, Laven! Darling, how are you?" She quickly approaches, leaning in she kisses both of my cheeks.

I smile. "I am good. How are you?"

"Fine as usual. Are you hungry?" She props a hand on her hip. "I did not see you at the dinner table."

"Oh, I ate." I press my hand to my stomach. "I was just wondering, Maivena; she is a servant here. I believe you are familiar with her?"

"I am," the smile that appears on her face proves it. "What about her?"

"I need a basket of food put together. May you do that for me?"

Her smile holds as she responds. "I consider I may."

* * *

When I arrive back at Maivena's, I knock on the unsecured wooden door before opening it. She is sitting at the table in the same place, eating more bread and food in the dish.

I walk towards the table and she stands as I set the large basket down. Lifting it open—her face beams as she sees all of the goods in it.

It seems Mrs. Patro also knows all of Maivena's favorite foods.

"When can you be ready?"

"What do you mean?" She looks up. "I cannot go with you. I do not have anything to wear."

I inhale deeply. "Maivena, you have clothing to wear. It is just up to you if you will wear them. Unless you would like for me to put coin in your hand, you agree to it being yours, and you pay the seamstress yourself."

She cuts her eyes at me.

"Wait outside," she waves to the door, shooing me away. "I will wear what I wore this morning."

"Yes, ma'am." I leave her to give the privacy she requires.

As I wait outside by the door, far out, I see two Wolves playing under the Moon; their play is gentle and daring. The way they move around one another, it is easy to tell they are paired.

Soon, the door is tugged open. I notice her hair is done the way it was earlier. Half contained up in a braid with curls falling around her face.

The bow and arrow brooch holds her cloak together. I reach out, centering it just a bit.

I motion forward. "Do not forget the basket."

She has cleaned the table; a small note is sitting in the placement of the bread and dish previously there. I know she is leaving it for her father, Kaden, and Ethel. Although, I am certain Kaden is located somewhere outside of this cottage waiting for me to walk away.

Maivena grabs the basket off of the table, and I take it from her.

"We do not need anything other than this?"

"No, I have a home in Gordanta that I built not long ago, Fonavyn House. The seamstress there will most likely have clothing hanging for you."

I witness the protest forming on her lips.

"You do not get to deny this anymore," I say before her lips part. "Not after you agreeing to this arrangement," I remind her.

"We do not have conditions set," she reminds me as well.

"Shall you go naked?" I suggest.

"Yes, if you do."

I chuckle and grab her hand. She yelps, latching onto my arm as I ascend from the step of her cottage.

"A forewarning would be appreciated next time!" Maivena beseeches.

She looks around us, admiring the movement of night shifting by. Wisps of white glow as I move higher into the sky.

That rapturing smile reappears.

"It is the stars," she mumbles.

"Reach out your hand." I urge her.

She is hesitant, but she does. White wisps swirl around her finger as we glide through nightfall.

"You should have ascended first with me."

She does not respond. Her hand that is still held in mine tightens. That is answer enough for me. She knows it too.

Her fingers that played with the stars are back on my arm, firmly holding.

I wonder if she, after all these years, has thought of me as I have of her.

We land at the castle gates of Gordanta; the stone palace sits near the water, lit in its magical candles. Maivena peers around, looking at the waves crashing upon the shore just under the moon and stars.

Guards approach the gates, and I can see Maivena's chin dipping.

"Look at me." Her eyes lift, green and submissive, not the woman I knew just moments ago. "You will look every person here in their eye, make it known that you deserve respect. Find the royal you were before being brought here; that is the only woman I will allow these people to know."

The gates pull open, and there is a square her shoulders form. Her chin does not dare to fall again.

14
THE NUISANCE

LAVEN HEPHAESTUS ARVENALDI, II
GORDANTA — WESTERN COURT OF VAIGON

Carmen and Lorena are hand in hand as they approach Maivena and me; they still beam as flirtatious as the day they met. Lorena's nose presses into Carmen's cheek as guards open the gates and the two of them walk through.

Their dark skin gleams under the magically lit candles strung around the palace, but their smiles glow even brighter as they near closer.

Carmen is attired in his usual green and blue topcoat, it is fitted perfectly to his arms and chest, and lined with a gold paisley print. His black hair is now faded and closely cut; the last I saw him, he had dreads down his back.

Lorena's dress barely touches the ground as she walks, two thin lace straps hold the dress up on her shoulders. The dress mimics the color in Carmen's coat.

The style here is different than on the citadel. The women's dresses are tighter and lower cut at the chest, only thin sheer and silk fabrics. Due to the heat that stays consistent in Gordanta it makes sense that they would wear rather less material.

A servant advances toward Maivena and me, asking to take the basket in my hand to my house not far from here. He is dressed well and glows in health. I know Maivena is observing this as well. I thank him before he gets on the back of a light brown Pegasus, he urges the Pegasus to run before taking flight into the sky.

Carmen and Lorena have always had that upper hand here, they treat their workers differently because they have sufficient control over their land. It is almost impossible for me to do what they do here with Lorsius still around. To Lorsius, it will always be *them* and *us*.

There is a grin on Carmen's face, his arm already held out. Our hands powerfully hit as he shakes my shoulder.

"What in the hell took you so long to come back?" He exasperates. "Is it always going to take someone terrorizing the land to get you here?" His lilac eyes are bright as he continues to pick at me.

I smile. "No, I already planned to come here in the summer when the others and I get a break. After Summer Solstice, specifically."

Carmen looks between Maivena and me, his mind is already working. "And who is this?"

He holds his hand out, and Maivena takes it. "I am Maivena; it is nice to meet you." Her eyes drift to Lorena. "You must be Lorena," Maivena nods. Their smiles are just as big as one another.

"I am. It is so lovely to have you here with Laven."

"Your gown is remarkable," Maivena says, finding that key to Lorena's heart. Well, other than sharp objects and Carmen—clothing is most definitely up there with Lorena's favorite things in the world.

A grin spreads across Lorena's face as she tucks her blue-black hair behind her ear. "I could show you around if you would like? They will just be prattling the entire time we tour. Who knows when they will talk about what needs to be handled." Lorena teases us.

Maivena looks up at me, and I nod. "I will find you."

Lorena's hand fills the place of my own before taking Maivena away.

"Look at you, you shining heir." He pretends to dust off my shoulder that is clothed in a black topcoat. "This is sleek," he smirks. "Of course, I am not surprised you still wear all black, even while being in the heat of the West. I think the only color your life has ever seen is the tunic given to you by Artemis, and even that is dark."

"You know I have never been fond of wearing colors."

He laughs as he hooks his arm over my shoulders. "Come, let us walk."

We gravitate toward the gates, and Carmen guides me to the dining courtyard. Servants are laughing and talking amongst one another as they clean.

Not one of them are captives from Old Quamfasi; they are all hires from local people searching for occupations.

I have longed to be here for months—to be with the smell of the water. Hear the sound of waves crashing onto the shore. But the dining courtyard I have missed the most. Candles with unmoving flames hang across the stone pillars that stand in a square around the courtyard; flowers and vines have grown along the body of the tan stone. Double hollyhock flower arrangements are in assortments of centerpieces down the long dining table.

Carmen sits on one of the benches near the large tree shedding its white flowers as I lean against one of the pillars.

"Your dick of an uncle left to help the Duchesses of Partalos just yesterday, I do not know how much helping he truly does. I can say I am relieved he is gone."

"And *I* can say I am dreading his return home." Tension is all there is throughout the citadel when he is there, but it all feels at ease when he is gone.

Carmen grabs a flower that has fallen to the ground; it is nearly dead and wilted. He holds it in his palm, and it disintegrates from a stem and petals to tiny black seeds.

Carmen has the power to give land regrowth or to demolish it whole with one touch.

"The Warrior we found," he drops the seeds into the ground and sways a hand over them. They sink, disappearing into the soil beneath. A green vine is already lifting through the earth. "Whoever he is, he is smart, but he is a pain in my ass."

"Was he here before the passing of the Dragons? That is why Roaner put a shield over the continent." This is a vital factor to know—if he and the other Warrior passed before or after Roaner's shield was projected.

His head drifts from side to side weighing the possibility. "That is plausible, but he leaves no indications of being here. So it is impossible for me to tell when he arrived. I believe in the possibility of them roaming before Roaner put the shield over, and they are stuck until it is down. But, Old Quamfasian people are brilliant. They most likely do have a way out and also a way in."

"What could they be here for?" Our previous war just years ago was about both sides laying down the line that neither can cross the border unless bearing news or severe matters only.

"That I am not sure of, he has not attacked. He seems to be fucking around on my land and tormenting those who chase him off. *But he keeps coming back.*"

We both nod to a worker as he wishes us a goodnight, leaving it to just Carmen and me in the dining courtyard.

"I have Warriors out to keep track of his whereabouts," he adds. "We will get rest before beginning our search tomorrow."

"Do you think they are looking to have another war?"

Another war within such a short length of years will put a strain on the continent more than the last.

He laughs. "I would not be astounded if that were the reason, but I do not think so. After all of these years, I am assured they have grown out of wanting back their land while some only ponder the debate to return for revenge. Now, I think they are testing us. Trying our strengths now that we have what was once theirs." He stands.

"As in?"

"As in sacred land." He responds. "There is power on sacred land, an upper hand. Bodies of the most powerful people lie beneath our feet. They could be inspecting if we have learned how to channel into them and gain our advantage over not just their people, but every realm."

"Having the ability to summon the power of the dead is rare, Carmen. Mostly because Hades does not bless many with strengths as deep as that."

He waves his finger. "Do not be so sure; someone must be able to. We are immortal, Laven. Everlasting. Even when we die, our souls live on because there will always be someone who can tap into us, even from the grave."

"You think smart, Carmen, but that is not why I am here." Our heads swiftly turn to the voice.

I know his face the moment he looks at us. His leather shoes are propped on the arm of the chair next to him as he eats fruit leftover on the table.

Carmen stands straighter. "High Prince Vorian."

"*Former* High Prince Vorian," he corrects, tossing a blueberry into his mouth. "I forgot how well fruit grows here; these blueberries are fantastic." His long golden blonde hair hangs over his red fighting leathers, crowding his bronzed face.

"Vorian, why are you here?"

"Well, colonizer Prince Laven," I narrow my eyes at him, and he smirks. "I cannot tell you."

"And why is that?" Carmen asks.

"Because," he shrugs. "It is a secret."

I raise an eyebrow. "If it is secret, why are you so excruciatingly obvious with your arrival?"

"I was bored. Do you have any strawberries?" Vorian asks while walking along the side of the table, his red eyes are searching for food.

"Vorian, enough of this nonchalant shit." My arms cross, and he cuts an eye at me.

"Or what?" He finds the chair he was previously sitting in and bites into a strawberry. "You will torture me like your uncle tried and failed to? Will you attempt to cut my cock off so I cannot have children? Or will you steal my sister and use her body as a vessel for bearing newborns of our bloodline?"

Carmen puts a hand on my shoulder as I take a step onward. "Vorian, you know he held no part in that. What happened to your people was horrific. Most of us did not wish for that to happen." He tries to reason, yet I know it is not worth it.

"What is it that they say? The apple does not fall too far from the tree. Birds of a feather flock together."

"*What* do you want, Vorian?"

Carmen's hand tightens on my shoulder.

Vorian grins. "You have always been such an angsty little fucker. By the way, those rogue things were roaming your woods. I killed them for you."

Carmen looks at me and then back to Vorian. "Did you kill them just as easily as you are saying?"

Vorian's eyebrows furrow, and his head juts forward. "Yes."

Of course, it would be easy for him. If we could not sense him here, the rogues surely could not either. As much as I hate to admit it, Vorian is one of the strongest and most intelligent fighters I have ever challenged.

"I should have trophies for how many of those things I have killed while being here."

"How much do you know of this disease?" Carmen asks more questions, but I know we will not be getting any answers. Vorian has always played this game; annoy you enough until you blather at the mouth and say exactly what he needs to hear without directly asking.

"I am not telling you," his face scrunches. "There is no reward here for me from telling you my secrets."

"Then what the fuck do you want?"

His eyes meet mine again and his face falls solemn, all irreverence leaves.

"What I want is to warn you." I study him as the words leave his mouth.

I find nothing, not a flash of lightheartedness is in his eyes.

"Something is coming. Something that could wipe us off the face of the earth. This is no disease. Someone has developed an infection, injected it into others, and it spreads from whomever they bite or harm. The creator controls them. I do not know how; I do not know what it is or why. But the only person they are truly conscious of is the creator of this mayhem."

I choose to keep quiet about my own experience with rogues, that is a private conversation to be had later between only me, Maivena, Carmen, and Lorena. Vorian does not need to know I had access to something that belongs to his land to save my life.

"Why should we trust what you are saying?" Carmen questions.

"Because your feet walk over the graves of my ancestors too. I will not watch their land degrade to ruins. Start training your people harder, a war is coming, and you all are not ready. The privilege you now hold has made your people soft, toughen them up, and expand your Mandems. You will need it."

Vorian is gone faster than the blink of an eye. Gone before I can question him further on who it is that has started this all. That is if he knows.

I look at Carmen, and he scratches his chin.

"Do you believe him?" Carmen asks.

I stand here a moment and nod. "Yes."

When it comes to his family and ancestors, Vorian fights harder than anyone I know. Years ago, he may have lost going head-to-head with me, however, it was a hard fight to win.

I refuse to remember the look in Vorian's eyes as the tip of my dagger was against his throat. I can still hear the uncanny screams of my uncle to kill him, yet, I remember the punishment that led after I did not.

"Oh," Vorian reappears, sitting in the same chair. "My friend, the red-headed woman. She and I can get through your shield. Tell Roaner if he wishes to truly put up a shield to keep everyone out, have Stravan teach him when he visits."

"How do you know Stravan is coming?"

Vorian throws a hand out. "He is my closest companion, of course, I know."

"Why not ally with us since it comes down to you and your people worrying for the land? Do Vallehes and Penelope feel the same as you?"

Vorian gapes at Carmen. "My parents and I would rather spit on our ancestors' graves than ally with you." With that he is gone again.

We wait a moment or so, presupposing he will come back again.

"What a joy it is to have him around," Carmen speaks, with sarcasm dripping throughout his words.

"I am sure he feels the same about us." I begin to walk through the courtyard and pick a white hollyhock from a vine.

"In the morning, we will need to assemble everyone, and we will enact new training." I advise. "Roaner, Amias, and Morano will arrive in the afternoon. We will give everyone more strenuous training, push them, make them train harder than they ever have. That is one thing Vorian is right about, and also something Morano has brought to my attention. Our people are weak solely because of privilege being on this land. Prepare General Vanytha; she may not be ready for all we will push onto them tomorrow morning. She most likely has not trained like this since the days of High Queen Penelope ruling Old Quamfasi."

15
SOUL OF TERROR

LAVEN HEPHAESTUS ARVENALDI, II

Lorena directed Maivena to the chamber I used to stay in while here at the palace, but this is not where we are staying while in Gordanta.

The balcony doors are shut, multiple candles around the room are lit, and logs burn bright in the large fireplace.

When I get closer, I see Maivena. She lies on the chaise in front of the fire, fast asleep. There is a book in her hand that hangs off the chaise; I smile and step closer.

Before I can approach, the book slips from her hand; the hard thud to the ground wakes her in fright. I flinch as she scrambles around panting. She tumbles from the chaise, and I avidly reach out to help her, but she clambers backward.

I do not want to frighten her any more than she already is. I can hear nothing but the loud panic in her breath as it forces itself from her.

She does not stop receding until her back collides with the wall. She coils herself into the corner of the chamber, her fingers nearly turn white from how tightly she holds herself . . . no, protects herself.

I stay where I am, and lower to the floor.

Her frantic heartbeat is like drums beating and echoing through the room.

I swallow. "Maivena?"

There is quiet weeping as her head buries into her knees. She is still asleep, still walking through a terror in the night.

I call out for her again, this time louder, but keeping my voice leveled and low.

Closing my eyes, I channel every sliver of power I received from Morano during the Blood Bond Ritual. I set out to reveal a small crack in her mind to force through to find her.

My mind begins to slip due to her low cries diverting me, a natural reaction, the need to save her from everything.

I dig deeper, focusing harder than I ever have to get into someone's mind.

There were many things Morano said would occur when I successfully make my way into someone's mind for the first time; the main occurrence, pain. Excruciating pain that envelopes your head from taking on not only your thoughts but theirs as well. And if you dig deep enough, it is possible to take on their emotions, which can turn out horribly if you do not have control over what you are doing.

I refuse to succumb to the pain. Instead, I fight it.

There is nothing here but darkness.

This darkness is not from me failing to get through to her. It begins to clear, clarifying the space her mind is trapped in.

She is there.

Curled, naked, and dirty . . . confined in a large, shaking wooden box.

Pegasi' hooves pound into the ground, carrying her away.

There is screaming. But it is not her.

Through a tiny hole in the wood, I see a little boy. He is chasing behind the broken carriage, yelling. His cries are painful, but she does not move.

He grabs onto the carriage, and I can hear his feet dragging to keep up with the speed of the Pegasi.

Ira.

It is her little brother.

Then, there is laughter from afar, vicious laughter as Ira's bellowing moves farther and farther away.

He could not keep up to get back to her.

"Maivena," I brokenly whisper. I am not aware if I fully spoke her name.

Her weeping continues.

"This is only a nightmare," I impel for more strength. "You have to open your eyes."

There is an ease to her cries. The girl in her dreams that I recognize well still does not move. She is as motionless as night.

"It is you, and me. There is only us. Open your eyes, darling. Look at me."

Immediately, I tear open my eyes to Maivena, and I intake a sharp breath as she quakes. She is crawling, her knees trip over her gown as she hastily rushes toward me.

She does not make it halfway across the distance between us before I gather her in my arms. Her body settles into my hold, and a gasp pulls at her chest as she finally breathes.

Her arms are tight around my back as she holds on to me for dear life. Her grip does not falter. She only holds me tighter, slowly seeking a regulated breathing pattern.

I secure my arm around her waist and smooth my hand over her neck, pressing my lips to the top of her head.

She stays here, unmoving and idle, searching for that small light of life she had before this.

And I give her every bit of life from me to fuel her in any way she needs.

I look down as she peers upward. Her eyes are big—as if asking if it is okay to stay right where she is. I pull her closer, and she settles further in. The warmth of my body calms the chills shaking her fragile frame.

"Fonavyn House is not too far from here. Do you want to go there with me?"

She sits up straighter and nods.

Still carrying her, I stand from the floor and grab her cloak that is lying on the arm of the chaise before ascending from the chamber.

Her head rests on my shoulder, and I know I could hold her here until death.

She stands as we land in the main chamber of my house.

Maivena turns, looking up at me and I trace her reddened cheeks. "Bathe with me."

Let me wash this terror from your skin.

I grab her hands and walk backward, pulling her in the direction of the bathing room.

She watches as I pull the lever that flows water through the stone tub. I light lanterns around the room to bring a dimmed brightness around us. Just above the tub the moonlight glows through the ceiling window.

Each button of my topcoat is pulled until it falls heavily to the floor. She releases my undershirt from being tucked into my trousers and I quietly laugh as she struggles to pull the shirt over my head as she is unable to reach. The moment I discard the shirt, I outstretch my arms and bring her closer.

She turns around and I move the thick curls flowing down her back. I pull the laces that hold her dress together, each tug of the white string reveals her smooth brown skin.

The satin slips down her hips, and circles at her ankles. I bend at the knee as she faces me, and remove the shoes from her feet. I am just below her chin as I kneel in front of her.

She slightly dips her head, and she grazes my forehead with her lips as I stare up at her.

I could faint just looking at her.

There is comfort forming in her eyes as her lips sweep from my forehead and down my nose.

I stand, and she draws out the laces of my trousers, grabbing the hem, she pushes them down my legs.

Her hands touch my hips, leisurely signaling for me to sit.

I find the edge of the stone tub and sit. I tightly grip the edge as she gets to the floor and sits back on her heels. Her fingers work to undo my leather boots, setting them side by side before removing my trousers.

I catch her chin, lifting her to stand with me as I realize where she is aiming to go.

She nears closer. "I want to touch you."

Trails of fire are left behind her touch as she rubs from my chest, slowly finding her way lower, and lower, *and lower*.

My breath hitches in my chest; she is nearly there, her fingers push through the dark hair leading downward.

I smile, and I shake as I speak. "Not yet," I reach down, lifting her from the floor. Her legs wrap around my waist, a kiss is pressed to my shoulder and up my neck as I step into the warmth of the water.

She sits between my legs and shadows of moonlight gleam over our skin.

There is a tear that glides down her cheek as she looks through the window. She quickly wipes it away, thinking I did not see it.

"Maivena."

She says nothing. She stays cast to the window, looking outward.

I tilt my head, watching her.

She is fighting weakness that she could show. Her eyebrows furrow, concentrating on removing all sense of emotion.

"This is not what an Intimacy Arrangement is," she finally says. "You are not supposed to be doing this for me. I am supposed to be doing this for you."

I do not utter a word.

Grabbing her cheek, I pull her to look at me.

"An Intimacy Arrangement is not only about what you can do for me," I say, "but what I can do for you. Every tear you shed is safe with me."

Her eyes fill. I know she wants to fight them, but the tears fall. They fall like a gentle rain down my fingers. Rain that makes the growing garden between our soul's flourish.

"You have the power to heal wounds, what of a soul?" She is barely audible.

There is a hollowness, a dark pain looking at the sorrow in her bosky eyes. "Your soul is yours to heal; I am only here to help it move."

PART II
PORTAL OF DERELICTION

16
SIX OF SPRING

ROANER KORSANA
VAIGON CITADEL

I SIT ON THE back of my Pegasus, Aryon, as we wait in the woods where Levora was last seen. Esme will arrive shortly so we may begin the course of pulling forth a portal.

It is more than discomforting to be in a place as this again. Although I have come here often to search and consistently hope for Levora's appearance, it is different here now. It could possibly be because of bringing someone else here outside of Laven and myself. I would involve Laven, yet he too deeply blames himself for her disappearance. It would be unfair to make him consistently relive that trauma. I will not allow him to risk his sanity again, Wyendgrev took enough from him.

Before me and our brothers, the closest person in his life was his sister. These woods hold darkness and will only shine light when she is found.

I am not only searching for Levora for myself, but for Laven. Peace should be his and mine.

After our previous meeting I was allowed to keep the book that contains the information on portals. If I am going to successfully open the portal to the realm she was taken to, I am going to need to consume as much information as possible.

It was nearly overwhelming to realize how much material there is to remember when practicing opening portals, but to get Levora to come home, I will manage.

One of the many traits I learned from the book is that portals will not be seen when closed but are still felt due to the immense energy required for creation. Once a portal is created, it can never be removed. It will not be visible but will appear if channeled properly. The appearance of a portal is either a door or you are shown the land you are being taken to.

I can hear the distant soaring of wings overhead as I wait for Esme's arrival.

Descending from the clouds in an expansive shadow, her Pegasus drives downward with Esme secure on her back. Esme looks below with eyes bright and silver, she is searching for open area on the grounds to land. When she sees me she directs her Pegasus to move to ground.

She is a rather large and muscular Pegasus with an entirely black body except for one small stripe of white along her nose. Whereas Aryon is walnut brown, solid, and sleek.

Aryon harshly stamps his hove into the ground, and I tighten the reigns to hold him from launching onward.

"Stay calm," I say to him.

Her Pegasus swiftly lands to the ground in a run and slowly comes to a stop before us. Her wings are expansive and strong as they shake out after landing.

Esme unmounts and touches the Pegasus before their heads connect and they both breathe in deeply. By the way they interact, she has had her for years. Only the longest connections between a Pegasus and their rider are this synced.

"What is her name?" I ask as Esme approaches.

"Oveila," she answers. "And yours?" Esme asks, looking over Aryon.

She is examining his muscles and stance as she stands before us, having left Oveila near the small flowing river. She sniffs the flowers growing near the water before hydrating after her flight.

"Aryon," I respond.

Esme walks to a particular area of the woods and stretches out her hand.

She is foraging for the portal we found the last time we were here when we first met to begin the search.

She gently moves her fingers feeling the energy of the invisible portal. She nods for me to approach, and I leave Aryon to drink with Oveila.

Gradually, as I move closer, there is a radiation of heat that grows and wraps around us as I reach where Esme is standing.

She walks around the portal to stand in front of me and she holds her hand outward once more. "It is still producing warmth from this side as well."

They created this portal to be accessed from both ends.

If the portal was created here, that does not mean that it is open wherever it led to. But, it seems that whoever opened this portal also created another in attachment on the other side to get back. The one way to know is that you will feel the radiation of energy from facing the portal, as well as standing behind it. This, fortunately, makes our task here easier to get there and come right back.

"Now," Esme begins. "Have you ever attended a Sorcerers Academy?"

"I have not," I shake my head. "Everything I know how to do was taught to me by my mother."

"Did she ever teach you anything about portals? It is usually a course that is mandatory when attending an academy."

"She did not."

Esme nods. "The book will be enough, but you must be reminded that this will not happen overnight. Summoning portals can take prolonged periods of time and you will fall short of strength after practicing. Bringing forth a portal will render your powers short; you must be aware of how much this will take out of you."

I do not have the time to fall short of strength. A life I promised to someone, and a life they promised me disappeared. This will be one thing in my life I will not allow to fail since she had never once in our younger years failed me.

Call it young love, pure infatuation, whatever people will say it was. Levora was the only thing to keep me from utter damnation.

'Laven!' That once quiet voice shouts. 'Laven stop it!'

The large boy above me is ripped away. 'Say it once more!' Laven shouts as his friend Amias holds him tightly around the chest with one arm and carries him backward.

He is put down and Levora rushes over and shoves him by the chest. 'What is wrong with you?' She screams. 'Hit him once more and I will tell papa!'

'Tell pa! Call him here, I will beat him in front of papa!'

'Laven!' A strong voice shakes the ground as his name is yelled.

Laven looks back to a man storming forward with long white hair. He looks at me and holds his threat to his sister, and Amias cannot hold him; Laven lunges from his grasp with his fist held in the air, just before his knuckles connect with my face again his father catches his hand right before my nose.

He is picked up by his waist coat and thrown to the ground in the opposite direction of me. He does not let up, he runs again, and his father braces him—his arms hook under Laven's armpits and his hands connect behind his head rendering him of all movement, but his legs still thrash.

'Should not have said that to him.' Amias stands in the distance with crossed arms.

Laven, the first, turns to Amias and Amias quiets quickly.

Laven's father looks down at his son. 'Are you done?'

He seizes all movement and is let go.

The large figure stands between us and looks between me and Levora as she sides by me as I come up from the ground.

He turns toward his son. 'You are going to stand here, and we are going to solve this without you retaliating with aggression . . . what happened?'

I do not speak; I am embarrassed to repeat what I said, nor do I want to let this man hear what I said about his family.

Laven does not speak either.

I wipe the blood dripping from my eyebrow, and he waits for either Laven or I to speak.

Amias does instead.

'He inappropriately called Laven out of his name and then challenged him,' Levora looks up at me, I do not look at her. *'And Laven retaliated.'*

He is hiding a piece of the truth.

When our eyes meet, Amias looks away and says nothing more.

Levora leaves my side and walks toward Laven, she grabs his hand seeing the blood that does not belong to him, yet she gently wipes it away as if it is a cut on his hand.

The four of them look at me as I stand here.

'I do not know what was said, I do not care to know what was said, but you,' he points at me. *'Will never speak to my son out of his name again, and you,'* he turns to his first-born child. *'You and I will speak of your immediate need for self-validation through operation of physical violence.'*

'No,' Levora speaks. *'What did you say to him?'* She stays put as she continues to nurture her brother's bloodied hand.

'Vora,' Amias steps over and pulls on her arm. *'Do not.'* He warningly speaks.

'Oh, but I want to.'

'Do not burden yourself to care,' Laven holds his sister's hand. *'He will not say it again.'*

'Where are you supposed to be, Roaner?' The eldest of us all asks.

'Walking to my dormitory at the academy.'

'Then walk to your dormitory,' he advises. *'This is done.'* His hands motion between Laven and myself.

I should apologize before leaving, but I do not see it possible. Could one have so much shame that he cannot apologize because he knows it would not change what he said?

So, I do not speak, I only walk on the path I do every day.

When I look back I see the four of them ascending as a whole to go home.

I pulled the hood of my cloak over my head when passing by the others in the same dormitory as me. We are youth, meaning we are nosy and prone to staring. That is exactly what I avoided.

I wince as I press the cloth against the wound on my eyebrow. That small attempt at fixing the cut has angered me enough to stop.

The door to my dorm pushes open and I sharply turn to see who it is.

She is moving swiftly across the room and towards me.

'I had a feeling you were too inept to comprehend cleaning a wound.' Levora says as she yanks away the cloth and begins to properly care for the gash in my skin.

'I do like you, Roaner.' She continues to speak as she leans down and her light eyes hold fury. 'But if you ever speak to anyone in my family like that again, I will allow Laven to kill you.'

I stare at her until I no longer see the anger in her.

Slowly, I smile. 'You would never let him kill me.'

* * *

You never truly know how far you can push yourself until you hit the ground in defeat.

I thought I could reach the ends of the universe in search of Levora. Nothing, not anything, nor anyone would stop me from getting to her. Why when I have the answers and the resources to find her, I cannot summon the strength?

I wonder if I have this fate because there are chances we are not mates and the person she is fated to be with is not me. I could be cursing myself by pursuing a woman that is already taken by soul.

I collapse to the hard ground fully weakened of energy and almost hope.

"You must learn to conserve your energy." A voice says through the darkness. They appear from ascension and the silver hues are recognizable.

Well, I knew her voice before she appeared.

"You cannot spend yourself so quickly. Take your time." Esme kneels in front of me.

She is not in her armor, she looks like she just left a gala.

Her dress is long and thin, wrapping around her in all sorts of directions.

"You look lovely." I say through heavy breaths.

"I know I do."

I nod. "I figured."

"And I figure you are ignoring what I am saying."

"No, I was listening."

"And are you still listening as I ask about your bargain with Vallehes?"

I nod again, still breathless. "My Emissary has found them. They were last seen in Terseius. They tend to be sporadic with their location, but they always return to the same Inn up North. Yet they have been hiding themselves, my Emissary will find out why they tend to fabricate soon."

She stands and holds her hand out to me. "Get up."

Our hands join and she pulls me from the ground.

As she tries to let go of my hand, I hold on tighter. "How did you know I was here?"

Her eyebrows furrow and slowly she looks upward. She shrugs. "I do not know; I just had an odd feeling you were attempting something stupid. And here you are."

"And here you are." I say back.

She looks at our hands just as I do.

Before I can speak again, she is gone.

17
LAVENDER OIL

LAVEN HEPHAESTUS ARVENALDI, II

I LOOK BACK TO the bed as I hear Maivena stir. I smile as she sits up; her hair is scattered in messy curls around her shoulders, leveling right over her bare hips. She observes me as I pull black leather armor from a box that Roaner brought with him.

"I do not think those will fit you," Maivena says, a deep rasp has overtaken her voice due to just waking.

"No," I shake my head. "They surely will not."

She crawls to the edge of the bed and sits back on her heels as I stand in front of her.

I lean down, pressing into the padding of the bed on either side of her. "They are yours if you wish to train again."

Maivena looks down at the leather now sitting next to her, and she runs a hand over them. I watch as she stares. I can feel it; her eyes express it. She is drifting off someplace else, somewhere that is not benevolent of her thoughts.

"Maivena . . . where are you?"

She does not say anything. Instead, her head just slightly lifts, eyes meeting mine.

"Somewhere," she slowly blinks, "but somehow right here."

I touch my nose to hers. "Come back."

Her lips curl.

That smile, dear Gods, that smile.

"Who will I train with?" She asks.

"Whomever you want."

"You?"

"Yes," I nod. "If you want me to."

Maivena looks down at the leather again. "Yes."

"You need to eat first, and then we will start after. What do you want for morning meal?"

Her head turns to the basket Mrs. Patro gathered. There are loaves of bread, cheeses, fruits, and jams. I walk away and grab it from the table.

Maivena's smile is untamed as I approach. I will never get over her love for food; she should have never been deprived of it for so long. Or possibly, I did not try hard enough to be sure she consistently stayed fed.

When I open the basket, I see she put her mother's scarf in it, along with the one I gifted her . . . and that wine as well.

She will want that wine after the training we go through.

Maivena grabs a loaf of bread and pulls off an end of it; she dips it into the jam and tears a piece of cheese from the block. She does not eat it, she holds the little combination outward, and I simper, shaking my head.

"You have given other people food over yourself for long enough. You eat first." I sit behind her, and she slightly turns with her eyes narrowed.

She forces it into my mouth with furrowed brows, and I loudly laugh. She watches me chew, analyzing my face to see if I like it. I do.

Sweet, salty, and almost savory.

We both sit in silence as we eat. She devours half of a loaf along with apples, strawberries, and cheese.

"How often do you train with your father?" I ask while wiping jam from the corner of her mouth.

Before she responds, her head turns to the door at the sound of quiet bickering.

She leans, focusing on the voices.

"Who is that?" She asks, lifting her finger to the door.

"Roaner, he brought someone with him. I am not sure of who it is, but when he arrived in the middle of the night, I know he had someone with him." Surprisingly.

The talking down the hall stops, and she goes back to eating more of the food.

"My father and I do not train often," she answers my question. "He usually does not have enough time, and more often than not, I am busy elsewhere."

"Then nothing too strenuous today." I clarify.

I had the opportunity to see her father on the training grounds not long ago, and he is fatal with every weapon. Without using his powers, he alone is death walking with a spear. The strongest of men and women fear him. So, it is no wonder to me why they attacked Maivena's home those years ago while he and his wife were away. An easy massacre is what that day would have been for him.

"We will only train to what you can handle. Do you mind if Roaner joins us?"

She looks at her arms now concealed in black leather. "I do not mind. He can help."

Maivena is skintight in armor from neck to ankle. I kneel before her to fix the boots' laces on her feet as Roaner recedes from the house to meet Maivena and me outside.

When I stand, I see the woman he brought with him.

Her face reads no expression as she looks past me and directly at Maivena.

She is in dark red leather with complex stitching along the shoulders and legs. These are Quamfasian leathers.

"Esme?" Maivena whispers.

The woman looks her over, analyzing Maivena's face and

roaming over her frame. Her golden eyes fill with a twinge of discomfort, an aching expression. "My Gods, Maivena."

They run to each other and their bodies collide as they desperately hold one another.

I look toward Roaner, and he fixes his gaze upon them.

"Who is she?" I ask.

He does not dislodge his sight from the two.

"Maivena's cousin, Esme Fondali."

I gape at them; this would be the first she has seen another family member in years.

Esme places multiple kisses upon Maivena's face as she holds her cheeks. "I did not know if I would ever see you again. Why did you not write me?"

"We were not allowed to," Maivena shakes her head. She holds her cousin firmly, as if she is afraid this is all a dream, like she will disappear in an instant.

"*Bouvestas**," Esme speaks in Quamfasian. There is a steam of some sort that moves from the leathers on her skin.

"Do not worry," Maivena tries to soothe her. "I have been fine."

The soothing seems to work as that peculiar steam coming from Esme retreats.

"Have you seen Ethel?" She asks.

"Yes," Maivena's posture slightly slumps. "Kaden came with papa. I found her on the grounds; we arrived the same day. Papa and Kaden were only allowed in because of Lady Apolla; they were turned away multiple times before reaching Apolla."

Ethel . . . she is whom Kaden came looking for.

Ethel must be Esme's sister.

"She is," Roaner confirms my thoughts but gives me no further elaboration and I do not question him.

"Gods, Maivena. Look at you, do they not feed you?" She examines her cousin's small frame. "Is their intent to starve you to your

---

* *Old Quamfasian: Bouvestas   Translation: Bastards*

grave? I brought food with me; we can eat first. Over my dead body will you train without eating."

"I already ate with Laven," Maivena says as she grabs Esme's hand to guide her to me. "Come meet Laven."

Esme's golden eyes are set in aggression as she swivels around to me.

Slowly, Maivena guides her across the ample space between us.

It is easily seen that she does not wish to be in the same environment as me. Understandable.

She looks me in the eye, and the steam I saw from just moments ago pushes forward and it circles me. Maivena grabs my arm and her head snaps toward Esme who stares at us, glowering at Maivena's hand on my arm.

At once, I see the realization in her eyes. Whatever this is she has encompassing me just alerted her of the mating bond. I want to advise her not to speak of it, but I do not know her, and it is not my place to tell this woman what to do.

"She will not tell her," Roaner calms my thoughts.

"Esme," she announces herself as she holds her hand out to me. Her nails are long, sculpted in a round point, and shiny.

I just know she has clawed eyes out with them.

I take her hand. Her grip is firm, a fair warning.

"Laven," I nod, and our hands disjoin.

"I cannot say I am pleased to meet you." Esme says. "Well, not with your scent all over my cousin."

She and Morano would be interesting in a conversation together.

"You and Morano would get along very well, I believe," Maivena faintly speaks.

I smile and pull her nearer. "I think so too."

Esme does not seem to be too impressed with us saying this. Once more, she frowns at us.

"Be careful, Maivena." Her cousin warns, looking between us. "Sometimes, your oppressor is nothing more than just that."

I narrow my eyes at her and she stares back with ferocity—virtually daring me to say something back to her.

"Esme, do not be so keen on incensing him." Maivena jumps to my defense.

She opens her mouth, and Roaner ascends, appearing near her. Immediately, she stops.

"Maivena," Roaner says. "If you would like, we all will train you. Esme said she would help," he says. Esme nods in agreement, and Maivena does as well.

Esme grabs Maivena and tugs her from my side; they walk down the large land area in front of the house. The ocean is still as I look outward and over the slope not far off.

"She is . . . intriguing," I say as Roaner stands beside me.

He nods. "You have no idea. Esme has been trying to process this for years. First her sister, then her cousin. She does not hate you; she is very protective over her family after everything that has happened. Seeing Maivena with you is a culture shock for her, especially ever since the division of our lands."

I do not know who this woman is to him, but they must have become close during his endeavors to New Quamfasi.

"I must warn you; she will challenge her," Roaner informs. "You will not like it, but Esme knows what Maivena is capable of. We may help, but Esme is the only one who is aware of how far Maivena can be pushed."

Cautiously, I watch the two of them.

"She is fragile, Roaner." I try to hide my perturbation as it builds. "She is not as solid on her feet as she used to be. It has been years since she trained to those depths."

"Trust her."

Trust the woman whom I know wants to claw my eyes out.

Esme begins plaiting Maivena's hair straight down the middle, starting from her hairline and down her back. A knot is tied at the end of her hair to keep the plait secure.

Widening the range of my hearing, I listen to what they are saying, but it is useless since I do not have full knowledge of the Quamfasian language.

They separate by drawing backward, putting multiple feet

between one another and they stop simultaneously.

There is a shield Maivena is holding, but only that, nothing more.

In the blink of an eye, they are charging at one another at full speed.

"She is making her relearn protection over herself with each weapon on its own," Roaner announces as I watch them move.

Every strike Maivena hurls is blocked, Esme moves too fast for her to keep up, and she knows it.

A hard punch is delivered to Maivena's stomach, and she does not remain steady on her feet; she falls backward on the ground and winces at the blow.

I step forward, and Roaner grabs my arm.

Esme looks back at us. "She can take a hit, do not let her fool you."

Swiftly, Maivena's leg swings out. It takes Esme off her feet, and I hear a chuckle pull from Roaner. "Do not take your eyes off your opponent." He speaks and quickly he receives a harsh glare.

They go at this repeatedly, resulting in the same ending as before. Unfortunately, each hit given by her cousin lands in a different place, forcing Maivena to grow short-tempered and tense.

"Has the General's daughter lost her touch?" Esme jeers.

Droplets of salt begin to drip down Maivena's neck, and through her posture I can tell she is growing exhausted.

"Come," Esme holds her hand out. "Get up." Maivena subsides her gesture and stands on her own. "Crotchety now, are we?"

"Fuck you," Maivena snaps.

"If she pushes her over the edge, Maivena will want to quit." I analyze the slumping of her shoulders; the shield is growing to be too heavy on the left side of her body.

"And you will allow her to?" Roaner responds.

I exhale heavily, watching her stumble again. *"No."*

"You would test her just as hard. Esme just has a harsher way of going about it."

A loud gasp pulls from Maivena as she falls to the ground, her hands flatten against the earth, feeling around. When I look at her eyes, they are clouded in white.

I move across the vast area in mere seconds.

Kneeling next to her, Maivena grips onto me the moment she feels me near.

"What the hell are you doing to her?" I growl at Esme.

"*Give me my sight back!*" Maivena shouts loud enough to make the birds flock from the trees.

"I would not have to use my powers against you if you fought better, which you can." Esme snaps. "Get up, Fondali. Use your senses."

"She has no real control over her senses; she has not ever shifted into her Wolf. Now give her sight back!"

Esme studies us as Maivena reaches up to me with her other hand, searching. Her fingers latch onto my arm, stilling the shaking moving over my hands.

I do not know if she is looking for support or keeping a hand on me to stop me from strangling her cousin.

"You need to get away from her, princeling."

I ignore her insults. "And why would that be?"

"Can you not see? You make her weak. Leave her," Esme's tone is crueler than before.

I grace Maivena's cheek, softly touching as I look at her.

Her words rattle in my ear, and I ignore Roaner as he tries to talk through the bond.

After years of being someone else's strength, it is horrifying to leave them alone in distress.

Esme's expression is teasing as she tilts her head at us. "Seems today's lesson is for two people."

"Am I to leave her stranded when she is being attacked while vulnerable?"

"No one said that. A war is possibly approaching, and you will not be near her every blinking second; she needs to do this independently. She has been able to fend for herself in the past, and she can again."

Maivena's hands slowly loosen, but she does not let go.

There is a slight smile that appears. "It is fine," she tries to diffuse the rising tempers.

I follow her from the ground as she stands.

"War or not," I look toward Esme. Roaner is now standing not far behind her. "You can chase me down with the strongest warriors known, but not a single person will stop me from being at her side the moment I feel her strength falter."

I reach down, grabbing her shield and fit it back on her arm. Esme opens her mouth to protest, and she stops when Roaner touches her shoulder.

"We said you could train her," I begin. "But I did not say I will sit back and not direct her. It has been years since she has trained like this; you should have had her practice stances before just punching her to the ground. A proper trainer would know this without needing to be told.

"Separate your feet wider," she listens. Her balance will stand firmer, and it will be harder for her to be knocked down. "Square your shoulders," as she does this, the shield lifts higher, guarding her greater than it was before. "Do not just use this as a shield," I tap the iron on her arm before I lift her chin and look into her grey filled eyes. "It makes one hell of a weapon. Use it as so."

And beat the hell out of her with it.

When I glance at Esme, she almost seems to be satisfied.

"Go," I step away.

Esme runs forward, but Maivena waits. I watch her ears flinch. She is listening to the pounding of feet coming toward her.

Still blinded, Maivena rushes forward and drifts around Esme with ease. The shield glides down her forearm and she catches it by the handle centered directly in the middle as she moves in a tornado around Esme. Her leg reaches back in a lunge, bringing herself to a steady stop. She punches Esme with the curve of the shield, right in the center of her back. The hit throws her forward, not only making her stumble to the ground in defeat but the punch nails her hard enough to knock her powers short, giving Maivena her sight back.

Before Esme can stand, Roaner shouts. "Again!" Maivena charges at her without hesitation.

She does not touch the ground again other than with her feet.

* * *

I sit down at the table in the kitchen as Roaner slides me a glass with dark liquor in it. The windows around us sit wide open, allowing in the night breeze.

I did not remember how much I had left to furnish in this house until I arrived here again for the first time in months. The kitchen is practically empty. Other than the bedchambers, everything needs more furnishing. I believe this is what the result is when you build a home out of an impulse.

"Who is Esme to you?" I ask Roaner as I drink all of what is in the vessel. I grunt at the burn as the alcohol settles.

He shakes his head. "Someone I met while moving back and forth through our lands."

"How did it come about you bringing her here?"

"She wanted to see if her old home was still standing from years ago." Roaner sips the liquor before continuing. "Esme resided here in our Western Court before the war. I told her she could stay with me after searching."

"And did she find anything?" I inquire.

"Yes," he nods. "Her old home is not far from here, so it was convenient for her to be here."

I smile. "Sharing a bedchamber with this woman?"

He smiles back, stands from the table, and starts a fire in the oven to avoid answering my question. "When will Amias and Morano arrive?" He asks.

"They are already here; they are at the Training Grounds with Carmen. They have been enlisting new methods of training. I will be visiting the grounds tomorrow to help."

"I will start a roast for supper, it should be ready by the time Maivena, and Esme are done bathing. You will most likely be taking the food up those stairs tonight." Roaner chuckles.

I saw the way Maivena walked up those stairs. Every muscle in her body is in agony after today. The only stop she had was to eat, and then she returned outside to swim laps in the large pond stretching along the pillars and trees out front.

"Either way," I say. "She is eating before she sleeps."

He stands and walks over to a small, black-leathered trunk. He retrieves a vial from it, and I can smell the oil before he tosses it to me.

Lavender.

He does not say anything. He dismisses me by looking to the hall that leads upstairs to the chambers. "Unless you need help navigating a home you built with your own hands?" He curtly says with amusement.

I ascend from the kitchen to the bathing room in my chamber.

Maivena's eyes are closed as she rests in the steaming water.

"I need help getting out," she mumbles.

I did not need to announce my arrival, she felt my presence as I feel hers.

I walk over and sit the lavender oil on the edge of the stone. She looks over to it and painfully shakes her head no.

She closes her eyes and her head leans back to rest. "I do not have the vitality for such movement."

"I do."

Maivena looks at me again. She wraps around my neck, and I reach through the water, lifting her. She soaks my bare chest as she clings to me, staring, admiring every inch of my face.

She stands on the shag rug in front of the tub and touches my lower abdomen, as I kneel, her hands gravitate over my chest and grip my shoulders. Grabbing the linen, I start by drying off her legs and lead up to her stomach. She looks down as I kiss along her legs. Her breathing falls short the higher I move.

I taste the skin along the curve of her breast, I ever-so-lightly touch her cinnamon-colored nipples with my lips, and fight the urge to bite down. Her eyes flutter shut, and I fear she may faint.

Then, I wonder how much weaker I can possibly make her.

I smile at the thought and finish drying her off before carrying her to the bed.

I return with the oil, and she stops me. "The oil will get all over the bedding."

"I really could not give a fuck." Finally, I breathe.

Maivena looks back as she lays on her stomach, her backside perches right below me as I straddle her thighs.

"What are you waiting for?" She whines while wiggling around.

Her ass lifts high enough to graze the outline of my length through the cloth of my trousers. "Maivena, you cannot–fuck," I tremble at such a gentle touch and grasp her hip, so quietly, she moans.

She hides the inert smile on her face by biting into her lip and leaning into my hand.

I grab the vial and pull the cork with my teeth; the popping of the cork makes her jump.

She flinches at the touch of the oil trailing down her back, and goosebumps raise across her skin as the oil drifts, pooling right into the dip of her back.

She moans out like a song as my hands rub over her skin. The golden glow in my palms works with the lavender oil, relieving the ache throughout her body.

Her skin coats in a sheen as I massage from her lower back and up her shoulders, gently squeezing and pushing my thumbs into the base of her neck. I see her body rest farther into the bed and her tense muscles find an ease from the pain.

I scoot backward and trail more drops of oil down her soft, brown thighs.

Maivena grips the bedding as I massage her inner thighs and up the curve of her backside. I smile, returning to that spot of her inner thigh. She tremors as the tips of my finger near where I can see her glistening. "God, look at you."

I close my eyes for only a second, and she turns. Her legs open and my mouth waters, looking down, I continue the slick trail up and down her thighs, and her eyes shut.

A groan tears away from me as I lean further down. "Teach me," I beg. Her cheeks heat as I look up to her from the position I lay in between her legs.

"Teach you what?" She sounds just as breathless as she was when training.

I smile artfully as she stares down at me, her chest rapidly rising and falling. "Teach me how to make you come."

18
CURES & FEARS

LAVEN HEPHAESTUS ARVENALDI, II

The moment her hand moves downward, there is loud knocking on the door of the chamber. Maivena turns toward the door, and a quiet laugh is given from her as the knocking continues. It proceeds to grow louder the longer I attempt to block out the sound.

"Laven," Morano says from behind the door. "I hate to interrupt, but you have King shit to give your attention to."

I yank the door open, and there is a smirk on his face. His smile vastly grows, and his eyes touch in the corners as he stifles a laugh.

"Morano, I swear, I will put you through the wall."

"Oh, I do not doubt it; you have once before. But *Your Majesty*," he taunts. "If Lorsius is not going to handle a King's duties, they are now the Heirs. Carmen and Lorena need you back at the palace, effective immediately."

I exhale heavily and turn to Maivena; her back is to me as she stands from the bed, and she secures a robe around her waist.

"You all have impeccable fucking timing." I bite out.

"I am well aware." He pats my shoulder with a heavy hand. "You can taste her for dessert, duties first." He mumbles his final words and I shove him down the hall as he hollers with laughter.

Maivena kneels in front of the fireplace, she pokes the wood with an iron rod, causing the fire to spark larger. She looks back at me as I put on a black undershirt and tuck it into my undone trousers. As I grab my vest, she approaches.

"Where are you going?" She ties the strings of my shirt hanging loose around my wrists. I raise an eyebrow as she moves on to tie the laces of my trousers tightly.

"Carmen and Lorena are asking for me," I answer. "I do not know what for, but I will return soon."

"Lorena," Maivena exhales while smiling. "She is lovely." She says as she unlaces my trousers and then perfectly relaces them together.

"Do not let her trick you," I watch her fingers as they work on the laces. "She can ruin someone's day if she chooses."

Maivena quietly laughs, nodding.

"There, you always have the laces improperly crossed. This is correct." She tugs at the waistband, and I lean down.

"Someone likes to pay attention," I lowly speak the words as I move nearer.

Her skin heats at the slightest touch. She pushes up from her toes, edging her lips closer to mine. Her lips chase after my own as I pull away and stand up straighter.

Maivena's eyes narrow as she looks up at me. I brush her bottom lip as I smile at her anticipation for our lips to finally meet once and for all.

Tensity, the forever builder of want and need.

"Just as you want to savor every bit of me, the feeling is verbatim, darling."

Maybe it would not be such a bad thing for us to be starved of one another, then when we grow excruciatingly hungry, we will not be able to eat enough of each other.

THE SONG OF VERITY AND SERENITY

* * *

As I walk into Carmen's study, the doors shut behind me. On a large table in the middle of the circle room lie two corpses—one of a Wolf and the other of a man. I quickly recognize Carmen's brother Carsten; he is wearing a white Healers topcoat as he observes two vials of blood sitting in a glass bowl of ice.

If I remember anything about rouges, it is the horrid smell their corpses release.

"I will explain," Carsten nods. "Come nearer."

"Thank you for coming on short notice," Carmen walks toward me clad in his black leather armor. "Lorena and I were on patrol and found these two dead—I am guessing they were from yesterday when Vorian went on his killing spree while here."

I walk around the table examining the bodies lying in front of me. "What is it that you are doing, Carsten?"

"Taking their blood," he lifts a vial before gently placing it back into the ice. "I am going to see if there is a way to reverse this disease, so to say.

"Use their blood, but against them. Then, if I can navigate around this and add my knowledge of medicine and herbs, I can develop an inoculation of some kind and give it to the people. But this will take many tests, possible weeks, months, even years. Depending upon the time frame it took for someone to create this infection, it may take just as long for me to develop a reversal."

If Carsten is forming an inoculation he cannot be the only Healer to have thought of this. The rogues have been trailing our realm for nearly six months now. If there are more Healers, they and Carsten need to work with one another on this.

"Have you contacted anyone else to see if they are trying to do what you are as well?"

The eyes of the corpse sit open, entirely black and drained of life as they lay limp. Even with life this is how some tend to look, the one that came after me when on the ship home from Terseius looked similar.

"I have, there are some, but not many have devoted their time to it. An assignment like this will take undivided attention. I will have to find someone who can truly give their time to help me develop—the more people I have to help me, the quicker I can cure and inoculate."

Maivena.

"I have someone in mind who can assist you."

His violet eyes brighten just as Carmen's do. "If they are willing, I will take any seconds or hours they can give to me."

I nod. "How far have you gotten with the process?"

"You are looking at it," he holds his hands out to the blood in the vials.

"I will bring her. I do not know how much knowledge she has of Healing, but anything you teach her, she will grasp quickly."

"Thank you, I will be here tomorrow, but now I must take these vials to the lab," Carsten says before leaving the study.

"Laven," Carmen calls from behind his bureau. "This is for Maivena. Lorena had them made for her," he holds out a white box tied with blue ribbon.

"All of you are invited to be here in the morning. I am hosting breakfast for us, and Maivena can wear one of these dresses then. Afterward, we will discuss more of the new training for General Vanytha. Vanytha is the main person who needs to know of all the current changes being put into place. Then she can teach the rest of our Mandem.

"Also, I hope I do not take away too much of your night, but there is a lot Lorsius, and I did not talk in-depth about before he suddenly left. It is about Misonva; he never signed the treaty confirming the extension of the border between our seas. We can read through it before you sign."

That would be because Lorsius is choosing to be stingy with land. I am not taken back by finding this out. We already have hell brewing on our land, us losing our vital connection with the Queens of Misonva is not worth the strain.

Carmen flips through the multiple papers full of information regarding the border between our realms.

As I grab a chair to sit down, I feel a slight tug on the bond between myself and my brothers. They say nothing, but just then, I receive visions of Maivena from three different angles, each angle they see is being sent to me. Her head is thrown back in laughter as she and Esme talk over plates full of supper.

I smile since there is nothing more for me to do but smile.

"Thank you," I say, searing this sight into my mind.

IT IS PAST MIDNIGHT as I look at the clock hanging on the wall, further than that—almost precisely an hour past twelve.

"Why must I stand like this, Amias?" I hear Morano ask. "I look silly."

"Because these rogues are fast and unrelenting with their strikes. Every second you need to be prepared for what can come," Amias says. "There is no structure to their fighting, they are fighting to kill within their first slash, and you need to be prepared."

I find all three of them in the undecorated drawing-room.

Roaner observes Amias intently as he moves and explains new training tactics. Suddenly, Roaner looks back at me as I enter.

"That took a long time," Amias says.

"There is quite a lot Lorsius did not do while he was here. And apparently, he is not in Partalos handling whatever he was supposed to. The Duchesses sent a messenger to the palace while I was there, and the messenger asked when the King was to arrive." Repeatedly, I move my hands across my face, trying to relieve the building of stress.

"When was the last time Lorsius visited one of our Courts and actually helped them when they were in need?" Morano asks, his arms cross as he turns toward me. "You are constantly called upon not even a day later to fix the shit of a mess he creates.

"Do not think we forgot about the week you were eating one meal a day because you barely had time to sleep, let alone feed yourself. You were too busy completing your duties and picking up behind Lorsius—you would think after he colonizes a land, he would do the work to upkeep it."

I can only laugh at what he says. If I go too far into thinking of everything I have done to save Lorsius's ass, I will see no end of rage.

"I am starting to think those white streaks in your hair are from stress, and not because you were born with them." Amias jokingly says.

"Believe me. I wonder that often," I nod. "We should discuss what I spoke of with Carsten."

"As intriguing as that sounds," Roaner raises his hand to stop me from carrying on. "You need to eat, sleep, and then we will talk of it in the morning." He walks forward, shoving me from the drawing-room and guiding me to the kitchen.

He leaves me to walk the rest of the way to the kitchen, returning to Amias and Morano in the drawing-room. When I enter the kitchen, I see Esme leaning against the wooden countertop with a teacup. There is steam evaporating as she blows on the hot liquid.

"Laven," she tightly greets.

"Hello."

I walk to the pot of food sitting on the counter. I almost question if I should skip dinner to avoid conversating with her, but I grab a bowl and carry about.

Scooping out piles of stew into a bowl, Esme speaks. "It is hard for me to entirely hate you."

I sit down at the table near the window in the kitchen, mostly to place distance between her and me just in case this conversation goes southward.

"Why the change of mind?" I ask, although I do not care.

She stills, her eyes lift from the tea in her vessel and to me.

"Because she looks at you as if you hung the moon, and you watch her as though the sun rises and sets on her shoulders . . . Maivena's happiness is one of the few things that means most to me. Do not ever let me witness this bit of joy she finally has after years of being subjugated slip by your doing."

I say nothing.

I say nothing because I do not make promises I cannot keep. I am not perfect, and I will not pretend to be for the sake of others.

Esme looks at me as if hearing my thoughts.

A knowing smile appears on her face before shaking her head and leaving the kitchen to return to her and Roaner's chamber.

Once I am done eating, I follow suit and go to my own chamber to sleep. Although, I do not know how much sleep I will get tonight.

* * *

I stare down at the grave.

LAVEN HEPHAESTUS ARVENALDI, I

'You mean to tell me,' I stop speaking as I look at my mother who stares down at the grave in front of us. 'You mean to tell me, not once did you ever come see me while I was imprisoned–'

'Laven,' she attempts to speak over me.

'No,' I sternly stop her. 'You do not prevent me from saying this. You told me your pain and now you get to listen to mine.' She is at a standstill waiting for me to continue. 'You came to see me not once, you never allowed my siblings to come see me, only my father came. Then, my father dies, and not even then do you come to see me, and now you bring me to an empty grave?'

'I wanted to tell you,' she begins to cry.

'You did not. Why?'

The sympathy I should feel for her tears is nowhere to be found.

'How could I tell you while you were already so torn with what was happening while imprisoned?'

'As my mother,' I step closer to her. 'As my mother you come and tell me. You figure it the hell out.' As much as I do not want to, I shed my own tears with her. 'How do you just not tell me?'

'I am so sorry.' She pleads.

'Are you?' I shout.

Just as I raise my voice she begins to speak. Yet, she fades within wisps of darkness that swarms around me like a hurricane. I fight to make my way through as I hear her calling for me.

'Ma!' I yell as I force through the gusts of wind that push me back to where I was previously standing. This is not just a push; I am being levitated back.

One step forward takes me another levitation backward.

'Ma!' I holler once more as I can no longer see a thing nor hear.

She is gone.

The empty grave with its carved headstone is gone.

There is nothing but darkness.

I am thrown to the ground as I take another step forward and the hard collision makes the area around me clear.

The wet, sharp stone is all too familiar to me, and so is that treacherous view of the dark woods as I look through the unrailed balcony of the prison.

My ankles are grabbed, and I am yanked across the rigid stone beneath me. Two of the guards are pulling me further to the edge of the open balcony.

I turn in their hold and reach out to grasp the ground. My chest rakes across the stone and I see the small lines of blood pulling from my flesh as I am being drug closer to the edge.

A rope is rung around my neck as we near the balcony and I am forced off.

As I fall from the edge I grab a loose end of the rope to stop it from hanging me. I am now swinging from the edge as my bloodied hands merely hold on for dear life. When I look up, the two guards are at the edge, waiting. Their laughter is widely heard.

Purely out of spite to live, I find the strength I still have to pull myself up the rope.

The moment I near the top of the balcony one of their boots connect with my face and I fall without a single hope for reaching the rope to pull up.

I only fall.

I fling as I wrench awake and shove the blanket away. I scurry backward so swiftly my head collides with the headboard in a direct strike.

"Stop! Stop, stop, stop—" I finally shout the words trapped in my throat.

The louder I scream; I begin to stammer.

A gentle hand touches my cheek as I pant.

Maivena is sitting next to me.

"Laven, Laven, shh," she coos.

She holds my face as she looks at me.

I grip her wrists as she gazes down at me. I hold onto her; a deep fear settles in that she will vanish. I am not ready to be taken back to that dreadful ache of falling so quickly.

"No, no, no," I plead as her hands loosen. "Do not let go of me, I will fall."

"Laven," she stills my head, and her eyes pour into my own.

Reality begins to fall into place the longer she stares down at me. Her hair cascades around us, curtaining me to see only her.

"There is only us." She whispers and I find security in her as we are bathed in a serene darkness. "You," she encompasses my face tighter. "And me."

I let her hold me until all previous thoughts of never having her are gone.

She once was untouchable for me. That tiny star you find in a sky full of black, and as you would reach for it; the clouds would hover, and the storm would begin—hiding the star until the storm would pass, clouds would rest, the star would be gone, just as she would be gone.

But she is here just as I manifested over that same star.

If there is one thing I remember my father saying, nothing meant for me can be taken from me.

Maivena lies down next to me as I turn to look at her.

She rests too far away. "Come closer, please."

I reach out and wrap my arm around her, tugging her across the bedding. She presses in so closely I can no longer tell if my breath is hers or mine.

As I shut my eyes, she quietly speaks. "Do you wish to talk about it?"

I only shake my head.

"You should, Laven." Her tone is soft and caressing, yet hesitant to push me too far.

I struggle to respond, but I do, nevertheless. "I cannot," are the only words I can muster.

She does not say anything back. I know she is not asleep. Her heartbeat is too unsteady. When she falls sleep I noticed she has the steadiest heartbeat, this is not that.

"It is not fair, Laven, for you to know my darkest dreams and I do not know yours."

I open my eyes, and she is staring at the tattoo on my chest.

"I want to tell you, but I just cannot. Not yet." I touch her chin and she does not respond to it. Instead, her eyes close as if I never said anything.

But she does not dare to let go of me through the rest of the night.

19
HER

ROANER KORSANA

I did not comprehend the ferocity of desire until I heard the melody of her voice and felt the rhythm of her body in my hands as it imploded wrapped around me.

I would be lying if I said I did not find gratification in assuaging someone with such a hard exterior. And I could not help but to continue assuaging her until I saw the sun peek through the slight opening of the curtains.

Even as she rested after no longer being able to continue, I was just as intrigued by her collapsing into sleep as I was in making her feel satiated.

But now, the blade set to my throat is making me swear to never speak of this again.

Hilarity.

"And the next times to come will not be spoken of?" The sharp edge of the dagger digs further into my skin. "Do it." I lift higher, forcing the blade to push harder into my neck.

It is an amusing thought that she thinks I am content with one night. I need more than mere hours, I fear I need years, possibly my grave. But what is six feet of dirt compared to the resonance of her voice?

Both of us are entirely naked as she sits straddling my hips with her plush and copious thighs.

"You are insane." She mumbles as I prop up on my elbows.

She yelps when I clasp around her neck and I ascend us. Her back is pressed firmly into the bed, the dagger now lost somewhere on the floor as it falls.

Those rapturing eyes roll as I sink into her.

Finally, I can breathe.

"I did not go insane until you let me touch you."

Her thighs shake as I gently connect us to that little place that makes her sing for me.

Tightly, she holds my wrist as I never let go of her neck.

No one should be this captivating as they come.

I slow my hips and she gasps as her gaze falls upon me again.

"No, please."

I smile.

Exactly what I wanted.

She knew better than to allow this, to talk to me like this, to touch me like she did.

She knew better than to let me taste her.

I gave my fair warning.

She did not listen.

Now how do I stop?

This is the danger of it all, I do not want to stop.

I just barely touch that little spot of heaven in her. I lower my face near hers. "Please, what?"

She lifts her knee, pulling me deeper. "I want to feel you," she pleads.

Our tongues dirtily play as I give her exactly what she needs.

So slow and steady that it alters the entire chemistry my body was once used to.

Now I am the one to sing for her.

* * *

I have heard of immediate sexual compatibility before, it is well known in mating bonds, but this is not that. This is starvation, and I cannot stop eating.

There is an immediate soul tie to the person you are fated to be with, along with the agonizing tensity; here the soul tie is not present, there is only tension pulling us together.

Unfortunately, most people who are hybrids tend to not have mates, and after all these years I am certain I am one. But I will never fully know until Levora is back.

There have been others before Esme but nothing as wild as this feeling.

No one has ever touched me and left fire blazing in their path.

Unusual is the only way to describe how we both were pulled so easily into one another.

It is peculiar how sharing a chamber with someone triggers you to think about so many possibilities and then you fulfill those possibilities. Both of us are contained in a room meant for intimacy so we completed what is done in rooms for intimacy.

I lie down a new undershirt next to me as I sit on the bed to tie my boots.

Two bare feet appear in front of me.

When I look at her she is now wrapped in her robe while holding a small vessel of tea.

I am well acquainted with the tea in her hands.

A brew specific for masking one's scent so others do not sense who they have laid with.

For a moment I stare at it. "We do not need it."

Esme does not respond; she holds it out closer to me with a determined expression.

"Our scents will fade by the time we are around others."

That is a lie, we both know it.

I do not want to get rid of the smell of us combined, something about it has trapped my mind. To avoid an argument, I take it.

She does not walk away until she sees that all of the tea is gone, and I have drank it.

Just as I finish dressing to leave for Carmen and Lorena's, Esme speaks from the tub in the bathing room. Her black curls are soaked and stick all over her skin as she sits up in the middle of the water.

"I will be sleeping in the chamber down the hall until we leave here."

I fix the bow and arrow brooch holding my cloak together.

When I reach the door to leave I glance at her over my shoulder. "No, you are not."

Maybe because we were so young, or maybe I am growing too tired and hopeless that Levora will ever appear again, I never felt this wild obsession with her as I do now with Esme.

Could it be the riveting feeling of someone who once saw you as an enemy now seeing you as a weakness?

Could it be I knew somehow I would already feel this way and it was only a matter of time before it happened?

There are one too many possibilities regarding this. And somehow, I know, without question, that Esme feels the exact same.

Although my obsession with her has found its footing, that does not subside my search for Levora. If she is still out there.

20
MOUNTAINS

MAIVENA FONDALI

It is mystifying to surmise where you stand with someone when you are suddenly bound to them by an Intimacy Arrangement. The arrangement consists of so many possibilities—you receive the life you used to have before enslavement, and in return, the provider keeps you as someone to talk to, someone to make love to, someone to abuse, or all three.

His tears are nothing but gold emanating over my fingers. If he will not allow me to understand them, that is all they are and all they will be. Golden tears that give me coin, fare, clothing, sturdy roofing, and polished wood to walk upon.

There are moments where I presume I can tell him anything—I could speak the permanence of the world right into his ear, and he would nod and tell me to carry on.

Possibly I think this way only because of the security that envelops me by just looking into his eyes. Or, I only feel this safety because he was the only one to protect me when I was an absolute damsel all those years ago.

There is a strength that pulls into my shoulders whenever he nears. His presence is the unwavering reminder that I, too, can be just as strong as he is.

And just as simply as he makes me feel this way, I am prompted with every thought that I once felt this way with another. I have once had these emotions and more with someone else before I was brought here, concluding I am chasing that within Laven.

As often as I force myself to forget, I can see him. I hold sight of his bronzed skin that always hinted darker in the Summer, and his golden hair that lightens in the sun, his scintillating mind that enthralled me every waking moment. I have surrendered to forgetting his touch, his eyes, the feel of him. Even his traits I despised to the marrow of my bones made me smile, I had to forget that too.

Only one question stands as to how far I am willing to go for the freedom of myself and my family. How deep will I dig for Kaden and Ethel to go home and start the family they wish to have? How far am I willing to go for my father to see my mother again? He does not speak of it, but I know how much he misses her.

I would climb the steepest mountain if it just purported that my family may have freedom. And if I reach the top of that mountain and my liberty does not lie there, I would not mind.

Sacrifice can mean anything to anyone. Yet, me staying and giving my family freedom is not sacrifice. It is the right thing to do. It is what will always be right for me to do.

Even if it were not Laven, I would sell myself to anyone to get Ethel, Kaden, and my father far from the mainland and to Xenathi. I know how to force myself into enjoying sexual affairs with someone, and I would do it countlessly for either of them. I was consistently told of my beauty growing up, or as my mother would say, *'you are exceptionally beautiful because of me.'* And I have learned to manipulate my beauty well.

Coming to Kaden's aid when he was sought out to be castrated was the first time I had ever given my body over to someone, and the second was for my father's saving. But the so-called doctors knew I would do it, which was why they came. That was the last time I laid in someone else's bed other than my own.

My father is the only one of the four of us who knows how to mask scents of all kinds, so no one other than us ever knew what happened with the doctors.

At that time, I did not care what was done with my body. After being taken, a thought never returned of leaving. The royals have rules set in stone that servants and foreign Warriors could never marry nor be mated to someone—unless previously married and mated before arrival.

If this is what it can be called—the only prerogative I and others hold is being tied to someone by an Intimacy Arrangement.

Although, Intimacy Arrangements always end. They have no choice but to end unless the man or woman you are arranged with decides to keep you alongside the mate they find, which is a rarity.

I am on borrowed time with the High Prince of Vaigon.

There is only a matter of days, months, and even seconds before he finds the person he is fated to be with, and I am back to being trapped on the servant grounds as well as my family. But if freedom is in my grasp before my time is up, Ethel, Kaden, and my father have a clear chance of going home, and hopefully so do I.

Yet, I do not think whomever I am mated to would accept the sexual affairs I have been in. I am considered a befouled woman to the prestigious. Even after knowing the reasoning behind my actions, I am convinced that for me to be wanted by people is a hard reach.

Then there is Laven. He has a right to know whom I have laid with before he and I do. I could not carry on in this arrangement in lies; it would be up to him to decide if he wishes to continue after knowing of this.

I walk toward a mirror, looking over myself in the dress Lorena had made to fit me. It is white and sheer with a thin layer of orange satin beneath the nearly see-through fabric. It cowls across my chest before fitting at my waist and it flows loosely around my legs, barely gracing the floor.

It is hard to deny the small amount of weight I have gained within just a few days with Laven and his brothers.

Like a brisk wind, Laven moves from one end of the room,

suddenly appearing behind me.

Roaner was not telling me a tale to make me feel like some special girl recruited by a Prince as his Intimacy Agrangee.

Laven has speed that I have never seen; maybe it was a gift from Hermes to be so agile when they were declared the High Four by Artemis. Or it is just the blood of the Orviantes in his family. The blood of an Original has high possibilities of making him so fast. His silver and white pieces of hair is the clear indication that someone in his family bloodline is a pure Orviante.

There is a smirk that pulls across his full lips as he comes to sight.

He is so pulchritudinous that it is painful to look at someone like Laven.

From the contrast of white in his dark curly hair to the beauty of his glowing brown skin, Laven could bring women to their knees, especially when that lazy smirk matches his hazel and blue eyes. One eye tends to flare in a light blue when his Wolf pushes for departure—like now.

Even in these tall shoes given to me by Lorena, I am still just below his shoulder.

"There is someone I want you to meet today; he is the Lead Healer here in Gordanta. He is looking for help developing a cure of some sort, an inoculation to protect the people. Would you wish to help him?"

Does he sincerely believe me to be so educated in healing that I could somehow help a Lead Healer?

I do not deny the opportunity. "I can," I nod.

His eyes do not leave mine. It no longer feels as if he is looking at me. Instead, he is reading through me and latching onto the tiny flash of doubt that I allowed myself to show.

Terrible is not the word to use when it comes to trying to guard my emotions with him. I cannot tell if he is impeccable at reading someone's feelings or if I am just this comfortable around him to allow my guard to falter.

"Maivena . . ." he says in that—*that* tone.

A vibrating, purring sound that moves down my spine, forcing me to stand straighter.

This is one thing I never experienced. The reverberations of someone's resonance have never shuddered me alive as his does.

"Are you certain? You do not have to say yes."

But I do have to say yes after the way I treated him those days ago. I am grateful not to have had my tongue cut out.

If they do not go to the Tree of Gods because of me, I have no choice but to help them find another way out of this havoc and create distance from the war we all know is coming.

"I am positive. I can help." Bringing a smile to my face, he studies that as well through the mirror ahead of us.

I turn, and he is already looking down at me.

Moments pass before he speaks, and I do not mind using this time to stare at him for as long as I can.

"Freedom suits you," he quietly speaks.

I reach, touching a silver button on his topcoat. "I am not free, entirely."

"As long as you are arranged with me, your freedom is identical to mine."

21
WESTERN SEAS

LAVEN HEPHAESTUS ARVENALDI, II

I watch Maivena and Carsten from the balcony of the dining room. They sit in the courtyard below as he presents different aspects of healing with her. Hopefully he is teaching her things she does not already know.

The book of healing herbs is extensive as he turns through different pages.

Maivena's eyebrows are joined together as she focuses on everything he is saying. Soon enough, she is communicating with him and asking questions.

"Well, tell me," Carmen says as he wanders out to the balcony.

"What?"

"Who she is. To you." His lower back presses against the stone rail as he crosses his arms. A smile rests playfully on his face. "And do not lie; you know I will see through it."

"We have an arrangement."

"Is that how we entitle mates now? Are people sick of the word?" His smirk meets the mockery in his tone. "Laven, you may be able to play your jests and secrecy with others, but not me. I can sense it.

Now, *who* is she?"

I look below us at Maivena and Carsten; they are now walking through the palace doors.

"She is one of our servants–"

"Laven," his tone is suddenly sharp. "Do not tell me this arrangement you have is the Intimacy Arrangement."

I sit next to him and he turns towards me while leaning in closely. "You are aware of the horrid Intimacy Arrangement my second father was in, hell, most Intimacy Arrangements are horrific. You saw how he treated her, you do not want to be seen that way. Those who once thought highly of you will begin to think poorly of you because of this arrangement alone."

I shake my head. "Not if I care for her better than other arrangements that people remember."

"Laven," Carmen grips my shoulder tightly. "No matter how well you treat her, no matter if she leaves the doors of your home without bruises, people will suspect the worst solely because it is an arrangement. You are paying her for her loyalty, and that has been highly looked down upon since the beginning of Intimacy Arrangements being known."

"Is that not how we function in day to day life?" I stand from the bench and look down at him. "Being paid for our loyalty in some form. Either it be in money, kindness, sex, gratefulness, anything. In some way we are always paid back for our loyalty. But, with Maivena, all she covets is her freedom. She may not ask for it, but I know that is what she is after."

"And you will give it to her?"

"Yes, if anything, it may make my situation much simpler having her free."

"Is she not aware that you two are mated?"

"No, she does not see value in shifting into her Wolf, and I do not want to tell her. I want her to find out on her own, not by me having to force her awareness." I would feel as if I were forcing it on her.

As much as I would love to be her only option in life, mates do not always fall in love. But, sometimes, a mate is just that—a dear companion you are bonded to and nothing more. I could never comprehend what agony Amias goes through. We vowed to never speak of him and Hua unless he does first.

"I can perceive that she has not shifted. She is taking a contraception, I suppose?" He sits down on a stone bench, and I lean my elbows against the rail wrapped in green vines and flowers.

"Yes."

"Now I see why you are in an Intimacy Arrangement," it all forms in his mind. "It is your only way to have her in every imaginable way."

"I am not the one who proposed it up," I hold up my finger. "She speculated that is why I am generous to her, and I said yes."

"Quamfasian women are always candid, and rather," he pauses. "I will just say straightforward." His purple eyes shift toward grief. Memories are flooding his mind of the woman he fell in love with before finding Lorena.

"When did you meet her?" He questions.

"I met her the day she arrived. The guards were on another raid under Lorsius's mandates, and she happened to be one of the people that were taken. This was seven years ago."

His eyes broaden. "And how long have you known that you two are foreordained?"

I clench my jaw. "Nearly all of it."

"Wait, all those years ago you went on a—killing spree—so to say." He grins.

"Yes, the only man not dead for her taking is Lorsius."

"And she is why you had that home built here?" Carmen smiles, playing with a flower wrapped around the stone pillar.

"That was extemporaneous," I laugh. "It is innocuous here, and there is nowhere else that I have been as prudent as this land. The vision you have for our Western Court is what I aspire to do when Lorsius is gone. Complete reversal of everything he has caused." Gordanta and the people here are a haven compared to my other Courts in Vaigon.

"Lorsius's translation of a Kingdom is never what mine has

been. Therefore, I refuse to allow a man like him to influence my decisions.

"And your choice to have a home built here was not extemporaneous, you were manifesting—and it served, in your own way. It has been years since I have seen a glint of light in your eyes. I know Levora would have loved to meet Maivena."

Pain overcomes me and I look out to the sea at the mention of my sister, hoping for the serenity of the sea to calm me.

"You understand you can leave Maivena here whenever you wish? I am sure Lorena is relishing in her company." He turns to the dining room through the open balcony doors. Maivena is walking in, and Lorena is already at her side.

I nod. "Thank you."

Maivena peers around the room and across the table where Roaner and Morano are sitting.

Carmen chuckles. "See how she looks for you upon entering a room."

"Leave it be, Carmen," I warn.

I fixate on Maivena until she can find me.

"Wait for it," Carmen whispers.

Her eyes drift to the balcony, and I know I am smiling like a fool. Maivena smiles as well and quickly walks across the room.

"Look at her, blooming like a butterfly, floating her way over." He teases. "Laven, her beauty is truly unusual."

Yes, it is. Her features are sharp yet somehow so soft and gentle. Old rich beauty.

She is charming in this dress, and the faint hint of orange behind the fabric does nothing but make her brown skin glimmer more illustrious than it already does.

Maivena notices Carmen, and she gradually comes to a stop. I can read that expression on her face—it is the same expression as the day my mother entered my chamber, and she did not know if she should have been submissive or open.

And just as she was then, she is now, unsure if she can approach the conversation.

Maivena turns toward the table in the dining room and finds the seat she was previously in next to Morano.

I furrow my eyebrows, and make my way to her.

As I sit in the chair next to her, she looks up at me with a vague smile and sips juice from a glass vessel.

"Why did you come over here?"

She swallows. "I did not want to intrude."

"You were not intruding on anything; he presumed you would come over."

Lifting higher, she is no longer slumped. "He did?"

"Yes, Maivena." I smile.

I intend to break her from this meek behavior.

Amias and General Vanytha enter the dining room and take the seats waiting for them.

"There are two nations of Wolves that do not associate with us." Vanytha pauses as she weighs what she will say next. "Well, they do not associate much with anyone other than New Quamfasi. Do you remember their names?" She asks me.

Maivena comes to attention.

"One of them lies on the outskirts of Xenathi; Nadrexi is their name." I clarify. "Ethivon has land claimed further North. Why do you ask?"

"Because there are many Warriors Xenathi acquired from Nadrexi that are the most influential Warriors known." Amias explains. "We could use their help in developing other effective war tactics, as well as warning them as to what is coming."

"We can venture there tomorrow evening," I decide. "We still have more to handle here before departing."

Maivena is fidgeting with the fabric of her dress below the table, an apprehensive tendency I have noticed of hers.

I reach for her, but she propels her hand for the glass of juice before I can touch her.

"Maivena," I speak quietly as the others begin to converse amongst one another.

She extorts a smile and looks up at me. "Yes?"

I say nothing and touch her hand, ascending us from the dining room to the sand where water rushes toward us.

She yelps and rushes backward.

"Laven!" Maivena exclaims.

I cannot help but laugh as she frantically gathers the dress's fabric in her hands to keep it from the sand and water.

Her eyes sharpen as she listens to my laughter while unstrapping those painful-looking shoes.

Maivena walks forward, her striking green eyes stare up into mine.

"You got my dress wet," her voice is low.

I smile and sparsely shrug a shoulder. "It will dry."

Even closer, she steps. Slowly nodding, she becomes devious. "So will you." She says all too mercifully.

My footing is lost as she jostles me backward into the water. I sink below, hearing her laughter as I drop under the sea.

I ascend from the water and back to the sand. She is still giggling as I stand soaked from the ocean.

I am the one to slowly nod this time while pushing a hand through my wet hair.

"Run," I say as I unbutton my topcoat and toss it to the sand.

"Run?"

The undershirt clings to my skin and it peels off as I remove it, leaving me in only trousers and shoes.

"I will let you get a head start before I throw you into the sea."

As the sun emits earthward, it ignites the hints of brown in her black curly hair.

Her arms sit loosely crossed beneath her chest. "You do not frighten me, Laven," Maivena says in her suave tone.

I hum. "You frighten me." I outline the sweep of her chin, leaving behind fragments of sand over her skin.

"Good."

Then, she rushes away in a run and I grin following behind her.

Like two children playfully in love, she bursts into laughter as she runs towards the sun and I linger in her shadow as she grins at me over her shoulder.

Her laughter grows as I catch her and she turns and her happiness stays, but it takes a turn. "Just borrowed time." She whispers.

"What is borrowed time?"

"You."

What if I told you, time is not relevant?
That what we have is infinite.
What would you say?

I do not ask, I stand in this moment with her and let her not know that we are the equivalence of eternity.

* * *

We have returned to the house, and Maivena is now in leather armor again. Today she trains with Morano; Esme has decided to cook dinner today, and I can sense that she is watching from the windows not far off. Roaner and Amias are on the training grounds with General Vanytha, helping seasoned and unseasoned Warriors gain knowledge of the rogues.

Maivena trained to strengthen her agility with Esme, and now she works with Morano to channel any power she could possess.

I stay near the house, observing from a distance. Morano and Maivena stand a great length through the trees near the steep slope of land leading to the water below.

As Morano begins to speak, I further my hearing, listening to everything he tells her.

"When was the last time you took the contraception to suppress your Wolf?"

Maivena is reluctant to answer. "Perhaps a week, if not more."

"How long have you been taking it?" His arms cross tightly over his chest.

She stiffens. "A few years now."

"And the dosage?"

"A tablespoon twice every week."

"Well, if it has been a week, it is working its way out of your system. Nevertheless, Maivena, you can put yourself in grave danger if you continue to consume that. Not only can you suppress your Wolf so deep she could never appear, but your powers could never appear as well." Morano informs her. "Do you know what your power could be? Have you ever felt or witnessed them beforehand?"

"Before taking the contraception, I was stronger, faster even. But no sign of magic."

"Maivena, this contraception could eat you from the inside out. Killing off organs you need to function in day-to-day life that are connected directly to your Wolf."

"I am careful." There is doubt in her voice.

"Which form of contraception are you taking?"

"It is called Pelven. It is in the form of powder you soak in tea."

"Do you think she would have any sign of power since she was taking it for so long?" I ask through the bond.

"It is hard to tell; Pelven is the strongest contraception. I do not even know how she got her hands on it—most of the people who have taken it must be set off into using their powers. I do not think it is the best option even to trigger her powers to come through. It may injure her because her body is not used to them; it will overwhelm her organs to have a shock of power unleash from her."

"Would it kill her?" I ask.

"No, but she would be weak for a decent amount of time. And that is not an option."

"Unquestionably not. Explain this to her." I exhale heavily, no longer listening in on their conversation.

Roaner appears from his ascension, standing next to me. "Is it true?"

"Is what true?"

"That Vorian got through my shield." His eyes hold no expression as he speaks.

Roaner took down the shield the moment he arrived in Gordanta. I did not know if he removed the shield because he knows of Vorian getting through or because we no longer needed it.

"So he says. However, you know Vorian is prone to lying."

Roaner says nothing more before ascending into the house.

22
ENDING SOLACE

LAVEN HEPHAESTUS ARVENALDI, II

"Laven, I have already bathed!" Maivena laughs as I tug her into the bathwater.

The white silk shift she is wearing immediately clings to her skin as she sits up after dunking under the water.

I smirk. "You will dry."

I pull the wet silk over her head and drape it across the ledge of the bathing tub.

"You opened all the doors," she smiles, gazing outward at the water crashing onto the shore. The floor-to-ceiling doors reveal the stars and moon from the tub, and she smiles.

"Tell me something," I push away the hair sticking to her face to see her more clearly.

"Like what?"

I lean in to perceive her face as she turns to view the sea again. "What was wrong at breakfast?"

She looks lost the longer she stares out at the stars hovering above the sea.

"That is where my mother is." She faintly replies.

As I recall morning meal, I remember the conversation of Nadrexi and then her sudden distance at the mention of it.

"I thought your mother and brother were in Provas?" I turn her to look at me.

Lifting my knee through the water, she sits between my legs and reaches out her hand, touching the scorpion tattoo starting at my knee and leading up my thigh.

"My mother who *raised* me is in Provas. The woman who gave birth to me is in Nadrexi."

I raise her chin, so her eyes join mine. "Keep going but stay here."

"My mother was a fiendish woman to my brother, he never stood up for himself, so I did. And she resented me for it. Every morning there was something wrong I did or was doing . . . her critiques of food I enjoyed that did not suit my figure, striking me when she felt I did wrong." Maivena forces a low laugh and turns around.

She lifts her hair, showing a deep scar hidden in her curls.

I incline closer, seeing the completely healed and lifted scar. "What happened?"

"Her temper happened," Maivena responds. "My mother is easily blinded by her own rage."

"How did that happen?"

Maivena shifts and faces me again, I thread through her hair, finding the bump.

"She struck me with my bow as I was leaving the house. I bent enough for it not to go through my neck. That was the last time I ever stayed there; my father had finally obtained a position in the Quamfasi Mandem. He did not stay long as a Warrior, and he was moved up to General relatively fast.

"The royals had given us rank my mother despised. When I would visit her in Nadrexi, she always made me feel dastard for having the luxury we worked for. Yet she had no quandaries asking me for coin when she demanded it. I was always ridiculous enough to give it to her. I think part of me still hoped that she would change after I did things for her, but she never did. No matter the length I went to for her, it was never sufficient."

It feels disproportionate to consume so much information about her, and I cannot even tell her what haunts me in my nightmares. There is already so much weighing down her shoulders. How could I possibly put my strains over it? She would go crashing with everything wrong with me.

I have looked over her all this time to now discover that her past was something horrid. I once thought that she was a woman at peace before this, a humble woman who had everything but wanted none of it to be at ease with her current state. When, all this time, she has been a prisoner of her mother once before, and now a prisoner of Vaigon. She is at ease here because she is familiar with her life as a prisoner.

How do you help someone flooded with such extreme amounts of turmoil?

Maivena abruptly shakes her head as if to disregard anything she said.

"You tell me something."

"What do you want to know?" I gently stroke the wound hidden in her hair.

She floats a hand over the water soaked in lavender. "What will happen after you find your mate?" I can see that portion of despondency crossing over her face at the consideration of returning to the Servant Grounds. "Would I go back?"

How else do you make someone apprehend that you will never leave their side? That you are eternally with them even when they do not discern it.

"You will go wherever you wish."

And I will go too if you would allow me.

That bit of hope returns. "And my family?"

"They will as well."

She continues to toy with the tattoo on my leg. An emotion takes over her face that I have not ever seen. "Have you ever had a lover before?"

There is no need to lie. "No."

The expression on her face is still unreadable to me.

"You are a liar."

I smile. "Did you not tell me to be a good liar?"

She smiles back. "Yes, but not with–" she stops.

But not with you, I silently finish for her.

"That is not real. You are a High Prince, the most sought-after man in our universe. *And*," she laughs. "Men are weak, you all easily cave under pressure when beautiful women are around you."

I lift her higher through the water and she settles in my lap as she straddles me. "Maivena," I say in a dramatically hurtful tone. "Are you saying I am like other men?"

She falls into laughter as I gently knead into her waist. "No!" She thrashes about. "But you could be."

I still, and she rests again in my lap. Her eyes sparkle with tears from laughter, and I wish there was a way to pause her in this moment. To forever see her glistening in happiness with the view of the stars and the moon hovering above her. To forever let her feel happiness like this.

"But you are not." She breathlessly whispers. "Why?"

Because of you, yet I cannot say that.

Or could I?

I think I could tell her anything and she would not be frightened away so easily. Plenty of men must have said she was the reason they behaved so they could have her in return. What difference would it make coming from me? To her, I am just another man bowing at her feet.

But I am not just another man, I am her forever. Therefore I am above them and I am above saying the things they say.

"Nothing has ever provoked me enough." I finally answer. "I have had plenty of women try to be the person I have casualties with, none of them have ever reached that little place in my mind to make me want to say yes to them."

She is nervous to ask the question I know lingers on her tongue. "And me?"

I exhale heavily and let my eyes fall to look over her body. Her wet hair hangs over her chest and covers her from my sight. I reach forward and remove her hair.

Just barely, I graze my thumbs over her nipples as I rub down and over her waist. "And you," I say just as breathlessly as her. "You because I want to be your favorite lover of all that you will ever have." I grasp her hips and her body responds just as my hips lift to hers.

Her hand grips the side of my neck as she looks down and her body moves with mine.

"The ways I will make love to you are endless." I cannot grapple with it.

She leads my hand up, begging me to play with her, and I do.

No.

This is too much.

I tug and pull at her nipples as she slowly rubs herself against me. Her back arches, a silent demand for my mouth. I give her everything.

But is it?

Is it too much? Or is it exactly enough?

She quietly yelps.

Fuck . . .

Her hips dig harder and I flick my tongue while using my fingers to tease the other.

So slowly, she continues with such need that I want her to never end.

I never want to not see her edging for a release she has wanted long for.

The deep furrow in her eyebrows.

The gasping and biting of her lips as she searches.

No.

It has to end here.

Impulsion is a horrid trait I must stop.

"Mai-" I choke on my words as she quietly moans at the feeling of us. "Mai, we need to stop before I lose every last bit of sanity and you will never leave this room again."

She does not stop.

"I never said I wanted to leave," she stares at how we could connect again and her eyes roll.

She wants this just as much as I do.

I build the strength to ascend, and we fall on to the plush rug laying in front of the fireplace.

"Enough," I warn.

She lazily giggles below me as I press her into the ground. "Fine, I will stop."

"I would think you are trying to kill me." I rub my nose against her wet neck and I can hear her heavy breathing thumping from her chest.

I stand from the ground to retrieve a bathing towel.

"Come," I nod as I sit down on the chaise.

Just as the nights before, I begin to dry off her body and she watches my every move.

"What would you say if I said we should no longer sleep in the same bed?" Her bright orbs are staring directly through me.

"Why would you want to do that?" I sit up straighter as she looks down at me.

"You should be lying in a bed with someone you are in love with, the person you are intended to be with."

She watches the rise and fall of my chest as I try to understand where this is coming from.

I could deny it.

I could tell her no and that we will sleep in the same bed no matter what she asks.

Except, I could never deny her wants—even within an inebriated mind, I could never.

"Is that what you want?"

She only nods.

"Say it."

"Y–yes," she stutters. "It is what I want . . . Intimacy Arrangements are purely sexual, and I feel we should keep it as such." Her words are hurtful, yet her tone is welcoming and soft. "Sleeping in the same bed as someone is above the laws of Intimacy Arrangements, which we still have not gone over."

She is correct, nevertheless, if this is what she believes she wants, then I will say yes as well. Either I like it or not.

Suddenly the entire atmosphere around us shifts.

Just as simply as we began, I so simply see the end.

We both are sleeping alone tonight.

23
PECULIAR

LAVEN HEPHAESTUS ARVENALDI, II

WE DID NOT SPEAK after she left the chamber last night. At morning meal, it was as if I never existed. If we did speak, it was brief, scarcely extending more than a minute.

I can understand her reasoning behind staying true to the original ways of Intimacy Arrangements, but not to speak to me at all seems as if there is more she is hiding.

Every moment I reached for her, she simply evaded it, brushing me over as if she did not apprehend that I was endeavoring for her.

Instead of challenging her, I let it be until we can have a moment alone again.

"What are the provisions for today?" Amias asks. He is approaching the kitchen carrying a vessel steaming with hot tea. He is only attired in bedwear, and his upper body is fully revealed, showing the sun and moon tattoo along the left side of his shoulder and chest. The same tattoo we share with Morano and Roaner.

"Morano is going home. He will be meeting with my mother and Axynth to enlist the new training for all of our Warriors."

He nods, adding. "Hua is on her way home as well; she will learn the new practices and go to Terseius to present them."

"You will stay here," I continue. "And Roaner will go to Wanora. Esme is coming with Maivena and me to Nadrexi, she was insistent on coming, and I will not be refusing her. I would prefer to keep my sight."

Amias chortles, sipping his tea. "I think she can do more than just purloin someone's vision."

"I deem so as well." I shift to the window, surveying Maivena and Esme as they talk amongst one another. "I am certain Roaner will be arriving in Nadrexi not long after we reach the destination."

"Yes, I will be," Roaner says while appearing from his ascension. Morano is next to him.

"Just how precisely is it that you met Esme?" Amias wonders while Morano sits down at the table with a mug of tea as well.

"She tried to kill me." He calmly states, glancing out the window.

Amias laughs. "When was this?"

"The last war between Old Quamfasi and us, she drove a spear through my chest and tried to drive an arrow into my head."

"Then?" Morano pushes for him to proceed.

"The spear drew from my shoulder, it went back to her, and I was left to bleed out until Hua found me on the battlefield."

"That is who did that to you?" Amias's laughter remains. "I recollect that moment of Hua locating you grappling on the field."

Roaner continues to focus on Esme and Maivena through the window.

"Maivena asked that we no longer sleep in the same bed." I belatedly recognize out loud not only to them but to myself as well.

They slowly turn to me.

"Why?" Amias asks. "The affinity she has for you is vociferous. This does not make sense."

"She thinks that I should be lying in a bed with someone I am in love with."

Morano laughs and smacks his knee. "Stop deceiving this poor woman and just tell her already."

Amias chimes in, in agreement. "You should, Laven."

"I do not want to. I want Maivena to find out on her own." My tone hardens. I glance at Roaner. "What do you say I should do?"

"I cannot tell you what to do."

I roll my eyes. "What do you *suggest*?"

He lifts a shoulder. "I suggest you do not say a word."

I hold my hand out as he validates my position. "Letting her determine this on her own is my most immeasurable decision. If I tell her, she could consider I am forcing it on her or perhaps lying. She needs to feel it herself, not be told it is there."

Roaner nods before he angles toward Maivena and Esme outside.

"What are they doing today?" I ask.

Roaner looks back at me with furrowed eyebrows. As if to ask, *'you do not know?'*

"They are trying to see if she can shift."

I look toward Morano, and he is now standing to leave. "She *cannot* shift yet; she will injure herself," Morano growls. He is briskly walking in the direction of the doors, and I promptly follow.

When he lands outside, Esme holds her hand up. "I am only getting her to find the essence of her Wolf, not to shift."

Morano's eyes flare then fade to orange, I step forward as he speaks, prepping to end any rising catastrophe. "I still do not advise it."

"I was not asking for your advice, was I?" Esme retorts.

Maivena seizes Esme, seeking to restrain her increasing furor.

"We can remain with strength exercises," Maivena meets Esme's eyes, inaudibly muttering to her in Quamfasian.

"We will train together."

Maivena swiftly turns her head toward me. Then, just as her lips part to declaim, Roaner speaks first. "Esme," he nods toward the house. Surprisingly, she follows, and so do Morano and Amias.

"You are not clothed to train," Maivena states, looking over my attire, or lack thereof.

I am only covered in my leather trousers and boots.

"Try."

"Try?" She edges for clarification.

"Try to find her, just a bit of her," I say, referring to her Wolf.

Her cheeks blaze in crimson. "I do not know how to."

"Close your eyes." I remember to keep my tone tranquil. If I learned anything through the help I was seeking years ago for mental clarity, it was to stay calm so others felt at ease in their difficult situations. Most moments I remember this, not always.

She regards me as I step forward. I reach out, lining from the heart of her eyebrows and to the round point of her nose.

Lastly, I receive a dainty smile. "Close them," I tap her nose.

Once her eyes shut, I round her and stop to stand behind her.

I move her braid to rest over her shoulder and I trail a finger from the bottom of her neck, over the leather armor, and down her back.

"Whenever you shift, you feel it here first." I press the base of her spine and there is a tremble that moves over her shoulders. "Your spine stretches, lengthening your upper body to create capacity for your organs to enlarge." I trail a finger back up. Tenderly I press against the most delicate part of her neck, and I rest my hand along the side. I curl my fingers, and I feel her growing pulse.

"After your spine, your neck and skull reform, so your brain has room for germination. The first time you shift may overwhelm you, but as the contraception leaves, your body will convert just fine."

She turns, and my hand eases around her neck.

I figure she will ask questions, but her eyebrows furrow, and she leans, observing the expansive land behind me.

Everything is unexpected after she grips my arm.

We ascend at her doing, not far but various feet from where we were. Her stability cripples and as we fall to the ground I do not know where to look for her first, when I do not see her, the panic settles in. She could still be ascending and get lost in the process and possibly end up anywhere.

"Maivena!" I shout, and I hear the doors to the house burst open.

I do not need to look to see that everyone is rushing outside.

An arrow soars over my head and finally, I perceive the three rogues assailing at us at full velocity and another arrow is shot.

"Maivena!" I scream again and I see her scrambling from mid air as she reappears from ascension and collapses to the ground, the fall does not affect her as she hurriedly crawls toward me.

Ferocious growling echoes around me and the sound of paws thumping into the ground follows the velocity.

Just as I see Amias in his brown Wolf form, I see Roaner in all black fur with the singular white stripe over one eye and then Morano. Esme is at the door of the house, her eyes are fully white and soon enough, the rogues are scattering due to going blind at her doing.

Before my brothers can get past us, Maivena grasps beneath my arms and hauls me toward her; the back of my head collides with her chest, and her arms barricade around me.

The rogues do not make it halfway across the depth of the trees before an excruciating scream belts over. As I look up to Maivena, her eyes are permeated in a gloom of orange and red as she bellows beyond the length between the rogues and us. The longer I stare at her, strikes of lines that mimic lightning move through her eyes and across her skin.

The sky eclipses above us; the currents of waves grow taller before crashing powerfully to the shore. All of the trees splinter in half; the fissuring sounds cut through her cry as she does not contain a measure of herself back.

The rogues disintegrate in their wake, descending to the ground in black ash and bones. In a trice, she falls quiet. The sea calms, the sky clears to blue, and the trees stand in ruin.

I turn to Maivena, and she is falling to the ground in a faint.

I catch her head before it strikes the ground. "Maivena, look at me. Open your eyes, love."

Everyone is gathered around us within no time, but Roaner still stands at a distance as he is now examining the burnt bodies on the ground.

"Morano!" I holler.

"She is fine. Everything that I mentioned yesterday that could happen is happening now that her powers have come through." His fingers press against her neck. "She still has a pulse but her body has gone into shock." He calmly explains. "Esme," he urgently motions her over. "Get her to a room, get these leathers off of her before she overheats. A fever is breaking all over her body and the last thing we want is her brain to burn."

"She just fucking burned those men alive; I doubt a fever will harm her." Amias says in a sharp tone.

"Who is more experienced in anatomy here?" Morano challenges.

"We do not have time for this bickering!" I shut both of them up.

I lift Maivena from the ground and Esme walks with me to the house. "I will change her, and you can gather cold cloths, it will help her cool down as much as possible. But we will need to replace them frequently."

I nod and we both ascend to my chamber where Esme begins to undress Maivena, and I gather as many cold cloths as I can.

24
NOW SHE RESTS

LAVEN HEPHAESTUS ARVENALDI, II

I sit in a corner chair of my chamber as Maivena rests. I look toward Esme. "What are these powers?" Given they are close family, there must be something Esme knows, possibly someone else in their family has a line of this magic that was passed on to her.

"I do not know," Esme declares with confusion. "No one in our family has them."

Roaner is leaned back against the wall with his hands tucked tightly into his pockets. "They mimicked the power of a Sorceress. Is anyone in your family from Galitan?"

Esme nods. "My mother is, but that in no way connects to her."

Roaner continues to stare at Esme who watches over Maivena. His lip's part to speak but he says nothing more.

"Is she part Banshee?" I ask.

"No, that is not what happens after a Banshee shrieks." Esme sits down on the edge of the bed, stroking Maivena's hair.

"The only conclusion there is for such strength would be her having blood from Galitan," Roaner thinks further before continuing. "Or a blessing from the Gods that she would not know of."

"We would have to ask uncle Naius." Esme refers to Maivena's father. "Only he would know of a gift from the Gods or some lineage we do not know of."

I cannot stop recalling the way her skin turned. How it looked as if her powers were appearing through her skin before projecting outward.

"Do you have a book on your family tree?" Roaner asks Esme.

"We do, but our grandmother would have it. She is old now and I would have to help her locate it."

"No," I stand. "Do not bother her with it. There are other ways to understand this without disrupting the elderly."

They both nod, but something tells me Esme was not going to let us see the book in the first place. Books on family trees are sacred and tend to only call for family to observe it.

"Esme," Roaner calls as he stands up straighter. "I need to leave soon for Wanora."

She rises to her feet and he waits for her to leave first before following her down the hall.

"Laven," Maivena quietly says. Her eyes are closed as she picks at the cloth on her chest—her face is bestowing deep distress.

I swiftly move from the chair and to the bed.

She seeks to sit up, but I do not give her an opportunity.

"My head," she whimpers. There is a tear falling from her barely open eyes.

"I know, love," I murmur.

I lift a hand, swaying the curtains all around to close, eliminating all light from the chamber.

Removing the rest of my clothing, I get into the bed next to her. "Come here."

Maivena's hand weakly grips my arm as I pull her closer.

Her legs lazily weave with my own as we lay on our sides.

Her eyes do not open again as her head lays on my arm.

Using my healing abilities to alleviate the increasing strain in her head, my hand faintly gleams as I do so. I trace circles over her temples until I see the furrow in her brows rest and her head grows heavier.

* * *

I could not stay with Maivena for long, but Esme took over in my place as soon as Morano needed me.

"Amias has gone to the Training Grounds with Carmen and Lorena, and he will not be home before you leave. I have already assigned a messenger to Hua, so she knows to be home when I arrive. As for Maivena, travel after she has gotten several hours of rest." He drapes his cloak over his shoulders before securing our brooch in place. "If it were up to me, she would not be traveling at all. What her body went through today was perilous, and plenty have died afterwards. You must be sure she never touches that contraception again."

"How did it trigger so suddenly do you think?"

Morano's arms cross and he looks me over. "You."

"Why me? I did nothing, I was only showing her what happens when her body shifts and we—"

"Laven," he interrupts. "For a man as intelligent as you, you are dreadfully obtuse. Her powers triggered because you were in danger. You had no perception of the rogues behind you, and she did. Her instincts have awoken and the first thing her mind thought of was to get *you* away from them. Ascension did not follow through, and her body panicked, forcing her powers to appear and it could have killed her. None of this is your fault, things happen, but you need to force her to realize the danger of continuing to take this contraception to tame her Wolf."

"Believe me," I say. "If I ever see it in her hands again I will burn it in front of her."

"As you should."

"Will she have struggles walking, eating, talking? Anything."

He simpers at my solicitude, and he shakes his head. "You are prepared for the worst, but no, she should be fine. I just checked her temperature as well as her pulse. She is all right for now. Although, I know you would happily spoon feed her and carry her if it came to it."

"Do not chaff." I smile. "It is only a matter of time before you encounter someone, and you are forced into the same fret as me when something happens to them."

Morano fastens his unruly black hair up in a knot, revealing his aureate skin and sharp features. "And when that day occurs I know you will never let me hear the end of it."

"Oh, I will never shut up about it."

He chortles. "I will see you in a few days."

I nod. "Be careful, tell me when you are home."

"I always do. Call upon me when Maivena wakes; I wish to know how she is feeling. Then, if you need me, I will come." Morano smiles before vanishing into a heavy orange mist.

25
THE PORVIENIA

LAVEN HEPHAESTUS ARVENALDI, II

As I enter Carmen's study, the six people who retain a position in his Circle are at a table. They are discussing the potentialities of war and making sure their people are prepared for what could come given recent events.

"I have layouts for you all while I am gone," I say, setting down a paper that is folded and sealed with wax.

At the table are General Vanytha, her wife Isaren, and Carsten. Then, Amorni, Carmen's Assassin and Emissary. She is also the woman who seeks out any information he may need—she and Morano are close confidants and look to one another when necessary for guidance on assignments. Amorni trained alongside Vanytha and Isaren yesterday and today. She will be commanding Partalos and advising the Duchesses of the reforms we are planning.

Lastly is Carmen's Right Hand, Stefan, and Lorena's Right Hand, Jain. They both take over if Carmen and Lorena are gone. Jain is being sent to Vaigon Citadel to attend to my mother. She is needed in the mainland so the government can operate placidly while I am withdrawn. Axynth would assist my mother; however, he will be too immersed in training with Morano. So, Jain will keep the continent under firm power when my mother is next to train for the coming days.

Carsten will be traveling through every Court within our realm for assistance in developing an inoculation. He then plans to comb through the other realms for expert Healers to aid him; considering I am unaware of who created such a virus, Carsten will be discreet in his search.

Although Vorian may have abolished most of the rogues here in Gordanta, he did not kill them all. I have coordinated patrol within the lands. If there were rogues near my home, I know they could be lingering elsewhere.

Because Gordanta is near the equivalent size of the citadel, it has compelled them to function as if they are their own continent– that making them my most vital Court. If I ever oblige any support on the citadel Carmen and his Circle is whom I go to; they handle their own and know how to defend it.

"When do you depart for Nadrexi?" Carmen asks as we walk down the hall leaving his study and the others to read over the layouts.

"I am waiting for Maivena to wake. There was an attempted rogue attack this morning near my home. It provoked her powers, and it has completely ridden her to the bed until she can sleep it off."

"That lucky contraception has side effects like that. Is there anything I can do to help?"

"You are already helping me quite sufficiently, Carmen." I could not ask him to do more than he and his Circle are doing.

Carmen prepares his hand. "Do not force me to slap you."

He walks to the balcony that presents the expanse of the sea. If I strengthen my sight, I can see the backs of the Water Dragons lifting through the water as they swim by. Now is the time they are migrating back here.

"Tell me what it is that you need my help with."

"Trees," I exhale. "Trees on the estate of my home were splintered in half when Maivena's capabilities erupted. Could you restore them? I do not want her to wake and see that there was carnage during her outburst. She would feel culpable for ravaging them."

Carmen's eyes widen. "She split trees in half?"

"Yes," I nod. "We are still determining the depth her powers can go to."

"Well, I will inform you now. If she was capable of splitting trees in half, she is an Elemental Bender."

"There is more," I add. "The sea rose to heights of waves I have never seen; the sky went dull as if it were about to hurricane."

Carmen's eyebrows furrow. "That is what that was?"

I do not answer him.

I begin to wonder just how far her powers expand.

"Laven, if she has the strength to make the tides of an entire sea convulse, break the earth, and change the weather over just one Court, she can do much more. Someone rarely possesses the power to dominate all elements of the universe."

"Wait," I stop him. "When Maivena killed the rogues, they fell like ash and bones." They did not have all their bones, but most of them.

Carmen promptly regards what I am stating. "She burned them from the inside out." He says in disbelief.

Fire.

"How did she do it? How did she wield her powers?" He urgently asks.

Carmen hastily walks away, and I follow.

"She screamed."

He chuckles. "I had a feeling," he waves a finger. "You need to teach Maivena to manage her powers and *fast*. If her anger rises, or if something—just the slightest thing ticks her off—she could assassinate someone with a simple fuck you."

"You know of her abilities?" I ask as we enter his library.

Carmen grabs my arm, ascending us upstairs. We stop inside a library and he pulls a book in one of the shelves and it pushes open, revealing another hidden library on the inside.

"This library was here when Old Quamfasi ruled." The shelf

slowly closes behind us after he motions for me to enter. "There is a book on her gifts; I will give it to you to take to her. It is written by the hand of the first person of her bloodline. They explain every possible way to manage her powers. It also emphasizes that there are plenty of accidents that occur; they could say something and unintentionally cause someone's death. I am surprised she was able to mutilate more than one body at once, but I should not be, her powers are extraordinary."

He continues around the small, squared library in search.

Small torches flare the further we move through.

"Do you know the precise title of her powers?"

"They were first identified with the Orviantes, the Originals." He roams through the books as he walks along the cupboards. "Here it is," he pulls a red leather book from the shelf. "Throughout time they were soon distinguished as Vaultai's. I will say, it is rare for our kind to have this power, it is usually only Sorcerers and Fae. This does not mean it is impossible for a Wolf to have them."

The cover reads THE VAULTAI in gold print.

"Let her view this. I am assured you would desire to know more, so you should learn as well."

As I sweep through the pages, various symbols of fire, ice, water, earth, and wind are drawn. Then an eerie picture of a screaming head that has been cut from its body and held by its hair.

THE ASSASSINATION OF NELDA
ELDEST DAUGHTER OF THE RUMASTI CLAN

I cringe at the drawn image and close the book.

I look to Carmen. "Do you think there are more books like this?"

"Most definitely. There is no possibility that other Orviantes from first origins have not written similar books; some could be more in-depth than this one. The only way to distinguish is to seek.

"I shall also add, there is only a matter of time before her powers reach outside of just mere elements and she finds everything that controls our universe and learns to bend that as well."

"The Gods?" I ask.

Carmen laughs. "Deeper than the Gods. Elements that created them."

This is when I need my father most. He was an Orviante and could help me uncover everything I needed to know.

"There are reasons her lineage was killed off or kept their abilities hidden. The Gods could never imagine ruling over beings that were stronger than them. And we all know how the Gods feel about being overpowered."

I nod at him. "Thank you for this." I say in reference to the book.

"Any time, it is important for you to be aware of her abilities in case matters are taken to the point of needing to keep her hidden."

As we leave the hidden library, I see the sun beginning to set. However, the sky is bright. There is still sufficient time to arrive in Nadrexi within an acceptable hour.

* * *

I enter the house after Carmen leaves. When I get to my chamber, Maivena is standing by the doors of the balcony. She is clothed in her shift and robe, staring undeviatingly at the trees. The trees that now seem as if she never ruined them.

"I did that," Maivena says in a sunken voice.

I had a feeling she was watching Carmen bring the trees back to life.

"It was an accident." I walk closer, hoping to close this distance. But, instead, I sit down, ignorant to if she still prefers to keep a distance between us.

She studies the book in my hands. "What are you reading?"

"It is for you." I elucidate.

Her walk is deliberate as she progresses forward. Ultimately, when she retrieves the book, I mark the recognition snapping within her eyes.

"Vaultai's," it is almost as if she is saying it to herself, coming to terms with her capabilities. She does not seem surprised by this book.

Has she known she has the power of a Vaultai?

"It is yours," I nod.

I wait a moment and let her absorb the first few details of the book before she slams it shut.

"Do you want to talk about what happened?" I dare to ask.

Immediately her head shakes.

Then, I remember her telling me how she felt it unfair that I knew more about her than she does of me. I do not push it. Instead, I stand and extract a small box out of my pocket. It is velvet, black, and tiny in my palm as I hold it out.

"This is yours as well," I speak.

Her eyes broaden, peering down at the box and back up at me.

I erupt in laughter at her apprehension. "Do not fret, it is not the sort of ring you are imagining . . . open it." I hold it out further.

I can recognize the hesitance in her eyes.

"Maivena, if you do not prefer to take it, you do not have to."

"No, I want it." She sets the book down as she advances closer.

I am uncertain if she is saying this to please me or because she genuinely wants the gift. So, I choose not to overthink it and wait as she opens it.

The tiny silver latch is pulled, and the box gradually opens in her hands.

A smile takes over my face as her eyes illuminate.

"Blue Tigers Eye," I declare. "It helps to soothe your mind and enhance mental dexterity. With you now being alert of your strength, I am hoping by wearing this it can help core you in some way."

Maivena's eyes well and she looks away from me to hide herself as she removes the ring from the box.

The ring is white gold—the engravings are labyrinthine with vines and leaves as the band leads to the middle to encompass the oval stone. There are even a few thorns along with the vines that reach to wrap around the Blue Tigers Eye.

She places the ring upon her index finger on her right hand. The fit is not ideal; this was deliberate. So, when she obtains the rest of her weight back, the ring is still comfortable on her finger.

"Thank you," she smiles, gazing down at the ring. "Wait here," Maivena says before hastening down the hall to the chamber she stayed in last night.

When she returns, she is holding her mother's scarf delicately in her hands.

"Here, I would desire you to have it."

Her mother's scarf?

"Maivena–"

"Please, I want you to have it. I know you would take care of it, you have before. I know it is safe with you. You can even pass it on in time to anyone, our men, women, and those unidentified wear them. It is well known for them to be given at birth to anyone. They are also given as gifts of gratitude." Her optimistic eyes glimmer as she holds it out to me.

There is no shred of doubt that I find when I look her over. She sincerely wishes for me to have this. I think it may even hurt her if I do not take it.

Leisurely, I take it from her. I have always been able to recognize how well she cared for this, the fabric still looks new, and the scent of her is intensely embedded in the scarf.

"My mother, who raised my brother and me as her own, gave that to me. In case you were querying." I was, but I was not going to ask. "In Quamfasi we call them Porvienia's." Her simper is playful as it emerges.

"I will cherish this." My smile grows to meet hers.

"I know you will."

26
THE SUNSET PROVINCE

LAVEN HEPHAESTUS ARVENALDI, II

Esme elected to ascend to Nadrexi on her own—this is not a shock to me; I supposed she did not wish to ascend with me. What I did not expect was for Maivena to go with her. She has been imperceptibly out of reach following last night. I would ask, yet I know she would lie or undoubtedly change the subject of conversation as if I never asked.

It could be plausible that Esme would take Maivena to Xenathi and not Nadrexi to free her of Vaigon, and if I were asked of it, I would lie. I would say I set her free from the shackles of my nation through the Intimacy Arrangement since that is the only way to allow a servant their freedom, but not without great argument from the government.

Unfortunately, my brothers and I may rule as the highest next to Lorsius, but there are specific particularities in our Court that must go through our entire government—releasing servants is one. If one is freed they all will want freedom, and that is another war that would beckon.

To get to Nadrexi, I must go over the Terseian Mountains. It will be simpler for me to go through Terseius and surpass the border to reach the lands behind Xenathi by the mountains. That is where Nadrexi will be. I have been there once before when my brothers and I went on a horizon run that we should not have gone on due to risking the chances of New Quamfasi locating us. They would have had every right to kill us upon sight.

If I recollect one thing about Nadrexi it is the sunset view from their ground area. That is how I know I am close, by the passing of deep oranges and pink through my ascension.

Nadrexi, The Sunset Province, is a land that has no governmental structure. They do not have legitimate protection other than the men and women who are their Warriors to guard the grounds. But then that makes me question governed lands. Nadrexi is a small nation of people who have lived on without a King or Queen for all these years. They prove there is no government needed for them to make it on their own.

The only qualm I have for Nadrexi is how open their land is to the rogues. Could there be a possibility of the rogues finding a way around the mountains and to Nadrexi? The journey from Vaigon Citadel to New Quamfasi Citadel alone is days' worth of travel. There are possibilities of the trip being a fortnight if you go by carriage—and that is without stopping. If you are proficient enough, it will be minutes, if not seconds, to ascend. That meaning, it would take a prolonged time to find your way to Nadrexi.

I cease my ascension when I know I have arrived. Then, not far off in the distance, Maivena and Esme are standing at a gate that was not there years ago.

Maivena stares at the initial on the black, iron gate securely between stone pillars leading to the palace doors.

A large H is what the initial on the gate reads.

There are Warriors behind the gates, intently watching the three of us. Maivena and Esme are hand in hand as they wait.

"A messenger went off to have the gates opened," Esme announces.

"Do you know whose initial that may belong to?" I ask.

"Hatsiverso, it is the last name of Lana and Jorja," Maivena answers.

The gate lifts upward, and two warriors are stepping in our direction. They are dressed in burgundy leather armor, similar to the design of Quamfasian armor. Except for their stitching, it is black and silver.

"You will be seen in the Throne Room." One of the Warriors speaks.

Without delay, he turns on his heel, directing toward the doors of the palace. The three of us quickly follow behind.

The construct of the palace is pristine, but it does not seem brand-new. On the contrary, the age of the stone appears only a couple of years old.

Exceeding the palace are hundreds of acres of land before you see a short view of a city, and I am confident beyond that are villages upon villages.

The floors are dark wood, but the walls are rustic and white. There are paintings strung on the walls of people I do not recognize; under the icons are names I also do not identify with.

We are led deeper into the mansion before coming upon a large hall. Above us, the ceiling is curved with carvings of the Gods implanted in it. Chandeliers hang from the top, and each is nearly six feet apart as they span across.

Windows span from the floor and up the walls before the ornamental ceiling curves. The windows allow a marvelous view of the sunset broadcasting into the hallway, hurling golden rays over the floor we walk on.

Finally, we reach the entrance of the Throne Room. The doors are pulled open, and a man is standing there with a female Warrior going over a map she is holding.

"One moment," he says, respectfully interrupting her.

The sleeves of his white undershirt are rolled up his arms, the strings of his collar are undone. It loosely hangs open revealing his brown skin and a portion of his chest. It seems as if he was busy before our arrival, but I have no messenger in Vaigon who can find the location of Nadrexi. I now know why since their small country appears to be wholly reformed over the years.

His eyes lock with Maivena's before approaching.

He is confounded the closer he steps; I deem it is because of her enthralling features. Yet, there is no denying the immediate connection between Maivena and him. It is tormenting, although captivating, to see the instantaneous bond between them, and they have not even gotten more than ten feet of one another.

"Zevyk," Esme speaks first. "Who knew you would want to become a King?"

He lustrously laughs. "I am no King, Esme."

If not a King, then what?

He smiles in my direction before holding a hand out. "Zevyk," he introduces himself. "You are?"

"Laven," I nod, taking his hand.

His eyebrows raise. "*High Prince* Laven?"

There is a wariness that takes over his posture.

Because of Lorsius, there will ceaselessly be a red flag hanging over my head due to his actions. It is impossible to compel people to understand that I have tried to be nothing like him for years.

I nod. "Yes."

"Well," His spurious welcoming smile continues to hold. "It is nice to meet you."

His gaze diverts from me and toward Maivena.

"Ivella," Zevyk graciously speaks.

Ivella?

He offers out his hand, and Maivena hurls into his arms as she races onward. She collides against him hard enough to knock a stray golden hair over his forehead. His eyes close, burying his grey orbs.

He is taking in every drop of her.

"If you must continue with what you were previously doing, we can escort them elsewhere to await your arrival." The Warrior who brought us here speaks after . . . *Maivena* and Zevyk part.

Ivella. I say to myself once more.

What am I missing?

"They are fine, Gavyn." Zevyk addresses the Warrior. "I will escort them wherever they need from here, thank you."

Everyone but Esme, Zevyk, Maivena, and myself leave the room. Maivena looks up at him as she steps back.

"What can I help you all with? Or were you only coming here for a resting stop?"

"Oh," Maivena turns to me. And I know for that split second, she forgot I was here.

There is a grin on her face as she reaches out and pulls me forward.

"Yes," I begin. "I require to speak with you on the matter of alliance."

"I would despise to deceive; I am not the one you would come to for alliance. Nadrexi is now a Court of New Quamfasi, their Southern Court. You would have to travel to Xenathi and speak with King Vallehes and Queen Penelope. Any matters that I would handle here would have to go through Vallehes and Penelope first. They ascended home this morning; they were here for a while helping me set several laws in place."

So he is the Duke of Nadrexi, a formal Leader in Vallehes and Penelope's Circle.

If I attempt to speak with Vallehes and Penelope myself, I know it would take days, if not weeks. There is a chance of never.

"It is nearly time for supper. Will you be staying?" Zevyk asks, glancing between the three of us and the small bags of clothes we brought along.

"Yes, we planned to." Maivena counters. "Does my mother still reside in the same house?"

His face turns to distaste after the mention of her mother. "She does. And the house your father owned is still prospering as well. I have an additional home for anyone to stay in if more people are coming."

"I will take the key to your additional residence, please." Esme swiftly declares. Maivena's eyes narrow at her, and Esme shrugs. "I want a clean home for my stay. Who knows when the last it was that your father's house was touched or cleansed. And I will kill your mother before I stay in that forsaken home."

Zevyk crosses his arms as he chuckles. "No worries over it. I have your father's home cleaned weekly, Ivella."

That affectionate smile Maivena distributes in moments of sheer thankfulness appears.

"Thank you." She modestly says.

"I would ask you where you have been all these years, but I will conserve that conversation for later." A hand runs down her arm, and it only leads her closer to him.

The movement is all too natural.

"Unfortunately, I do have to meet with my General again, she is who just left us. If you need me, send word, and I will be there." He steps to leave but stops before turning to Esme. He holds out his hand, and the key to the home he spoke of appears in his palm.

"Thank you," Esme says before taking it from him.

"I will inform my mothers of your arrival," he tells Maivena. "I am sure they will be itching to see you. I will direct them to wait until tomorrow so you can settle in for tonight."

* * *

The home that belonged to Maivena's father, Naius, is a stone built mansion secluded in the vast forest and just near a waterfall that calmly blankets down. It replicates a cottage, but largely more expansive.

The inside is intricately embroidered; the brick walls are painted over in a cream wash. The fireplace is a relatively generous size to warm the entire home. First, there is a small shelf with books filling it to the brim, then there is the reading corner in the windowsill that outlooks the waterfall.

I can envision Maivena sitting there rendering nearly every book on the shelf while carelessly gazing at the water every now and then.

Maivena bestows a chamber for me to stay in. Not far down the long hall is her room and two others.

"Did he call you Ivella?" I eventually ask my itching question.

Maivena nods after looking around the chamber. "Yes. I did not want to be known as Ivella while in Vaigon. Although I valued my time as Ivella, I felt like a radically altered person after being delivered to the servant grounds. That was when I knew I would be distinguished as Maivena."

You were forced to become a different person.

I nod and sit down on the bench in front of the bed I will be sleeping on.

"Is Ivella what you wish to be known as now?" *Even to me.*

I regret asking; perhaps I am envious of Zevyk discerning a side of Maivena I do not know. Maivena is all I know and I hold on to her admiringly. I want to be able to address her as the person he does not know.

Setting my possessiveness aside, I wait for her response.

She appears disinclined. Then, all her own, I see it. I see her. That profound vigor I knew was always in her.

Ivella is her strength.

"Yes, I would like for you to call me, Ivella."

* * *

We did not speak again after she told me she wished to be known as Ivella.

And I did not ask who Zevyk was to her.

27
BEACON OF LIFE

ROANER KORSANA
VAIGON CITADEL

IT IS LATE, TOO late.

The portal is just within my grasp. The moment it appears, I see the darkness of woods on the other side. Even through the darkness it is like a small light opening.

I know I can fully open it.

But I do not.

I need more time . . .

I once wanted all of this time I have had to be gone. Now I want time back. If I wanted to, I could make it happen, I could very easily turn back time. But that calls for ruining fate as well as calling for my ruin because I chose to change destiny.

Now, I want nothing more than time.

I am a Sorcerer with a bloodline connected to the greatest Sorcerer known to our world, it is only natural that I can open a portal with ease. I just needed to know how to, and now that I know how to, I do not wish for it to be open just yet.

There is more for me to figure out. More for me to understand before Levora comes walking through the other end.

My mother is my voice of reason and always has been. Between my father and my mother, she is a gentle breeze, and my father was a tornado ready to rip through homes. They leveled one another out faultlessly. My father gave me textbook intensities of chaos to level out my gentleness I received from my mother.

"It is past midnight," her hand gently touches my cheek as I fix the wood in the fireplace.

I do not answer her. I continue to rearrange the wood, and I can feel her eyes boring into my back as she prepares tea.

Her voice is soft as it travels across the room. "Why are you silent?"

I stand from the fireplace, and she suddenly appears with tiny teacups.

"Confusion."

"Come, sit." She waves her hand before disappearing in front of me and reappearing on the chaise not far from the fireplace.

When I sit with her, she continues to gaze at the fire. "Confusion, you say." She begins. "Why?"

I had sex with a woman and now I want to know everything that is in her head. More than I wanted to know with Levora.

She could listen in on my thoughts if she wished to. One thing about my mother, she will always make me say it, either she hears it in my head or not.

"A woman."

She laughs. "We are confusing individuals, are we not?"

"I cannot say she is confusing; she is rather blunt. I am the one confused. Inflicted feelings, so to say."

My mother slowly turns and she stares at me for a prolonged period of time, I cannot look at her, so I keep my eyes on the sparking fire.

"You have never spoken of a woman to me other than Levora . . . have you known her long?"

Have I?

What possible past life have I known her in other than the now?

"How long does it feel that you have known her?" She rephrases her question.

When her eyes close and she is quietly resting next to me, I think I have seen it before.

Have I not?

"Years."

"And Levora?"

Who is Levora now?

What kind of woman is she?

Who has she become?

"What of her?" I ask over the cracking wood.

The longer I stare at the fire, the more I see Esme in an erratically joyous state laughing with Maivena over supper.

"Oh, Roaner." She quietly breathes. "Darling, sexual connections live with you forever, you must be careful. I have told you not to lie with women you do not have intention of staying with for a prolonged period of time."

"Who is to say I do not wish to?"

When I look at her again, her tattooed, light brown skin is flashing in the hues of the fire. I can see the disappointment growing on her face.

"Do you?"

I shake my head. "I do not know."

"What will happen when Levora comes home?" I was dreading this question. "You will have to stop seeing this woman if you plan to be with Levora like you originally hoped. There will be no way for you to have her in your life nor you in hers. It will need to be like she never existed."

"That is a far stretch." I challenge her.

"It is not," she demands. "This woman has you confined somehow. So deep that you are coming to me for help. I am willing to help you if you are honest with me."

I put down the undrunk tea on the floor and rub my eyes searching for some form of clarity. "I do not know why I am so consumed."

"Desire is a thief in that way." She responds. "What are you going to see through? This woman, or Levora."

"I will not just leave Levora where she is." I retort.

She smiles and her head tilts. "I did not say that. Did I?"

No, but as much as I want to bring her home, I need her to stay where she is for the sake of my sanity.

"Levora has been gone for years," she cautiously speaks. "I feel it is only natural that you are scratching at the walls in anticipation to have forms of intimacy, and the moment you receive it you think it is something more than what it is."

No, something that is unreal does not feel like this.

"If I bring Levora home, that means never knowing what will come of now." I weigh the options before me. "If I know what will come of now, there is a chance I would never want to bring her home."

I will lose my mind if I do not know what could come of Esme.

My mother sets her tea on the ground next to mine, as she leans in her long braids fall around her thin shoulders and she encompasses me into her warm embrace.

"Have you spoken to this woman about how you feel?"

"No," I force a laugh. "I am not ready for her to run away yet."

"You are forgetting one thing," she says as her hand places upon my head that is pressed into her shoulder.

I look up to her. "What is that?"

Her dark eyes are bright as she stares down at me. "Either you bring Levora home or not. What is meant for you will never get lost on its path to you. It will always come home."

She is feeding a thought about Esme that is not real.

A thought I have had plenty, and I will continue to avoid that thought.

I stand abruptly and my mother looks up to me. "Where are you going?"

"Although it is late, I do have business to tend to." I lean down and kiss her forehead. "I will see you again soon."

28
WAR & WOMEN

LAVEN HEPHAESTUS ARVENALDI, II
NADREXI — SOUTHERN COURT OF QUAMEASI

Sleep did not find me well last night. Each close of my eyes soared my mind into sauntering restlessly with irate thoughts, and those irate thoughts woke me every hour. And each moment I awoke, I searched for the body that used to sleep next to me.

I lift from the mattress and rub the tingling sensation from my eyes before I look at the sunlight coming through the windows.

Then the emergent sound of the waterfall rests my mind so intensely that I almost believe I have gotten days' worth of sleep.

"Oh, you are awake."

Being rapt with the view of the waterfall ahead of me, I did not realize she was here.

Ivella.

"I brought tea." She tells from the door.

I hear the soft pad of her foot step into the room.

"Wait." I call, forcing her to a standstill. "I am bared."

"Oh, I-I can leave it on the dining table."

The door does not close behind her. As I turn, I can see her holding two teacups in her hands as she moves down the hall.

You dullard. She was trying to have morning tea with you.

I hear the door to the cottage open and leisurely close.

After I tie my trousers, I leave the chamber to find where she has gone to.

"Laven."

Roaner walks through the forest and toward the house.

Ivella is crouched near a garden of flowers where hummingbirds which were previously feasting on nectar are now playfully circling her.

"Lord Zevyk and his mothers' said for the two of us to meet them at the palace. I just met with them so I could be allowed entrance."

He enters the home and I look back to Ivella, who still holds the attention of nature itself.

"You are here earlier than I supposed." I say to Roaner after closing the door. "I did not expect that you would be here by this hour; I presumed you would not arrive until tonight."

Roaner shrugs. "Wanora learns steadfast."

I smile and gape at him.

Wanora learns new training fast? Or Roaner briskly demonstrated to be here with Esme?

"I heard that."

"Oh, I am aware that you did."

I would push for more information on who she is to him, but I could not pry for information on his life when he never does with me.

* * *

Zevyk and his mothers requested that we discuss our arrival over morning meal to discover any possibility of persuading Vallehes and Penelope to allow some form of alliance once more.

The probability of Vallehes and Penelope denying us an alliance is high. I want to stay hopeful, but there is no chance to secure myself within hope. What Lorsius did to their people to rule the mainland is unforgivable. And no matter who I ask, this may continue to be denied.

If Vorian was conscious of the beckoning war, I am sure that the rest of his people are preparing or perhaps already prepared.

Roaner and I walk into the dining room after our escorts open the doors. "High Prince Laven, Lord Roaner," Lana greets. "It is lovely to meet you. I am Lady Lana, this is my wife, Jorja."

Lana is welcoming as she approaches. Her dreaded white hair is pinned half-up, revealing her radiant dark skin. Next to her, Jorja nears with an outstretched hand, also introducing herself.

Her handshake is firm before her fair-skinned arm casually circles Lana's waist. Jorja is attired in trousers, an undershirt, and a vest that is untied. The opposite of what her wife is wearing—a dainty light blue dress with navy trimmings throughout the fabric.

"Let us dine together while we talk. I hope you have not eaten yet," Lana looks to the table. "The kitchen prepared a lovely morning meal for us to consume."

"We have not. Thank you for accepting us in this way." When Courts welcome you with a meal, it is known as the utmost respect for the person coming.

The dining table is full of fresh fruit, bread, cheeses, jams, eggs, and a few foods I do not recognize. However, it is disrespectful not to try nearly everything, so I will be eating it no matter what.

After we have gathered food onto our plates is when Lana begins to speak first. "Zevyk informed me that you were looking for a union. I believe this is because of the intrusion of rogues?"

I nod and swallow my food before speaking. "Yes, do you all know of them?"

"We do," Zevyk responds. "Vallehes and Penelope were here speaking of them before they left for Xenathi. We have yet to run across any here on our territory, but that does not mean we could not."

"Agreed." I speak.

"Laven," Lana continues. "We could speak with Vallehes and

Penelope; still, the chances of reconciliation between our nations are very slim unless your uncle is dead. And your mother."

Out of nature, I sense Roaner go on defense, I do as well, but I decide for the both of us that this is not the place nor the time for the both of us to murder three people very high in New Quamfasi's Circle.

"My mother had nothing to do with the crimes Lorsius committed so I would direct you to keep her out of your blames."

"She may not, but she has not left her position as a Ruler high in stature in New Vaigon, and neither have you. Therefore, it would be challenging for the rightful heirs of the Throne to trust you. Yet, even after all the crimes your uncle committed, you and your mother both still stayed, and your father is nowhere to be found. So, how far would Lorsius have to go to make you leave? And why has he not gone far enough already to make you flee?"

Because I could never flee without Maivena.

I ignore her mention of my father, that is a conversation that we will not be having today.

"A nation can only be as strong as its leaders." Zevyk adds.

I force myself not to reach across this table and choke him. "I have my reasons."

"I surely hope there is a good reason." Zevyk says before sipping the juice in his glass vessel.

"My mate."

His eyes sharpen as he looks at me.

"Then your reasoning for staying is poor." He targets. "She should have been all the more reason to leave that God's forsaken land. But, possibly, you do not care for her enough to get her out of such turmoil."

Before I can respond, Jorja casually intervenes.

"I am sure there is much more lying behind it than we are being given, Zevyk," Jorja looks in his direction. "Rest, my child." She removes her vest that matches her trousers before sitting. "What specifically is there that you need help with, Laven?" Jorja asks.

"My Warriors and people need to be trained, and Nadrexi is

known for having the most substantial Warriors of all time. That being said, I was seeking you all out for aid in war training. We have been implementing as much training as we can, but it is not extensive enough."

Jorja responds first again, knowing that her quick-at-the-mouth son and wife are treading too heavily. "I will speak with Penelope and see what it is that we can do."

"There is word that the High King of Provas is to come to New Vaigon?" Lana asks.

"Yes, Stravan is to arrive during Summer Solstice."

"That is soon," Lana nods before biting into a piece of bread.

Roaner's senses are on high alert, but he continues to eat quietly next to me.

"You will need to hold a meeting with all Leaders of Voschantai Universe. Call all arms, gather all Warriors. If war is coming to one of the largest realms, it will come to all realms."

"Correct," I begin. "But it is not safe for us to hold a meeting with all leaders. What if one of the leaders from outside realms is the person who crafted this disease to destroy us?"

Jorja nods. "I thought of that," she adds.

Zevyk leans back in his chair as he bites into a slice of an apple. "I will train you, and in return you can train your people." He announces.

"I will kill him if he hurts you," Roaner says. *"I will make it seem as if it were self-annihilation."*

"As much as I would love that," I fight the smile threatening to grow. *"We cannot do so."*

"Why is that?"

"Because he means something to Maivena. I would not wreck her in such a way." I would not do to her what she would not do to me.

"If you wish to train together, that is fine by me."

Zevyk only nods and continues to eat.

"We will discuss the further matters with Vallehes and Penelope." Jorja says. "Although you may feel as if you are leaving with nothing, you just may not. I will see what I can do for you both."

Jorja gives a faint smile.

* * *

That dreadful morning meal has ended and Zevyk has cleared the Training Grounds specifically for us. He requested that Roaner not attend or be near; I understood because I know he could sense that Roaner wanted his soul for morning meal. But Roaner is never far, I can feel him here, but Zevyk cannot.

"No use of powers." I say to Zevyk as I toss my undershirt aside.

"No worries," he smirks, throwing his undershirt aside as well. "That is not how I was trained."

I quietly laugh. "And neither was I."

Looking over his build, I try to examine just how resilient he could be—discover what muscles protrude more than the others to determine where his strength lies.

"Was there a reason?"

"I was born with basic abilities," I stand straighter. "All my life I had no choice but to use hand-to-hand combat as my strong suit, that is until the Blood Bond Ritual when I was gifted partial power from each of my brothers. It just enhanced everything I already had."

I see that façade of bumptiousness over his frame falter.

As I grew up, my father taught me to fight in the dirtiest ways, especially against those I despise with a burning passion. He taught me enough to kill multiple men, but I will not attempt to kill Zevyk, but I will be using what I was taught.

"Shall we?" I take a step backward, and he does as well.

As we advance forward our swords immediately clang loudly through the forest far out.

This may not be an ideal situation for us both.

It is only known for men to duel for training, war, or to kill the other for the woman they love. However, I cannot let this duel go too far. Ivella will most likely have my head in the end if Zevyk is harmed.

I soar my blade downward, yet I can feel the point of his epee coming toward my skin. The rush of his sword sends a signal of air over my skin, alerting me of what is coming.

Rotating, I shift my sword in my hand and ram the handle of the sword in the middle of his neck. He falls to the ground gasping and coughing.

"That my mother taught me."

He stands. "Your mother fights grimy," he pants as he speaks.

"My father trained her."

"And I trained Ivella." His superciliousness returns.

"No wonder I needed to teach her so much."

His rapier slashes outward, and I promptly dip my shoulder, evading his foray.

"How is that you know Ivella?" I ask.

Zevyk smiles. "She was to be my wife."

Then, again, our swords are crash down into one another, both of us fighting for the intent to kill, but neither of us aiming for death although we wish to.

"You are aware she will wish to stay with me." Zevyk says breathily as my sword knocks his out of his hand.

Our chests heave up and down as the freshly sharpened edge of my vane presses to the side of his neck.

"We are done here."

"What will you say when she tells you so? Will you deny her? Or will you demand her to do as you say so she will keep put by your side?"

I fit my sword back into the sheath strapped across my chest.

"You know, I would like to believe that she would stay with me." I admit. "Yet, I will not tell her what to do nor where to sojourn. That is all her own choice."

"And you would let her go? No interference from you again." He tightly crosses his arms, sweat drips from his golden hair and down his arm within the taught motion.

"No," I shake my head. "I would still be within her vicinage."

A shudder of resentment streaks within his eyes.

"Why?" His tone is strident as he demands a response.

"Because she will want me around, and I will come."

"And what if it were only her bed that she called you to?" He asks.

He walks toward his undershirt lying on the ground and pulls the dark fabric over his shoulders.

I should be shocked by such a question, but I am not. I grasped that this was one of the reasons Zevyk feared me. This duel was nothing but an antagonization. I distinguished this going in, and I will not allow him to believe he could bid my bluff.

I know Maivena, and I think I know Ivella as well. Neither of them would crave for another other than the person they are wedded to because she will be smart about who she marries.

"If that were the reason she was to call on me, then that would mean you are not fulfilling her in ways that she knows I can."

He laughs. "So, then what? You become High Prince Laven, the paramour." He continues to dig a hole that he will not find me at the bottom of.

"For her? I would become anything she wanted me to be. In the end, it is still me she is asking for it from." I stand in front of him once more. "You are trying to test me, Zevyk, but what you do not know is that I have grown up with an uncle that has seen me as competition all his life. It will take a long time before I allow you—someone, I do not know—to bring out the vilest side of me.

"If Ivella desired to be here with you, then that is what she chooses. I do not tell Ivella what to do because I want her to do what her mind calls her to. Not because I want to secure her to my side out of pure possessiveness. Nevertheless, Ivella can easily trigger my possessiveness. However, I keep it subjugated."

He continues to stare through me as I grab my undershirt and throw it over my shoulder.

"Mates are not always sure to stay together." This is precisely what I expect every man to say who throws themselves at her feet, coveting for a morsel of her time.

I am the one to laugh this time. "You are telling me things I already know. Let me know when you have something to tell me that I am not already aware of."

"Ivella does not know what she wants, she never has," he quickly speaks as I begin to ascend. "Only a fool would walk away from making her see what she could have."

A grin appears on my face as I turn around. "No, only a fool would force her to see a future that is not there."

"And you see what her future holds?"

"I do not. But I also do not influence myself to be in someone's future unless I am meant to be in it."

"And if you are not meant to be in her life?" He steps forward.

"Then so be it."

Losing her will be my ruin.

* * *

When I arrive at Ivella's home, she is wrapping a large bathing cloth around her chest as she recedes from her swim near the waterfall.

As I enter, the house is quiet, alerting me that Roaner and Esme are not here like I thought they would be.

"You are back," Ivella says as she enters. A shift and robe now replace the bathing cloth that she wrapped around her.

She looks over the secured sheath across my bare chest, and then next, the black handle of the sword sitting at an angle on my back. "Were you dueling?" Her eyebrows furrow as she steps closer. She is observing, searching for a wound.

"No, just training," I say, removing the sheath. "Are you hungry? Roaner said he perused the city on his journey in this morning, and there is a small bakery that sells pastries of all different kinds."

She glows. "That bakery belongs to my father's close acquaintance. I used to go there when I would visit here during Winter and Summer Solstice."

"Would you like to go now?"

"Oh," she looks around before her eyes meet mine again. "I am meeting Zevyk soon, but I could take you another time. Possibly tomorrow?"

I smile and shake my head. I was expecting Zevyk to send a messenger here while I was gone to ask her for a day of her time.

"Tomorrow, I plan to leave."

With you or without you.

She walks away to busy herself in the kitchen, and I stay where I am. But then, the subject of our conversation quickly diverts.

"I will be going to the market to buy vegetables for supper. Lana, Jorja, and Zevyk plan to come along to see me."

"Do you need coin?" I ask.

She responds with the shake of her head as she makes another cup of tea, not meeting my eye any longer.

"No, I will be fine."

Instead of asking whose money she will be using, I walk to the chamber I am staying in to change clothing.

As I change, I can hear the padding of her feet against the floor outside of the door. I wait to see if she will open the door, knock, anything. Yet, she is only standing there. Contemplating. She does nothing. She only leaves.

* * *

Roaner shouts out my name as I swim by the waterfall; he is standing at the cottage door, motioning for me to meet him inside.

After drying off and putting my trousers on, he sits at the dining table, sipping a glass of dark liquor. Next to him is a freshly opened bottle of whiskey. He reaches for the bottle and fills the crystal glass, and slides it to me.

"What will we do?" He asks.

I do not need to suspect what he is speaking in reference to.

"We wait," I quietly grunt as the smooth liquor gives a satisfying burn in my chest.

"Do you believe Jorja will be able to persuade Vallehes and Penelope?" His finger trails over the edge of the glass as he awaits a response.

"No," I confidently respond. "When Stravan arrives we will speak with him of the matters, see if he may be adept in the persuasion of New Quamfasi or if he will come to our aid. No matter what, I am asking for something in return of whatever it may be that he wishes for us to do to find Dyena."

Roaner removes his cloak and vest, stretching out his arms and resting back into the chair. "Stravan will know we will want something in return. Make him indebted to it."

"What if it is him spreading this vile disease?"

"Doubtful," Roaner puts his glass down. "Morano and I both do not believe so. He may have been on rampages over the years, but do not let that skew your vision into believing he would be so hateful he would spread infection. His rages are through desperation. He will do anything to find Dyena, and we will do anything to prevent or win a war."

I huff. "War and women."

"They go hand in hand." Roaner says in a deep tone after swallowing the liquor. "Speaking of women. Where is she?" He asks, referring to Maivena.

Ivella.

"She is off with Zevyk, and I am fathoming that he is courting her all over again."

"You did good," Roaner nudges his knee against mine. "Do not give in to such pettiness as his. If Maivena knew of what he did, she would not have gone with him."

My eyebrows raise. "I do not know; I think she still would go with him. Or, in some way, he would convince her to. They have been apart for a long time and were to wed before the guards took her. Nothing could stop this indisputable time they want together."

"That is interesting to me." Roaner precariously says as he swirls the liquor in his glass.

"What is?"

"Their relationship." He clarifies. "Maivena and Zevyk."

"How so?"

"Something must have transpired between them beforehand. He

can cry and complain about how you should have taken Maivena and left New Vaigon, but he should have been searching for her before her father was. That is *if* it is true they were to be married. If she had as much meaning in his life as he deems, he would be trapped with her in Vaigon, not her father. Just as Kaden followed Ethel, Zevyk should have followed Maivena."

I strain to not speculate too abundantly about a situation I do not copiously know.

"Naius was the only stable male figure in Maivena's life," he continues. "I understand it is natural he sought to save his daughter, but Zevyk, her awaited husband, that is odd he was not searching before Naius, did not find her, and did not stay. Yet you have tallies of bodies on your hands for men just taking her."

"Everything within this is very nebulous. And there are one too many questions to ask without intensifying tantrums after every query."

"Will you tell her now?"

I distinguish that he is hinting at the mating bond.

"No, that would be too evident. She would claim it as me only saying it because Zevyk wanted her as his wife again."

"Laven," Roaner leans forward. "What if she marries this jester?"

I throw my head back in laughter. "If I cannot probe her to stay with me without a mating bond, what makes you believe I could when she knows?"

"You doubt yourself. You have barely had time—mere weeks." His hand throws out as if to gesture the time.

"Well," I breathe, agreeing. "I am not completely leaving her life."

"Explain," he urges as I tilt back the rest of the liquor in my glass.

"Vuamsati Academy, she still holds a place there; they are just awaiting her arrival."

"And she will need a way there without complications of crossing borders." Roaner smirks, adding it all together. "What if she chooses to go no longer attend?"

I lift a shoulder. "I will cross paths with her again soon enough."

Roaner reaches behind his chair, and another full bottle of whiskey is in his hand. He grabs the other that is open on the dining table and gives over the fresh liquor to me.

He stands and leads for the door; I follow behind him while holding the whiskey low at my side.

There is a smile on his face as he gazes out at the glorious view of the Nadrexi sunset.

He nods for me to pop the cork concealing the liquor, and I do.

"What do you dream of?"

I grin. "You know what I dream of."

He holds out his vessel to mine, and they clank together. "Now kiss it to the Gods."

Our heads tilt back, taking a deep drink to the Gods in the hope of our reveries being heard and gifted to us.

29
THE GRAVITAS

LAVEN HEPHAESTUS ARVENALDI, II

ONCE AGAIN, I HAVE found myself not receiving any form of sufficient rest.

Ivella sent word to Esme relatively early before the evening could begin that she would not be returning to the house. She has been entirely absent since I last saw her yesterday.

Waiting around with my thumb up my ass for her to return is all my morning and afternoon have been. Then, I begin to question if she will return at all. I know Zevyk would be capable of such a thing, but Maivena would say before leaving me.

As much as I would like to despise being here, there is nothing to detest. On the contrary, the cottage is consoling in its own ways. The waterfall continues to give my mind a form of rest that sleep has not been giving it. Everything here is irrevocably restful.

I could use this relaxation I am receiving but lying around for such a prolonged time is immoral. There is still much to be done on the citadel that it is impossible for me to truly rest.

My waiting does soon come to an end.

Now a letter is being delivered by a messenger.

A fragment of me does not wish to pull off the wax seal as I already know what will be written.

Laven,

Ivella has informed me of her situation over the past years. On behalf of myself and my family, we would wish for you to ultimately grant over her freedom as well as her father Naius, her cousins Kaden, and Ethel. With the Intimacy Arrangement intact, you hold all power in wholly freeing herself and her family. And since you hold high placement in your government there should be no issues in the process of this.

If you request to deny this plea—which you hold the right to—the messenger should still be there to send us word.

Ivella & Zevyk

As I fold the letter, the door to the cottage forces open to Ivella storming in. The letter is snatched out of my hands, and I raise my eyebrows at her.

"And what was that for?"

"He was not to send that," her sharp tone could slice this entire home in half.

"Why not?"

"Because I am no coward," with each word she grips the letter in her hand tighter and tighter. Soon a slight flare of smoke begins to form. "I wanted to speak with you myself."

I reach for the letter, and she breathes, allowing me to remove the paper that is about to catch fire in her hand.

"Well," I initiate. I would rather not stand here and waste our time. "Is this what you want?"

"I need to get my family home, they—"

"That is not what I want to know," I interrupt. "If you crave your family's freedom, say the word, and I will have it done instantaneously. But you, what is it that you covet for?"

Those quiet seconds go by as she debates with herself as she did yesterday when at my door, chose not to say anything and left. As I know she is now. I give her the time to answer, although I know what it will be. Still, I wait—letting her decide on her own without my influential force.

"The same."

I nod. "That was all you had to say."

Standing from my chair, I walk to the chamber to gather my things.

* * *

I should not be angry with what she chooses. Nevertheless, I am. That bitterness I have been suppressing since being here is sitting on an edge, and I am afraid anything will tip it over that edge toward anger at any moment. And that is what I will not allow Zevyk to have. He will not receive the delight in knowing he unequivocally pisses me off.

When I leave the cottage, I see Ivella and Zevyk quietly speaking near the kitchen.

"Will Roaner meet you here to leave?" She is quick to ask.

I turn on my heel to face them. "No, I will go on my own. Roaner and Esme will spend however much more time here that they want."

"Why do you not stay and take a few day of rest with them?"

Nearly laughing at her question, I cover it with a smile. "No days off for me. Morano is going to the Servant Grounds to collect your family and bring them here."

"Thank you," she smiles, stepping forward. I lean slightly away and look out the window as a decoy of my attention. She does not come any closer. She has caught the hint.

"I should be going; the clouds are darkening."

"I spoke with Esme," Ivella announces. When I look at her, there is a twinge of ire circling within her eyes. "She said you will still come here to retrieve me for Vuamsati Academy."

"Yes, if you still want to attend." I counter.

Zevyk finally attempts to speak from the corner of the room, she is fast to shoot him a glare, and he shuts his mouth.

"I do," she nods. "You will come here tomorrow morning, and

you will show me around the academy. I know they wish for people to arrive earlier in the morning like last time." Her hands hold together in front of her, resting over the white fabric of her dress.

"Then I will arrive when the sun rises."

I ascend before having to bear any more of this conversation with a brooding Zevyk in the corner of the room.

GORDANTA — WESTERN COURT OF VAIGON

Upon arriving at Fonavyn House, I find Hua and Amias with one another in the kitchen. Hua points the knife in his direction with a glare and he leisurely backs away from her.

"You are nearly on time; we are struggling to prepare a shitty supper." Hua hurries over to hug me around my shoulders tightly. Her eyes drift behind me and through the window in search.

"Where is Maivena?" She asks while tucking her brown hair behind her ears.

Roaner ascends into the kitchen and Esme is not with him. I look to them both and nod. "Feel free to explain where Ivella is. I have someplace to be."

"Ivella?" Amias asks, but I leave before any further questions are asked.

My ascension ends in Carmen's study.

"You are back. How did it plan out?" He asks, standing from behind his bureau.

"Not as well as I thought." I dryly say. "They are now a Court of New Quamfasi, I did not ask why, but I am conjecturing it is for protective matters. The Lord of their Court will send word to Vallehes and Penelope in attempt to request that they ally with us again. Yet, I am sure they will say no."

Carmen exhales heavily. "I am sure they will say no as well. What of Ethivon? Do you believe it would be worth the travel to their continent?"

"I do not think so. We will wait for Stravan to arrive during the week of Summer Solstice, fulfill his wishes and ask for his aid in the war."

"An astute High Prince." Carmen praises. "Now, what is wrong? You are brooding as you speak." He analyzes my face before walking around the bureau and leaning against it.

He removes his black topcoat and waits for me to speak.

Instead of telling him what is on my mind. "I need a friend and a saloon." I say in replacement.

His eyebrows furrow. "Laven, what is wrong with you?" He laughs.

"I will explain it after we get a drink."

"Emotional drinking is a bad habit to develop."

I cut him a glare. "Do we genuinely desire to go down that path? Shall I remind you of all the times you would drag me into town, emotionally drink, and cry about Lorena not wanting to–"

"My Gods, all right!" He interrupts, not wishing to backtrack too far into the past when Lorena denied their mating bond and they had to be tied by the Blood Bond Ritual.

Carmen grabs his topcoat and flings it over his shoulder, holding it there as the other hand shoves into his pocket.

The moment I touch his arm, we ascend to the city and walk toward Korna's Tavern.

We are greeted upon entry, and Carmen leads me to a more private area of the saloon.

"Dark and two glasses," he nods to the young boy who has approached.

"Well?" Carmen urges.

"I said *after* the drink," I bite out.

He chuckles at me and leans back in the cushioned chair.

The tavern is dimly lit, and with the sun receding, a woman moves through the area, lighting more candles and lanterns.

The interior is elegant. This is one of the newer taverns built since I have last been here.

When the liquor is brought out, Carmen pours a fingertip full, and I wave my hand in small circles for him to run more, only causing him to burst into laughter.

"Oh, I cannot wait to hear about this while you are shittily drunk." He brings his glass upward as I give him a vulgar gesture.

* * *

"And she will marry that bastard, then what?" The glass in my hand slams onto the table.

"You become High Prince Laven, the paramour." Carmen laughs, teasing me.

"No, she would never ask that of me." I struggle to pull off my topcoat with the rising heat in the tavern.

"Possibly not." He considers.

"There is no *possibly*," I say as I pour more of the liquor into my glass. Then, I burst into laughter as I miss the glass, and the bourbon goes pouring onto the table. "There is no possibly because Ivella is a devoted woman, and she wants others to be devoted as well . . . oh, Gods, she will marry this fucker." I whine into my hand.

Carmen's laughter pulls my head upward.

"Fuck you," I flick the liquor at him after I dip my fingers into the glass. "You were me not so long ago. Mourning your desperation to the fucking moon thinking she would hear you."

"Trust me, my friend." He wipes away the splash of liquor on his skin. "That will be you tonight."

I grunt at the sharp downfall of the liquor in my throat. "No!" I shout. "I am not crying to the moon. I am not that despaired."

"You make yourself think you are not that despaired." He leans across the table as I drink from the bottle. "Just wait until we get out those doors, and you see the bright shine of grey and white. Then you will scream at the stars."

I slump in my chair, throwing my hands lazily over my face. "The stars! The stars! I took her to those fucking stars. And what will he do? He will only show her them. He will not be as romantic as me. He will not be as gentle and caring with her as I would."

Carmen snorts. "I am sorry. It is just very entertaining to watch you spout this way. I never thought I would see the day."

"It is not *day*, Carmen. It is *night*." I can hear the slurring of my words, and I reach for more alcohol. "That little shit had the gravitas to tell me he knew she would stay, and she fucking did."

I shift to the door, measuring the distance I must walk from here to there.

As I look away, a woman is entering the tavern. Her hair is light, and it stops at her ivory shoulders.

"No," Carmen instantly says, yanking my chin in his direction. "I know what it is that you are thinking, and the answer is *no*. I am taking your drunken ass home and to your bed. The bed you were sharing with Maivena just nights ago."

Maivena.

"Maivena? Maivena is nonexistent. Maivena, the one who wanted me, is gone. Shot into oblivion. There is only Ivella, and there is no having her. So, I will entertain myself elsewhere."

I turn to the woman who still stands near the tavern's door. This time she is looking at me as well. She is tall and slender; her long fingers clutch a small bag.

"You halfwit!" Carmen harshly whispers. "Are you even attracted to her?"

I purse my lips together as I look back to Carmen. "No, but she is convenient. And it seems I am convenient for her as well. So, leave me be," I stand from the table.

"Laven, I mean it. You will be revolted with yourself in the morning. Let us just go home."

Snatching from his grasp, I step farther away from him. "I am going home. With her."

His eyes widen. "Do you dare to bed a woman in a house meant for another? You are drunk out of your mind and not thinking properly."

"That house I made is no use. My manifestation is shot to hell. I may as well turn that hell house into a brothel. That may be my finest idea yet."

He reaches for me once more, and I step back again. "Do not touch me; you will ascend us away and ruin my night."

"I am trying to save your idiot ass from a enormous mistake." He points. "Or are you too drunk to remember what I went through the time our roles were reversed in this exact situation?"

I shrug. "Honestly, friend. What is the worst that could happen?"

"You are absolutely impossible!" Carmen plucks me on my forehead, and I swat his hand away. "Fine, go off. Bed that woman, and when you wake up next to her, your realization of the mistake you made will hit you harder than your hangover."

He ascends away, and I hesitate to walk toward that door where the woman stands. Instead, I tilt back another glass of bourbon, thoroughly washing away the hesitance.

A RUSH OF COLD water yanks me awake, nearly drowning me in my sleep.

Hua is standing there, ready to pour another bucket of water, and I quickly hold my hands out.

"Hua, what in the Gods name is wrong with you?"

"You do not get to ask what is wrong with me!" Her voice towers above my own. "You brought this woman into this house drunk out of your mind and obnoxiously bedded her. Roaner had to put a shield around your chamber so we could get some fucking sleep. I get to wake you up however the hell I want!"

Her shouting sends a roaring pain into my head.

Woman?

What woman?

I look next to me at the shuffling that draws my attention.

I look to Hua and she grips me by my hair, I wince as the pain soars over my head.

"Felicitations to you, Laven." She yanks my hair harder as I close my eyes, forcing me to reopen them. "If your strategy was to make Maivena miss her first day at the academy, you succeeded. Get some fucking clothing on, go downstairs, and apologize to her."

"And you," Hua looks to the woman hurriedly putting her dress on. "Get the fuck out of this house."

"We ascended here," she says, panicked. "I do not have a

carriage to take me to my home." She says.

Hua's eyes flare in a deep purple as she turns to the woman. "Then fucking walk. It is what you have legs for. Use them."

I nearly trip over my trousers as I try to pull them on.

"Ivella is here?" A sharp stab of terror strikes through as I connect the multiple dots from last night.

"Yes, she is here. Roaner went to Nadrexi to retrieve her since you were too busy fucking this woman until the sun came up. By the time they made it to Vuamsati, it was too late." Hua strides out of the chamber, and just as I stumble into the hall, I see Ivella walking down with her belongings.

She looks toward me and then to the woman walking out after me.

"Do not make her walk," Ivella says. "Take her home."

I follow her down the hall as she glides down the stairs.

"And who will take you home?" I reach out to catch her arm when we are on the first floor.

She stares down at my hand in disgust and then up at me. "Do not lay your hand upon me; I know where they have been. Go clean yourself and take that woman home." Her voice is curt as she speaks.

I am nailed to this place on the floor by the development of hatred blaring in her eyes.

"There is still tomorrow," I quietly speak.

"No, there is not. You will not retrieve me tomorrow or any day after that. You humiliated me in front of the leaders at the academy by making me late. It is already enough that I am not a woman of Vaigon attending that academy. You handed them the chance to talk down on me by doing this."

"If you let me speak with them, I can resolve it." I try to reason, but I know it is no use.

"I do not need you to resolve anything." The cold expression over her exterior is unmoving. "Roaner," she calls.

Immediately he appears at her side.

"I would like to go home." Her voice is low.

"Just wait," I step forward, and she grips Roaner's arm sliding closer to his side, nearly hiding. He lets her, and he stands his ground between the both of us.

"I am sorry, I can—"

"I do not need your apology either. Zevyk will find me an education elsewhere."

That is low, and she knows it. I cannot defend myself any more before Roaner ascends with Ivella clutching his arm and the few items that belonged to her.

I rush to the chamber she was staying in during her last night here, and I see the dresses neatly stored in the wardrobe. The scarf I gifted her sits folded on the corner of the bed as well.

She took absolutely nothing that I gave her, nothing other than the pieces of myself that she stormed away with.

30
STATE OF DILAPIDATION

ROANER KORSANA
NADREXI — SOUTHERN COURT OF QUAMEASI

"Maivena, my brother can be very pernicious. Even with those he loves." Her sharp green eyes stare in my direction as she ferociously makes tea in the kitchen of her father's home in Nadrexi. "He never means it but I am helping him work through not reacting on the first emotion he feels."

She does not respond, instead she brings me a small vessel of tea.

"Unless you would prefer wine like me," she says after noticing I do not sip the tea.

I look outside and the sun is still high in the sky while she drinks her tiny vessel of wine.

When I shift my eyes back to her, she is still intently staring at me, daring me to mention the time of day that she is consuming alcohol.

"Your brother tends to have a streak in him when he does not get what he wants."

"Do you remember the saying about the Orviantes?" I ask. "How they all used to be quick to anger at inconveniences. I believe Laven has that streak."

Maivena sits on the chaise across from me and stares down at the small vessel of wine in her hands. "Was his father like him?"

I smile. "Laven the first and Laven the second are exactly that. The first and the second. Laven is the clone of his father with streaks of black in his hair."

She laughs before looking up. "What was his father like?"

"His father was strong, calculated, quiet, and had a soul like I never knew. I admired him because he reminded me of my late father. When I came to Vaigon I was a fatherless child that looked for trouble in every corner until I crossed paths with Laven, and his father became a parental figure to me that I easily realized I was craving. The second son he lost is what he called me."

"Why is that?" She asks, entirely absorbed into the conversation.

"Apolla, Laven's mother, miscarried their second son, and when I came into their life Laven's father swore I was the child he now holds in his heart as what would have been."

"It is eerie," Maivena observes. "You look like them, but your skin is slightly lighter."

"Plenty of people believe that it is from the Blood Bond Ritual," I explain. "Although, Laven and I mimicked one another before then. Many people thought we were brothers before the ritual."

"Your doppelgänger."

"Something like that," I say. "Laven and I are similar in many ways which is why I tend to understand him much quicker than the rest. Although, he hated me when we first met, nearly beat me until I died." Maivena's eyes widen, and I laugh. "Oh, I deserved it. I forced his hatred to appear out of jealousy, I wanted his life, the life I knew I would have had with my family before my father died. But now, both of our fathers are gone and that leaves us, just me and him. Laven and his father saved my life at such a young age when all I knew was rage, just like my brother. And I will do anything within my power to make sure he finds the peace he deserves, and I am going to be sure the both of us turn out to be the men our fathers were for our sons."

"The both of you will make amazing fathers," Maivena says

sipping her wine. "I enjoy hearing these details about you and them. I do not think Laven would have ever told me."

"Laven does want to tell you," I correct her. "He had no time."

No time before you left.

She does not answer, she only nods. Instead of answering me she returns the conversation to where it was. "I am afraid I see you being an all-girl father."

"I think so too." I chuckle in agreement. "What about Laven?" I urge her to read her own future and his.

She takes a moment, pondering on the thought. "Boys," she quietly speaks. "And one tyrant girl. The girl will be his favorite, but he will not forget to love his sons."

"Yes," I smile. "That does sound about right."

"Nothing tells me otherwise." She laughs. "How did you and Laven come about to like one another? Let alone be bonded by blood."

Tracing back to those times, it was all because of Levora. "A mutual acquaintance, Levora was her name, she brought us closer by forcing us to be around one another. She was a dear companion to both Laven and I." I choose not to speak too much about Laven's life especially about Levora, a story he wishes to tell her on his own. "She gave us no choice but to tolerate one another and I thank her deeply for it. If it were not for Levora I would not know the love of a brother let alone a sibling."

Maivena nods. "The love of a sibling is quite different. You feel obligated to give them the world and some days you chase to take it from them."

I cautiously continue this particular conversation. "Have you missed your brother?"

"Every second I was gone I missed him . . . but I will see him soon." And with that, she quiets.

I look to the small table sitting between us and the book Laven gave her is sitting on it. "I will make a pact with you."

"What pact?"

My head sways from side to side. "Not technically a pact, but a benefit for you."

"And that is?"

I point to the book that says THE VAULTAI in large letters. "We begin training and I teach you everything important to know about controlling your powers and more."

"And nothing in return for your dues?"

"Nothing."

"Not even time with my cousin?" Maivena smirks.

"You are funny," I wave my finger. "No, not even that." I lie.

* * *

I put my hands in my pockets as I stare at the portal gradually appearing in front of me. Purely through mind work, I open the portal.

Regret.

To the pit of my bones I can feel the regret that will brew every day if Levora returns now. There is no certainty that she will be found immediately after it opens, but the time I spend looking for her could be spent understanding my purpose with Esme.

'Do not let your life be filled with regret or what could have been. If you need time, take your time and keep that portal shut.' My mother's words repeat in my head, yet it all feels selfish.

All of this endless searching, sleepless nights looking, illegally crossing borders of multiple realms in search. All of this turmoil I have put into Levora only to end it and leave her where she is after years of searching just because I need to know if this woman I have only known for a short period of time will mean everything to me or nothing.

The portal continues to expand, and I see the peaking view of the woods I have previously seen when opening the portal.

And gradually, it closes, and I leave.

VAIGON CITADEL

As I walk down the stairs outside of the palace I can see Amias and

Morano talking with each other over liquor at the large stone table. All around them sit large floral trees, statue fountains of Laven's grandfather, Vaigon, and pavement to walk around on that now has grass growing around it.

"Brother," Amias holds a drink outward for me to take.

"Keep it here," I nod for him to place it on the table. "Where is Laven?" I ask, although I am certain I know.

"Chaos Chamber." Morano proves my thought correct.

"Keep my glass, I am going to check on him."

"If you can get in there, you know no one has ever seen that room." Amias says before tossing back the rest of the alcohol in his glass.

When I get to the highest floor of our home where Laven's Chaos Chamber is the door is cracked open, which it never is.

I step nearer to the door, and I can see the destruction done to the room.

The artistic destruction.

Plenty of beautiful pieces of art lie around the room, then there is the destruction. The torn wallpaper, the broken windows, and somehow he managed to draw on the ceiling though I see no ladder lying around.

Laven has always had an artistic soul, but none of us knew how deep the passion was.

'What would we be if not royals?' Amias asks as me and my brothers sit on the mountains that hover atop Nadrexi.

We fall silent, pondering on the thought of who and what we would become or if we would even be alive.

'I would have taken my mother home to Galitan,' I begin. 'And I would be seeking guidance from my relative Martana to be a greater Sorcerer to care for my mother. I do not know if I will ever have a mate, but if I do, I will care for her and her family as well.'

'I would be dead.' Morano quietly speaks.

'No you would not,' Laven instantaneously speaks. 'Even if we were not royals, I would still discover a way to keep you from pursuing that form of work.'

Morano does not elaborate further. 'And you?' He asks Laven.

Laven stares far into the sunset and wonders.

'If I were not a royal I live on the countryside not far from the city, I would be an artist, and Mai—' he stops speaking and is slow to continue, but we wait. *'I would lead a simple life, quiet and poetic. My father said there will never be anything more to life than the people who love you and how you treated them. In my dreams I live an unpretentious life, and I would still live it if I could.'*

Amias shifts and smiles. 'Hua and I would still be Warriors in the Mandem, but we would live a much more hidden life than what we live now. But a Warrior is what I was born to be, some days I believe that is all I was meant for, then Hua comes along and proves me wrong. If I am certain about anything in my life no matter the outcome, it is her.'

Looking back, I now know exactly who that was he nearly mentioned to us and seeing this room full of death and beauty, I know this is what he feels on the inside.

The humbleness of being thankful for his life yet loathing it in the same moment. That is what this room defines. The chaotic phases of his life and how he copes with his existence in such a ghast world.

In the distance I can hear his boots dragging through the grass, when I look through the windows I see him approaching in the distance below. To keep from being seen, I ascend back to the courtyard with Amias and Morano.

"Well?" Morano speaks first with a worried expression. "Did you get in?"

"He was not there." I exhale heavily as I remove my cloak and undo the strings of my undershirt beneath my vest.

"Here," Amias taps the rim of the glass with liquor in it.

I do not disclose what I saw. What I experienced felt too personal to see and I could not let anyone know that I witnessed what truly is going through my brother's soul.

"Hopefully this was a lesson for him." Amias says before drinking what is left in his glass.

"No," Morano knocks the edge of his empty glass against the stone table. "This was no lesson for him to learn. That was not something Laven would do, that was very out of character for him to bed a woman he does not know."

"What if he is going through it again?" Morano asks staring into his glass.

Amias and I both look at each other and then at Morano.

"We are older now," Morano continues. "Yes, we have a closer eye on him, but you heard what the Healer said all those years ago after confinement for so long—after being tortured for so long. He was declared manic due to his state. What if he stays in that chamber for so long we find him as we did years ago?"

'What has happened to him?' Morano asks standing near the door, he grips the doorknob behind him as he watches.

When I look at Laven, he is sitting in the corner of the room whispering mumbled words as he picks at his skin in one particular place on his arm.

Amias slowly walks forward, and I grab his arm. 'No, I would not.'

'Something is not right.' Amias whispers. 'He has never acted like this his entire life.'

'That is not Laven.' I warily speak.

The Healer stands nearby. 'Due to the disturbance from incarceration, his mental state is tremendously fragile. I have seen it in the past with others who were . . . tortured in Wyendgrev Tower. There is a slight possibility that he may not recover from this, and there is a chance he can.'

'He will,' I say. 'He will recover.'

'You are young, child. You do not have the education to be certain that he will be fine after such trauma.'

'Then I will learn,' Morano says as he gently approaches Laven. 'I will learn,' Laven's head twitches as he tries to look up at Morano now crouching beside him. 'I will learn what it takes to help someone come back to themselves.'

Morano grabs Laven's hand that is picking at his skin, and he holds it.

'It is not that simple.'

'I did not say it would be.' Morano snaps. 'I said I will learn. I will not let him stay like this, he does not deserve to be physically trapped and now mentally trapped. He would not allow it to happen to any of us. We will heal him!' Morano shouts at the Healer and I can see the tears falling down his face and landing on their hands that are conjoined.

'What-wh-wha–"

'Shh,' Morano hushes Laven. 'Do not worry, you will be fine. Let us lie down, you should not sit in this corner for long, your wounds will not properly heal this way.'

It is difficult, but Morano gets him to stand, and his frail body is still wrapped in bandages due to his wounds the Healer is mending. But I cannot say this Healer knows what they are doing when it comes to the mind.

'Ma-M-Mai-Mai–' Laven tries again. 'Sh-sh-she-she is–'

'Who does he speak of?' Amias asks.

'We do not know, he cannot fully speak her name yet, but his mother and I have tried to probe him to speak further.'

'Not necessary,' I say. 'Just let him mumble and we need not to worry. We will care for him, learn his disabilities, and work with him until he is Laven again, until he is our brother again.'

Laven's legs give out and Morano cannot hold him. Amias and I ascend and catch him.

Amias is crying as he looks down at Laven's lifeless body still mumbling gibberish we do not understand.

'You both hold his upper half, I will take his legs, we need to take him to the bed. He should have never gotten out of it.' I emphasize my final words so the Healer is aware that I do not believe he is performing his duties well enough.

When he gets into the bed I look at Morano and Amias. 'He will be fine, we will be sure of it.'

Amias grabs Laven's face, forcing him to look at him. 'Remember who you are. You are Laven Hephaestus Arvenaldi, second of his name. You are an Heir to the Throne of Vaigon. The blood of Orviantes courses through your veins. You are our brother.' His voice cracks. 'I am Amias, your Right Hand. Roaner is your Assassin. Morano is your Emissary. We are The High Four. You are the Head of House Arvenaldi. You are to be King. Strong souled, Laven. Forever your bloodline will reign.'

Laven's blue and hazel eyes stare into Amias's as he speaks and his breathing is ragged as he opens his mouth to respond.

I hover above him, next to Amias. 'Say it.'

He struggles.

We push him.

For the first time, I have the opportunity to attempt to use our mind link. 'You are capable of it, now say it.'

He rapidly blinks as he looks at me and his hands begin to twitch. Morano grasps his hands again to calm his nerves.

He rapidly blinks as he looks at me and his hands begin to twitch. Morano grasps his hands again to calm his nerves.

'We need you.' *I plead to only him.* 'Now say it unless you dare to leave us.'

His body jerks and Morano does not let go of his hands and Amias is still grasping his face.

'Say it.' *And this time, I am not begging. I will not lose a brother.*

His pale lips tremble as he searches for the words, his body continues to strain as he attempts to speak, nevertheless, he prevails. 'S-st-str-str-strong s-sou-souled.'

Just as his father intended him to be.

Nothing will compare to the harrowing days of believing the person who brought us together would be leaving us.

"You think this will push him back there?" Amias asks.

"No," I answer. "Not this, but now that we are aware of why he was imprisoned, we need to be aware of how much he is willing to put himself through for her alone. The name that he was calling that night was hers. He is in pain," I can hear the deep resonance of my voice after a sip of the alcohol. "Today he thought he and Maivena were done with, so he acted out to be spiteful. If he learned from anything, it was that spitefulness will solve nothing, it will only result in worsening an already problematic situation. Yet, I do not see Maivena keeping away from him for long."

"Ivella," Amias mumbles. "Ivella Fondali."

"Did you know she had a streak for winning The Quamfasian Games?" I ask. Their eyebrows raise before they both explain they did not. "Her streak only ended before being taken captive and brought here."

"That does not take me by surprise," Morano smiles. "Ivella is the daughter of one of the greatest Generals alive. She *should* reign as the greatest Warrior next to her father."

"I would not expect Naius to raise a non-Warrior child." Amias laughs.

As I go to continue our conversation, Ezra appears from ascension with Heshy.

I wave my hand for them to come closer and they approach the table we are sitting at in the courtyard.

"You both know Heshy," I say to Amias and Morano. "This is Ezra."

"Pleased to meet you Ezra," Amias nods.

Morano and Ezra both exchange only a glance and say nothing.

I ignore it and stand from the table and Ezra follows me down the large path within the courtyard.

"Current status?"

"Complete," Ezra confirms. "Within weeks they have arranged to meet me here in Vaigon Landing to watch the races of the Pegasi. I will continue to monitor them until they are officially here."

"Excellent," I reach into my pocket and give him his coin.

He glances over his shoulder at Morano but continues to walk with me to the exit of the courtyard.

"Keep me updated no matter the fact that we have a date set for them to return. I want to know their every footstep."

"I will be sure to report it."

Ezra begins to leave the courtyard, but I call out his name once more. "If you continue to thrive as an Emissary over the course of this season there is one more position for you to obtain."

"And that is?"

"An Assassin," I smile. "House Arvenaldi could use a second."

PART III
CARVING A KING

31
RETURN OF SPRING

PHYV
THE MORTAL LANDS

PAINTING HAS BEEN ONE of the few things to keep my sanity under control.

Besides the comfort of my family that I found after being dumped here in the Mortal Lands, art is all there is. Those simple strokes from a brush that turn into beauty, pain, love, and even death. In the past, my creations turned into all four. Now, the art seems to only be enraptured by beauty and love.

My time here has not been the worst years of my life because I have Levora and Greyce, but by hiding who and what we are for the sake of the Immortal Lands, our true home, we have struggled immensely to blend in with the humans. To be among them is still as foreign to me as it was on the first day, and we are now approaching six years of living here.

I watch precariously as the face unraveling beneath my pencil begins to divulge slowly. At first it does not resonate with me, then the long curls in her dark hair, the almond shape of her light eyes, the warm skin. It all becomes identifiable as to who the woman is.

It is the same woman as usual. I toss the sketch book onto the paint-stained coffee table.

Nyt, my dog, looks up to me from the floor with his usual head tilt. "I am all right," I smile and pet his head as he worries.

When I glance down at my sketchbook, I retrieve it and flip through the recent drawings. I hold the tip of my pencil between my teeth as I look down at the multiple renditions of one particular woman. That beauty and love in my art is her.

Just when I reach to grab an old sketchbook, I ascend to the balcony of the stairs as I hear the doors to our home soar open. Greyce has come rushing into the house and immediately she looks upward. "Phyv! Come on, the portal is opening again!" She shouts and frantically gathers many of her belongings, first her precious romance book, Nyt's leash, and her favorite cardigan.

I ascend over the balcony and down to her. "Calm down, Grey!" I plead as she repeatedly ascends around our home. One moment she is near the window, the next she is upstairs, then in the kitchen. Levora's cat, Salem, hisses at her as she continues to cause chaos. "How do we know it will stay open this time?" I ask as she now gusts around the living room to gather more of her things and many of Levora's.

"Because," she looks up to me with hope. "It still has not closed! This is the longest it has ever stayed open."

I grab her face as her breathing grows erratic. "I do not want you to get your hopes up if we return to the woods and the portal is closed."

She only smiles. "But Phyv," she shakes her head. "I know it will stay open. Please, gather everything that has meaning and let us go home."

Whenever Grey says that she knows something, she has never been wrong. When I was applying at multiple different jobs to earn a wage to provide for the three of us, my good friend, Heath Carlisle, whose family is very much old money rich, came along with a position at their law firm. Greyce swore that the job was perfect for me and that she knew I would be accepted. And I was.

Then there was the time we were searching for a home fit for the three of us and the lifestyle we choose to maintain. We were shown two homes to purchase that were hidden in the countryside closest to society and the firm. One was only a three-bedroom home, manageable amount of space, but not enough to house Nyt and Salem, the acreage was too scarce, and we all knew we needed enough space for privacy to be who we are without the risk of public eye.

The second home was the home we are in now that Grey knew was ours. I thought she was wrong because I was afraid we would not be accepted. The home houses six rooms, a large kitchen, enough land for three horses and for us to be free. There are many other qualities about this house that we loved upon entrance—tiny pieces of this home are aged so finely that it reminds us of our true land.

Greyce calls it Pinnacle Sensory, but only a form of it, a power that alerts the mind of danger, truth, and more. She has never been taught to fully embrace and understand her ability since it takes great practice to be cognizant of Pinnacle Sensory without putting yourself in harm's way. In spite of that, Greyce is rarely erroneous, but I fear this is the first time she may be mistaken about something. Mostly, I fear her disappointment in her abilities failing more than that portal not being open.

I leave the disagreement be and do as she is imploring me to do.

Nyt is first, then, in a duffel bag, all of my art supplies, sketchbooks and multiple favorite pieces of clothing although I know I would not need them. Then, my camera and everything needed for it to properly function.

I can hear the rummaging of Greyce downstairs as she continues to gather different belongings of hers and Levora's.

The words I will say to her if her abilities have failed begin to form in my mind just in case she is wrong.

We meet at the doors of our home and Greyce looks around at everything we have built here for the past four of the six years we have been in the Mortal Lands. I may struggle to live here, but the girls do not. They have thrived here. It took time for them to grow accustomed to the human ways, but once they did, they became the best versions of themselves I have ever seen.

Levora broke out of her timid shell and learned to stand up for herself without the interference of neither me nor Grey.

Greyce became free of an arranged marriage that held her hostage.

"We do not need to leave this behind." I tell her as I now look around at the beauty we created here amongst the pain.

A tear falls down her face and she stares up at me with puffy, red eyes. "We need to get you home."

I smile. "I am fine, Grey, truly."

"No, you are not." She grabs my hand while Salem sits in her arms and Nyt is right next to me. "After six years of Levora and I living the fullest life, it is your turn. No longer will you be satisfied by giving happiness to others and not have all that happiness and more given back to you. You will be happy at home in Voschantai, you will thrive, you will find a wife and you will make me an aunt so I can spoil every child you have." Her chin quivers and Salem licks the tears falling down her chin. "And I will be sure that those children and everyone who stumbles into our life knows how amazing of a person you are."

Love is not an adequate word to use to describe what both Greyce and Levora have meant to me these years. We found each other within the same vicinity of each other in the darkest night we had ever known in woods that were uncharted to us. All three of us were so young and ignorant. Everything about this world was new to us and we had not a clue of where to go, nevertheless, we knew we were staying with each other. And then our family formed, and we crafted bonds thicker than bloodlines.

"Home," I whisper.

Greyce nods. "Home."

Out of everyone we know, our closest friend Heath will come looking for us first when I do not appear at work or our usual family dinners—I have explained a false family emergency in a note for him to find and I asked him to care for the house and our horses for however long we will be gone. I do not think we will be away for an extended period of time. I know for certain that we will be back soon. Just as Levora, Greyce, and me were thrown here on the Mortal Lands, we cannot be the only ones.

Grey keeps her hand in mine before ascending and we leave behind our little life built here to meet Levora in the woods.

When we land from ascension Levora is staring at the portal very slowly closing. It looks nothing like I thought it would. I do not know what I expected it to look like, but it was not this. The portal is in comparison to a circle of silver and blue electricity hovering in the air.

"Hurry!" Levora shouts. "It is closing!" She turns to me and I run towards it, just as I reach my hand out it grows massively and I can see the opposite end of the portal.

The woods within are dark, but the moon in our universe always shines brighter than the moon in the Mortal Lands. This is how I know this portal leads to exactly where we last were.

Without a thought, I push Levora through first along with Greyce. They both begin to shout at me, but I cannot hear a word they are saying as I haul everything we brought through the portal and lastly, myself, Nyt, and Salem.

Just as I step through the portal it lunges me and our pets forward and I collide to the ground next to Levora and Greyce.

"You stupid idiot!" Levora shoves me. "You could have gotten left behind!"

I look down to Nyt and Salem as they hesitantly glance around their environment.

We look back to where the portal was, and it is gone.

I stand and breathe in deeply.

Levora smiles up at me and Greyce takes her hand. "You are home."

Home.

32
A FAE KING

LAVEN HEPHAESTUS ARVENALDI, II
VAIGON CITADEL

WEEKS HAVE PASSED SINCE I last heard from Ivella. I have sent countless letters in different forms of apologies and each one has gone unanswered. The last I have seen of her was that final day in Gordanta before she left for home with Roaner.

Now, it is the week of Summer Solstice, and Stravan is arriving soon, just hours now until his arrival.

We have sent search parties out in quest of Lorsius. We are approaching more than two months since he has been heard from or seen. Neither Amias's father, Axynth, nor my mother know where he has gone to. The Duchesses of Partalos informed us that he never set foot on our Eastern Court after he left Gordanta.

To make matters worse, Lorsius never set a Right Hand in place, which now leaves everything up to myself and my brothers. There may be many tasks to be completed that belonged to Lorsius, but most of the matters *should* be left up to only myself, Roaner, Amias, and Morano to solve. My mother has her own duties as the Highest Lady in Vaigon, yet no matter what, I would never allow everything to be held over her head. She would argue I have my own duties as well while taking over everything Lorsius has left behind, and she has picked up after him many times before. Only an imprudent son would throw such taxing work on their mother.

* * *

It is unusual for a High King from an outside realm to be welcomed without both the High King and High Queen of the realm he is visiting. Today, Stravan is welcomed by a High Prince and his Leaders.

"I say wear it; you should be the one wearing it." Morano says from beside me.

We are looking at the crowns—Lorsius's and mine. Both crowns sit on the white velvet cushions, beaming under the sun shining through from the glass ceilings.

The crowns are pure Black Tourmaline, the bits of golds and oranges in the Tourmaline brighten as the sun catches them.

"I will not put his on. I will wear mine and no others."

"Oh, come Laven. Wear it, try it on." Amias antagonizes.

"No," I reach out and touch my own crown. "I will wear Lorsius's crown when he is dead."

Roaner's head tilts. "That could be arranged."

"Again, no." I chuckle. "If we are to kill Lorsius it will only be done out of needing a perfect reason to do so."

"There have been perfect reasons to do so." Morano says.

"Yes, but not to the people." I remind him.

Roaner, Amias, and Morano all have their own crowns placed upon their heads.

Their crowns are all alike—similar to the intricacy of my own but in white gold, with shorter peaks circling around. Their crowns each hold a single Black Tourmaline stone in the center.

I place my crown upon my head, leaving Lorsius's in its place.

* * *

We stand outside on the Welcoming Grounds. Stravan is arriving here along with his children, the Dragons. Our Welcoming Grounds are vast in green land before the trees in the woods hover far in the distance, and through those woods is the path that leads directly here. Stravan will not need that path, but he will need this acreage for the Dragons to land.

"And how long is he to stay?" My mother asks.

Her long box braids are upheld in plaits that secure her tiara on her head. Leisurely, she adjusts the sleeves of her white gown that splays out across the ground behind her.

"Until after Summer Solstice, possibly longer." I am unsure myself. "We shall see."

"Straighten your spine, Morano." Ma gently speaks as she sends him a glare. Nothing but a pure mother look is being sent to him.

Instantaneously he stands up straighter.

My mother smiles before looking ahead and waiting for the sight of wings in the sky.

When I met Morano, Amias, and Roaner we were very young. All of us were born on the same year but different months. When we turned eight and ten I decided to give them position within my Circle I had yet to develop, and when I decided this, they moved into the palace.

My mother and father became their parental figures, especially for Morano and Roaner who did not have true stability with family before we took them in.

Morano no longer associates with his family and Roaner only has his mother.

Roaner's father was slain while protecting him and his mother, they were under attack by a group of men during their travel from Galitan to here. There are plenty of things that happened that day that I could never fathom having to witness at such a young age.

I look at Roaner now and my mother places a hand upon his shoulder before gently squeezing. A habitual loving gesture she always gives.

"Laven, where has Maivena been?" My mother asks. "Her placement at Vuamsati Academy is still open and I have not been told that it has been filled."

Amias releases a deep chuckle and Axynth looks at me with raised eyebrows.

"Oh, Ma. Did Laven not tell you of his debacle?" Morano speaks without a bit of remorse, a gruesome smirk is plastered on his face.

"And what debacle do you speak of?" Axynth asks.

"I will tell you later," I lie.

"Yes, you will." Both Axynth and my mother say at once.

"I absolutely hate you." I snap at Morano through the bond.

He only laughs and looks ahead.

"He is coming." Hua announces as she stares into the sky with beaming purple eyes.

One of Hua's powers is that she can see what others cannot; especially what is coming.

My mother quickly walks toward Hua, fixing her tiara so the pear-shaped Black Tourmaline drapes perfectly down the middle of her forehead. Next, she corrects her cloak draping over her black leather armor.

The moment she moves back to her placement, strong gusts of wind from forces overhead compel us to stand steadily.

Seeing the Dragons so closely would seem frightening to some, I believe Amias is shitting himself as the four of them land in front of us. To me, they are more ethereal than I could have ever imagined the closer they appear.

The hooks of their long claws dig deep divots into the ground as they move forward.

Tuduran lowers his wing and Stravan comes smoothly down from his back, landing perfectly on his feet.

At my height, I am barely the size of their teeth, if anything, I am smaller than that.

Three of the Dragons bow before us, all but one. Nara, the beautifully white and iridescent Dragon. She is who Dyena used to ride.

Stravan looks back at Nara and she takes to the sky avoiding a bow. Tuduran takes off after her and so do the others.

I had thought that being in the presence of someone as Stravan to be fear-provoking, it is beyond that. Being in his presence is riveting, it makes me stand taller. He is hundreds of years old and contains power from the Orviantes, the originals before our time soar through his blood. This power I feel in him is the same power I have felt in myself as we both share blood from Orviantes.

"She is a stubborn child," Stravan says in reference to Nara. "Just like her mother." He watches the four of his children play in the clouds, nipping playfully at one another's tails and wings. "Thank you for having me for Solstice." He says turning toward us.

"You are welcome." I nod. "We looked forward to your arrival." Partially the truth. But I watch my thoughts around him, Stravan could barricade my mind at any given moment.

"Lady Apolla," Stravan tilts his head to my mother. "And where is High King Lorsius?"

He looks between all of us, his bright blue eyes search.

"My son will be holding placement as High King until Lorsius's arrival."

I nearly gape at my mother, but I hold my posture.

We did not speak of this. Since when did she decide that I am High King while he is away? It has always been me picking up his slack while he is gone, but never taking his place.

"He should be home within time." I add. "He sends his apologies for missing your arrival, we apprehend the severity of a High King or High Queen's presence during a welcoming of another." I attempt a casual lie since it is unknown as to where the hell Lorsius is.

"Theoretically, by your mother's word, a High King is here. If I am honest, I am content that you are receiving me instead of Lorsius, he is known to be quite a pain. And I did not wish to meet such a colonizer as him."

I know Morano and Amias are fighting their laughter. Stravan has been known for being brutally honest.

My mother only gives a smile and a nod. "Shall we go inside? Supper has been prepared upon your advent."

"Yes, thank you." Stravan nods.

My mother and I lead him in first and the rest fall in line behind us.

"I told you to wear the crown." Morano teases.

Internally I begin to laugh. *"And I told you I will wear it when he is dead."*

"How do we know he is not dead already?" Amias asks.

"Highly doubtful." Roaner says. *"Lorsius is too stubborn to die."*

"Yes, he is," I dryly reply in agreement.

* * *

"How long do you plan to stay with us, Stravan?" My mother asks as she cuts into the roast on her plate. "You are welcomed to stay any length of time that you would like."

"I would say nearly two weeks. The week I was to spend in Xenathi is no longer an option." He swirls the red wine in his glass before taking a long sip.

"Oh, why is that?"

"A wedding I was invited to was called off."

Amias begins to choke on his wine as I stare blankly ahead. I finish chewing and reach for the vessel of wine to pour more into my half full glass mazer.

I swallow deeply before speaking. "Whose wedding?"

"The Lord of Nadrexi and the General's daughter of New Quamfasi—Ivella and Zevyk. I may still visit; I am not sure yet."

"Trouble in nirvana?" Morano jokingly says down the bond.

"Roaner, did you know of this?" I ask.

"Yes."

"And you did not care to tell me?"

"Ivella made me swear to keep it to myself, at least I upheld my end of the promise and you found out from him."

Axynth speaks. "Did they explain why it was called off?"

"I asked my close acquaintance, Vorian—that little comedian—he said he could hear them arguing. I know nothing more than that."

And just that fast, all of the wine in my mazer is gone, and I am reaching for more.

"I am sorry to hear that." My mother says, her eyes softening.

"Not all marriages are meant to be. They are not mates anyhow." He waves a hand dismissing their faulty engagement.

"Do you believe everyone that is a fated pair stays together?" I ask while pouring the last of the wine from the vessel.

A servant quickly replaces the vessel with one that is full, and I give a nod of thanks.

"Yes," Stravan replies confidently. He wipes the corner of his mouth with a cloth before going on. "It is rare to marry someone other than who you are destined to be with. If you do not marry them, it is habitually because of radical matters and dissimilarities. Although, Ivella and Zevyk will realize where their fate lies sooner or later. It is doubtful that it is within one another."

"What was their dispute about, Roaner?" Amias asks.

"Laven. She was caught trying to leave and Zevyk stopped her."

Caught? *"What do you mean caught? Why would she be caught leaving?"*

Before Roaner can respond, Axynth speaks again, drawing my attention away from what was just spoken.

This bastard is *keeping* her from me.

"So, how may we aid you in finding Dyena?" Axynth asks Stravan.

"I would like to start with search parties, my Dragons will also search. If they suspect, we look wherever it is they may sense she could be."

"And if you do not find her after the search parties?" I ask.

His eyes meet my own. "Then I roam your lands and look myself."

"Romantic," Morano speaks sarcastically, and I send him a sharp look.

"Dyena is far from romantic," Stravan laughs. "She wants loyalty, and that is exactly what I will give her by never ending my search."

After biting into more food, I propose the aid I need as well. "It is only customary that I ask a favor of my own." I speak.

"We are allies now, what do you need?" He asks.

"There seems to be a war beckoning over our land. Someone is spreading a rabid disease over our people, turning them into carnivorous beings, ruthless even."

"Yes," Stravan nods. "Vorian was telling me of it. Whoever it is that created this most definitely wants power. Your realm is very strong and agile, your realm is also one of the largest, it is no wonder to me that this is where they began. Vorian explained that some of the rogues he fought were expert in fighting, and some were just fighting with the intent to ravage. What exactly is it that you would need from myself?"

"If the war is sure to begin, we would necessitate all of the help we can obtain," I say. "Who knows how many others this person has allied with them? We would need your Warriors to fight alongside us. As well as training, *thorough* training. Lorsius did a poor job with his previous General. Now that Amias and Hua hold title as our Generals they are open to any further training you could provide. We do not have allyship through other nations within our realm so I would deem you to be our best choice."

"I will speak with Vallehes and Penelope," Stravan offers. "I will see if there is anything I can do to persuade them, nonetheless, they are most likely going to say no. But if war were to break, yes, you do have the stance of my Warriors with you."

"Thank you. And I do not see it necessary to attempt at persuasion with New Quamfasi, they have made it vividly clear that they will not ally unless Lorsius has no part or is dead."

"And I do not blame them," Stravan begins, "yet, they may have no choice. War here means war there, either way, I am speaking with Vallehes and Penelope. I will not allow my closest friends to be ignorant to this. I will go to them while I am here and deliver word to you on their response."

THE SONG OF VERITY AND SERENITY

* * *

"I see you escaped your mother and my father before they could get their hands on you." Amias chuckles as he sits in the courtyard with me, Morano, and Roaner.

"Yes, I did. Axynth is showing Stravan around the palace."

Roaner reaches across the circled stone table to knock the ash from his cigar.

I look to Roaner. "Is he holding her from coming to me?"

"Yes."

"Do I need to kill him?"

He smirks. "No," He says as a swirl of smoke escapes his lips. "Ivella has attempted his murder and he learned a lesson."

Good.

She should have followed through.

"She has not answered any of my letters. How is she coping with her powers?"

"She is doing well." He says with uncertainty. "She is still learning them; it will take some time for her to wholly fathom and wield them, but, she is strong."

Morano leans back in his chair looking up to the hanging candles over the courtyard. "Did anyone discover if someone in her family has the power of the Vaultais?" He asks.

"No, that is still uncertain. Her powers seem to only mimic that of a Vaultai." Roaner shakes his head. "Her mother who raised her, Stelina, dug into the roots of all families who have the power of the Vaultais—she found nothing of Wolves wielding them. These powers are solely hereditary, only the Fae are still known to have a strong bloodline of it. Even the Sorcerers do not contain those powers any longer." Roaner's eyebrows raise as he speaks. "And we also know for certain that Ivella is not Fae."

Abilities are ever-changing in our world. Dependent upon how far your lineage goes back is dependent upon the powers you have. Someone could receive abilities from an ancestor from hundreds of years ago that have not been in the family for centuries. Anything is possible.

"Maybe she will pop a pair of wings in due time." Amias jokes and I roll my eyes at him.

"We should speak with Stravan of this, before he can go to Xenathi would be best." I play with the small white gold hoop in my ear. "This earring, by the way, is the last time I allow all of you to convince me into doing something while we are drunk." I point.

"Let us not get into what you do when drunk." Roaner teases while simpering in my direction.

Morano half smiles, touching his ear. "I think it suits us rather well."

Morano thought it would be a marvelous idea for all of us to get one ear pierced while drunk, and of course, we did it out of pure stupidity and peer pressure. Now we have a tiny, thick hoop in our left ears.

But he is correct. We do not look horrible with them in our ears.

"And it flatters your new haircut," Amias nudges my shoulder.

"Enough of the haircut." I hold up my hand. "All I did was get the sides and back trimmed closer to my head." And the stylist left a bit of length on the top, not much, but a decent amount.

"You know the women love hair like that," Morano chortles. "I identify what you were doing there."

"I will put my cigar out with your skin if you do not shut your trap."

He rolls his sleeve up and shoves his arm outward, and across the table. There is a grin plastered on his face as he grips the cigar between his teeth.

"Will we really not discuss it?" Amias asks, looking around the table.

I disregard what he is trying to aim our conversation for given I am already done speaking about that wretch I should have killed weeks ago.

"Laven," Amias's mien turns for annoyance. "Ivella is repudiating marriage with this man. We all comprehended it would not last anyhow! Go with Roaner to Nadrexi next week."

"If I go to Nadrexi next week, I will commit another murder." If I ever hear of him holding her hostage from me again, it will be his death.

Morano gives Amias an unsatisfied glare. "You rush things," he says as he tosses back the liquor in his glass. "Let it burn, Laven. Let it burn until it utterly fucking explodes. Why do you think Amorni from Gordanta and I get along so well?" He winks an eye.

"Good Gods," I shake my head and look toward Roaner.

"I do not like how he worded that, but yes." Roaner nods in support. "However, not yet, not any time soon should you go to her."

Morano boisterously laughs. "Wait until she finds out Laven has fucked half of Vaigon's women."

I sit here waiting to see if he will say another infuriating thing.

He raises his eyebrow waiting for my response.

"I am debating if I will slit your throat now or in your sleep." I tell him.

"You whore," he continues to torment me in his playful manner.

"All right," I give in. "I have had sex with quite a few people. It meant nothing and there have been no ties devoted to any of the women, and I have never laid with any of them more than once."

Morano's head tilts. "That might be worse."

"Can you count how many there are on your hands anymore?" Amias tags in after a large flare of smoke releases into the night air. "Or have you started to count with your toes as well?"

This time, I flick the ashes of my cigar at them, they hiss in pain and Roaner chuckles as he leans back in his chair.

The sounds of running feet jerk us away from our conversation and guards are rushing towards us.

"What is it?" I urgently demand.

"Your sister, my Lord. Levora," he pants heavily. "Princess Levora is home."

Roaner and I both look at one another and his cigar falls from his mouth and tumbles to the ground where dead flowers lie. "That is not possible." He shakes his head.

"I can promise you, Your Grace, Levora is who stands outside of this courtyard right now."

33
OUT OF THE WOODS

LEVORA APOLLA ARVENALDI

*L*aven!' *I scream over the distant sound of deer running around me, within the trampling of the deer I can hear my voice heavily carry through the woods.*

I scramble to my feet as nothing but darkness surrounds me, and the very dim shine of the moon holds no guidance. As I look upward I faintly see small bats scurrying across. The more I observe my surroundings, I perceive a small circle formed of lightning hovering in midair multiple feet away from me, and through it, I can witness Laven running about and shouting my name into the void of the woods. The realization sets in that I am no longer home and Laven cannot see nor hear me.

The circle begins to close, and I hurriedly run towards it with all ambition to make it through, but I stumble as sharp sticks dig into my bare feet. I can still hear him calling me, but he is moving in the wrong direction. 'Laven!' I cry out and my voice cracks the louder I scream, and slowly, he is fading as he moves farther and farther away while searching for me in all the wrong places.

The world moves slowly the closer I get, and just as I reach to touch the circle, it repels my touch and soars me backward. I collide with the ground, and gasp for air as the collision takes all my breath away.

When I look again, the circle has entirely closed.

The tears that have welled in my eyes fall as I relentlessly scream. I beat into the ground as if in some way if this circle will reappear, I will see my brother, and go home.

Slowly, I stop bellowing when I hear an unrecognizable voice calling for help. I stand again and pull the knife from its sheath wrapped around my thigh.

'Trust not a soul. Wield weapons against anyone you do not know.' I do as my brother taught me.

The person hollering for help appears, and it is a man in a torn undershirt ripped from the laces and across his shoulder. He stands extremely tall, nearly the height of Laven, with dark glowing skin.

I hold out my dagger before me in warning.

His hands immediately hold up and he stops in his tracks. 'No, no worries. I just heard you and came to find the voice.'

'Why?' I step farther away and continue to blink away the tears.

'Because I am guessing you were thrown here through a portal just like I was.'

I say nothing and keep my dagger forward.

'I am Phyv,' he points to himself. 'I am from Provas, the Realm of the Fae. You are?'

I am hesitant, but I answer. 'Levora, House Arvenaldi.'

'You are of the Realm of the Wolves.'

I rapidly nod my head.

'Whoever you are looking for—'

'My brother,' I interrupt him. 'And he will kill you if you touch me.'

'I do not doubt it.' Phyv stays put where he stopped.

An arrow whistles from afar and we soon see it as it veers between us. We turn in the direction the arrow came from and a young woman appears dressed in dark grey leather armor.

'Greyce, Realm of the Hybrids.' She immediately introduces herself. 'Now how the fuck am I to get home?'

Home. I had grown used to calling Phyv and Greyce my home in the Mortal Lands, only out of the thought that there was no way home—there was no way of getting back to my brothers, my mother . . . Roaner.

Yet, as I look at Roaner, he does not seem to have the slightest reaction to my return.

"Vora?" Laven whispers ever so quietly. And all I can do is cry.

Before my body can fully register with my mind, I am running to him. And just as he used to, he catches me. He holds on to me the way our father used to, and the tears fall quicker, harder—like the rain pouring down windows in a frightful storm. But the thing about Laven, he catches every raindrop and fights the storm with his sword.

'Want to know something?' Laven whispers as I sit curled next to him.

I scoot closer as loud thunder strikes. 'What?' I ask while looking at the storm raging outside and clinging to his arm.

'When Pa gave me my sword he had it made to fight off storms just for you.'

'Did you?' I look back at Pa as he reads a book in one hand and in the other sits Mama falling asleep with a swollen belly.

Pa smiles. 'I did.' He answers as he props his feet up on the ottoman in front of the fireplace.

'Should I do it now?' Laven asks.

'Oh!' I stand. 'No! You will get hurt!'

'If I have that sword, nothing can hurt me. I will fight all the storms that dare to frighten you, Vora.'

Just babies.

That was all we were during that time.

And even now, having been gone all this time, I have not a doubt that he will still be that pugnacious force in my life.

Quickly after, I am surrounded by Morano and Amias who hold on to me just as Laven did. Roaner continues to keep his distance.

"Where the hell have you been? And what are you wearing?" Laven asks as he looks me over. He glimpses at Greyce and Phyv as they stand not far off.

I look down at my jeans and so does Laven.

"Mortal clothing," I say.

"Mortal clothing?" Morano shouts. "How in this world did you end up in the Mortal Lands?" He glances down at Nyt who is leashed next to Phyv and continuously cuts his eyes at Greyce who is holding Salem.

"A portal," Phyv steps closer and Morano and Amias step backward. I grab his hand and Greyce's pulling them both next to me to show that the animals are harmless.

"This is Phyv and Greyce," I introduce. "And these two pets are Nyt and Salem. Nyt is a black German Shepherd," I lie. He is a hybrid wolf-dog, but I will never tell them that. "And this little black cat is all three of ours," I take Salem from Greyce and he clings to my arm out of fear of his new environment. "While Greyce and I have been in the Mortal Lands, Phyv took care of us like we were his own family. We found each other the night we were left on human territory."

"How did you possibly conceal yourselves from the mortals?" Laven asks.

"It was very difficult, but thankfully, we all have very average features according to the humans, so we did not stand out too immensely." Phyv informs them all. "When it came to shifting and using our powers we stayed hidden on our land far from society. I kept a fabrication over our features that were too out of the ordinary for humans, mostly my ears that would bring attention."

"Your land?" Amias asks, crossing his arms over his chest.

"Yes," Greyce answers with her usual sharp tone when she feels one of us is being wronged. "The land he purchased for us where our home resides."

Roaner stays quiet as he stares off into the courtyard with a rapidly rising and falling chest.

Laven steps nearer to Amias and places a hand on his shoulder. "It is visible that you were very well taken care of," Laven turns to Phyv. "Thank you, truly. This is a debt I will repay for eternity. There were never moments that passed when I was not thinking of where Levora went or what possibly happened. And thank you for getting her home safely."

"Coming home is not something that I can take recognition for," Phyv does not take credit, although he should. Greyce and I both saw how easily he opened the portal. If it were not for him, we would not be here. "Levora was the one who went back to the exact location of the portal and saw it finally opening again one day. Ever since, she went back daily to be sure it was the portal that took us from here. When she was sure of it, she monitored it."

"You let her do that alone?" Amias cuts in once more.

"I am not a child any longer, Amias. I am capable of having a task such as that now." I take offense to his assumption that I am still some weak young girl, yet I too cannot forget it has been years since we have seen one another, and he is not used to me looking out for myself while alone, he is still used to always being by my side.

Amias's eyes soften before leaving the conversation alone.

"Levora did very well with this, if you cannot see, we are indeed home." Greyce commends as she rubs my back.

"We are worried is all, we are well aware that our sister is capable, but thank you for your input." Laven says to Greyce.

I take Amias's hand and he smiles down at me before tugging me into another hug. "And I had Nyt," I say looking up to him. "He was always there to watch over me before I got comfortable enough to be on my own."

"You mean the Wolf you have roped?" Morano says stepping away from me again while glaring at Salem.

"Oh, Morano—"

"No, Vora!" Morano interjects. "You know I do not like cats, and can you please take the Wolf off the leash?" He says to Phyv.

"I am sure you did perfectly fine monitoring your way home," Laven chuckles as he side eyes Morano. "Ma will be elated to hear about it."

I smile at the mention of her. "Where is she?" I urgently plead to know.

Of everyone, my mother, my mama, I have missed her in times when I have needed her the most and had no one to turn to other than Phyv or Greyce—they could always calm my thoughts and be there for me in only ways they know, but no one will ever replace the love my mother gives and the knowledge she holds in her enthralling mind.

"I am unsure where Ma has gone to. I am certain a guard has already found her and told her of your return."

When I look to where Roaner is, he is gone, without a word he has already left.

I do not stop to think of him and I turn to the ever so familiar voice approaching.

"Axynth!" I give Salem to Greyce before assailing toward him.

"By the Gods, Levora where the hell have you been?" He takes a quick glance over me before his eyes grow bigger and he is pulling me into another hug and multiple kisses are placed over my face, he stops and looks me over once again in disbelief. "These are mortal clothes," he looks back at Laven and Laven nods.

"They are," he says.

"Mortal Lands?" A man hovering behind Axynth asks.

"Vora, this is High King Stravan of the Fae Realm." Laven introduces.

The Realm of the Fae.

"I am pleased to meet you; I am Levora Arvenaldi, this is Phyv, he is also from the Fae Realm."

"What exactly were you all doing in the Mortal Lands?" Stravan asks.

"It was not willingly that we were there," Phyv begins. "We were sent there non-consentingly and were stuck there for six years. We only have found our way home through the portal we were sent through."

"So there was you," Stravan points at me. "Of the Realm of the Wolves. Phyv, from the Realm of the Fae, and the young lady standing not far off with the dog and cat?" He glances at Greyce.

"Yes." I nod.

"And where are you from? If you do not mind me asking." Stravan asks Greyce.

"Ramana," she answers. "Realm of the Hybrids."

Stravan slowly guises over us. "You all are three of six. There are three others that went missing at the same time and day as you during the season of Spring. You have been known as the Six of Spring since it happened."

I knew it, the three of us knew it.

"Did you already suspect this?" Stravan asks.

"We did." Greyce responds.

"Well, when the other realms discover you all have returned, societies will not stop talking about it until the rest of you are found."

"They will want us to travel through the portal once more to find them." Phyv concludes and Stravan nods as he continues to observe Phyv.

"What year is it in the Mortal Lands?" Axynth asks.

"Year nineteen eighty-five." I answer.

"Not to forget the other realms will demand this search while we have rogues roaming." Morano says.

"Yes," Laven nods.

"Rogues?" I question. "What rogues?"

"While you have been away there has been a recent outbreak among our people. A rabid mutation of some sort that has altered them mind and soul. There is no cure, and we do not know who it is that is spreading such a disease among our land, but we plan to find out before it can go too far and we approach war."

"War began when they plotted an attack on our kind." Amias says.

"Unfortunately, yes, it did." Stravan agrees.

"How can I help?" I ask looking between them all.

Laven smiles walking forward and grasping my shoulders. "You can help me by resting." He kisses my forehead before the same eyes of our father look down at me. "You have just returned home, and you should take time to grow accustomed to Vaigon again before being thrown into the strenuous tasks we have been taking on. Although, I would like to speak with you, Greyce, and Phyv privately."

34
A MOTHER'S ADORNMENT

LEVORA APOLLA ARVENALDI

Laven leans back against his bureau as Phyv, Greyce, and I enter. Something in Laven is unlike before, still just as caring, but darker in a sense. It could be the years we have spent apart and that we are now both fully grown adults that must get to know one another again, but what I feel in him is what I felt with our father. Strength and stability.

Before I was taken to the Mortal Lands, Laven and I scarcely had moments together due to his imprisonment in Wyendgrev. His release was very shortly before I was taken. During his imprisonment our mother refused to allow me to see him in a place as Wyendgrev, mostly because of the horrid history behind it and how my brother was treated as a prisoner similar to one detained from Quamfasi. My mother and father held great hatred for my uncle due to this. They never understood how Lorsius was capable of allowing Laven to be treated just as those who were taken hostage from Quamfasi and not as one of his own blood.

When Laven was released he was a tiny thread hanging from death. The procedures that were done on him by the Healer should have had him screaming in agony, yet he was already so near to death he could barely comprehend anything happening around him. It took months for him to heal, and when he was finally healthy again, our time was removed once more.

One thing I never understood: why he did what he did to be imprisoned and live through that pain.

As I look at him now, it is almost as if none of that happened. Or it did, but it shaped him into someone I did not get to watch grow through the agony.

"I do have questions of my own that do not require the ears of others." Laven says as we settle into our chairs. "Firstly," he says directly to me. "I care mostly about how you are coping with what has happened."

"I have been coping fine," I smile. "Truly, I have. The night everything happened I found Phyv and Greyce, and from that day and on we took time to know one another and then we took the time to know the new world functioning around us. It was difficult, but we did it, and we made good friends in the making of our life there."

"And do these friends know about us? Voschantai Universe," he further elaborates. "Or those of Lorvithinan Universe."

"No," Phyv answers. "Not even our closest friends know who or what we are. They only know us as we are on human territory, and we kept quietly to ourselves while allowing our bodies to remember functionality as we used to here."

"You are aware that no matter how careful you are, it is still possible that you were seen?" None of us answer. "There is no such thing as allowing yourself both worlds. You either entirely deprive yourself of it or let there be a grave risk of being caught."

"Have you been to the Mortal Lands?" Greyce questions.

"No," Laven calmly responds. "I do not need to experience the Mortal Lands to know how to conceal a secret. There is no such thing as clandestinely living in a world with mortals. They operate much differently than we do and for you to even suspect that you have not been monitored is asinine."

Greyce does not respond.

"Whoever took you and dropped you there could more than likely be monitoring your every move, and if they are not, you still never know. Which is why I say that there is no such thing as trying to keep secret and still believing you have the availability to show who you are on the same territory. Anyone with sight is capable of seeing something they should not."

He waits for one of us to continue, and we do not.

"I am glad you are safe, not only you, Vora, but all three of you. I am certain your families have been searching for years now. We can only hope the others still on the Mortal Lands have the same outcome as you all."

"If they begin a search I would like to be a part of it." Phyv says to Laven.

"A search will begin for them now that you are home. The guards here have large mouths, Amias is most likely holding them all by secrecy to not speak of this or entirely wiping their minds clean of what has transpired so Levora can have her privacy while home. But, with all of this aside, you three have a long night of settling in before you."

"And I must go home," Greyce says with a saddened smile. "As much as I love you both I do miss my family."

"I will take you home." Phyv immediately declares.

"Wait," I stand, and Greyce does as well. "When will you come back?"

She cannot just leave me so suddenly.

"Oh, angel," Greyce smiles while holding my face. "I will see you every moment even while here detained by borders."

"Six years do not so easily get washed down the drain." Phyv says as his arms hang over our shoulders.

"I will send Amias with you on your journey to be sure you get to where you need to be safely, he knows Voschantai Universe like no other." Laven stands up straighter from leaning against his desk. "Where did you say you reside, Greyce?"

"Ramana."

"Amias knows the way."

Greyce does not let go of me. "Tomorrow, and if not tomorrow I will see you within a week's time."

"And you will return here after taking her to Ramana." I say to Phyv, and he bows before me, the gesture looks odd given our current mortal attire since I am only used to seeing a gesture in clothing suited for someone from this universe.

I look down at Nyt and Salem as they sit by the fire brewing in Laven's study. "I will keep them here with me while we wait for you to return."

Amias appears next to Laven through ascension and with one more hug and a goodbye to Nyt and Salem, Greyce and Phyv follow him out.

Laven sits down in one of the chairs near the fireplace and I do as well.

"Seeing you in this type of clothing is odd." He laughs.

"The attire here is much different than it is on human ground."

Laven nods. "I have done some research of my own regarding the Mortal Lands, they seem to age rather fast there. Though, how we dress here is what they used to dress like years upon years ago. What was it like there?"

As I recall many of my moments there, I think I recall most the immense cultural differentiation.

"Well, there is quite a large difference between us and them racially."

"Blacks and whites." He mumbles. "I read about this, how they are divided by race just as we are now divided by realm. How did you cope with that?"

I think of the ways I was treated there versus here.

"I would never want anyone to experience the things said to me, but most especially Phyv . . . the names they called him, Laven; what they mean. In the Mortal Lands many other people who look like Phyv snap and let go of all anger they hold due to so much agony building up over centuries, and rightfully so. Looking back on the origins of our universe and seeing the people that it started with makes Phyv one of the most beautiful men. Yet, in the Mortal Lands they treat him as if he is some creature merely existing. Then, there are those who are paler skin and hold hatred for him for succeeding in so much that they didn't, and they retaliate by thinking he owes them something for having such a high-ranking job. Phyv pushed on no matter the pain because of me and Greyce. I think that is why I clung to him so much and why we have the relationship we have. He reminded me of you, and even though we had Ma and Pa, you were always the most prominent in my life and Phyv replicated that. And what is even more worse, the people of that world do not hear the cries of the minorities until violence transpires. If speaking is not loud enough, then . . ."

"Violence will make them hear." Laven finishes. "It is intriguing how the world of humans takes action, though, I will not be adamant about us being much different. If me speaking to you does not get the word across to need radical change, then my actions will. In some way how we function here will always be different from how the human's function. They have no other choice but to divide based on race and gender because there is no true power for them to hold to divide by anything else. There are governmental statuses that they divide by, but color is something they see so greatly there. We do not need ethnicities nor a pale face to proceed in our world, and that is something we will always hold above them, either we have our strength and abilities or not, what they will struggle with for eternity is something we will never have to face, and I am forever grateful for it. Dark skin will always be prosperous on our land." He pauses and thinks. "Although, I cannot say I am as strong as you deem. I have had plenty of moments of severe weakness that I have caved in and done things I should not have."

"That is what you believe of yourself, and you know I will never agree with you."

"Agreeing to disagree," Laven smiles. "I have missed you."

I stand and pull him from his chair to hug me once more and he smells just like pa. "I have missed you more."

*\ *\ *

I feel unidentifiable in these clothes. I do not remember the last time that I have worn a shift and robe to bed. Yet, the clothing is not the only thing I am growing to remember here. My inabilities are also very prominent. Inability to bend magic of any sort and having strength that mimics the strength of a mortal. That is my undoing here in Vaigon and Voschantai as a whole.

I am considered weak here. There is nothing that I can do that matches the abilities of my family. Despite all that Phyv, Greyce, and I went through, I did not hate it in the Mortal Lands because I felt normal to that world. Whereas here, the place I am supposed to know as home is nothing near it. Well, I am not someone built to be in this world. But when you love someone, you are willing to make as many sacrifices as possible to be sure they are happy.

So, I will endure for Phyv as he endured for me all this time.

The doors to my chamber burst open and I see my mother standing in the doorway with two of her ladies behind her. They bow before quickly leaving us.

She stares at me, as if to be sure it is actually me that she is seeing, and I too with her.

Her chest rises and falls in her corset as she slowly approaches.

One hand hesitantly reaches outward to touch my cheek and I fall into her.

"Ma," I cry out and I can hear the sweet whisperings of *'angel'* as she cries into my hair.

"My girl," she smiles down at me with tear-soaked cheeks. "Mortal Lands?"

I wipe away the tears on her beautiful skin that was deemed horrendous where I previously lived. "Yes, Mortal Lands."

She exhales and nods. "I will begin a bath for you, and you will tell me all about the mortals and their way of life."

* * *

I step into the warm water and Ma rolls up her sleeves and rubs shavings of soap into a soft cloth. She sits on the ledge of the bathing tub and begins to cleanse my back. I close my eyes as the warmth of the water and the soap is rubbed along my back.

"Laven is different."

I hear a soft exhale followed by a gentle laugh. "Laven is a grown man now. Very different from when you left."

"Is there no woman in his life?"

She chuckles again. "There are many women in Laven's life," I sharply turn to her in surprise. "But," she holds up her finger. "There is one prominent one, he no longer speaks of her, but I know his soul can only speak to her."

"What is her name?" I turn back around as she continues to clean my back.

"Maivena."

I smile. "Pretty."

"She is a beautiful woman. Very brave heart."

"And your relationship with Laven has been mended?"

Before I was taken, Laven and our mother were nowhere near speaking terms after the death of our father. I blamed my mother for a long time for not telling Laven sooner, but we all were grieving the most important man in our lives. I believe it is true that we all do grieve differently.

"We are mended, we mended after you were gone. He realized he did not want to lose me too, although, he is my first child, my first son, he could never lose me if he tried."

I grab her hand and turn around in the warm water to face her. "I am glad to see him healthy."

She smiles. "Those years of his mind not being with us are gone. Laven has flourished from who he was previously, he did it with the help of all of us, even you when you were still here. The old rhymes you would sing to him to help him sleep he still tends to hum every now and then."

"And everything else that has happened while I have been gone?"

"What do you mean?"

"The rogues."

Her head shakes. "No, my love, that you will not be worrying yourself with."

I want to be worried by it. I want to help, I want duties, I want tasks, I want quests. I am capable. I am labeled a High Princess then I am not allowed to act as Princesses do in other realms. High Princess Hekva of Misonva, the Vampire Realm, has a history of being a great Princess to her people and will prosper and reign. There is even a young Warrior I read about years ago while here, she had won every Quamfasian Game starting at the young age of sixteen, her name is Ivella Fondali, and her streak most definitely continues, and I am certain she was stellar in the war. That is what I want. Now that I am home I must make them promise me that I will not be kept small. I do not want to be known as the pretty Princess that did not know how to defend herself and called like a damsel for protection.

"Then what am I to be worried with?"

"Making sure you are settled before taking on extremities." She waves her hand for me to turn around again so she can finish my back, and I do.

"Laven was never expected to settle before having extreme duties bestowed upon him."

"That is because Laven needed to be shaped to become High King when Lorsius no longer rules."

That name sends shivers down my spine.

"Laven needed to be molded and carved to fit his coming position, whenever that may be. Even now Laven is still being molded to fit the role of a High King, but he is nearly there."

I no longer wish to speak of me and turn the conversation back to my brother.

"And what do the boys become when Laven is High King?"

The hot water slowly drifts down my back and as I close my eyes I see the distraught look on Roaner's face at my arrival and I tear them open.

"They keep their title and move higher. They become more

prominent in House Arvenaldi and in our citadel as a whole." Her head lowers near mine. "I do not want you to fear what you will become. Not every High Princess nor High Queen must be vigorous to make history, Levora. Be *you*."

35
WELCOME HOME

LAVEN HEPHAESTUS ARVENALDI, II

"Can he be trusted?" Morano asks as we wait in the courtyard for Amias to return home from taking Greyce to Ramana with Phyv. "And where has Roaner gone to?"

"I am unsure of both. Roaner will appear, he is in shock, we all are. As for Phyv, time will tell."

"And if time tells us that he is untrustworthy?"

"I would like to say we would kill him," I ponder the thought. "But he means too much to Vora to commit to that. So, we shall see."

"Where are you?" I ask Roaner down the bond.

"My mother needed me immediately; I will return home shortly."

"Is she all right?"

"Yes," he calmly states. *"I will inform you of everything later."*

"Roaner is with his mother. She called on him during Levora's arrival."

Morano's eyebrows knit together. "What is the matter with Ma Kansyna?"

"He said he will inform me when he returns home and that she is all right."

Morano slouches back into his chair and his knee begins to bounce. "I did not sense anything wrong with him upon arrival." He says in reference to Phyv.

"Neither did I." But there is something about him that I cannot quite understand.

"And he kept my sister alive and well." Morano adds.

I smile. "He did indeed."

Morano sits up straighter and looks me over. "How have you been?"

"I spoke with Levora for—"

"No," he interrupts. "How have you *been*?"

He means Ivella.

Slowly, I shrug. "There is nothing else for me to be but fine. If she is choosing to not speak to me, there is nothing I can do. Their wedding may have been called off but that means nothing if she does not speak with me."

"Laven," Morano leans forward and shakes his head. "You are everything she could ever want and more. She will come home. In the meantime, I want you to stop being so sexually available for women you do not know. This is not you and I know you do not enjoy it; you are just participating in sexual acts with others because the tiny sliver of you that gave up hope is trying to take over when Ivella still exists. You have been patient for years, just wait a little longer for her. Her life has been flipped upside down and she is readjusting to her life as a royal and it is easy to get lost in that process, you, and I both know this well enough. Be the patient man you are and continue to give her time. She called off the wedding, I am certain that she is coming to her senses."

In the distance we both can hear footsteps approaching.

Amias and Phyv appear before us and Phyv stops as Amias walks to the table and sits down.

"She is home safely?" I ask.

"Yes, but it took time. They are royals in Ramana. Greyce is the daughter of a General and her mother was not easy to access, even with word that her daughter had returned."

"Thank you," Phyv says to Amias.

I look at both Amias and Morano and nod for them to leave, they both stand and ascend.

"Do you drink alcohol Phyv?" I ask as I pour myself a fingertip amount into a short glass.

"I do."

I pour him one as well.

"Do you have a last name?" I hand him his glass and I motion for him to sit.

"In the Mortal Lands Levora and Greyce gave me their last names. Here, no, I do not have one."

"Just Phyv?"

"Just Phyv."

"Well, just Phyv, I want to thank you again, but personally. My sister spoke very highly of you, and I do not know what I would do if I found out she had any fate other than the one she had with you and Greyce."

Phyv beams. "She spoke of you when we first met in the woods where we were left. She told me if I touched her you would kill me, and I had no doubt about it."

Remembering that day and scavenging through the woods to find her nearly sent me back to the person I had just recovered from being.

"She is not wrong." I smile as I take a sip from the glass. "And she is still not wrong."

He nods, understanding where the conversation will go if he disagrees. "And I too still have no doubt about it."

"She also spoke with me of your struggles while on human territory and I do commend you for what you went through. You are better than myself, I would have revealed myself all too quickly handling their kind."

Phyv takes a small drink from his glass and sets it down. "It was a culture shock, yes, but I would go through it all again for both Greyce and Levora."

"You have a strong mind, Phyv. Some cannot call themselves so lucky."

He is slow to speak but says what is on his mind. "I can say the same of you."

"No," I lean on the table. "I had my brothers, I had Levora, our mother, and Axynth. I made it through because of them."

"Just as I made it through because of Levora and Greyce. We are one and the same."

"We seem to be."

Phyv drinks the last of the alcohol in his glass before standing. "Please tell Levora I will come find her tomorrow."

I do not respond to him, and he begins to walk away.

"Phyv."

He turns to me.

"Where are you going?"

He faintly smiles. "Home."

"Where is home?"

He does not have an answer.

"You will house here, there are plenty of chambers for you to reside in and I am positive my sister would lay her hands on me if I allowed you to leave knowing you do not have a home to return to."

"That is not necessary, I can assure you."

"I told you that I am indebted to you for the care of Levora, and I mean that. You have a home here for however long you wish for it to be."

"Thank you." He bows.

"And Phyv," I add. "Please go and claim your *hybrid* wolf-dog," they cannot believe me to be so dense about the animals of the human world. "He has shit in my study and I was not too fond of cleaning it."

36
ANCIENT BLOOD

STRAVAN PROVANSEVA

"LAVEN," I GREET AS I enter his study.

It is early in the morning, and I knew he would be in this room drowning in duties before we dine for morning meal. As much as I am unsure about my stay here, it is evident how much Laven does just as a High Prince, as a High King he could be fearful given the knowledge he already has and the knowledge he will gain. I need to understand as much about him as possible. I would scour through his mind, but I have already attempted, and he is the only one out of all of his brothers that can keep his head so guarded it nearly hurts me to break in.

"You are an early riser," Laven says as he stands from his bureau.

He is donned in all black and his leather vest has tiny stitchings of dark blue in it—very similar to the cloaks given to them by Artemis.

He dresses well for a child known of the night.

"Oh, do not mind me. Please, continue to sit," I wave as I sit across from him. "Tell me about you." Since I cannot find out for myself.

I am already aware of his past because word spreads easily in this universe when you are declared manic as both he and I were. One thing is, psychosis never truly leaves, and it can be activated to return by anything that hits that nerve to send us over the edge. Being fucking insane is the only factor that we relate on, but I do not know what initiated his outrage to fall into insanity.

Laven leans back and waits. "What is it that you wish to know?"

Everything.

"Tell me about your beginning as a royal." I know a slight amount about his upbringing, but not enough.

Laven's eyebrows raise. "I was raised in a royal family. My father was a Duke, and then I was declared Heir as my uncle does not have children. He no longer has a mate to have children and he did not want to pick a woman to have a child with and he does not believe in adoption—nevertheless he has many illegitimate children he does not claim. So, me being his own blood and the white in my hair signifying I am an Orviante without question, he chose me to be his Heir and neither myself nor my parents had much say. Then he made my sister Levora second Heir."

"He does not speak with his illegitimate children?"

"None."

"Why is that?"

"They were all conceived in brothels, that is why."

Children of a High King whose mothers are sex workers are not permitted in royal lines, none at all. Even being bastard children, this does not mean they could not come after Laven for a royal placement.

"And after becoming Heir?"

"After that was when my life sharply rotated."

"How so?"

He chuckles lowly and does not respond.

"The twelve men." I continue for him.

"I do not speak of that." He puts a stop to this particular topic proceeding any further. "My life was altered because I was thrown into being a High Prince that I did not ask to be. I was fine as a

Duke's son; I did not want for anything more, even then I desired for less."

"You were still always meant for royalty. Your father was well known for his strength, and I can very much say I feel it in you. Your uncle, I cannot say the same, but somehow these tend to be the men who rule."

"And yourself?" Laven turns the matter toward me. "Are you a ruler like my uncle or my father?"

I smile. "With my many years in this world, I have been both, but only an outrageous person could commit to what your uncle has." I have not always been a great High King. Many moments of trial and error have shaped me into how I rule now. Which is still not considered great to most.

"May we pray he pays for his outrageousness."

"I hope so as well, my companions did not deserve what happened to them. If they would have allowed me to intervene like I wanted to, he would be dead. "But, I did want to speak with you of something else as well." Laven nods for me to continue. "Phyv."

Suddenly, I have piqued his interest more. "Other than what your sister has told you, what else do you know about him?"

"Nothing too particular, I did not consider last night to be the finest occasion to plunge into exactly who Phyv was before he was taken to the Mortal Lands."

"Phyv is an orphan," I inform him of my own research I have done in such little time. "Although he is an orphan I am unsure of why he has such a . . ." I drift off as I search for the word.

"Why he has such a power held behind his eyes."

He noticed it as well.

"Exactly," I point. "No orphan has the demeanor of Phyv, it could be worrisome to not wholly discern a person. This pushes farther than just worrisome. It could be hazardous, I feel, to not be comprehensible of his past. He mimics the grace of someone with truly ancient bloodlines and it will be worth it to search who he is, even if he himself does not know who he is."

Laven nods. "I will have Morano look into him with me. He has been accepted here because of my sister, but I will be keeping a close eye on him."

"Anything you learn, bring me aware of it. If it ever came to his execution, it would have to be on Fae land so you may avoid having more hatred bestowed upon your nation."

* * *

"Phyv, is it?" I say as I approach the younger Fae on the way to the dining hall with his large dog.

Now attired in rich clothing, Phyv looks even more regal than I imagined.

He bows before speaking. "Yes."

"Where were you born, Phyv?"

His dog sits at his side and I see his nose wiggle around in the air as he smells me. He sneezes and I raise an eyebrow. "Trust me, I am not too fond of your smell either."

"I am unsure," Phyv laughs. "I have been an orphan since I have had the mind to remember anything."

"Oh," I fake an apologetic expression. "I am sorry to hear that."

"No need for pitying me. I have been content with my life." As he says the words, I can tell that it is a lie.

"No other way to live but contently with what you have." I nod. "Though, if you wish to see where you are from, do not fear to ask myself nor Laven of your upbringing. We have access to archives you may not, but now that you have been accepted into this citadel you may seek with us."

"Phyv!" The pretty little Princess beams as she runs down the hall in a light pink gown and the dog begins to wiggle around as she approaches. "You stayed." She grins up at him before giving the pup the attention he is craving, down the hall she came from slowly walks the black cat that belongs to the sister. "King Stravan," she greets me, and we both bow before each other.

"I will let you two go ahead of me, I am sure there is nothing of your morning conversation that will concern me."

As they walk away to the large doors opening to the dining room for them, Phyv glances over his shoulder at me and nods.

A tiny sharp wind wisps by my ear, it is almost ignorable until Laven appears. I heard not a footstep, nothing at all.

'This one,' Sloan points to the name within the Arvenaldi family tree. 'The shining Heir.'

The moment I declared my visit to the Realm of the Wolves will be commencing, Sloan began research on each man in The High Four and each individual in House Arvenaldi. First, we are to learn about The Head of both. I would have thought The Head of their House would be the High King, but as we look upon the data now, the High King certainly is not The Head.

'Laven Hephaestus Arvenaldi, the second. He is told to move at the speed of an expert ascender. He is strong, intelligent, and he was born with basic abilities but after the Blood Bond Ritual with his brothers one power developed. He learned to project force fields strong enough to move mountains.'

"Well?"

I gaze at Phyv once more as he continues to walk down the dining hall with Levora. "He smells ancient." I admit.

"Ancient?" Laven's eyebrow raises. "How could that be? Given his age and the records at the orphanage, it states he arrived as an infant some twenty odd years ago."

"Yes, but his blood. His blood smells of those from before my time. And, technically speaking, not many of them are left after the first Domestic War in Voschantai, meaning Phyv should be much older than he is being predicted to be." I turn to him as he now watches the dining room doors open before his sister and Phyv, and they shut behind them. "You may have worry over the rouges and the people from other realms that will demand for their family members to be found on human territory as your sister and Greyce were, but add Phyv to that list of worries. Someone like Phyv should not exist, Laven."

37
THE LAKE

LAVEN HEPHAESTUS ARVENALDI, II

Stravan and I have begun planning for investigative parties. I did not expect him to want to arrange something such as this for Dyena's search, I figured he would want to comb through this land himself. It was my last thought that he would trust others to say they found her. I would not trust anyone to search for Ivella without me there.

"Explain what is being spread. Just how exactly the rogues become rogues." Stravan speaks as we mark all pertinent areas to search on the map of Vaigon Citadel.

"It is by a scratch, or you are bitten. Depending upon the size of a person is how long it would take to spread and entirely take over your body with no return." I explain as I draw a large red X over the Terseian Mountains.

"Is there anyone you know that has been bitten?"

"Yes," I nod. "Myself."

His eyebrows raise and he looks up from the map. "And how are you still yourself? How are you not a rabid being like the others?"

"I had an expert Healer." I leave it at that.

Stravan stands with his arms crossed over his chest. "Is that so? Then why has this expert Healer not been able to heal others?"

"They did not have the power to get to every person."

He quietly hums while nodding. "And is this Healer of Quamfasian descent?"

"No, they are from Nadrexi and lived a short period in Old Quamfasi before the war."

I continue to trail along the map marking all places to search for Dyena while he speculates who it could be that healed me.

"You had them use the Tree of Gods, did you not?"

Of course he knows the tree is a viable source for healing.

"I did not have them use it; they chose to use it. I had not thought of it," I respond honestly. "And I will not ask the Quamfasian people for the tree because I know the harm that will come their way after my people and other nations know that it is still standing and was never destroyed as they said."

"No matter what you will have to use the tree."

I look up. "And why is that?"

He smirks. "Because during the war the only way to save those bitten and scratched is to use the moss from the tree. That is if people can be taken to the Healing Tents fast enough before they are killed to be put out of their misery. No matter what, that tree will have to be used. I have my own way of protecting it, I will place a shield over it only myself and Vallehes know how to get through."

"Speaking of shields. Would you mind teaching Roaner more about shields?"

Stravan laughs. "Why? Because Vorian told you he got through it?"

Through my silence, he can sense my confusion.

Stravan nods. "Comprehensible."

"Roaner is cautious of those who are around his mother as well, I would not be the one to ask. There could be a possibility that he would take you to her, but it will be under supervision."

"No, it is fine. I will not contravene boundaries while I am here." He sits down at the table in my study and glances out of the large windows and through the woods. His eyes slowly begin to narrow.

"Laven, does the Lady by the Lake still reside in the Northern Woods?"

I cringe at the thought of that woman. "She does."

Stravan chuckles. "I know, she is a peculiar one, but she is older than time. What if we went to her? Do you believe she will have knowledge of who is starting this war?"

"As much as I would like to avoid that eerie woman entirely," I exhale heavily. "I do believe so."

The Lady by the Lake knows and speaks all futures, pasts, and presents. Nevertheless, not without a cost.

"What will we bring her?" I ask.

"Oh, trust me. We will be enough. Agivath and I have quite the history, as long as I am there with you, there is no gift needed."

He smirks as my eyes widen.

"Not the history you think. My mother brought Agivath something no one else could after her home was attacked centuries ago."

"And that is?"

"Beauty. An assembly of people from a newer generation that were afraid of Agivath set her home on fire when her prophecies they did not like the result of followed through. You see, people are petrified of things they do not understand. They were terrified by her aptitude to vision all life, so they ambushed her. They thought it was impossible for her to see so far into a being's life, but when she proved them wrong, they attacked. They set her home to fire, and Agivath had nearly burned to death before my mother got to her cottage. My mother asked her what she wanted in return for her pain, and it was the beauty of a hundred women—that strength of beauty can make one eerily attractive. It is no wonder that people are startled by her, only Agivath has never harmed. She tells the truth and *that* is what is horrifying." He stops and warily gazes at me. "When we go to her, I want you to be very careful with the questions you ask. And be sure you are prepared for the response."

THE SONG OF VERITY AND SERENITY

* * *

Our Pegasi's hooves pound into the earth as they dip between the trees, following the trail that will lead to Agivath's cottage. Their wings tuck in tightly as the deep woods narrow and widen.

The woods to Agivath's home are the grounds that no one has touched. Some were too afraid to come near her grounds and some say they knew better than to try to take land from someone who has been here longer than any of us.

"Whoa, Axvin," I call to my Pegasus.

Stravan comes to a stop next to me as I see Agivath near the lake, she is wholly naked as she scoops up a bucket of water.

As she stands her long black hair falls down her back in heavy curls. Her pristine dark skin radiates from the water cascading over her rather buxom body.

"Ah, you brought a High King with you," Agivath says in delight. Her eyes are filled with a clouded orange as she looks between Stravan and I. "Not just any High King, a High King that will always live and die by principle."

As we come down from our Pegasi. I tilt my head to her.

"Yes, I am aware you are familiar with Stravan."

"I was not speaking to you," a smile appears on her face. "I was speaking to Stravan, the King with hair white as winter."

"I am no High King, I am—"

"You will be a High King in due time. By the drive of a Queen's golden blade, you will be King." She is staring at me—*through me*—like she is reading my fate through the depths of my eyes.

The moment I go to speak, Stravan raises his hand.

"Remember what I told you, Laven." He warns me. "Be cautious of the questions you ask and the form you ask them in."

"Oh, Stravan, how lovely it is to hear your voice." Agivath sits down her wooden bucket of water and holds her hand out to him.

He places his palm in her slender hand and her other palm covers the top of his hand. Her eyes close and she smiles.

"Your bloodline will run strong." She calmly speaks.

She lets go of his hand and with her eyes still closed she gestures for mine next.

Her hands engulf my own. "As will yours," her clouded eyes open and she turns over my palm. She traces the lines in my palm before moving toward the cut in my wrist from the Blood Bond Ritual. "Watch over your brothers. Four can become three."

A sharp stab pinches in my chest. "When?" I demand to know.

"When what?" She asks.

"Laven," Stravan pulls me away. He shakes his head. "Agivath, we are here because we need help discovering the person who created this disease being spread across the Realm of Wolves."

Her head tilts with a smile. "Your family is from great leaders of Old Voschantai, but not all are great. Not all have the purest of hearts as your mother who is the first of nine. That sixth has always had a way about him."

As he takes in her words, he stands there, pondering. "Sixth." He mumbles.

"That wretched sixth child." Agivath says as if she knows him well, which she may as well given her ability to see all life. "He did not keep the best companions around him, did he?"

"Do you know the person spreading this, Stravan?" I step closer to him.

He takes a moment to respond. His jaw clenches. "Unfortunately, I believe I do. Although, I have not seen him in nearly twenty years."

Lifting his head back up to Agivath, Stravan begins his next question. "Dyena is missing. She has been missing for the past twenty-four years. By the time Summer is at its hottest is when it will be twenty-five years. Can you tell me anything that will help me find her?"

Agivath clicks her tongue as her finger ticks from side to side. "Oh, finding her is a depth of powers that mine do not even reach." She exhales slowly before giggling. "Two Mad Kings that have raged for love stand before me; how delightful this day has become."

Stravan looks in my direction and I ignore him. "Who is to be

Queen when I am King?"

She only smiles and shakes her head. "I do not reply to questions you already know the answer to."

"I do not know the answer." I push harder to hear the exact name.

"But you do, you just do not know how it could be possible with her *predicament* and your failure to realize you have overcome your past. Having bad days does not mean you are unhealed, beautiful Laven . . ." she pauses and her eyes close again as her hand presses to my chest. "There is a sweet song that plays in your heart, but your soul thunders."

I look toward Stravan and nod for us to leave.

"Thank you, Agivath." I say with a tilt of my head. Stravan does the same next.

"I do hope to meet her; you will come back here, and I will need no payment. I wish to see into the child blessed by the God's, or I will come to you myself."

Child blessed by the God's?

"Yes, I will be sure of it." I promise and choose not to question any further.

As we top the Pegasi, Agivath calls out my name one last time.

"You must embrace her for dear life. In destruction, in beauty, at the end of the world. She will always be the last one standing."

Leisurely, Agivath reaches down, grasping her bucket of water before trailing toward her cottage.

38
REVERIES ARE HEARD

ROANER KORSANA

"Has Ezra returned?" I ask Heshy as he rushes to keep up behind me.

"He has not, my Lord, I believe he will return tonight or possibly tomorrow. I will send him for you once he arrives."

I shake my head immediately as we race down the halls of the palace that lead to the exit doors. As we advance further, the doors push open, and Levora makes her way through with Phyv and their pets. I look away before either of them can see me.

I stop and turn to Heshy. "You both will leave me alone tonight and tomorrow morning. Everything I need to speak of with Ezra can wait until I have returned."

A heavy breeze looms by in their passing, and I refuse to make contact with either of them.

My plans for today and tomorrow are final, no one is interrupting them. Not even Levora.

Heshy nods. "And you will be home when?"

"I will be home tomorrow evening," I motion forward for him to follow me through the doors. "I will come find you once I arrive."

"Well, have a pleasurable day, wherever that may be."

I chuckle. "It will be."

* * *

I ascend to the gates of the border between Xenathi and Vaigon. The border stands hundreds of feet tall, and within the stone-built wall is heavy iron, making the border sturdy enough to stand for years upon years. When I am seen through the peep holes, the gate rises, and I am allowed through from recognition. Patrol is waiting there with spears held tightly in their hands. They are dressed from neck to toe in burgundy armor, ready to fight immediately if anyone dares to pass unwarranted.

"Lord Roaner," one of the men says in a greeting. "Why have you come back?"

"I need to speak with Lady Esme about plans arranged through King Vallehes. Donvarsa Manor to be exact of her location."

"Lady Esme is in the final hour of her meeting with Prince Vorian. Philip will gather the horses; he will take you there." The guard nods to a man walking toward a stable, and he grabs the reins of two horses leading them to me.

No matter what, I will never be allowed to ascend within their lands unless supervised. I must be seen to where I am going, and I must be retrieved from where I was last taken.

Philip hands me the reins of a black horse before he saddles his own; I follow suit, and my horse chases behind his the moment he takes off.

Not the slightest commands from me can be made while using their horses, only commands from Philip can be made, it is my only job to sit and be along for the ride until we arrive.

* * *

I am back where I was previously, the same Consultation Room where I was once begging for help to find Levora, and now I am here for the opposite.

Philip is before me as Esme and Vorian stand at the table in the middle of the Consultation Room overlooking what seems to be a map of a sort, it disappears in a flash at Vorian's doing. "Lord Roaner of Vaigon is here for you, Lady Esme. If you are not finished with Prince Vorian I will have him wait in the hall."

Vorian looks at Esme who is stoic, a woman who contains no emotion on her face and does well at hiding her reactions. Too well.

"Roaner can stay, Philip. Thank you, we are done here." Vorian nods and Philip leaves.

"What did you need?" Esme questions sharply.

"I need to speak with you privately."

"You could shield the room after I leave so no one will hear your conversation, since you perform so well with shields." Vorian teases.

Esme laughs and turns to Vorian. "Put this lie to rest."

This time I am the one to chuckle given I already know the truth of that past situation.

"Vorian was trapped in your shield. He never got through it, nor did he get out of it until after you removed it. He would not shut up about how he could not leave Vaigon because of you."

"I do plead my apologies, but I am very glad to know of this."

Vorian smirks. "I am sure you are glad." He moves from the table and nears closer to the door to leave.

"Do not travel too far," Esme says to Vorian. "We are not done here."

Let this man leave, Esme.

"Come find me after you are done. I need to speak with my mother and father, and I will tell them that Roaner has arrived if they do not already know."

They say their final goodbye before Esme's eyes lock with my own.

"What are you doing here?" Rage. "More specifically, what are you doing here *unannounced*?"

"Hi," I walk the vast distance between us. "How was your morning?" I ask. "My morning was fine, how was yours?" I continue.

"Yours was fine as well? That is good to hear." I stop directly in front of her, just an inch from touching. "You look lovely."

The tiniest bit of her hard exterior softens.

"I know I do."

"I figured."

Her dress is long and silk, it wraps around her body except for one side where her entire waist is revealed down to her hip.

"Why are you here?" She asks again, this time softer.

"You have not let me see you since we have been in The Sunset Province, the only way to see you is to catch you off guard it seems." I reach out to toy with the sheer pieces of fabric on her dress.

"I have been occupied."

"You are occupied no longer." I declare. She glances from my hand and up. "We are going somewhere. You are not allowed to ask questions. All you will do is take my hand and follow me."

Her lips itch to protest, to demand to know where we are going, when we will be back, and how we are getting there.

I wait.

She looks down. "I cannot take your hand if you do not give it to me."

Foolishly, I smile. And damn it. She does too.

"You stand correct, Lady Esme."

Our hands move in unison, the second her fingers lace with mine I ascend.

When we land, we stand outside of my home far from Vaigon.

GALITAN -- THE REALM OF THE SORCERERS

Esme peers around our current environment before she turns to me. "Are we in Galitan?"

"When was the last time you were here?" I ask, knowing one of her parents, possibly her mother, is a Sorceress.

"Never," she observes the beauty of the land before us.

"Your family has never brought you here?"

"No, when my mother met my father she stayed with him in

Old Quamfasi, and they made their life there together." She turns to the large cottage behind us and then she is gazing at the vast forest lingering beyond the home. "She left her life here and never came back."

Galitan must not bring her peace.

"Even the air here feels different than the air in the Realm of the Wolves." Esme observes as she inhales deeply.

"Fresher," I nod.

"Why are we here?"

She has not let go of my hand since we have landed so I lead her into my home. "This is my home away from home. I had it built a few years ago as a place to escape to when I cannot handle the burdens that lie in Vaigon." I shut the door behind us as she enters. "I had a dream many nights ago that I brought you here."

"Fulfilling your reveries." She simpers.

"No," I chuckle. "This was a reverie that was heard and gifted. I merely wished and it was given."

"Roaner," her voice is so soft and supple. It pulls me closer, and I watch as that wall she carries around comes tumbling down. "We should continue to keep this strictly about the bargain between–"

"We are not speaking of any duty to be completed while here, just ourselves. By the end of tomorrow night, I want to know everything about you and you will know everything about me."

She attempts to respond while staring at the button on my topcoat. "I do not want to only talk about ourselves."

I smile. "If you would have answered my many messengers I have sent to Xenathi it would be possible for us to have more conversation than usual."

"Strictly business."

"I will be damned before we are strictly business again."

"We will have to be soon," I know she is hinting at Levora, and I do not allow our day to turn toward her. This is about us, and only us.

"I do not think we will."

Her chest dips. "I am not meant for longevity, Roaner."

My eyes flutter as I try to listen to what she is saying given the seriousness of this conversation. "If you say my name once more I will be entirely lost with no return." Her hand graces my cheek, and it is my undoing. "Esme, I have not touched you in far too long and you will truly experience how insane I am if you deprive me any longer."

"Roaner," her voice purrs as her finger trails over my lips, before she can say it again her dress is gone, and her body is pinned below me in my bed.

"Take off your clothes," she begs as her body writhes beneath me.

Her thighs open wider, revealing more to me that I have missed other than her stark attitude and stubbornness.

I trail my hands up and down her inner thighs and she deeply moans. "Roaner," she moans again, unable to finish any words.

Nothing, all we have to do is nothing to be so ready for each other.

I sit up between her legs and she is tearing at the buttons of my topcoat, and I fight to undo the strings of my trousers. My undershirt is hanging off of one shoulder before I grow impatient and sink into her the moment she gets my trousers just below my hips.

* * *

Esme quietly exhales as she dozes off in front of me. I reach upward and run my finger down her nose. "I am awake," she mumbles.

"Then open your eyes," I cup her cheek and she lazily looks at me. I smile as she struggles to open her eyes. "What did you mean earlier?"

"About what?"

"That you are not meant for longevity. What did that mean?" I trace small circles on her cheek to keep her awake, but I fear it is helping her fall deeper into sleep.

"Love."

"Why do you think that?"

"Nothing ever lasts forever, Roaner." She utters. "Nothing lasts, I do not last. You consider that you want a certain life with me until you tire out and leave wishing you never made the choices that you did."

"You do not know what goes through my mind when I see you, do not think I am so comparable to the boys you have had in the past."

Suddenly, I must meet the man who ruined the woman that I am certain was built for me and no one else.

"Do you not have a wife waiting for you? A wife you have been searching for while pursuing me."

There it is.

"She is not my wife, I lied to push Vallehes for help, Levora is Laven's younger sister that I grew close to while we were young and stupid thinking we would marry knowing well enough it would not prosper. I was not finding her solely for myself, I was finding her for my brothers as well. Then you decided to appear again."

"And when she comes home, and you realize you still want her you will prove me right that I was not built for the longevity that you seek with me."

"You are wrong," I say just over a whisper.

"How so?" She challenges me.

I hold her cheek tighter. "She is already home, and I am here making love to you and trying very hard to create it with you." I gently kiss her hand as she stares blankly. "Now, tell me how you will attempt to run away from me again so I can prove you wrong once more."

39
AT HER EXPEDIENCY

LAVEN HEPHAESTUS ARVENALDI, II
VAIGON CITADEL

I HAVE ASKED STRAVAN yesterday and yet again today who it is that he knows, specifically, who it is that is spreading the mayhem over my land. Just as yesterday, his response is the same. Yet, at least today I am receiving a more in-depth answer.

He has an inkling of who it is but refuses to guess or speculate and false claim someone—which is comprehensible. Just because Agivath says that it could be his uncle or the companion close to him, does not mean it is accurate. Visions of the future are always subjective as are visions of the past.

There was a letter he sent to his sister, Savarina, in hopes of her doing research across their realm while he is away. I wrote out specifically when and where our first outbreak began. Next, I wrote out the process the body goes through after being bitten, clawed or both. All words from my own experience and also what I have witnessed.

I do not state in the letter that these are words from my own experience because I do not need word to spread too far of my having been healed by the Tree of Gods.

"Laven, what do you consider?" My mother asks as we walk the area outside of the palace, making sure all decorations for Summer Solstice are in place.

Inside the palace decorations are nearly complete. All of the gold strung candles make everything appear more ethereal than it already is.

Now we are outside aiming for the same, but she is incorporating flowers and greenery through the gold and neutral shades.

I give her a smile. "It looks lovely as you have it now."

There are decorators moving across the span of the balcony wrapped around the palace, they are twining strings of leaves and flowers across the tan stone.

"Apolla," Axynth calls for my mother as he stands in his black leathers and cloak.

"Oh, Axynth." Ma gasps as she walks toward him. "Do fix your hair before we leave!" Immediately she is forcing her fingers through his white hair, lifting the pieces hanging over his forehead.

"You and Amias both seem to forget what a brush is." She scolds. "Stravan will be coming with us to our Southern Court, he will learn the land of Wanora as we arrange the search parties. I cannot be certain we will arrive home before Solstice, so come." She holds her arms out to embrace me before she and Axynth leave.

"And who will you be spending your Solstice with? One of the women on your list?"

"Ma," I say in shock.

"Did you think it was hard to understand the smirks on the boys' faces? Especially my sons." Axynth raises an eyebrow as he watches me.

Amias could not have a poker face if he tried.

Axynth has always been able to sense when we are getting into something we should not be, especially myself. When I lost my father, Axynth became the father figure we all were missing.

"They mean nothing." I declare to him as my mother rushes off to aid a decorator.

"All the more reason to not spread your legs." Axynth reaches out, fixing the string on the collar of my undershirt. "You are not getting any of these women pregnant, are you? Do you know what it means to pull—"

"My Gods," I interrupt him. "I am afraid Morano beat you to that bit."

Axynth smiles, his chest gently jumps up and down as he laughs. "So, you are pulling out and praying?"

There has not been a reason to pull out. I do not know if I remember what it feels like to have that rush of pleasure any longer.

"All of you behave while we are gone." His hand roughly pats my cheek before finding my mother again and ascending.

Then, soon enough, I see the Dragons overhead taking flight to Wanora after Stravan.

* * *

"Ethivon," Morano says as he enters my study with Roaner and Amias.

"What of it?" I ask looking up from the stacks of letters Lorsius avoided from the small villages and cities within the citadel.

Salem sneaks into the study through the small opening in the door, he prances through the room and leaps on to my bureau taking Morano by shock. "Is no one monitoring these animals?"

"He is harmless, Morano." I laugh as Salem stretches across the papers. I pick him up and place him on the chaise near the fireplace; right after, Nyt enters to find Salem and he lays on the ground next to the fire.

"We still need to go there soon," Amias sits down on the chaise near the bookshelf. "We need to speak with them, warn them of what is coming while also asking if they have had any encounters with rogues."

I nod while leaning back in my chair. "We do. I have been thinking of this for some time now, but I cannot seem to find a way to Ethivon."

"We also need to ask for allyship." Roaner says as his arms cross.

Alongside Nadrexi, Ethivon stood the strongest next to Old Quamfasi in the war. Ethivon was one of the many reasons Lorsius conceded in our final war.

Ethivon alone could have demolished our men and women.

"And do any of us truly know the location of Ethivon after the war?" I look between them all.

Amias's eyebrows furrow. "Do not look my direction."

Morano chortles at Amias as Roaner leans against the window, he stares far into the woods before his head turns toward me. "Ivella does."

"Oh, Ivella." Morano sardonically sings.

"Send a messenger to her, she will respond." Roaner urges.

I do not know what would make him think she would answer this letter out of the many I have already sent, but I pull out a paper, quill, and ink.

Ivella,

Roaner brought it to my attention that you have the location of Ethivon.

I would like your assistance in finding their whereabouts. We must look to them for allyship as well as sending warning to them about the possibilities of war if we cannot get the spread under control.

  Thank you,
  Laven

After handing off the letter to a messenger, I look at Roaner. "Why would she respond to this if she has not responded to anything else I have sent?"

He shrugs. "She will."

"I think this would be a quest to assign to Levora. She wants duties, and immediately. She is still getting used to being home, yet she is adamant about wanting work."

Morano quickly agrees. "After all she went through, I *know* she is capable of it."

The four of us decide and set it in stone that Ethivon will be Levora's first ever task.

* * *

Roaner was not wrong.

    Our messenger has returned and bears a letter in his hand.

    "From Lady Ivella of Xenathi."

    I take the letter from the messenger, thanking him before he ascends from the study.

    Morano leans across my bureau, his chin is propped on his palm as he smirks at me. "You should see how red your cheeks are."

    I shove him away before pulling the red wax seal.

    Amias peeks over my shoulder and I push him away.

    Roaner chuckles from the window, his smirk ignites the green in his blue eyes.

    "I should strip all of you of your placements." I sneer at them.

    "You would not dare. Your life will be unfulfilling without us." Morano smiles.

    The words from Agivath slip into my mind and just for that split second, I wonder who it would be. Whose life am I making sure stays on this earth as I offer my own. Agivath was not clear if this would happen, so I continue.

Hello Laven,

    I do know the path to Ethivon, Roaner is correct. I will speak with you soon.

        Ivella

    Quickly, I am writing another letter to send.

    I am desperate and I do not care that I show it.

    As I write, I can see Morano practically jumping in his chair.

Ivella,

    Thank you for responding.

    When do you plan for us to speak?

        Laven

    "Now we wait again." Morano simpers as I seal the folded letter.

* * *

We did wait, and we are still waiting.

I am unsure if she will even respond again—forcing me to wait in angst for a short letter.

"And what was the problem here?" I ask Farsven.

Farsven is Lorsius's Auxiliary and informs him of issues within our towns and cities.

By the high stack of papers in his hands, again, there is much Lorsius has put off out of not caring to provide our people with what they beg for and need.

"There have been multiple sellers in our markets who tax the Quamfasian people more than what they tax the people of Vaigon, that is if they tax the people of Vaigon at all. Two days ago, there was a brawl between a shop owner and an Old Quamfasian Warrior. This is not new information; this has been going on for years now. Lorsius does not care to tell them to fairly tax everyone. In his eyes, the Old Quamfasian folk are being fairly taxed, when we can see they are not."

He continues, feeding me more and more information of everything within the mainland that has been avoided. From Lorsius not properly serving our people, to the extreme legal matters that are not being met within Vaigon's highest societies—illegal enslavement, assaults, building on land without contracts and deeds, fake coin production, contraband, treason, illegal trade, and somehow even more the longer he sits with me.

All of this will take seasons upon seasons to clean up, as well as needing proof to charge everyone properly.

I allow Roaner, Amias, and Morano to listen in on everything Farsven explains. And as each problem is explained, each of us pick up a task as it is said.

This week I granted Roaner and Morano the ability to have as much say as Amias and I do. It was the best decision I have made thus far. Both Roaner and Morano now have the position to handle all the matters they took on from Farsven and will hand out demands to our highest of societies as if they were mine.

If I am to be High King, the people of Vaigon will learn now what I will demand of them, or they will lose everything they have by my word. There is enough they have gotten away with, and when I am to reign, they will be given no choice but to forget the treacheries they once were able to commit or serve the consequences. I have endured pain, suffering, and agony at the hands of this nation. My citadel. I have been a victim, I have been a prisoner, I have been a patient, and I will never allow this same nation to see me weak ever again.

IT IS MUCH PAST midnight as Roaner, Amias, Hua, and Morano sit in my study with me.

Mrs. Patro had mounds of dinner brought to the study, there is still much left as we all deliberately work and eat at once.

"Do any of you believe I have failed in some way for not knowing any of this?"

Roaner's eyebrows deeply furrow. "How were you to know of any of this if he did not tell you? None of this work we are dealing with is of your duties."

"I understand that, but what if there was some way that I should have known of this?"

"Laven, stop." Hua says bringing me another plate filled with food. "Lorsius took over these tasks for a reason. He hid them from you because he did not want you to do what was right and most importantly, what was legal. There is so much here he has done that qualifies him as a High King of treason within his own continent. None of this is your fault. Now eat, you are the only one left who still has yet to eat."

She gently grips my shoulder before returning to her chair.

Morano rolls up a wad of papers before reaching across the table. He draws back, whacking Amias across his face, jolting him awake.

"Stop it!" Hua scolds Morano as she snatches the paper from his hand and hits him back just before he can duck.

"Fuck you!" Amias hollers. "You diminutive bastard!" He grabs a vessel that still contains wine in it.

Roaner reaches out, stopping him. "Leave my wine, it did nothing to you."

As I roam across a letter from a mother pleading for her son to not be drafted in any coming wars, I remember the group of enlistees Hua and Amias met with weeks ago.

"Since I have you both here, how has it been training the new enlistees?"

Hua laughs but Amias is stoic. "Those children are arduous and indolent." Amias sneers. "They spoke a great deal about what they think they can handle, and when tested they flee. Some have egos and I do not even understand what they have accomplished in their short life to have an ego of any sort."

"I will join you soon and speak with them."

"High Prince Laven is going to attend the Training Grounds?" Hua teases.

I point a warning finger at her. "Only to mend your indolent teenagers."

"Is there anything I can help with?" We all turn to the door and Levora is standing there in her night attire.

Roaner looks away continuing his work.

"There is quite a bit for you to assist us with. Tomorrow morning I will explain it all?" I ask.

She nods and looks toward Morano. "Behave, Amias knows where you sleep."

They chuckle and before she leaves, she looks at Roaner who is busy in his papers. She opens her mouth to speak but chooses not to.

As she leaves down the hall there is a messenger walking up with a small letter in his hand. Before he reaches the doors he bows before Levora who smiles and continues on her way out. As he hands over the letter to me, I ask when it was that this was sent, and he tells me just now.

She must be having difficulty sleeping.

"She is," Roaner says through the bond while gathering more

food onto his plate.

I would ask why, but I am sure I already know the answer myself.

Laven,

You will see me at my expediency.
Ivella

40
SUMMER SOLSTICE

LAVEN HEPHAESTUS ARVENALDI, II

DAYS LATER AND IT is finally Summer Solstice. The first Solstice I am spending in my study raking through the mounds of papers to go through.

The sun is nearly setting, so the entire citadel will be bustling with excitement. Music, dancing, drunken minds, and possibly Blood Bond Rituals.

"Laven Hephaestus, I do not think so!" Levora waves a finger while walking in.

I smile at her as I see her beautiful dark orange gown.

"The world is alive like never before and you are in here going through paperwork!" She grips my arm, and I am shocked by her strength as she pulls me out of the chair. "Come! Get ready, there is Brovita sitting in a stemmed glass waiting for you in the Throne Room. Wear your nice vest and topcoat, and for goodness' sake, wear something other than black!"

I erupt in laughter as I move down the hall from my study and to my chamber to change.

"Vora," I call and she turns to me. "You look stunning." I smile.

A grin pulls at her face. "I know, now go get dressed so you can look stunning with me!"

* * *

The Throne Room has been opened and decorated for our highest members on the citadel. The floor to ceiling balcony doors sit open, allowing in the music and chattering from below. Overhead you can see the sunset through the ceiling windows. The decorators have strung the candles and greenery, it hangs like moss from a tree on the ceiling, and a golden hue emits throughout the Throne Room.

I find Amias, Morano, Roaner, and Hua, who sits on the edge of the table. They are beaming with laughter as Morano tries to drink the Brovita in his glass without hands.

I would join them, but there is something nostalgic about this.

Will this be the last time all of us have moments like this?

Ever since Agivath spoke of the possibilities of losing a brother, it is nearly the only thing I can think of. Who? When? Why? Where?

Roaner looks over his shoulder.

"What is wrong?" He worries.

I smile and shake my head. *"Nothing."*

After moving through the crowds of people, I reach the table and my glass of Brovita is immediately forced into my hand.

Brovita is a drink we only consume on holidays, it is strong, sweet, and only meant to be drunk with those you love. It is also the main drink at ceremonies of all kinds. It is known as the Nectar of Intimacy. Brovita truly holds up to its name.

"Now that he has decided to join us, we are getting shittily drunk tonight." Amias holds his glass up in the middle of the table.

"To whatever the Gods bring us until next Solstice." Hua grins.

Our glasses cheer in a clank before it touches our lips.

Levora shouts for Hua and she quickly hops down from the table and over to Levora and Phyv.

"I am guessing you will somehow disappear before the night

comes and be in a certain someone's bed?" Morano teases Roaner.

There is a smirk that appears on Roaner's face. "Abso-fucking-lutely."

"After a bottle of Brovita it is elated sex like no other." Amias says with a grin.

"That is only because Brovita is a high, not a drunken state. It *feels* euphoric–" Morano's words begin to trail off and a smirk pulls at the corner of his mouth. His eyes are directed to the open doors of the balcony where the stone steps lead into this room.

Inch by inch she continues to appear up the stairs, there is a woman alongside her that I have never met, both are hand in hand. I could not have told you she was there if Morano was not instantaneously asking who she was.

I can see one woman and one woman only.

A presence like a thousand-piece orchestra.

Her skin glows in a smooth sheen of oil, catching the bits of golden light strung above us.

The sheer cream dress on her is long. It reveals her from hips to ankles, and in the middle, it drapes downward, covering the area just between her legs. Her shoes are rich gold, and they lift her multiple inches higher. Her breasts are revealed through the white material, showing the hint of her cinnamon-colored nipples that caress the fabric above them. There is a deep V cut in the dress from her neck, stopping right above her navel.

The hair I only knew as curly is now done in long, dark knotless braids that flow with every step. Every braid lays over one shoulder, grazing right above her hip.

Her entire back is revealed—the white dress cowls above her lower back before falling to the floor. Bits of tan and gold are laced throughout the creamy fabric igniting her skin.

As she approaches closer, I can see the seams of tan and gold along the edges of the fabric that lines the tops of her hips.

Each connect of her shoe against the stone floor raises me to life, bringing me more aware that she is here and vastly approaching.

Her body is plentiful and antagonizing. Across her hips, she is etched in soft lines signifying fine thickening.

Splendor as this is not quotidian.

Woman.

Ivella is a religion standing on its own, and I go to my knees to worship her every night.

"You blessed piece of shit," Morano grumbles through the bond.

"How am I of the blessed? Regrettably, I cannot have a crumb of her." I dreadfully remind him.

"You lie. You could have her. You make stupid decisions, that is all."

The longer I look at her; the deeper my chest begins to wound.

"Ivella!" Hua calls and Levora is staring wide eyed at her.

I cannot bear to look at her again, but still, I can feel her approaching.

That same scent I smelled all over the letter from days ago rushes through me.

Fucking citrusy sweetness.

"Look at you!" Hua says. "Who is your friend?"

Suddenly, Morano is smoothly on his feet walking toward them to find out the name of her companion.

I finish chugging the Brovita in my stemmed glass before pouring more.

You will have to speak with her at some moment, you idiot.

"This is Lourdes, she has been my companion since birth." Ivella's smoothly deep voice speaks and my eyes flutter. "Lourdes, this is Hua, Amias, Morano, and Laven."

Fuck.

I turn and quickly pass my gaze over Ivella and to Lourdes.

"Lovely to meet you," I nod.

Morano attempts to intrigue Lourdes. She overlooks him with a soft smile. "You are charming, but I am here to accompany Ivy and nothing more. We must get back home to attend the Solstice Gala."

Oh, Gods.

She has not a clue what she has just started. Morano will never give up after being denied.

"Laven," Ivella calls.

I could fucking cry.

"Yes?" I answer as I pour more Brovita into my glass.

"A word?"

I nod and stand from the table.

By the Gods I will burst if I look at this woman.

I walk toward the balcony where we are far from everyone, but still in view.

"You wanted a map for the journey to Ethivon?"

Staring down at the crowds of people gathered and dancing seems to hold my attention now as I listen to her speak.

"I do, if you do not mind, would you be able to lead Levora to them?"

I do not even realize I brought the bottle of Brovita outside with us until I am bringing the glass spout to my lips.

She reaches outward and I see the form of her long and perfectly sculpted nails. They meet in a rounded point, just barely a natural shade of white.

Finally, I look down at her as she drinks from the bottle my lips were just over.

She hums. "Nadrexi's is better." She shrugs, handing it over. "Who is Levora?"

Looking down at her hand, the ring I bought her containing Blue Tigers Eye still sits on her forefinger. But upon her left hand, not a single jewel sits.

The harder I look; I see the faint tan of where a ring used to be.

Is the wedding ceremony truly off?

"Levora is my sister, I do not believe you two have met." As I glance back at my sister she is still staring in amazement at Ivella.

Ivella waves, and in her daze, Levora finally waves back.

"I did not know you had a sister. I do not mind taking her there. Yet, allyship is not going to be their decision." She explains. "Ethivon is now a Northern Court of Quamfasi, you will have to go through Vallehes and Penelope first."

Our eyes meet this time and I lean against the stone of the

balcony rail to playoff my weakening knees.

We stand here, her holding the bottle of Brovita low at her side as she observes the people below.

"I should visit Mrs. Patro." A smile finally appears on her face.

"Why have you not answered any letters I have sent to you?" I cannot resist asking any longer. "Why answer that one letter but not the rest?" I try to avoid irritation but as she looks at me with perplexity, I cannot help but to wonder why she is about to form a lie.

"What letters?" Her tone rises.

"The letters I have been sending nearly every day the past month and a half."

She glances away from me, her eyebrows furrow as she falls into thought.

I am no fool. It all aligns.

"Unless someone has been accepting those letters and forgetting to hand them over to you." I scoff at the thought. "He is such an idiot." I cannot keep the thought to myself.

"And why is that?" Her agitation clearly comes through.

Gaping at her, I carry on. "Because he has you. I do not. That is why he is an idiot." I point.

"I did not come here to speak of this," she turns to storm away. I catch her arm. Her head whips around as she stares directly through me.

"So, you admit it?" I smirk.

"Admit what?" She says through gritted teeth.

"You know *what*." I let go of her arm and straighten.

That it was not as easy as you made it seem to walk away from me. Otherwise, your marriage to this fool would still be intact.

"I do not read minds," she fixes her long hair that is flung over her shoulder. "I will not guess what it is you are trying to hint."

Again, she walks away.

"There is a difference, Ivella." She stills, turning, looking at me over her shoulder.

"And what difference is that?"

I laugh and all this does is agitate her further.

"A difference in what, *Laven*?" She says my name with a sharpness that transfers her anger to me as well.

I step closer to her and clench my jaw. "There is a crucial difference between someone who will show you the stars and someone who will take you to them."

There is a challenge I can tell she is willing to put up, instead she walks back to the Throne Room to find her companion and to meet my sister who is itching to talk to her.

I do not follow her in, I head down the stairs of the balcony, letting my feet carry me toward a clearer mind.

41
VISIONS OF RUIN

PHYV

Vaigon is a dream I have dreamt. Sometimes, I think I have seen it before, though I have never been here other than now. The people of Voschantai Universe, old and new, speak of the beauty of Provas towering above all nations, but there is something darker and mesmeric about Vaigon that calls me home. I have always coveted to be more; in Provas, where I was known as my weakest due to my upbringing in the orphanage, is not where I feel I can be more. Here is where I feel it.

Summer Solstice was never something I truly celebrated with great intent like most here are doing. All Solstices were just a day to consume high amounts of alcohol without remorse and to bed multiple people because the Brovita has filled us with such a sexual high there was no one else more meaningful to lie with.

Here, they all celebrate Solstice together as one. They use this time as their moment to just be with one another, laugh, eat well, and mingle with loved ones. Although Solstice only comes twice a year, they take this time with one another and spend it well because who knows when you will have moments as this ever again.

I could not deny the strong brotherhood between Laven, Amias, Morano, and Roaner. Their brotherhood is not built on just silly interactions from their past. Most of the people in Levora's life are close because of bonding through trauma and building beauty from it.

'Laven met Amias first. Axynth, who is like an uncle to me and my brother, is Amias's father.'

'Yes,' Greyce nods. 'I remember you mentioning that your father and Axynth are brothers through the Blood Bond Ritual.'

'And then Laven and Amias became brothers through the Blood Bond Ritual. They grew up together so closely that they vowed to stay together all their life. Next they met Roaner, and their original interaction was not what you think would build a bond as strong as theirs. Some people think that Roaner and Laven have known each other longer than Laven and Amias have. Sometimes, there is no time frame for an unbreakable union to be built.'

'How did they meet?' I ask.

'In passing on their way home from Vuamsati Academy. Roaner and Amias had met in previous days beforehand, but Laven and Roaner met that day. This was during the time my brother was still carefree and living happily. He was playing around on their walk home and bumped into a grouchy Roaner that was already having a bad day. Roaner called Laven out of his name and Laven retaliated with his fists.'

I laugh imagining it. During my time in the orphanage many fights like this happened daily.

'What made them grow closer?' Greyce wonders.

'There was a gathering at the Orshe Waterfall in the Eastern Woods and there was cliff diving. The friends that Roaner had at the time were not true to him. He told them that he could not swim and the friends said they forgot, but only after pushing him over the ledge. No one other than Laven dove in to save him. Even through his hatred for Roaner, Laven always lives by what is right within his own measures.'

'Live and die by principle.' I nod.

'That is him,' Levora smiles thinking of her brother. 'And from there they worked on their friendship, promised each other a new beginning and grew to *where they are now. Through time they both discovered they are more alike than they thought, but still, in their own ways. Right at the time that Laven and Roaner's relationship was on the mend was when my mother miscarried our youngest brother. And through that my father felt like Roaner was that child they missed out on, so he proceeded to be the father figure that Roaner lost.'*

'And Morano?' I ask about the last.

Levora weakly smiles. 'Morano was found. His parents were selling him.'

Greyce quietly gasps as her hand presses to her chest. 'Not in the way you mean?'

'Sexually,' Levora nods. 'They had a beautiful child, they were pinching for coin, and did not have a care in the world about what they put their child through. All they knew, was that they needed money and they had a gorgeous son.'

'How did Laven find him?' I ask.

'Laven was walking the streets of Precydes, our most busy city. He was fetching me my favorite bread from a baker and while leaving he saw a young boy hiding in a short dark alley. He was naked and filthy, Morano was nearly flesh and bone and nothing more. Laven approached him with ease, he was afraid he would frighten him off. But Laven offered him his cloak and Morano urgently took it, then he offered him the bread, that he took too. It was not easy for Laven to persuade Morano to leave with him given his past, and Morano did not want anything to do with our mother when Laven brought her. He feared adults deeply and rightfully. Laven gained Morano's trust through protection and teaching him combative skills. It was only until then did Morano finally come around others because he now knew how to fight.'

'Where did Morano stay after Laven found him?' Greyce asks.

'Ryverian House, our safe house when it was small and nothing but the size of a shed. The safe house became larger when my father realized Morano was there, and he turned it into a home for him and that home turned into the safe house for all of us. It was called a safe house because Morano named it that, that tiny shed turned into a large mansion was what he knew as safety.'

'Any word of his parents through that time?' How could you just give up your child to anyone and everyone?

Levora smiles. 'No, his parents chose to have nothing to do with him after realizing he was in the hands of Royals, my father gave a firm threat that if they came after him it would be their execution. Besides Amias who has amazing parents, my mother and father became Second Guardian of Morano to hold him as their own. Even Roaner, who still has his mother, was inducted into the family because during this time his mother was still making her way through the trauma of losing her husband and my parents were there for him in every way he needed until his mother was better.'

It is interesting to see four almost entirely different personalities flow so well together in a bond. It is not the Blood Bond Ritual that makes them so tightly knit with each other. They were meant to be brothers and live on together. This I crave.

Ivella who was previously with Laven on the balcony has returned after what seems to be a quite heated conversation.

"Ivella, darling, you look ravishing." Morano says as he hugs her. "How have you been since I have last seen your beautiful face?"

"I have been fine, and yourself?" She asks while embracing him.

"Same as well," he nods while holding her hands. "It is good to see you well, Ivella, I mean that."

"Move over, I want my hug as well," Amias pushes Morano and Ivella laughs as he bear hugs her with his large Warrior frame.

Levora stands quickly, waiting for one of her brothers to introduce her.

Instead, Ivella turns to Levora herself and this gives her all the more excitement.

"Hello," her voice is soft and deep. "I am Ivella—"

"Fondali," Levora urgently interrupts her, and I smile.

Ivella's eyebrows raise, and she simpers as she looks over Levora trying to identify her face. "Have we met?"

"No, I–I read about you years ago in past morning papers. When I read the many articles about you and your winning streak in the Quamfasian Games it inspired me. I was speaking of you to my mother not long ago, I had no idea Laven knew you."

That may be the most impressive piece of information I have heard since coming here.

Winning repeatedly in The Games is not something that happens often, if I am certain, The Games are no longer held unless other nations still use them as training tactics.

Ivella grins at Levora's tiny ramble. "Yes, Laven does know me," she regrettably speaks. "Too well, if I must say."

"My brother is a handful; I am sorry if he has ever rubbed you the wrong way."

"Rubbed the wrong way?" Morano laughs. "That is one way to put it."

Ivella sharply turns to Morano, and he quiets.

It seems while Levora was gone these four men found a new ring leader, it is hard to not see the respect they hold for Ivella.

"Your brother, Levora, is an amazing man. A man that did a considerable amount for me in life that it will be impossible for me to pay him back for it all. There is not much that your brother could do that I would consider inexcusable."

Levora smiles and I see her drift into profound thought. She shakes them. "I am glad to know you hold him so dearly."

"Ivy," her friend Lourdes calls. "We must be going; the Solstice Gala in Xenathi is commencing. Our Courts are arriving as we speak."

Morano cannot keep his eyes off of Lourdes, and quite frankly, I understand him.

Lourdes has the beauty, I would die a thousand lives to see. Similar in height to Ivella, she is built just as thick, but firmer in shape, dark skin and eyes, and hair of the night with curls like tunneling waves.

The women here on the Immortal Lands are by far more appealing than the humans I consistently saw.

"But you," Ivella turns to me, and looks me over. "What is your name? I have not seen you before." Next, she examines my pointed ears and my face once more.

"I am Phyv, pleasure to meet you." I stand and she takes my hand.

The moment her hand touches mine visions of multiple different elements cloud my sight. Fire is first, then oceans that rise high and crash deep, after, the deep cracking of the earth and strong gusts of wind that turn into lightning and thunderstorms.

I quickly blink away what is ripping through my mind.

"You as well," she precariously gazes at me, and Levora takes my hand that Ivella was holding.

"I hope to speak with the both of you more when I am not being bombarded." Ivella laughs.

"Oh, when do you plan to return?" Levora asks.

"Soon," Ivella touches her hand. "I hope the rest of you enjoy your Solstice."

She says one final goodbye to Morano and Amias before taking her friend's hand and ascending.

"You have finally met our soon-to-be sister." Morano hangs his arm over Levora's shoulders.

She looks up at him perplexed. "What do you mean?"

"Ivella, Laven. Laven, Ivella." Amias connects the dots for her.

"Are they arranged? Laven swore he would never be an arranged man and that he would only be with his mate." Levora searches for questions and answers all at once.

Neither Amias nor Morano seem surprised by this, they just smile.

"She *is* Laven's mate, but she is unaware of it." Amias explains. "In time she will know."

"Then who is Maivena that my mother spoke of?"

"Ivella was Maivena." Morano clarifies.

"*Was*? What does was mean?"

"This will all make sense one day little sister." Amias laughs. "Now, as we were." He raises his glass.

"Oh, Phyv, I see an old friend! Come meet him." She grabs my arm and pulls me in the direction where he stands waving.

"Are you all right?" Levora whispers as we make our way over.

I smile. "Why would I not be?"

"Because I know you just had another vision." She stops walking and stares up at me intently. "You can tell me what you saw."

"I will, later. Let us go meet your friend first, then we can go find where Nyt and Salem have run off to." I can hear him running around in the distance below now.

42
THE CAVES

LAVEN HEPHAESTUS ARVENALDI, II

My brothers are looking for me. Neither of them have checked through the bond, yet I can feel them on the search as I walk around the courtyard. I am greeted by various people who tend to talk badly behind closed doors but play nice when in front of you.

"High Prince Laven, another beautiful Solstice." Mrs. Yeshti says as she places her hand on mine. "Most beautiful Solstice I have seen, did the High King arrange the decorators?" She pretentiously asks.

"No," I smile removing her hand from mine. "My mother arranged the decorators, they are our servants from Quamfasi, stunning is it not?" I ask while looking around.

Her face falls at the mention of who the decorators are, but she catches herself. "Yes, pretty it is."

"Laven!" Amias hollers from a distance behind me.

"If you would excuse me," I hold my hand up to her and she leaves.

When I gaze back, the three of my brothers are standing there with Stravan.

As I look in their eyes, they are all filled with tension, even in their stance they are on edge.

"What is wrong?"

"We all have a short venture to go on." Stravan aggressively grips my arm, and before I can blink, we are ascending at his doing.

When we land, we are thrown to the dirt in the woods.

Glancing around I come to the realization as to where we are. "Why are we in the Terseian Mountains?"

Roaner is also on high alert. His eyes dance through the woods, searching for any outsider on the attack under Stravan's orders.

"You tell me, Laven. Why are we here?"

"Stop playing some guessing game and just tell me."

Stravan turns to look at the tops of the mountains.

"Why would my children act out of their normal when over these mountains? What is up there?"

He cannot truly believe that Dyena will be hidden within the mountains.

"Stravan, there is no possible way that Dyena is within here." I begin. "We–"

"Ah," he holds up a finger, stopping me from continuing. "Why do you doubt it so quickly?"

"Because we would know if she were there. It would have been brought to our attention that she is roaming the mountains all this time."

"And who is to say she is roaming freely? Who is to say that she was not put there?"

There is a rise of anger within him, it is accelerating at a speed I cannot keep up with.

"I see it this way," he slowly paces back and forth in front of us. "Either you can tell me the truth, or one of your lives can be taken."

We look between one another.

"Stravan, none of us know of her taking. Ever since we were children it was spoken of as some tale to tell before bed. How would we as children know where she has been taken to? Let alone be part of her capture."

And just as I finish, there is a soaring pain that rushes through every part of my body. It is crippling, bringing not only me to the ground but Amias, Roaner, and Morano as well.

I stiffen as I try to move and that stiffening turns to torture.

There is a chuckle that comes from Stravan as he continues to pace.

He looks over at us.

"You are even weaker than I thought." He mumbles.

Roaner grips the ground, one boot slams into the earth as he struggles to his feet. He falls back to the ground, but again he is up and I struggle to follow, but even through the pain, I do.

Stravan looks to us. "You two are stronger than the others."

I try to speak, but any bit of movement sears a deeper pain throughout every part of my body.

"How about now?" Stravan waves a hand and Esme appears on the ground. She is curled and dirty, her clothing is shredded to nearly nothing as she lies limply on the ground. "Will you tell me what sits in the mountains now?"

The deepest scream of pure agony tears through the woods as Roaner's magic erupts through Stravan's.

He weakly crawls across the ground, but the moment he touches Esme, she fades away as if she was never there. Frantically, Roaner looks around. He is gasping for air as he stumbles to his feet.

"The imagination works mysteriously does it not?"

"You can torment us all you wish. We know nothing."

Roaner comes falling to the ground again at Stravan's will.

"I can do this all night until one of you collapses to their death. If I am smart, the first I will get rid of is this one." He points to Morano who cripples further to the ground. "Then I get rid of the High Prince's hand, and then the rest of you one by one."

"Stravan, stop!"

I cannot move to see her, but I can hear my mother yelling through the woods and coming closer.

"And you," Stravan domes a shield around her, it radiates in through the darkness in a bright grey. "Apolla, you and I will have a word."

"They know nothing, I swear it. Let them go, I am the one who knows everything, please." Her words break the more she speaks. "Let my boys go home, they know nothing of what occurred here. I have not spoken a word to them."

It begins to strain too hard to think. Just to form a word to speak draws more strength out of me. Yet, it could just be Stravan taking more life from me by the second. I have felt pain like this once before and prospered through it, I can do it again.

"And what is it that you know?" Stravan urges for clarity.

His blue eyes flare like hues the more his fury rises.

"Let them go and I will tell you. I give you my word, let them go, and I will tell you everything." It is a rarity for my mother to swear her word.

Something is shouting to me that she should not be telling him what she knows.

There is nothing I can do about it in my state.

Stravan is now only focusing his powers on myself and Roaner.

"I swear it, I will give you anything you ask." My mother offers more and Stravan studies her.

Suddenly, the pain is gone.

It does not gradually leave; it is taken away immediately as if we never felt what happened and this sends me into a short shock. Amias is quickly catching me as I stumble.

"Go, I will be home soon." Ma looks to us behind the shield still trapping her.

"Ah," Stravan warns as I stand up on my own. "You will want to stay."

I struggle to breathe. "I would not dare to leave my mother with you."

"Not for your mother, for her." He points through the woods. "You may come out now."

"Do not jest me." I snap at him.

Roaner grips my arm as Ivella appears.

No, it is not possible . . .

"How do I know this is not another one of your little tricks?"

I look over her for a single sight of something being out of place.

The moment I step forward, there is a hard shield placed in front of me.

"You do not go near her. Not until I have this all solved."

"What the hell does she have to do with this?" I demand.

"You will see . . ." Stravan turns to my mother who is still trapped beneath his unmoving barrier. "Care to speak?"

She glances between Ivella and me.

"Dyena has been transferred from multiple different hiding spaces. Artemis is who took her those years ago because she wanted the strength of the Vaultais to hold a bloodline within our realm—the Realm of the Wolves.

"The day Artemis took her she had Hermes capture her soul. They divided it and had it put into Ivella the day she was born. Artemis gave Ivella the bits of Dyena's soul that contain her powers. Through the pits of our souls is where our powers lie, no matter your kind or the realm you are from, your powers are not just an ability, it is who you are in your soul. There are still parts of Dyena's soul that Artemis left within her to preserve her immortality, but she gave Ivella her strength and gifts.

"It has nothing to do with someone being chosen or specially picked. It is by pure coincidence that Ivella was the child to be birthed twenty-four years ago. She was stillborn and then given life again by the transfer of souls."

My mind runs rapidly trying to position every word my mother has said.

Then it occurs to me.

When we get to Dyena, Stravan will demand Ivella's life for hers.

"Over my dead body will he do so." Morano says. "There is a way out of this."

"How?"

"The Blood Bond Ritual. The moon is finally beaming, we have time."

"And what if even through the Blood Bond Ritual she dies?"

Morano does not respond.

Ivella is staring at the ground. It seems like she may faint right in front of us.

"Then explain to me why their features favor one another." Stravan demands. "You have seen Dyena before, and now you are looking at Ivella. Explain why they look nearly identical!"

"It could be because of the transfer of their souls." My mother stays calm. "That is the only answer I can form for that. But Ivella looks like her parents, they could be doppelgangers, plenty of people within our world look exactly alike with no trace of being related. The same goes for Laven and Roaner, they have looked similar all their life and are not related by any mean other than by ritual."

The shield is removed from my mother and slowly she stands.

"Where is she?" Stravan asks.

"The Caves, I am the only person that knows the way in. It is locked by magic."

"And does your brute of a King know of this?"

My mother immediately shakes her head. "No, Artemis strictly arranged this with me. No one else knows."

"Take us there," Stravan nods for my mother to go first.

I make a fast line for Ivella, but death grasps my shoulder. "All of us go." I snatch out of Stravan's grip and go to her.

The moment I am near, she continues gazing at the ground still as the night.

Finally, she adverts upward, as I reach to touch her cheek Stravan shouts.

"Move your feet, Princeling. And do not even dare to think of ascending her from here."

* * *

We have moved farther up the mountains, reaching the depths of the caves.

Ivella stumbles up the uneven ground as we trail around the mountain. I grab her arm to prevent her from going over the edge and Stravan tensely swivels around.

"I am preventing her from falling, if she is the answer to all of this, you want her protected, correct?" He only stares at my hand now wrapped over her arm. "This ground is wet, cracked and pebbled. Her shoes are not meant for it."

I reach lower and he observes every movement from me leaning down, lifting her from the ground, and into my arms.

"Get moving," he demands.

I hold her closer and she wraps around my neck, tightly gripping, and reluctantly we carry on.

She does not talk, though she does not have to. I see the desperation and defeat in her eyes as she stares at me. In her eyes, that green I know well transforms the visions of every beautiful life I once saw into never-ending nightmares with threatening verisimilitude. I am now forced to no longer see her in fanciful fabrications. This is real, and she may perish, and I could leave this mountain carrying a body bereft of life.

Have we not equally lived through enough pain in our short time of life?

Must death be layered on top of it all?

'We are not exactly the luckiest nor the most loved beings the Gods have created. We are given mates, someone specifically crafted and created only for us. Either we fall in love with everything about them or not—there is always that deep-rooted connection that holds our soul to the earth. When they perish, we do as well; we may still be here, but it feels as if we are dead—a walking, living corpse. We have the chance to hold on to immortality and youth if we continue to phase into our Wolves, yet all that means is merely living, being here as just an object. When they die, a part of us dies as well. We can either live with the emptiness or end it all to be with the person destined for us. Those are our options. We carry on cut in half or die to be whole again. There is no living in-between the two after someone so dear to you is ripped away.'

I have spent years being assured that her life lives on for the sake of my own, and in my own ignorance, there is that regretful fragment of the unknown that prevents my certainty.

She is the reason for every breath I take and every last.

Her head rests against mine and she presses closer.

The path upward grows steeper and my brothers close in tighter.

Amias treads directly in front of me with Morano and Roaner behind me.

The rigid stone alongside us grows wetter the farther we walk, the air is growing tighter as we reach the most open the mountains can be. It is pivotal to see such grime burgeoning when we were just lavishly celebrating a night that is to be considered our most reverent.

Ahead, I see my mother begin to slow down and Amias stops. He outstretches his arm, preventing me from walking any further.

He too is aware.

Ivella lifts her hand, and with a gentle squeeze of his shoulder, urging him forward, Amias intakes a sharp breath before proceeding.

My mother has come to a full stop in her lead.

"She is behind here?" Stravan asks pressing his hand against the wooden door. His eyes widen and his ear presses to the door. "I can hear her breathing, open it, now!"

My mother nods, making haste to open the door that has not a single handle or knob connected to it.

There is a desperation in Stravan as the door lifts.

Each second, I see his hands tremble more.

As much as I try to visualize him as the villain, I see myself in him. I would react the same if someone did this with Ivella. It is a different kind of loss that I could not ever understand, nor do I wish to.

Just as my mother said, Dyena is here.

She lies flat on her back with a large bed stone beneath her.

"Dyena!" He shouts as he engulfs her cheeks standing beside her. "She is still in the same clothing," he says in relief. "Dyena?" He pleads once more.

As Stravan said, it is nearly frightening how close in similarity Ivella and Dyena are. The longer I look at her, the more I begin to see Ivella.

His eyes lift to Ivella and this time, I do not care what he says.

"No," I tug her away from him.

Stravan's eyes narrow. "A life for a life, Laven."

Ivella's hand grips my own as she peers around me, fixating on Dyena.

I hold her tighter. "You can go to hell."

"There is an alternative for this." Morano urgently announces. "It is Summer Solstice, the only known time to perform a Blood Bond Ritual. The ritual is known to heal the weak and even give life. It is the only method closest to the Tree of Gods to bring a life that is just hanging by a thread back to earth."

I will go as far as begging this man.

He should know. He can tell.

Just by looking at us, you know we are a part of one another.

"All right then," he gazes between both me and Ivella. "I am not wasting any more time than I already have." Stravan motions for Morano. "We do it now."

* * *

I already know it now. If she somehow departs from this life in the process of the ritual, I will find my own way of parting as well.

"Are you all right with doing this?"

More. I should be asking so much more, and I cannot.

How are you processing all of this?

Did you know?

Have your parents spoken of this with you?

While nodding she continues to stare at the woman on the stone bed.

"Yes, I am fine with it." As the words are said, I hear that hint of ambiguity in her voice.

She does not want to, no one would. She is doing this for the sake of our lives.

"We need a High Priest or High Priestess; we cannot perform the ritual without one present." Morano attempts an excuse.

It is a lie. We do not need a High Priestess or High Priest. There are plenty of people in the world who have done the Blood Bond Ritual without them because they could not acquire a Priest or Priestess.

He as well seems too afraid of what will happen.

We cannot avoid that there could be a likelihood of this going unbearably wrong, not only for me, but for Stravan as well.

What if all the life within Ivella returns to Dyena?

If Ivella was stillborn, what are the potentials of her returning to that?

Deteriorating to her original form of never being meant to exist.

"Do not fuck with me," Stravan aggressively speaks at Morano. "You will perform this ritual whether you want to or not."

Ivella looks around the cave, her eyes land on a small sharp rock. She retrieves it from the ground and holds it out to Morano.

"The only choice there is, is to try." Ivella aims to reason with Morano.

Giving a slight nod, finally, he takes it.

There is a great deal I should be saying—words that should be tumbling from my mouth as she walks away from me. Yet, I cannot bring myself to profess love at the last moment, there is not enough time in the world to utter a syllable about the depths that my love reaches to for her.

Even in death I hold hope of being with Ivella as I should be.

My grave could not hold me from coming back for her.

"How is it done?" Stravan asks.

Morano explains the process to him while holding Ivella's hand behind him. He further explains that even with Dyena being of Fae blood, the ritual is still possible.

Ivella's eyes are blown like a doe in astonishment. I have ever seen her go as pale as she is now looking at Dyena.

I step nearer to them. "When this is complete what comes next?"

Stravan's eyes find Dyena's almost lifeless body. "She will decide." He then turns to Morano and gestures for him to perform the ritual.

"You do not command me around." He says through clenched teeth.

Stravan raises an eyebrow. "Right now, in this specific moment, yes I do."

Morano opens his mouth to reject his orders again, before I can stop him, Ivella does.

"Morano," she quietly speaks.

As he turns to her, there is a smile on her face, as confident of a smile as she can give him.

"What if you die?"

He is worried. I knew he would be.

"What if you die?" She asks in return.

He says nothing.

"Come now," Ivella steps closer to Dyena and she tightens her grip on Morano's hand to subdue the tremors trailing over her fingers.

She holds out her wrist to Morano, stiffly, she lifts Dyena's hand showing her wrist as well.

As the sharpest edge of the rock pulls blood to Ivella's wrist, I can hear my mother trying to edge into my mind.

"Remember to breathe, my love." She says in the calmest tone I have ever heard.

I continue to stare ahead of me.

Secrets, so many secrets she has kept yet I struggle to hold them over her because she is my mother.

"If anything happens, get Ivella to the Tree of Gods. I can hold off Stravan long enough for you to get there." Roaner spews a plan to us all.

"It will have to be Morano to take her, he is the only one who can pass the border." Amias adds.

"I will get through that fucking border, even if I have to blow it into a million pieces. I am the one who will take her." I put in the final word as we anxiously observe Morano connecting Ivella and Dyena's wrists.

Ivella gently wraps her fingers around Dyena's forearm to keep their wrists intact.

"It is working," Morano speaks as he rapidly looks between their conjoined wrists and Ivella.

Still fine. Still alive.

Stay, Maivena. You have to stay.

The veins in their hands begin to ignite gold, nearly as bright as the sun at its most golden hour. This is the transfer of their blood mixing within one another while giving Dyena life to her soul as well.

There is gentle movement in Dyena's fingers and Stravan hovers over her face, waiting for her eyes to open. Yet, I am waiting for Ivella's eyes to close. Praying the strongest prayer I have ever given to the Gods.

Dyena's lip's part, intaking short breaths as we watch life return to her.

And then, there they are. The beaming green eyes that replicate Ivella's.

The golden hues radiating from their skin begins to diffuse and we know the bond is complete.

As Ivella pulls her hand from Dyena's, the small cut to her wrist heals over, leaving a fine small line.

Her thumb rubs over her wrist, staring at it.

"You played the song." Dyena speaks in a tone that is hoarse and rasped.

Stravan has no words to respond, he only nods as tears pour down his face and drip to her cheeks.

He is gathering her from the stone bed and into his arms, cradling her so she does not have to walk. If she stepped a foot onto the ground, she would topple over given how many years she has been held solitary.

Dyena looks around at us, her eyes fall upon Ivella.

"I could hear you all here," she says continuing to glance at the faces surrounding her.

"I am sorry, deeper than that if there is a word for it." My mother pleads. "I was not given a choice. There were repercussions if I said no to Artemis, she held a threat over my bloodline if I decided to deny her holding you here. Even now I do not know what will happen. I am sure she is aware of you holding parts of your soul she wished to keep wholly within Ivella."

"Did you deny her when she first asked?" Stravan questions.

She nods. "Yes, then she threatened to take Laven for my denial. I had no choice but to do as she demanded. I was not going to allow her to take my only child."

"Before you condemn her once more," Amias speaks. "Let us not forget that there is no such thing as denying a God without grave risks attached to it. And the Gods are liars. I am sure Artemis planned to do more than just take Laven if she were denied."

Did my father know of this?

Dyena gazes at Stravan. "You of all people perceive what it means to be pressured into dark tasks for the Gods with a threat lying behind it."

"That was when I was a naïve teenager. We are all–"

"Naïve or not." Dyena struggles to be gracious, her glare set on my mother is deadly, but even she comprehends the severity behind an ultimatum from a God. "No, I am not of the same mind as Apolla, but her reasoning was grave. Your vengeance and mine is with the Gods, not her." Nevertheless, Ma will never be trusted nor fully welcomed by the Realm of the Fae standing alone.

"Thank you," Dyena looks to Ivella with a weak smile. "You knew the risk of your life and still you chose to aid me. I will owe you for eternity."

Ivella does not need to say it. But she did not do this for Dyena. She did this to spare our lives even if it meant hers being lost.

Ivella only nods, returning the smile.

"And you will not treat these men as you did outside." Dyena scolds Stravan. "I heard you down there. You will teach them to strengthen and wield their powers as you do. These young men had nothing to do with this."

"You have only been back for mere minutes, and you are already reprimanding me." Stravan stares at her with the yawning endearment as she glares at him.

"You would not have it any other way." She says knowingly.

Turning her head to us again. "We will see one another soon enough. Thank you." Dyena bids once more as Stravan leads the way out of the cave.

The Dragons are swarming above us when we reach the opening, they are elated at the sight of their mother.

As I turn to Ivella, she is walking away—moving farther into the woods and then, ascending before I can call out for her.

43
PURPOSE & WORTH

LEVORA APOLLA ARVENALDI

The arduousness within the unknown.

The unknown factor if you should go to someone to learn if they need help coping or if they cope better alone.

I cautiously watch Laven as we sit in the Ryverian House far in the Western Woods.

The others are speaking quietly amongst one another in the kitchen. Laven sits slouched in the large armchair as he rubs his finger over his lip that holds his teacup.

"Vora," he mumbles, and I urgently walk towards him. "You will start training again soon. Possibly tomorrow. Do you still have your dagger?"

"Yes."

"Start carrying it around again. Tomorrow you will come with me to the Training Grounds, and we will craft you a sword and a spear. Then you will begin training with Amias and Hua."

Suddenly, everything I have wanted is before me and I am frightened of it.

"So soon?"

He looks down at me as I kneel next to his chair. "I need you to train and carry lethal weapons and know how to use each of them, for my sake. This world is full of threats, and you came home to a clustered and disoriented nation. There is too much transpiring for me to sanely allow you to walk around untrained and unarmed."

"What–what if . . ." I shake my head. "What if I am no good at it?" I want this but I am now afraid of the outcome. The discovery of truth. The discovery if I am capable.

"Levora," he leans in closer. "You are not weak. You are fully capable of being the version of yourself that you dream of. Your mindset regarding your lack of abilities must change if you want to succeed. And not only for my sake do I need you to realize this, but for you. Neither of us inherited father's gifts. I overcame that by learning to be a weapon and it is what I need you to do. Train daily, educate yourself in all areas of life, trust your intuition, know your Wolf, eat copiously and well, test yourself in forms you never imagined you could handle."

"Strong like you is what I crave."

"What about being strong like Levora?" His hand holds mine as he speaks. "Comparison is not only the thief of joy but a thief of prosperity. You are not me, and that is your power. You are you and you will be strong like you. You have always seen strength in everyone else and wanted their strength, now I must urge you to see that vigor in yourself. I can no longer enable you to see so much in everyone but yourself. You are not in the Mortal Lands anymore, you are here in Voschantai during the ages of war, Vora, and because of this environment you must learn. I cannot handle the possibilities of losing someone again."

My chin quivers as I stare down at his hand tightening on mine. "What if I fail?"

His forehead presses to mine. "You will never fail, you are an Arvenaldi. We have history of the Old Voschantai in our veins. Strong souled."

I nod as quiet sobs release hearing the words our father used to say. Yet these words were always told to the boys, Laven is the first to ever say them to me. And as I say those two words, I feel the ancestry of past Arvenaldi women move through me.

"Strong souled."

PHYV LOOKS ODD IN the black leather armor. I never thought I would see the day that we train together here in this realm, but time has come for it to happen.

"No matter how your training ends today," Phyv straightens the cloak over my shoulders. "Do everything with intention and you can leave the Training Grounds everyday knowing you gave it your all."

Nyt aggressively sniffs our attire before huffing and throwing himself to the ground next to Salem who is laid on the chaise next to the fire.

"Come, Laven is waiting downstairs."

When we breach the doors of the palace Laven is speaking with Axynth who ascends before he can see us.

"Remember," Laven knocks a knuckle against my chin.

Strong like Levora.

"I did not forget," I say. "How are you this morning?"

By the look in his eyes I can see the lack of rest.

"I will be fine," he tries to lessen my worry. "Good morning to you, Phyv. I am glad to know you will be joining us."

"If there is anything I enjoy most about Voschantai Universe, it is the way we fight. Warriors here are much different than the soldiers on human territory."

Laven snickers. "You can say it if you like."

He is dying to hear that they are weaker than us.

Phyv only laughs and touches Laven's shoulder as I do, and we ascend to the Training Grounds.

As we walk through the grounds, far in the distance stands Hua and Amias delegating hundreds of rows of men and women.

There are one too many pairs of eyes looking over us and Phyv and I follow Laven in his path toward Hua and Amias.

"High Prince Laven holds to his word," Amias smirks.

"I do when my General complains about inconsolable new

trainees." Laven nudges Hua.

When Laven overlooks all of the young people before us, he lands on one who is reaching across his line to push his friend who does his best to hold his composure.

"What is your name?" Laven asks the boy causing commotion.

"Vargas Yeshti." He says all too proudly.

"Yeshti," Laven's eyebrows raise. "I ran across your mother yesterday at Solstice."

"I am certain you did; my family holds rather high rank, so it is only natural that she is on the Palace Grounds for such an event."

If there is one thing about the Yeshti's, they have always been the snobbiest of the rich in our highest societies. Many of our Gala's were, and possibly still are, hosted by their family and there were many people who found their gatherings to be tedious and uptight.

Laven laughs at the boy's cockiness. "What is your strong suit, Vargas?"

"As the largest man in this subdivision, I thrive in all areas."

Even at his current large size, Laven still topples over him.

"Oh, then you must be a great Warrior already. Would you mind showing me?" Laven steps backward letting there be space. "Choose another upcoming Warrior to challenge."

Through his confidence, I see him waver, but he covers it with a laugh. "I do not need to show you that I am qualified to be great."

"Great?" Laven speaks with surprise. "How old are you, Vargas?"

"Eight and ten."

This time, both Phyv and I get a chuckle out of this. Even as someone who is not qualified to judge any upcoming Warrior, I know he has had no training powerful enough to qualify anywhere near great.

"Funny is he not?" Amias speaks and I can see his annoyance rising.

This is the problem child Hua was speaking of.

"Very," Phyv nods.

"You are eight and ten, and believe you are a great Warrior.

Why?" Laven asks.

He does not answer Laven out of humiliation of so many thriving Warriors before him.

"Is this the one you said was all talk when we spoke the other day?" Laven asks Hua.

"And a few of his other companions as well."

"Very interesting . . . So, you want to be a great Warrior, but you do not want to put in the effort to become one and will not show me that you are capable. Your family's wealth, Vargas, has generated a lot for you, but it will not secure your name as greatest Warrior. Your family's money will secure you as a *privileged* Warrior, and those are two entirely different titles. You need to suffer and understand your abilities before claiming you are great for anything. Since a child you have never known what struggle is, and this will be your weakness."

As cocky as this young boy is, he seems to listen to Laven and crave his words. Maybe because he is speaking with a High Prince or maybe he secretly wishes to impress Laven and is afraid to embarrass himself. Vargas is vividly defiant and lacks discipline. Laven has been known to have discipline in his life but with our brothers and people around him as well. Sometimes his discipline is his downfall, nevertheless, there is no other person fit to speak with Vargas than Laven.

"Fight to find your purpose and then you will know your worth." Laven continues. "As of now, your purpose is nothing, as is your worth. You will heed my orders to succeed, or you will pack your things and go home. And I do believe your father would not be too pleased to see his only son standing at the doors of his home because he failed to become a Warrior."

Vargas still does not respond.

He has been humbled.

"Stand up straighter when I speak to you." Laven's words shock the young boy and he takes his place in line.

Now fear has been instilled.

"Amias," Laven sharply turns to him. "Train them as we were trained by our fathers." The methods used in the Quamfasian

Games. "Find the tallest trees in the woods located here on the Training Grounds; remove their branches and secure rods into the body of each tree—make them learn true strength by carrying themselves to the top and then carrying another on their back. From there make them learn stability by turning the trees into pillars and they will practice in the Pillar Race. Take them to Terseius daily to climb the mountain where stray Dragon's roam. Then lead them to Gordanta where our waters go twice as deep as the Terseian Mountains are high—where the currents are so strong even mature Water Dragons struggle."

"Riveting," I hear the voice of a young woman say from afar, our eyes meet mine and we smile at one another.

She is small in comparison to everyone else here. Small yet mighty. Her leather armor is thinner in comparison to the others, this makes it easy to tell a commoner from the rest by the leathers they have to fight in. Not all armor is built the same, some are built lacking in protection so that people of lower income can afford them.

"That is torment!" Vargas exasperates.

"You are a man. Is that not what you said? Men can accomplish these tasks, so prove to me how this is torment." Laven dares. "Unless you are unequipped for the wrath of war?"

He does not speak again and chooses to cling to his worthless pride.

"You all will learn to be swift, vigorous, and sturdy before you are allowed to touch a weapon again. A real Warrior knows that the weapon is not in their hand, they are the weapon." Laven observes the rows upon rows of young men and women training to be like him, Hua, and Amias. "Only three-hundred enlistees?"

"Yes." Hua answers.

"And this is all of them?"

Amias nods in response.

"I will give it two fortnights to have three-hundred more enlistees, or we begin drafting."

Hua smiles, the word draft is music to her ears.

"The Spartans succeeded quite well with three-hundred." I say.

Laven smiles. "Unfortunately, little sister, not all three-hundred of these young men and women are built for their profession to be a Warrior. I can see plenty who will be attending Vuamsati Academy instead of pursuing a title here."

Since the beginning of time, the greatest profession to have has been to be a Warrior. There are plenty of other well known professions to have, but to be a Warrior, you are the mightiest of mighty.

Hua tops her Pegasus before it trots through the rows of upcoming Warriors, and she selects the girl with the most urgency. The one who was most excited to participate in the trials of the Quamfasian Games. "You will aid me in building the courses, come." Hua nods her head, and the girl is quick to saddle the Pegasus with Hua.

44
PRINCE OF RANCOR

LAVEN HEPHAESTUS ARVENALDI, II

THE WEEK OF SUMMER Solstice has come and gone. We have not truly known how to talk about what happened. I think Amias would rather forget it ever happened, Morano fills his fear with laughter, Roaner seems to not have a care in the world, and my mother has been quieter than she usually is. I have asked her if she is all right, and she gives a mere response before carrying on about her day.

There is nothing I have truly felt other than the wonder of where Ivella is, and how she is processing this rush of information. Processing her new life. When I have asked Roaner how she is coping, Esme told him she has secluded herself from everyone—burying herself in her studies at Vanlaxa Academy in New Quamfasi, while running off to her father's home in Nadrexi whenever she gets the chance.

A thought has come to send a letter to her, see if I can be taken to her, even under supervision I would do it. Although, letters seem to be out of the question. There is the chance of her jealous awaiting husband butting in and hiding the letters once more. She did not confirm that is what he did, yet it is not hard to solve it was him who was not giving her my letters.

All the night of Summer Solstice did was make me realize that I have no choice but to push my people and those close to me to be experienced in combat. Especially those who have no establishment of powers.

I cannot say it was fear that was instilled in me. That night I was forced to be a greater High Prince and in addition I must force those around me to do what we should have been doing all along. I cannot only be a great High Prince to a weak nation. It needs to show within my people and our citadel that Vaigon is altering, and it is altering for the better.

"Could you imagine how Lorsius would have handled Solstice?" Amias's voice pulls me from all thoughts.

"It is better Lorsius did not handle this. Stravan would have ended our realm with an easy lift of his finger." Morano answers.

"That is the problem." I sit up from my slouched position in the chair. "There could have been strong possibilities of that. If Lorsius were here we would be dead, there is no avoiding that outcome. He does not make the rational decision in these situations. His first thoughts are always irrational."

I stand and begin a tedious stride back and forth. "Do any of you think I would be able to cross the border?"

Morano laughs and I glare in his direction.

"First, please stop pacing. You are making me anxious." Amias says. "Secondly, no. I do not think you could cross the border. Even if you begged and gave over everything you own, there is not a single possibility of you getting past that wall."

"Laven," Morano pleas. "Roaner said Esme will keep you informed of Ivella. And if Ivella is not around often enough, there is not much Esme can tell you."

Our messenger, Ezra, who Roaner promoted, enters the study and greets us before placing a letter in my hand.

"Thank you," I nod to Ezra before he ascends.

"He is always so quiet." Amias whispers.

"No, he is not." Morano clarifies. "He just does his job and leaves."

Amias turns to him. "And how would you know he is not quiet?"

Morano smirks. "Because I have been with him, on more than one occasion."

"I should have known," Amias says, shaking his head and returning to the papers in front of him.

"And I am the harlot?" I ask with an arched eyebrow.

His brown eyes sparkle in orange as they taper. "Just read your letter and tell us who it is from."

The wax seal is imprinted with a P engulfed in wings, I know exactly where this has journeyed from.

"Stravan . . ." I exhale and they both stand.

Laven,

We would wish for your presence in Provas within the next seven days. We are holding a celebration in honor of Dyena's return, without you and your brothers, this would not have been possible. Each of you may bring anyone along with you that you want.

Alongside the celebration, the following day we will be holding a conference with our Circle and yours as well. If there is anyone else you see pertinent to knowing any information regarding what will be spoken of, bring them with you.

We are delighted to show you and your closest companions the beauty of Provas.

With chasmic respect,
Dyena and Stravan

I hand over the letter to Morano.

He laughs. "This bastard tries to kill us, then invites us to Provas for festivities and a conference."

"I am not surprised," I take the letter as he hands it back over to me. "I knew a letter as this was coming soon enough. I will send word to Carmen and Lorena; they are the only others I can think of that would be major figures to know of this."

"Has Carsten had any further luck with the inoculation?" Amias asks while moving through the multiple papers and letters regarding illegal enslavement.

"Unfortunately, no. He has only found a few Healers with the same expertise as his. But that is more than nothing. Carsten will need all the help he can get with this."

"Did Stravan tell you who it is that he knows that developed the disease within the rogues?"

"I am suspecting, from the letter, that the conference Stravan and Dyena invited us to has to do with that." If it is not, I will be bringing it up.

Amias lifts his head. "Did he include Lorsius's name in the invitation?"

"No," I smile. "Stravan does not favor Lorsius enough to invite him."

"There is not a single High King and High Queen that would want Lorsius's attendance or company at any event." Morano chuckles.

"When does Roaner return?" Amias asks.

"Today, possibly tonight."

After the night of Summer Solstice, Roaner took Esme to my home in Gordanta to spend the rest of Solstice there with her. It is officially the end of the week, and Roaner should arrive home before nightfall. I am sure the sudden urge to take her away was due to Stravan feeding Roaner a thought of Esme being taken captive.

Then again, after a scare as that, who would not run off with the person they love and cherish them for as long as they can?

We all thought it was Esme we saw that night, but for Roaner, he saw the end of the world.

"I have the dates set for questioning those who committed treason, and now we move on to setting trial dates and hearings for those taken into enslavement without permission." I walk toward the table and set down the official letters to be sent out when Ezra arrives.

Ezra may have been moved up in rank, but he is still my most trusted messenger. I cannot quite let him go from his position just yet.

"Here are more letters," Morano hands out. "Last week Roaner and I went out to the acres of land claimed without payment. The homes that are being built are rather extravagant when we were shown the blueprints. I reason it is also vital to note these homes are near the size of mansions and are being constructed by servants, which they also did not have the permit for.

I grab a wooden box and pile all the letters into it.

"I will have them torn down and pay the servants for their work. I have to head out of that side of town to visit my grandparents." Amias announces. "I will deliver the people their letters."

"What is next?" I ask, looking over the table still flooded in paper.

* * *

"Stop trying to drink away the thoughts of her." Axynth says as he enters the courtyard.

He grabs the bottle of whiskey and looks down at it. "Strong shit," he laughs while shoving my shoulder.

"Your mother spoke to me of what happened on the night of Solstice." He sits down and pulls the cork of the whiskey, drinking it straight from the bottle. "Your mother usually tells me of secrets she keeps, but not this one." I turn toward him, and he is staring out—gazing at the flowers twirled around the pillars of the courtyard.

"How is she?"

He smirks. "She is fine, although, she worries. Nevertheless, it does not seem to be for herself that she worries for." Axynth drinks more of the liquor before turning to me. "And you. You are heartbroken."

I look away from him, avoiding this conversation people continue to force me to have.

"Trials are soon, and hearings." I divert us away from Ivella and to the issues occurring in our land.

"So I heard. If Lorsius would give me a stronger hand over our continent, I would be able to keep these legalities under control.

Nonetheless, he strips me of all my say, and puts me so far down the line of royalty, I have no rule over anything. I am simply a General's father."

Growing up my father, Axynth, and Lorsius were all so close it was as if they were family, and when Lorsius began ruling, he treated Axynth differently when he discovered that Axynth was another person that disagreed with his ways of ruling. Lorsius left Axynth high in rank but took all say from him.

"Regarding the trials, Lorsius does not care about what we do with the Quamfasian people. He could care less about however it is that those in the higher societies use them. As a High King, even he has committed his own treasons. There is only no way to prove that to the people who do have healthy minds."

"You are more than just the General's father," I begin. "You are a father to all of us and you did all you could to prevent Lorsius from turning into the person he is now. As for the ways of Lorsius, there is nothing else for me to do than grin and bear it."

With everything Hua, my brothers and I are doing, it will be a shame when all our hard work is reverted. Knowing Lorsius, that is exactly what he will do.

"You are doing well," Axynth says. "No matter what happens and whatever it may be that Lorsius says to belittle you. You are better than he will ever be, and that will always be why Lorsius has seen you as his most robust competition. You are identical to the person your grandfather, Vaigon, was, and it frightens Lorsius because he is not."

* * *

I have returned to my study again, if I cannot sleep, I may as well put my time toward completing work that is left to be done.

Roaner is entering the study just as I sit.

He is quiet.

He is always quiet.

But this quiet is different.

"How was your trip?"

He sits down at the table across from me, he forces a laugh and shakes his head.

"Roaner," I urge him to speak.

He shakes his head again.

"I will not be going on another short trip any time soon, and I ask that we leave the conversation at that."

I nod, not pressing any further.

"Ivella is still not talking to anyone," he updates me without me needing to ask. "Even when she spoke with her father, he told her he knew nothing of Dyena being involved. Artemis only told them that she wished to gift Ivella with life. Out of pure elation her parents immediately accepted. But they knew nothing of exactly *what* life it was that Artemis put into her. After meeting with her father, and speaking with him, there is not a chance he would have accepted such a gift if he knew it was the life that belonged to Dyena."

I would not think so either. I have never spoken with her father, yet by the way he raised Ivella, it does not seem he would commit to something as this.

As I am more often told that Ivella wishes to keep to herself, the more I see the large reg flags of warning that she is not fine and that she is not coping well. However, I cannot force someone to speak with me if they are not ready.

I have thought often about going to Xenathi to visit her, just to see if there is a chance I can be there for her in ways others cannot. My only problem is, there is not a chance Vallehes and Penelope are letting me cross that border. If she moves between both Xenathi and Nadrexi, Nadrexi would be my only hope of getting to her. Just maybe.

"Laven," I lift at the voice. "Roaner."

From beneath the table, Nyt quietly growls and I stop him before there is a retaliation.

There is a leering simper as he looks from us down to the mounds of papers in front of us.

"This work can be left to me now that I am home." Lorsius smiles.

45
THE HIGH KING IS HOME

LAVEN HEPHAESTUS ARVENALDI, II

The moment Lorsius declared my work was over he had Farsven move the paperwork from my study and into his. Then, all of the trials that my brothers and I arranged were canceled, and every person being prosecuted was released with a small smack on the hand.

This is how it has always been. Those on our land that he favors get away with acts others would not. I cannot say his hatred only persists for the Quamfasian people, even the poorer folk of Vaigon Citadel are neglected, though not as harsh.

His own people, he tends to hate. If they cannot carry the weight to be high earners, he will look down upon them as if they are ill-equipped for life itself. Yet somehow, he does not look down on them as much as he does the Quamfasian people. When our people requested to work for the palace, he told them there were better earnings elsewhere because jobs as those are meant for the Quamfasian's.

He sees ruling over the Quamfasian people as power. Having a form of strength above them when in previous times, they were untouchable given they are Orviantes but do not look the part, just like Lorsius, he too is an Orviante but inherited no abilities and gifts other than a deceitful mind.

"Where is it that you have been all this time?" My mother asks Lorsius.

"I yearned for some months away, so I left after I finished in Gordanta." He says as he cuts into a large helping of chicken on his plate.

"Finished?" Axynth challenges. "You finished nothing in Gordanta, Laven did."

Lorsius smirks. "Because I knew he would."

"It is a good thing you have him, otherwise you would not be the High King you are today without him cleaning up your messes." Axynth attacks again.

This is exactly why Lorsius stripped him of his rights to being high royalty. Axynth will challenge Lorsius any given day knowing he will win and Lorsius will not retaliate in any other way than taking his rank. Axynth still means too much to him as a Blood Bond Ritual brother. Taking his rank is as far as Lorsius is willing to go.

"You are wrong again, Laven would not be the High Prince he is without me leaving these tasks for him to fulfill. I am only preparing him to be better."

I nearly laugh at him, but instead I go back to eating the food on my plate.

"So you figured an unexpected leave of absence was necessary without a word?" My mother questions.

"I would not have taken the leave if I did not need it, and I knew the citadel was under control. I have done the work to sustain my land, and the people in it. There is no requirement for me to announce when or why I must need a leave of absence."

No one else says anything back to him. We linger on eating supper in silence. Even the servants make barely a sound when approaching, they too feel the discomfort of his arrival home.

* * *

I figured I was done with Lorsius for the rest of the night, but apparently not.

He has sent a messenger for me to come speak with him.

Lorsius can never let it go when being put in his place, nor can he handle being shown where he is wrong without retaliation.

I would not be taken back if this little meeting he has requested is to strip me of all my say in what happens on Vaigon.

"You made quite the mess while I was gone." He already begins showing where I am wrong in his eyes, but not to others.

"By mess, do you mean clearing the treason and illegal enslavement our highest societies have been committing?"

He smirks and turns to the fire. "The people in our societies have choice to do what they wish–"

"Even illegally? Not one of them has permits for the land they are building on. None of them have had permission to take servants as their own and do whatever they wish with them."

"How I run this citadel is up to me, not you." He stands straighter, stiffening his spine and stance. He does this as intimidation and I find it comical. He has not fought a day in his life in years which is why he requires Kings Sentinel and I do not.

"You operate our citadel slovenly." I declare. "The other Courts laugh at us. They taunt you behind your back because you are an incompetent High King. If you think they do not know who truly rules this citadel, you are out of your fucking mind."

He erupts in laughter. "You think you are proficient enough to be a High King because of the light labor I have given you?"

"It seems ever since I was seven and ten I have been competent enough to rule better than you have."

"Do you presume you have knowledge that I do not? You forget, Laven, who has laid foot on this ground longer than you have. You have a long way to go before you can ever apprehend anything someone of my age has."

"Since when must you be an exact age to have experienced

unfathomable aspects of life? Age holds no ground in what someone experiences at any time within their life–" I stop and reflect for a moment. "I would expect someone as you to know that you do not need to be of a particular age in order to retain a level of knowledge, expertise, trauma, or anything of the sort, given your past. Age is nothing but years we have walked earth, it has not a measure of intelligence. You will find, if you seek, that there are plenty of people among this world much younger than you, and wiser.

"It is no insult to an older person to retain further knowledge, nor is it an insult to learn said knowledge from someone younger than you. I pity you and many others who act so obtusely and act as if you are being told what to do by a child. I am no child; I am a grown man and so are you. Either take the knowledge I can give you or exile your poisonous mentality."

Lorsius walks toward the windows, gazing out at the moon in the distance.

"You sound like Axynth," his face turns with disgust.

"Is that all you have to say? You have listened to everything I have said, and this is your response? Did you even hear a word I said?"

Lorsius shrugs before sitting down in his chair.

No . . . he cannot respond because he knows I am correct. He is well aware that I will always have the time to confront him.

"What High King cowers away?" I continue.

He runs a hand through his hair. "Laven, you will not be High King. This is what you wish to prove, but you will not rule. Immortality is mine, and I will hold it by its chains for the rest of my life."

By the drive of a Queen's golden blade, you will be King.

"Just because we hold immortality does not mean it cannot be taken away."

He props his boots up onto his bureau. "And who will take my immortality from me?"

I shrug. "You are right," I say, leaving this conversation where it is. "By immortality you will continue to reign." Until the drive of a Queen's blade. "I think from now on it is best I ask for forgiveness rather than permission."

His eyes narrow. "And what does that mean?"

"Exactly what I said."

"Do you see yourself as high and mighty all of a sudden because of taking my place when I was gone?" Lorsius asks.

"No." I sit down in one of the chairs across from his bureau. "As of late, I have pondered the thought of leaving."

I watch the growth of fear within his eyes.

"Leaving what?"

"The Throne. You will be reigning for eons; you are King enough to handle these lands on your own." I stare deep into the woods as I speak.

Lorsius laughs. "You will do no such thing, you are born to be royalty, Laven. There will be no other lift suited for you other than what I have given you."

"Then confess it," I stand.

"Confess what?" His tone sharpens.

I lean against his bureau, our eyes bore into one another's. "Concede to this tediousness and profess that without me you would not be half the High King you are. Just by me breathing you prosper greater as the High King, and before me the reason you prospered was because of my father and Axynth. They too who you shot down when you discovered they could be stronger leads than you. Who is next? Will you find a Right Hand to then dethrone?"

Lorsius leans in. "I will dethrone anyone in my way."

"Then I will gladly watch the fall of your reign."

* * *

As I ascend to the courtyard, Amias is already holding out a cigar to me.

"I am plotting the death of Lorsius." Morano's tone is laced with malice as he takes a long sip of the red wine in his glass.

"You will not," I say as the stream of smoke disperses from my mouth. "Let it happen on its own."

"I wonder how much of my power within our land he will try to take from me after our conversation."

"What was the conversation about?" Roaner asks.

"I told him he is who he is because of me and there is no denying it."

Morano nods. "Hell yes you did." He says as smoke leaves his mouth. "Just how much of our say got revoked?"

"All of it. I at least hoped for him to be gone long enough to take those bastards to trial."

Morano's slams his hand into the table. "I want them hung!" He dramatically shouts.

"Shut up, you dunce," Amias laughs. "You will wake the entire citadel if you shout any louder."

"No matter what," Roaner speaks lowly. "You will be King. There is no escaping that." He says with resilient assurance.

"Are you prepared for all of the women that will throw themselves even harder at your feet?" Amias asks before he places his cigar back in his mouth.

"There will be no space for them to believe they can do so." Gentle flares of smoke flow from my mouth as I speak.

"And why is that?"

"I will prefer my reigning High Queen over a damseled mistress."

Morano pours wine into a glass before handing it to me. "When did you know that she would be a fit High Queen?"

"The moment she was willing to lay her life down for us over rescuing herself."

"She is a General's daughter," Roaner says. "Before any High King or High Queen there is the General standing before all to defend their people—it is what they are bred for. Her vigor for protecting her own and her ability to stand with grace in the grasp of death is what makes her High Queen."

46
THE WAY I DID BEFORE

ROANER KORSANA

"DOES THIS END?" LEVORA asks as we sit on the swing that hangs between the two trees hovering above the river.

I reach across to move a long wavy curl dangling in her face. 'Does what end?'

She is lost in a trance as she stares down at the water just barely touching her feet but encompasses mine.

'Us,' she whispers. 'This feeling. We are not mates; you would know by now. It is said that mates always tend to stay together unless drastic measures occur to make them drift apart. What will happen when one of us finds that person.'

I scoot closer to her and she leisurely looks up.

'Do you really believe I would allow anything to come between us?'

'No, that is not what I meant. I know you would not, I am only thinking hypothetically.'

'Even hypothetically, the answer is no. We built our connection together, that does not so easily die. I see a great difference between building a connection and having a fated connection. Most fated pairs do not put in the effort to build what we have, and that is where we always win. What we have will never see an end.'

EIGHT SEASONS LATER

'I know what a Snapdragon means, Roaner.' Laven sits across from me in the dining room as we have finally made it home from searching for Levora through night and day.

He waits for a response but I cannot give him one.

'You proposed.'

'No,' I shake my head. 'We collectively agreed that marriage is what we wanted and to keep tradition alive she was going to respond with the Snapdragon and then—' I stop and look at him. 'I believe I have loved her since the day we met at the academy, and—'

'And you did not think you could ever imagine a life without her existing in it,' Laven's eyes fall as he speaks, as if he has experienced exactly what I am feeling.

'However long it takes.'

Laven nods. 'However long it takes.'

"Heshy," I request as I hesitantly fold the letter in my hands. "I need you to deliver this. I will be in the Ryverian House if you need me."

Taking the letter, he observes the name, and still stands in front of me.

"Are you sure?"

"Yes."

Before he can question me any further I ascend from my study and to the Ryverian.

* * *

The door to the Ryverian House opens and I lean against the balcony of the stairs.

"Hello friend."

Levora stares upward.

"Hello."

I travel down the stairs and her hands gather together in front of her.

"How have you been settling in?"

Levora is hesitant to answer, I see the fury building in her. "I have settled fine."

I walk towards the drawing room where I see the mural painted of me, Laven, Morano, Amias, Hua, and Levora. It was strung pristinely on the wall by Apolla herself. Levora does not speak as she stands a distance behind me looking at the mural as well.

"You know, I always thought I had everything under control. I could *never* be miscalculated. I knew my occupation, I knew who I would love, I knew how I would love, I knew down to the final coin how much money I would obtain." I look at her over my shoulder. "You would not recognize who I am now."

"I do not."

"Years of separation does that."

"No it does not," she retaliates.

I wait for her to continue. No matter what this conversation will turn into an argument.

"It is true, Roaner, that distance makes the heart grow fonder."

It was not true for us.

"But your fondness for me has died?"

"Fondness has many forms, and I will not answer this without knowing exactly what fondness you are speaking of."

"Love!" She shouts. "Love, romance, the dying need to be with someone. And that someone is no longer me, is it?"

I will not lie to her. "It is not."

Her chest slightly caves in hearing the words. "You could not even wait until I returned before searching for someone else?"

"You speak as if you know any of what I have gone through while you have been gone all these years."

"I speak this way because you have not spoken to me at all since I have returned home! You do not even look at me and you avoid me as if I am one of the rogues you all speak of!"

"Because I am avoiding this!" I shout back at her as her eyes fill. "I am avoiding your hurt and pain due to the realization that I do not love you like I once did."

"I am done with everyone trying to protect me from everything! I am a woman, and I can handle all emotions that swarm me. I do not need you nor anyone to hide something from me out of what you call avoidance of my hurt and pain. It is my hurt and pain and I choose when and where I wish to feel it. If you loved me at all, you would have spoken to me of how you have been feeling the moment I came home."

"If I love you?" My voice raises higher than hers. "I am the one who opened that fucking portal, Levora! It was not opening by itself. Not anyone else but me. I had to plead for help from a source I had no right to be working with behind my brother's back, only to ensure you came home in return for what they wanted!"

She flinches at my words.

She does not speak.

"Every day I went to that portal and saw it opening, that was you?" She asks in disbelief.

I nod.

"Then if you were so diligently looking for me that it caused you to hide your bargain with whoever it is, why did you not continue to wait for me given I would be returning shortly?"

"I–" the words trap in my throat. "I do not know how it happened. One moment I am looking for you, and the next I meet her, and I lose all rational thought. The love you and I share now may not be the same as it once was, but I love you, Levora, and that is undeniable.

"I knew you in a time of my life where I needed someone to cling to and so did you. You and I both know that what we shared was not love; it was comfort. We allowed one another to be who we thought we were at the time when we were just children still trying to understand what our purpose was. Even now we are still understanding our purpose. I love you deeply for all that you acquired for me when we were just teenagers. But young love is not all that we will ever be. We will grow to have a strongly bonded friendship like I have never known. But that is all we will be," my chest tightens as I watch the tears fall down her face, but I must continue. "You were my heart, but I feel her in my soul. I touched you and I saw everything gentle about the world, I touched her, and I saw a home. And to continue pursuing you when we could love someone else more would be torment."

She stares at the floor between us. "Just children trying to build a safe space when neither of them were the right safe space for each other to begin with." Her eyes lift and I see all the peace I once thought was mine.

"We had too much growth to go through before we should have thought of marriage at such a young age. I was not looking for someone when I was seeking you out. She fell upon me twice at the most inopportune moments, then by the force of bargain we had to work together."

"What was the bargain? Find me in return for what?"

I shake my head. "I cannot tell you that, I cannot discuss those matters with anyone. If I could, I would tell you."

"Then can you tell me if this woman is your mate?"

The burning question that strangles me. "No, I do not know what she is to me."

"When did you meet her?"

"On the battlefield of the second war between us and New Quamfasi."

Levora's eyebrows furrow. "She is not a person of Vaigon?"

"No, she is from Old Quamfasi."

"Her name?" Levora asks as she fiddles with her fingers.

"Esme Fondali."

Her eyes widen. "Queen Penelope's Right Hand?"

"Yes, and she is the cousin of Ivella."

"Strong women."

"What is that supposed to mean?"

"Exactly what I said. Men here crave women who thrive in all areas of life. Esme and Ivella are both one of those women to be held in high demand."

"Levora," I exhale heavily. "You will find someone who will hold you in high regard for exactly who you are now and who you will grow to be. Do not force yourself to be something you are not, the fates do not align with those who try to be someone else other than who they intended you to be. The Fondali cousins are very different from you solely given their past and upbringing. Esme and Ivella had to fight all their life to be who they are now; you have lived life softly whereas they lived in a hell that felt inescapable. And you know something?" I take a step toward her. "There is nothing wrong with either. Live as you are supposed to, just as they do."

"I did not want to come home," she admits. "Well, I did. I wanted to come home to my family, but I did not wish to stay here nor to live here again. I developed fine amongst the humans since I am practically just as they are. Average, a normal being that walks their earth. Yet, here, I am not that. I am high in royalty but low in power. That is the most belittling aspect of being here, although I do not hate it. I came home for the relief of the people I love, as they lived in a small world with me for my own relief."

"There has never been anything wrong with that, Levora. You are not an unwanted woman in this universe because you do not possess gifts. You have a way of showing your strength without needing to flaunt power and magic. You are *more* than what the God's have given us."

Our family has expressed this to her in many ways, there are only so many ways you can tell someone something before they hear it.

"I should have spoken to you sooner," I continue when she does not respond. "And I did not speak to you, and for that I am sorry."

"I love you too," she finally says.

I rest my hands on her shoulders and she gazes upward. "I hold you in high regard, it may not be in the way you once knew it, but I will always hold you highly in my life. Nothing is changing that."

47
BIRTH OF TWINS

LAVEN HEPHAESTUS ARVENALDI, II

"REMIND ME OF YOUR name?" Amias asks Ezra as we eat morning meal in the courtyard.

Morano's eyes widen as he looks at Amias, his cheek is full of food as water drips from his wet hair due to our previous swim in the East Lake.

Summer is creeping over our nation by the day, and the heat is already harsh. None of us dared to put our undershirts on after our swim.

"Ezra," the messenger responds as he hands me the letter.

"Do not go just yet," Amias says as Ezra begins to leave.

"Leave him be, Amias," Roaner chuckles.

"Thank you, Ezra." I nod to him, giving him leave from pestering Amias.

Morano chucks a piece of bread at Amias, and I smirk.

"You like him," Amias grins. "He makes you nervous."

"I am not nervous." Morano shouts, but his cheeks are coated in red, and it is surely not from the growing heat.

"Morano, even the tan covering your skin cannot hide the heat of a blush on your face." Roaner announces as he uses his spoon to crack into the top of his egg to dip bread into it.

"Not everyone can have a complexion as beautiful as mine," Amias smirks, rubbing a hand over his dark brown skin. "It hides every blush."

I laugh and pull at the seal on the letter Ezra brought.

"Laven gets as dark as you in the Summer." Morano nods with a mouth full.

Laven,

I am staying at my father's home in Nadrexi. I would like to speak with you soon, sometime today to be specific. If you are occupied and cannot meet me today, please send word before the sunsets.

Ivella

Everyone flinches as I rush from my chair.

"What in the Gods name is wrong with you?" Morano asks as he watches me tug my black undershirt over my head.

I move at a pace so rapid I messily tuck my shirt into my trousers and I do not give myself the short seconds it would take to tie my collar.

Amias picks up the letter and smirks. "I knew it would happen within due time."

"I will return shortly." I announce just before ascending.

NADREXI — SOUTHERN COURT OF QUAMEASI

This is the fastest I have ever ascended anywhere for a distance as far as Nadrexi. It was like a flash before my eyes, short seconds.

As much as I may hate what occurred in this house the last time I was here, this corner of heaven brings me as still as I could ever be.

The beautiful white and tan stone of the mansion now has ivy growing along its build, giving the home even more character than it already contains. The trees that line the perimeter of the home are brighter, greener than they were the last I was here.

Once I knock on the door, I hear Ivella's feet padding against the wooden floors.

The locks on the door unlatch before she opens it.

She looks up at me. "That was fast."

"I was not busy."

"You look messy . . . and wet." Ivella examines my damp hair and disheveled undershirt.

"And you look like you woke up not long ago." I gesture to her night shift and dark blue robe. The rich silk slips down her shoulder and she quickly pulls it back up. "We went for a swim," I say as she steps to the side allowing me entrance.

"You and your friend?" She pushes for clarification. "Did you bring her?" Ivella looks outside in search.

"No, me, Roaner, Amias, and Morano." I elucidate. "I have not seen the woman you are thinking of since that day."

She only shrugs and responds with a quiet hum.

"How long have you been here?"

"A while." She moves away from me and to the fireplace where a black teapot boils.

Sitting down on the chaise, I continue to watch her venture through the home.

"How have you been?"

Another shrug. "I have been fine," she simply responds as she makes tea at the wooden island in the open kitchen. There is a plethora of fruits and vegetables sitting in baskets along the island counter and multiple vials of some red sauce.

Leaning my elbows against my knees, I sit, waiting to see if she will tell me why she summoned me.

"Why am I here, Ivella?"

She pours the tea into a small vessel and sips the piping hot liquid.

"Did Stravan and Dyena invite you to Provas for a gathering?"

"Yes," I answer—trying to stay patient. "Why am I here?"

"How are you coping with Lorsius's return?"

"Speaking of Lorsius with you is not a conversation I crave to have." After the words leave my mouth, I hear how rude it sounds, but she is quick to respond before I can correct myself.

"Right, I am sorry. I forgot that we only speak of the worst of my life and not yours."

"That is not–no," I begin to stammer. "That is not what I meant–"

"Then what else could you mean?" She interrupts, knowing I do not plan on explaining. "You never speak about yourself and it is *odd*, Laven. As someone who wants to know so much about someone else you surely do not reciprocate it."

"I am trying," I breathe.

"Where? Where are you trying? Who are you trying with? It is not with me. Every time I speak of what troubles you or I try to be there for you, *with* you, you push me away."

Rapidly, I bounce my knee to avoid pacing, and she waits, when nothing is said, she speaks first. "You can leave now."

"No," I panic and my hands begin to shake, I contain them by standing and forcing them into my pockets. "You asked me here for more than a conversation about Lorsius. I do not speak of Lorsius with you because there is too much damage that he has done that involves both you, and me and I am begging for us to not relive it. So, no. I do not want to speak about him."

What I say does not matter. I have already pissed her off.

She does not answer and swirls her tea in the vessel.

"Are you going to continue playing around with that cup of tea or are you going to speak to me?"

Her head snaps so hard in my direction her hair flings over her shoulder, knocking the blue silk from her shoulder again.

"You do not get to patronize me." Her words sharply throw across the room. "*You can leave now.*" She is no longer offering my exit, she is demanding it.

"No, I would like some tea, if you could be so *kind*."

"*Kindly* make it yourself in the company of your own home."

I gape at her and quietly laugh while rubbing my hands over my face.

"Just talk to me, Ivella."

"No."

"Why?"

"You do not tell me anything about yourself, so you do not deserve to know anything going on within my mind."

"Ivella, there is a lot of time it will take for me to tell you many things," especially the shit clawing at me in my nightmares. "If you could spare me a few months I could tell you. But this does not mean you should not tell me what you feel."

She still stands there, sipping on that fucking tea in her hands.

Fine.

I breach across the sitting room and toward the kitchen, she continues to ignore me. When I stand before her, I take the teacup from her hands.

"Since I cannot have my own, we shall share." I take a long sip of the tea, draining half of it from the vessel.

"I do not share." She glares.

I reach out and lift her chin with my finger. "And neither do I."

Both of our eyes gaze upon each other, and within it, I so easily see how everything right in the world works just in the scape of her emerald eyes. Then, the danger as both our eyes drift downward to lips, and I hear the shredding of clothing and breaking of wooden bed posts.

"Last I heard, you are shared upon many." She turns her head away from me and begins to cut the vegetables on the table.

I put the tea down and lean against the sturdy wooden table, bracing myself for whatever will be said next.

"No woman wants a man who is for every woman. It is ugly, and embarrassing."

I laugh through the growing pain. "Believe me, I am the only one embarrassed." As I touch the fabric of her robe, I am given a warning.

"And if you touch me again one of your fingers will end up in my stew tonight," she continues to cut the potatoes. "And I do not think either of us want that."

The sharp edge of the knife rapidly slices down and I mind

myself.

"Other than Lorsius," I divert the conversation because I do not think I can handle hearing any more of her distaste for my previous choices. "There are a few things I can tell you about myself." She nods for me to continue. "My favorite meal is whatever it was you made the first night we had supper together. My biggest pet peeve is people who cannot chew with their mouth closed—the sound agitates me so deeply I want to slit their throat. I have a fear of falling but I still climb to the highest point of the Terseian Mountains to overcome my anxiety. If I could live the life of a minimalist I would, but my lifestyle does not call for that." I stop to think up more rubbish about myself to blurt out.

To my surprise she asks me a question. "What is your favorite color?"

"You."

Her eyes narrow and she puts down the knife. "You are dumb."

"I am rather irate too."

She smiles and I do as well.

"I also wanted to tell you to keep to safe places tonight since Lorsius has returned." She says putting down the knife and looking up at me with large doe eyes. "His return could cause the anger of many."

"What does that mean?"

"It means you must promise me something."

"Anything." I simply respond.

"Whatever you do tonight, do not fight and have sanctuary."

"Ivella," I furrow my eyebrows. "You cannot beg me not to fight without an explanation." What on earth is she getting at?

"You said you would promise me anything."

I let go a breath. "Why? Please, just tell me that. What is happening tonight that would make you plead for me to not fight?"

"I cannot tell you, but if you promise me this I will give you whatever you want in return."

"That is excessive to think I will want something in return. But you need to answer me this." I grab her hand as she tries to busy herself once more. "Are you in danger? If you are, Ivella, I will not say this promise will be kept if your life is at stake."

"I am not, I swear it."

Watching her for a few moments, searching for any hint of a lie, I see none and leave it as is. Though she is incorrect if she thinks I will not have some watchful eye over her tonight. I am sure I can send Roaner here to see what has her out of sorts. If I must, I will return here tonight to be sure of her safety myself.

"Do you fear him?"

I do not need to mention his name for her to know it is Lorsius I speak of.

She plays with my fingers. "He should fear me."

From a distance I hear slight cracking. It draws my attention upward, though as I look up, it is not the roof.

"What is that?" I ask as it carries on.

"What is what?"

"That cracking sound," I glance around our surroundings. "Do you not hear it?"

She fills with shock and runs across the room and toward a corner. When I follow, she is leaning over a wicker basket with a black cushion. The closer I approach, I see a large, scaled egg.

I kneel next to her in amazement.

"Where did you get this from?"

"It was a gift from Stravan and Dyena." Ivella mumbles.

She lifts the basket and carries it closer to the fire. As the hues of the fire gleam over the egg, I see the silver brindle that ignites within the black casing of the shell.

"Ivella, Dragon eggs have not been gifted in hundreds of years." This is extraordinary.

A gift of life for giving life.

There is another quiet crack of the shell, and we watch it split down the middle in an uneven break. Then, one small head breaks free of the large shell.

She quietly gasps as the Dragon pushes free. "Laven, look." She tugs me forward. "There is another behind him."

My eyes widen as the other's head slowly lifts through the shell.

They stare up at us, black as night with a white brindle over their bodies, and eyes blue as the sea with swirls of hazel encompassing the blue. I lean in farther as they hesitantly step out of the casing of the shell.

"Twins . . ."

"They look like you," Ivella says in a daze.

Both of them scurry in her direction, clinging to her and hiding behind her robe that has fallen down her shoulders.

"They are so small compared to how large they will grow." I observe their wings that are nearly transparent.

Within time, their wings will grow firmer. So sturdy even the greatest spear cannot penetrate them.

One with a white birthmark down its head peeks at me, it gives a quiet screech before hesitantly moving toward me.

Its tiny talons are sharp as it walks into the palm of my hand.

"He likes you." A slight smile appears on her face. "Name him."

"Me?" I ask.

She nods. "Name him."

I aim to deny her again, but as the little Dragon looks up at me shaking out his wings a name for him comes to mind.

"Vaigon."

"Your grandfather," Ivella softly responds.

"My grandfather is one of most the amazing men I know, and I want to do right by him. It was not fair that Lorsius named a nation after him but did not create a nation that would uphold to his name. My grandfather, Vaigon, and grandmother, Reynai, are Orviantes. They are who my father got the white hair from, as well as the blue and hazel heterochrome eyes. Then, those genes passed on to me, but the white is only in streaks throughout my hair since my mother was a commoner." I can see my grandfather so clearly as I stare into the orbs of the Dragon playing in my palm.

I look down at the other Dragon resting calmly in Ivella's lap. "Is that a boy as well?" I ask.

She nods. "Vorzantu." Ivella touches the fragile neck of the

Dragon as he rests his head in her hand.

"What is Vorzantu?"

"The maiden name of my mother who raised my brother and I. Stelina Vorzantu."

I wince as Vaigon sinks a little tooth into my finger. "I believe someone is hungry. And I do not think they will cooperate well with fruit and vegetables." I say looking back at the abundance on the island counter.

"Oh," Ivella stands, lifting Vorzantu with her. There is a black leather chest next to where the wicker basket with the egg was sitting.

When she opens the chest a form of mist flows out.

"What is in there?"

"Dyena sent a chest of ice with meat for them to eat when they hatch."

"A chest of ice?"

The strong scent of blood forces outward and Vaigon clumsily flies from my hand and toward Ivella. He does not properly take flight and I just barely catch him as he falls to the floor.

"Here," Ivella laughs. She hands me a glass bowl concealed with a wooden lid full of fresh meat. Immediately, Vaigon goes insane.

I give him a little cube of meat and he devours it, urging me for more as his head nudges my hand. I smile.

"Do you think you will be fine alone here with them?"

Having two newly birthed Dragons could contain a bit of havoc in this house for her.

I see the mounds of textbooks on the table behind me, but I also see the stress in her eyes from Summer Solstice still wearing her down.

"They will be more than enough company to keep me occupied." She smiles looking down at them both as they feast from a bowl of raw meat.

"And if they become too much?"

"I will call on you if they do."

The longer I watch the two tiny children, I begin to wonder.

"How many people know of you receiving them as a gift?"

"No one. Only us."

"People would kill for ownership over a Dragon."

"And I will kill them if they touch my children." She simply declares.

Their mother.

"No one will harm them. They are not a property of ownership; they are little lives that grow to be even more intelligent than us. Why do you think it was Dyena's children that found her in the Terseian Mountains? Just as a mother or father raises a Dragon, they develop a strong form of protection over their parents. They have a grave hatred for those who are enemies, and they will attack without a thought. A mother or father does not need to tell a Dragon of who their enemies are, they know and easily protect. They will grow to know these lands and they will have a fundamental understanding of defending it and guarding the people who reside. Any outsider who comes along wishing to take my peoples land again will wish they never did. I will allow them to burn armies to their graves and feast on those who threaten."

Moving closer, I tug on her chin.

Those big, sad eyes stare upward.

"If anyone dares to take another thing from you, you will burn them with nothing less than vengeance."

Fear clouds her eyes. "What if I get lost in my rage?"

"Then that is when I come in . . . from now and on, you will no longer ask for approval, you will take whatever it is you want and only ask for forgiveness."

VAIGON CITADEL

When I walk into the palace, I ascend to my study where Roaner, Morano, Amias, and Phyv are waiting. Hua and Levora clearly hold agitation on their faces.

"What is wrong?"

"I believe you instilled enough fear into Lorsius." Amias says. "And I do not mean the fear of leaving, you instilled the fear of overpowering him."

"How do you mean?"

"He stripped you and may as well count us in on it," Hua says through her clenched teeth. "Any legal matters within Vaigon no longer allows our say or input. From now on, we are to sit about like trophies to him. Small fillers in his lineage that have no say."

"It may as well be as if we are just pretty royal faces roaming about the palace." Morano's anger coats the room.

Roaner stands. "Do not worry over this. He will be gone soon enough."

"*Now*, Laven." Morano says from the corner of the study. His hands are shaking as he stares at me. "Now is the time that you allow me to rip Lorsius to shreds."

I should be concerned. I should feel something about us being stripped of our say in all of the important matters our nation goes through, but I feel nothing of the situation.

Roaner continues to look at me. *"Trust me."* He says to only me.

And I do.

48
FALLING STONE

LAVEN HEPHAESTUS ARVENALDI, II

"Did Ivella speak of Ethivon with you?" Levora asks. "You should tell her that it is no longer an option to travel to them."

"We spoke of Ethivon on Summer Solstice. They are now a Court of New Quamfasi—they needed growth in numbers after the wars, so who better to ask than the two largest and strongest nations outside of us? With Nadrexi and Ethivon on their side, New Quamfasi has enough power to overtake us and rule again." Although, I doubt that is anywhere near what Vallehes and Penelope want. Vaigon may hold the graves of their ancestors, but the trauma of living on this land again is too strong for them to return.

I decide against telling them of Vaigon and Vorzantu. I will only tell them if Ivella wants me to. If she did not tell anyone other than me of them, I am sure it is not my place to tell my brothers.

The door of my study opens to my mother, and we look to her, wondering if she bears any news of Lorsius. Behind her, Nyt and Salem leisurely follow behind.

"I will tell you now that I know Lorsius's word is not final. He knows well enough that without all of you he will not be able to rule strongly." She begins.

"Did he say that?" Morano asks as Nyt sits next to him. Morano looks down at him and smiles. "You know, I like you. We are alike but in very different ways." He pokes Nyt's nose and his tail begins to wag from side to side.

My mother smiles and shakes her head. "No, he did not, but after our screaming match, I could tell he is worried."

"What of all the training we put in place for the Mandem's in our Courts? Did he just stop it and revoke that as well?" Amias questions.

"They need this training desperately, Apolla." Hua stresses. "He cannot revoke this."

"*That* I did not allow him to have a say in, we must continue to train and prepare for war. It is hard to ignore what is in the air, the attacks of rogues have minimized but there could be specific reasoning behind that."

I nod in agreement. "I was thinking of this the other night when I gathered how quiet it has been for the past month regarding the rogues. The more the rogues flood our nation, the more ways we find to kill them. If their numbers are too short they will never be capable of holding their end of the war to win. When we go to see Stravan I will be sure this is the first thing we speak of." There is no time to waste if they are gaining their numbers.

"May I?" Phyv asks raising a hand.

I nod.

"It could be perilous; however, you should still hold a meeting with the High Queens and High Kings of all realms. We should not risk one of the Leaders being the person who created this plague and hearing our resolutions, but it will be worth it to have a deeper alliance than within only our realm."

"We can have this meeting safely," Morano speaks. "I will go to the conference in the form of a servant to Laven and rummage through their minds."

My mother shows the approval of this on her face. "Will we tell them to invite their Circles as well? Would that not be too many minds to barricade through?"

"I will do fine," Morano assures her. "Invite everyone and their Circles, act quickly."

"Do you forget that we were just stripped of our say in matters as this?" Amias sarcastically speaks and my eyes cut at him.

"Lorsius does not need to know what we do; he will thank me for this later."

Amias turns to my mother. "Will we be given our say back?"

"Soon enough, I believe so. And I know you will be given tasks and duties again. He is not strong enough to do this on his own. He has no Right Hand to help him, I am sure word will be sent asking all of you to help him with something."

Roaner's eyebrow raises, agreeing with my mother.

"We will not dine with him." Amias declares. "At least I will not."

"None of us will. I will ask Mrs. Patro to bring our afternoon meal and supper here." I say relieving us all of a torturous dinner with Lorsius.

"Do what you wish." My mother says placing a hand on my cheek. "Lorsius always will, and so will you. It is only fair."

"Ma Apolla, how do you feel about murder?" Morano asks.

She only smiles at him and waves a finger before leaving the study.

"Was that a yes?" Morano questions.

Amias throws a bulky book at him from the shelf and Roaner stills the book midair. He walks toward it, grabbing it from the air, and places it back on the shelf.

"Throw a dagger, not a book. Have some respect." Roaner reprimands.

"Come," I say, walking to leave the study. "With Lorsius here or not, he will not hold us back from our training."

* * *

"No, absolutely not." Morano shakes his head stepping backward.

"I will not commit to hand combat with a Vaigosian Warrior as you."

"Oh, just train with him." Amias pushes him forward.

Just as I step onward, Morano shrinks inches below his height as shifts into a different body. *Ivella*, specifically.

"Hit me now," he dares.

I cringe at hearing her voice come from him and I step backward.

Roaner is bursting into laughter as he sits by the lake. Quickly, Morano shifts into Esme, shutting Roaner up immediately.

Instead of changing his voice to Esme's, Morano speaks to Roaner in his natural voice.

"Stop," Roaner says as Morano begins to walk toward him. "Stop it!" He shouts as soon as Morano begins to chase him with an eerie giggle.

Amias catches Morano by his arm as he runs by. "Stop giving them sights they will never forget." He cannot help but to laugh as he talks.

Morano shifts back to his natural form and stands next to Amias.

"Why not you two?" Morano looks between Roaner and I. "Hand to hand combat."

"No," Roaner smirks, remembering the first time we fought. "Someone will have my neck if I hurt the High Prince of Vaigon."

"That someone has yet to reveal feelings. So, that someone has no right to feel any kind of way if I am hurt. That is only if I allow you to hurt me."

"Oh, please." Roaner rolls his eyes. "You will curl into her arms at the slightest scratch and let her weep over your wounds any given day."

"Ha!" Morano laughs. "The both of you are hilarious. You both would curl into your woman's arms at the prick of a nail."

"I have no woman," Roaner bitterly responds.

"And neither do I."

"Esme is in denial that she is falling for Roaner," Amias observes. "And Ivella is oblivious."

"Has she shifted yet?" I ask Roaner.

"No, not yet."

"The contraception is still leaving her system then." Morano says. "When she does shift, she may have difficulties shifting back into her bodily form."

I look to Roaner. "And that is when you will come get me."

"Now," Amias looks between Roaner and I. "Back to training shall we?"

* * *

"I do not know how long I can do this." Morano says as he begins to trail around the room.

Supper has been brought to the study, but he has become so angsty that he can barely eat any of his food. His eyes cast upward, staring at the moon hanging over the framed glass ceiling.

"We will have work to tend to in no time. We all are rather aware that Lorsius struggles to hold his own."

Before Morano can respond, the doors of the study burst open.

A guard we know well is panting at the door in fright. "An ambush, Your Highness," he struggles to get out the words. "Every Court but Gordanta and Partalos are under attack. The numbers are grave, we do not stand a chance."

We rush to our feet and ascend from the study to the grounds.

He was not lying.

People are running, fleeing the area.

As I look around at the growing chaos, I recognize the Quamfasian leather armor immediately.

Every Court but Gordanta and Partalos are under attack. Gordanta and Partalos are the only lands not containing captives from Quamfasi.

They are here for their people.

"What do we do?" Amias asks while grabbing a stray sword from the ground.

Then, what I spoke of earlier with Ivella comes to mind.

"Ivella," I whisper as I frantically search around me.

'Whatever you do tonight, do not fight and have sanctuary.'

"We stop our people from retaliating." I shout over the small war erupting around us. "I will have no Quamfasian blood on the hands of my Warriors."

Amias lunges onward, repelling a blade from driving into a young Warrior of New Quamfasi and Amias looks back at me.

"Protect the young of New Quamfasi, at any length." I command. "Tell our own to stand down."

People have shifted into their Wolves; savagely fighting one another for the blood in their throat. The visceral sounds of snapping teeth sound off, then the loud cries and whimpers lead after.

The main problem here, who is who in Wolf form?

"Find me by the Servant Grounds, be sure no one enters the palace!" I say to Morano and Roaner before they ascend.

The moment I come to a halt near the grounds, I see Ivella defending the entrance.

Two Vaigosian guards charge towards her and the smile that forms on her face is one of excitement for death. She runs onward and they phase into their Wolves as they leap toward her and just as swift as the wind, she falls to her knees, gliding beneath the long span of the Wolves still lunging through the air.

Ivella rotates on her knees and smoothly stands, a dagger is held in her hand dripping in blood. The sharp edge is stabbed through an intestine ripped from the Wolf now lying limp on the ground.

The epee is thrown to the ground, and she draws her spear. The moment she lays a finger on the spear, it ignites in a glow of dark orange.

A force field is thrown at her, and her spear repels it.

The anger in her eyes flare, and that bit of magic I witnessed in her long ago returns.

The anger in her eyes flare, and that bit of magic I witnessed in her long ago returns.

"Weak men use their powers." As the words leave her mouth I watch the Wolf begin to cripple and yelp as he claws at the ground. His cries sound gargled the more he yelps.

Water is thrown up and his eyes begin to swell.

She is drowning him from the inside out.

Ivella walks over the dead bodies and back to the line of the Servant Grounds.

The grounds are solely under her protection as I see Quamfasian Warriors help their people flee from the area.

"Laven!" Morano shouts down the bond. *"Come to the gates of the palace!"*

At the fright in his voice, I ascend immediately through the chaos.

When I arrive, Esme is in battle with Lorsius.

"If he weakens her, I am stepping in." Morano warns.

"You do not know Esme enough," I say. "She will kill you for intervening, she is fighting for blood. Do not dare to step in."

Her foot collides strongly with his chest, throwing him multiple feet backwards. Lorsius grows frantic as he shouts for his sight to return. No mercy is held over him. Behind him, Penelope appears, catching him by a grip of his hair. Then, I recognize his clouded eyes filled with white. Esme walks toward him with a grin. Like prey, they circle him, taunting him in his most vulnerable state. They weaken him until he falls to the ground, searching for a weapon that is not there. Penelope draws her sword, and the beautiful, golden blade appears.

'By the drive of a Queen's golden blade.'

As the sword rises up, it drives down just as fast, splitting right through the top of his head. She yanks the sword down like a lever, ripping directly through his face and chest. His blood, intestines, all of it pours to the ground and so does he.

Penelope gazes at me as she rips her sword from his body and his corpse falls.

"You now have our alliance." She says with blood all over her face.

Her blade lifts into the sky, ricocheting a beam of gold into the night sky. The Quamfasian people go still.

THE SONG OF VERITY AND SERENITY

"Hathasna!" Penelope shouts.

And in the distance, I can hear the breaking of the border and chants echoing through the night—it moves through the wind in a song.

The boisterous sounds of stone falling echo far and wide.

"What are they saying?"

All around us the Quamfasian people begin to chant along with those far beyond the dwindling border.

"They are singing to the fall of the border . . . and getting their people back." Roaner stops, listening farther. "Raise your voices, sing across the border, wave our flag wherever we go. Let them hear us from the depths of nations unknown."

They chant and sing, some speak in happiness, some speak in sadness of those they lost here years ago. I can feel the passion pouring from their voices as their hands press to the ground where their loved ones died so long ago in the influence of Lorsius.

Ivella is in the distance, looking me over. She does not meet my eye before ascending.

* *Old Quamfasian: Hathasna   Translation: Victory*

49
DIRT OF THE DEAD

LAVEN HEPHAESTUS ARVENALDI, II

People are gathered around the corpse of Lorsius as he is set ablaze.

"You are a King . . ." Amias says in a quiet gasp.

He watches the burn of Lorsius as he stands next to me.

"I do not care to see this," Morano speaks as he stares down at the linen sack that holds Lorsius's decapitated body now set to fire. "Summon me when you need."

I cannot find a proper response to give him nor anyone.

I would think after the man who has done nothing but ruin my life leaves the earth for good, I would have a lot more to say than saying nothing at all.

Then it dawns on me, as High Prince I always knew where to begin when it came to my nation. But, with multiple servants gone, no workers, and our people in fright, I do not know where to begin to level out the growing chaos.

"What now?" I ask as my mother holds my arm.

"You become the High King that Vaigon needs and bring grace back to your grandfather's name. Lorsius is gone and now there is you. You will rule as you see fit."

Slowly she turns back to the burning corpse of Lorsius. I watch as her shoulders finally rest for the first time in years. We all have now found rest for the first time in years.

"I will direct the cremators where to go next." Axynth says. "This is a pivotal night for us all, process it however you must. Everyone else will be."

When I look into his eyes I see the blankness, the misunderstanding, and the loss of a Blood Bond brother, but I do not push for him to speak.

Even I cannot. Though, there is one person I must see to settle the thoughts raging in my mind that I cannot process alone.

I go back to the Servant Grounds in search of Ivella.

I have never heard it so quiet here. No one is left, every Quamfasian is gone and back in their home.

Roaner is coming toward me and nods for me to follow him. "We will handle what goes on here. Speak with him."

When I look to Vallehes he is still striding toward the palace, and I enhance my speed to catch up to him.

"You will be helping me?"

He glances in my direction. "My qualm was with Lorsius, not you."

"And?" I push for further clarification.

"And when my General's daughter swears me to a promise, I follow through." He comes to a stop and turns to me. We both stand head on. "There is a fine line I draw between my women and your men. You two will be nothing more than mere acquaintances and every visit between you two—from now and on—will be monitored. This, I give you no say in."

"Now just wait a moment," I hold back my retaliation as my mind spins from one too many things happening at once.

Lorsius has died just moments ago and now I am being told I must see Ivella under supervision as if I am some visceral threat.

I stop thinking too far and try to form a response before reacting.

"Do you not think that is intrusive? Monitored visits are overbearing to say the least."

"No," his head shakes. "I do not. With Ivella home we will do everything to watch over her and provide protection within her boundaries."

"She is safe with me."

"Not in my eyes. After the day she was taken, and how they took her, that made every man on Vaigon a threat, even you."

"I am no threat to her, Vallehes, I do not need question that she told you about me."

"She did, and my Queen and I will decide within time if I believe you are not a threat, then my Circle will dictate, and I will consult with my people."

He begins to walk away again, instead of protesting his words once more, I follow along.

Our people intermingling with one another I can see as a problem, but it is unfair to those who mean well about one another. There could be slews of mates that are found between my people and theirs now that the border is removed, and they are denying a right that we are given at birth—to be with the person we are fated for in whichever way we wish.

I lead the way to my study and Vallehes shadows my guide.

"Firstly," he begins as we step into my study. "Your people will demand my people back, especially your people who are lazy and most definitely those who used my men and women as sex slaves. Some will riot over the death of Lorsius because they will not want you to be King, but there will be those who do want you to reign and make change. You will not be able to satisfy everyone, and those who rebel against you will be fierce. I advise you put strong demands in place and make it known who rules this land. Your people will try to override you, weaken you, and try to turn this nation into what *they* want it to be."

"Conservatives." I speak.

Vallehes nods. "Precisely. Do not listen to people who are afraid of change, they hold nations back from prospering because their minds are so tightly shut off by fear and prejudice."

"Amias and I will put orders into place."

"You may put orders into place but what of the people who do not listen nor follow?"

I sit down in my chair as he sits across from me. "They will be given an ultimatum."

"Life or imprisonment." Vallehes questions.

"I have no want for prisoners, however, there is enough room for graves."

"I figured you would say death." Vallehes simpers.

"Why?"

"I am well aware of your infamous killing sprees from years ago . . . of your own men."

"I had my reasons." The only reason being the woman you are saying I must have supervised visits with.

Vallehes shrugs. "With the border being torn down, we continue to protect the line. No one shall pass without consent from myself, my wife or any higher up in my Circle. I am certain there are plenty of people on my land that wish for revenge, they want blood of any kind in return for those we lost to your uncle. So, I will watch over who enters your side as well."

"And not every court was ambushed?" I ask for certainty.

"No, we went to the lands that still held our people captive." He stands.

"I have already told you the most important things to do in the meantime. Control your people before they get reckless—anyone who dares to cross the line to abduct my people will be slain. They will receive no other option but death."

I nod in agreement, and he continues.

"As for the rogues, sightings of them on our lands will grow when they appear again. We have yet to cross paths with any, but my son, Vorian, he has killed plenty of them while in Gordanta. He put training in place of how to fight them off once he arrived home. So, when they do come to our side, we are prepared. I will come back in the morning . . ." he pauses. "I do not know what your relationship was like with your uncle, but I will apologize for your loss if you cared for him."

"No, Lorsius and I did not get along well. He has ruined me in plenty of ways," ways I am still working on with our palace Healer I must see more often; given the chaos, I have not been to a mental session in more than two months. "Shock is mostly all that I feel."

"Understandable. Sleep well after speaking with your Generals, you will necessitate it."

Standing from my bureau, I try to say something more. Add on how I also necessitate Ivella.

"I need her," I announce as he walks for the doors of the study. "And she needs me too. Not physically, but mentally and emotionally. You cannot deprive us of that."

Vallehes looks at me over his shoulder. "You will earn your right to be alone with her."

"And how is that?"

His dark eyes light up. "The Quamfasian Games."

He attempts to leave again.

"We have children," I blurt out.

Slowly he turns toward me. "That she did not tell me."

"I did not think she would."

"What are their names?"

"Vaigon and Vorzantu—twins." Twins with wings, claws, and sharp teeth.

His jaw tightens. "How old are they?"

"One."

One day old.

"Those children are your only exception to pass, nothing more or less."

"You do know that you and I are not that different from one another." There is a smile that appears on his face. "We both seek the same wants for our people. When my family were the Leaders of Gordanta all those years ago it was their vote you had to stay as High King. What do you think I did with the men that took Ivella?"

"I had a thought in my mind that you would reveal the answer to my wonders about your . . . massacres. I will believe that you protect Ivella when I see you defending her myself, not by the words of others."

Just as I think he is done, he stops once more to speak.

So this is who Vorian gets his never-ending talking from.

"Prepare your seamstresses." Vallehes warns. "You will need to be fitted to wear the Regalia of a High King—your Coronation is soon."

* * *

Ezra delivers the ashes of Lorsius to the Throne Room as Levora, Amias, Hua, and I speak of what Vallehes told me to arrange. Roaner and Morano are still off keeping the people under control.

Ezra stands there longer than I intended. He wants to say something more, but instead, he only leaves.

We stare at the urn filled with his ashes. The ashes rest in an urn of the purest gold I have ever seen.

"I would like to be left alone."

I do not know if any of them heard me until they begin to walk away.

"Laven?" Hua calls from the doors of the Throne Room.

"I am fine, Hua."

Amias whispers to her before she is taken away with him.

As the doors close and I hear their footsteps fade farther and farther away, precipitously, all of the immersed rage I have hidden for years pushes forward.

I grab the urn from the pristine box it is sitting in and soar it to the floor.

The gold shatters into pieces and dents the floor at its collision.

As I stare at his ashes scattered across the floor, there is nothing else I can do but scream at them in the way I have wanted to all these years.

I need to belittle him as he belittled me. Blame him for the taking of Levora as he blamed me. Admit that I know the reason those guards were able to torture me so was because he allowed it. I let every tear fall onto his ashes, every tear he once told me to hold back to make me more of a man.

The unrelenting screaming does not ease. I let it continue until I feel my chest will give and my voice will die with him.

I can feel the bond trying to strengthen. They attempt to speak to me, but I shut them out.

This I must do alone.

"Laven!"

I stare at the doors of the Throne Room in fear and the bellowing of my name grows louder.

I try to remember how to shield a door from opening, yet my powers are faulty, my mind is too far gone to function even a slight bit of my powers.

By the struggling behind the doors, I believe I was able to summon a sliver of my strength.

It is not enough—the doors burst open and I cry harder.

Ivella searches the room before seeing me. She glances down at the broken urn, the ashes, and me.

The closer she steps, the quicker I realize I am sitting on the floor.

She kneels in front of me still dressed in her leather armor.

Her eyes bore into my own and a gentle smile appears on her face as she scoots closer.

My lips tremble as I try to speak and she shakes her head, stopping me from attempting to utter a word.

Then all there is, is guilt. The guilt of having to let someone ignore everything they are going through to cater to me.

"I am a burden to you," I say through the sobs shattering my words.

She is not offended by what I say. If anything, she seems hurt. "When have I ever said that?"

"You have not . . . you manage enough of your own suffering to have to accommodate my own with it."

Again, her head shakes, and that soft smile does not leave. "You are not burdening me. You would only be voicing your griefs and we would sort through them."

Say it you coward. Tell her . . .

Ivella looks at the floor and the mess of Lorsius around us.

Grabbing my hands, she pulls me to stand with her, and I do.

She stares up at me and dusts me free from the dirt of death and places a hand on my cheek. "You do not always have to be the hero."

"If not me, then who?"

Her hands tighten on my face. "You know who."

I grip on to her wrists as her hold is unrelenting and Levora appears at the door.

"Put him to bed, please." Ivella says and Levora nods.

Levora replaces Ivella's hands with hers and leads me away. When I look over my shoulder I see the hue of orange fading as she has ascended.

50
CRYSTAL CLEANSE

LAVEN HEPHAESTUS ARVENALDI, II

MY ACCESSION COUNCIL WAS held first thing in the morning. I had to make my formal proclamation to claim the Throne wholly as my own.

The crown was rightfully handed over to me in the end, and I did not wish to place it upon my head just yet. Morano said he wants to cleanse the crystals in the crown before I am to wear it. Yet, I did not want to wear it out of spite of Lorsius. I am not prepared to wear anything that he once wore as his own.

Quickly after my Accession Council, I was asked when I would be arranging my Coronation Day, who is to be High Queen, and when I will begin my lineage. I wanted to be a prick and schedule the Coronation for tomorrow, only for some reason, I still try to have some form of respect for Lorsius and hold the celebrations off until the people have calmed down. It is customary to wait a prolonged time to have your coronation after the death of a royal. This is why we have the Accession Council, still claiming the Throne, but without celebration. In the past, Coronations were seen as a vile event. It is great to celebrate a new royal taking the Throne, but not without connecting the celebration to why there is a new royal overtaking.

I stand before the people of our land, most of them conservatives demanding back what once was theirs. And by theirs, they mean ownership over the men and women they claimed as their own by illegitimately writing agreements over the Quamfasian people.

There are so many shouting voices that I have stopped trying to keep up with what the people are saying. The mostly quiet people are the guards and Warriors I have disguised as conservatives to take charge of anyone who attempts to begin an uprising.

When I look to my mother who stands off to the side with Axynth, she seems declined to want to acknowledge anyone.

She has not spoken much, if at all.

I cannot tell if she is saddened by the death of Lorsius or stunned by his absence.

"My word is final!" I shout over the people standing below the balcony of the Throne Room—they all fall quiet to listen. "There will be no more use of servants from Quamfasi in any form, and you will not cross the line to find the men and women you criminally claimed. The leaders of New Quamfasi and I have made a treaty this morning stating exactly what I am saying, and if that treaty is broken, it is their decision of what to do with you next."

"Leaving us to our death by another nation?" Someone shouts angrily, as I look, it is the father of the Yeshti family.

"No one is leaving you to your death. This is your warning that if you dare to cross, that is what waits for you. It would be your own inanity that leads you to your death."

"Lorsius would not allow this!"

"We never wanted you as our High King!"

They all shout the same displeasure but each person speaking their hatred for me and my ways of running a land in different words.

"And we never wanted you weaklings as our people, yet here we are!" Hua hollers in my defense.

"If you choose to go against the reforms, that is all your own doing. The new laws are being sent out to you currently, when you arrive at your home the letters will be awaiting you. Do not forget that your actions will always have consequences."

I turn to Hua. "Have them all sent home. I will not allow them to bombard the palace like this all day, anyone who disobeys will serve time in Montgem Penitentiary."

There is a smile on her face as I leave the balcony and she ascends down to the people with the guards.

Roaner appears at my side as I walk down the hall to the new study we all share as our own. We each individually have our own study, but now we have the opportunity to claim Lorsius's old study as ours. And it is now identified as Marl Study, the combination of all our initials together, another place solely meant for us and our family.

"I am going to have Ezra send word to Vallehes and Penelope, we need to follow through with the conference between all realms." He informs us as we sit down in the study with Morano and Amias. "We may not have had sightings of the rogues in some time, but this does not mean to fall back, this means to stand firmer."

It is eerie how low the rogues have been lying, it is worrisome, but there is much to do in their absence.

"We just finished rescheduling the trials for the people who committed treason under Lorsius's rule." Amias says as he and Morano arrange the papers splayed across the large table.

"Thank you," I say.

They look at me confused.

"For trying to reach me through the bond last night."

All three of them continue to stare at me blankly.

"We did not try to reach you last night . . . we knew you needed that time alone." Morano clarifies.

"It may have been your mother," Amias announces. "She and my father were looking for you when we were walking to the West Wing of the palace."

I gaze at Roaner—who is already looking at me.

"Does she know?"

"Not that I am aware of."

Ezra enters the study as I make the attempt to ask another question.

"This is for the King and Queen of New Quamfasi, it is urgent so deliver it as quickly as possible. It contains information on the rogues as well as a conference that must be arranged between us and them."

Ezra nods before taking the letter and ascending from the study.

"My Gods, Morano. Close your mouth." Amias teases.

"He is just so painfully beautiful." Morano says within ascension as he and Amias leave.

Roaner sits across from me at the large wooden table intricately crafted with glass throughout. This very table belonged in my father's old study that I do not visit often, in fact, none of us visit it. That is the one room in this palace that we do not touch given its sacredness.

"When you said to trust you, did that mean what I thought it meant?"

Roaner leans back in his chair, nibbling on his lip. "What did you think it meant?"

"I think it meant you arranged his death."

"Drastic times call for drastic measures."

"The bargain I signed stated I could speak of this with no one other than the people involved."

"And who arranged this bargain?"

"Vallehes Valendexi."

"We did not only plan this solely for the death of Lorsius," he leans closer. "But because we need a fit High King, and Lorsius could never have been that. I will let you see the day I signed the papers." And he projects the vision from that day to me.

After the execution of High King Lorsius Ouranos Arvenaldi, the only of his name, High Prince and Heir, Laven Hephaestus Arvenaldi, the second of his name will commence The Throne.' I read aloud from the bargain before me. I look up at Vallehes who stares down at the paper between us. 'You want Laven to take The Throne? You do not wish for it back?'

'Tell me why I would want it back?' He asks with nothing but pure curiosity.

412

'Tell me why you want Laven to have it.' I reply with the same tone.

'Because I need a High King who will prosper and one I can work with. My son, Vorian, pays close attention to our land and Vaigon's. He can feel a difference in the air ever since the intrusion of the rogues. Given his ability of Counterintuition, I take heed of his every word, that being said, I need a fit High King to rule next to in war. Prophecy says Laven is to be the strongest High King Vaigon and many other nations will know and I need him sitting on that damn Throne sooner rather than later.'

I furrow my eyebrows. *'Prophecy said by whom?'*

'Agivath,' Vallehes crosses his arms. *'She tells no lies and only truth and can read every future brought to her.'*

'How did you even make it on to Vaigon to speak with her?'

'I have my ways.'

'And you were explicit in the way you asked her these questions? You are aware that a question can easily be asked erroneously and answered erroneously. Without specifics Agivath will answer incorrectly.'

Vallehes takes offense to my questioning. *'I believe I know how to speak with Agivath given how long she and I have known one another. So will you fulfill prophecy, or will you deny it?'*

Before I say another word, I am signing my name.

"You have your doubts about yourself ruling and I understand them." Roaner calmly speaks as I process. "Now you know. You will reign as King of Kings so by prophecy, and no one can take that from you. You will forever be the best ruler Vaigon has ever had."

"I would only be the second ruler. There could be many after me."

Roaner smiles. "And those rulers will be your daughters and sons. But you," he points. "You and Ivella are the two that will begin a lineage that is indestructible. You have been carved for this, your failure is not in vision because it does not exist. *Rule*, Laven, and rule how you believe it best."

* * *

When I find my mother, she is sitting in the courtyard staring up at the greenery encasing the statues around us. A beautiful scarf is wrapped around her as she rests.

"I used to come here at night, especially on occasions when Lorsius and I would have arguments. He hated that you were so attached to me," she forces out a laugh. "He thought that I made you soft—weak, even. When we were young he would tell me and your father he always coveted a son that was just like him. Then that son never came, and there you were."

I stand next to her, and she looks up to me while rubbing my arm.

"I think there was something much deeper. All my life I have known him as a hateful person."

My mother nods. "Only deep searching will give us those answers."

"What made him tolerate you more than others?"

"I nearly killed him when we lost your father, and he realized he had no choice but to have a form of respect for me or I would execute him myself."

She should have, yet that would have resulted in her hanging.

"Do you need anything?" I kneel beside to her.

She places a hand upon my cheek. "All I need is for you to be the High King Lorsius could never be and *always* be that King no matter what these people say . . . promise me." A single tear falls down her skin.

"I promise."

Morano calls out my name and there is a letter he is holding in his hands. "Vallehes and Penelope have responded. They would rather not wait to discuss arranging a meeting with all of the Realms, they have requested our two nations meet today."

Ma stands from her chair, showing no interest in the letter. She moves for the doors of the palace before I focus on Morano.

"Tell Ezra it is final. Have him send word that we meet at sunset."

PART IV
VERITY

51
TWO NATIONS

LAVEN HEPHAESTUS ARVENALDI, II

Vallehes and Penelope requested to hold the meeting on our land, it is usual for conferences such as these to be held in the Throne Room. But, this Throne Room has a past that I did not believe they wished to relive, so I made sure our meeting would take place in the dining courtyard outside.

Each person within my Circle is here. Amias, Hua, Roaner, Morano, Levora, and even Phyv. There has been no need for me to watch over Phyv like I have thought. He is quiet, keeps to himself, helps my sister train, and goes about his day. To busy him outside of that, I chose to give him tasks within our Circle. This will also call for a closer eye on him just in case he is someone we are not expecting as Stravan has explained.

My mother chose not to attend, I also can read in her posture that she wishes to no longer have anything to do with the Throne or royalty itself.

Axynth has chosen to stay by my mother, so every decision that happens today is all on myself, Levora, Hua, and my brothers. Though, no irrational decisions should be made today. In the past we used to always need the approval of someone else to follow through with a decision that we make, now there is no one to tell us what we may or may not do.

Ezra is leading toward us—escorting Vallehes, Penelope, and their Circle to the courtyard. When they reach where we stand, there is a stiff greeting between us all.

As Penelope introduces their Circle I already recognize four people among them. Fucking Zevyk, the dipshit Lord of Nadrexi. Esme the Queen's Right Hand—which I had no idea of. Naius, Ivella's father, and now again a General of New Quamfasi. Next, the woman clinging to his side with red hair that is hard to ignore.

She overlooks me as I do her.

Turning down another path, I stop.

I tilt my head to a scent that is not of the Fae. Then, I narrow in on a woman far out. She is covered in burgundy gear; one arm is clothed while the other is left free. Her red hair is in a tight braid, and a spear is concealed against her back from the left shoulder to her right hip.

I can see the brightness of her grey eyes as she smiles. But it is no welcoming smile.

I let go a deep growl as she steps forward. Digging my rear into the ground, I hold my head downward and release a force field that rattles, shaking the trees and earth beneath us. Her spear is drawn swiftly; it ignites in a glow of blue as she holds horizontally. The force field bounces off of her spear, and it retreats; soaring back to me.

Running forward, I bear my head down, shattering through it.

She is who Hua was chasing down when she and Vorian were trapped under Roaner's shield after the passing of the Dragons. They both had to of been looking for Ivella, Naius, and their other family members.

Vaughn and Nina, the Duke and Duchess of Ethivon are the only two I have not met until now. In the past, Ethivon was the first nation of our Realm to branch off on their own. They had a rather weak nation and it took time for them to reform after having no worth on their land, now, they are prospering and a Court of New Quamfasi.

We all walk around introducing ourselves to each other, especially Phyv and Levora who have not met any of the people from their Court before.

Standing face to face with Naius is intimidating. No matter how young he may look, he exudes the strength of hundreds of years of intelligence and vigor.

I can see that he is who Ivella gets her sharp features from.

The redheaded woman outstretches a hand to me as everyone moves to seat themselves at the table. Her eyes are cuttingly grey, and her hair is pin straight.

"Nice to finally meet you," she says in a soft tone.

"Other than when we were trying to kill one another?" I jokingly ask.

"Your force field dented my spear."

Naius looks in her direction with tapered eyes and she smiles. He must not know she was roaming the lands that day.

"If I wanted to kill you, I would have, King Laven. I am Stelina Vorzantu."

This is whom she named Vorzantu after.

"You are Ivella's mother." I smile.

Well, the mother who raised her.

"I am in fact." She does not deny the title nor does she try to change it, Ivella is her daughter, no alterations must be said.

"It is rather apparent that you failed to tell me this detail of you two battling." Naius nudges Stelina closer to his side and she giggles. "I would have liked to know you were near me when I thought I would never see you again."

"Oh, my love. There is still more for you to know, but you are home now." Ever so gently, she rests a hand over his chest and he places a lithe kiss to her forehead.

After years of being apart, there will be much for them to know of one another again.

They both walk away and take to a seat, and I do as well.

"We discussed the advantages and disadvantages of going to every Realm for aid in the war—that is if it happens." Penelope announces after we all are seated. "And we collectively decided it would be best to arrange the conference soon."

"You believe the war may not happen?" Hua asks, meeting Penelope's eye.

"I have my doubts, although, Vorian has expressed his thoughts. He truly feels it is upon us, he cannot tell when, but he can feel it nearing."

"When would you advise we send out word to the other Realms?" I ask. "We have spoken with one another about Provas being our meeting ground. It is centered directly between all the Realms."

Penelope looks toward Vaughn and Nina.

"We would not send a request for a meeting until both of our nations are prepared for the possibility of war beginning *that day*." Nina pauses and a flash of disgust runs across her face. "Your people need training in strength and agility, we must discover the strongest and the weakest. Meeting with all realms runs the risk of too many secrets being revealed if one of them is causing this."

"Laven has put courses into place. We have nearly five hundred new enlistees and they all will run the course." Amias informs Nina. "You would know the course well given it has obstacles similar to that of the Quamfasian Games."

"It is the method our fathers used to train us," I add. "And we use it now to establish who is capable of being a Frontline Warrior."

"If you would like for them to have more extensive training we can arrange chaperones to guide your people to where we now hold The Games." Stelina offers.

"Stelina and Ivella are the two who judge The Games and discover who is strong enough to lead in war. Ivella pursued The Games at a young age and won multitudes of times." Penelope gloats with a smile.

"Oh, please." Esme rolls her eyes. "She cheats, she pushed me off the pillars during The Pillar Run."

I see Roaner smirk from the corner of my eye.

Stelina grins. "You were in her way, and any matters can be taken to win, Esme."

Ah, so that is why Esme trained her the way she did in Gordanta. She was using that moment to get back at Ivella.

"Where is Ivella?" I ask.

Vallehes looks directly at me. "Tending to a Game with Ira and Vorian. Everything that will happen now I will inform her of later this evening."

I choose not to fight him on why she is actually not here. Then, I wonder if he knows of Roaner and Esme's little moments together that would make him worry more about his Right Hand than my small moments with Ivella.

"We suggest that you and your Circle tour The Games within the dome." Nina says. "You will be allowed to tour the competitions, then train to how you believe you will succeed in the obstacles."

I nod and hold my hand up. "Only my Circle, our strongest Warriors, and guards will participate in this. We do not have enough time to train all the people within our nation before traveling to Provas to meet every Realm. We could be wasting our time."

Vallehes shrugs, contemplating it. "I understand, but you will still need to have as many people as possible to go through The Games. It is the best way to challenge your people to be better."

"Then we will train the weakest here on our obstacles until we see them fit to compete in The Quamfasian Games." I declare.

"And what if one of us fail?" Roaner motions between us.

"Then you are weaker than we thought." Zevyk remarks.

Esme whips her head in his direction. "Coming from the man who failed his first time competing."

Zevyk replies with nothing.

"You are Zevyk Hatsiverso." Levora speaks.

He nods at my sister.

"You also did not win your second game."

Roaner chuckles and Esme glances between him and Levora before looking away. Roaner has not looked at Esme once.

Levora cannot keep her eyes from glancing back and forth

between Roaner and Esme who sit across from each other by accident because chairs were quickly filled.

"Could I request to have Esme train some of my people?"

Penelope grins. "Esme has a wedding to plan so she will be busy for some time, but I can assure you that you will have great trainers."

And finally, Roaner is looking at her.

Esme's head is turned to Penelope and she smiles weakly. "It will be quite the celebration."

Roaner attempts to speak, but Vallehes does first. "We will give sixty days for everyone to prepare and participate in The Games. At the end of those sixty days is when we will send word to the outside realms to arrange a conference. If we are to ally with not only you, but also the people of Vaigon; there will be plenty of give and take on both ends. Have your nation begin to train, and send your strongest to tour the dome before it is time for them to compete."

* * *

It seems there will be plenty of visits to Provas within a short period of time. There is the conference Stravan is still holding for us to attend for the celebration of Dyena and to discover who he knows that is spreading this disease. Then, we will return within a short period of sixty days to meet with all realms.

"I have the trials to attend to for the treason committed, if you need me, call and I will come back."

I thank Morano before he leaves, and I stand from the table in the courtyard.

When I reach the entrance of the palace doors, I hear a faint shriek from afar. The longer I stand here listening, the louder it grows.

It is hard to ignore the young Dragon messily flying towards me in fright.

Vaigon . . .

"How in the hell did you get all the way here?" I curse under my breath as he continues to loudly shriek.

Just within a short period of two days he is twice the size he was, still rather small, too small to be flying such a long distance away from his mother.

He flaps his growing wings, nearing closer to my hand that is outstretched. The moment the tips of my fingers land on his head, a vision soars from his mind to my own.

His thoughts are flooded with images of Ivella nearly drowning in her bathing tub, she is thrashing, struggling to recede from the tub. Something . . . someone is holding her down.

Before I can see anymore, I grab Vaigon and ascend directly to her father's home in Nadrexi.

NADREXI — SOUTHERN COURT OF QUAMEASI

I fall to the ground as I clumsily end my ascension in front of the bathing tub.

Vorzantu struggles on the edge of the tub as he holds her head above the water with his neck.

When I look closer, I see them.

Large wings that weigh her down and sink her into the water. Without shifting properly and naturally, her body's strength is not where it should be to hold a pair of wings this size. From a child the Fae are taught to hold their wings, Ivella has never in her life had wings.

My clothing soaks and clings to my skin as I scramble into the water.

"Laven," Ivella quietly cries as she looks up at me.

Curling her into my arms, I lift her from the water and Vorzantu goes flying. Water flicks from his wings and onto us as he soars away, but not too far.

"I cannot sit up with them, they—"

Quietly, I shush her before she can overwhelm herself.

"Do not worry too much, it may interfere with your ability to make them go away." Her cheeks are flushed as she shivers.

Her hands tightly grip my topcoat to find warmth, and to find relief from the wings weighing her down. The wings are heavier than her if she cannot hold herself above water.

"I took it off," she says as tears trail down her skin. "The ring you gave me."

When I look down at her hand, I realize she did.

"Why did you take it off?"

"To bathe . . . but I was angry about something, and then this happened." She can only motion with her eyes to the beautiful white and beige feathers.

The ring truly does act like a shield of protection to control her mind from spiraling about.

"Where is it?" I ask.

"On the ledge of the bathing tub."

I lay her on her back across the bed, quickly pulling the large duvet over her for some form of warmth after being trapped in water for who knows how long.

After retrieving the ring, I put it back on her finger.

"How do I make them go away?" Ivella peers up to me as I lean against the poster of the bed.

"It must be similar to a form of shifting. All Fae can summon their wings just as we summon our Wolf when we must shift."

As I graze a finger over a white feather she gasps and swats at me. "I can feel that! Do not touch my wings!" Her face heats in red and I force myself not to laugh.

Interesting . . .

Sitting next to her, I reach out my hand and she takes it. Her long nails dig into my skin as she grasps onto me.

"I will help you sit up, you will want to be standing to do this."

She slowly nods as I swoop in to assist her back—her forearm bears down onto my own for support as I hold her up against my chest.

"Are they not too heavy?" She asks.

Although, I believe she is only looking for validation that she is not weak.

"Not to me. The only reason they are weighing you down is

because you have yet to shift into your wolf and develop the strength our kind bear."

"Would I not bear the strength of a Fae to hold them?"

"Technically, you should. This does not mean you do not, I have heard plenty of stories from others who have wings that they appear in the most inopportune times and because it caught them off guard it is difficult to manage them. Do you remember what I taught you about shifting?"

She nods.

"It is exactly the same for Fae, but you only need to learn control from the tip of your spine, directly downward to your feet. Everything from the spine and down you must control."

"Not only my back?"

"No. When you can manage your wings—in due time—you will realize that every bit of your strength for supporting these will come from spine support, core support, and a solid stance on the ground."

I may have done quite a bit of research of my own for this exact moment.

I did not know I would be the person to help her through this, but I learned enough to prepare for the *just by chance* moment.

"How do you know so much? Did Stravan teach you this?"

I smile and shake my head. "Stravan and I are not as close as you may think. I have a library, and I put it to use."

"As you should."

I lowly laugh. "Close your eyes, try to focus as much as your mind allows it. Feel every strain in each muscle that supports the wings. Breathe through it until you feel weightless, even with the heaviness of the wings molding you to the ground."

Her breathing pattern grows erratic as I let her stand completely on her feet; only supporting her by the press of our forearms.

Vaigon and Vorzantu linger closely by, watching her every move. They look from me, to Ivella, and back to me.

I do not say a word as her eyes are shut, focusing on making the wings form back into her body.

Her knees buckle and she falls to the floor. I let her.

I can see those tears welling again as her hands press into the floor to support her.

I kneel in front of her, and she is quietly weeping at the pain the wings cause. "Look at me."

She shakes her head and continues to watch the tears falling from her eyes and onto the wooden floor.

I grab her face and her swollen eyes look into mine.

"You can do this, Ivella."

"There is too much faith you have in me." She weeps.

One of us must be the stronger one here; I will not force her to be that one.

Be strong and she will be too.

"If I have too much faith in you, you have too much faith in me. Here, right now, there is no such thing. You will stand because you can, and you will hold your wings as the mightiest do."

Slowly, she nods.

"*Stand*, Ivella."

Her round chin quivers before she nods again and forces to her feet with quiet grunts.

Her toes begin to dig into the floor.

"Easy, do not focus too much on one singular body part." It could harm her more than help her to put so much stress into just one body part.

She quietly hums in response.

"Square your shoulders . . . breathe into every muscle . . ."

The wings shudder and she lowly gasps.

"It is all right," I laugh. "I will not let you go soaring into the roof."

"Very funny." Her voice is almost inaudible. "You let me fall." She says in disbelief.

I laugh again, this time harder. "You needed to."

"Are you saying I need to be humbled?"

"Never."

"Liar."

She stops speaking to flow back into her focus that helped the wings move.

This is good that she is finding enough concentration to even move the wings. By the time she shifts into her Wolf she will already have full control over the wings, as well as an understanding to control shifting back into her human form after her Wolf arrives.

Her hands grip my forearms even tighter, and the Blue Tigers Eye begins to glow. I smile as I look down at her and the wings begin to slowly recede. The light cracking of bones move into place to accommodate the beauty of her wings.

I grab her robe that lies on the corner of her bed to cover her now that the wings have fully receded.

"I do not want anyone to know." She declares, peering upward to me with wary eyes as I tie the robe in a knot—securing the satin fabric around her.

"I did not plan on telling anyone." It will be hard for her to hide these new cute ears.

"No," she shakes her head. "I know you will not tell anyone, but . . . I do not know. I feel like I said that to say it to myself."

There are questions I want to ask, yet I am afraid to. I do not want her to push me away so quickly with no level ground of how much we both share with one another. Although, it always seems I know more about her than she knows about me.

Now.

Now is the time I speak because I crave to.

I begin lightly. "Technically, I am not supposed to be here. And if we are caught I do think Vallehes will want my neck for it."

"Vallehes is afraid. No matter how often I tell him we are fine it is as if it pushes him deeper into worry."

Rightfully so it seems.

"I want to tell you about my sister, the real story about—"

Ivella's head quickly shifts as knocking on the door pulls her from me.

She glances back up to me and I nod, quickly catching the slight hint of trepidation in her eyes . . . Zevyk.

She tries to speak, but it is already too late as I ascend from the home and back to mine.

I cannot risk being seen and I do not wish to see nor hear of their bond together as I am finally capable of telling her what she wants to know. What she should know.

* * *

When I return I change out of my soaking wet clothing and lead to the dining room where Roaner is beginning our meeting with Carmen and Lorena. While we are away in Provas for the conference and celebration—or lack thereof—they both will be taking care of the mainland while we are gone.

Carmen looks back at me with a smirk. "My King, I grovel at your feet." He sarcastically says as he bows before me.

Lorena rolls her eyes as she embraces me. "We arrived early, but I figured it would be fine so we can have a full discussion of everything you all have been rearranging in the citadel." Since Lorsius's death.

"Yes, it is better you arrived earlier than later. Thank you for being considerate of that."

"Where were you?" Carmen asks.

Roaner is staring at me as well—brother or not. I will not be disclosing where I just was nor what I was doing.

"I was with a friend."

Lorena's eyes roll again. "Another one of your chambermaids?"

I laugh. "I do not have chambermaids, thank you. We currently have no maids nor servants. We are in the process of hiring people to become workers within the palace."

"The ambush," Carmen nods. "Were any of you harmed?"

"No, no one was harmed unless they attacked Quamfasi first. There are very few of our people who died. We tried warning them to stand down, and they did not listen." I shrug.

"Come," Lorena motions toward the dinner table. "Let us eat before we discuss anything. I will not be able to bear political talk unless I am on a full stomach."

WINGS OF SUMMER

LAVEN HEPHAESTUS ARVENALDI, II

MY MOTHER LOOKS TOWARD me with soft eyes. "No, I will stay here." She says after I ask once more if she will be going with us to Provas.

She may have not been formally invited to Provas, but I was told in the letter I could bring anyone along with me, and because she is my mother, I will still ask out of respect.

"Do you wish to have anything to do with the royal line any longer?"

"I never wanted to be a royal at all. I led a simple life before your father, and I will continue to live a simple life now that you are where you should be."

Axynth is closely near her as she declares her want to discard the royal line from her life completely.

Axynth has not spoken to anyone much since the death of Lorsius, outside of my mother he has only spoken to Amias. No matter how horribly Lorsius treated Axynth, I am aware that there is something to be felt on losing someone you are bonded with by the Blood Bond Ritual. My father and Axynth always tried to lead Lorsius away from the path he was going down, I can only see the guilt of failure in him as he stands before me. I recognize that guilt of failing a sibling well.

"This is up to you, ma. I will not try to convince you otherwise."

Her history as a royal has never been a history she is honored to hold, nor is it the history she wishes to live on with. There were plenty of times my mother had to do what she did not want to . . . and there were also plenty of times she could not do what she wished to. This was never the woman I knew as a child. My mother was a carefree woman who lived simply in the world of commoners and relished in her life as one. Quick with wit and sharp tongued, that is not who I know now. This is not the woman my father fell in love with. As I ponder on who she was then, I see that she is who I get my want for freedom from. Most importantly, my freedom from the crown to lead a life of leisure.

"I still want you to feel comfortable coming to me for help." Her hands clutch onto mine as she speaks to me. "Just because I no longer want to be in the line of royalty, does not mean I do not want you to come to me for aid in decisions."

Smiling, I nod. "I will only come to you when needed or for urgency. I do not want to pester you too often . . . where will you stay?"

"My father's old home," Axynth announces. "And wherever else she wishes to go."

My mother looks at the clock on the wall. "Oh, it is nearly time. Go find your brothers and sisters so you all arrive on Provas in a timely manner. Is the gentleman Levora brought home going with you as well? He is a nice young man."

"He is. I will see you both when we return." I nod to them before ascending from my mother's old study and to the gates of the palace where everyone waits.

Phyv and Levora stand closely together next to Amias, Roaner, and Morano.

"Just how long are we to stay in Provas?" Morano asks with an arched eyebrow as he pets Nyt's head.

Out of us all, Morano would stay home and never leave if he did not have to, in fact, he hates traveling but does so because he must. And, although he is not his dog, I am certain Morano would request that Nyt stay with him as the two of them seem to be a match made in heaven.

"As long as it takes for Stravan to tell us who is trying to conquer our land and people with a rabid mutation."

"How does it feel to be visiting home, Phyv?" Morano asks to make conversation with the awkwardly quiet man.

Phyv shrugs. "Provas was never truly a home when I was there, it is just a nation I was born into." He picks up Salem who stretches upward along his leg to be lifted.

"Well," Levora begins. "We will make the best of it."

"Why is that?" Roaner questions.

"I was born an orphan."

"But you have a family now," Levora takes his hand and then holds the other out to me.

Her fingers curl into mine as my brothers place their hands on my shoulders and I ascend us to the Realm of the Fae.

PROVAS CITADEL – REALM OF THE FAE

The gates to enter the main palace are large and intricately engraved white gold. If I look closely enough I can see the wings and vines encompassed with leaves, and small flowers.

We formally wait in our specific order for the guards to return from telling Stravan and Dyena of our arrival.

When I turn, I see Ivella approaching with a man I have never met nor seen before.

He is tall, extremely muscular, and their faces favor one another. His skin tone is just a shade darker than hers, and his eyes are exactly the same green.

This must be her little brother, Ira . . . well, not so little anymore.

Vaigon and Vorzantu come rushing toward me with low yelps and screeches.

Amias flinches and shouts as Vorzantu's wing nearly touches him and he runs to be closer to Morano who stands the farthest away.

"Amias," Morano consoles him. "They are small Dragons, they are not going to hurt you."

"Say that to the Water Dragon that tried to swallow me whole when I was out at sea."

Vaigon and Vorzantu settle upon my shoulders as Ivella approaches and Ira cautiously looks between us.

My brothers are already trying to ask questions through the bond, and I block them out.

Amias looks warily at the Dragons as they stare him down.

"They can sense your fear," I laugh.

"And just exactly why do they take to you so well? Not to mention the strong resemblance between their scales and eyes to your hair and eyes."

I do not answer them as Ivella reaches, touching the chin of Vorzantu with little caresses.

"They take to him because they chose him as their father." Stravan announces from the opposite side of the gate that is now opening for us.

"Dragons yield the appearance of the male or female they resonate with while in the egg. And that male seems to be Laven, as for Ivella," he smiles. "They just love their mother. It only makes sense that they chose to cling to you, Laven. You were named after the Greek God of Fire—it is only natural that this happened . . . unless there is other reasoning behind them choosing you."

I narrow my eyes at him, and he smiles.

"Ivella," Dyena grins, rushing toward her. "You look different," she says as she lovingly tucks her hair behind her ears.

The tiny, sharp point above her ear lobes are revealed. The peaks of her ears are not as sharp as those of the Fae, but it is noticeable now that her hair is not covering her ears.

Dyena quietly gasps, and pulls her hair back down, quickly comprehending that no one knows of her developing Fae appearances.

Wait until they find out about her wings.

When I glance at Ira, he is still standing there stone faced without a sliver of emotion to be seen. He must know as well.

Stravan and Dyena exchange a wary glance and he gives Ivella a slight nod. His eyes meet mine before glancing away. A fair warning that he will want to speak with us alone.

"What was that?" Morano asks after witnessing the small exchange between Stravan and I.

"It may have to do with Ivella."

"And her Fae ears?" Amias chimes in. *"I knew she would pop a wing."*

Once again, I block them out.

"Phyv and Levora, correct?" Dyena warmly greets as she looks between the two standing next to each other.

"Yes," they say in unison.

Levora shakes her hand but Phyv keeps to himself after he bows before her.

"Good to see all of you given our last interaction." Stravan tries to lightly joke.

"Yes," Morano sarcastically responds. "How funny of you."

"We will dine in Du Porva Plaza." Stravan chuckles as he speaks to us all. "There is a celebration being held in the Plaza this afternoon, but first we will show you all to your chambers, then attend."

"What of our meeting?" Morano asks.

Stravan smiles, knowing he would ask that. "That will be held tomorrow. I would like for you all to enjoy the beauty of Provas before we talk politics and war."

This man is completely different from the man I knew weeks ago.

He is . . . softer?

There is a quiet laugh that bursts from Amias and Morano, even Roaner has a smirk on his face. They were listening to what I said.

Vaigon and Vorzantu fly from my shoulder and to the ground. They both sit face to face with Nyt and Salem and the four of them cautiously smell one another.

"What an odd interaction." Ivella says as she tilts her head at them.

Slowly, they seem to take to one another, but that is until Salem hisses and Morano points. "Now you see why I do not like the feline."

"When the human world meets the immortal realms." Dyena laughs.

"And Phyv," Stravan addresses and Levora grasps Phyv's arm. "Welcome home."

* * *

Beauty is the foulest way to describe the view from the balcony of my chamber. This is impeccable. It is spoken among many how Provas in the Summer captures you. It is hard to look away from anything. The large fields that span across the horizon, spouting out the brightest poppies one could ever see. Then there are the fields that lead to waterfalls and waterfalls to oceans. Even farther out are the small villages, towns, and cities.

The part of the palace we are on has glass ceilings that can be opened if you wish, as well as a balcony that circles directly around the chambers on this floor.

Vaigon and Vorzantu still sit on my shoulders as they watch Stravan's fully grown Dragons play in the sky. They both begin their own play in the chamber, following the exact lead of Tuduran and his brother Calypton.

Just down the hall from me is Ivella. I wonder if Stravan and Dyena did this on purpose—placing her and I on the same floor, stunning views, and putting no one else on this level of the palace with us. Even her brother was shown to a different wing of the palace below.

If Ivella were to bring anyone with her, I would have thought it to be Zevyk. The only way to know if they both are wholly finished with one another is to ask and stop wondering by searching for a ring.

We are only given the opportunity to speak with each other when something drastic happens, never because we both seek one another out. She made it clear that night she found me that she does want me to come to her, and that she too wishes to come to me. Yet neither of us do.

They flock to her, but they begin to fight again over who will sit in her arms.

"Wait until they realize they will grow to the size of oceans and never be able to cuddle in your lap like pups again."

Ivella nods with a smile. "I wish I could keep them this small."

"They are rather adorable to be known as the largest predator in our world."

When they calm down Ivella looks up to me. "Stravan and Dyena have sent a messenger for us. They want to speak with us now."

"Will they come?" I ask looking toward Vaigon and Vorzantu.

"No, I asked Ira to stay with them while we are gone."

"He does not need to come with us?"

"No, just us," she lays down the Dragons on the bed. They leisurely roll into a ball beneath their wings before falling fast asleep on the duvet.

* * *

We are led to Stravan's study where he and Dyena await. They waste no time clarifying why they called us here.

"So," Dyena begins. "When did you discover your wings?"

Ivella swallows before speaking. "'Twas the night before yesterday."

"You should have sent someone for me," Dyena speaks in a warning tone. "And you were able to summon them to leave?"

She nods. "It took time, but yes. Laven was with me."

"And what of your Wolf?" Dyena continues after glancing at me. "Did you shift into your Wolf when the wings summoned?"

"No, only the wings appeared."

Stravan stands. "Within time you will shift. If you were able to summon your wings—accidental or purposeful—you could phase into your Wolf any day now."

"It is good your body is beginning to shift into itself before the war can come." Dyena soothingly says. "Even though you and I will be in the Healer's Tent it will be good for us to be on the watch for those who try to get into the tents with ill-intent."

Ivella will be in the Healers Tent?

Stravan scoffs. "Some Healer you are." He mumbles beneath his breath.

"Oh, hush." Dyena snaps. "You really must let that go, Stravi."

He gapes at her. "You dug your nails into my wound, forcing me to tell you it hurt before you would heal me!"

She smiles. "Because you refused to admit that you were in pain, and I knew you were."

Ivella and I quietly laugh before the conversation continues from where it began.

"There are very few people who are half Fae and half Wolf. It used to be seen as abominable because people did not understand it, or they wanted them to breed, or hold them as trophies given you are beautiful creatures in full form." A Wolf with wings. A creature of only imagination, a creature told in children's stories, until those imaginations and stories became real and the world grew too scared and curious causing harm.

Dyena nods at Stravan's words. "It was not until recently that Stravan and I have come across a Hybrid of any kind in a long while. For myself, there is you and Roaner. As for Stravan, there is Roaner, Esme, Greyce, and you, Ivella." Even now to this day, given how protected the Realm of the Hybrids is, there is still fear of a Hybrid like Ivella being taken and used for show.

"The strength and abilities bared by a Hybrid can be immense, nonetheless, unordinary. You inherit powers from both sides that strengthen one another every day." Stravan explains. "We want to warn you to be careful because self-destruction is possible if you do not have your abilities under control."

"Would she be affected as a bred Hybrid would?" I ask. "Essentially, she was given life again through Dyena, she was not truly born a Hybrid."

Dyena nods, understanding. "Yes, but her being a stillborn and being brought back to life through me, made her a Hybrid. As if she was born a Hybrid. It is important you stay careful. We are unsure of how many people are still out there that wish to do what used to be done with Hybrids."

"You know I do not leave my home often. I am either here, training, or at the academy."

Here?

Why would she be here?

"Is Roaner still helping you train in wielding your powers?" Stravan questions.

"Yes." Ivella nods.

"With your father's impeccable agility and strength; he can change the earth into water and water into earth. Within my mother's bloodline, they are Caliothen's."

Stravan's eyebrows raise. "It has been some time since I have met a Caliothen."

Caliothen's can use their voices to sing or talk their way into anything they want or need. They have the ability to talk or sing someone to commit murder, fall into delusion, chaos, and even lead them to their death. Which is why many of them were slain in past times. Even to this day they are still broadly seen as a danger to societies. Then, there are the Vaultais that are also within her powers. Vaultais voices bring pure death, and it is easily triggered by anger or protection, but a seasoned Vaultai is capable of wielding such powers whenever they see fit. The type of the death their opponent suffers is based solely on the wielder. This bloodline still runs strong in the Sorcerers Realm and the Fae.

"Those who can speak or sing nations into sleep or death . . . it is no wonder you were who received half of me. My powers from the Vaultais and yours fit like a match, but in its own ways. Through our voices alone, we can make continents crawl."

"And," he chuckles. "We want to be sure you and Roaner are taking the correct measures in your training."

When I look to Ivella she is holding a guarded expression. "I have not attempted to wield any of my mother's powers."

Stravan attempts to question, but I shake my head, stepping closer behind her. She should not have to speak of her mother, let alone why she chooses not to channel into a power she received from her most profound abuser.

"No one else would be capable of teaching you other than a Hybrid themselves." Stravan says. "As long as you and Roaner continue your training, you shall thrive."

Faintly, I give a smile. "She already does."

Stravan simpers as he looks between the both of us. "I do know of a trainer in Ramana, the Realm of the Hybrids, that could keep your training more consistent if you would like. There are others that are half Wolf and Fae that she has helped. She trains in all brackets of strengthening, controlling, wielding your powers and also trying to understand them."

Ivella gives a slight nod. "I would consider it. When could I meet them?"

"Whenever you would like, just let me know when you are ready."

"You have bloodlines of many strong Orviantes, Ivella." Dyena begins. "There are the Caliothens, the Vaultais, and what else?"

"My father can bend water and earth."

"And I am guessing other members of your family can also bend elements?" Stravan asks.

"Yes, most of us are Elemental Benders."

"As does she," Dyena refers to Ivella. "Your powers from the Vaultais and the Caliothens together are great. Though, to bend elements within it make them all the greater."

"Unfortunately, we do have a celebration to prepare for tonight." Stravan says as a hand rests over Dyena's back who is smiling up at him. "So, we must end this here. In the morning, after morning meal, we can continue."

* * *

"How has training with Roaner been?" I ask as we walk down the hall that leads to both of our chambers.

"It has gone well, though it is not often. Only when I have the time. If I am not training with Roaner, I am training with my father, mother or Ira."

You could ask me to train with you, is what I wish to say. But, instead. "You learn from their training well." Is all I say.

She smiles. "They train well, although most of the training I am going through I have already learned. I must now relearn them."

"Did Roaner know of Vaigon and Vorzantu?"

"No, only you and my closest relatives know . . ." slowly she drifts off with her words before glancing upward, staring directly into my eyes. "What was it you were going to tell me the other night? You were going to speak of your sister."

"Do you know of the Six of Spring?"

"Yes."

"Levora was one, as was Phyv and their friend Greyce. There are three left to be found, and I fear pleas from Galitan, Misonva, and Vosand will come soon. It is just too close together with what is currently happening."

"How were they taken?"

"Through portal to the Mortal Lands."

This takes her by surprise. "How did they survive?"

"They are lucky they survived." I add. "They kept themselves hidden, but I do not know how hidden and this worries me. They say they were careful, but—"

"But how careful?" Ivella finishes.

I nod.

Ivella smiles at this tiny bit of progress. I do not need to know this is what she is smiling in satisfaction for. I can feel it.

Grinning like a fool, I look away from her, and toward the setting sun that beams hues of orange and pink across the sky.

She turns as well, and the golden hour catches her opulent skin that has darkened since the first heat of the sun.

"How does it feel to be a High King?" Ivella playfully asks.

I laugh. "No different than when I was a High Prince, surprisingly. Possibly because I have always picked up after Lorsius and did duties that he should have done. I think all my life I have felt this way—now that I hold the title, nothing feels different. Just a singular piece of paper giving me my ownership over the Throne."

"You have had your Coronation already?"

"No, you would know of it."

She smiles again and I think of a thousand more things to say to keep that smile. "Do you think you would ever truly feel like a High King?"

"I am not sure when that would happen. I am not sure I want to feel like a High King at all." There is too much to change within Vaigon for me to feel like a King. Especially not with the people under me. This is a generation of people that praised Lorsius, not me.

"What do you wish to feel like?"

"That I am unsure of as well."

"And that is fine too."

"Is it?" All my life it has been made out to seem as if you need to know at every moment what you must be in this eternal life we are given, I have never truly felt the pressure until now.

"You move at your own pace, Laven." Her tone deepens, searing her words into my head. "Not at the pace others expect you to."

And what I hate the most, every interruption between us when we are furthering our relationship and strengthening our bond before we can proceed any farther to more.

Her brother exits her chamber with the Dragons swarming in our direction.

Ira does not give a single glance nor a word before nodding to Ivella and ascending down the hall.

"We did not get to speak of this with Dyena and Stravan because we ran out of time, but today is Dyena's Coronation."

"Oh," I was under the impression that Dyena has been High Queen all this time.

"And also mine, in a form."

Oh . . .

"How do you mean?"

There are two ladies making their way towards us with a dress draped over both of their arms as they approach.

"I am now the Right Hand to the Queen of Provas."

53
A BOND GROWS

LEVORA APOLLA ARVENALDI

The doors to her chamber are pushed open by the two men standing guard, Queens Sentinel. They both wear a sigil made of a Wolf and Fae wings, these are Ivella's protectors. I may not know why I am here, still, I want to be. Ever since the day that I read about Ivella in the morning papers I have craved to meet her. Now I have the chance to know her, and soon enough, she is supposedly going to be my sister.

Ivella sits at her vanity toying with her hair, immediately upon seeing me, she turns with a smile, urging me to come closer and the doors close behind me.

Her robe is a rich night blue and so simply I see her donned in our Vaigosian blue cloaks and dresses.

"Do you braid, Levora?" She asks as her hands rest on my shoulders.

"I do."

"Would you like to braid mine for the Coronation? I cannot properly braid the back and I am growing displeased with how it is turning out and I now wish to find a cutthroat's razor and shave my head."

I laugh seeing how her curls are messy from fussing with her hair. "How would you like it braided?"

"I loved how you plaited your hair for solstice." Her eyes brighten through her previous frustration. "Would you be able to style it as so?"

I touch her hair feeling the soft yet slightly coarse curls.

"Come sit down," I urge her back to the satin bench at her vanity. "I think it will look beautiful given how long your hair is."

Ivella smiles at me through the mirror. "I am nervous." She speaks lowly, so low I nearly did not hear her. "I am speaking lowly because I do not want your brother to hear me." She stops once more before carrying on. "He will come in here and then I will cry and look a mess for today."

I smile. "He is good at eavesdropping, but I did not see him in his chamber as I arrived at the doors."

"Good," Ivella playfully grins. "I can speak freely then."

I grab small pieces that frame her face and pin them at the back of her hair. "My brother and you know one another well?" I reference the last time we spoke at solstice.

Her eyes fall. "Laven has known me since my arrival in New Vaigon years ago. We were young, I believe he was seven and ten at the time."

During the beginning of Lorsius claiming Vaigon.

"How old were you at the time?" I cautiously ask knowing well enough this topic of conversation treads heavily on trauma.

She struggles to speak. "I as well was seven and ten."

"If you do not mind me asking," Ivella turns to me. "Why was Lorsius such a hateful person? How could he allow the imprisonment of his nephew and chosen Heir."

I exhale, hearing the story my father told me countless times as a tale but it was all truth. I sit on the bench next to her. "My uncle grew up differently. You see, we come from a family of white hair. Meaning–"

"You are Originals—Orviantes."

"Yes," though sometimes I do not ever feel like I am one. "Lorsius was the only son born with darker hair. It was always a mystery as to why since no one in our family has dark hair other than my mother who was a commoner and married into the family. Lorsius was treated differently by the people around him because we were a family of a pure bloodline, either we had mates or not. My grandfather did his best to live by his father and all those before him, but sometimes–"

"The pot boils over." Ivella quietly interrupts.

I laugh. "Exactly. My grandmother laid with a man that was not my grandfather, but was her mate, she had one upon many secret visits with him and one day, there was a slip. And came Lorsius. My grandparents swore to never tell him why he looked as he did. And in this secrecy my father, who was the second eldest after the death of my aunt, my namesake, he promised to stop the purity of our bloodline because it was not fair that the truth was withheld from Lorsius."

"He was not born with white in his hair at all? Not even like Laven."

"No, not a single streak of white. Growing up my father did his best to protect Lorsius. He was his little brother but even through the love and protection my father gave him, Lorsius still grew hatred solely because he looked different from the rest. As well as the others high in society who looked down on Lorsius made him angry. He tried his best growing up to be a man like my father and grandfather, but, as you said. Sometimes the pot boils over, and that hatred never goes away. Then, after time, Lorsius found a mate and she was not an Orviante, she was a commoner."

Ivella's shoulders stiffen. "In those times commoner mates of an Orviante were slain to keep the bloodlines pure." Even when there were complications with birth due to inbreeding, that never stopped the reigning royals from keeping things within the circle they saw fit for a crown let alone a Throne.

I smile softly. "She was taken from him before they could flee.

Their plan was revealed by someone who overheard their conversations, then it was revealed that she was pregnant, and not just pregnant but showing, and that made it all the worse. She was the only person who brought Lorsius his happiness given his circumstances. She made him feel needed in the world and it was taken away."

"And Laven, the first, and Apolla stayed together. Why is that?"

I smile thinking of their gentle yet crazy love. "My father met my mother after this all transpired, and for my grandparents to avoid this happening again they pursued to have the law changed."

Ivella's head tilts. "That is why Lorsius would not allow my people to be mated. It was out of spite."

"*Deep* spite." I carry on. "Then, my parents were allowed to stay together and live the life Lorsius prayed for. And in this, he took Laven and made him his Heir and then me."

"You poor children had nothing to do with his need for reign. Did Lorsius grow to hate Laven's father as well?"

"He never said yes, but I feel that he did. I never knew my uncle as a good man, though I do not think he ever was. All I hope for people like him is that they are paying for their dues when they proceed to the afterlife. Lorsius took my brother as Heir and treated Laven the way the people wanted to treat Lorsius when he was born out of wedlock. That I will never forgive him for. My brother was happy, and free, and careless, and fun. He wanted all the riveting aspects of life." Ivella gently places a hand upon mine as tears fall down my face. "Not only after imprisonment was Laven a drastically different person, but before then, when he was declared Heir, something in him altered to someone I did not know. Lorsius deserved to rot for what he did to Laven and your people. He did not deserve a quick death. Everything he did to the people around him should have been done to him."

"Revenge is lovely, is it not?" Ivella weakly smiles.

"I think my brother and I are similar in that way. Sometimes, I wonder if the reason Laven killed all those men was for revenge, but he never said to anyone why he did what he did . . . the deliverance of twelve heads and three missing bodies without reason? You murder this way out of revenge and hatred."

Never in Laven's life did he have enemies nor did he seek out people to eradicate. This was out of sorts for the man who was so happily free.

Ivella pauses and her eyes drift. "Say that again. The *deliverance*."

"The deliverance of twelve heads?"

She is captured in thought.

"Are you all right?"

"I–I never knew what it was that he did to the men." Ivella forces a laugh. "He is creative in his killing, is he not?"

"He is." I chuckle.

I stand to finish her hair and as I am doing so it is hard not to notice how distant she grows and how quiet she has become.

Then, by surprise she speaks again.

"He saved me . . ." she swallows and looks up at me again through the mirror. "He saved me. That is a debt to be paid for eternity."

"There is no debt to be paid," I assure her.

Within her eyes I can see the deep-rooted love for my brother that she holds. Their love that I can feel was built on nothing less than trauma.

"Laven will want nothing from you other than knowing you are safe. That is another downfall of my brothers."

"Constantly needing to be the hero." She whispers.

"But who saves the hero?"

She seems afraid to speak, the hesitance grows, yet she continues. "Me."

"Tell him that over and over until it is all he remembers."

Ivella nods and a smile appears.

"Thank you," I say. "For being there for him after the cremation of Lorsius."

"He fell." She says both literally and figuratively.

"And you caught him."

Ivella hums. "I will catch him for the eternity of my life."

"And he yours."

* * *

When I find Phyv in the same place as before, the boys leave so I may speak with him alone as he very shyly requested.

"That took a while." He begins.

I tilt my head as I see his angst. "What is wrong?"

"I think now is the time to speak with you about what I saw when I touched Ivella's hand."

"Phyv," I heavily breathe and pinch the bridge of my nose as I sit next to him. "You pick the most opportune moments."

"No," he holds up a finger. "I have just now discovered how to explain what came to me in the vision."

"And that is?"

"Her standing in the midst of all elements of the world and war raging around us. I believe she may be the key to winning the war, but if not controlled she could do more damage to those around her and herself if she does not have her powers in check."

I knew Ivella held strength, but I did not think she held old strength. It has not been known for someone to possess powers of all elements since Old Voschantai. But this is only a vision, he could be wrong about this. All visions hold the opportunity to change as the future does.

"What elements, specifically?"

"Fire, water, earth, air, ice, lightning. All you can imagine."

I nod. "I will speak to Laven, it is also time you spoke in depth with my family of your powers. You could learn a great deal about yourself and help others in the process."

"The Coronation is beginning." A guard says from the doors of the drawing room.

"Let us go and enjoy ourselves before we think too rashly."

54
WHITE ROSES

LAVEN HEPHAESTUS ARVENALDI, II

White petals are splayed across the stone ground where Dyena is being sworn in as High Queen of Provas. Those same petals take you to the stairs that lead up to the balcony of the Throne Room. Along the sides of the path of petals stand the people of Provas.

Those around us are singing for the prosperity of Dyena, through their words they are sending prayers over her reign to fill for eternity. Some are whispering small thanks of her return.

Along the curve of the walls below the balcony sit orchestras encasing both sides of the stairs. Violinists in the front play slowly before those in the back encompass the symphony to make it grow and echo through the land surrounding us. A pianist that resembles Stravan joins, giving the symphony depth and life to welcome the Right Hand to the Queen.

"Laven," Morano speaks in a low whisper as he stares in awe of Ivella. "Did you know of this?"

"Yes," I respond lowly. "We spoke of it prior to the Coronation."

Ivella's eyes stare strongly forward, her shoulders hold that firm square I recognize.

A little girl gazes wide eyed at Ivella. "Mama," she whispers. "Can I wear a dress like hers when I am older?"

Her mother smiles and gives a slight nod before refocusing on Ivella.

There are two men holding the train of her gown as she recedes down the stairs toward Dyena.

Her hair is pulled back and lowly gathered, revealing every bit of the dress that covers her. Diamonds trail down the dress in expanding lines to enhance the curves of her natural body, then, at the flat of her chest her skin is revealed up to her shoulders that are donned in diamonds covering her like armor.

Having her hair worn up shows the small, sharp point of her ears to the people. Signifying, in some form, that she is of the Fae.

Her brother, Ira, is standing not far off in the crowd of people watching Ivella approach Dyena.

An Orb and Scepter is placed in Ivella's hands. As she bows before Dyena, the tiara is placed upon her head—it is crafted in the form of branches twined within leaves and embossed in white gold.

It is stupefying how well a crown suits Ivella. Well, the crown does not suit her, she suits the crown. I imagined for years what she would look like decked in royalty, but I also imagined what we would look like if I left the royal line and ascension. We would be commoners outlying in the lands, working, and raising children—if that is what we chose.

"We must ascend to the balcony and wait for their arrival." I say to my brothers. "All those of royalty are expected at the balcony to sing their Continents Chorale."

"Even visiting royals?"

Amias and Roaner both nudge Morano forward. "Yes, even visiting royals."

"Just go," Levora says with a tone laced in annoyance.

Phyv chuckles as he follows us.

I shake my head. "Cannot bring him anywhere." And Phyv

continues to laugh.

Stravan is waiting at the top of the stairs for both Dyena and Ivella's arrival after being crowned. He looks back at me before his eyes return to the women.

I step forward. "What is your Continents Chorale?"

His sharp blue eyes meet mine again before gazing at Dyena. A simper appears on his face as he watches her. "She *is* the Continents Chorale."

As they both glide up the stairs I return to where Morano, Amias, and Roaner are standing.

A High Priest leisurely walks forward before stopping at the top of the balcony and his large voice bellows above the orchestra. "Dyena Provanseva and Ivella Fondali, High Queen and Right Hand of Provas."

Ivella and Dyena both place a hand on Stravan's arm as they stand on either side of him. They walk directly to the Throne where a seat on either side of Stravan awaits Ivella and Dyena.

* * *

"Laven, this is my sister, Savarina, her mate Daevien, and my brother Sloan." Stravan introduces my brothers, Levora, Phyv, and I to his family one by one.

All three of them take after each other vigorously; the bright eyes, dark brown skin, and hair that is as white as snow. The same features of my family.

"King Laven, correct?" Daevien asks me.

"Yes," I nod, still not fully comprehending that I am now a King, nor am I used to the title, but I do not correct him, nor do I tell him to only call me Laven as I prefer.

"It is lovely to meet you," Savarina smiles, "if you will excuse me." She says before taking off to where Dyena has entered from, alongside her is Ivella.

Daevien and Sloan give one another a smile.

"Sava is not much of a talker with those she is unfamiliar with."

Stravan quietly forces a laugh.

And it seems she is not too fond of Ivella either.

She does not greet her at all, she just barely skims by her and goes straight to Dyena. Ivella barely pays attention to this at all, but I surely notice it.

"Jealousy," Morano says. *"She wanted the title of Right Hand."*

When I look at him, his focus is directed away from Savarina, but it is easy to tell he has seeped into her thoughts. It has been a bit of time since he has last done this.

"Let us go sit and eat." Stravan leads us to the table filled with fresh fruits, vegetables, meats, side dishes, assortments of bread loaves.

"What happened to no longer entering thoughts of others unless needed?" Amias chuckles as we follow Stravan to one of the dining tables.

"This was needed . . . I do not trust the way she looked at Ivella, and neither did Laven."

No, I did not. There are one too many eyes over Savarina for me to watch her too intently. We all would become suspect for prolonged staring.

"Why in the world would she be jealous? She is High Princess of Provas." Amias questions in disbelief.

"Because," Roaner begins as we sit at the table. *"Right Hands have word over Princesses and Princes. She most likely feels obligated to have the title of Right Hand by blood or other reasonings."*

"No matter what," I speak to end this conversation before we eat. *"I will keep watch tonight. There are one too many things a person would do to another to secure a position closer to the Throne."*

As I sit, Ivella continues to eat in silence with her brother next to her. He too seems to glance at Savarina every now and then. Next to Ira sits Levora who sends me a questioning look. I nod at her, signaling I will speak with her later, she nods back before turning to Phyv who is already devouring the food along the table.

I can relate with him on the need to have your home food again after a prolonged period of time.

When I look at Ivella, she is already looking at me.

I drift my eyes to the chair next to me and back at her.

She smiles and nods.

There is a small exchange between her and Ira. Next, he is introduced to Levora and Phyv before she ascends to the chair next to me.

"You put one of the most talkative women with one of the quietest men." I laugh as I turn to her. Her leg presses flat against mine as I scoot closer.

Ivella cackles as she looks across the long table at Ira who sits in discomfort as Levora talks his ear off. "Maybe she will break him out of his shell, and he will converse with someone other than me."

I rest my arm along the back of her chair as I settle further in. "Are you saying you are growing tired of your brother?" I look down at her as she plays with the bow and arrow brooch on my topcoat.

"No," her smiles fades. "He needs companions who can understand him. Ira has been quiet all his life, and some people do not understand it or find him to be disrespectful. He has just always been in his own little world, and he does not want it disturbed. Someone like Levora would be a good friend to him, she seems patient and that is what Ira needs—a patient person who does not give up. He cannot continue his life with just me, our mother, our father, and Iysha."

"Who is Iysha?"

"Our little brother, he was born while me and my father were in Vaigon."

She traces her finger over the arrow, and I grab her hand. "And if Ira does not want to have a companion outside of his family?"

Ivella looks up with a worried expression. "And stay sheltered all his life?"

"What if he enjoys being sheltered? What if he wants to keep a life small and intimate?"

She slouches into my side as she stares at Ira and Levora.

"It just does not seem right."

I smile and pull her closer. "It does not seem right to you, but it seems right to him."

She looks up at me. "And that is all that matters."

"Yes."

"Ivella!" Dyena calls. She turns her head, and her smile returns. "Come meet, Hecta!" Dyena waves a hand for her to come and before I can speak to her she ascends.

"Brovita," Stravan appears next to me as he sips sparkling liquid. "Here," he fills my glass with Brovita before handing it to me. "Provas has better Brovita than any nation you will go to."

"Is that so?"

"So it is," he nods. "But now that I have something in your system, I wanted to speak with you, add more hell into your daily life."

"Because that is exactly what I want."

He smirks. "You can handle it." He finishes what is in his glass before leaning closer in. "The other Realms have sent their inquiries. They want to know where the people of their nations are now that Levora, Phyv, and Greyce have been found."

This time, I am the one to drink. "I was hoping we would have a bit more time than this."

"So did I."

"I already have people in place for it. Levora, Greyce, and Phyv will go back in search. And if you have others who can fabricate themselves like Phyv did while in the human world feel free to send them along."

"I do, but for starters we send only them. If needed then we will send others. We can talk in further depth tomorrow during the conference. It will be worth it to bring this up, and I will have someone send for Greyce so she is caught up on this information and it is not sudden that we are sending them back."

"For now," I stop this conversation from proceeding further. "Let me enjoy this Brovita."

"Quite delicious is it not?"

I do not let him have verbal satisfaction, I only continue to drink.

* * *

After the celebration ended Ivella was taken in all sorts of directions. But, I have an undying need to see her again. When I find her, she is sitting on the balcony in her chamber. One foot dangles off the edge, and one knee is pulled to her chest.

I slowly near the edge of the balcony next to her and sit.

The beautiful dress from earlier today is hanging in her chamber over the bathing room door. Now, the dark blue robe I last saw her in, she is wearing again.

One end of the robe slips over her shoulder as she holds a bottle of wine up to me. By the label that reads FONDALI VINEYARD, I know it is wine that her father has made.

"So," I start after taking a sip of the wine. "What was it that persuaded your agreement to becoming the Right Hand of a High Queen? A High Queen of the largest Realm in our entire universe." I laugh with my final words and Ivella does as well.

Her eyes form that glint of happiness, yet even smiling I can see something is missing to make her whole. Although, I never knew her when she was truly happy and elated with life. I question if she has ever been happy. This small bit of desolation seems to guise naturally on her.

"Dyena and I have become close with one another over the past couple weeks since the night of Solstice. She does not have many companions and she felt we would understand each other the best—and we do. I did not understand how strong the bond is between people after being tied by a Blood Bond Ritual. I have my close companions, but there will not be someone so close to me as Dyena is."

A mate would be . . .

"Was that the only reason she chose you? Because of the bond through the ritual." I cautiously sit next to her, and her eyes advert to the stars clouded in the sky. I choose not to look too long at the drop off the edge of this balcony.

"No," Ivella smiles. "The more we got to know each other the more we realized our strategies to build reformation are the same."

I hand the wine to her, giving her a reason to have to look at me again. Just as before, I can see those tiny specks of deep orange appearing within the boskiness of her eyes.

"Reformation?" I ask in a form of disbelief. "We need reformation?"

Ivella shoves me as she quietly laughs. "Yes, reformation."

"And what are these plans of reformation?"

After taking a long drink of the wine, she answers. "Unwavering allyship. I did not become Right Hand for the sole purpose of she and I agreeing on multiple different aspects of life. But for the security of our people. We need consistent backing by a resilient army, and Provas can provide us that. Along with Provas, comes the coalitions they have as well.

"The other Realms will not be sturdy enough on their own to deny us allyship; repudiating us means tearing their allyship apart with Provas, and that is what no Realm wants. The worst enemy of enemies does not want the greatest Realm in the world against them. The Provasian people will always have the armies and Mandems you want on your side.

"Now, we all are legitimately secured together again. By the Coronation of Dyena and myself; it is as if we are one nation again—so to say. And you now have New Quamfasi, New Quamfasi has Provas, and Provas has every Realm. We are tied in more ways than one. Even if your tie to New Quamfasi were to be broken, it would not matter, you have me binding us forever."

Roaner missed one thing about Ivella being fit to be High Queen. Her intelligence and ability to strategize a crucial plan with ease.

"I wish I was gifted enough to devise a plan as this."

Ivella hands the wine to me again, sarcastically rolling her eyes.

"You are intelligent enough to think of something as this. But I did not think of this alone—Dyena was the deviser of this plan, and my family, and then I decided it would be the most tenable decision to tie our lands together in the form of me being Right Hand. Our Blood Bond was just an extra piece to the puzzle."

"Speaking of bonds," I say as she takes another sip of the wine.

"Have you spoken much with your family?"

"Yes, I have been going home more often than before, but I still stay at my father's home in Nadrexi. That is where I officially reside."

"What is with that brooding sister of Stravan's?" I finally ask about Savarina and Ivella's eyebrows raise as she laughs.

"She is not too fond of me."

"I gathered that," I begin to laugh with her. "It looked as if she was ready to lunge across the table any given moment to stab you with her bread knife."

Her head falls back and the harmonic laugh pours from her chest, I cannot help but to grin as I watch.

"Savarina does not understand the companionship between Dyena and I. There are things Dyena tells me that she cannot tell them, she believes Savarina is jealous, but does not understand why. Dyena has told me of the times where Savarina makes them seem closer than they are."

"Untrue friends." I take the wine bottle as she places it in my hand.

Ivella begins to stare out in that same way I have seen before when her mind takes her somewhere that is not welcoming to her.

I near closer and her head lifts—our skin just a mere inch from touching.

I *need* to be just as close as we were earlier, if not closer.

"What is it?" I probe.

She begins to soften as she watches my lips move with the words I speak, and the more she cracks that hard exterior, I see Maivena.

"What if I cannot do it?" Her eyes meet my own and as if it is so natural to her, she slightly leans, falling in closer. "What if I am not capable of being a Right Hand to a Queen? What if my mother was right all along?"

"Do not listen to her." I plea.

That voice of her mother is roaming through her head. I can nearly hear every repugnant abuse being said to Ivella as if it were me.

Ivella's hand falls, toying with the label on the wine bottle. "I try not to," she stops speaking and bites hard into her lip repeatedly.

"It will not be easy to forget, but you must remember that everything she said to you was out of jealousy and hatred for herself." Just as my uncle was with me.

Her hand moves from playing with the label on the wine bottle, to playing with the sleeve of my undershirt. I can hear each beat of her heart the closer she gets to our skin touching. Can she hear mine? With a quiet hum from her throat, a smile appears over her lips.

"I do not want to sleep alone tonight."

Just as my words leave, she looks up at me again. "But we have to."

And like a poisoned arrow moving right through my back, knowing of it, seeing it, then feeling it—I remember.

A Right Hand must always be on the verge of marriage or . . . *already* wedded.

That soar of anger I am acquainted with pushes forward.

Snatching my arm away from her, I move so swiftly to my feet I see her hair fling at the rush of speed.

Her chin quivers as she looks up at me and I shake my head. "You are not allowed to do that to me." Tears flood down her cheeks—staining the robe covering her skin. "Ivella, I am telling you this once and never again. *Stop* giving me fallacious hope."

"Laven—" she calls out, but I leave before I can hear a word about why she will always pick him over me.

55
DISCOVERING THE OPPONENT

LAVEN HEPHAESTUS ARVENALDI, II

"SO SHE DID POP a wing like I predicted would happen." Amias smirks as I meet him, Roaner, and Morano in the hall. Alongside them stand Phyv and Levora.

"She did," I say forcibly laughing before I change the subject of our conversation. "The meeting with Stravan is in almost an hour, we can have morning meal first or we can wait to dine after the meeting."

Morano sighs. "We finally get to know who it is that has spread this infection among our people?"

"Possibly, as I mentioned before, he is not positive of this, but he has an inkling. Although," I turn my attention to Levora and Phyv. "Stravan has sent for Greyce to attend our conference."

"Why?" Levora worriedly asks.

"The letters are in; the other Realms are now looking for the other three of the Six of Spring."

"It was only a matter of time." Phyv nods.

"Will we still go back to search? Me, Phyv, and Greyce."

"Yes, the task will be yours and we will join you if we must."

They all nod in agreement. "Since when did Ivella have Dragons?" Amias questions with a cringe of discomfort over his face.

"No," Morano laughs. "The question is, since when did you become a father to hellfire breathers?"

"I did not know I was their father until Stravan made it clear of how a father is chosen. It did not look like Ivella knew of that either."

We turn toward the length of the hallway as we hear footsteps approaching. It is Ira scaling his way toward us, not a care in the world to speak.

"Ira, is it?" Amias asks.

"Yes," he nods.

"You should tour the city with us after the conference." I offer, but he quickly declines.

"No, thank you. I am only here to be sure my sister makes it safely to wherever it is she goes."

"She could have walked with us." Morano politely tells him.

By the look in Ira's eyes, he does not show a want of anyone other than himself being around his sister. Even if she has told him we are safe for her to be around—which I am sure she has. Although, after last night, I do not think she wants to be around me just yet.

"No, I will walk with Ira, thank you." I hear that deeply smooth voice speak.

She is dressed perfectly in black silk and lace. Half of her back is exposed as the dress falls in tiers of lace along the silk revealing one leg and is held on her shoulders by thin straps. Both Vaigon and Vorzantu are sitting on her shoulders, and quickly, they both swarm in my direction. Their growing talons nearly punctured the thick material of my topcoat.

"Ivella, dear." Morano playfully greets. "You look stunning."

Sarcastically, he bows to her, and she gives him a caveat glare.

"Lady Ivella." Someone calls from a distance.

As I look, there is a messenger approaching with a small letter in his hand. His large, black wings just barely graze the floor as he approaches. After Ivella retrieves the letter, he bows his head before ascending.

Her eyes glance over the paper, and a strong appearance coated in fear floods her face.

"What is it?" I ask.

"Nothing that concerns you."

I narrow my eyes at her as she folds the paper back up.

"I must meet Stravan and Dyena at the balcony of the Throne Room." She announces.

"Why?" Ira asks taking the letter from her and reading over it himself.

"They wish for proof that I am truly half Fae."

Amias's face goes stone. "Were your ears not enough?"

"Most likely not," Morano answers and I already see him thinking of a solution to this.

"They want to witness her bearing the wings." Phyv says in a distant thought. "In order to be accepted, they want to see that you can properly hold yourself up while carrying the weight of wings that are hundreds of pounds."

"Ivella," Morano begins again. "Fabrication is what anyone could use to look like something they are not. A glamour." He is plotting to go in front of the people as her.

"That fucking sister," Levora scoffs. "I know it is no one but her demanding this, and I am sure she got other people of their land to demand it as well."

"No, you will not be forced to harm yourself in front of all those people just for the satisfaction of a jealousy." Morano shakes his head. "I will go as you, I have shapeshifted into the body a Fae once before, they would never know."

Ivella smiles at him. "Thank you, yet I will not allow you to do that."

"You can hurt yourself." I finally speak.

"Truly, Ivy, this is not a good idea." Roaner tries to convince.

"Then so be it," she snaps, and I witness her eyes almost turn dark orange and fade back to green. Ira grabs her hand, and she lets him. "If I hurt myself, oh well. I will not be made a coward to her nor the others questioning me. Either I fall down as those wings appear or not, she will not insult my capabilities."

The sharp points of her heels hit loudly against the floor as she pushes through us to leave, and we follow behind her.

* * *

The people waiting below the balcony of the Throne Room speak amongst one another quietly as Ivella stands next to Stravan and Dyena.

Dyena grabs Ivella's hand, and I can see the silent conversation they both are having. She is reluctant to release Ivella, but she does after a smile of affirmation is given.

"How can I help her?" I ask Roaner.

"Find the will to channel your strength into her."

I nearly look at him to question why he would suggest this, then I remember the crowd we are in front of that are not only watching Ivella, but the men behind her as well. *"How could that be possible without our bond established? Do you think she will know I am doing this?"*

"I am unsure, but it is worth it to take the chance and bare the wrath to come after or you let her fall."

"Over my dead body will she fall in front of these people." I reply.

Savarina stands far off alongside us looking directly at Ivella's back waiting for her wings to sprawl.

At an attempt, I try to envision the crowds through her eyes.

"I do not see this wise," Amias quickly says. *"The strength she holds as a Hybrid is gravely different from ours. You could hurt yourself attempting this."*

"Then so be it."

"No, it is not just then so be it," Morano snaps. *"If you fall out while this is happening then what? The entire continent will put us at question, but more so Ivella than us."*

"Then help me." I suggest. *"All four of us are capable to do this together if one cannot do it alone."*

My mind goes quiet, and I recognize the surge of invincibility move through me. There have been countless times that the four of us had to be strength as a whole by channeling it into one another.

Now that I have the vigor, I need it to go to her, and quickly.

"Search for the bond between the both of you." Roaner speaks. *"If she holds the form of her wings, she can feel you if she recognizes it or not."*

Just as the night I had to search for her in her nightmares, it is no different than now.

That small sliver of her I can connect to, I latch onto it, placing every bit of my strength in her while my brothers hold me to the ground.

Ira is intently watching Savarina, not caring a bit if anyone sees him glaring in her direction. He is ready to lunge at her any given moment.

The beautiful wings I saw just days ago flare—white and tan feathers shake out, producing the beautiful sound that birds do as their wings move through the wind but at a much stronger force.

Stravan smiles while glancing over her and then at me. "I believe that concludes what all of you wished to see." Stravan's voice booms over the people and he looks over his shoulder at Savarina.

The wings recede back, leaving Ivella standing with her back bare again. I could beg to see her bearing the wings again. Hair of the night, and wings of the day—a beautiful nightmare.

Ivella turns sharply in her heels, her eyes meet Savarina's, and without a word she starts for the doors, nearly bumping her shoulder as she walks past her.

The four of us follow behind her, and I can hear Morano mumble beneath his breath, but Amias pushes him onward. There is nothing more that needs to be said to her, she now has made a fool of herself in front of her own people for questioning Ivella, and convincing others to do so as well.

* * *

Stravan's study is large enough to hold a table to fit nearly forty people, but there are only enough chairs for the fourteen of us that are needed for this conference.

His Circle is already seated, and Savarina and Sloan speak

quietly amongst one another. Daevien and Dyena watch from a distant end of the table, but, be that as it may, it seems they are monitoring the conversation more than they are listening. Ivella and Ira sit near one another and the chairs alongside her are open near the head of the table.

Levora, Phyv, and Greyce take a seat first. Then, my brothers and I take to the open chairs next to Ivella.

"When you described what it was that was taking over your people," Stravan speaks as he sits down. "I was incredulous to what you were telling me. My uncle's closest companion was against all the Realms splitting off into their own continents when we were known as Varlesan."

"That was centuries ago," I say.

Daevien nods. "Yes, Stravan's mother and father were forced into turmoil because of the choices Sythin–Stravan's uncle–allowed Yaro to make. Yaro saw no reason for the lands to split, but only for the purpose of power. Power to rule over every Realm since he was high in House Provanseva due to a Blood Bond Ritual."

"Like I am to Laven," Amias says.

"Yes," Stravan nods. "My family knew that it was logical for all the Realms to split off. Not because of differences, but it only seemed right to allow those of the same bloodlines to be able to make choices for their people that they saw fit. There were plenty of times we thought we were making proper choices for certain bloodlines, but really, we were not." Stravan sits up straighter and holds out his hand. In his palm appears a portrait, as I read the name beneath it, it is a portrait of Yaro.

Ivella leans in, examining every curve of his face.

"Why do you think it is him trying to spread this infection among our people?" Levora asks as she takes the portrait from him.

"We think he went mad, a possible imbalance within his brain after the death of Sythin." Sloan says. "He had this insane thought to spread this disease over the people to force them to believe they wanted to stay, that they craved to stay controlled by one leader in particular."

Morano looks down at the portrait and back at Stravan. "He confidently verbalized this to your father?"

"No," Stravan laughs. "I discovered it because I was the Royal Spymaster to my mother. She suspected something was off with him, although no one knew what it was, we figured it was grief as we all were grieving Sythin. So, I was sent to discover what was truly wrong. I found his journal where all of his plans were, and I delivered the journal to my mother. Then we found out that he had fled when he knew the journal was missing. No one knew where, and no one knew where to find him."

"He abandoned us in a war he started." Daevien says.

"The first Domestic War," Ivella says in deep thought.

"Yes," Daevien continues. "He tried so vigorously to keep all the lands together, that he developed a war he ran from after his thoughts were revealed."

"Who would have thought all the lands would have to come together again to fight him off in another war he is beginning?" Amias sarcastically speaks.

"A war we are trying to avoid," Dyena adds. "You spoke with Vallehes and Penelope of arranging a conference with all the Realms?" She asks me.

"Yes, I called the meeting between just our Circles, mine and New Quamfasi, before we arrived here yesterday."

"Good, follow through with the universal conference, we must have this meeting soon. We cannot sit around any longer, everyone must train, and all doctors and Healers must prepare." Dyena looks toward Ivella, and she gives her a slight nod.

"When do we expect this war to happen if it does?" Amias asks.

As General, he and Hua must be ready, as do our Mandems. This is why it was pertinent for us to instill the vigorous training we did.

"Yaro had a fascination for wars in the winter." Savarina finally speaks.

"When will we bring the other Realms aware of this?" I ask. "It must be soon, there will be no need to wait any longer than we have to."

Dyena and Stravan gaze at one another, weighing the options. Then they look to Ivella.

"We still have yet to tell them of my induction," Ivella starts. "We will send word of that first, then ask for a conference here since Provas is the center of the universe."

"We would not have to wait so long to arrange a conference if we inducted a Right Hand that was already of our continent."

"And you will watch the snide remarks that come out of your mouth." I accelerate my voice as I stare through Savarina.

"Sava," Daevien grabs her arm.

"I will gladly slit her throat," Roaner casually says down the bond.

"Since we are now allied, there will be boundaries set for respect." I announce. Savarina goes rigid as she never lets her eyes move from my own. "I will not sit here and allow you or anyone to speak to Ivella, myself, or someone in my Circle the way you just have."

She ascends from the table without response and Dyena looks to Daevien.

"I will speak with her," he nods, but his expression reads tiredness.

"It should not be a problem getting Ramana on board," Greyce speaks before this drama can carry out any further. "For those of you who I have not met, I am Greyce Rovech, first daughter and first child of General Gordyn of Ramana."

"Lineages born with a daughter as the first child are known as the strongest lineages to live." Stravan says with respect.

Ivella smiles. "It is nice to meet you, Greyce. I too am a daughter and first child of a General, it is not often that I meet fellow first daughters of Generals."

"Seems as if you and I will have a great deal of talking to do after this meeting." Greyce smirks.

Eldest daughters amongst eldest daughters. This very room is filled with power.

"Greyce, if you can speak with King Neryus about this, do you think you could get him and his House to appear at the universal conference?" I ask.

"I do, he knew of my coming here and Neryus already has some insight on what is transpiring here with the mutations. He is expecting an enquiry for a universal meeting."

"Good," Stravan says. "I agree that we must send word soon, just as important as it is to bring the Realms aware of the alliance they now hold with Vaigon through us."

"That should play out rather interestingly." Sloan laughs as he pushes a hand through his curly white hair.

"It will play out just fine," Dyena speaks in a warning tone, and Sloan smiles. "They cannot thrive without the alliance of us, and they would not wish to break that. The Realms may know of Vaigon being under new ruling, but all may not know. Hopefully, they will be more inclined to you than they were to Lorsius."

"We may only hope."

"I will have messengers sent to the Realms now," Stravan begins. "And Greyce, thank you for offering your assistance. Once we get back our responses, I will bring you aware, Laven."

"And when I have a response from Neryus I will come back here and go to Vaigon to give Neryus's answers." Greyce nods.

"I think we all must be aware that there is no *if* when it comes to this war." Sloan says as he leans his elbows on the table. "This war is going to happen, and it will not be for the weak to battle in—who knows what Yaro put into those mutations to enhance any abilities the people he mutated already had. We can hope to stop the war from happening, but the more we convince ourselves that this will not occur will weaken our guard. We must be ready at any given moment to fight. All Realms will now become a target after this meeting."

"We would be foolish to believe that if he has crafted a septicity to control our kind that he is not developing another for other Realms." Roaner adds. "His goal is full control over the world. We have seen what this mutation can do to our people firsthand." He says motioning between our Circle and Ivella as well. "I can only imagine what he would do to someone of the Fae, or even the Hybrid Realm."

"If he so crosses that path my father will seek him out in the war and personally kill him himself." Greyce smiles.

Dyena warily looks up to Stravan and then toward Amias. "Would you mind training with Sloan? He is our General and all new training you have found or developed, we would like for it to be passed on to him and our Warriors."

Amias slightly winces. "There is not much training I could pass on to him since I do not know the agility of an infected person of Fae. But I can teach him what it would be like to challenge a rogue Wolf as well as reminding you to implement the old games to discover the strongest and weakest."

"They have an arrangement to train with my mother. They will participate in the Quamfasian Games and afterwards they will be given advanced training." Ivella tells Sloan.

He happily gazes at her with every word she says, and I taper my eyes on him when his glance drifts to the movement of the words coming from her lips.

"I will send my own warriors as well to participate," Sloan stands and looks to Amias. "Come, I will introduce you to my frontline."

"If this war truly happens by the time winter comes, Vaigon and Vorzantu should be old enough to fight." Dyena informs Ivella. "We will be preparing Tuduran, Nara, Calypton, and Vion."

"Would they not be too young?"

Daevien nods. "They would be, but young Dragons can fight if given the proper training and armor since their skin would not be proofed of weapons just yet."

"We could bring them here?" I ask. "For proper training."

"Yes," Dyena says. "And it will be important that we use all Dragons that contain a rider."

"Why is that?" Morano asks.

"When Yaro fled he took his Dragon and I know he will use her. Daiga is Nara's sister and she has always been a very well trained Dragon for battle as is Nara, and I am certain that their bond will be weak when entering the battlefield. This war will be gruesome for all."

"Are you certain they will be large enough to ride by winter? They still fit on our shoulders."

Stravan laughs. "Believe me, they will grow before you realize it. Dragons have sporadic growth spurts and by winter they should be perfectly capable of being ridden."

"We will bring them," Ivella announces, although I know she does not wish to train them so early.

"And you both will learn to ride, you will use Calypton and Vion. Ivella has already met both, Laven, you can meet them later this evening."

"As for the Six of Spring?" Levora asks.

Stravan heavily exhales. "Yes, that as well."

"What of us?" Greyce asks.

"The other Realms have discovered our return," Phyv informs. "They know we went missing the same day and time as the others, now that we are home, they want the others of their nation found."

"That means we go back," Greyce's eyes fall.

"Only if you want to." I say. "There are many other options we have that does not enforce you going back."

Greyce shakes her head. "No, I will go back."

"If it means finding people who are in need of coming home we will do whatever it takes." Levora says.

"I can only imagine what someone of Misonva is going through in a world like the Mortal Lands. Vampires were never built to last in that universe," Daevien counters. "Though, none of us are built to be there."

"This search may take months if even years." Phyv explains.

"Do you still have a home on human territory?" Ivella asks.

"We do," Levora responds. "We have a close friend watching over our home while we are away for a supposed family emergency. If any of us go there is plenty space for us to live."

"I may have to go with you on one of those trips." Ivella smiles. "But however you fabricated your ears, Phyv, you will have to do it to mine."

He laughs. "That will not be a problem."

"We would go together," I say and Ivella only looks at me with a gentle expression.

"So it is settled. Universal Conference is intact as well as our search for the others on the Mortal Lands."

Dyena recalls everything.

I look around at everyone sitting at this table. Every strong and resilient being. "Welcome back to the ages of war."

MOONLIGHT IN PROVAS

LAVEN HEPHAESTUS ARVENALDI, II

"For you," Dyena is standing next to me with a glass of wine.

"Thank you," I nod to her as she sits at the table across from me.

She follows to where I am looking, and quietly laughs as she pulls at a piece of bread from the basket on the table.

"Ivella," she whispers as she watches her as well.

Ivella . . .

She and Morano are walking down the stone path arm in arm as they look at the different shops within the city of Provas, Du Porva. They stop in front of a small jewelers shop and a necklace with a Sun and Moon pendant catches her eye. Ahead of them walk Phyv and Levora and the others have gone off to other shops and cafes nearby.

Dyena and I are sitting at a table outside of an eatery that gets plenty of consumers. Stravan, Daevien, and Sloan have gone inside—talking, and laughing with their people as if it is a normal day to day occurrence for them. But, then again, I see exactly how comfortable I wish for my people to feel around me. This place reminds me of a more city-like environment of Gordanta, but nothing will top Gordanta. That is a home like no other.

"She is an intelligent woman. Quiet, though." Her chin lifts as she speaks.

I laugh and bring the wine to my lips.

"Why do you laugh?"

"Give it time." I say just before sipping the dry wine. I watch her continue to admire the necklace through the window before moving along. "There will come a day you piss her off and you will realize she is not so quiet."

She chuckles. "You would know."

I cut her a look, and I cannot help but smile. "Yes, I would know."

"Nothing is perfect," Dyena runs a finger over her wine glass while she stares through the window of the eatery and at Stravan. "We did not agree on much, but we did agree on the level of respect there must be for one another, and how we wanted to treat, and be there for our people."

"Loyalty."

"And love grows from loyalty."

"I have given someone loyalty, respect, and security for years. That is not always true."

She smiles. "You never truly know what someone is going through, do you? You may provide exactly what they want, although you could be providing it at the wrong time, but when time comes they will shower you in everything you have ever wanted."

To be showered in any form of love by Ivella is all I would need. It would not even need to be in the way I want, if it is her, I want it.

"When did you both become close companions?"

"Not long ago," she sips her wine before setting it down and toying with the rim again. "Through the Blood Bond there was a lot we saw within each other accidentally, but that is only because we did not know how to control our thoughts when it came to a Blood Bond. Every night terror I had, she had. Every night terror she had, I had. Though, both were oddly similar. Solidarity in darkness. It drew us together. I knew which nightmares were mine and which were hers. So, I then reached out to her to truly understand what it was that haunted her, she did not immediately tell me, of course. Nevertheless, we reached that point, talked through each others trauma and realized we never had a companion that quite understood us like we did. Some relationships do not need measures of time to be valuable, our first personal meeting I think we both knew we would be close for years to come. Just as you wish to keep her, I do too."

Knowing that Ivella has someone she confidently confides into brings me a form of peace I did not know I needed. I always wanted that person to be me, even though it is not at this moment, I am grateful that Dyena is there with open ears and arms.

"Thank you."

Dyena smiles. "She will always have a home with me Laven." Gently, she exhales before looking over her shoulder at Ivella and then back at me. "She knows you love her, you have been patient, and I am asking you to continue to be patient just as you ask her to be patient with you."

"Does she know we are . . ." I drift off.

Dyena realizes quickly what I am implying. "No, she does not."

Behind Dyena, Stravan appears with his hands placed on her shoulders. "Miss Yunha is asking where you are, she said she wishes to see you tonight."

Dyena's hand places on top of one of Stravan's as she looks up to him from behind her. "Ah," she hums. "I will go see her now, keep our brooding High King company."

"I will," Stravan laughs.

"I was talking to Laven." She teases before kissing his forehead and going into the eatery Stravan was previously in.

"Humorous that one is." He chuckles.

"She is."

"So," he turns his head to me. "When are you going to have the big day? Or am I not invited to your Coronation."

I smile. "You are invited, I will have a Coronation but I will decide when. I am not interested in having it just yet. I do not want a large celebration since I do not see a real need to celebrate ruling Vaigon just yet. Whenever I do, I will plan to keep it small."

"When I first became High King I did not have a Coronation."

"You were the first and only High King I know of to not have one."

I remember reading long ago about his succession and that a Coronation was not held.

"Coronations are seen as more of a celebration for you moving higher in the monarchy after the death of the one before you, when we lost my father I did not see that as a celebration, that was a tragedy. So, I do not exactly see Coronations as necessary unless they are for someone being inducted into the royal line like the Coronation we had for Dyena and Ivella. Otherwise, no. As for you, you do not want to celebrate having a sullied land, which I also understand."

"I am wondering if the hatred will ever end." I force a laugh.

Stravan simpers. "Sometimes it does, sometimes it does not. It took a long while for me to enjoy being High King."

I believe I will be the exact same.

"I will also help you and your brothers learn how to wield your powers like I can, it is important that we train our people and yours so they are prepared, but we cannot forget about ourselves."

He is right, it is easy to think of what all must be done for those around you and forgetting what to do for yourself.

It is odd, really, that after our past he now hopes to help us after aiming to kill us.

"That will be greatly appreciated, thank you."

Off in the distance there is dancing and music erupting through the streets. I smile as I see Levora being led in a dance by Daevien. She bursts into laughter as she stumbles around, for the first time, I see Daevien smile too. Levora rises to the tip of her toe as Daevien spins her, the dancer she once was so many years ago is now shining through.

I stand when Ivella and Morano are far into the city. "Excuse me," I say to Stravan and I walk over to the jeweler Ivella was looking at.

The sun and moon pendant is small enough to fit perfectly in the center of my palm with room.

"Hello!" The elderly seller approaches. "A beauty is it not?"

"It is," I smile at him. "How much?"

"Three-hundred gold dollars."

I nod. "I would like to purchase it, could we have it wrapped?"

"Of course, come in and pick your box and wrapping!" He hobbles his way back into the shop and I follow behind him.

* * *

I purposely have arrived at the palace much earlier than the rest, when I reach the wing Ira is staying in, he is sitting in a drawing room by a fire with Vaigon, Vorzantu, Nyt, and Salem. A book is in his hand as he diligently reads. The pets and the Dragons sitting next to each other sleeping is an odd sight to see, but something we will need to get used to.

He looks at me as I stand here with the small box containing Ivella's necklace.

"I need a favor from you, if you do not mind."

He does not answer, he blinks and I take that as opportunity to continue.

"This is for Ivella, I do not want her to know it is from me, would you mind giving this to her but say it is from you? She will not accept it if I say it is from me."

I wait patiently and his eyes drift down to the box and slowly back up.

"It is not from me, it is from you."

"Yes, you are right." I nod. "But would you mind saying it is from you? She will not accept this if it is me she receives it from."

Once again he stares but nods. "Put it here." He nods to the table next to him and I do.

"Thank you." I nod.

Ira does not answer, he only returns to his book and I return to my family in the city.

These joyful moments they are experiencing are pertinent given how quickly this world could turn to war again. I too join them knowing my moments are running short before the time comes.

I CAN FEEL MY arms tugging to be suspended outward at my sides. The pain is nearly unfelt as I slump down to my knees in the filth below me.

Not far away, I faintly hear feet stepping into the grime along the ground and suddenly, a body falls to its knees in front of me. They grab my face and force my head up.

I know this touch.

I know these hands as if they are my own.

Ever so quietly, she sings, she sings a melody so gentle my mind chases after it and I no longer feel trapped in this stone cell that is never ending in pain.

I open my eyes and I am no longer in the cell, I am home, my old home. The first home my family ever had.

I can hear the tiny multiple feet around me, when I look, it is a very little me with wild curly hair chasing after Levora.

'Gotcha!' Pa shouts as he catches us in his arms.

'All right you three,' Ma says as she emerges into the drawing room with a large pregnant belly. 'You know, you are nearly just as bad as these children. It is like having three children already.'

He rubs a hand over her perfectly done goddess braids and pulls her closer. 'Now you get to have four children running rampant in your home.'

She laughs loudly and this makes my father grin.

The little me in his arms ruffles his white hair and he gently rubs his nose with mine as Vora laughs in his arms.

'Supper is ready,' Ma wipes dirt from my face. 'Let us go get you both cleaned and then we can eat your favorite meal!'

'Venison and potatoes!' I dramatically sing and I quietly laugh at myself.

Pa puts both Levora and I down and chases us up the stairs and laughter bursts throughout the house once more.

I wake from a dream I never thought I would see again and now hearing a voice that is a never-ending melody in my mind.

Sitting up I look around the moonlit dark room. The balcony

doors still sit open as I left them before going to bed, the curtains gently blow inward as the wind rushes over the sea and pushes the slightly cracked chamber door.

I stand from the bed and venture across the hall to Ivella's chamber.

She is sound asleep and both Vaigon and Vorzantu lift their heads as I enter.

"Go back to sleep." I whisper, but this only makes Vorzantu fly in my direction and gently land on my shoulder. Vaigon stays in bed with Ivella, and tonight, Vorzantu sleeps with me.

When I lay back down Vorzantu curls next me and as my eyes close that same melody I heard leading me from my nightmare returns and I allow it to push me to a sleep so peaceful that for the first time I do not want to wake up.

/

57
CALL BLUFF

LAVEN HEPHAESTUS ARVENALDI, II
VAIGON CITADEL

Upon arriving home, I go to the Marl Study where Carmen and Lorena wait for me.

There is a letter Carmen is holding. "From Quamfasi," he says as he hands it over to me.

The wax seal is dark red and imprinted with a Wolf encompassed by the letters V and P, this is specifically from Vallehes and Penelope.

Laven,

we are requesting you and your Circle's presence tomorrow afternoon. You will tour the dome where The Games are held and it will be up to you and your leads to train your people as you see fit. In the next sixty days, we plan to see you and your people competing.

Vallehes & Penelope

"It is a letter from Vallehes and Penelope. They are making sure we are following through with our commitment to tour the amphitheater to compete in The Games so our people are prepared to fight next to theirs."

Lorena laughs as she sits in my chair and props up her feet. "He is calling your bluff."

"He is," I point before I put down the letter.

"We all will do fine competing in The Games, it is how your father trained you, both Lorena and I have competed as have the other Dukes and Duchesses."

"But our people," I add. "How will they do?"

"They should train just fine," Lorena says as she reads the letter. "We have sixty days after the touring, within in that time frame we can solidify many to succeed. And if we find out some are weaker than we thought, so be it, they get put to the back."

"Your mother is looking for you, she is in the dining hall." Carmen advises. "I did not know she was not only leaving the royal line but the palace as well."

I put the letter down and nod. "Yes, I am not looking forward to it, I will go find her now, thank you."

When I arrive in the dining hall Levora is sitting at the dining table with our mother, Roaner, Amias, Morano and Axynth.

"Laven," she smiles while swarming in my direction.

She embraces me and I hold on to it, unsure of when the next day will come that I have this again.

"How was Provas?"

"Lovely, you would enjoy it there."

"Well," she brushes her hands over my shoulders. "You all will take me one day, I look forward to seeing everything Provas has to offer. Let us eat." She guides me to the table.

"I am not ready for you to leave yet," Levora says and our mother smiles.

I have gone my entire life with my mother except for few prolonged periods of time. How do you naturally carry on without the person that taught you everything? It feels like losing another parent as we lost our father. Though she is just a short travel away, this palace will not feel the same without her in it.

But she cannot stay here forever. This was never a life she wanted and she only stayed until I reached the point where I am now. She swore to never leave us alone with Lorsius and promised to stay only for us after the passing of our father, now that Lorsius is gone, there is no need for her to stay any longer. And for the sake of her peace, we must let her go.

"You know where to find me and you can come to me whenever you want. All of you," she touches Morano's cheek and he latches on to her hand.

"Take care of my mother, Axynth." Morano speaks warningly.

Axynth laughs. "I think Laven, the first, would come back from the dead and kill me himself I did not."

My mother laughs. "He would indeed."

"Do you need help packing any of your belongings or fathers? I am only guessing you are taking pa's belongings with you as well."

"We took care of that while you were gone, my love. We did not want to add that to your list of worries. Everything is packed and ready to go, I only wanted to wait and say goodbye in person."

"Vaigon would not have had a sliver of decency if it were not for you." Amias stands to embrace her and she grins as his large frame envelopes her.

"Oh, that is not true when you boys are here. You all did much more than I did."

"You raised us to be the people built to lead and have decency," Roaner is next to say his goodbyes. "You are owed more than you believe. I may have had my mother still, but you always loved me like a mother and you were there when I did not know I needed you. Thank you, Apolla, I could never repay you for such a life you gave all of us."

"It was not always perfect," she begins.

"And neither were we, but you dealt with it with ease." I remind her.

"A mother like you is what I wish to be." Levora rests her head on her shoulder and I witness for the first time in a long time how identical Levora is to our mother. Though her skin is lighter than our mothers, she is a replica.

"You will mother how you are meant to mother with only my influence. And I cannot wait to see you be the mother you should be." She stops speaking and smiles at all of us. "Oh," she quietly gasps. "I will miss you all." The tears begin to shed and Levora wipes away each one.

"And do bring these adorable pets when you come," she smiles at Nyt and Salem who devour raw meat in wooden bowls we keep for them in the corner of the dining room. "They are quite the company."

"I will be sure of it," I say as I approach her once more and that same adoring look she has gazed at me with all these years holds. "I love you, ma, never forget that."

She holds my face as she stares into my eyes. "Always remember what your father said. *Strong souled*, you are an Arvenaldi, born of great leaders, there is nothing you cannot do. History is in your veins, live as so."

* * *

Greyce sits down with Levora and Phyv in the Marl Study, the study my brothers and I claimed as ours after Lorsius was ridded of.

"We are trying to discover good timing for you all to go to the Mortal Lands again, though with everything currently transpiring there is much you three should not miss out on, most importantly, training. You do not want to leave and then return to war unprepared. Yaro's army is still quiet, but that could mean anything. We do not want to risk either of your lives."

"The sooner the better, you think?" Levora asks.

I tilt my head back and forth. "We could, but tomorrow we tour the dome to train for The Games to understand what our people can and cannot handle. And I want you present for that. Have you begun preparation yet?"

"Yes," Greyce says. "It would be best to start where we all were first dropped on the human territory and search for clues or remnants of anything that could have been left behind by others, from there we lead out."

I nod. "Have either of you checked to see if the portal is still functioning? I say for you three to even go through it once more just to be sure. Have Roaner go with you if you must."

"I was able to get it open after our return from Provas, but I did not try to go through it." Phyv confirms.

He was capable of opening it without Roaner?

"Try to get through it today, see if it still allows you through. For now, I see it best we keep here, continue to plan, and wait until training is over to search. We do not want to move too suddenly and fuck this up."

58
SUITORS

LAVEN HEPHAESTUS ARVENALDI, II

I CONTINUOUSLY DRIFT BACKWARD, avoiding the ferocious swing of a new trainees blade. It may have been a mistake to give her a real sword instead of the makeshift wooden swords.

I stand up straighter. "All right now," I stop the young girl from nearly stabbing me in the chest.

"The aim is to *kill*," she says with ferocity rolling in her childlike eyes as she points her sword at me. I begin to wonder if this little girl is Amias's child and he did not tell me.

I stifle a laugh as her expression grows in fury.

Even the youngest children we are training, not to the same extent as others, just enough to know how to wield a weapon against someone who means harm. This little girl will know exactly how to defend herself with confidence. She seems very willing to take my life right here although this is just training.

"Watch," I motion for her to follow my lead.

I pull my sword from the sheath wrapped around my hips and steady my feet apart.

I look back at her from the corner of my eye and she does the same. I cannot help but to smile at her determination to be great.

I settle down into a lunging position and angle the handle of my sword at my hips with both hands before slowly rotating the blade forward.

Each movement I make, she replicates.

"And again, this time by yourself."

Her face goes stone as she separates her feet, gradually lunges forward while simultaneously bringing the handle of her sword to her hip and rotating the blade outward. She returns to a stanced position before repeating the same motions over.

All around the sounds of war training ricochet on the Training Grounds, but none of it distracts her as she continues down the squared off area specifically for sword practice. Once she meets the end I stop her. "Now backwards!"

And with ease, she does.

"An intelligent child," Hua smiles.

"Very much so."

"What is her name?"

"Lilyana, she and her family are here today to train. They are commoners from the Southern Villages. Very nice people."

"Where is Roaner?" Hua asks after looking around the grounds and not seeing him.

"He is in Xenathi telling Vallehes and Penelope of our visit to Provas."

"Laven!"

We both turn to the voice calling my name, knowing who it is by sound.

"Well look there, speak his name and he shall appear." Hua says as Roaner approaches, she nudges his shoulder before ascending toward Lilyana and guiding her to the Archery Unit.

"Goodbye Laven!" She says with a grin as Hua takes her away.

"Bye Lilyana!" I call back and she grins, continuing to wave.

"How did it go in Xenathi?" I ask Roaner.

"It went well," but quickly he ventures the conversation elsewhere. "Did you know Ivella was accepting suitors?"

I almost did not hear him properly. "Run that by me once more." I lean my head further out to be sure I am hearing him correctly.

"High King Neryus of Ramana was in New Quamfasi while I was, he was fully courting Ivella for what seemed to be marriage."

"You cannot be serious." I cross my arms as I force a laugh.

"On my life, Laven, High King Neryus is pursuing Ivella."

Does he not have any fucking Hybrid women to pursue out of the thousands in Ramana?

"What on earth were they doing?"

She will accept suitors but not accept me, someone who has tried to be a suitor and much more for years now.

"She dined with him in the courtyard, they went on a horseback ride through the countryside, he met Vaigon and Vorzantu–"

"He met *my* fucking children?"

Roaner's expression turns wary. "It was brief, but yes, he did."

"Where are they? Right now in this moment where are they?"

"He was leaving when I was."

"Good," I fix my sword into the sheath before walking away.

"Laven, wait!" Roaner catches my arm. "Do not think too harshly just yet she could deny Neryus."

"Do not think too harshly? Either Ivella has lost her damn mind or she wants me to. To introduce Vaigon and Vorzantu to someone that means to be in a position that is mine is a threat standing on its own. What she did *is* harsh, I am merely reacting."

"Shit," he mumbles as he looks down the way to the entrance of the Training Grounds.

Ivella is vastly approaching in the distance, donned in a long dark and light orange dress that flows with each step. The moment our eyes meet she ascends across and grabs my arm taking me with her, when we land we are in my personal study.

"You told Vallehes we have children?" She shouts as I look down at her.

"Do we not? Or are you planning for Neryus to father Vaigon and Vorzantu?" I respond just as aggressively.

I could not care that my half-lie has caught up to me, what I care about is that she has allowed not only Vaigon and Vorzantu around Neryus, but also that she did not tell me that suitors were lining up at her door.

"Laven, that is not the point! You told Vallehes we have children and that was the reason that we needed to see each other. You could have told him more specifics or at least tell me that you are relaying this message to him so I am aware of it. He is walking around believing I have *birthed* twins that belong to you, that is not what happened. And Neryus has *nothing* to do with this conversation." Her anger is rising with each word and I can feel the heat from her body forcing outward and directly on to mine.

But neither of us take a step away. If at all, we have moved closer.

"Should I have lied? No." I make an effort to calm down, though I am finding it nearly impossible. "Vallehes was threatening that I would never be allowed to see you unless supervised given the history of our people, my immediate thought was to tell him that we have children since it was not a complete lie. And Neryus has everything to do with this conversation and I will not let you avoid the fact that you did not tell me you were accepting suitors."

"Firstly, I was not expecting Neryus, he just arrived and asked to be a suitor. When a woman becomes a Right Hand she naturally gains suitors, especially if she is not already married. I was never expecting this nor accepting and I did not turn Neryus down after he came all this way. Above all, not now given the time we are in and any wrong move could trigger a bad reaction from any realm."

"Ivella," I heavily exhale as I pinch the bridge of my nose before looking at her again. "I do not care." I honestly speak. "I have been the utmost patient man with you and I am done. I am telling you now what I want and it is you. I do not want you to marry anyone and you are aware of why."

If these words do anything, it builds her anger encompassed by passion. "An ultimatum is below you, Laven."

"No, not an ultimatum. I am telling you how I feel and I am allowing you to choose what you wish to do with what I tell you."

My father said *'pain is inevitable, what it is you choose do with that pain is what matters.'* I believe this applies to all things in life and not singularly pain.

"Just because you do not want me to marry does not mean I will not!" She retaliates once more. "And as a High King I am sure you will be searching as well given High King's have a time frame before they find a wife."

"So then we both are to explore all options but each other?"

"I guess so."

"Then leave," I nod to the door. I lift a hand and it opens.

Hesitance.

She stares up at me as her chest rises and falls and I greedily watch as this dress perfectly extenuates her most glorious parts. And the sun and moon necklace she saw while in Provas sits prettily upon her neck.

Still, she has yet to leave because she does not want to.

'I am asking you to continue to be patient just as you ask her to be patient with you.'

Finally, she turns and the moment she reaches the door I breach across the room and shut it just before she can leave. I tighten my hand on the knob as she reaches for it.

Her breathing goes ragged as I press my body against her back.

My eyes roll at the sensation of her being so close again.

I lower to her ear and her entire body shudders as I inhale deeply.

"Leave this room knowing that a marriage to him or any man will not keep me held away. *Universes* are not far enough apart to keep me from finding my way to you. If you think a silly marriage will do it, you are wrong. I am the doing and undoing of everything we are as you are too. Go and marry him Ivella and watch how much more unbearable I will become for you. I can get much worse than this and I have not even begun yet."

As I stand straight, she ascends from the study and back home.

When I arrive back to the Training Grounds I find Amias and

"We train. Now."

Immediately he can tell something is the matter and does not question it as he grabs his sword and we gain the attention of many as he lets me battle through every emotion I do not know how to process.

59
THE PAST

PHYV

"ARE YOU TRULY READY to go back to the human world so soon?" Greyce asks. She sits next to me on the chaise and puts a small cup of herbal tea in my hands.

Something about the human world always made me feel so incomplete, here I am finding my place and somewhat enjoying it. But to have it interrupted by going back to the Mortal Lands so soon was not planned, I knew I would go back at some point in time, not within the matter of weeks. Nevertheless, if it means finding others who are like us and crave to return home, I am willing to go back.

"I do not mind going back if I can bring the other three out there relief by coming home."

"And the people of the Realm of the Banshees and Realm of the Vampires, I think about them often and how they are able to live in a world amongst humans."

"It will be good for Nyt and Salem to return home for some time?" Greyce says as more of a question than statement.

"I do not know," I say as Nyt rests his head on my lap. "He seems to love it here, the food does both Salem and Nyt well. They are getting more nutrients from the meat here, the water is much cleaner, and they take well to everyone they are around."

"Although Morano has a favorite," Levora chuckles as Salem cuddles into Greyce.

"Give it time, I am sure a moment will come that they grow to like each other."

"When will we attempt to cross the portal?" I ask. "We all have varying schedules and I'm uncertain if we can find the right timing to attempt crossing."

"Nights work best for me, unfortunately. I would much rather cross during the day, although my schedule will not allow it."

"Same for us," Levora waves a hand between her and I. "As long as we are together we should cross just fine."

"There is one thing I do miss about the human world and it is that damn pizza and pasta."

"Yes!" Vora gasps as she agrees with her. "We must figure out a way to make that here, I know it must be possible."

"Honey, if I can make jam I can make sauce, it is possible." Greyce winks.

"Phyv, Vora," Amias says from the door of the drawing room. "Hello Greyce," he nods to her in greeting. "We are ready for you both on the Training Grounds."

"Thank you, we will be there shortly." Levora says before Amias leaves. "Do not go yet," she tells Greyce, "stay with Salem and Nyt and we will be back for supper."

"No running rampant around the palace today for you two." I say over my shoulder as both Levora and I leave.

* * *

Levora is on the Training Grounds first, she is training with Hua in the Archery Unit far in the distance. Closer is the large development for experts in the Sword Unit, where Laven and Roaner are. Laven's movements are sharp and precise, just on the verge of murder but not exactly pursuing a kill. For someone of Laven's size, he is agile and quick—he is much thicker in body and well shaped, though not as chiseled as Roaner, who is lean and large, but not as large as his brother. Their skin has darkened under the beat of the sun, Roaner has now taken on a much more brown complexion as Laven's already brown skin has turned dark. From afar, I can see the faint scars that sit all over his back and discomfort grows the longer I look at them.

The tattoos along the length of the right side of their bodies are identical: a Wolf sigil formed by the initials L, A, R, and M. That is their brotherhood tattoo.

I narrow in, as if in slow motion, I watch the sharp edge of Laven's pristine sword nearly take to Roaner's neck, as he leans to dodge it. Laven sweeps his hand down, knocking Roaner's sword from his hand. Then, his forearm forces forward and a light blue hue projects and a force field rushes Roaner's body across the field they practice on.

"No cheating," Roaner coughs through the pain as he sits up from the dirt paved ground.

Laven turns toward me and I shake my head. "No."

Laven laughs and approaches me as Roaner leaves to go where Vora and Hua are. He grabs his black undershirt from the ground and tosses it over his shoulder.

"Who trained you?" I ask as he signals for me to follow him.

"My father and mother both. As well as Axynth, Amias's father."

"How long have you been a Warrior?"

"Interesting enough, not long. A considerable amount of years, not nearly as long as Amias. I did not become a Warrior . . . well," he stops and corrects his words. "I was not considered a Warrior until after I led the second war against New Quamfasi."

At his current age he would have been newly seven and ten at that time. "You led that war?"

"I did and I did not have fun doing it. Lorsius used to say that the reason I conceded so quickly in that war was because I did not want to participate in it. We were getting our asses handed to us and I had no choice but to put the war to end, sign a treaty in Lorsius's name and leave the war where it was."

The further we walk down, the closer we get to the Archery Unit and an arrow clumsily shot by Vora makes its way toward me and Laven. All too smoothly, Laven pivots and catches the arrow soaring by.

"Sorry!" Vora holds up a hand with a wary expression and Laven cannot help but to laugh as he tosses the arrow back into the square of the Archery Unit.

"You led a war as a practical High King when only a High Prince?"

"Want to know something hilarious?" He chuckles. "I was not even a High Prince yet. Just the nephew to a High King."

Lorsius began a war he did not fight in. How many more Leaders must Voschantai Universe see like him?

"Now you are High King."

"That I am." He simpers.

"Laven!" A little girl beams from the Hand to Hand Combat Unit. She is jumping up and down with her small hands waving over her head.

"Hi again Lilyana," Laven grins as we continue to walk through the Training Grounds.

"Have you grown used to hearing that yet? Being called a High King."

"The longer I ponder on that question, I realize I have the same answer forming."

"And that is?" I say over the veering sounds of spears letting loose across the Spears Unit.

"Even when Lorsius was alive, when was I not a King? When was I not fulfilling duties that belong to a King? Unfortunately, as much as I did not want it, I was bred for this role given my family's history of leading all their lives—it is in my blood to lead as it is in my sisters. My father used to call me the brown duckling among white swans. I was the first of our family to openly admit to not wanting to be a Leader."

It is odd to hear someone say they did not wish to be in a royal line of some sort. Royalty gives you an automatic form of wealth in every aspect of life. People kill for this, yet Laven wanted to run from it.

"I always knew I would lead, but that did not mean I wanted to."

When we reach the large premises for the headquarters of the Training Grounds we sit on the wide steps stretching across the establishment.

"And now? Do you still want to lead?"

He looks at me from the corner of his eyes. "There is more at stake now. I have a large family that I hope to grow, I have important people in my life to provide for and all of those people rely on my placement to continue in the royal line so they are secure in life."

As I recall the stories of Roaner and Morano specifically, I know that without Laven they would not be where they are now, if anything, their beginnings sounded like outcomes for death.

"It is my duty to carry on for my family, either I enjoy where I am or not."

"You make me see royalty in a way I have never imagined."

He turns to watch all of the people training in the units yards ahead of us. "Because I am living a royal life not as people imagine it to be. When people think of royalty they see crowns and gold and luxurious clothing and twelve-foot tables full of food. When we see chains and poverty and slavery and famine—this does not mean that the people do not also see this, but they see what we see in a much different light because they are living it. While we are monitoring it and coveting to solve it. Two very opposite sides, yet both on the same side.

"You see what we allow you to see. It is important you know these things before you are properly presented a position in House Arvenaldi. It is not easy here, war will rage, deception and propaganda are important and you must be good at it, and strength is needed in every area. We thrive on brotherhood and sisterhood. Family, blood or found, is to kill for and we protect each other's mates and spouses as if they are our own. If you fall, one of us will be there to aid you and you must reciprocate it. Then, and only then, will you be a suitable fit."

"If I am honest, this is a placement I never even dreamed I would have. I always sought a way to just get by. Having so much handed to me makes me want to work for it since that is all I have known."

"Never unknow it. Always know what it means to be diligent. This war will call for nothing less now, during, and most importantly after, when for months on end there is nothing but rebuilding and depression."

The aftermath of war is what many Warriors have said is the worst. Searching for your family or companions, turning over multiple dead bodies in hopes that it is not someone you love dearly.

"As I study the people around me and the multitudes of abilities they have, it was easy to add together that Yaro is starting a war in the age of some of the strongest people this universe has known. He wants more than to just rule all the lands—"

"He wants to rule the strongest people in all realms." Laven finishes. "As long as I am living, High King or not, he will never know what it feels like to rule me nor anyone of our world."

I look at him as he still stares out at the people ardently training to fight for this realm.

"Forever may you reign, Laven."

60
VEHEMENCE

LAVEN HEPHAESTUS ARVENALDI, II
XENATHI --- QUAMFASI CITADEL

"WELCOME BACK TO QUAMFASI," Stelina greets as we stand where the previous border once was. There are two large carriages waiting for us being led by four Pegasi each.

Her dark red leather armor is thick and slightly lighter in stitching than the others, this discloses her as someone prominent in House Valendexi.

"We are in bad timing here at the moment, there is a current game occurring so we must make the journey there quick, so we will ascend. We had the Pegasi prepped but it will take too much of our time we are already short on."

"Thank the Gods." Morano mumbles.

"Morano has a fear of a tipping carriage," Amias clarifies when he notices Stelina's face turn for confusion.

Stelina laughs. "Well, one day you will have to ride the carriage there, but today we will not be able to."

"Why is it that we usually go by carriage and not by ascension?" Levora asks.

"The Games are held in a sacred area, correct?" I ask.

Stelina nods. "In order to reach the dome we must enter through the Hashthyna Forest where the Tree of Gods is protected. The Hashthyna Forest is the only land outside of Xenathi and the only land Lorsius was unable to touch because we kept it hidden through fabrication."

"How was that possible?" Roaner asks.

"We made it look as if it were useless land and he left it to us. But only our people knew what was really there. Something sacred that not all can see."

"Did he never question it?" Morano chimes in. "Someone like Lorsius would not let the Tree of Gods slip through his fingers without a fight."

"When I say useless land I mean destroyed. In his eyes, he saw only a stump of a tree that was burned and everything around it had perished. There was nothing left to it for him to have use of."

"If we were to ride there we would also cross the Vaisenya River." I add.

Levora's eyes widen. "The Prayer River?" She translates.

"Yes," Stelina smiles. "It is one of the most beautiful and venerated waters known to this world. Not many lands were blessed with these rivers, in those waters lies nothing but beginnings when someone truly covets for change and miracles that they deserve."

I can see the wheels turning in Levora's eyes as she drifts into deep thought.

I touch her shoulder and she jerks from her thoughts as her eyes lift.

Stelina holds out her hand to me and I take it and behind me everyone gathers to rest a hand on my shoulder and as Roaner touches last, we ascend to the dome.

We stop within what seems to be a small town but it is an area designated to crafting weapons, armor, and multiple appointed quarters to enlist.

I follow behind Stelina's path and as we move through she sharply turns her head toward the large shop where workers are crafting armor, one piece of armor in particular is being crafted in black leather with blue stitching. It mimics the leathers we wear in Vaigon.

"Is my daughters armor ready yet?" Stelina's voice booms across the vast distance.

The man crafting the armor briskly looks up with large eyes. "I am getting there, Stel!"

"Get it done!" She snaps at him as we continue to walk.

The farther we walk through, I see the tip of the open dome appear and bodies jumping and lunging through the air to reach the other end of the course that seems never ending. The more the dome appears I see all of the near thousands whom watch The Games as they occur. Their cheering and shouting grows all the more louder the closer we get.

We walk through the stone entryway and I see Ivella standing in the open space as the next group of people line up to race toward obstacles at her command.

She slightly turns her head over her shoulder, she does not look at me, but it is that acknowledgment of knowing I am here.

She walks to the row of people readied to take off.

Her leathers are tight up her legs but hang loose around her waist with her upper body only clothed in a white thin strapped shirt under the beating sun that has turned her skin a shade darker. Her hair is tightly braided down her back. I have never see her face so clearly in all the years I have been around her.

She stands before the next group avoiding all eye contact with me.

"Ivella," Stelina calls. "*Desva je nuat hesa*.*"

Ivella lifts her chin. "*Esu*?*"

They walk toward each other and exchange a low conversation before Ivella approaches all of us.

"This is incredible." Hua mumbles as she watches each person

---

* *Old Quamfasian: Desva je nuat hesa*   *Translation: Do not start yet*
* *Old Quamfasian: Esu*   *Translation: Why*

take to the courses.

"It is," Ivella laughs as she and Hua embrace each other.

"I want to do it today." Hua looks down at her in question if she can.

Ivella nods. "You can, it would be with Lourdes."

Hua finds a smile. "Even better."

Ivella greets everyone from Vora to Amias.

Everyone but me.

"I have to leave but I will return shortly."

"Where are you going?" Amias asks as she leaves his embrace.

"I have to test my armor."

She walks away to leave and I speed across the distance and stand in front of her stopping her hard in her tracks. She collides with my chest and I catch her before she stumbles backward.

"And me?"

She glares upward with reddened cheeks. "Hello Laven," is all she says before pushing from my arms.

Just as she tries to walk away I catch her chin with the tip of my finger and her eyes draw upward.

"Hello to you too."

That familiar gaze of defiance appears. "If you dare to be unbearable so can I."

I smile. "You will be giving me exactly what I want."

Quickly, she turns away before ascending from the grounds.

"Laven, the next game is beginning." Stelina says and I walk back to where I was.

She now stands where Ivella was before sending off the next group for the courses.

From the observatory at the very top of the dome sits Ira and Naius who are monitoring everyone as the people who have succeeded forward now race through a tunnel at the end of the dome on horseback. Ira walks to the edge and Naius jumps down from hundreds of feet and lands smoothly on his feet. He tops his horse before following the last person out of the dome, through the tunnel, and they head for the outlying forest behind the dome.

From the crowds multiple names are being shouted as Stelina's arm raises and a loud horn bellows across the dome. Then, the competitors race toward the start.

"Pay attention closely," Stelina shouts over the screaming onlookers. "Watch every participant, study every course. You may learn ways to win The Games through them. Even those who do not win have intelligent tactics."

"What is outside of this dome?" Levora asks.

"The courses that mentally, emotionally, and physically challenge you."

I walk further ahead witnessing the first competitor dive into the large pool that spans the distance of fifty yards. Each person fights through the water as Ira stands from the top of the dome and as his eyes close, he intakes a deep breath before his eyes reopen and forces his hands downward and through magic he creates currents and waves that have effect on their performance. I can hear the soaring winds rip across the water and move towards us causing us to stand steady on our feet.

Esme appears next to Ira and they chuckle about something, then, her eyes are flooded in that recognizable grey, and Ira takes a step backward.

"She is not going to blind them is she?" Morano wonders.

"No, but come this way, we must stand under cover unless you care to get wet!" Stelina rushes over to an awning under the seating of the onlookers and we all follow behind.

Esme turns her head to the sky and the clouds begin to darken. Her hands hold out from her sides, and slowly, she rises, and as she does, the thunder rolls, rain begins to pour, and the lightning strikes the edge of the pool. Some this throws off guard, others stay right on course toward the end.

"Since when could she control the fucking weather." Morano's eyes sit widened at her abilities.

"My husband's family comes from Luveshtan's, Elemental Benders." Stelina smiles.

"Who all can bend what?" I ask her as she steps closer.

"Naius can turn water to earth, Ira can bend air, Esme can create storms, Ethel can bend water and ice, and Iysha we have yet to discover, though I believe it to be fire. He is quick to anger like his sister and he was born during the season of Sagittarius just as the God of Fire."

"Hephaestus."

"Recognize the name?" She simpers.

"I do indeed."

The tips of Esme's boots touch the ground first before leisurely landing flat on her feet. As she recedes from the air the storm slowly comes to an end and the rising sun returns.

Ira and Esme ascend to the ground, and on either side of the dome under the awning sits a lever on each side. Before the competitors finish the first obstacle in the water still rushing with waves, they pull the levers at the same time and the next course rises. Uneven balance beams rise up by hundreds of feet and the first person to exit the pool looks vaguely familiar.

"Who is she?"

"That would be Ethel, my niece, Esme's older sister. You may have seen her when she was with Ivella in Vaigon when they were servants."

"Does everyone in your family thrive well in The Games?" Phyv asks.

Stelina tips her head from side to side.

"That is a yes." Levora whispers as she watches Ethel leap up to the tipping balance beam, she swings her body up the rising beam and she begins to run across the narrow way as it slowly swings like a seesaw. Just as the beam falls down in front of her, Ethel rotates to slide down the beam as it recedes.

"After The Beams, no feet are to touch the ground until after The Ropes to reach your horse!"

As the balance beams rise so do The Pillars that stand by five hundred feet with rods along the length of them to the very top. Beneath the pillars lie a pool of water to catch anyone who may fall. My father was not so kind to me and Amias when it came to us running the pillars as children. Many broken bones occurred, we were healed, and told to do it again. Although, the pain of falling made us more aware of our balance to not fall from such great lengths again.

"Who is that catching up to her?" Levora asks.

"Kaden, her husband and mate."

The moment Ethel lands on the ground from the beams she begins to heave up the rods along the pillars. The truest test of strength; carrying your weight up hundreds of feet. As Kaden begins to catch up to her Esme shouts from the top of the dome. "Come on, Ethel! *Vashla** Nadrexi!" Drums begin to sound off and specific areas of the crowds begin to chant Nadrexi while waving a light blue flag back and forth. And where Esme stands from the top, Ivella appears and they both wrap their arms around each other's shoulders and begin to jump with the beat of the drum while waving the Nadrexi flag.

Ira continues to intently watch as this pushes Ethel to proceed, and she catches Kaden up the never ending pillar and her strength increases.

She reaches the top of the pillar as others behind her still struggle on the beams but they are gaining on both her and Kaden.

Ahead of her lie twelve more pillars to run across.

"Balance Ethel," Stelina whispers under her breath as she watches her niece take long leaps to get from pillar to pillar.

To prevent Kaden from catching up to her, she takes strides in front of him to reach the ropes that hang from centerpieces of the dome.

Screaming louder than before breaks out as she leaps for a rope and slides down to the ground and toward her horse that takes her to the tunnel door that opens for her to proceed to the next course outside of the dome.

"What exactly lies outside of this?" Hua asks over the shouts of the people above.

"Upon exiting the tunnel you reach the forest where you must go

---

* *Old Quamfasian: Vashla   Translation: Chant*

through four more courses. Bows and arrows while on horse, spears and swords, hand to hand combat, and lastly the Forest of Fears."

"What is that?" Morano stands closer.

"It is a forest that brings forth your most deepest fears and makes you confront them. If you have already conquered what haunts you it will be easy to pass through, but with slight difficulty. Though, if you have not, that will be the day you meet them face to face and seek your way out. Mental clarity is the goal, it does not determine if you have won The Games but it determines if you are ready to conquer your greatest fears."

"Ma," Ira approaches. "Ivella is ready to test her armor, it fits her well when I looked over it just now but we must have her train in them to break them in. Also to be sure it enhances her abilities like planned."

"Ivy!" Stelina calls from below.

Ivella looks downward from the top of the dome and she ascends to her mother.

"We will go to the training grounds so you can test your suit," Stelina then turns to us. "You all may come as well, you will meet with Vorian after who will set the date for your next arrival to enlist your people to compete in the games."

As I take in her new armor, it is a dark blue with light blue stitching in it. These were the leathers I saw upon entrance.

"I will train with you," I step forward. "We can go now and I am already dressed in my suit."

Before she can protest, Stelina grabs our hands and we all ascend to their Training Grounds not far from the dome.

We now stand on their Hand to Hand Combat Unit. I remove my cloak and Roaner takes it from me and drapes it over his shoulder.

"He fights dirty Ivella," Morano smirks.

She does not answer him. Instead, she suddenly rushes onward and I do as well. She breaches halfway across the distance between us before she leaps and one leg angles down in a direction right for my hip.

In a drift, I dodge her foot and catch her armor, throwing her into the air. White and tan feathers fall to the ground and her wings sprawl as she steadies herself in the heights above me.

I simper at her control. "So it is true that God is a woman?"

Her wings oscillate, carrying her higher just before she soars down in a sharp line. She grips me by the hair dragging both of us to the ground.

We roll across the field fighting to see who will pin the other first.

She grips my neck and ascends across the ground forcing me down, her dagger is drawn and pointed right at the center of my face.

"Still refusing to be my Queen?" I ask through a strangled breath.

Fury builds in her beautiful green eyes that move with specks of orange.

Her hand tightens and her wings fall around us, cascading over me like blinders. Even in this position with a dagger narrowed in on my face, I feel entirely safe here.

"Still bedding half the women in your nation?" She fires back.

I ignore that dig, though it is hard not to. "Prophecy, Ivella. You will be an Arvenaldi, you will be a High Queen, and you will be great. *We* will be great."

I ascend from her grasp and the dagger she was holding releases across the distance between us, and in my distraction to avoid it, she instantaneously stands. Her arms draw backward before her wrists collide and her hands draw apart. I watch the magnificence of fire swirling through the span of her hands.

The blue stitching in her armor ignites as the fire soaring between her palms grow.

The armor is working.

Behind the fire I see all the pain and agony she holds, it just so happens to be me she is taking it out on, but I am the only person built to handle every demon that follows her.

"Calm, Ivella." Esme has arrived and she grabs her arm before she releases everything against me. She consoles her cousin with a calm voice, a voice I have never heard her use. It seems the stone woman has a soft side for those she loves deeply.

Naius appears next to her and he touches Ivella's wrist and the fire dulls until it is gone.

Naius looks at her hands. "Where is your Tigers Eye ring?"

"I do not have it with me. It is at home." She is short with him as she speaks.

"I thought we agreed you would not take it off?"

After I speak, that temper of hers creeps back in.

"Go home and get it." Naius gently speaks before she can retaliate at me.

"I will go with you," Esme offers and Ivella accepts as they grab each others hands.

Ivella and Naius exchange a final glance with one another before he smoothes his hand over the back of her head and pats her back.

"Now that you have witnessed The Games," Naius shifts his attention to all of us. "You may plan accordingly for the next sixty days. If you need help, call upon me or Stelina. We will aid you with anything you may be in assistance of."

Before they leave, Esme acknowledges everyone but Roaner who continues to stare her down.

"Esme," Roaner attempts to walk to her but quickly she interrupts him.

"Come, Ivy, let us take a little trip to Nadrexi to gather your sanity."

Without letting Ivella say goodbye, Esme ascends them both.

I turn to Naius. "Where can I get a suit like that?"

"I had a feeling you would ask." Naius laughs.

"I have a question," Hua takes to Naius. "May I participate today?"

"Are you looking to compete or have a trial run with The Games?"

Given they have already trained together in the past, Naius would be first to know that Hua is absolutely ready to participate in a game without training. We all are, but out of all of us, Hua keeps the most fit and agile.

"Compete."

Naius smiles. "Then I will have you enrolled into the next game."

VAIGON CITADEL

I have sketched the perimeter of the dome and within it the trials. First, the large space where the race toward The Pool begins. After, the span you must run across before reaching the balance beams that rock like seesaws. Then, the strength test up The Pillars that lead to The Pillar Run. And lastly, The Ropes, the final jump toward reaching your horse that will carry you to the final rounds.

"The jump from here to here is quite a distance," I point from The Pillars to The Ropes. "People will have to put their all into the leap they take from that length."

"I will make it one of the most necessary practices." Amias confirms.

"Let me take this to the city for printing," Hua motions for me to give her the sketch. "Sign your name in the corner so the people know it is you who crafted this sketch and they can learn the courses visually before practicing physically."

I roll the sketch before tying it off and handing it over to Hua and she is gone.

"Did you see the way he tried to drown them in that pool?" Morano asks from the corner of the study.

Roaner chuckles and sits down.

"Morano," I chortle. "He was not trying to drown them. He was making their swim more difficult to test them. Not drown them."

"Laven, if you can, practice controlling your force fields in motion. You could create those same waves that Ira did with air as you could with force fields." Phyv explains.

"This is true," Roaner says. "After the pool is built on the Training Grounds we will attempt then."

"Oh," Levora says standing after seeing the sun setting. "I must meet a friend in the markets. I will see you for supper?" She asks and we nod before she is off.

"We should have asked her to get vegetables for supper. I plan on eating at Ryverian House tonight." Amias says.

I smile. "It has been quite some time since we have dined there."

"We have not had the time to." Roaner regretfully speaks.

Due to everything transpiring over the months, we have not been able to spend the time we would like in the Safe House. There are one too many memories there, both good and bad that give that mansion character similar to Fonavyn House in Gordanta. But Ryverian House will always be greater than the rest as that is the house my parents raised all of us in.

"I will go to the market and get what we need," I stand from the table and remove my top coat. "What meats are you making?"

"My dear companion," Amias grabs my shoulders as I undo the laces on my undershirt. "You will be cooking the meats, not I. We are having fish, plan accordingly." He pats my cheek.

I stare at his stupid grin he shows when he wants someone to do something for him. His dark skin beams under the sunlight and his eyes crease in the corners as he begins to chuckle.

"Get out my way." I playfully push him so I can leave.

61
NADREXI NIGHTS

LAVEN HEPHAESTUS ARVENALDI, II

When I reach the markets I go to the best baker we have, though he is farther past the markets that reach city grounds, Jeshtyp Bakery is where I need to go first.

As I enter the bakers shop, Jeshtyp is already smiling my way. "Ah, Laven! Your sister was just here, she was purchasing her favorite loaf."

"Yes, she told me she was in this area meeting a friend. I am here to purchase for supper, what breads do you have today?"

"She was with a friend, very nice woman! Come this way, I will show you what I have that is fresh. Just pulled it from the stone."

I follow him through the dim bakery where plenty of others are dining with cheese and wine made by his wife, Mrs. Patro, the chef in our main palace.

"Her friend was very sweet," he continues. "She bought an abundance from me, I do believe she is from New Quamfasi. She wanted a basket full of jams, cheeses, thin meats, and loaves. I was happy to see her, I knew her from previous months and this is the first I have talked to her in awhile. I gifted her a loaf and in return she gave me wine."

When I walk by the paying counter, that pristine bottle of wine is all too recognizable.

"What did she look like? I may know who you speak of by description."

"Old rich beauty. Freshly dark skin from the sun, slightly rounded nose, curly raven hair, light eyes—green!" He shakes a finger as he recalls entirely.

Ivella.

Ivella, Ivella.

Of course she would not ask me to bring her here, she asked Levora, her newfound companion.

Mr. Patro ties his dreads away from his face, cleanses his hands in a small water fountain, and next, he moves to the fire where a cast iron skillet sits closed with hot wood on top. He sweeps the wood off the top of the skillet, removes the lid, and reveals freshly baked sweet rolls.

I press my hand to my chest. "Mr. Patro, you must have known we were eating fish tonight."

He laughs before pulling the skillet from the fire and places it on a wooden table nearby to wrap the rolls in cloth. After I receive the rolls and give him his pay, I make my way to the fresh markets where I know they must be now.

How I can get Levora to leave is the question.

Then, I hear the melodic laughter led by the grace of wild summer beauty.

And with the utterance of her voice my entire soul responds.

How is someone capable of shining like diamonds and pearls?

I approach closer to where they stand gathering fruits right in front of the stand where I need vegetables. I gravitate closer and through the people striding by I see her face appear and fade within all, but I never lose sight of her.

"Hi, Peter." I smile as I reach the vegetable stand.

Ivella's head lifts from the other side of the market and she looks around, searching.

I smile.

"Laven! What are you in need of today?"

Still she searches and Levora begins to pull her to the next place, a small stand full of candies, but she is . . . distracted.

"I need everything for a fresh vegetable medley. Cucumbers, tomatoes, lemons, onions." As I name everything off he is gathering it. "As well as sweet potatoes, asparagus, and broccoli. I believe my brother already has carrots and zucchinis at our home."

Ivella cannot pay attention to all the sweets Levora is pointing out, her eyes are still rapidly searching.

In a basket, Peter has everything ready and I take it after giving him coin.

I begin to walk down the way as she is taken down the other side of the market again.

"On your right, between the stands."

Her body jolts and her eyes expand.

She turns and through the passing of people, she too sees me through the crowds.

It worked.

I have access to her mind.

"Get rid of her."

And in the confusion her eyes hold, defiance returns.

She continues on with Levora who has her smell a jar of honey.

Ivella's eyes flutter and she nods.

"We will be getting this too!" Levora grins as she hands over her coin and Ivella places the jar of honey on top of the small basket of dark cherries.

"Get rid of her or find me in your dreams tonight."

She does not listen, instead, she carries on with Levora who readily shows her more of her favorite sellers and their goods.

* * *

"Man of the hour!" Amias shouts as I enter the Ryverian House.

"Start the fire in the kitchen would you?" I push him away from me.

He smirks. "And you got the sweet rolls." He says after rummaging through the baskets. "I knew you were perfect to cook dinner tonight."

"What is on the menu tonight chef Laven?" Hua asks while looping her arm around my shoulders while eating strawberries from a basket.

"Fish, that Amias so kindly caught for me to cook. Fresh vegetable medley, roasted potatoes, roasted vegetables, and sweet rolls."

"You know, you all could learn to cook." Roaner says from the drawing room as he and Phyv play a game of chess.

"Why?" Amias and Hua ask in unison.

"Why cook when you all exist to do it for us," Hua squeezes my cheek as she takes the vegetable basket to the sink where she pulls a lever and water comes pouring out.

She grabs a soft bristle brush and begins cleaning the vegetables.

"Very funny," I force a laugh as I grab a bowl and prep the food.

"And what about wine?" Morano asks.

"I have that," I turn over my shoulder and Ivella is walking into the house with Levora.

This I was not expecting.

She looks me over as I cut the vegetables that Hua has washed.

"Ah, so the friend you were meeting was Ivella," Amias smiles. "You get to enjoy Laven's finest cooking."

"Oh, I did not know you were aware of how to use a pan over fire." Ivella teases.

"Now, now. I am capable of many things that you do not know of."

She only hums in response before walking over to Phyv and Roaner. "Although I would love to stay, I cannot. I promised Ira I would dine with him in the city."

"Next time!" Morano shouts as he picks off a broccoli stalk and tosses it into his mouth.

"Yes, but I want Ivella's cooking next time." Levora vouches. "I have heard you make an amazing tender venison."

Ivella laughs and promises she will cook for her as long as one of us catches the deer.

"Levora, I will walk Ivella out. Keep cutting this for me."

"Oh, do not worry yourself. I will be ascending. Have a lovely dinner."

Her greatest ability, avoidance. And she is gone.

"I will go get the fish," Morano leaves for the backdoor where he was gutting the fish outside.

"Remember mother used to make this?" Levora smiles as she helps me cut all the vegetables.

"I think that is why I am so good at making it." I smile, and she nudges my arm and continues to chop.

XENATHI — QUAMFASI CITADEL

I ascend past the gravel line where the border between Xenathi used to lie. The second I am through, patrol is standing there, spears held tightly in their hand. They are dressed from neck to toe in dark red armor, ready to fight on hand if anyone dares to pass unwarranted.

Given it is now night, this visit could turn out to be monitored.

"High King Laven," one of the men says in a greeting.

"I need to speak with Lady Ivella. I must cross to Nadrexi to be exact of her location. The visit will be short," I add for hope of me getting through.

"Philip will ascend you there." The guard nods to a man walking toward us.

Even after our newfound trust; the Quamfasian people allow no outsider to ascend on their own, we must always be escorted. They must see you to where you are going and retrieve you from where they left you.

Philip touches my shoulder and takes me to Nadrexi.

NADREXI — SOUTHERN COURT OF QUAMFASI

The waterfall is even more beautiful in the night and the stars in the velvet sky reflect on to the water flowing around her home.

"Have Lady Ivella send word when you are ready to be retrieved," Philip says as I walk up the stairs to the doors.

I look up at the small mansion built in tan stone. Ivy has grown along its corners and edges, trying to claim the space that was once rightfully theirs. Far through the wild trees opposite of the home lies the sea that takes you straight to Provas. This land is the only land near the ocean that crosses to the Realm of the Fae.

Philip walks farther through the trees before vanishing; the moment he is gone, I ascend into the home, stopping right inside her chamber.

The double doors to her bathing room are open; I can smell her. The scent of wild citrus and salt of the sea reels me in.

Ivella moves with alacrity, her green eyes fade into a deep orange; staring directly through me. She sits in the smooth stone tub, roses, and lavender floating in the warm water around her.

The windows that scale from floor to ceiling lay open, the Summer breeze sings through the trees, and in the night the woods are vast and seen right from this room.

She watches as I circle the large tub while loosening my cloak, the dark blue fabric falls to the floor, and her eyes do not move from my own as I remove all my upper clothing.

I stop in front of the tub, mere feet away from her. The steam in the water grows; she is deliberately making it hotter, thinking I will not make it through.

Once I remove my topcoat, I lean on the edge of the stone, watching her just as she watches me.

"Ivella," I lowly call. She does not come; she only sits up straighter, rose petals sticking to her luscious brown skin.

She plays with the water.

"Come here." I hold onto the stone tighter.

Her full lips finally part. "No." Her soft tone is of fire.

"Ivella, come *here*."

She sinks under the water.

I cannot see her past the petals. I do not move, waiting for her to recede from the water.

Two hands reach upward, pressing to the stone right below me. She gradually lifts through the water, flower petals cling to her skin and hair; small pieces rest over her face as her nose just grazes mine. Water falls slowly down the curve of her breasts.

Lower my head, searching for her lips, I close my eyes. She drops lower into the water, causing me to quietly whine.

"You do not tell me what to do." She whispers.

I chase her lips blindly; she is just there, a short hair away.

"No, I do not. But when you are naked, I do." I slide my finger up her chest, stopping right at the length of her neck, squeezing enough to guide her back up.

I could maneuver over her body through pure muscle memory.

Opening my eyes just enough, I see that defiant smile and the shut of her eyes—she is groveling at the touch of my skin to hers.

I reach downward, gripping the plush curve of her ass, hoisting her from the bathing tub. The water drips from her hair and skin as I lift her. I can hear the flapping of wings from the birds entering the room and diving into the water.

Her full legs wrap around my waist as she grips my chin, biting my lip with the sharp point of her canines she brings forward, then, gently tugging.

I rest my forearms under her thighs as I rub my fingers toward the softest spot I plan to devour through the evening.

She withers and moves, searching, hoping for one little touch of my fingers where she wants. But, instead, the more I tease, her moans grow louder, sending vibrations across my skin.

Her forehead presses to mine as my teasing her becomes my own torment.

"If we do this now, you must be prepared for how insatiable I will become with your body." I warn.

"Starving," she mumbles against my skin and my knees weaken.

The heels of her wet feet dig into my ass as I walk to the bed; the wind purrs through the room, sending the white fabric from the canopy bed to flow through the air and fall back into place.

I slowly put her down, her feet finding the floor just as I drop to my knees. Then, lifting one leg to hook over my shoulder, her foot trails up the tattoo on my back, opening herself to me. Her back presses to the poster of the bed as I immerse under. There is a tremor of a moan as my tongue explores her in places I have only dreamed of. The moment I taste her, my eyes close, I know no return to willpower.

As supple as biting into perfectly ripened fruit. You cannot help but to nip for more and ravish her until she coos as the morning dove in the Spring.

A high-pitched gasp echoes as I gently suck on the tiny nerve that is setting her wild. I smile as she tugs at my hair as if it were possible to pull me any closer.

She wraps tightly around my finger as I slowly push inside of her. Her leg shakes as I gently caress that spot right inside her.

Ivella gazes down, as I drag my tongue over her sweetest spot. Her eyes flutter shut and her moans dance with the chirping of the birds.

My hand reaches up, grabbing her chin. "Watch how much I enjoy what is mine," I groan as she drips down my fingers like honey. A little trail flows down her inner thigh, and I follow it with my tongue.

"Laven," she cries out.

This alone I could get drunk off, my own personal sweet white wine, drinking her in until I am addicted. The only liquor sitting at the top of my shelf, the first I reach for.

I look upward as she watches me lick up her thigh and back to where I belong.

Gripping her round hips, I tug her forward, and flick my tongue against her at a rapid pace. It is her undoing.

The rose petals still latch on to her skin. She looks empyrean standing above me, glowing in the moon beaming through the doors.

Her leg still draped over my shoulder tugs me onward as she meanders over in pleasure and her soft stomach curls in small bumps.

With the quiet chants of my name, the melodic moans; I have been desperate to have her. She does nothing but everything to make me crave her in every form possible.

I move toward the bed and she perches below me, sitting gracefully upon her knees. Across the room I see the cherries and honey from earlier.

I retrieve it.

She watches while I tilt the small jar full of honey. The sweet candy of nature slowly flows down her shoulder like a waterfall, gliding across her chest in an uneven slope. I lean down to her shoulder, gently kissing the first droplets of honey; her head tilts backward, exposing her neck, igniting my tastebuds to the flavor of this delectable woman. The salt of her skin combines with the honey, providing me my own flavor not another will know.

Tracing from shoulder to neck with my tongue, she is panting by the time I grace her ear with a soft bite. Rolling my finger down the center of her chest, I stroll to that hidden place sweeter than the honey etched across her skin.

Everything I have felt in the luxury of my dreams, I need to feel tonight and not another day can go by. I cannot avoid the way I need to feel her hands move like satin over my skin. How her lips will press to mine, pouring the saccharine heat of her mouth into my own, drowning me into inebriation.

I smile as her eyes roll to flutter shut; a quiet exhale escapes both our lips as I find that delicate place of her pleasure. I take in every moment as it comes. Keeping this seared into my memory—afraid, that somehow, I will forget it all.

Each breath, each touch of her hand to my own; it is remembered as if it is my own breath, my own hand to my skin.

Leisurely pushing her to her back, Ivella eagerly gazes up at me as I grab the linen bag filled with dark cherries. I pour a few onto the bed, holding one; I dip it into the thick golden liquid, tracing more lines on her body. The honey falls from the cherry, taking to the heat of her nipple, gliding down the curve of her breast. I watch how she glistens under the honey, squirming in a lovely sheen as I do the same to her other nipple. I bite into the cherry before savoring the taste of the woman beneath me.

The next to etch into my memory is every way her body responds to the touch of my skin to her own. How each breath from her chest is my guide to the next place my tongue will taste, and the next thick curve my hand will stroke.

I squeeze a handful of cherries, watching the red nectar pour. She gasps at the liquid taking to her hot skin. Her head plummets back as I rid the now bruised cherries, only to find every inch of her, painting her skin in another delicious coating.

"I need you inside me," she pleads for it as if her life is at stake.

Unhinged, I go into unending hysteria at those few words I can finally fulfill.

Those supple fingers tug at the laces of my trousers before they fall to the ground with the rest of my clothing.

A deep groan and sighs of relief fill the air around us as I guide her hips to my own. I trace my hands up and down her chest as I watch the dearest connection given to us. I tightly shut my eyes as I feel her licking the red taste of cherries from my fingers. I am too overwhelmed to focus on just one moment at a time. Happily overwhelmed in every astonishing way possible.

Her tongue curls around two fingers, sucking, and . . . Gods.

Prayer.

I need prayer.

Her skin rubbing against my own is like velour; I knead at her breasts before I flip her body to her side. She yelps at the swift movement, a smile appearing on her lips.

I hoist her leg as I straddle the other pressed into the bed. Having her this way is the utmost desirable. I can see everything . . . the form of my length perfectly fitting her, her round ass, the curves folding in her waist, the tantalizing shape of her breasts, the enchantment of her face.

Caressing all over her body as I align my hips and tenderly thrust inside of her, I am already coming undone. Touching her, looking at her, hearing the moans that she breathes as I begin to helplessly thrust into her is every bit of my defeat.

I slightly lift her leg, rubbing that spot between her thighs.

Her nails dig into my arms as her moans grow to match mine. She is warm, dripping wet, snug around my length, and she is entirely my own.

She moves beneath me; her legs wrap around my hips. I can feel her pushing her strength forward. Then, finally, she flips us, her Wolf glows in her eyes, either she knows it or not I too respond.

This is exactly what I have needed for years.

She smiles, and her hips swirl in a spellbinding wave. An impenetrable state of nirvana as she rides me in this angelic form.

Her hands press to my chest as I lowly growl at her slower pace. The way her arms push together extenuate her ample chest as she moves faster. I bite into my lip, wishing she was not pinning me down so my tongue can reach those delicious nipples.

"My Gods, Maivena." Gentle spasms move through me.

She sits, bearing me inside her, causing me to fall farther into the pillows. Her hips move back and forth generously as she holds me so deep.

That familiar sensation is more vital than ever; I growl at her, well aware of what she is doing. She will not make me come before she does. It is my only rule that will never die when we make love from here and on. She will always be first; if I struggle through it, then so be it.

"Do not dare." I shake as I fight the sensation, but I cannot move. I am enraptured by this woman of mine; there is no escape from this.

"I want you to." She moans as I push her to her back. I grip my cock as I close my eyes, trying to calm myself.

She turns to her stomach with her hips lifting upward. I smirk and straddle her thighs. I steady my arms on either side of her as I cavernously dig inside of her; she cries out as I bite her shoulder and place a firm smack against her ass.

"It is my only request." I groan as she tightens around me. "You will know a never-ending swarm of pleasure whenever I make love to you."

I curl my hips, finding that trembling place inside of her that makes her wither and shake below me. I sit up, and gather her hair, tugging at the root. She grunts as I pull her to her knees, yanking her head backward.

With my other hand, I trail up her chest, gripping her neck as I pound into her. The most glorious sound is resonating through the room as I move through her.

I moan sonorously in her ear, and her thighs quake at the oscillation of my voice. I smile and bite down as she releases strangled sounds from her throat.

"Feel me, Maivena. All of me." I pull her head back further and caress her neck as she finds that euphoric release.

Slowly, our lips finally find each other for the first time. It is gentle yet carnivorous. I flatten my tongue against hers, licking, tasting her moans as she comes.

I wrap around her body as my orgasm chases hers. Her back pressed firmly to my front as her fingers reach back, threading through my hair as I let go deep inside her. She giggles as I whimper in her neck when her hips press backward, moving in small deep strokes sending chills through my bones.

* * *

She lays on top of me—her finger traces the outline of my face. Moments have passed while we stay just like this. Both of us inching closer every now and then, wondering just how much closer we can get than how we were previously.

"Why did you stop calling me that?"

Lazily, I open my eyes to see her gazing at me.

"You told me–"

"I know," she interrupts and shakes her head as her cheek presses against her arm over my chest. "But I–I enjoy it. I *miss* it."

I stroke her chin. "Maivena," I whisper. "Maivena, Maivena, Maivena . . ."

She grins and covers me with her body. "Yes."

And just as easily as she is fire from hell, she is the divine water people wish to find the Gods in.

She sits up, straddling my waist. I sit up with her, flower petals that were once on her skin now sit all over mine.

I look over her face, holding the back of her neck as she smiles. The black curls in her hair dry beautifully, falling down her arms in a soft coarse texture.

Her lips press to my fingers as she holds on to my palm. I watch each move and kiss her lip's trace.

I pull her forward, her nose plays with mine as the sound of the wind sings around us. I can feel them whispering, *'home, home, home, home.'*

I ever so lightly touch her lips with mine.

"We must stop running from each other. It will be the end of me."

"Time, Laven."

And patience.

I stand from the bed and head to the bathing room with her held tightly in my arms as her lips move against mine. The birds fly from the water as I step into it; they too seem to sing in our presence.

"MAIVENA?" I WHISPER AS she now sleeps on top of me. We did not make it to the bed and I knew it would be a problem the moment we fell here on the chaise. I will not let her sleep on this. She is unmovable in this rest that has overtaken her.

Slowly rotating upward, her head falls to my shoulder and she lowly groans. She wraps around my neck as I stand and take her to the bed.

She maneuvers about the bed in her sleep to get comfortable as I dress.

Leaning in, I kiss her forehead.

"I will see you tomorrow." I delicately speak.

She does not wake and I quietly laugh against her ear.

On a small paper, I leave a note next to her for when she wakes.

62
TRUSTED CIRCLE

DAEVIEN JORDESQA
XENATHI — QUAMFASI CITADEL

"Ivella?" I aim to grasp her attention as she watches the sun sink below the trees ahead.

Vaigon and Vorzantu play fight in the sky, just in front of the setting sun. The young Dragons have grown large in size, larger to the capacity where their play fighting in the sky seems much more aggressive than before.

Her eyebrows are furrowed as she sits deep in thought.

As I observe, the new armor she now wears fits her well, and it seems already somewhat broken in.

"Ivella?" I call once more.

She turns and she brings a smile to her face. I laugh and she does as well after realizing she was here yet somewhere else at the same time.

She is brighter in appearance and looks extremely well rested, though beautiful, she has always had an appearance of tiredness and stress. Today, this is an entirely altered person from when I last saw her just a day ago. Funny to think of it, I know that aggressive smell of Laven all over her must have something to do with this. She no longer just smells like herself, there is a combination of both of them celestially intertwined.

"What was it that you wanted to speak of?" She walks away from the balcony I have met her on and she takes down the large hallway.

"Dyena and Stravan wanted me to speak with you of forming your own Circle. As you are now considered someone high in multiple royal lineages, it is pertinent that you discover who to keep closest to you to handle any and all matters you cannot."

"Oh," she waves a hand. "I am fine on my own, or at least I would like to believe I can manage well enough. Do you think I cannot?"

I smile. "Ivella."

She laughs and nods. "I know it is not that you nor Dyena and Stravan think I cannot, I spoke with them of this already and I was unsure of it, I am only guessing that is why you have been sent here." She nudges my arm as we walk.

"It may have something to do with that." I laugh.

Not only has Ivella formed a well rounded relationship with the Provanseva's, all except one, we as well have formed a grounded friendship. Since the beginning of her arrival when it was only a small supper to thank her for choosing to bring back Dyena, it turned into them learning more about each other and then all of us. When one welcomes one, we all do.

There is something about the way she is so readily there for those she cares for that reminded us of how grounded we used to be. After Dyena's disappearance all of our relationships began to falter and weaken. Stravan was absent, Savarina and I began to struggle, Sloan barely spoke to anyone which was out of his character, we all were not who we once were. When Dyena returned and Ivella arrived, we began to see how we could strive for the stability we once had.

This is what makes it all the more difficult when Savarina does not see what we see. Though, someone could ask what it is that we do not see that Savarina does. The conflict between the both of them could form dissension between our family if they do not mend.

Ivella has made many attempts to reconcile with Savarina, when Ivella does not know what she did to require reconciliation.

Amongst many other issues above this specific one, we all have a relationship to rebuild with the High Princess of Provas.

"If I have a Circle combined of my people, Vaigon, and Provas it will make the other nations see that we are not only joined by me becoming Right Hand of Provas, but by me putting full trust into those around me despite prior differences. We cannot just be *seen* as united," she stops and turns. "We must act as so. And I have already put thought into who I want, well, who I need."

"And they are?"

As she forms the words to speak a terrorized voice shouts from below the balcony hall. "Ivella!" The child continues to scream.

Ivella moves like a blur, and she is running to her little brother Iysha as he frantically rushes toward her.

"What is it?" She urgently seeks answers as she sees his ripped undershirt. The lining of his small vest is torn across the shoulder and his curly hair is more disheveled than it usually is. "What happened to you!"

He jumps into her arms and her eyes fill in the fiery orange that electrifies from corner to corner.

She is searching the woods far from us where he came running from. Her senses are heightened, searching for a threat.

When I ascend to where they are I see the dirt all over his face and the small cuts on his cheeks.

"Iysha," I kneel to his level. "You must tell us everything that happened."

"I-I-I was—" he begins to cry over his words and Ivella's eyes return to normal as she focuses on her little brother.

"Slow," she places a hand on his chest and her other hand slowly rises up and down as she helps him regulate his emotions before speaking.

"Four men!" He yells. "They were in the Hashthyna Forest while I was there with my companion and we ran to lead them away from the forest."

"What did these men look like?" She rests her hands on his shoulders to weigh him down from spiraling more.

"They were–" he stops, looking for the words. "They looked wrong! They looked similar!"

I visibly see Ivella's heart drop.

"Did they touch you, Iysha? Did they touch you or your companion? Are any of these scratches on you from them?"

She grabs his face, leaning in closer to examine every scratch on his body, soon she is turning him around to check his back and legs.

"They did not touch us, Ivy. We ran away. But they took a Norpheyen, it was a large one! They took it from its baby!"

Ivella looks up at me worried.

"Ma and Pa are not here, but I will take you to Esme, she will watch over you while I am gone."

"No, no, no!" He shakes his head rapidly. "I want to be with you!"

"Iysha, I have to go into the forest to see where they are now. I promise I will be back," her hand rests on his bruised cheek. "Now come, we must go to Esme and she will clean you up."

Iysha grunts and looks up at me. "You will go with her, she should not go alone!" The young boy shouts at me.

"Yes, I was already planning on going with her. I promise I will return your sister in one piece."

His eyebrows furrow just like Ivella's were moments ago. "You better."

"Come, Iysha. You must get cleaned and examined before we leave, you will be just fine with Essi."

* * *

Ethel and Ira come with us after hearing of the attack on Iysha. One of Ethel's abilities outside of being an Elemental Bender, is the gift of Pinnacle Sensory.

After smelling what was on Iysha she is able to locate who and what attacked him and his companion. According to Ivella, she believes it to be the return of the rogues that were created by Yaro. Tonight will be my first time encountering them.

Although there are four of them and four of us, they are considered outnumbered. Given the four of us and our strengths and abilities, it's as if it is six of us against three of them.

"The forest has gone dark," Ethel says as she looks at the moon. "They could still be lingering here to hide."

"When I took Iysha to Esme he said that he does not remember them following him outside of the forest lines," Ivella walks closer to the end of the forest that turns to large fields reaching the Palace Grounds.

Ethel walks toward the last tree before the fields, her hand places on the tree. Her eyes roll to the back of her head and rapidly move from side to side as everything that last transpired between Iysha and the rogues crawls through her brain.

Her lips part to speak and she blinks. "They never left."

Just as the words leave her mouth, one by one, the rogues briskly run by and head for the opposite end of the forest.

Ivella is quick to chase, the first to dart off like sharp wind through the forest. We all follow behind as we center our vision around us and on the rogues heading for an escape. Her vengeance to catch them is visceral, they tried to take the youngest child in her family, more specifically her little brother. This time, the people who attempt to take her family from her do not get to be free.

"What if they get too far!" Ira shouts mid run.

"When we get to the border patrol should be there!" Ethel hollers as we now veer through the trees. Moving at a speed so quick even Vampires would struggles to keep up.

Ivella and I gain closer in and at her sides, I see her hands form two flat spheres of fire electrifying, waiting to be thrown.

The first is released like a sharp frisbee that has no return, it strikes the ground beneath the rogue lagging behind tossing his body forward and Ivella releases another and this time, it slices directly through his body and he falls in two halves.

"There is another!" Ethel yells.

And from the left where the others are, the next rogue rushes ahead.

We exit the forest and reach the woods that lead to the border of Vaigon.

"We have to tell Laven!" Ivella shouts as we briskly make our way through the border.

Just as Ethel said, Vaigon's patrol is there in Wolf form, riveting growls echo as they take after the rogues invading their land.

"Find Laven!" I yell over the wind whipping through our voices at the speed we run through the woods. "We will continue to track them!"

And through ascension, Ivella is gone and we cross the border.

63
NEVER A DAMSEL AGAIN

LEVORA APOLLA ARVENALDI
VAIGON CITADEL

I lift my hand from the ground and wipe away the falling tears. I can feel the grittiness of the dirt swiping across my face as I rub over my skin.

'No! I can do it!' I shout at Roaner as I attempt to climb the pillar again.

'I said that is enough!' He screams and I am pulled from the pillar and he stands me in front of him, taking me by the shoulders. 'You are going to harm yourself worse than you already have. There is nothing wrong with trying again tomorrow. You do not need to be perfect at everything on your first try.'

I stop the words daring to tumble.

I can no longer think about how Roaner or my brothers and Hua have been perfect at everything they have done within a day.

'We have tomorrow.' He grips my shoulders harder and I turn away from him. 'Levora! Where are you going?'

'Just leave me, I will be fine.'

Strong like Levora.

Strong like Levora.

I repeat the words in my head and say them aloud.

"Strong like Levora. Not strong like the others, like Levora."

I dust off my training gear and stand.

It is now entirely dark in the woods.

Out of desperation to get away from everyone and the raging world around me, the woods tend to be a small sanctuary right where I can see through the opening of the trees where the moon loves to shine.

I look down at my training suit and my chin begins to quiver.

Not allowing myself to wallow in self pity, I walk on.

'Discovering your strength is comparable to understanding your tastebuds.'

'Tastebuds?' I exasperate. 'Of all things you compare it to tastebuds!' It feels like second nature to laugh as he does.

'Yes, I mean it.' He chuckles as he bites into the food on his plate. And within his black eyes I see white granules bouncing like stars. 'You try everything and discover things you enjoy, and that translates to you understanding what techniques fit you best. It is easy to be powerful, but it is about how you can be powerful. Just as you figure out your favorite foods, figure out your favorite ways to conquer. There will always be more than one.'

'You have an odd brain.'

He smiles. 'You have no idea.'

Each moment of falling, losing balance, tripping over my own feet, weakening each movement, it all continues to nip at my brain as I recall it.

Tomorrow will either be another day to improve or another day to fall short.

Loud cracking of branches thrum through the woods instantly grabbing my attention. Turning in small circles, I observe my surroundings. Yet, I can see nothing.

"What is a weeping High Princess like you doing alone in these woods?" I hear a sinister voice vibrate through the trees.

I search again.

"It does not seem that she speaks." Another says and his voice travels like a slither to my ear.

Two disheveled men appear from the darkness of the trees.

Two of them, and one of me.

I would not last fighting off one, let alone two.

As their faces appear, their eyes are identical. Wholly blue . . . the blue Laven has warned me of when explaining the appearance of rogues. These men could not possibly be rogues. They are too well tamed.

The clearer they narrow in, I see no scarring upon them, yet there is a peculiarity about their skin and how it is tinted gray.

Two more men appear. They all hold the same sinister smile.

Rapidly, I look between them. I may not make it out alive, nevertheless, I will attempt to.

Run, a quiet voice speaks in my head, and I do.

If I am one thing, I am light on my feet.

Just as they begin to close in I run.

Given their slow reaction time to follow, they were not expecting me to be brave enough to begin the chase.

My heart batters through my chest over the sounds of their heavy feet pounding into the ground behind me. I know these woods, even without years of being here, I remember every placement of the trees here like the back of my hand.

That is my advantage.

These woods grow wider and tighter at multiple random points, making it that much more confusing for them and that much more navigable for me.

When I reach the wider span of the woods is when I run faster, but the moment I do I am hauled into the air and held tightly with no release.

I know it is him solely by embrace.

Daevien.

I am flipped over his shoulder and onto his back as his wings span out, gliding us through the trees. We come to a landing point and he looks at me over his shoulder.

"Finding you getting chased down by rogues was not on my agenda tonight." He smirks.

"Trust me, it was not on mine either."

The rogues gather around us as I stand.

Daevien's spear is drawn and is held in front of us as one black iridescent wing circles around me.

Nothing can touch me here.

"I do not have all goddamn night." He snaps at the rogues who dance around us.

"If I run–"

"You are not going anywhere that I cannot see you. You do not leave here unless it is with me."

A dark shadow is cast overhead and Daevien smiles.

I look toward the sky, and the dark figure is soaring toward the ground, aimed directly at us.

Their arm is sharply angled downward and they land in front of us in a perfect kneeling position, their fist simultaneously punches the ground as they land. The moment their knuckles collide with the earth, the ground as they land. The moment their knuckles collide with the earth, the ground cracks, knocking us all unsteady and Daevien nears closer.

A circle of magic surrounds us, and it propels every man outside of the circle.

Their head slowly lifts.

Ivella.

"I have formed the shield, they will not be able to pass through it to reach her." Ivella informs Daevien. Her arms swarm upward, crossing in front of her chest. The stitching in her dark armor ignites in a glow of red, and as her arms uncross, a knee lifts and she soars back into the sky. As she disappears, feathers begin to fall around me. Each one igniting against the ground in that gentle blue hue of her magic.

Wings.

The rogues begin to search for her but are also unsure of who to watch. Ivella or Daevien.

Through the woods we can hear her running circles around them, then, a laugh so taunting comes from her as they struggle to see Ivella.

The men that were once around us lie scattered, the first to stand begins to run directly at me.

The strong sound of a spear veers right across my cheek, just missing me by a hair. The spear drives through his shoulder, entering through one end of his body and fully exiting through the other. As he falls, Ivella is standing behind him, and in a slight lean, she dodges the sharp point of the spear and catches it directly in the middle.

Blood drips down her face from the drive of the spear through his shoulder, but she does not bother to wipe it away.

I turn and Ethel is there drawing both swords from behind her back. The shrieking sound of the silver wakes the lying men even more.

She waits for them to stand.

One down, three to go.

The second rogue to rise runs away just as the other two gather their strength.

Ivella's eyes widen as she decides whether to chase him, or to stay.

"He will get away!" Ethel shouts as she focuses on the man standing.

Daevien's black wings span outward as he charges down the path to the runner. He ascends and reappears directly in front of the rogue. Daevien's body veers upward propelling ahead in a direct line, his feet are aimed forward, driving right into the man's chest. As the rogue is thrown the sound of his bones breaking cracks through the air from the force of Daevien's strike.

Before Ivella and Ethel handle the last two, Ira appears and places a shield around the two men, holding them in a small prison, then he does the same to the others that are injured.

Now they have nowhere to go, even if they knew how to ascend, they would not be able to get through it.

"We will hold them for questioning," Ivella announces.

"And who is to say we will give you any information?" One of them grits through their teeth.

She steps closer to the shield. "While your skin is being peeled off bit by bit we will see how long you will last before snitching."

Ivella turns to Ethel. "I will have a transport arranged to take them to Unalave. I will tell Laven."

One tries to spit on her through the shield, but it only retaliates on him by flinging back on to his own face.

"You are just as much of an imbecile as you are weak." She says before ascending.

Daevien grabs my hand and we ascend from the woods and into the palace where Laven is sitting in his study with Stravan.

Upon seeing Ivella, Laven's eyes widen as he assesses the blood drying on her face.

He is immediately inspecting her for a wound.

Quicker than ascension, his feet project him across the room and toward her.

Nyt and Salem gather around my legs and I smile through the stress we have just been put through. "Place," I nod to their new beds that Laven had made for them, but it seems they both like to sleep in one bed together next to the raging fireplace.

"Dae," Stravan calls. "What happened?"

"Rogues, possibly?" He questions himself as he answers.

Stravan looks down at our looped hands and I pull away before questions may arise.

"Yes," Ivella responds as Laven is wiping away the blood on her face with the fabric he tore from his shirt. "They are very . . ." she struggles to find the word. "Aware."

Laven's eyebrows knit together. "Aware?"

"They spoke, they were agile, they understood their surroundings, they were nothing like the previous mutations we saw when you were attacked."

"You were attacked?" I gasp at Laven.

"Yes, but it was some time ago, shortly before we stopped seeing the rogues roaming."

Stravan heavily exhales as he and Laven make eye contact.

"He did it." Stravan mumbles as his fingers scratch at his chin.

Phyv steps forward concernedly. "Did what?" He asks.

"He created a mutation to make them aware of themselves, but somehow under his control." Laven says as he places the dirtied fabric on the table, Stravan's face scrunches before he looks at it, sways a hand, and it is gone.

"That means this just got much more difficult." Ivella says.

"But they were weak." Daevien announces.

Laven's nods from side to side. "Not necessarily. They could have been weaker links that were sent here. We do not know what kind of extensive training he could be putting the others through."

"I noticed that the previous mutations we saw are no longer around," Ivella sits in a chair and Laven does not bother to move from her side. "Do you think he got rid of them because of their recklessness?"

"Possibly, possibly not." Ethel looks out the floor to ceiling length windows, searching for her cousin Ira who still holds the men under his shield. "He could be using them in the war, but we will stay prepared for it."

"We will need to tell the others." Laven speaks. "I will have Ezra send word in the morning."

"Do you think they wanted something?" I ask.

"If they wanted something they would have sent their strongest, and you would not be here my love. But," she slowly looks up at Laven and Stravan. "They took a larger Norpheyen."

"What is a Norpheyen?"

"A Norpheyen is an extraordinarily large bird with a colorful body and four wings. Both predator and prey, though, mainly predator given its size and sharp talons." Laven explains. "Young Dragons tend to hunt large birds as Norpheyen, if too young, the Dragon could easily become the prey. In Misonva, the Vampire Realm, Norpheyen's grow to similar sizes of Dragons. Just as Xentigons do that reside in the waters of Provas with the Water Dragons. In Misonva, Norpheyen's have riders just as Dragons do, and so do Xentigons.

Here, Norpheyen's will grow to be the span of a small cottage. They strictly live in the Hashthyna Forest given the environment they need, when winter arrives, they take to the Forests in Gordanta."

"He is going to use them for war," Phyv counters. "That bastard." He forces a laugh.

"How many did he take?" Laven asks.

"As far as Iysha saw, just one." Ivella answers. "He said they took the Norpheyen from its child, but we did not find a young Norpheyen anywhere. So I am only suspecting he had two taken."

Stravan looks over his shoulder at Ivella. "Where are the rogues now?"

"With Ira in the woods, he put a shield over them so they may not escape. I said we should take them to Unalave for questioning." Ivella makes eye contact with Laven to be sure this is fine, but he is already agreeing with her.

"I will have Hua and Amias hold them there."

"What is Unalave?" Phyv wonders.

"An underground prison where no one escapes, we will only keep them alive for questioning. Some are injured, but it is nothing that they could not heal from." Ivella says as she rubs her dry, bloodied, hand against her leathers.

"You just want to torture them," Stravan simpers.

She smiles staring off through the trees. "Maybe."

"How were they found?" Stravan questions.

"They were trying to capture Iysha and his companion while they were playing in the forest. So, yes, I do want to torture them for trying to lay a hand on my brother."

"Play nice," Stravan gently kicks her foot which dangles as her legs are crossed. "I will go home and speak with Dyena tonight. Tomorrow, have Ezra come to Provas and I will give him the letters to inform the other realms that the search for the remaining Six of Spring will begin.

Laven nods and Stravan is gone.

If I am not strong enough to fight a rogue, how am I expected to find missing people of our world? Quests such as this require agility in fighting, not just brains, and if I am ever alone I cannot depend on someone else to always rescue me in an ambush.

I need to want it more, I need to want it for me.

No longer will I want strength only for others, but for me.

"I will go too; I need to speak with my father." Ivella stands.

She and Laven exchange only a look, but Laven stands there confused as she does not say anything to him other than giving just a glance and leaving with Ethel.

"I will see if I can be of any service to Ira in the woods." Phyv offers.

"I will come with you," Laven nods and they both ascend to where everything transpired.

When I look up at Daevien he smiles.

"Try not to get yourself killed while I am gone."

"I think you may be asking for too much."

A grin appears on his face and through it he gravitates closer than before.

The man with stars in his eyes.

The faintest feeling overcomes me as I stare at how strikingly beautiful he is.

Dark silky hair.

Brown skin.

How his smile replicates how gentle his heart responds.

Captivating. Enchanting. Everything of the sort.

Daevien is the most rapturing man to enter this world.

Then, the expression of terror takes over his face. Terror and sadness that turns him into someone I want to save. Someone I know I could save.

"Why did they bring you there?" He says in a harrowed whisper.

Immediately, he ascends.

64
ANGEL UPON WATER

LAVEN HEPHAESTUS ARVENALDI, II

"WHEN YOU HAVE FALLEN deep in thought you look like the angriest man I have seen."

I smile at Stravan as he approaches me on the dining room terrace, he fixes his fitted vest as he walks over, the silver lining in his clothing just matches his neatly styled white hair.

"No, not angry, just confusion. But that seems to translate to anger does it not?"

"It does indeed." He sits down at the table and gathers a small plate of food. "How is the Princess this morning?"

"Levora is well, she has been carrying along. She is now training with Roaner and Phyv again. Nonetheless, I saw the heaviness in her eyes when she was here moments before you arrived."

"She will get through it. Levora is a quiet force, her determination and capability to retain knowledge and memory is a gift she is unaware of."

Below, I hear the loud barking from Nyt as he chases Salem through the courtyard beneath us and they race up the stairs to here.

"He has done exactly what we thought," I speak and Stravan lifts his head from his plate. "The first rogues all those months ago were tests. They were little pets to practice with before discovering how to properly craft something that can be our greatest end and his greatest rise. Those men that attacked my family last night are perfectly capable of conversation and agility like someone skilled, Hua said so herself when she spoke of them to me. What is next? Skilled Warriors with amped strength and speed?"

"May I get you anything?" Abyl, our dining hall servant, who is a new hire from our land approaches.

"Tea, please." Stravan nods. "Thank you."

And when he is gone, Stravan begins. "Laven, there is nothing that Yaro could do that is undefeatable. We are doing everything to prepare for what he has. We are crafting indestructible fighting gear that our ancestors would come back from the dead to fight in, instant cures are in the works, we have thousands upon thousands of Warriors across the universe. We have allies who, if they are smart, will not break their allyship. He does not yet have an army of rogues built strong enough to properly defend themselves."

"From a young man to now being almost six and twenty, I have built too much for this nation to go to waste. Do I particularly agree with the way the land was acquired? No, but that does not diminish everything I have done to be sure we stood steady even while Lorsius was alive—"

"And we have a grand amount of time to be sure we defeat this fool of a war bringer," he interrupts. "And we will be certain that you continue to live on as the High King you are ready to be."

'Prophecy says Laven is to be the strongest High King Vaigon and many other nations will know and I need him sitting on that damn Throne sooner rather than later.'

"How long do you and Dyena plan to stay?" I leave my thoughts and focus on him.

Abyl returns with Stravan's tea and sits it in front of him with a small jar of honey and thoughts begin to eat my brain.

I rub my finger across my lips as that taste in my mouth from two nights ago returns.

"I am unsure yet, if that is fine with you to accompany us for an unknown amount of time?"

"That is fine with me."

Last night during Stravan's visit he mentioned staying for a period of time to teach me and my brothers how to wield our powers to the depth that he can. After what transpired with my sister, Iysha, and the rouges, I want to waste no more time to be better and gain more knowledge.

But, Stravan wants to know more about Phyv before they are sent back to the Mortal Lands to find the final three of the six.

I have tried to explain to him that there is nothing about Phyv to be on alert of, in his eyes, that does not stop him from questioning why Phyv is so unexplainably ancient in looks and powers. Levora spoke with me of a few of the magical abilities he has, they are extensive, extensive to the degree that only those of ancient origin had. When I discussed this with Stravan it just made him even more on edge.

"And what will you be doing about your Coronation?"

I sit up straighter and grab the bowl of strawberries. "I do plan to have a coronation, but I do not want one that is a large gathering of all the high people in our nation. I want it to be intimate and small. I will only have a traditional Coronation if Ivella chooses to be High Queen. If not, then no."

"I had a feeling you would say that." He smiles.

"Where is Dyena?"

"She is with Ivella, I was going to ask you to show me the way to her home. Dyena has already gone there since she knows the location by heart, but I do not."

"Ivella stays at her fathers old home in Nadrexi." And I hate that she stays in that small mansion alone so far away and too close to her mother that needs to be kept away.

His white eyebrows rise. "Nadrexi is quite the distance away."

"It is," I walk away from the terrace and to the dining table. "I try not to think about it too often, nevertheless, here I am."

"Well, let us put your worries at ease and go see her."

He grabs an apple before holding his arm out to me and I reach across the table ascending us to The Sunset Provence.

NADREXI — SOUTHERN COURT OF QUAMFASI

Arriving at Ivella's home, we find both Ivella and Dyena sitting wholly naked on the short dock that leads to the waterfall next to her home. Their wings are sprawled out behind them as they sit with their legs entangled laughing about whatever they may be while eating figs.

I nearly cannot tell them apart from behind, but Ivella has one tiny beauty mark on her back that is slightly offset from the center between her shoulder blades.

Next to them sits Vaigon and Vorzantu who hurriedly come my way. I kneel to their level as they are now too large to fit on my shoulders. Stravan was not exaggerating when he said that young dragons can go through growth spurts within the matter of days.

"Your mother is rather naked," I say to them and they both let out a quiet noise that rumbles in their chest. Vaigon opens his mouth to produce that same sound again, and in the back of his throat, I see the flare of fire circling and as his mouth closes it is gone.

How did they go from tiny beings to predators so instantaneously?

Both children are now at the height of my knees, by next week, I expect them to be at the height of my hips. The span of their wings are comical, they are much longer than their height, placing them in that odd stage of growing. At first, their wings were too small, now, they must grow into them.

"Ladies," I begin.

They both turn with smiles on their faces, reeling down from whatever little words they were telling each other.

"Dyena do you not remember what clothing is?" Stravan immediately asks.

"Do you not remember what free will is?"

Ivella stifles a laugh and I narrow my eyes at her. "Please, get dressed." I politely plead. "We must get back to Vaigon."

"You and Laven have training before I meet with him and the others."

We have training?

"What training?" Both Ivella and I ask Stravan in unison.

"You will learn how to ride a Dragon. I have Tuduran and Nara ready for you to train with and we will bring the littles, they must be there observe and this can be step one to prepping them for war. The fastest way a young Dragon learns is by visually seeing and hearing the commands given."

"Must we go now?" Ivella asks.

"Yes, please. Go dress." Before I do not know what to do with myself.

"I have a session at the academy to attend after so we would have to make it quick."

"That is fine, Ivella, please get dressed." I attempt to rush her.

They both laugh at us before ascending into the house.

Stravan turns me and shakes his head. "I did not need to know they looked exactly alike."

I pinch the bridge of my nose, finding the words to say unless I choose to hit him. "Just get in the house." I shove him.

When we enter the home, Stravan slowly makes his way in and I guide him the rest of the way through.

"The house is mostly an open concept. Kitchen is here, drawing room is across, there is a nook there," I point to the corner where the window reveals the waterfall. "Books to read are there as well dependent upon how long they need to get dressed." I take across the long expanse of the house and go toward the kitchen.

A wide window stretches across the entire wall of the kitchen from the counter and stops beneath the first shelf that has plants of all sorts hanging over it.

I grab a large vessel near the sink and pull the lever that allows the water from the well. As I reach to water the plants drying out, I hear Stravan chuckle from behind me.

"You move about this home as if it is your own."

Setting down the vessel, I smile and turn to him. "I have just been here often, that is all. If there is anything I see may need to be done, I do it."

"You said this house belonged to her father?"

"Yes, Naius had this home built years ago, it is now Ivella's."

"Good, he should keep something as this in the family." Stravan walks toward the hall. "And down this way?"

"Down this way leads you to a larger library, a private drawing room, and a study. Upstairs is a level with three chambers and a study, above that floor are more chambers and another study that is combined with a library."

"Perfect home for a family and to house guests." He nods.

And down the stairs Ivella is first and Dyena strolls behind her.

Ivella's dress crosses over her chest, covering one shoulder and leaving the other bare, and just opposite to that, her entire side is revealed. Just over her hip, the dress is tied in a little knot that reveals one full leg down to her sandals.

"Will you be comfortable enough to ride in that dress?" I ask.

"Laven," her hands smooth over the cream colored dress that hugs her body. "Anything you may do in trousers I may do in a gown." Dyena pulls Ivella's wet hair away from her shoulder and ties it half up for her.

I turn to Stravan as Dyena reaches him, I tilt my head to the door and he smirks before ascending, Dyena in hand.

"Ah," I say in warning as she aims to get away from the conversation I have been wanting to have since that night. "Did you not see my note?"

"I saw it."

"And you did not want to respond?"

Her eyes propel up. "You think I wanted to wake up to a note instead of you? I wanted you to stay with me and you did not and I woke up in the—" she abruptly stops and shakes her head, she is fighting the urge to speak with me.

Just as I have with her.

"Let us just leave."

"No," I jump in front of her. "What do you mean you woke up in–"

"I mean nothing by it." Her tone turns harsh. "I am leaving now, you know your way to Provas."

"Ivella, please–"

"No!" Her voice reaches its peak and I see pain begin to ruin her face. "You–" she struggles to speak and she searches for the words before she can say them. "You lie in bed with me and then you left me!"

I flinch at the porosity of her voice, but mostly the terrorized expression taking over her face that was once so happy.

She slowly inhales and her eyes close for a moment before re-opening.

"I am sorry, I tried to wake you but you were already sleeping so deeply that even when I moved you, you did not wake. You looked peaceful so I wanted you to stay that way."

She looks down at the floor between us and takes a single step backward.

That distance, that wall she builds guarded by the strongest Warrior known, has returned.

When I see, or believe that I see we are moving forward, we take ten steps back.

"Peaceful," she hums. "What is that?"

"Something is the matter, Mai. And you need to tell me."

She stares upward and a smile appears, a smile to cover fear, a smile to cover pain, a smile to cover every burden still feasting on her limb by limb.

"We need to meet Dyena and Stravan. I am going to take Vaigon and Vorzantu with me, you may ascend there alone."

65
VYLORDA VANOX

LAVEN HEPHAESTUS ARVENALDI, II
NESVYNHA, PROVAS — THE DRAGONS DENS

Ivella and Dyena are speaking quietly out on the mountain where they stand near Tuduran and Nara. We are right outside the Dragons dens. Below us is a vast dip off the mountain that spans thousands of feet before there is another steep upward slope that leads to the next flat land. I can see the many skeletal bodies that have tried to travel across and were most likely burned on their way.

Dyena is sternly speaking to Ivella, who is distant from the conversation though she is listening as Dyena rips into her. Near them, Vaigon and Vorzantu look the size of Nyt next to Tuduran and Nara. I would have thought they would cower away but they seem to curiously near closer to the large Dragons who look down at them from the corner of their eyes.

"Her stubbornness is excruciatingly familiar." Stravan looks over his shoulder at me. There is no comical flare to his words, he seems to be just as annoyed as Dyena.

"Her stubbornness will be my end."

Something deep.

Something so monopolizing is holding her hostage.

I have always been told all my life how secretive I am, but her— Ivella is a level of secretive even I cannot bear.

"You know, do you not?" I urge him as he continues to watch the two women very far ahead of us speak. They know exactly what she is not telling me.

"I do," he nods. "And so do you. She just has not told you to what extent."

"Stravan, if she is in some form of danger, you need to tell me this instant."

Knowing they are listening, he answers. "She is fine." But below he signs with his hands six letters.

N-E-S-Y-R-A

Nesyra?

Ivella climbs up the side of Nara using the saddle wrapped around her white and silver scaled body.

Stravan and I approach closer and Ivella seems like the tiniest being as she sits upon Nara's back on the large saddle.

"Now, to ride, you must give all commands." Dyena explains. "Since Nara is grown, you will not need to guide her much, but you will mostly be saying the commands for Vorzantu as he follows. Nara is aware that he is young so she will keep next to him and act as his guide as you will. The same is for you, Laven, when Vaigon is with you."

"Ivella," Stravan motions for her to begin.

Ivella grasps onto the handles of the saddle and with a pull, Nara stands straighter and she towers above us. Spanning larger than two hundred yards, her wings flare and Vorzantu, who sits next to Ivella on Nara's back, stands taller as well.

And by slightly leaning forward, settling into the front of the saddle to sit steadily, Ivella speaks. "*Avanya*.*"

At his first command ever heard, a small twitch shakes through

---

* *Old Voschantai: Avanya*   Translation: *Fly*

Vorzantu's head. So young, but now prepared to be properly ridden when the time comes. This day will shape both him and Vaigon.

Nara's large spiked head that meets to a rounded point lifts. She bellows out a loud roar that shakes the mountains and causes rocks to crumble down the steep wall. Nara walks on and with one oscillation of her wings she takes down the steep mountain and all of us near the edge, watching as Ivella directs both Nara and Vorzantu.

Vorzantu soars right above Ivella's shoulder as Nara takes a swift upward turn. She turns her head to Vorzantu and a smile appears on her face as she watches him follow with ease.

Next to me, Tuduran rumbles quietly and his head bows and my chest grows tight seeing such a magnificent being welcoming me toward him.

I have seen the day of riding a Dragon in my dreams.

Now, the opportunity presents itself in front of me and for the rest of my life.

Tuduran nudges tiny Vaigon with his large nose and Vaigon leisurely makes his way up Tuduran's large wing, over his back, and sits next to the saddle waiting for me.

When I take the long stroll up Tuduran's sharp back, I sit in the saddle and position myself forward.

"Now, just as Ivella did." Dyena nods. "Do not be afraid to fall, Tuduran will catch you."

Mighty.

Mighty is the feeling that overwhelms my entire body as I sit so high up that Stravan and Dyena seem like small horses down below.

I can feel the rising and falling as Tuduran breathes in deeply and exhales slowly. And next, the heat that radiates from his thickly scaled skin that cannot be penetrated by even the sharpest spear. The thickness of this skin speaks volumes of his age.

"Are you ready?" I look at Vaigon and he leans down, nudges my hand, and searches the skies for his brother and mother. He is ready to be with them.

With one pull of the black leather saddle, and a single command, Tuduran glides into the sky to find Nara.

In the past, I would have been frightened to be taken off a cliff, now, it is exhilarating.

As we rush down the mountain, Vaigon's wings are sharply pointed outward as he takes with the sharp wind whipping over us. Even in the wind, and far in the sky, I can hear the quiet laughter of Ivella

"*Vylorda**."

And with a turn up, I hold tighter on to the saddle and Tuduran takes to the horizon.

Vaigon slightly lags behind, but with two beats of his wings, he is next to my shoulders again. He lets out a loud call that alerts his brother we are near.

I pull up on Tuduran's saddle and Vaigon observes my movements as well as Tuduran's as he moves higher into the sky at my gentle commands.

In the clouds.

Never have I ever been this high up before other than by ascension, but even through that it is only a mere second, not for however long I wish.

Taking one more flight higher, I see Ivella soaring steadily with Vorzantu and Nara.

"*Lasevni**."

Tuduran levels out and we reach Ivella as we slide over and through the clouds.

"Ah," I stop Vaigon from losing focus as he aims to playfully attack his brother.

Nara's head turns and she lowly growls as she sees them misbehave.

"Vorzantu," Ivella calls and his focus realigns.

"Oh, they have done well," I recognize the voice as Stravan's as he rises from below on Vion's back. "Let them play." Vion rises

---

* *Old Voschantai: Vylorda*   Translation: Skies
* *Old Voschantai: Lasevni*   Translation: Steady

higher, causing slight competition from Tuduran who is most definitely dominant above his siblings.

Calypton comes sharply soaring from below and is far ahead.

"Show off." Ivella remarks and I see a smirk appear on her face before she nods to Vaigon and Vorzantu to play freely. They both turn and look at me and I too agree.

Then as if we both had it in mind, Ivella and I tug hard on Tuduran and Nara's saddle edging them forward at a speed so fast, Tuduran nudges Nara and she nips at his side.

Ivella gasps and her eyes lock with mine.

She smiles before veering Nara higher and in an easy flow she circles around me and Tuduran. Beneath me Tuduran rumbles as I launch him on to chase and behind us Stravan laughs and Vion too follows.

Just as our Dragons round about and play, Vaigon and Vorzantu follow, keeping close for when it is time to go.

Up here, worries do not exist, torment is released. In the skies there is power, there is freedom of a sort that few know.

But, even sometimes the highest skies see torment.

The Dragons begin to stop playing and I feel Tuduran stiffen beneath me.

His eyes are searching.

Stravan and I now ride behind Ivella and Dyena and they begin to search for what has suddenly set the Dragons off to be on alert.

And below the clouds a dark shadow looms under. A shadow much larger than the four of us now squared off. I grab Vaigon and tuck him under my arm but Stravan reaches his hand out, nodding for me to release him.

This is a moment for learning how to flee when trouble nears, as it is now.

I release him and he stays close.

Stravan brings his hand up to his mouth, telling us to be quiet until the entirety of the shadow below is gone, then, in Dyena's lead, we take back to the Dragons Dens.

"What the hell was that?" I slide down Tuduran's back and he and his siblings urgently take to the skies quietly.

"Vanox." Stravan says as he monitors his children who now patrol the skies.

"Vanox, the largest and eldest Dragon to this universe. She is nearly one-hundred years old and will most likely live another hundred." Dyena says as she grabs Stravan's hand.

His hand rises to the sky and it closes into a fist, the clouds still and as his hand reopens, the clouds desiccate, revealing how far Tuduran, Vion, Nara, and Calypton have gotten.

Under the cast of the sun, Calypton's brindle red skin glistens. This could call for him to be too visible, and I believe that is why Stravan and Dyena worry as they hunt Vanox.

"Why are they going after her?" Ivella asks.

"Just to monitor, to be sure she is not attacking. She most likely sensed us and was searching, but she did not travel high enough. When you are above a Dragon it is difficult to be found. We were lucky today, nevertheless, when these two grow older," Stravan looks down at Vaigon and Vorzantu who watch the elder Dragons leave. "Watch them, you never know when she may appear."

"She does not have a rider?"

"No, her last rider was my mother." Stravan turns to us. "After my mother was gone she no longer had a rider."

Ivella connects the information in her head. "Did Vanox have a rider prior to your mother?"

"Yes," Stravan smiles. "In order to ride a Dragon that has a previous rider you must conquer it. By that, you must kill it and when it wakes, it will be yours–this may only happen three times, after the third the Dragon will never wake again. Given Vanox's current size, it will be nearly impossible to ride her now. No one is capable of bringing her down other than herself."

66
VAGUE PROPOSALS

LAVEN HEPHAESTUS ARVENALDI, II
XENATHI — QUAMFASI CITADEL

THE OFFICIAL TREATY BETWEEN Vaigon and New Quamfasi has been written by me. We are now legally declared allies. Even as our allyship is now solidified, we have chosen to keep to our own lands and to not intertwine our people. Vallehes, still, is against those of Vaigon and those of New Quamfasi to wed. I can understand his great fear, but his fear has shifted into resentment, and this is another way to keep us apart while still together.

We stay on our side, they stay on theirs.

If visits to each side must be made, it will now be easier to pass, but you must state your reasonings for entering either nation and names will be taken before passing through and identification will be held until returned. This is large progress since just a day ago no one was allowed to pass through to New Quamfasi other than myself or those in my Circle.

I sign my name as Vallehes and Penelope do, and Stravan, Ivella, Dyena, and Esme witness and place their signatures next below ours.

Two treaties were written of the same information, one for

myself and one for Vallehes and Penelope.

"Now that this is complete," Ivella starts. "We can arrange a meeting between all realms to discuss your treaty being final. With this treaty intact, all realms are finally united through Dyena, myself, and this."

"How well do we think that will go?" Vallehes asks. "In the manner that Lorsius left his relationships with the rest of the world they may not take well to this."

"It should go well," I answer. "If they have a negative retaliation, that would have an impact on their alliance with Provas, and that they do not wish for. Through Provas' unification with New Quamfasi, and now Vaigon's unification with New Quamfasi we are whole again. If they attempt to argue it in someway, Stravan, Dyena, and myself will create a treaty of our own."

"I have already formed one," Stravan opens his hand and the treaty appears. "We will sign it now since we already have witnesses."

"With this, there is no gateway for denial." Dyena says while neatly adding her name to the treaty. "Now, nothing Lorsius has done is impossible to undo."

"I do not only want us to be seen as rulers in separate lands. We need to moderately interact in a form that makes sense to others." Vallehes begins.

"I spoke with Daevien recently about not just saying we are now united, but to act as so." Ivella stands straighter in her formal attire, and right over the dark red fabric of her gown rests the Sun and Moon necklace. "Vallehes and Penelope and I have agreed that it would be best for you and everyone in House Arvenaldi to witness our first blessing to occur in quite some time, it will be held at the Tree of Gods. We are inviting you to attend, to relearn the ways of Quamfasi. When Lorsius ruled he formed a nation for people to be nonspiritual whereas we never forgot our spiritual upbringings."

"I can tell you now that we all will gladly agree. Tell me the time we must be there and I will be sure we are ready."

It has been quite a long time since Vaigon has seen religion in some form, now it is time to reawaken that lacking factor.

As we are signing again, there is a knock on the door of the Consultation Room.

Two women enter through the doors with a letter in hand. The wax seal is a dark purple engraved with flowers and in the middle the letter *I* and *F* are pressed in perfect cursive.

Ivella Fondali.

"Lady Ivella," one of them smiles with a blush. "It is for you."

Her eyes widen as she overlooks the wax seal.

Dark purple.

Galitan, The Sorcerers Realm.

"It is from High Prince Ozias. He is arriving this afternoon." The two women say in unison.

Ivella signs her name on the treaty, urgently takes across the room, and the women leave with her.

"Interesting," I chuckle.

"Excuse me," Dyena says before taking down the long hallway after Ivella. And the doors slowly close behind them.

"What is interesting?" Vallehes asks.

I bear a grin. "Nothing."

Vallehes face turns for distaste and I can hear the remark he wishes to say before he says it.

"Laven," Stravan interrupts, knowing his friend is about to cross a line. "Let us go to the bakery we saw on our way in."

Vallehes rolls the treaty into a scroll before Stravan and I leave.

Stravan ends our ascension in a busy city and his arm links over my shoulder.

"Ignore Vallehes," he says as we weave through the people of New Quamfasi.

Suddenly, couple after couple appears around us. They are flirtatious and affectionate with one another and I am here under my companion's arm. But, one thing I notice of all the couples, the men are wearing scarves around their top coats or over shirts and vests.

"Why are they all wearing scarves?"

'In Quamfasi we call them Porvienia's.'

Although there are many men walking through with Porvienia's, each one seems to be sewn in a different print, not a single one looks similar. Even if the colors are the same, the pattern varies.

"Ah, the Porvienia's." Stravan examines them as we sweep through the city full of people.

Many are walking in and out of shops and bakeries with baskets full of goods.

"The Porvienia is given at birth, when you grow older the woman or man pass it on to their spouse, mostly it is the woman who passes it along, or if you are in a same sex relationship or mating bond you give it to them. Which is why you may see two men wearing each. A Porvienia holds great significance to family and love, since it is gifted at birth, passing it on to a spouse is like passing on your life, your trust, your everything. It is known as the greatest gift to give. During weddings the man will wear it and it is customary for your wedding to match the color scheme of the Porvienia."

When she returns, she is holding her mother's scarf delicately in her hands.
'Here, I would desire you to have it.'
Her mother's scarf?
'Maivena—'
'Please, I want you to have it. I know you would take care of it, you have before. I know it is safe with you. You can even pass it on in time to anyone, our men, women, and those unidentified wear them. It is well known for them to be given at birth to anyone. They are also given as gifts of gratitude.' Her optimistic eyes glimmer as she holds it out to me.

There is no shred of doubt that I find when I look her over. She sincerely wishes for me to have this. I think it may even hurt her if I do not take it.

"You have it." Stravan smirks as he looks at me. "And something tells me that you did not know what it meant when you are given a Porvienia. Do you not love it when women vaguely propose first?"

I shake my head, lost for words.

"She does not know."

"It is not about if she knows or not, fool." Stravan laughs. "She gave you her Porvienia because she knew that her life is always in safe handling wherever you are." He continues to look around at all the men donned in the Porvienia's given by their spouse. "If I were you, I would be wearing it right in this moment. Wear it every day, sleep with it next you, she gave it to you, act like it."

"Technically speaking," I recall. "I gave her a Porvienia first."

He bursts into laughter once more and amusement is full in his bright blue eyes. "So the both of you have vaguely proposed to one another. For the love of Gods, you two get more interesting by the second. You are hers and she is yours, stop letting these men come here asking for her hand when it is already taken."

* * *

Ivella's chamber within the main palace of New Quamfasi is relatively similar to that of her father's home in Nadrexi, though here, it is larger and holds too much space.

"What are you doing here?" Ivella asks as she sits at the vanity.

Through the mirror before her, I can see both of us so clearly.

Then, she sees it.

The Porvienia, given to me by her, rests neatly over my shoulders. The cream and tan Porvienia matches quite well with my black attire as I see it over me.

She is at a loss for words as I play with the fabric.

"Do you know what a Porvienia is, Mai?"

Stoic.

"I was today years old when I learned."

Not a word.

"Giving someone your Porvienia is similar to putting your life into that person's hands." I walk towards her and kneel. "Sacred." She stares directly into me. "Then there is the aspect of love and marriage behind it."

Now, she stands. "A Porvienia can be taken back."

"Then do it," I stand and accelerate across the distance between us. "Take it from me. Take away what is rightfully mine and give it to another."

I wait and she can only glance between my face and the Porvienia wrapped around me.

"This is mine, forever. I was born to have it and I will be buried with it. Put me against those men and watch who will come out winning. Do not make me revert back to the days of men killing one another for love, I will do it, and I will be fucking good at it." I turn away and aim for the doors.

"You are pretentious," she mumbles.

Slowly, I turn to her, and seeing such an exquisitely angry woman standing before the allure of nature lingering through the windows is spellbinding.

"*Confident*, I think you meant."

"And what makes you think you can hold yourself so highly above the rest!" Finally, she snaps.

"Because you are mine!" Fluently, it all explodes. "I am a pretentious, arrogant, asshole because you are mine! By every fiber of my being, you are mine. From the soles of your feet to the curls in your hair, you are mine. By the way you roll your eyes to the way you laugh, is mine. From the tears that fall down your face to the pain in your soul, is mine. *This* is why no matter how many men you allow to beg to become a suitor, I will always be at the head of the line either I joined first or last. I have a born *right* over these men and I will be damned before you allow another."

In an instant, she beams across the room and I collide hard with the door.

Insanity, greed, unhinged, covetousness. She would eat me alive, and I will let her.

But not today.

I grasp under her arms the moment she falls to her knees before me.

I stop before this reaches a point of me being unable to say no.

"We," I heavily exhale as her green orbs turn just as orange as a sunset. "We will not touch each other again until we are both ready for what fate has aligned." It was my original plan that was shot to hell, but now, I will not let us messily fulfill desires until the day comes that we are sturdier than the stance of mountains.

I lean downward and our lips graze, her eyes shut, and when I pull away they reopen to the green I know all too well.

"There she is," I whisper within my ascension to leave.

VAIGON – UNALAVE PENITENTIARY

Phyv closely follows behind me as we walk along the large field that leads to Unalave.

Immediately after my visit with Ivella, he informed me that one of the rogue prisoners had quite the information to speak about Ivella.

We reach a halfway point in the field, and within the grass lies a wooden door that will lead to steps to reach underground.

With three particular knocks, a moment passes and the door is opened by a guard who makes way for both me and Phyv to enter.

Candles rapidly flare as we walk down the steps, but the small square of light from the door still cascades our shadows forward, as we reach the bottom of the long flight of stairs the natural light is cut and all there is to guide us are candles.

There is a small dark room rounded off in a circle, in the center sits a small table with a book that holds the name and location of every prisoner here. There are not many, but this is where we hold some of the most dangerous people known to our world. We are not the only realm to have a prison like this, grave danger lies everywhere, and if you are capable, you can catch it and harbor it.

Given the severity of the rouges, all four men that attacked Iysha and Levora, even the injured, are here.

Three halls span from within the circle room. One ahead of me and two on a diagonal on either side.

"The left hall." Phyv points.

It is always eerily quiet in this prison. Possibly because everyone here is kept so far from one another in walls so thick there is no interaction possible. But even so, the quietness here has always been different. There are doors of steel and stone to keep the prisoners contained, then behind those are the barred doors for them to see.

As we take down the hall, this time, candles do not light. We must use our own night vision to be led.

"The last cell in the back right corner is where he is." Phyv leads.

"What is his name?"

"He goes by Jaxyn, he could be lying."

"Is he quite the talker?" People who talk at great lengths do so to con information out of you by speaking amply.

"Only when provoked."

Treading lightly and hearing every word is vital.

Jaxyn was not sent here accidentally.

Phyv presses a hand to the door of his cell and gradually, the heavy stone lifts, and multiple feet behind it the barred door stands firm.

Jaxyn sits slouched with his elbows propped on his knees. His head lifts and in the darkness of his cell his rogue blue eyes beam, then a lazy smirk appears. "You brought the High King."

"Laven and Ivella. Ivella and Laven." He tauntingly speaks.

"What do you know of Ivella?"

"What do you want me to tell you that I know?"

"Do not toy with me. What do you know?"

He chuckles. "The girl who was made."

"Ivella was not made, she was born different."

The prisoner clicks his tongue amusingly as his head shakes from side to side. "No, Ivella was *made* different. There is a vast aberration between being born a Hybrid, and being made a Hybrid. Oh," he smiles. "I could talk about this little story all night. The touch of the Gods to her soul made her stronger than an average Hybrid. Ivella is not like the rest of us. She bears an imprint of the Gods, making her nearly as strong as them. But, it is not natural, the body she was born in was not made for such powers."

I look over my shoulder at Phyv who is glowering at Jaxyn.

"Who told you this?"

He tilts his head and his ear twitches. "Not who told me this. What told me this." He continues to smile as he looks around his cell

"I hear it in the walls." His fingers spread and his hands shake with excitement as he talks.

"You are a Wolf?" Phyv asks.

"I am a mutation."

"Of what?"

"You would love to know, would you not?" His head rapidly shakes as he laughs.

"Where are you from?"

"Galitan is my home."

Has he possibly spread this mutation all the way to the Sorcerers Realm?

They would have said something by now.

Though, just because Galitan is home, does not mean that is where he is from.

"Do not speak to him again unless I am here. Close the door." I nod to Phyv.

"Goodbye, High King Laven!" He all too happily shouts as the door comes to a shut.

"I need to arrange a conclave."

"With whom?"

"Agivath."

67
BE AS ONE

LAVEN HEPHAESTUS ARVENALDI, II
VAIGON CITADEL

STRAVAN SETTLES INTO THE chaise before the fire. "He said all of this?"

"Yes, I can only suspect he can see things similarly to Agivath, he spoke of people as if he already knew them like Agivath does, but he did so freely. He asked for nothing, he said he would speak the story of Ivella all night if he could. Behind those doors when they are shut and only he can hear himself, I am sure he does."

"It is natural for women to have stalkers," Amias contemplates as he closes his book. "He could be one."

"A stalker that far away? He said his home is Galitan," I continue. "But I refuse to believe him."

"Galitan would have mentioned if Yaro's mutation reached their land, if anything, Galitan would be capable of ridding the disease the moment it would spread through their nation." Roaner says in addition. "My mother still goes back to Galitan often to teach and she has said nothing of the mutation being there."

"He is fabricating the truth," Morano stands in the doorway as he tosses a bronze coin in the air. "It is easy for one to say one thing and mean another. I say take all he says with a grain of salt."

"Also," Levora speaks next to me. "It is not as if Ivella is an unknown individual. I knew of her in the papers all those years ago as the girl who never lost The Games, that is a huge statement on its own. Those papers are not only printed in our realm, the daily papers here are sent to every realm just as papers in Galitan or Ramana are sent here. She is the first born female to a General, she has just become the Right Hand to Provas, she holds placement in three Houses, well, soon to be three Houses. She is well known to say the least."

"Someone, anyone, can take her name, story, whatever they learn and turn it into anything." I add. "Though I will not ignore the fact that he is correct that self-destruction is possible. I have spoken with Ivella in the past of her powers, and I gave her a book on her abilities and it states that her powers can destroy her."

"If what he says is true about her being made, that book will be no use and Laven will need to speak with her soon." Phyv says as he sits next to Stravan and Nyt comes rushing over to him.

Hua scoffs. "That bastard is always speaking nonsense whenever food is taken to his cell." She sits in my chair at my bureau and eats the copious amount of food on her plate.

"It is true, in a sense," I tilt my head. "She was stillborn, brought back to life through Dyena, and we do not know if Dyena is the only person Artemis took power from to bring Ivella back."

"I did not contemplate that." Stravan scratches his chin as he looks at me.

"That means one thing," Levora looks up at me warily with large hazel eyes. "You and Ivella must ask Artemis yourselves."

"*If* Artemis will tell the truth," Morano crosses the study and sits at his bureau by the corner window. "I am better off going to Unalave and discovering where this rogue got his information from."

With Morano being a Mind Bender it will be possible for him to get any information needed, but if the prisoner is a Mind Bender as well, this could end badly. Plenty of Mind Benders have gone against one another in the past and have been crippled in their head and have found no return from it. I cannot let that happen to Morano, nor will I put him in the danger of it.

"No," I deny. "Not unless we know exactly what this prisoner's powers are. Ivella and I will call upon Artemis and speak with her. She created Ivella, she will tell us what exactly she crafted."

"When was Artemis last here?" Stravan asks and Salem takes a leap on to the chaise between him and Phyv.

"Summer Solstice when we tied our Blood Bond." I wave between my brothers and I.

Stravan's eyebrows knit together. "There was a blessing she placed upon you four, correct?"

We nod.

"Do not call on her until I have trained you four to bring forward the gifts she gave you. There may be a reason she has not returned here since." He stands. "I must find Dyena. After the events in New Quamfasi tonight, speak with Ivella of this, she needs to know immediately."

XENATHI — QUAMFASI CITADEL

The sun is setting, we are exactly on time for the events tonight in New Quamfasi. Passing over the boundary line that used to exist between our lands I lead us past a row of trees and stop where Kaden, Ethel's mate, waits with two carriages with four Pegasi in front of each.

There are stables lined down to the woods where horses and Pegasi are kept to travel into Xenathi and a small headquarters where I see people inside laughing over something the other said. These are the guards of New Quamfasi that will be on patrol after we are gone.

"Welcome back," Kaden greets.

"What exactly will be happening tonight?" Levora wonders.

"Tonight is Iysha's blessing, Ivella and Ira's little brother and my cousin by marriage. At the age of seven every child is prayed over under the Tree of Gods for hope of prosperity and health. We have not done a blessing in years. After the wars and our people being taken, those who were still here did not see it right to continue them. So, blessings occurred privately until recently. Now that all of our people have returned home, this will be the first spiritual celebration New Quamfasi has seen in years."

When Quamfasi reigned before Lorsius, my family was high in society and part of the Circle that ruled the West which is now known as Gordanta. There was not much I remembered about spirituality as a child. As I got older, the wars transpired, and I was never taught anything more. This will be the first celebration like this that I have attended.

"Aunt Stelina informed me that you all did not have the opportunity to be taken through the Hashthyna Forest when you came to overlook The Quamfasian Games?"

"We did not, there was not enough time between our arrival and making it to the next Game." I inform.

Kaden nods. "Well, let us go now. The sun is setting and it will still be light enough for you to see the magnificence of the Hashthyna Forest. Come, let us go." He motions to the carriages and I take Levora to the first and secure her in.

Next Phyv enters and behind him Hua follows.

"These fucking carriages makes my anxiety flare." I hear Morano mumble as he walks away.

In the next carriage now sit my brothers, but Kaden does not join either carriage.

"You will not be joining us?"

"I will be leading the Pegasi." He shifts into his Wolf and his black fur shakes out before he nods for me to enter as he trots to the front.

The moment I enter the carriage it shakes and Morano grips the door.

"For the love of the Gods," he stresses. "Amias, Roaner, switch so the weight is even and this damned thing does not tip over."

Roaner stares him in the eye and aggressively shakes the carriage with his body.

Just as Morano reaches out to grab him by the neck, the door of Levora's carriage forces open and Hua is sticking her head out.

"I will snatch one of you from that carriage if you do not stop. We need to leave."

"We need to leave," Morano mocks her.

Quickly, Hua barely appears in our carriage through ascension and smacks him before leaving.

Kaden's eyes are playful as he watches us, then, he begins to jog forward and the Pegasi follow.

"Oh Gods," Morano breathes as he grips the handles.

Amias rolls his eyes before holding his hand out to him, Morano urgently takes it and Amias winces at his grip.

"All it takes is one rock," he whispers. "Over we go."

"Morano, please, I am begging that you shut your mouth." Roaner pleads.

"No, you just tried to shake me out of this hell box."

"Maybe it needs to topple over so you can grow past this fear and realize you will be fine." I laugh.

"I am not like you, Laven." He slowly breathes. "It will just get worse and prove me correct."

We make a wide turn towards the woods that grow more expansive the farther we are carried through them. The trees here stand taller than those in Vaigon and wider, the Pegasi tighten their wings to their bodies as we are pulled through the more narrow paths.

As the sun sets, the golden hues beam through the trees and into our carriage as we pick up speed and the Pegasi begin to run through the ever expanding woods.

There is gradual change in the trees as we progress through the path. The trees appear finer, vines begin to sprawl from tree to tree, and just as the atmosphere grows more ethereal, so do the animals we surpass.

The carriage shakes as a strong gust of wind soars above.

I think Morano may cry.

"A Norpheyen." Amias points as we see what it was that shook the carriage.

One of the majestic animals that Yaro had taken just nights ago.

The Norpheyen lands on a tree next to another Norpheyen and they intently watch as we rush by.

Then, we cross paths with the land animals that are nearly as large as us in Wolf form, some even larger.

"Valgeners." Roaner lifts his chin.

Valgeners, possibly the largest land animal in this world.

Their bodies are great and firm with the silkiest short coat. Under the light of the rising sun, the iridescence of their dark coat gleams.

"Oh, it is chasing a little Norpheyen!" Amias leans to watch.

The small Norpheyen is a brindle of shades of green, just as every Norpheyen is born to blend in with its environment, and over time they develop their own colors. By the looks of it, this one has already started to develop his colors as I see a stripe of orange along its long head. This would be why it was seen by the Valgener, it is developing its adult features while still small enough for an attack.

Just as the Valgener stealthily chases the young Norpheyen up the tree, its mother swiftly soars through the forest and the young escapes. Her large mouth opens, revealing teeth near the size of my legs, as she attempts to latch on to the Valgener, whose claws protrude from its expansive paws to catch her long blue face, and a fight between the two breaks as we continue by.

Nature, the circle of life stops for no one.

The forest begins to clear and, in following, the Pegasi race across the water of the Vaisenya River behind Kaden.

"Oh my days," I mumble.

There is no bridge, by the grace of magic or more so the blessing of these grounds, we cross the water as if crossing along land. When we reach the ends of the river there is a waterfall that cascades between two large walls of rigid stone.

The water is clear enough to see the movement of the tall grass beneath it flowing like multiple tiny waves with the motion of the river. The waterfall is bright and clear and within the rush of falling water, I recognize the speckles of sparkling blue that lie in piles beneath the water. On the other side of this wall lies the Tree of Gods.

These waters dare to bring fairytales to life, nonetheless, I can only imagine the prayers these waters have heard. It gives it a history of not being the fairytale-filled dream it looks, but visuals that are fabrications of the worst, just as we are. Beauty may reside on the outside, but on the inside, there is terror we pray to rid.

Kaden disappears through the waterfall first, then each carriage one by one follows and the waterfall heavily cascades over us before we are taken on an upward hill through a wet and dark tunnel. The tunnel is wide enough to pull us through, but with an easy reach of my hand, I could touch the walls.

"This is never ending," Morano says in the darkness. He lays his head back against the seat with firmly shut eyes.

"Tighten your grip again and you will be holding Laven's hand." Amias speaks.

"He will break my hands, I need them." I chuckle within my angst to be out of the tunnel and see the tree that Ivella used to save my life from being in the hands of Yaro.

"He needs his hands to touch Ivella." Morano peeks an eye open at me and I gently shake the carriage again.

"These poor Pegasi." Roaner mumbles, and quietly, all four of us fall into a fit of laughter and the light at the end of the tunnel begins to appear.

The Pegasi take a turn to the right and gradually it is like everything appears at once. The people who sit around the roots of the tree talking amongst one another, others on the opposite end praying, the children who run freely through the forest.

The tree stands hundreds of feet tall and wide.

Many vines of moss hang from its branches as it glows in its radiant blue and white.

It is hard not to recognize that small sliver inside of me that pulls toward the tree.

Ever since the day that Ivella used this to save my life it has lived in me as it does now.

Then the carriage comes to a stop and Morano darts out first and the rest of us follow.

It is horrid to believe that the rogues were remotely close to here, but given the sacredness of this land, the Vaisenya River and the Tree of Gods are monitored so heavily that the moment they would have come closer, they would have been killed.

As I walk farther away from my family and closer toward the tree, I reach out, just craving a touch of what brings life to this forest and has brought life to me.

The hanging moss is soft yet durable in my hand, but as I release it, it leaves behind the bright blue and white particles on my hand.

"Enchanting, is it not?"

I turn to Stravan as he touches the tree. "What is even more riveting is the feeling of the actual bark of the tree against your hand, some say they can even feel the heartbeat of the land within it."

"It is much larger than I imagined." I mumble.

"It is, I am always taken back whenever I come here. Every time I see it, it is like seeing it for the first time."

Vaughn and Nina, the Leaders of Ethivon, appear not far from me and gently cut pieces of the tree and place it in a wooden bowl, then, I watch as each Leader uses the moss to mark their people down the middle of their forehead. The moss is further drawn over the eyebrow and down their bare arms. They begin to glow in the dark, moving like fireflies as they all move to stand around the tree and slowly everyone goes silent.

"They are being painted with the moss as a way of truly embodying the Tree of Gods, some consume it, but not all. Mostly, you are just painted with it."

The people begin to move to create space for Naius and Stelina who carry a sleeping Iysha in their arms.

He is laid under the hanging moss and over his body he is encompassed with markings of the tree.

"Each mark on his body is done by a family member and it is only placed upon him after they have put a blessing over him." Iysha's entire body is sketched in blessings, he is loved and cared for by many.

After Naius and Stelina sit back on their heels next to him, Ivella and Ira proceed down the open path toward their family.

Ivella's dress is wrapped intricately around her body and on some of the parts revealing her skin lie small markings from the tree over her.

"We must move back," Stravan says and we find the distant area where the rest of my family stands.

I look at the small hundreds of people before us. They are now set apart, but close enough to reach their arms out to meet; each gripping the forearm next to them. They sit against their heels before bowing, all of them are in a curved row of people falling forwards like a game of dominoes, still holding on to one another. There is a deep vibration from the tree and the ground below us, it is not disturbing, it is calming and tranquil as they sing.

"They are asking for safety, love, strength, patience, agility," Stravan whispers to us. "All things needed for a future Leader of their nation."

Where Iysha lies before his family, roots push from the ground and wrap around him from the tips of his toes to the strands in his hair. Some of the roots glow in the blue and silver from the tree and some in their natural brown, completely concealing him.

Their singing strengthens and they all sit up and move in a circular motion as their heads direct to the sky.

There is a bright light that glimmers and Ivella smiles as the roots wrapped around Iysha shine before desiccating into dust against his skin; laying in a thick layer over him and through his hair. Their singing slowly turns into a harmonic hum before ending completely. They fall down into the bow they started in; never releasing one another until Iysha's hazel eyes appear.

Iysha wakes in slight confusion, he does not move but his eyes flow around from the people and then to his family. He grins as his eyes settle on Naius and Stelina before slowly sitting up and the layer of dirt over his body falls away.

Looking at the five of them, I notice how each of Naius's

children take after him in features. Though, his two eldest are darker in complexion and hair than him and Iysha, who has lighter skin and brown curls that have their own mind.

The moment Iysha sees Ivella, he leaps into her arms and her head buries into his curls as she breathes in deeply and her smile grows.

Leaders throughout New Quamfasi herd around Naius and Stelina to greet them after and within the crowds, I see Ivella step away. Her smile begins to fade and she is gone unnoticed.

MISERY OF VERITY

LAVEN HEPHAESTUS ARVENALDI, II

By scent alone, I navigate my way through the main palace of New Quamfasi to where Ivella has come.

When I enter her study she is sitting, curled in her large chair with her knees tightly pulled to her chest. Her eyes are cast upward, staring at the moon as it shines down, cascading a gentle ray over her.

"Are you all right?" I ask, slowly approaching her.

She smiles and nods, not making any eye contact.

I cannot get through to her, although, I realize it may not be my place to try to reach her through any form of mind link.

"I am fine, just leave me be."

"Something is the matter; you can tell me." The nearer I step, the more unwelcomed I feel and the more distant she becomes.

She continues to smile. "No, I cannot . . . I will not." She looks at me with eyes brightly filled with sadness. "Not until you can give me exactly what it is that you ask of me."

The one major factor that will burden our relationship.

Then all there is, is guilt. The guilt of having to let someone ignore everything they are going through to cater to me.

'I am a burden to you,' I say through the sobs shattering my words.

She is not offended by what I say. If anything, she seems hurt. 'When have I ever said that?'

'You have not . . . you manage enough of your own suffering to have to accommodate my own with it.'

Again, her head shakes, and that soft smile does not leave. 'You are not burdening me. You would only be voicing your griefs and we would sort through them.'

How do you see someone in such grave depression and add yours to it?

How do you recall all that you were without returning to it?

"I do want to tell you . . . but this conversation will not be as easy as you think. I cannot," I stop, searching for the right things to say. "Anamnesis of those days are the most difficult. I have no way to speak of it without feeling as if I am falling back into it and appearing as that person I know as my weakest."

"It is that you believe you still need to fake your true feelings around me that proves you and I cannot pursue anything farther than just an alliance."

I knew my past would cloud over us, but not like this.

"That is not fair to hold that against me."

"Why?"

"Because I cannot control what happened to me to make me how I am now."

That smile turns into a forceful quiet laugh. "Do you believe me to be stupid, Laven?"

I do not answer her as her eyes fall deeper into mine.

"I am just as much yours as you are mine. And we both know the reasoning behind why that is. We both know what it is that holds us together so tightly."

I can feel the falling of my face at her words.

When?

"When did you know?"

Her nails gently scratch against her knees that are close to her chest. "After I discovered the wings, but, I think I always knew. I was never certain, though, after you left Nadrexi when I first went back home I think I knew for certain. Then I became Fae, and I knew it the moment you walked into the bathing room."

Large wings that weigh her down and sink her into the water. Without shifting properly and naturally, her body's strength is not where it should be to hold a pair of wings this size. From a child the Fae are taught to hold their wings, Ivella has never in her life had wings.
My clothing soaks and clings to my skin as I scramble into the water.
'Laven,' Ivella quietly cries as she looks up at me.

"Knowing the connection is there and feeling it is much more different than suspecting it. Which makes it that much more incomprehensible that you still think you cannot tell me everything from your past that has brought you to now. The trauma of our backgrounds brought us together, what a grotesque way to form love, let alone a mating bond, but how beautiful it is when you aim for the better together through it."

"Why did you never tell me that you knew?" There has been so much for the both of us to see and experience since that time, still I am not sure how much more a solidified mating bond would change given our current circumstances.

"I am angry with you," she responds. "I have been for quite some time, why would I tell you?" I do not answer. "You speak of *nothing* with me. You did not tell me that your imprisonment was because of me, you did not tell me what happened while you were there, you do not tell me of your father who passed, you love your mother but I can see a disconnect and I do not understand why. Why is that?"

Nibbling on my lip, I begin to aggressively fumble about with my fingers.

Because I do not want you to carry a single burden of mine nor yours but I will proudly carry it all even if it incapacitates me. But there is nothing other than inequality when that person loves you enough to do the same and you do not let them.

"If you cannot speak to me, about any of it, then what are we doing? I am supposed to be the person you can tell anything to, yet I barely know you. Yes, I know you, but I do not know you. The you no one else knows or sees. The person you so greatly hide from the world.

"I do not only wish for the best parts of you, I want the worst of you. It may seem anomalous or peculiar to others, it is not to me. It is gratifying to know someone can give you every morsel of themselves without being sensitive to what you think, they just let you hold them through their worst fears knowing you will protect them in their most vulnerable. I could not care at all about those who value only the perfection in their spouse. That is not me, it will never be me. The worth is in the foulest fragments of you and how you cultivate through it. That is what the value is—having someone who is so broken flourish right before you. This is the splendor of love. The laughter is beautiful, the riveting adventure, lovemaking that cripples you from mind to limb. But the *ugly*, the distraught, the fear, the dreadful pieces of love is what nurtures it. It teaches you the differentiation of choosing to stay and feeling indebted to stay."

And she speaks exactly what I am afraid of.

What if I give her everything and it no longer is her choosing to stay, she feels obligated to stay because of what she now knows? I could never hold her hostage in a way such as that. Then, she continues like she has heard every word.

"It is as if you are terrified to fathom that after it all I would still be here because I *want* to be here—despite the ruin in you. The way I can love you terrifies you, and I cannot push you to comprehend how I feel for you. That part must be done on your own . . . I choose you, Laven, because I want to give you those pieces of myself, not because of fate, because *I* say so. I do not want to let anyone else know me in the way you should. Yet, if I have to, I will. If you want to talk of fairness, I am the only one who is not being treated fairly.

And you know well enough that I will not stand for anyone to treat me unfairly. Even a mate."

She waits. She sits there so patiently waiting for a response.

Ivella looks over the tears gliding down my face, that fall to stain my shirt. Just as I look at hers.

"I–" coming to a strong halt, she continues to wait. "I do not know if I could ever say it."

The gentlest smile appears on her face. "And I cannot accept that."

PART V
NEVER SURRENDER

69
CORONATION DAY

LAVEN HEPHAESTUS ARVENALDI, II
VAIGON CITADEL

I STARE AT THE food on my plate as I hear footsteps make their way to the dining room terrace.

"Laven?" Roaner speaks. "Are you all right?"

"I decided my Coronation will be tomorrow afternoon."

He sits across from me, glances down at my untouched food, and then at me again. "Why? You said you did not want one."

"I do not. I will follow tradition and have one."

"The planning of your Coronation is not why you were trapped in the Chaos Chamber all night. Was it?"

"No," I answer honestly.

And in the silence between us I can hear every single word from last night repeating in my head. The distraught way she spoke that she cannot accept what I cannot give her. My greatest defeat, not being apt for what I so desperately have wanted, turned into a need.

"Ivella said no." I say over the thoughts that have environed my head.

His dark eyebrows furrow. "No to what?"

I gather my hands in my lap as they begin to shake and he watches. "To me."

Placing my hands in my lap, I begin to pick at my trousers as I used to when I did not know what to do with my hands in stressful situations.

'But the ugly, the distraught, the fear, the dreadful pieces of love is what nurtures it. It teaches you the differentiation of choosing to stay and feeling indebted to stay.'

"When did this happen?"

"Yesterday evening."

I watch it come together in his eyes as he realizes that is why I was mentally absent from all conversation that transpired last night and why I have been physically absent all day.

Roaner contemplates what to say and I have now torn a small hole into my trousers with my nails.

"Place your hands on the table." He says delicately.

Reluctantly, I do.

His hands firmly press over mine as I now scrape the table with my nails. "What do you need?"

What I need is no longer obtainable.

It will forever be right in front of me, never within my grasp.

And somehow, I am to carry on around her as if nothing matters any longer.

"Nothing." I stand. "I have planning to do."

"Laven," Roaner follows. "It is late, rest. You can pick up wherever you left off in the morning."

What makes him think I will sleep. I will not know the difference between night and day after time has passed.

"Help me plan for tomorrow," I say to get him out of my hair. "Amias sent out the letters to the people that my Coronation will be tomorrow and where it will be. I need you to make sure everything is in place."

I do not know what that specific everything is that I speak of, I just need him and everyone away from me.

"YOU ALL MUST LEARN to work in sync," Amias's voice is loud and boisterous as we stand before the trainees on the Training Grounds. "There will be plenty of chances that all of you may come across one another while on the battlefield and if you are not properly aiding each other, it will be pointless to help."

"As a unit," Roaner says. "Where one lacks, we all lack. Where one falls the other must naturally be there to pick them up."

"It is vital." I announce. "We will show you one of the many ways the four of us learned to operate in the same pace and discover where the other is weak to support."

Morano and Amias walk across the Training Grounds with a twelve-foot log and place it on the ground in front of us.

"Watch carefully," Hua advises as Morano, Amias, Roaner, and I stand on one side of the log. "Four people lifting this log at once is not as easy as it seems. Height must be equal, and if it is not, learn where to adjust and how to adjust."

Roaner stands behind me. "Be careful stronghold, you like to toss this log around like a game of ball."

"Do not worry, Princess Roaner, I will catch you if you cannot balance it." Amias chuckles.

"And you better not fall after catching him," I hear Morano grumble. "I do not want four hundred pounds falling on me at the start of my day."

In their fit of laughter, Hua begins.

"Down boys," she commands.

The four of us squat with our backs straight and place our right hand under the log.

"Up!"

We stand and the log heavily sits in our hand.

"Been working on your back muscles as of late," Amias teases Roaner as our upper bodies are exposed except for the leather arm covers that stop at our shoulders.

"Fuck you," he mumbles as we shift the log to hover over our shoulders.

"The log should never touch your shoulders," Hua speaks to the trainees. "It should only be just above it."

Hua moves to stand in front of us. "Down and over."

We gradually move down into a squat and back up. "Watch how the shortest adjusts his height to go down and lift at the same time as the tallest."

Next, we all shift the log from our right shoulder, over our heads and catch it with our left. As the log sits in our hand on our left, we repeat.

Down, up, over.

Down, up, over.

Down, up, over.

"How many more times are we to do this, *General Hua*." Morano asks as we squat for the fifth time."

Hua lazily grins. "As many times as I want you to."

I know he is holding up a finger at her as she gives one back and the young trainees around us laugh.

"Now, you all will try." Hua nods for us to place the log down and she selects six trainees of similar height to try first.

The log drops from our hands and slightly bounces at the collision to the ground.

"Thank you for your assistance boys, now get off my grounds." Hua dismisses us.

"I love you too," Morano jokes before we ascend.

* * *

"For you," Stravan enters the Marl Study and places a folded letter on the table in front of me as I prepare a speech for the Coronation.

"What is it?"

"It is from myself and Dyena." He says as I reach for the letter.

I pull the wax seal and read RENEWAL OF THE VOSCHANTAI GALA, on the other side of the invitation my name is written with the location of the festivities.

"We will be holding the first Voschantai Gala since the split of our nations long ago. This is also our opportunity to show the other realms our unification."

"Clever," I nod.

His arms cross as he looks me over. "So you decided to have a Coronation? On my way in your brothers informed me of your plans."

I nod again.

I am sure that is not all they informed him of.

Dyena most likely knows what happened the other night and has told him to come here.

"What happened to you not having one unless Ivella—"

"Do not finish what you are about to say," I hold up my hand and return to writing the speech. "When you know exactly what happened."

"Laven, this will be short-lived."

"How are you so sure? Did she tell you this?"

"No, she did not tell me this," he becomes defensive. "But I know Ivella and I have grown to know you as well, and you *both* are fucking stubborn. I do not know who it will be, but one of you will come to your senses and realize there must be some form of give and take in love. It is never perfect and that is what the both of you must learn. You do not need to show up perfect, and you can have your boundaries while still properly caring for one another. I have gone through this Laven, and until you both come to terms with this there will be no progression."

He stands. "Now, you may continue with this Coronation as you have planned, I will attend and smile and wave and greet and remind you that without a High Queen, a Coronation will be a futile event."

* * *

As Stravan leaves, I finally find the courage to write the letter that I should have written first thing this morning.

Ivella,

There is something we must speak of soon regarding the rogues that attempted an attack on Iysha and Levora.

Please respond as soon as you can.

House Arvenaldi

I sign the letter without disclosing my name and stamp it with the Wolf sigil of mine and my brother's initials. She may be more inclined to respond to me and my family, but not likely just me. No matter what has happened between us, she must be told of what has been said by the prisoner.

"Have it sent immediately," I say to Ezra as he takes the small rolled letter. "It discloses information that must be responded to right away if she may."

Ezra nods and before he leaves, he and Morano exchange a glance and he ascends.

"The Coronation is still on?" Morano asks while removing his topcoat.

"Postponed," I nod. "As of now, it will happen when it is supposed to."

"Publicly claiming a crown is gratuitous. All it is, is a celebration for commencing when everyone knew you were next in line."

"Well, now the people are demanding my Coronation. They find it odd that I have not had it yet and are questioning. We all know the rigid nation Lorsius bred, they do not find change to be convenient and when customs are not followed they become irritated."

"Lorsius is no longer here to wash their backs," Morano pours himself a glass of dark liquor and then one for me. "They can get over it or go fuck themselves." He quietly exhales as he eases back into his chair after sipping the alcohol. "How is our little trinity? Levora, Phyv, and Greyce coming along well with their plans to return to the Mortal Lands?"

I take a long sip from the short glass and close my eyes. "Fine, but they are focusing primarily on training before I allow them to be sent back.

Whoever it was that took them there will know the rest are being searched for and we cannot risk them being unprepared. We do not exactly know what lurks in the human world, but if we must, we may go with them as reinforcement."

Morano smiles as his finger runs over his glass. "I just want to go for the experience."

"I had a feeling, I think we all do."

In a sudden rush, Morano and I turn as we hear heavy boots running down the hall, when I turn, I see our guards frantically approaching the study.

"My King, it is Quamfasi! They are under attack, and if we do not act quickly it will reach here. The rogues have returned in large quantities and they are stronger than before."

Morano's glass knocks to the floor as we stand. "Ezra," he mumbles before ascending.

"Prep the guards, gather the Warriors and find Hua, lead them to Quamfasi now!"

XENATHI – QUAMFASI CITADEL

The moment I arrive, the battle is growing just before the boundary lines where the border used to stand. Horses and Pegasi run wildly through the woods to flee, some Pegasi are looking for their rider. I see Ivella standing multiple feet away from a Warrior with a bloodied sword. Behind her, she is guarding Ethel and Kaden, who is struggling to heal the gushing wound to Ethel's chest.

"She jumped in front of me," Kaden cries out as his hands shake while healing Ethel.

The battles transpiring around us look far too familiar to what our war will look like. The rogues are fighting intelligently, some in Wolf form, others in silver fighting leathers.

I rush toward them, adding in my own hand of healing until another can aid us. "Kaden, you need to get her to a Healer, we will not be able to do this ourselves. There is but only so far that our healing capabilities can go."

Just as the Warrior attempts forward for Ivella, I see Roaner running behind the Warrior who caused Ethel's injury. A force field projects from Roaner throwing him to the ground and just over my head an arrow is let loose, barely missing the Warrior as he stands. I turn and Hua is running over.

"I will take them," Hua kneels beside me and she slides her bloodied sword into her sheath, gently Hua and Kaden lift Ethel from the ground as she gasps for air.

"Ivella," I sharply call from below her as she and Roaner stand on both sides of the Warrior. "Kill him."

They charge at each other and the battle rages louder.

Just as they near, Ivella slides to the ground and between his legs, as she rotates in her glide, she stands and her fist punches directly into his back knocking him unsteady. Her arm forms a chokehold around his neck and he topples over, throwing her to the ground.

She dodges his punch that drives downward and his fist connects with the earth and with the curve between her thumb and first finger, she jars him in the neck repeatedly and he falls back. Out of the corner of my eye, a rogue plows in her direction, without a second thought Ivella draws her dagger from her thigh and using the leverage of a dead body below her, she jumps from it. When the rogue nears, simultaneously her knee rams into his chest and her dagger protrudes through his head forcing blood through his ear.

She moves to the Warrior as he uses this opportunity to attack with her back turned.

Knowing his next move, Ivella turns and the entirety of her eyes fill in an electrifying orange, not a single hint of her green eyes are to be seen within the power overtaking her. That sadistic smile for blood is something I recognize well from the last time I saw her fighting in an ambush. But, this—this smile is different, and this power looks stronger, something unknown to our world. Something that is much more vigorous than anything I have ever seen.

She walks only a few steps before one knee lifts and the depths of the earth below us convulse in a profound vibration. Splits are sent through the ground as she rises into the sky with orbs that circulate in her hands like lava and lightning. Across her skin her powers ignite like they did when she first saved me from a rogue.

In a scurry, the man falls back.

He was not expecting a challenge as this to be at hand.

Ivella's hands come together expanding the orbs before she soars back to the ground. Her hands punch through the earth, shaking him and his to go unsteady. This is when she seizes her moment. Orb after orb fly from her hands, colliding into his armor, eating away at the fabric until it reaches his skin—devouring his flesh to the bone.

Her large wings appear, and his eyes widen as she tortures him to the ground.

As he falls, so do the rogues around us.

Anything that happens to him, happens to them . . .

"Ivella!" Esme shouts as she and Roaner stand back to back over a corpse. "The rogues!"

She pays no attention to her; she is solely focused on disposing of this Warrior.

One wing draws backward and forcefully drives forward. A strong gust of wind from her wing flings his body backward and into a tree.

As I look around us, piles upon piles of ash lie on the ground from the bodies of the rogues.

Ivella moves nearer to him as he cripples on the ground, she kneels lower, her mouth just above his ear as he thrashes beneath the power holding his desiccating body to the ground.

Supplely, she speaks into his ear with death laced in her words. "You have lost." And the final pieces of the Warrior that are left disintegrate.

I look up as we all see a red electric sphere slowly opening on the opponent's end of the battle. It is a portal.

A man slowly appears behind it, his eyes are drawn wide as he stares down at the man suffering below Ivella. The longer I look at him, I recognize his face.

Dark skin, stark white hair, black eyes, and one crooked eyebrow. Yaro.

And through the portal he stares at me.

Then, the portal shuts and he is gone.

Ivella stands over his body and grabs a gold ring from the ashes of the Warrior.

"What is that?" I ask.

"I do not know."

There is a thin dark blue line through the middle of the ring and Stravan appears next to me examining the ring.

Ivella overlooks the ring next, and on the inside we see Yaro's name written.

But not just Yaro, YARO, II.

That was not just some Warrior.

He was Yaro's son.

70
TIME & HEALING

LAVEN HEPHAESTUS ARVENALDI, II

Esme sits next to Ivella as we wait in the Healers Infirmary, the hallway we sit in is lit with candles and the flames flash over the stone walls and windows. At the end of the hall stand two doors that take you to the Healer's Rooms where Ethel is.

Esme's knee begins to rapidly bounce in anticipation.

Ethel should be on the mend, but that blow to her chest is deep, not even our healing powers could mend it.

For the third time, I see Ivella's arm twitch, she tries to cover it by grabbing Esme's hand but I can feel that something has happened to her that she is hiding.

"I am fine," Ivella swats at me as I kneel in front of her and grab her arm. Ignoring her, I tear the leather of her suit; revealing the inflamed skin and darkening veins.

Looking up at her I rest my hand over her forearm and she flinches as I heal the damage done. "How often has this been happening?" I ask.

"First time."

"Second," Roaner aggressively corrects as he stares at her from his leaned position against the wall.

"You informant," Ivella grumbles under her breath.

"This has happened before?" Esme takes the words from my mouth. "Have you spoken to uncle Naius?"

She tugs away her now healed arm and Esme looks between us before I stand.

"We need to speak of this," Roaner says for me. "You cannot continue to reach this point and think nonchalantly of it. Control, Ivy, you need to learn to control how you allow your powers to overtake you."

That is the downfall of having great strength. Sometimes we never know how strong we are until it reaches the point of harming ourselves while harming others.

"And the rogue prisoner that spoke of this."

Ivella looks up at me. "What?"

"Phyv said he was talking about you and I went to go see what it was he spoke of."

A Healer comes walking down the hall with Kaden and Esme darts from the bench we sit on.

"Your sister will heal just fine. Her sternum was broken and it nearly punctured her heart, it was possibly just an inch away. A few more days here and she will be back to normal. It may take some time before she operates as she used to but she will be just fine in due time."

Esme sighs in relief. "May I see her?"

"Yes, she is not awake, but you may come see her if you would like."

"I can go with you." Roaner steps closer to Esme, and to my surprise, she accepts him.

"Laven," Amias urgently calls down the bond. *"We must meet with Vallehes and Penelope in the Consultation Room. The ring has been examined, this was not just any ring Yaro's son was wearing."*

Roaner hears this as well and I hold my hand up as he contemplates if he will stay with Esme, or come with us. *"Go with Esme, we will be fine."*

"Inform me later."

Kaden and the Healer lead Roaner and Esme down the hall, and they walk closely next to each other before I see their fingers gravitate to each other.

Now, only I and Ivella are left.

"Vallehes and Penelope are calling for us," I say.

She stands and ascends without me.

Vallehes tosses me the ring as I end my ascension at the door of the Consultation Room. "You will hold this ring in a safe place, and as you have rogue prisoners, ask them what the ring does."

"I believe it controls the rogues, or creates them. In some way, this ring has everything to do with what he has created." Stravan says.

"If Ivella killed Yaro's son," Amias begins. "Would that mean the rogues we have imprisoned have died as well? We all saw it, when his son was being defeated so were the rogues. Then, as he died, they did too."

I look at Stravan and at the same moment our heads sway from side to side.

"This ring he was wearing had possible control over the rogues, that could mean he only had control over the rogues we battled, not all of them."

"Now the question is how many have that ring?" Penelope heavily exhales and sits in one of the chairs at the large table.

"I will speak with the prisoner again, he said his name is Jaxyn, but that is debatable."

"I can see if it is true that he once resided in Galitan." Morano says. "It will not be difficult to find him in their books, I know it is not possible for there to be one too many Jaxyn's."

Stravan nods. "Galitan will need to be looked into. If Jaxyn is truly from there, we will need to scope their land."

"That is where he said he is from?" Vallehes questions.

"Doubtful. He was mouthing quite a lot when I spoke with him." I choose not to go too in-depth. I know Ivella did not read my letter yet and I am unsure if this conversation is one she wishes to have in front of everyone here.

Even then, she is very quiet as she stands in the corner of the room looking down at her now healed arm and rubbing a hand over her skin.

"If he is telling the truth, Galitan has been breached without their knowing we will need to speak with them promptly." I add.

"Ivella," she looks to Amias who is scratching his chin and he does not look at me. "You received a letter of proposal from Prince Ozias of Galitan?"

I know exactly what he is to say next.

"Yes."

"And did you deny him?"

"No."

"Good." I say and her eyes narrow at me. "We will use that as leverage to see if they are part of this mutation, or if they truly do not know that someone who says they are of their land is infected."

"And then what from here?" Her tone is dagger sharp.

I tuck the ring into my pocket and look at everyone. "We will mourn our dead and be thankful for our triumphs. It will only get worse from here and on."

71
EVERYTHING AT ONCE

IVELLA FONDALI

'You were not right nor wrong. There is no such thing as right or wrong when you are learning, what I will tell you is that the entirety of our infinite life is about lessons.' Ma says she rubs her hand over my hair.

I turn and she is already smiling looking down at me as I lie in her lap.

'Misperception is a thief. We go into love thinking we know what must be here and that is it, all or nothing. When that all or nothing can ruin something pivotal. I always said that I wanted a husband who had a past with no one. I wanted my own children, I wanted to be the only person in his life that mattered because I deserved it. But, the universe is funny. And she gives you what you need. Not what you covet for. Then, I met your father, I met you and Ira, and all of those thoughts I had about what I knew I wanted was formed through ignorance.'

I open my eyes as I lay at the bottom of the tub and lift through the water.

As I look at the stars that burn in the sky, I see him.

I see the shape of his eyes forming.

So easily his face is outlined.

And within the shooting of the stars, they dance, forming his black and white curls.

The longer I look at the star given eyes, I see all the reverence and adoration he once looked at me with, and then, the distraughtness, the pain.

I stand from the bathing tub and wrap the linen around my body.

The doors to my chamber open and Dyena enters, I see the backs of two guards at the doors and instead of them turning to close the doors, she does instead.

"Ivella?" Dyena calls.

"Here," I say from the bathing chamber.

She smiles. "Hello sister."

"Hi," I say, still standing in the tub wrapped in the linen.

"Are you all right?"

I think so.

Thinking is not knowing.

Am I?

Will I be?

"Come out of the tub," she holds her hand out and I take it.

She walks me to my vanity and grabs the small jar filled with the cream for my hair that my father made specifically for my curls. Then, she combs her fingers through my hair and our eyes meet.

"Your mind is raging."

"Are you hearing every thought?"

Dyena laughs. "No, but the energy is pulling."

"How many bodies were there?" I ask.

"Few, thankfully. Yaro's son was ridded of before the rest of the rogues could ambush." She pinches the side of my neck and I smile.

"Battlefields aside," Dyena uses the end of my linen to wipe remnants of the cream from her hands. "How *are* you?"

"Fine."

I am not fine and I will not say it.

"Ivella, you are a mirror of mine," she delicately speaks. "Yet also an entire opposite of me, still, I know when something is the matter. And I know when you are lying."

She waits.

THE SONG OF VERITY AND SERENITY

She will wait forever.

"You are giving up."

I tilt my head higher. "I am not giving up."

"Then what are you doing?"

The stiffness grows. "I do not like this."

"I know you do not, and that is why we will speak of it right now."

"Speak of what?"

"You know what. You are angry, are you not?"

Another pause.

"Yes."

"Why?"

"Because I love him." And in saying it, I feel that tiny crack in what I have fought to avoid. "I love him and he is not ready for it." Making all of the progress I have built to be with him into nothing.

"Just because he is not ready at this moment, Ivella, does not mean never. Men are fragile, they do not admit it, but all they truly want is to be loved, adored, and cherished, and held. They want everything we want and sometimes they want it more than we do, and are any of us ever truly prepared for that?"

No, none of this makes sense.

Love does not make sense.

"He needs time to . . . to heal, to alleviate his—"

"Since when must one heal alone, Ivella? I think after all these years have passed of him not prospering through his trauma is sign enough that he cannot do it alone. He cannot do it without *you*. He has his brothers, he has a loving sister, he has close people around him. But you," her voice softens as she kneels in front of me, and her hands tightly grasp my own. "You bring him elation that no one else ever has. You make him forget those years of his life ever existed, no matter how you came into his life, you did. And you changed it for the better."

He is young, he must be my age.
He has white in his hair.

He is an Orviante.

His cloak is thrown around my shoulders, the fabric is heavy and velvety. Most importantly, I am covered.

For how long?

How long will he be nice to me before he forces me to be a chambermaid like my companions who have been taken?

No, he is not like the others.

I could be wrong.

'I–I am Laven. What is your name?'

Finally, I breathe and I can hear the fading screams of Ira as I am rushed away in that godforsaken carriage.

Ira . . .

How will he be without me.

'What is your name?' *I am asked, after all, I do believe I heard him asking for my name, but the screaming. The screaming, wailing Ira is trapped in my ears.*

Ivella, but I cannot tell him that.

The first name to come to mind is what my father said he wanted to name me before coming up with the name Ivella.

'Maivena.' *It hurts to talk.*

Maivena.

Yes, Maivena will do.

He is so soft spoken.

'Did they–did any of those men touch you?'

The hard hands gripping my shoulders reappear and as if I am reliving it all over again, I can feel the tearing of all of my clothing as Ira is held before me to watch.

I shake my head of the thoughts, not realizing he will see that as a response.

'Please, do not feel like you have to lie to me.'

I cannot say it.

I cannot say the way I was touched in front of such an innocent soul.

I shake my head again. 'They only took my clothes . . .' *I do not hear myself speaking as rabid thoughts race through my head.*

A tear that I have been fighting sheds, but only one, I will not let anyone of this bastard nation see me cry over the putridness of man.

'One day,' *he whispers,* 'I am going to kill them.'

A great promise from such a young boy.

How will someone like you ever conquer the power of twelve men?

Instead, I ask, 'why?' Why harm your own?

I can hear the tightening of his jaw just before he speaks. 'Because they touched you, and you will learn fast here, Maivena, that I do not tolerate men touching women outside of their consent.'

Finding the courage, I lift my head.

As he stares at me I see truth in his pretty eyes. 'Laven,' I mumble. 'You are kind.'

His smile is lazy. 'Let us see if you still find me kind when I deliver their heads to their families.'

"Do not," Dyena exhales slowly as she wipes away the fallen tears along my face. "Do not be so keen on knowing everything. Sometimes, not much good can come from knowing the entirety of a situation. You have gone through far too much for a woman who is only five and twenty. You have been forced to live above your age, you have been forced to overcome trauma, you have been forced to do many things you have not wanted to. Now, I am begging you, as your sister, to just be happy and love him, Ivella. It is what you both need most and that is all he is asking of you . . . to just love him and to let him love you, unless you would like for your greatest regret in life to be letting him go."

YOU & ME

LAVEN HEPHAESTUS ARVENALDI, II
VAIGON CITADEL

'What is in that chamber?'

'Nothing,' I guard the doors and he smiles.

'Let me see,' Pa aims forward and I continue to stand my ground.

I attempt to stay calm. 'It is nothing.'

'Laven, let me see.'

'It is messy, and you do not like mess.' I warn him.

'I will live.'

I deny him again, and this time he forces me aside.

Opening the doors of the chamber he comes to a stand still. I worry that he will be upset with the cluttered room, but that does not seem to be why he is taken back.

All over art supplies lie on small tables, easels are randomly placed about with undone art work and brushes that have dried paint.

He peers around the chamber from the entrance. I push past him and he catches my arm. 'An art room, no wonder you like to spend so much time in here. Why do you hide this?'

I shrug.

'It is your mother,' he smiles, seeing the portrait. *'Perfect lighting and shading.'* He runs his finger over her glowing dark skin. *'Even the eyes are perfect.'* He takes it off the small easel and looks at me. *'I will give you coin for it if you allow me to have it, I would like to put it in my study.'*

I smile. *'You look at Ma every day.'*

He smiles too. *'I will never not want to look at your mother. But this was made by my son, and I would like to keep it.'*

I nod. *'I do not want your coin, keep it for yourself.'*

He loudly laughs as his head falls. *'Unfortunately, no matter what, my coin will always be yours as well. I will give you pay for your work.'* Turning in a circle to observe the chamber farther, he stops when seeing a larger portrait on the balcony. *'Who is that?'*

I speed across the room and hide the undone painting beneath a large linen cover.

'A girl,' I look at him over my shoulder.

'And you know this girl?'

I do not answer. I do not really know her at all. I would like to.

But I am not allowed to.

He does not press further. *'My son is an Artist. Out of you, the boys, and Vora, I thought it to be Roaner, though, I am sure he has his own hidden artistry just as you do.'*

'Poetry.'

Pa nods. *'I should have known.'*

He turns to me still smiling. *'I will be taking this, and this is for you.'* He places a large golden coin in my hand, before he pulls me into his chest by my head. *'Never stop,'* he grips my hair. *'Art, poetry, music, it all sets off dreams, and for sanity to exist, we need those dreams to give us something to look forward to through the chaos. We need the Artists, the Poets, we need them to live so there is ease. Do not ever stop creating, even if it is not beautiful. Life is just as hideous as it is pulchritudinous.'*

I twirl the coin through my fingers as I sit in the middle of the Chaos Chamber.

From the center of the room I can disclose the worst of my days versus the best. Just through the destruction all the way to the most pristine pieces I have created, I can see it.

All around me lie incomplete sketches done in charcoal with stark black lines that trail off to nothing, many of those paintings were from the beginning of my years learning art. Then, there are the paintings, the portraits, the ripped canvases that have paint bleeding down the torn fabric that dried in that way. So much in this room are captured moments from my life, moments I have wanted to keep immortalized when some day we may not remember any of this. Even the worst of moments I have drawn, Amias crying and then the transition to happiness, Roaner filled with rage that turns to meekness, Morano shy and hidden and then boisterous and loud, Levora shouting her happiness to hiding her face in her hands. So much this room encompasses what I can never imagine letting go no matter the emotions held within.

On nights like tonight, my innermost feelings have a ruinous effect on all that I create.

This chamber does not only bring peace, it brings process, the process of all thoughts that I struggle to say even to those I trust the most, but maybe that is the worst of this place, it enables me from prospering through my worst traits.

Throughout my hours spent here, I realized that the only way I could ever fall back into who I was years ago would be by losing her. I would rather struggle to speak to her about every suffering I have faced than to turn into who I was at my weakest and not have her at all.

It seems we both have come to learn this.

A scent that has grown to be my favorite circles around the room and its warmth environs me. And then I am thanking every God for its arrival.

"Ever since I was young, I had to learn to be the barrier." Once more, I question. "How do you so easily let that go and turn into the person who now needs to lean instead of being leaned on?"

From heel to toe, I even know that.

She sits next to me on the floor.

"It does not always have to be that way."

"But it is what I am used to."

She turns and sits between my legs.

"And we are ever changing, learning new ways to simply allow others to be there." Her voice shifts into that deep, soft tone that saves me from every fear. "Ask for help."

"I have done everything, Maivena." Little by little, it falls apart. "Doctors that recklessly care, Healers who have worked holistically, everything that exists, I have done all that I can possibly–"

"Laven," she grabs my face as my head rapidly shakes. "There is *you*, and *me*. There is only us." I desperately look up at her as I slump further down, and she lifts me higher. "If either of us exist, there will be nothing to burden us alone."

Not a heartbeat goes by where she lets me go.

With the lift of a shaking hand, I draw my fingers down my chest and then over her forehead.

The ancient way of saying, "my soul knows yours." I speak.

Her chin quivers as she nods, then, she repeats that same action with her hand. "And no one else's."

A bond that even love does not know.

This woman was built to bring this me back to earth when I begin to drift into a world full of terror. Just as I am built for her. Mated. Not mated. Neither of us will know a bond like we do right in this moment.

"Through your worst days I will love you. There is no amount of trauma you can go through that I will not be able to handle. But you have to let me in. There have been few to carry you at your worst and I will be the last and greatest."

Within our tears, I gently kiss her, tasting the sweetness of her lips encased by the salt pouring down our faces.

Her existence is given from the God's, a riveting being they permanently attached to me. Nothing but remembrance is needed here and the endearment we share. Now that I hold knowledge of what it feels like to lose her, I will be indebted to all of our contretemps, and all of our blessings.

Taking her hand, I ascend, and she laughs as we fall into my bed.

At the end she sees the Porvienia lying over the corner.

She crawls across the bed, grabs it, and comes back to me.

There is joy in her eyes that I do not think I have ever seen. The joy of being with me.

She wraps the Porvienia around my bare shoulders and I smile. "Now what?"

What do you do after your dreams come true?

I have spent the past seven years inheriting my dreams from the shape of her face.

Now what is to come next?

She smiles rubbing her thumb over the short hair on my cheek. "Whatever you want."

I grin and wrap us both in the Porvienia as everything I have coveted for tumbles from my mouth. "I want you to be my wife, I want you to be High Queen of Vaigon, I want a house we can turn into a home, I want children that look exactly like you." She laughs again and I add that to the list of the many things. I thread my fingers through her hair, holding the nape of her neck. "I want as much peace as a High King and High Queen may have."

Her smile turns warmer, and she nods. "I think I can accept that."

"Maivena . . ." I whisper.

She kisses my hand and smiles. "Only to you."

MOURN YOUR DEAD

LAVEN HEPHAESTUS ARVENALDI, II

I PULL A BOOK within the Marl Study and the floor to ceiling bookshelf heavily turns.

"The ring is within here?" Maivena asks.

I step into the hidden room and bring her with me. "Yes, only you and I know of its placement."

The bookshelf closes behind us and we enter through the secret drawing room my father had put here years ago.

Maivena circles a hand and the candles flare around the room.

"It is held in my fathers favorite book." I lead her to the next bookshelf and grab for the poetry book he would always read to us over a bonfire. "Poetry of Nuemasy."

"Nuemasy still writes some of the best poetry to this day."

"He does." I smile. "Even in his hundreds of years."

I open the book and in a small corner where no words are written, I have a cutout where Yaro's ring is placed. I pull it from the poetry book and tuck it into my pocket.

"Now, we see what else we can learn from that rogue. There is no way he does not know what this ring does. He likes to talk, and we will need to make it quick."

"The funeral," Maivena nods.

"How many recognizable bodies were there?"

"Sixty-three of the eighty. Twenty-nine injured. Ten were not possible saved."

Not able to be saved like me since their time ran out.

"How has Ethel progressed since last night?" That wound was horrid and I feared there was no return from it.

Maivena smiles. "She is on the mend as the Healer said, but she will have a ways to go before she is active again. Forcing Ethel to be still will be the hardest."

"Forcing a Fondali woman to be still is a task all its own."

Maivena shoves my arm and holds her hand out to me and I take it.

* * *

We walk through the dark hall of Unalave and down the left hallway where Jaxyn is. Two guards are at the end of the hall standing before his cell where the door is lifted, but the barred door is intact.

"Jaxyn," I speak first.

Maivena steps closer to the bars and Jaxyn easily takes interest in her.

"Ivella Fondali," she holds her hand out to him through the bars and I step closer, as do the guards behind us. These are the Queens Sentinel given to Maivena through Stravan and Dyena. The same guards from her Coronation in Provas.

Jaxyn examines her hand before standing, taking it, and smiling. "Hair of the winter, skin of the summer, eyes of ice and fire, Orviantes. One with hair of the raven. You may have lost two Dragons, but you gained two more in their place."

I touch Maivena's shoulder. "What are you speaking of?"

He lets go of her hand and she looks up at me.

"What of our Dragons?" Maivena demands.

Jaxyn does not answer her. "I would like a gift the next time you see me."

Just like Agivath, but how to know he speaks the truth as Agivath does is the standing question.

"I have one now." Maivena turns to me and I reach into my pocket revealing the ring. Her urgency grows as he now speaks of the danger to Vaigon and Vorzantu.

The moment he sees the ring, he stumbles back into the farthest part of his cell where we can barely see him other than the brightness of his blue eyes. "Where did you get that!"

"Your *kind* ambushed us last night and this was left behind."

Good, do not tell him everything.

"You should not have that!" Jaxyn shakes his head. "Whose?" He points. "Whose name is written on the inside of that?"

Neither of us answer him.

He knows these rings well.

But it seems it instills the fear into him that I hoped for.

"We will discuss that later," Maivena responds.

"Boy!" His eyes transition from Maivena to me. "You need to tell me whose name is written in there, you can do great harm with those! One ring is the strongest, the others are additions and not as powerful. They all are seeds of disaster!"

"How many are there?"

"Three and one in the making. One for each Leader and if that ring belongs to who I think, you can ruin this nation if it lands on the wrong hands."

I look down at the ring sitting in my palm. "Do not worry about that."

"Oh, I will!"

"Tell me about our Dragons and I will tell you the name engraved." I offer.

"Tell me the name in the ring and I will tell you about your Dragons."

He is fucking impossible.

"Unfortunately, we do not have all day to stand here and go back and forth. We will be back tomorrow to see if you will change your mind and tell us what this is you are sputtering about our Dragons."

To my surprise, Jaxyn is shooing us away. As we move backward the door to his cell closes and locks.

"We must find them, now." Maivena grabs my arm and we take down the hall to leave Unalave and find the children.

XENATHI — QUAMEASI CITADEL
DONVARSA MANOR

"Ira!" Ivella shouts the moment she enters her family's large home. "Ira!"

He ascends directly to her and she looks up at him with urgency while grabbing his shoulders. "Where are the Dragons?"

"Hunting, I was just with them." Confusion takes over his face at her question.

Before saying anything else, she takes us to the woods just outside of the home, and at our sudden appearance, it startles Vaigon and Vorzantu who were hunting large birds in the tree.

Vorzantu turns and lets out a scream at us as the large birds flee.

Maivena releases a breath as they come swarming in our direction.

They hover in front of us as their wings flare to keep them at our level. Vaigon leans his head forward and Maivena smiles as their heads connect. Touching Vorzantu's growing head I am shown his avid hunt for the large bird that turned to failure through a vision he shows me. I smile. "You will catch another, we had to be sure you were safe."

Looking over their current size, their heads are nearly the same size as mine, and by tomorrow it could be bigger. The free rein they both have is giving them room for growth that Dragons in the past did not have due to being held in caves.

Dragons form bonds, and it is pertinent that they have as much interaction with us as possible. The relationship between them and us will continue to grow, and since we have been around them since hatching, they will have no connection with another rider as they do with us.

There is not only us for Vaigon and Vorzantu to know, they must learn bonds between our family's and our children that will be Heirs to the next Dragons.

In their eyes I see the life of every Leader in my family.

These Dragons will not see an end as long as Maivena and I are here.

We are now one of the strongest Houses to live in Voschantai Universe solely because of Vaigon and Vorzantu. Lorsius may have begun to ruin, but by naming me Heir he set his ruin for failure as I now hold a new reign in my hands. Maivena and I have brought fortune and greatness back to my family name.

"Watch over them, danger may lurk." Maivena says to Ira and he shifts into his wholly black Wolf to follow them.

Maivena holds on to my arm as we watch Vaigon and Vorzantu set off toward the sun, and I hear them release a loud and deep roar over the land, their land.

"Come, the funeral awaits." As I turn to walk away, Maivena stands there, watching them until she no longer has sight of them nor Ira.

Grabbing my hand, we leave for the burial of those lost.

XENATHI BORDER

Rows of families walk by carrying the body of their loved one in dark caskets as we stand exactly where the ambush occurred.

Maivena approaches the rows of caskets, and with a gentle prayer said she touches the first casket of many and fire flares from her hand taking each casket to flame.

"In light of this," I say to my family that stand quietly near me. "We will use their erratic methods of fighting to enlist harder training. This was the first ambush of what will be many more to come."

Over the fire Stravan and Dyena stand with those of New Quamfasi, as we stand with our people.

Stravan looks at me and nods.

"This outcome shall not be for any of us." I turn to them. "Promise me."

Levora attaches to my arm and we all stand closer as the cries from the families around us blend with the ever growing flames of fire.

Maivena returns at my side and the families of the dead throw orchids into the fire after a prayer is sent.

As a whole, we all walk to the fire. "For reign, for blood, for us."

MORTAL LANDS

LEVORA APOLLA ARVENALDI
VAIGON CITADEL

I OUTSTRETCH MY SWORDS before me and Amias stands a distance away.

"Position," he calls.

Greyce observes intently while standing near Amias.

Settling lower, I curl my left arm and my elbow points outward. Aligning the edge of one sword along my forearm, the other guards one side of my body.

"Perfect," he smiles. "Now hold position, come up the balance beam and walk. When you are battling, you will need to know your center, and in your center you must be aware of your surroundings to guard yourself. You cannot focus too long in one area, tunnel vision will cause your death."

I walk across the narrow beam solid in position. "Now on one leg, lower, and rise up." Greyce advises.

Amias raises an eyebrow at her. "The trainer here is whom?"

Greyce crosses her arms not making eye contact with him. "I am a trainer, if you would like to be technical."

"Stop, I cannot focus if you two are going to bicker."

I stare ahead at a tree, using it as my focal point, lifting one leg, I hold my guarded position while slowly sinking.

"Hold it," Amias says, witnessing my leg shake. "Now move your arms out to your sides and guard yourself again, feel every muscle and control it. Now up."

In a struggle, I move my arms outward. Keeping my focus ahead, I sink down and within my motion upward, I guard my body again. Then, I repeat this once more.

"There is the dancer we all know well." Amias teases.

"I did not know you danced." Greyce looks up at me with widened hazel eyes.

I point my sword at her. "Used to dance."

Amias chuckles at the image of us before him. "Your background in dancing will aid you well in war. You know good balance and can move your body within it, keep practicing this, little sister, you will do well with this before moving forward."

Dancing. Of all the crafts I tried as a child I excelled in dance and would use it as my gateway for peace and clarity. After being taken to the Mortal Lands, my love for movement ended, as I no longer felt like myself.

I have not danced in years, now I am relearning those days to conquer the dance of war.

"We will do it again, this time, train your right leg."

"And this time, the both of you will be quiet." I say to them.

Greyce nudges him playfully and Amias fights his smile but his happiness wins.

* * *

We stand before the portal that opens for us with just the reach of Phyv's hands. The sharp, crooked strikes of lightning through the portal grow larger and I can gradually see the view of the woods behind it.

A place so comforting, and all the same, traumatizing.

The day of a new life and the leaving of old.

Greyce stands beside me as Phyv's outstretched hand expands the portal to the height of the trees in the Hashthyna Forest.

"Nyt and Salem are missing out." Greyce chuckles.

"Oh, only due time before they come back with us. I am sure Morano will enjoy his time with Nyt, I am not so sure about Salem." We are only going home for a short visit and coming back. Just to be sure that the portal still properly functions from both sides.

"Ladies, now would be the most opportune time to enter before it closes."

Greyce smiles and I grab her hand as we go back to the place we once called home.

When the three of us enter Phyv draws his eyes around the area of the sunlit woods.

"I have always hated the smell of the Mortal Lands." Greyce scrunches her nose.

"And somehow, you endured quite a few years of it." Phyv teases here. "We are not fabricated," Phyv says as his black wings slowly tuck inward. "If there is anything either of you need we must act quickly."

"Trust me, we will be done soon." Greyce says observing the woods and sniffing. "I would like to attend the Voschantai Gala tonight."

Thinking of the Gala only makes me wish to be here past the time we must be home, I do not want to face Daevien again after our last interaction.

What did it mean?

'Why did they bring you there?'

"I am sure you are dying to be dressed prettily and flaunt it." Phyv chuckles.

There is a quiet rustle in the woods before it grows louder. "Holy shit!" A young voice shouts.

Swiftly turning, we see a group of young children in the distance.

"He has wings!" A little girl screams.

Before they can make a run for it, Phyv projects a shield that stops them in their tracks and keeps them in place.

"He has wings?" One of them exasperates. "They just came here through that thing!" He says referring to the portal.

"Oh my god, we're going to die here. I'm so young." Another cries as she tries to punch her way out of the shield.

"Enough!" Greyce shouts over them. "What are you doing in these woods alone?"

"What are you doing in these woods coming through that thing!" The little girl with large curly hair shouts back.

"They will talk," I say. "Phyv, we cannot risk it."

I will need to find Amias, their memory must be wiped clean in order for us to pass through consistently without danger.

"No! We will not say anything!" The little boy holds his hand out.

Greyce analyzes them. "I do not trust children."

"You can trust us, pinky swear! Our friend is like you!"

The two girls eyes widen as they look at the boy rambling off at the mouth.

"Just like us how?" Phyv asks.

"He can cast spells and they work! He turned a boy into a frog!" The boy continues.

"Shut your mouth before you get us killed!" One of the girls shouts and pushes him against the wall of the shield.

Simultaneously, me, Phyv, and Greyce look at one another.

"Galitan," we say in unison.

"Galitan?" The girl with pin straight black hair asks. "That is where he said he is from. Are you from where he is from?"

"We searched maps all over to find Galitan and there is no such thing."

"There is no such thing to you." Greyce corrects.

The children within the shield begin to hit each other as they stare behind us.

Phyv quickly ducks as something veers over our heads, turning around, a young boy stands in the distance.

In a precise motion, his hands curve in front of him, forming a purple sphere that continues to grow between his palms.

"Leave my friends alone."

THE STRANGEST DREAM

LAVEN HEPHAESTUS ARVENALDI, II
NADREXI — SOUTHERN COURT OF QUAMFASI

"I HAVE READ SOMETHING like this." I smile at Maivena as she leans over the stone railing of the balcony.

"Have you?" Her voice is a low hum traveling from so high up all the way down to me.

"I have. Except, you and I are quite different from the lovers written in the pages."

Maivena shakes her head and a grin grows on her face. "How so?"

I ascend from below and up to her. As I latch onto the stone she gazes at me and her nose gently caresses mine.

"*She* saves *him*."

Her laugh echoes in the night. "Our love is not for books."

"Why is that?"

"Because it is real."

"That is *exactly* why it is for books."

Heat exudes from her skin as her eyes lighten. "What about the part they do not write of?" And her finger trails over my cheekbones.

"What part?"

"The part when you are in my bed."

That familiar fire chases behind her touch. "They would burn books if they wrote of what I will do to you in your bed."

Her hand curves around the back of my neck and through my hair. I ascend us to the hard ground of the balcony, and she giggles in my ear. "They would burn it twice."

"Why?" I groan, licking up the curve of her neck.

"Because I begged you to do it again."

Ascending to the bench in front of her bed, she stands before me. I lean back, spreading my legs wider and Maivena smiles as she tilts in. Wrapping my fingers around her neck, a playful smile appears as she rubs a hand up my thigh, gripping my length.

"Take off your clothes."

Standing up straight, there is nothing short of defiance in her eyes as she slowly tugs one tiny strap of her silk dress down her shoulder. And just as slowly, if not slower, she glides her hand across the bridge of her chest to the other strap waiting to be pulled.

"Do not be so cruel."

She diabolically laughs, as if to say, *'I can be crueler'*. The dress catches around her hips, with a gentle push the dress circles around her ankles and she steps out of it.

A thing of vivacious beauty, from every curve and line around her hips.

She turns and I tilt my head as she bends over to undo her heels.

Vivacious indeed.

The dimples in her thighs are like pivots for diamonds over her skin.

A woman made from a goldmine.

"Fuck," I writhe about staring hungrily at every inch of her.

Reaching out for one touch, she pushes my hand away and I lazily grin as she stands facing me again.

She ascends and I can feel her nearing closer behind me as she crawls across the bed.

Her teeth bite down on my ear and I fall into her shoulder as her hands caressingly move up and down my chest and abdomen.

To be touched and cherished by the person you love the most has a way of pulling you deeper than you ever thought possible, some days it turns twisted how dirtily you want to take them in every corner of a room.

Her fingers play with the laces of my trousers and the warmth of wetness moves up my neck as her tongue finds my ear. "Still lacing your trousers wrong?"

I smile.

'Lorena,' Maivena exhales while smiling. 'She is lovely.' She says as she unlaces my trousers and then perfectly relaces them together.

'Do not let her trick you,' I watch her fingers as they work on the laces. 'She can ruin someone's day if she chooses.'

Maivena quietly laughs, nodding.

'There, you always have the laces improperly crossed. This is correct.' She tugs at the waistband, and I lean down.

'Someone likes to pay attention,' I lowly speak the words as I move nearer.

"Purposely." I try to laugh but it only turns into a deep groan. "Teach me to tie them again."

"I want to teach you something else instead."

Naturally, I lift my hips at the suppleness in her voice as it gravitates from my ears and downward.

She snakes around me and goes to her knees.

This is what will declare me mentally insane again.

With a lift and tug, she removes my trousers and her eyes darken before she greedily leans in.

Instantaneously, it all becomes too much, but overbearingly perfect.

I want to feel unending hysteria.

I want to feel debilitated.

I need to feel everything and not know what to do with myself.

I need to be crippled by the magic between her legs.

I pull her up and our lips fight.

Deepening the kiss, she goes back down and continues to give me everything I want until I can no longer handle the grace of pleasure, and even then, she does not stop.

"You are trying to kill me."

She giggles and comes to a stop.

Each touch sends tingles through every body part. Then she touches my scars with her supple lips and slowly stands in front of me.

"As much I would love to go on with this all night my love, I am getting rather impatient with this tease of your body while I am not pleasuring it."

"You can have me whenever you want." She dances her finger through the dark flood of hair above my length and that is all it takes.

I quickly pick her up and our lips dance at a leisure pace. I kiss down her neck as I get into the bed pulling her up to the pillows. As I straddle between her legs I marvel at the way I fit so damn perfect. "You were made for me. And me only."

I uniformly move with her touch as she gently bites my neck and I grip her thighs.

Her body is like a map marked with trails that lead me to all the ways to pleasure her, but I have a favorite path of my own.

"Laven. . ." her fingers tangle through my curls and I smile.

I slowly rub over her clit and her body rocks as she turns her head and pushes into the pillow as I carry on the glorious act of making her come. I push one finger inside of her, curling and edging. Then, I add a second, searching for that sweet spot that will make her go–

She lets out a quiet cry and I grin looking up at her.

She quietly mumbles while forcing her head into that pillow again. I push it away. I want her screaming for me.

As I taste her, she grips my arm and her moans become uncontrollable.

"Yes, come for me." I beg.

I quicken the action of both my fingers and mouth, like a gradual rise and fall, I slow and quicken repeatedly—teasing her in the most dreadful way possible to build her orgasm to explode.

I want her to feel like she has never felt.

"Oh–" her voice catches as she claws at my arm.

I flatten my tongue against her rubbing up and down and she gasps.

In one swift motion, I sit on the bed and fling her over me. Grabbing her hips, I turn her around and her legs hook beneath mine as I drag her closer.

She reaches back, perfectly angling us together and I escape to the place where magic is made.

Groans of relief flood through the room as she eases down, then back up, repeating this until I am blinded by the ecstasy of pleasure again.

The winding of her hips grows harder as she rides me into oblivion.

Her ass moves in ripples, tempting me to touch. As I grip, her riding slows and I rub my thumb just over another secret place. Her moaning has no restraint as I continue and the feeling of her dripping down my cock is answer enough of where I will take her body next.

So slowly, I can feel her tightly pulling with each stroke.

"Who knew a pretty little thing like you enjoyed such lascivious ways to have love made to her." Her thighs are shaking again as she still moves at this slow pace, trying to move faster. "Slower," my voice comes out in a low growl, gripping the curve of her ass. "Feel *every* inch made for you."

A strangled sound catches in her chest as her hips stutter, reaching, I pull her arms behind her back and hold as I thrust my hips up.

Deep, long, strokes.

Slightly shifting to the right, I can see us through the mirror, her body ricochets as I thrust harder and I can see how captivating she looks as everything bounces. "God you take it so well."

And she withers. "Laven," she harshly shouts.

"Come all over me," I need to feel her orgasm just as much as she covets for it.

As the words leave, she messily topples over that peak I bring her to, but I do not stop. I continue riding her through it as she too watches us come undone in the mirror.

The rise and fall of my chest is heavy and rapid as she pulls one of her arms away and reaches between her legs, touching her clit and then gently groping me as I move through her.

"Please come inside me," she begs and in those few words, one more gentle squeeze, I now make more of a mess over us than she did.

She giggles as she presses her hips down and I jerk at the aftershock.

Again, she continues, and I now wither beneath her as her moans are soft, enjoying making me cry out at the hysteria of unending pleasure. Now, she is just enjoying the feeling of us combined, sweet, slick sounds.

My eyes roll. "All right," I pant.

She lifts and I see all things sin.

Sin all over an angel.

I pull her into the bed and she laughs. "We need to bathe."

Wrapping around her, I cuddle in. "Mhmm."

Letting me rest for only a few moments she sits up. "Come," she pulls me along with her.

"I already did."

She smiles and pushes me into the bathing water.

"Do not worry, you will dry."

* * *

There is rustling within the sheets and then the padding of footsteps.

I maneuver around the bed, I open my eyes when all I feel is the leftover heat of her body in the bedding.

"Mai?" I sit up.

Dressed in her white night-shift, she continues to walk away and quietly mumbles.

"Maivena?"

She exits through the doors of the chamber and down the hall.

Leaving the bed, I find my trousers and quickly haul them up my legs as I chase behind her.

"Mai?" I call out once more, and still, she does not answer me.

The closer I get to her the more unaware she seems of her surroundings as she walks unevenly through the hall.

I slowly pass by her as we proceed.

There is distance in her eyes and she keeps on as if not seeing me.

Sleepwalking.

'You think I wanted to wake up to a note instead of you? I wanted you to stay with me and you did not and I woke up in the—' she abruptly stops and shakes her head, she is fighting the urge to speak with me.

Just as I have with her.

'Let us just leave.'

'No,' I jump in front of her. *'What do you mean you woke up in—'*

'I mean nothing by it.' Her tone turns harsh. *'I am leaving now, you know your way to Provas.'*

'Ivella, please—'

'No!' Her voice reaches its peak and I see pain begin to ruin her face. *'You—'* she struggles to speak and she searches for the words before she can say them. *'You lie in bed with me and then you left me!'*

I flinch at the porosity of her voice, but mostly the terrorized expression taking over her face that was once so happy.

She slowly inhales and her eyes close for a moment before reopening.

'I am sorry, I tried to wake you but you were already sleeping so deeply that even when I moved you you did not wake. You looked peaceful so I wanted you to stay that way.'

She looks down at the floor between us and takes a single step backward.

That distance, that wall she builds guarded by the strongest Warrior known, has returned.

When I see, or believe that I see we are moving forward, we take ten steps back.

'Peaceful,' she hums. *'What is that?'*

'Something is the matter, Mai. And you need to tell me.'

This is exactly what she meant.

She is frightened to be left alone in her sleep, not just sleep, but sleepwalking into who knows what when she is alone.

The dangers that lurk due to sleepwalking are horrifying. Nonetheless, I should not wake her.

'I will never try to wake you from sleepwalking ever again.' Amias grumbles as Axynth places a cold compress to his son's eye.

'I told you to never do that.' The last time my father tried waking me from sleepwalking I accidentally hit him too hard and he went into the wall. 'You are never aware of the outcome that can come from it.'

There are low words she speaks, words I cannot make out even as I walk right next to her.

Maybe, if I try, I can gently guide her back to the chamber and no harm will come.

Directly down the hall the doors to the balcony sit wide open.

She comes to a complete stop and eerily, her head tilts. "The woods," she whispers.

I look over the balcony and towards the woods. In a flash, she is running directly to the open doors.

"Maivena!" I shout, frantically racing behind her.

Just when she reaches the railing I catch her and swing in the opposite direction, she begins to fight and I hold her tighter.

"Mai, you must wake up!"

Out of pure shock and terror, I force us to sit on the ground as the deep fear I had of heights returns because of this exact moment.

Soon, she goes limp and her eyes close.

Every possible place she could have ended up while alone ransacks through my head.

Watching her nearly fall to her death is enough for me to not allow her to be alone ever again.

Languidly, she blinks, barely making out my face as she looks up.

"Laven, darling," she says in a silent gasp. "I am having the strangest dreams." And just after the words are spoken, she faints, falling back into the sleep she was in before we ended up here.

I hold her closer and stand from the ground.

Far out, I hear the rattling of the trees. When I turn, I see nothing.

"Amias," I say through the bond.

Surprisingly, he responds. *"Are you all right? It is late."*

"I am fine. I need you to come to Nadrexi, Maivena's home. Something is out here and I cannot leave her."

"I am coming now, give me a moment."

Laying Maivena down in the bed, I touch her cheek and the stress between her eyebrows releases. This goes beyond sleepwalking, she was nearly taken to what could have been her death and I can feel that whatever was in those woods was luring her.

Something so monopolizing is holding her hostage.

I have always been told all my life how secretive I am, but her–Ivella is a level of secretive even I cannot bear.

'You know, do you not?' I urge him as he continues to watch the two women very far ahead of us speak. They know exactly what she is not telling me.

'I do,' he nods. 'And so do you. She just has not told you to what extent.'

'Stravan, if she is in some form of danger, you need to tell me this instant.'

Knowing they are listening, he answers. 'She is fine.' But below he signs with his hands six letters.

N-E-S-Y-R-A

"Who is Nesyra?" I whisper as Maivena turns in her sleep and her head lays in my hand against the pillows.

Outside of the house I hear a sonorous howl echo in the night. Amias.

"Someone was here," he says. *"I can smell them, the scent still lingers strong."*

"Search until you find them. What happened tonight cannot happen again."

"Is Ivella all right?"
"She will be."

MEAN BOYS DIE EARLY

LAVEN HEPHAESTUS ARVENALDI, II

MAIVENA STIRS IN THE bed and slowly rises when realizing I am not there. I smile as I remember this exact look from many mornings ago.

Standing from the edge of the bed I crawl closer and she wraps around me, forcing me into the bed to lie on top of me. Her hair falls in my face as she places her head in my neck and deeply inhales.

"Can you breathe in there?" I laugh as I move her hair from my face.

Her head buries deeper and I laugh harder.

She places a lazy kiss against my neck. "I only need this."

Wrapping around her she presses closer.

"How did you sleep?" I ask the impending question.

She only hums.

I rub up and down her back and she exhales. "Did you know you sleepwalk?"

She lifts her head.

Hesitantly she responds. "Yes."

"Strange dreams, are they not?" She is afraid to speak. "When

I used to sleepwalk, I would end up in the most random places of all." The distance in her eyes tries to appear, but easily fades as I tell her a bit of my own story. "The most dangerous place Amias ever found me in was Wyendgrev Tower. The *same* cell I was kept in for the time I was there. These dreams are dangerous if not monitored or understanding what triggers them."

"What stopped it?"

"Redemption," I roll over and she smiles below me. "The act of absolution."

"It is real?"

"Redemption?"

She nods.

"Redemption does find the soul." I travel my hand up the curve of her stomach and toward the middle of her chest. "It is a feeling," I press on the spot where my hand rests on her chest. "You recognize the warmth of serenity here," she deeply breathes inward and I press my other hand against her stomach. "You are reminded of the security of verity here. You fall into calmness like lullabies—a song of ease."

"You have felt this?" She asks, breathing into the exact placement of my hands. She is searching for the calm.

"It took years, but yes. I know that if it is possible for me to experience this, you will as well."

VAIGON CITADEL

The trainees position as they are told and ready for advanced sword dexterity. "I do not know whose scent it was," Amias says. "Their scent did replicate something slightly similar to Ivella's. Possibly it was a family member? But a family member watching her jump to her death? Not likely."

"Maivena's family protects her more than they love her, though I guess protection is a form of love."

"Nesyra is the name of the woman Stravan says that she fears."

His arms cross as he thinks.

Nesyra?

As I process what Stravan said, I think of every person in her life that I know, then there is the one I do not know.

Her birth mother.

Amias looks at me as if connecting the pieces together the same moment I have.

"Nesyra?" He asks once more.

"Yes."

"I will look into her now and try to find her exact location, I will also add Morano to the task, knowing him, he most likely already knows of her location. Where is Ivella now?"

"Preparing for tonight." His eyes grow and I can tell he forgot. "The Voschantai Gala is tonight."

"Yes, I remember." He dreadfully speaks. "Why did Stravan have to reintroduce the gala?"

"Oh, be quiet. Maybe this is your opportunity to court a new woman."

He laughs and his shoulders jump. "I do not think I am ready for such a commitment yet, I thank you for the suggestion. I will see you tonight at the gala." He says just before he ascends.

When I focus on the trainees again, I see young Lilyana, her raven hair is spilling from its braid and around her reddened brown cheeks. She forms the position I taught her and the boy before her laughs, but he does not find it so funny when she expertly targets him with her sword.

His laughter stops as he repeatedly jumps backwards and falls to the ground. She points her sword directly in his face as the sole of her boot presses into his chest.

Seeing the little boy closer, I recognize him.

"Get up, Iysha." Maivena says. "I told you not to taunt anyone while you are here, now look at you."

Soon, Iysha smiles at Lilyana as she presses the blade into his nose. "You are not funny, you are a mean boy." His smile fades. "Mean boys die early."

"Lilyana," I fight my laughter, her eyes fill with tears and she stomps over to me. "It is all right." I say as she wraps her arms around my neck and little tears fall between the crease of my leathers and neck.

"Look what you did!" Maivena shouts. "You will not cross borders with me if you will act like this, I told you to be on your best behavior, you are going home!"

"What? No! I was going to apologize!"

"Were you?" She questions. "Or do you now only feel bad for your actions because you have gotten in trouble?"

Iysha repeatedly glances between me, a hiding Lilyana, and Maivena. He stares at the back of Lilyana's head as she will not show him her face. "I am sorry, I did not want to make you cry."

Lilyana holds on to my neck tighter.

"Iysha, I do not think she is ready to talk to you right now, you can apologize again later."

Maivena nods at Iysha. "Go back to headquarters with Roaner and when he asks why you are there, tell the truth."

He attempts to argue but Maivena steps nearer to him and he quiets. "Headquarters, *now*."

Iysha looks at me and Lilyana once more before turning around and going where he has been told to.

"I do not like him," Lilyana says as she looks at me. "He is ill-mannered and ugly."

From behind me, I hear stifled laughter. Looking over my shoulder, Morano is there covering his mouth. "You know what? You should tell him that when he apologizes again." Morano says.

"If you do not shut your mouth." I glare at him and he walks to Maivena and she swats his arm.

"He is not always like this, Lilyana. On behalf of him, I am sorry he was teasing you."

Lilyana nods and I wipe away her small tears.

"I do not like it at the orphanage." As she speaks, I furrow my eyebrows. "The boys are mean there like him and one of them pushed me because I am small and I hurt my head. I wanted to hurt Iysha for teasing me."

The red mark in the corner of her forehead seems to have drawn blood and as I move her hair it is barley healing.

"What do you mean the orphanage? Why are you not with your parents?" I ask.

"Ma and pa are gone so I stay at the orphanage until they come back."

"My love, where did they go?" Maivena asks.

"I do not know, but the lady at the orphanage says they will be back soon!" Her dark eyes brighten through the redness. "And I get to go home and not be with sticky boys." Her shoulders scrunch as she visibly cringes thinking about them.

"Do you have any siblings?" I question.

"No, just me."

Hua makes her way over and stops our conversation.

Morano holds his hand out to Lilyana and she takes it. "We will stick to archery for the rest of the day." He says and they walk away.

When they are farther away, Hua begins. "Her parents passed in the ambush, Laven, there is only Lilyana left from her bloodline. No one else."

"And she is being abused while she is there?" Maivena points.

"That is what it seems. I had her head checked this morning by a Healer who was on the grounds and he said that her wound was not properly cared for."

"She is not staying there. I will have a room and guards arranged for her, she is not living in an orphanage." No child should live in a place like that, and I know of the horror stories that are deeply rooted in orphanages. She will not see another day there.

Hua touches my arm "It is not that easy. You cannot pull a child from an orphanage without adopting them."

"Then we adopt her." Maivena says for me. "And we will explain to her why she lives with us. No child, no matter the age, should be lied to about their parents."

Maivena revs up in anger and I reel her back as I hold her closer.

"From short experience," Maivena begins. "Those places are not an environment for children. She does not need to only worry about the little boys, but the big boys as well, and the men. They are all there, there is no division because the people that run those places do not care what happens to children they believe should be killed off with their parents. Her last day at the orphanage is today."

"The adoption process—"

"I am High King, Hua, I need to follow no process. Lilyana is not going back there, adopted or not. What I say, not what the people at the orphanage say, *what I say*." This is the first time I have used my privilege in years, and I will use it again for Lilyana if I must. "Those leaders at the orphanage will not tell me what the fate of an innocent *girl* will be that means harm upon her."

Hua smiles. "I did not know what it would take for you to force your hand. I am glad to know my future nieces and nephews will be in great hands."

"You would have them taken if they were not." I say.

"Adopting Lilyana means beginning your lineage, overturning Levora and Amias, and that also means the people will question."

"Not only question," Maivena adds. "They will have ill-will towards her given she is not of Arvenaldi blood. She will need to be protected, she will need to be taught many things about this harrowing world and being a Leader of it. Shaping Iysha has not been easy, and by the defiance that lights in her, it seems she will not be easy to shape either. It will take commitment, but we will be fine."

"Maybe you can learn to teach her to tame that defiance." I tease.

Maivena holds up her finger that has the Blue Tigers Eye ring. I smile and touch it.

"I do believe that goes both ways." Maivena teases back.

"Ouch," I smirk.

"I guess little Lilyana needs one of those rings as well." Hua chuckles as she crosses her arms. "Are you ready to take on being a mother and a father within such chaos? War is brewing and we do not yet see an end."

"She is already growing up in war, she is a young girl learning to wield weapons and defend herself when she should be running through fields with her companions and picking flowers. Her life will be no different, she will just have more responsibility as she grows." I look down at Maivena as she looks up at me. "Waiting to be ready holds life back. Now."

* * *

"This is the right thing to do, but what if we set her up for failure? What if I am not fit for her? You have spent time with her here, but not I. I was desperate to remove a child from a grave predicament before it could worsen."

I stand next to Maivena on the terrace of the headquarters and she watches Lilyana train with Morano. "She is a fierce child, smart for her age, quick to learn, she is small and feels big," I bump Maivena with my hip and she smiles. "There is passion in her eyes with everything she does even though she does not know what such a word means. Lilyana was built to have more than a life led for common routines. She has ambition and vehemence just like us." All of us, even my brothers and sisters. She is just like us all.

"We are just beginning, Laven, what if we do not get to enjoy our time together before adding a child to it? What if—" she stops and I can hear the words she wanted to say brewing in her mind.

'What if I am just like my mother?'

"Are you more worried about the time we will have together, knowing there are many of us who will be taking care of Lilyana, or are you more afraid of being as your mother was?" I pull her attention from the Training Grounds and toward me. "You are never going to be like her, ever. You know the affliction of your mothers actions too well to project that on to a child."

"That is just it, what if I know her affliction too well to not be just like her?"

I grab her hands and she gazes at how they join. "There is nothing we will go through alone."

"I have short patience." Her eyes well. "And—"

I lift her head. "And we will work through it. Just as you wish to be here for me, I wish the same."

Pushing forward, her cheek rests against the leather covering my chest. As I press my lips to her head, she speaks. "She will be the first Heir, the first Heir that is *not* an Arvenaldi, you know what the people will call her, how they will retaliate to naming someone not of your blood an Heir. They will let the word roll off their tongues as if waiting all their life to call an illegitimate child that is above them a bastard."

"Do we not take tongues for that?"

Maivena laughs and her body rumbles against mine. "We do."

"We will teach her that she is just as much a part of us as we are of her. We are not the parents who made her but we were meant for her."

When we look down, Morano and Roaner are guiding Lilyana out of the Training Grounds and to the exit. She is happy again as she skips between Morano and Roaner and twirls on her toes.

"You can always depend on Morano to lift a sour mood." Maivena smiles.

"We must meet them," I say. "Where is Iysha?"

"Here," he mumbles as he walks on to the terrace with a quill and paper full of letters.

"What are you writing?" I ask.

"Roaner made me write Mean Boys Die Early over and over until the paper was full." He aggressively shakes the paper and I laugh.

Maivena smiles and touches Iysha's cheek. "She is right, you may want to get your act together." She gently squeezes his cheek as he hugs his eldest sister.

"I apologized." His voice rises and he holds Maivena tighter.

Her fingers run through his wild curls. "And we said she was not ready to accept apologies."

"Go put that paper down," I nod. "We need to leave so we can prepare for the Voschantai Gala tonight and when we get to the exit of the Training Grounds maybe she will be ready to accept an apology."

At the exit waits Roaner, Morano, and Lilyana. The closer we approach with Iysha I see Lilyana's nose scrunch with anger and her arms cross.

Maivena kneels to her level with a smile. "Iysha would like to say something to you, are you all right with that?"

"No."

Iysha goes to speak and Roaner holds his finger up and he quiets.

Given the amount of time Roaner has spent in Xenathi in recent days helping Maivena train, I am certain he has spent quite the time with the little brother who clings to his eldest sister.

"What if we try?" Maivena continues. "He can apologize, you do not have to accept it, but I would like for you to know that he is sorry."

Lilyana swings her head in his direction, waiting.

Iysha does not waste time. "I am sorry, I did not want to make you cry. I thought I was being funny."

"Well, you are not funny, you are rude and act like the boys from my orphanage. I do not like boys like you." She turns her head but then quickly turns it back to him. "You are ill-mannered and ug–"

"Lilyana," I stop her from finishing her sentence that Morano was adamant she say to him. "Do not influence that." I say to Morano and both him and Roaner are acting foolishly. "Some uncles you will make."

"I am merely telling the child to voice her feelings."

Maivena shoves Morano. "Not if it brings more harm to the situation."

"Lilyana," I kneel next to Maivena. "How would you feel about spending the night in a big palace tonight?"

Gradually, she smiles, and her mood shifts. "Like a High Queen?"

"Yes," Maivena laughs. "Just like a High Queen. You will have your own royal guards, you will wear pretty dresses, eat lots of food, train whenever you would like, and even spend time with Dragons."

"Dragons!" Lilyana jumps. "I want to meet Dragons!"

"You get to meet two," Iysha smiles at her excitement and wants to join. "They are fun to be around."

Her eyes narrow at him. "How would you know?"

He is growing timid around her and is lost for a response. "Because they are my sisters Dragons, Vaigon and Vorzantu."

"They are your Dragons!" Lilyana looks at Maivena. "You ride Dragons!"

"We both do," Maivena motions a hand between me and herself. "Vaigon and Vorzantu are not large enough for Laven and I to ride them."

"Are they big enough for me to ride them?" Lilyana fills with more intrigue.

"Light steps," Roaner chuckles. "You must train to ride Dragons."

"I will learn!" She jumps. "I want to see them!"

We all chuckle at her ever-growing excitement.

"First," I rest my hands on her tiny shoulders. "We will show you the chamber you will be staying in and let you grow accustomed to your new environment."

"And then I get to meet Dragons? Can my Ma meet them when she comes home? She has always wanted to see a Dragon."

Roaner and Morano warily gaze at the child.

Though, we all are conscious of the fact that now is not the time to tell her that her parents will not be returning home.

Swallowing deeply, Maivena grabs Lilyana's hands. "What if I told you your mother and father are living out all of their wildest dreams *right now*?"

"Even Ma's dreams of Dragons?"

I faintly smile. "*Especially* her dreams of Dragons."

77
OLD KINGS & QUEENS

LAVEN HEPHAESTUS ARVENALDI, II

Side by side, the seamstress has placed our attire for the gala on figures built exactly of mine and Maivena's shape. The figures sit in the middle of the Throne Room on stands and as the sunsets, the light catches the tiny dark blue jewels in Maivena's gown projecting blue light over the walls.

Her dress was built for a High Queen as my topcoat was built for a High King. Near the figures sit our crowns that I have had remade. We will wear nothing that once belonged to Lorsius, only our own.

"Your arrival together will cause great commotion among all, not in just the Realm of Wolves." Stravan says from beside Maivena and I. "You will be seen by all the Leaders of every nation attending this gala. The new history of Vaigon and its beginning has made it impossible for other realms to side with you in any occurrences where you need aid."

Lorsius was known as the High King who was a treasonist. One moment, he was fighting for placement in House Valendexi while being the brother to the Duke of Gordanta, my father. He signed an oath to them, he promised loyalty, and then, over time, after securing his placement in the House, he turned on them, and used all he knew to receive their land and rule. This is what caused other realms to turn on him and what made it difficult to establish trust. Now that I am ruling, I must show that I am the divergent of Lorsius.

Maivena is my partner for life and our bond will give us the opportunity to raise Vaigon to the prospering nation I intend for it to be. As an Heir turned High King of the land stolen from his High Queen who now reclaims what belonged to her people. After the signing of the treaty, this will be the next significant propulsion for global alliances before a war can transpire. Arriving together and exposing our mating bond will be the utmost pivotal turn for Vaigon and Quamfasi.

Reclamation but civilly.

We are not searching to have one leader again, but to be joint as we were before the domestic war.

"And then you will make the realms quake at your presence as you defy what was known as the inevitable. You are not the only Realm known to have split into multiples and not see reform as a possibility. The end goal is unifying the Realm of Wolves before pushing for unification among all, that is where your influence across Voschantai Universe will begin—the return to the ways of Old Voschantai, within limits. Alliances during those ages were stronger than blood, we must get back to that to survive what is coming. Just as I brought unification back to the Realm of the Fae, you will do the same." Stravan grabs our crowns from the white velvet cushions they sit upon and walks towards us, Maivena is first to receive her white gold crown formed like twigs surrounding Black Tourmaline.

The moment the crown is placed on her head I witness the shift in her from Lady to High Queen. "And you," Stravan crowns me next. "You will be the first High King that looks like an Orviante since my crowning. Bloodline matters, but looking the part is just as vital. The white in your hair will get you far, and for the both of you to wear regalia similar to old Kings and Queens will be a moment all its own. You did not need a Coronation because that is what this day is for. After tonight, the people will see you in the shape they saw yours and my ancestors. And along with that, you have your Dragons that make your Houses stronger than what existed before."

This moment is larger than life not only for me, but more for Maivena who will be crowned as High Queen of the land she was once enslaved to.

On the balcony of the Throne Room sit Vaigon and Vorzantu who overlook the land below them. They are growing more instinctual by the day and has resulted in us being a Dragon House. Some of the strongest Houses to ever live, including Stravan's family, is example of this. The Realm of the Wolves have never been Dragon riders until us.

"Go prepare now, I will have your clothing taken to your chamber. The sun is setting and time is commencing. You will be introduced into the gala last so you have time to prepare."

* * *

In the same prosperous blue as mine and my brother's cloaks, the neckline of her dress meets above the collar bone and is trimmed in golds and tans. Long, elegant, and sequined with diamonds and blue crystals that form as a corset around her body; then, the flat of her chest is exposed beneath the lines rowed with gold. The dark, sheer fabric lays over her arms and meets the floor. The dress is that of Old Voschantai, the fabrics used in those times were used to craft what we now wear.

Her hair is intricately braided to hold the crown steady upon her head.

Maivena turns to me with a smile and adjusts the pins on my black top coat and then the chains of the bow and arrow brooch holding my blue cloak together.

"We are ready." She says.

"Are you certain?"

She looks at me confused.

"One detail is missing." I pull a tiny box from the pocket of my cloak. "The solidification of my proposal to you."

"Laven, I do not need a ring for solidification." She places her hand over mine, stopping me from opening the box.

"But I want to give you this."

After she sees my unending desire to give her this ring, she agrees.

Opening the box, the pear shaped moss agate ring is revealed. The gold band twirls like vines and leaves, some leaves are donned with tiny amber stones that meet the moss agate in the middle.

Every detail of this ring was formed from the colors in her eyes.

"I had it made quite sometime ago when I thought things were going how I imagined, but when it did not, I still chose to keep it out of hope."

Hope got me far even when I thought it was failing me.

"You should not make me cry before we leave, you will ruin my face before we are seen in front of hundreds of people." She laughs as her tears build.

Our eyes meet and through the growing bond between our minds, I show her exactly what I see. She sharply breathes and her hand tightens over mine. She is now seeing herself through the eyes of the person who will cherish her more than anyone else will for the rest of her life.

"Even shrouded in tears you are breathtaking."

"I want to do that too," she says as her mind clears.

I grin. "It will take some practice."

Ever so lightly, she touches my cheek and smiles.

Taking her right hand, I place the ring on her fourth finger and her smile widens as I kiss her hand.

"I do believe it is time we leave."

Turning, she looks at the darkening sky and the stars that begin to glitz. "I believe so too."

We walk to the balcony of our chamber. She looks up to the night sky and her grin softens. "Take me to the stars again."

She looks around us, admiring the movement of night shifting by. Wisps of white glow as I move higher into the sky.

That rapturing smile reappears.

"It is the stars," she mumbles.

"Reach out your hand." I urge her.

She is hesitant, but she does. White wisps swirl around her finger as we glide through nightfall.

And just as before, I admiringly watch as she twirls her fingers through the stars as we soar through them.

"The stars will always be ours." She whispers.

"Forever."

PROVAS CITADEL — REALM OF THE FAE

Upon landing at the entrance, guards stand on either side of the long flight of stairs that lead up to the open doors of the gala. The exterior of the palace is decorated in bouquets of flowers and small candles that string from window to window. Overhead, the Dragons swarm by and into the sky; their roars grow distant as Vaigon and Vorzantu try to keep up with them. Tuduran slows, and waits until the two children are ahead of him and he follows behind, guiding them through dark skies.

Up the flight of stone stairs, candles line along the sides and guide to the entrance.

"Thank you for your arrival, King Laven," a guard nods. "Lady Ivella, lovely seeing you," he greets as well.

"Hello, Jaymes." Maivena smiles at one of the guards of her Queens Sentinel.

"You will be seen up the stairs and wait by the door for your summoning."

"Thank you," I say to Jaymes before I turn to Maivena and guide her up the steps with me. Her hand tightens around mine, and gently, I squeeze hers back.

The announcer of tonight's gala stands at the top of the stairs, and next to him, the trumpets blow rhythmically into the night.

"Do not let me fall up these stairs."

I chuckle. "Never."

As we reach halfway up the steps, the announcer turns toward the gala filled with people. Even at this distance I can hear the clinking of glasses, quiet talking, the laughter, everything transpiring in the room resonates right to my ears.

"High King Laven of Vaigon, the Realm of the Wolves, second of his name, Head of House Arvenaldi and Head of the High Four. Lady Ivella, awaited High Queen of Vaigon, prominent in House Valendexi, House Provanseva, and Head of House Arvenaldi, and Right Hand to Provas."

At his final words, the announcer steps aside.

I can feel all of the eyes lying upon us before I see them.

Below us, on the next flight of stairs that lead to the floor stand every High King and Queen of all realms.

We are the Sovereigns of Voschantai.

Stravan and Dyena stand at the front, angled behind them are Vallehes and Penelope and everyone after.

The High King and Queen of The Realm of the Sorcerers, Galitan.

The High Queens of The Realm of the Vampires, Misonva.

The High King of The Realm of the Hybrids, Ramana.

The only not in attendance, the High Queens of The Realm of the Banshees.

In the crowds of the people standing around the tables, I see my mother with my brothers and sisters. Her hands are held in front of her as she smiles through the tears brewing in her eyes.

Everyone in attendance tonight are the highest of people that you can possibly locate across all lands. Most in attendance are Heirs—Princes and Princesses, Dukes and Duchesses, Houses and Circles, and after them the most profound doctors and Healers, alongside Generals, Emissaries, and Assassins. Any extra bodies are guards people may have brought with them for safety measures.

"Welcome to the first Voschantai Gala in ten years, we are delighted you all have arrived. May you enjoy your night, and mingle among one another like we once did, supper will begin now."

One by one, we recede down the long flight of stairs and to the floor after the announcer completes.

On either side of the room are long tables where supper is served and throughout the floor tall tables are sporadically placed with large floral arrangements centered on every other. And overhead the dome ceilings are made of glass and stone. Every three windows in the ceiling, gold chandeliers hang with candles lit in them.

The stares from many in the room are due to hatred, jealousy, or awe. Either way, Maivena holds tighter on to my arm and we continue as we should.

The moment we get to our table, the people begin to talk, and the low cluster of voices sets an ease to the room brewing with tension.

At our table sits Esme with Stelina and Naius, who I wave to in passing.

Vallehes looks ready to cut my head off.

And Ethel and Kaden are the only missing.

"King Laven, Lady Ivella."

We turn to the voices and the High King and Queen of Galitan stand before us. Enora and Javan. Enora's braids are contained from her face, revealing the gold essence across her dark skin and her dress is the darkest of purples and silver. When meeting Javan, his eyes are the lightest color of blue with skin the same as Enora's, his topcoat was meant to fit her dress as mine and Maivena's do.

He holds his hand out to Maivena and she greets him by taking it. Wrapped around his first finger, as well as Enora's, is the Sorcerer's Clasp. "Pleasure to finally meet you both."

"The pleasure is ours," I say to him after we both bow before one another.

"It shall be a lovely night," Enora smiles. "Let us hope we can all bear being in the same room for a prolonged period of time."

Looking about the room once more, "I see no reason for us not to."

"The return of the gala shall be just as enjoyable as the celebration of Summer Solstice." The voice is smooth as the words are spoken, and by ascension he appears. High King Neryus. One of

Maivena's prior suitors. He bows before us as we do. "Ivella, you look stunning," he smiles.

"Thank you, Neryus."

Neryus's purple eyes brighten and his bronzed cheeks hint red.

"I see Jes has arrived, let us go to him." Enora says to Javan as more people arrive in the room either through ascension or they are led into the room by guards.

With a final goodbye to us and Neryus, they leave.

"It is good to see you again, Neryus." I say.

His smile maintains as he looks at me. "You as well Laven, I am sorry for your loss." He says in reference to Lorsius.

"Not a drastic loss, but I do thank you for your condolences."

"Neryus!" A man calls from across the room. He waves over the multiple heads lingering around him to be seen.

"Ah," he rolls his eyes. "I did not remember that coming to this gala meant running into to people you no longer associate with that believe you are still companions. If you will excuse me."

Maivena laughs. "Not a worry."

Neryus forces a fake smile and goes to the person still calling his name.

"Tonight will be good," Maivena looks up at me as her arm wraps around my waist.

"Yes, as long as everyone stays on their best behavior." I tap her nose and she giggles.

"Who let Wolves mingle with Vampires?"

Misonva.

The High Queens stand hand in hand dressed in deep reds and black. Sasenys and Margeau.

Sasenys and Margeau both grab me for an embrace. "It is great to know Vaigon is now in good hands." Margeau says.

The two of them, knowing my father well, stood beside us in war only because of their respect for my father and family before Lorsius was ruler.

"Your dress is stunning, Ivella," Sasenys touches her shoulder. "I need one in red."

Sasenys smoothes her hands over her red gown made of different sleek fabrics and around her waist is a corset that completes the dress. On the other hand, Margeau is dressed in her fighting leathers and strapped with weapons. One thing the Vampires will always wear, their Moonstone amulet or either their Moonstone ring that protects their dark pristine skin from the sunlight.

"Are you fighting tonight?" I make fun of Margeau and she laughs deeply.

"I need to be prepared for anything when we are amongst *these* people."

Sasenys holds Margeau's arm and shakes her head. "She is always ready to throw a dagger, it is a trait we are aiming to exile."

Maivena laughs. "That trait can be useful." Her knuckle sweeps under Sasenys's chin causing a shy grin.

"It is," Sasenys smiles. "You know, Ivella, you may visit Misonva whenever you may like. Anyone Laven holds in high regard we do as well."

"Thank you, I have always wanted to visit, so I will take you up on that offer."

Sasenys squeezes Maivena's hand before glancing at the table they are to sit at. "Our son has just arrived but please send a letter when you plan to visit, Ivella."

They ascend across the room and Leacayne, their son, holds his glass up to me in greeting.

Maivena hums. "They are sensational."

Then, from the table, my mother makes way. "My boy," she coos as she approaches with Axynth, who was just with Amias.

Her embrace is warm as she wraps her arms around me. "Ivella, darling." Ma hugs her tightly after looking over her face. "It brings me joy to see you look well, and well for the role that Vaigon has long awaited for."

High Queen.

"The regalia of your grandfather fits you well." Axynth says with a saddened smile.

And in bewilderment, Maivena and I look down at my topcoat.

"This was the topcoat Vaigon Arvenaldi wore to his last Voschantai Gala when he was a ruler. I asked of Stravan to be sure it was placed upon you. I still have your grandfather's pins saved. I will have them sent to you to wear with the rest of your pins." Ma adjusts the Wolf sigil crafted from mine and my brothers initials and smiles.

"You may want to bring the pins yourself."

"Why is that?" Axynth asks.

"There is someone you will want to meet," Maivena informs. "After the gala we will tell you," her voice lowers. "Now may not be the most impromptu time given the amount of ears lingering."

Lilyana will love my mother, and I know my mother is craving to have a grandchild racing through the large ranch she now lives on.

"Fair enough," Axynth laughs.

"Ivy!" Maivena is called by her close companion Lourdes who sits at the far end of the table. She stands and races over.

"We will leave you two," Ma kisses our cheeks. "There are others we have not seen in quite some time that will be disappointed if we do not speak with them." She grabs Axynth by his topcoat and pulls him with her.

Lourdes takes Maivena from my arm and they tightly embrace one another.

"Hello, Laven," Lourdes flings her dark hair over her shoulder. "Great seeing you again given the last time we spoke you could barely make eye contact with me."

"Lourdes," Maivena warningly speaks as she runs her fingers through her friend's straight hair.

"I am sorry," I laugh. "I was rather out of sorts that day."

"I could tell," she continues to make fun. "Ivella was stunning on the night of Summer Solstice, I would have been choked up as well."

Maivena playfully shoves Lourdes before looking about the room and her eyes fall on the terrace where Dyena stands with Daevien, Stravan, and his siblings. They are talking to people she does not seem too happy to be speaking with. Turning her head, Dyena mouths to them both. *'Help me!'*

"I think we must save Dyena," Maivena laughs.

"I would want to be saved if I were talking to a rat like Sava—"

Maivena covers her mouth. "We cannot speak like we usually do, we are around very high stature people we do not know. Choose your words wisely tonight."

"I like you more now that I know we have a common hatred, Lourdes."

The companion smirks. "I will take that Orviante on any given day."

"All right you two." Maivena stops us from speaking about Savarina.

Lourdes rolls her eyes and with a glance at me Maivena leaves with Lourdes.

In topcoats similar to mine and wearing our cloaks and brooches, my brothers come smoothly walking in my direction with Carmen who is donned in the darkest of red and a pristine purple cloak. "High King Laven, I bow at your feet." Carmen teases and they chuckle as he improperly bows before me.

I push him away and he chortles. "Say that again and you will, and not because you want to."

"Because he will take you out at your knees first." Hua says from behind me.

She is dressed in her leather armor meant for special occasions and her cloak bearing our Wolf sigil.

"It takes your opponent down rather quickly." I smirk.

From behind Amias, a finger taps on his shoulder, he turns and Greyce is behind him dressed stunningly in black. Amias, lost for what words are, weakly smiles at her.

He says nothing and quickly looks away from her.

Dissatisfaction is written all over her face and she looks at me.

"Levora and Phyv are on their way here, but I must speak with you about what happened while we were gone. Timing is not too great, but it is important."

"Important enough to say it around all these people?" Hua remarks.

Greyce's eyes turn for anger. "I was not speaking to you. Mind where you stand in this conversation."

Hua tries to respond but I quickly place a hand over her arm. Amias steps in front of Greyce, shielding her from Hua. Not once in my life have I ever seen Amias and Hua stand head to head like this.

I have never seen Amias defend a woman other than his mother since Hua . . .

Though already annoyed with him, Greyce steps to the side, ignoring Amias.

"Laven," Greyce nods her head to the terrace where the stairs lead to the spans of courtyards.

She walks away, I meet Amias's eye and he turns away.

As I follow Greyce we stop when we see Stravan, and he trails in our shadow.

"What is wrong?" Stravan asks when we reach privacy.

"When we crossed through the portal we ran into children who were in the area. I suppose they were hiding when we crossed."

"And?" I urge her to continue.

"Levora and Phyv stayed behind to be sure the children were in good hands."

Stravan holds up a hand. "Greyce, those children could say something."

"They will not," she instantly shakes her head. "One of the children is from Galitan and he has powers already. I can only suppose he attended Neseryk Academy where young Sorcerers are taught by the greatest professors. But the age does not add up, he is a young boy and we all were taken there years ago, he would have needed to be a tiny child at the time he was dumped there. He was also wearing the Sorcerer's Clasp on his finger when summoning his powers."

The Sorcerer's Clasp is similar to a ring but it is a metal material that covers your entire finger and is flexible. Bevinium, a crystal only meant for Sorcerer's, lies within the metal and enhances their power. At every academy in the Sorcerer's Realm each clasp is designed different. In the room, all from Galitan wear them.

"If he wears a Sorcerer's Clasp he is important, not all are fortunate to wear one. He also could be someone that was taken there more recently." I say. "Given the amount of time it took to bring you all home, we run the chance that whoever has been dropping immortals on the Mortal Lands is still doing so."

"What is his name? How long has he said he has been there?" Stravan asks.

"His name is Evryn, and I am unsure of how long he has been in the Mortal Lands. I left to come home as soon as I could. Levora will be back soon to report more information. I came to immediately tell you what is happening."

"When Vora is home I will speak with her." Regretfully, I carry on. "It may be best that one of you stay in the Mortal Lands until this is solved."

"Phyv will be, he will come back and forth until we know for sure what all of the children know. While Phyv comes back and forth Levora and I will look into Evryn and be certain he has family to come home to."

On the terrace above, we can hear laughter from the people above as they converse.

"Our privacy is running short," I observe. "We must get going."

Greyce leads us back up and on our way through the room I can hear the muttering of those around me. Some speak of what it feels like to be at the return of the gala while clanking their glasses full of Brovita. Some say how they would have decorated differently. Others talk about the people they are dreading to have to speak with.

Then, I see Levora far out and she smiles as she waves at me.

She is attired in a gown I have seen once before, the longer I look, I realize it is a gown passed down to her from our mother. A stunning cream gown sequined in blues and golds.

In the distance, Daevien desperately overlooks her through the crowds with his hands tightly behind his back. He is contemplating an approach, but his pained expression does not leave and he stays where he is.

"How interesting it is when the chambermaid enters on the new King's arm." A man says nearby amongst all the people. "More specifically to an event where all eyes see everyone who enters and leaves."

I stop and Greyce looks over her shoulder when I am no longer following her.

"What was that you said?" I ask.

The man does not answer me, he continues to walk to his chair and sits down knowing I heard the words meant to be an insult towards Maivena.

"I do not answer to you," he throws the words over his shoulder.

"Laven," Axynth says from across the room. "Laven," his voice is growing closer and louder as I grab the arm of the chair the man sits in and I fling him across the floor. The people rush out of the way as his chair comes to an abrupt stop in the middle of the room.

"Laven!" Maivena shouts as she fights through the small crowds. Lourdes and Greyce grab her, keeping her still.

I walk in front of the man and I immediately recognize his face. *That* doctor.

The doctor who was known for conning many of Old Quamfasi's women into saving the men from castration and being bedded in return for his *graciousness*. This is a man of Lorsius's nation, not mine.

"Laven," Maivena says once more and Dyena stands before her, guarding her with an arm as the doctor's guards approach, and the sounds of weapons bounce through the room.

Jaymes stands largely before Maivena and Dyena with sprawled wings in a Knight's armor. "Touch the Right Hand and it will be your head I have in return."

Around me, I see my brothers' swords drawn at the guards who dare to crowd around me.

Another guard tries to approach. Right away Stravan steps in front of him and he stops.

The darkest of magic dares to pour from Roaner as his hands are held outward at his sides. His fingers have faded to black as he smiles, hoping to use the Dark Magic taught to him by his mother. Esme comes closer to him, guarding his back, within her hands orbs full of fog form.

"Do not come near him." Sasenys warns as she and Margeau point their weapons directly at the others who attempt to close in.

"Laven, think wisely." My mother says.

I ignore her.

Leaning in front of the doctor, he realizes he is out numbered as everyone stands ready. "Say it once more." I grip the arms of his chair tighter.

I can feel his quick hot breaths as I close in on his face.

He is quiet as his fear grows.

"Tonight was supposed to be a grand evening, now look at what you have done, you have caused a scene because you cannot keep your mouth shut and your hands to yourself."

His lips tremble, fighting the words that dare to fall from his mouth.

He looks at Maivena and in a brisk motion, I grip his face. "Do not look at her, look at me!"

He tries to spit in my face and I tighten my grip.

"I have lived through three High Kings and I will be damned before I bend for an amateur King who dares to have an awaiting Queen that is a *whore*!"

He says it.

I look to Maivena. "By your call, my love. Does he live, or die?"

Her chin lifts higher, her eyes darken, and curtly, she nods.

I smile down at him. "And I will be your last King."

Without a thought, I force my hand into his mouth grabbing his tongue, he struggles and I quite enjoy it knowing all of the harm he has placed upon not only Maivena, but others. Using all strength, the length of his tongue rends from his throat and he falls to the floor scrambling. His body jerks about on the ground, and an arrow is shot directly through his head stopping all movement.

Naius gives Hua her bow and kneels next to the lifeless body. "That is for the depredation of my daughter." Seven years too long to wait for the death of this doctor and the others who still live. "And you will not be the last to die for it." Naius stands.

I throw his tongue to the floor next to him and look across the room at Maivena who only sees me. I step over his body and walk towards her. I outstretch my blood coated hand, without hesitance, she takes it and leaves the barrier of her companions and Queens Sentinel.

My family does not put down their weapons until the guards do, and all at once the guards recede backward, some advert their eyes to the ground, frightened of the sight before them.

"Someone clean this mess up," Stravan says over the quiet room. "The night must go on," he turns. "Orchestra," he waves a finger and they continue playing while the body is removed.

THIS OVER EVERYTHING

LAVEN HEPHAESTUS ARVENALDI, II
VAIGON CITADEL

"Oh, spend the night with me, Grey!" Levora clings to Greyce's side as we all collectively arrive home. "We will be lighting a fire at the Ryverian House and enjoy what is left of the rest of the night. Given what I walked in on during the gala." Levora cuts her eyes at me.

"Maybe he should have kept his mouth shut." Amias crosses his arms.

I raise my eyebrows. "That too."

Though, there will be repercussions to be served. Whatever family he has left, which I am sure must be quite a few, will ask questions or demand there be payment for loss of their family member. I can only speculate this is what the might of a High King must be, needing to serve no repercussions for your actions given you are the law.

"Well?" Levora waits for Greyce to say yes to her pleas to stay with her for the night. "Morano and Roaner are already waiting at the house for us."

She is reluctant to answer and I feel it may be because of the reaction she received from Amias tonight, thankfully, she does not let that be held over Levora's happiness. "Why not? I do need to go home first, I will change my clothing and come back."

"I can go with you!" Levora beams.

"I will be fine," Greyce chuckles. "I promise, I will return soon and I will bring you one of my sweaters to wear that I brought with me from the Mortal Lands."

"You know the way to my heart." Levora smirks.

"What is a sweater?" Maivena and Amias ask simultaneously.

Levora laughs. "It is like a men's undershirt but thicker and much more comfy."

"I will bring you back one as well." Greyce winks at Maivena. "I will go now."

To my surprise, Amias speaks to her. "Are you sure you do not want anyone to go with you?"

"I am very certain, I do just fine on my own, thank you."

Ouch.

Maivena hides her smile as she sees Amias's face wrench in annoyance.

It has been years since Amias has merely shown interest in anyone since his separation from Hua. I fear my brother is making stupid decisions based on feelings that someone else has inflicted and now carrying it with him into current relationships that could thrive.

"All you had to do was tell her she was beautiful tonight." I privately speak to him.

Ignoring me, he watches Greyce ascend home.

Finally, he responds. *"I cannot breathe when she is around me."*

And fear encompasses his eyes as he looks at the tiny remnants of magic left behind from her ascension.

"Let us go then," Levora holds her hand out to Amias and he finds the vivacity to compel a smile for her and together we ascend to the Ryverian House.

* * *

In the back of the house Roaner, Morano, and Ezra are being guided by Esme as she points out where to put all of the cushions on the ground around the fire pit. The cushions are placed near or in front of the chaises they have brought outside. It seems we will be here for quite some time, they have placed enough cushions for us to all fall asleep comfortably.

Within the darkest part of the forest, I can hear the rustling of wings and quiet purrs of a Dragon. After, I see the eyes that are exactly of my own, then, beaming through the trees, Vorzantu is first and directly behind him is Vaigon.

Maivena smiles as they settle on the ground near us. Now, they know where to find us without needing to guide them. They are learning that both Vaigon and New Quamfasi are their homes.

"Your wings are strengthening," Maivena touches Vaigon who nudges into her hand.

Vorzantu leaps up to the back of the chaise and sits while curiously watching Roaner, Morano, and Esme lie down the rest of the cushions for us to sit on.

"I need to change my clothing, as much as I love this gown, I must get out of it." As Maivena walks away, I trail in her footsteps, she needed help getting into this gown and she will need help getting out of it.

Leading up the stairs of the back of the house, Maivena smiles looking around. "Has this home always been this stunning?"

"Not at all, it started out as a shack, it was a safe haven for Morano until my father had it turned into a larger home."

"You mean a mansion," she casually corrects while entering through the doors and observes the area around her. Once in the drawing room, she finds the portraits of all my siblings and I posted on the walls. "I remember that young face."

I roll my eyes at her as she stares at the portrait of me when I was seven and ten.

Not long after this portrait I met her. Who would have thought in a short period of time after that my life would be drastically changing?

"Come along," Maivena closes in and the gentlest smile is there. "Let us change."

* * *

Maivena has put on one of my black undershirts that fits her like a small dress then she wrapped the dark blue Porvienia around her shoulders. Just as she has, I place my Porvienia over my shoulders.

From upstairs I can hear the quiet laughter from below and I follow the sound.

"Make way, I come bearing Brovita." Stravan says as he walks down the steps and to the firepit where everyone cheers, awaiting him with small wooden vessels.

Turning, Dyena hands me a bottle to open and I fill mine and Maivena's vessel.

"Brovita is for special occasions!" Morano shouts, but willingly takes some.

"Is tonight not special?" Levora asks, looking around the pit at all of us.

I sit on the chaise behind Maivena who sits on the cushion placed in front of it on the ground. She leans her head against my knee and settles in.

"Sweaters anyone?" Greyce says through ascension holding five pieces of fabric that looks soft to the touch though heavy.

Ezra puts down his guitar and helps Greyce by grabbing a couple and giving one to Maivena and then Levora who adamantly demands one in particular that is light in color and has buttons.

Hua plops to the ground near Morano and tilts back her vessel of Brovita until it is gone, Morano laughs and fills her cup again.

"Sweaters," Levora holds one up and we pay attention to this human attire. "Also known as cardigans, say which ever you would like, they are the same thing, do let anyone tell you otherwise."

"It is a cardigan."

Turning at the voice, Levora and Greyce grin. "Phyv!"

"When was someone going to tell me that children are not as fun as some people make it seem?" He asks while looking drained.

"How is that immortal child coping in the mortal world?" Stravan asks and gives Phyv what is left from the bottle of Brovita.

Ezra begins to play a lovely melody from his guitar and by magic, Stravan brings forth his own guitar and plays with him.

"There is a child from our universe on the Mortal Lands?" Esme questions as she observes the cardigan given to her. "How are they surviving?"

"By sheer luck." Phyv sits next to me. "And his friends."

"I enjoy the feel of this." Dyena smiles as she puts the dark green cardigan on.

Vaigon and Vorzantu hesitantly smell the fabric on Maivena, but they are quickly distracted when they hear Nyt barking on his way over to everyone. Behind him slowly trots Salem who hops into Greyce's lap as she sits on the ground where cushions lie.

Nyt, being playful, antagonizes Vaigon and Vorzantu, urging them to chase him around the perimeter of the house and they fly lowly behind him as he speeds away.

"Dragons and domestic pets intermingling." I laugh.

"Odd," Roaner quietly says from across the fire and we all fall into laughter.

Amias sits next to Morano on the chaise and it is impossible to avoid how often he has looked at Greyce since her arrival. He stares at her like she is the tiny glimmer in the night that leads him on his way.

"We will talk of the child on mortal land tomorrow." I start. "Nothing that involves our duties shall be spoken of for the rest of the evening."

"Agreed," Maivena says as she looks up at me.

The dark blue sweater in her lap attracts Salem and he curls on top of it and purrs.

"That is the sweater he would sleep on when we would not be home," Greyce chuckles. "I figured it was only a matter of time before he saw it and gravitated towards you."

Phyv stands and holds up a small book. "I brought a book back with me, it is full of the poets from the human world. Some of their most profound poets are in this book and I figured I would share it with you all."

"Come sit," Levora motions him over to the large chaise she sits on. Phyv leaves my side, then both Levora and Greyce sit on either side of him and cuddle in. I can see how often they must have done this in the past because of how natural it is for them to lean on him and he opens the book.

Nyt, finishing his lap around the house, stops at the feet of his people. Levora pets his head and Vaigon and Vorzantu land on thick branches of the trees nearby.

Phyv flips through the pages in the book, searching for a poem, as he does so, Maivena adoringly pets Salem who enjoys her touch and rolls around in her lap.

Esme and Roaner, who sit on the other end of the fire pit near Hua narrow in on Phyv, waiting. It seems we all are rather intrigued by the entice of poetry. Or, maybe, in this world brewing with battle, for one night we want rest.

Greyce points at the page as he turns and Phyv smiles, nodding at her.

"A poem written by Allen Ginsberg," he begins. There is a quietness that settles around us and all we can hear is the melody of Ezra and Stravan's guitars, sparking fire, the slight breeze dancing through the leaves on the trees, and now Phyv's calm voice as he recites. "The weight of the world is love. Under the burden of solitude, under the burden of dissatisfaction. The weight, the weight we carry is love . . . and so must rest in the arms of love at last, must rest in the arms of love."

POEMS LED TO TEARS, and tears led to more Brovita, and more Brovita led to dancing around the fire until we tired out.

Now, Maivena curls her legs through mine as she turns to her side.

The touch of her hand to my cheek forces me to open my eyes and she stares up at me doe eyed before she lays her head over my chest.

"Hold me all night. Do not let go, not once."

I do as she asks, and she too holds me.

The restfulness of love in only our arms.

THE WAR HAS BEGUN

LAVEN HEPHAESTUS ARVENALDI, II

"Lilyana?" Maivena gently wakes the sleeping child.

Lilyana's black hair is sprawled over her face and pillows as she sleeps. Finally, she stirs, awakening to the voice of Maivena.

Maivena quietly laughs as Lilyana rolls over in the large bed and pulls her blanket over her head.

"Is there a little girl named Lilyana under that blanket?"

Lilyana giggles quietly and Maivena quickly pokes her head under the blanket and Lilyana erupts in laughter before sitting up in bed.

I sit on the edge of the bed and smile as she grins at me. "Are you hungry?"

"Yes!" Lilyana stands on the bed.

"Let us wash this little face and get you fed." Maivena pushes her fingers through Lilyana's mane of hair repeatedly and her eyes close as she does so.

Lilyana pretends to fall backwards, and I laugh as Maivena catches her and she erupts into giggles again.

"All right, you." Maivena smiles as she stands from the bed and

Lilyana jumps down.

"Let me see this head of yours." I nudge for the child to come closer and I fish through her hair to examine.

I could heal the tiny wound for her, thankfully it is already mending on its own without the need of an extra healing hand.

"Did you sleep well last night?" Maivena asks her while I check her head for any other injuries unseen.

"I did," she nods. "Can I eat morning meal now?"

"Yes," I laugh. "We can eat now before Ivella leaves."

Quickly, Lilyana's eyes turn for sadness. "Where are you going?"

"I will be back," Maivena crouches down to her level and taps her nose. "I have to go home first, see through quite a few things with the Leaders of my Circles and I will be back."

Lilyana looks around the large chamber and gazes through the windows of her balcony and back at Maivena. "You do not live here? This is not your home?"

"Not yet, but it will be." Maivena smiles.

"You will come back?"

"Yes," Maivena chuckles.

"You promise?"

"I will come back, I promise."

* * *

Stravan looks on with satisfaction as he examines my new leather armor. The same person who built Maivena's armor has built mine as well but in black with more stitching and firmer padding around my shoulders and knees.

"This is very well made." Stravan says as he touches the leather stitched like the skin of a Dragon. The leather suit is now on the same figure that my attire to the gala was so we may see it. Next, I must put it on and move so the suit can be like a second skin.

"Have you tried using your force fields to bend elements?"

"How so?"

"Instead of just projecting a force field, learn to hold it, similar to a shield but you control it to move. Say you project a force field and knock down your opponent. You can do that same thing with water, fire, air, anything."

Never in my life have I considered how far force fields have gone until now, I always saw them as a basic ability, now with Stravan here, he will be able to teach us a grand deal of what we never knew we could do. And now is the time for all of this.

"The abilities I have are sporadic ever since the Blood Bond Ritual with my brothers, there are powers I have that I did not know of until it comes out, though force fields will always be an ability I thrive at."

"And your speed."

"Is that really a power?" I turn and walk out of the Throne Room and he follows.

"Of course it is, the speed you run at is craved by many, you have like no other. That is a power. Some think you must have an extraordinary gift in order to be considered vigorous."

"My father used to ask, *'who would escape a barricaded room first? The strongest person or the person with the most knowledge?'* When I was young, of course, I told him the person who is the strongest. Then, he explained, you can put the physically weak person who has the most knowledge in a room with the strongest person and the one with the most knowledge will make it out first. They do not need to rely on their physical strength to get them far. Their knowledge will carry them through anything." You can have strength, truly, anyone can. Though your strength is useless if you do not know how to use it properly.

"Your father sounds like my mother," Stravan says as we walk down the hall leaving the Throne Room. "She would tell tales very similar to that, but ours was written in children's books."

"The Unlikely Warrior?"

Stravan laughs. "Yes, that exact book."

"I spoke with Phyv over morning meal and he told me more about the child, Evryn, trapped on the Mortal Lands. He said that Evryn was not brought there, he landed there by accident. One moment he was playing with his friends the next he slipped through where the portal was drawn to take immortals from Galitan to where he is now."

Stravan flinches out of perplexity. "If he has accidentally fallen through that portal he was not the only one, this could be happening all over Voschantai."

"And that is what we need to find out. From the time that Levora, Phyv, and Greyce went missing with the others, how many more mysterious disappearances have happened? This revolving around the intrusions of rogues is not ideal. What if one of those rogues ended up in the Mortal Lands? What if the humans have found their way here by accident while walking through a portal?"

Stravan rubs his face as all the words process. "We need to get to the other realms, immediately. We need to find these portals and have them guarded. Portals should not just stay open, they should have to be opened."

With a world as ours, there will never be such thing as anyone knowing exactly what transpires, especially when it comes to the realm of magic that can warp universes. There will never be just one way. "Whoever created them must have discerned a new way to form portals to stay open. Unless they are closely monitoring the portals and opening them when certain people near it."

Leading us back to my study, I draw a piece of paper from the drawer of my bureau and the quill and ink.

"I will find Ezra and have this sent directly after it is written," Stravan speaks beside me. "And I will find where Levora, Greyce, and Phyv are. They shall not go back to the Mortal Lands unless more of us go with them, we should not risk them being there alone without knowing of this." He says just before ascending in a rush.

To Whom It May Concern:

Galitan, Ramana, Misonva, and Vosand, your presence is immediately requested in Vaigon where the Leaders of Vaigon, Provas, and Quamfasi will await. Grave matters regarding the Six of Spring must be discussed immediately. It seems more has occurred since the time of their taking to now.

Please send a response as soon as possible, this must not be taken lightly any longer.

Laven Hephaestus Arvenaldi, II – High King of Vaigon

Rolling the paper, I reach for another to write the next three letters to be sent. As I begin writing, Ezra walks into the study with Esme at his side, who stares at me with a horrid expression overtaking her face.

"When did you last see Ivella?"

I furrow my eyebrows and swiftly stand. "This morning when we ate morning meal with Lilyana, why?"

"Because," Esme heavily breathes. "I cannot find her and she was supposed to meet me long ago. I have already asked our family if they have seen her and they have not and no one knows–"

"All right," I try to calm her as I feel my own build of perturbation. "She must be somewhere and has just forgotten."

"Laven," Esme's voice rises. "I have searched everywhere, I know my cousin, she would not just forget. You and I know this well, Ivella does not just not show up. She says something!"

Just as she shouts, Roaner falls from ascension screaming in pain.

His leg has been slashed through nearly to the bone and blood already coats the floor.

"Roaner!" Esme shouts as she and I tumble to his side to examine his leg, and Ezra helps Roaner to sit up as he grows lightheaded at the loss of blood.

"Roaner," I grab my brother's face and force him to look at me. "What happened?"

His bright blue eyes are dull and he tugs at his vest while grunting at the pain encompassing his body, Esme quickly rips the vest off of him revealing another wound and her hands begin to shake as she sees all the ruin over him. She attempts to heal him but his wounds fight against being healed.

"Ivy," he coughs and blood seeps from his mouth. "Laven, they took–they took her. They took Ivy and the Dragons."

Esme looks up at me and I rapidly blink as the words burn into my head.

They took Ivy and the Dragons.

"Who, Roaner?" Ezra asks while pressing against the gash in his stomach.

I go stoic, unable to comprehend any thought.

War.

War.

War is the only raging thought.

My brother.

My wife.

He chokes on his blood once more and grips my vest, yanking my attention, even on the edge of death, Roaner still has that fury in his eyes and I hold his cold wrist.

"Yaro."

A name has become the worst thing to ever happen to me.

Holding Roaner tighter, I stare down at him.

"The war has begun."

ACKNOWLEDGMENTS

Nectar of War is Leilani's largest novel she has ever written. Taking nearly five years to complete, plenty of this would not have been possible to finish without the many people who helped and motivated her over time. She gives great thanks to everyone who has supported her, as she knows it takes a village. Below are the main people who helped finalize this process.

This debut novel and *The Nectar of War Series* is dedicated to Grace Rached, a strong souled woman, a movement all her own. Grace was one of the first people to read the rough draft of *Nectar of War* before it met the public and she was one of the first to share her personal thoughts about what she read. Afterwards, she always reminded Leilani of the power her writing held, and after her passing, that reminder lived on in Leilani and was a driving force in publication. Within her relationship to Grace, she met Bec Scholten who she is eternally grateful to have in her life.

Thank you to Alyce Brown, the Founder of Evening Edits and the Head Editor of *Nectar of War: The Song of Verity and Serenity*. Through it all, Alyce worked tirelessly with Leilani on perfecting her debut novel and giving it the life it needed. Without Editors like Alyce, novels would not be where they are today and this series would have never been published.

Thank you to Allison Edwards, the fantastic Cover Designer. With just the book cover alone, Leilani did not see all that her book would become until the beauty that Allison brought to life. There were many covers that Allison graciously came up with for Nectar of War, then, both Allison and Leilani knew that there could be nothing more timeless than creating a classic and elegant cover to tie this series together.

Thank you to Dorothy Colodro, the marketing genius who helped Leilani develop her first website dedicated to her novels. Dorothy, even through her own busy schedule, was the first Editor to see Nectar of War before there was Alyce, if not for Dorothy, Leilani would not have sought after Alyce.

Finally, thank you to the readers. Without readers, novels would not have succeeded thus far. They bring education, clarity, joy, and ammunition to Authors. Sometimes, all a book needs is a reader to drive a novel or series to its succession, that is something an Author can never do alone.

Since Two Thousand and Eighteen Leilani promoted *Nectar of War* on Bookstagram (when it was known as a previous title), met mounds of people, crafted beautiful relationships that inspire this novel, and some of those friendships still last to this day. There were many fellow Authors she met, and many readers she met—as mentioned above—who helped her believe in herself. To you all she is forever grateful for.

Thank you.

THE STORY PURSUES IN . . .

RANCOR OF FATE
THE RING OF REIGN AND RUIN

A SNEAK PEEK AT THE NEXT NOVEL IN THE NECTAR OF WAR SERIES

IVELLA IS THROWN BEFORE the people who have been awaiting her. She is bound by silver rope disabling her from tugging too hard on the restraints. Silver against a Wolf is deadly to skin, she stops yanking her wrists and lifts her head.

She sits on the tan marble floors of a Throne Room, a Throne Room that is unrecognizable, as are the men in it.

Her chest slightly caves in as she is trapped in a room containing one too many men.

But one face in particular stands out before the rest.

Yaro.

He sits in the large stone chair with eyes narrowed directly at Ivella. Alongside him stand three others.

Only one has white hair that mimics that of Yaro.

All she can remember from when she was at home to here is the person capturing Vaigon and Vorzantu, chasing them down with Roaner, then suddenly blacking out.

Yaro looks toward the man who stands tall next to him and Ivella looks at him as well. His eyes are dull and his skin is light brown with messy straight white hair pulled into a low knot.

Yaro nods at Ivella and the white haired man breaches across the room.

Deeply rooted in the refusal to appear weak, she stays put and does not cower away from him.

He lowers to her level and grabs her hands that are tied together. Upon his hand sits a black ring with blue within it.

This is another ring.

His harrowing eyes fill in darkness as he holds her hands.

Ivella stares up at him, not daring to take her eyes off the man grasping on to her that could ascend them from this exact place to anywhere he wishes.

His hands tighten and she winces at his grip.

Quietly, he gasps.

"Anything, Venny?" Yaro asks.

Venny's eyes rapidly blink and when they open again, his eyes appear brighter but all the more worried. Gently, he puts her hands down and he stands.

"Nothing," Venny says as he gazes down at Ivella. "Her thoughts are entirely unheard and I cannot see into her past."

But, Ivella was not guarding her thoughts at all. If anything, her mind is raging.

Where are Vaigon and Vorzantu?

Where is my husband and my family?

Where am I?

Yaro stands when Venny is back at his side.

As Yaro places his hands in his pocket, she sees a gold ring with a thin stripe of glistening blue right through the middle.

Another of the four rings with one more in the making.

And we have one.

"Ivella Fondali," he says as he recedes down the stairs. "Did you know that was my son?" He asks as he approaches her still sat on the floor. "My only heir."

She does not answer him.

She refuses to say a word to any of the men in this room. Not out of fear, out of resilience. Silence can get someone far. Silence causes the unexpected.

"And you, you will give me another."

"Yaro!" Venny shouts. "This was not a part of the plan."

Ivella is immovable.

This threat to be impregnated by a man she does not know is not the first time she has heard it. In fact, she had a feeling that was why she was here.

"And those well growing Dragons will be mine as well." Still, Ivella only stares. "Does she not speak?" Yaro snatches Ivella by her hair, yanking her head upward and their eyes lock.

Ivella spits and within the fluid is a raging fire that catches his left cheek.

Yaro hisses in pain as he steps backward trying to wipe away the spit from his face.

His boot draws back and connects with her face throwing her body backward.

Finally, there is a sound that comes from her.

A cunning, dark laugh.

Laughter . . .

Laughter after being kicked directly in the face.

She sharply turns her head to them and blood pours from her nose and down her mouth. She appears frightening, laughing within such a state. Blood coats her once pristine teeth as she grins in her laughter. "You have not an ideation of the war you have awoken by my taking."

Then, so sharply the laughter ends. "Ivella Fondali," she continues, for Yaro as he did not formally introduce her. "Daughter and first born to General Naius Fondali. Right Hand to the High Queen of Provas, *your* home. Awaited High Queen of Vaigon. Lady of House Valendexi, House Provanseva, and *Head* of House Arvenaldi. I am the doing of every Realm in Voschantai coming together. I am a progeny of superior lineages, nothing will subjugate me."

Yaro glares at her and slowly he looks over his shoulder to Venny who is stoic. "You saw none of this?"

"None, her thoughts were blank."

Ivella stands as Yaro walks away.

"Take her out of here." Yaro says to a man opposite of Venny.

Before Ivella can speak, he ascends across the room, she is in his grasp, and they are ascended to the cells in the pits of the palace.

From the ascension, she falls to the grounds that are murky and filled with grime.

"Oh no, no!" An estranged voice from the cell diagonal of her speaks. "A Vaultai is in here! She will speak and turn us into dust!"

Ivella pivots away and stays put in the corner of her cell.

The prison is very dimly lit by fading candles, faint sounds of dripping water is the only resonance outside of the murmuring voices from other cells and in the distance she can hear the screams and cries of the people being tortured for whatever they have done. Though, even the innocent end here.

Within the cell she attempts to cast her powers but nothing comes of it.

"Help!" The stranger's voice from the other cell shouts. "Help!" He relentlessly calls out. "She is trying to use her magic! She will kill us all! This building will burn down! She will curse us all! We will be no more!"

"It will not work," a man says from just outside of her cell.

Ivella's head lifts.

Venny.

"Pruvania is laced within the cells bars that hold you, meaning—"

"My strength here is useless." She finishes for him.

He leans against her cell, and as he does so, she feels she has seen it before but she cannot pinpoint where and who.

"I will strike a bargain with you."

"Strike a bargain with me in front of this loud mouth?" Ivella turns her head to the man who does not stop screaming. "And of all people, why would I bargain with you?"

She knows he hid her thoughts.

But why?

And does she truly care to know?

"I am the only person who can get you home. I am sure this is what you want, right?"

Ivella laughs. "I am not leaving here unless I have Yaro's head on a sword."

He smiles. "That is exactly why you and I must strike a bargain."

Ivella stares at him.

He will be so easy to fool if he is so willing to bargain with a prisoner whose mind he cannot see into . . . use him, manipulate his stupidity, find my children, and burn this universe to pieces for ever thinking they could take me like the rest have.

Ivella nods and stands from the dirty floor, all the wet grime clings to her dress and feet.

It has been quite the time since she has felt filth as this. Maybe it was the time when she was locked in the dirty cellar of Nesyra's home, comparable to when she was in the dirty carriage that took her from her brother, which was not just coated in dirt, but blood, feces, and all sorts of bodily fluid.

Venny stretches a hand through the bars of her cell.

A handshake.

A handshake to seal a bargain.

Yes, Ivella thinks to herself, *a fucking imbecile.*

She firmly shakes his hand and as their hands disjoin he pulls a set of keys from his pocket and unlocks the barred door. As it slides open he takes a step backward and Ivella takes a step forward.

'The first step to freedom is knowing it is yours, there is a grand amount that happens in between, but the final step is execution.' Her fathers words chime through her ears and she smiles at Venny.

I am a High Queen that will never know isolation.

"My name is—"

Ivella's hand thrusts forward and a force field propels Venny by the ten feet between his back and the wall behind him.

As his back connects with the concrete wall, his body rises higher up the wall as Ivella's hand stays outstretched, holding him by the warp of magic still growing in her.

Green vines lace around his neck and wrists, holding him hostage as he fights to escape.

He attempts to speak again and the vines around his neck tighten more and more. The other prisoners begin to shout around her as they are trapped in their cells. Lifting her other hand, her fingers clasp into a fist and suddenly, they go silent.

"Where are we?" Her voice is all too calm as she speaks.

"Lorvithinan!" Venny gasps for air. "Lorvithinan Universe!"

Portal, she says to herself. That is the only way to reach other universes.

'Long ago when Lorvithinan came to aid in the first Domestic War the only way to enter was through a portal.' Esme reads to Ivella and Ira from an old history book. 'It was not the first portal opened, but it was the largest and it spanned over hundreds of yards that reached thousands to allow all armies to enter at once. It takes an educated Sorcerer to be capable of opening a portal that expansive.'

"Yes," he answers after seeping through her mind. "After you blacked out you were taken through the portal." He gives her answers she has not yet asked for. He is in her head. "I promise, Ivella, I will give you the answers to everything you want, but we must leave here soon."

Ivella walks across the multiple feet before her still holding her hands in position and Venny's eyes begin to water as the makeshift rope made of vines chokes him more. Now, he can barely breathe.

"No!" He strains for air, and he forces the one name he knows will stop her. "Laven!"

He watches the name shake her.

"The fi–" he struggles. "The first!"

She lets the rope around his neck slightly loosen so he may speak. Her eyebrows knit together.

"Laven," he breathes. "The first."

"What of him?" She demands more information, not comprehending why he is speaking of Laven's father.

"Me."

Her head shakes. "Laven the first is dead." Ivella says through her confusion.

"I would not lie about this . . . Look at me, Ivella, *look* at me."

And she does.

She already has and that is what frightens her.

'Name him.' Ivella urges.

Laven tries to deny her again, but as the little Dragon looks up at him and shakes out his wings a name for him comes to mind.

'Vaigon.' He says.

'Your grandfather,' Ivella softly responds.

'My grandfather is one of the most amazing men I know, and I want to do right by him. It was not fair that Lorsius named a nation after him but did not create a nation that would uphold to his name. My grandfather, Vaigon, and grandmother, Reynai, are Orviantes. They are who my father got the white hair from, as well as the blue and hazel heterochrome eyes. Then, those genes passed on to me, but the white is only in streaks throughout my hair since my mother was a commoner.' He can see his grandfather so clearly as he stares into the orbs of the Dragon playing in his palm.

Venny is still held to the wall, and Ivella nears closer.

Staring directly into his eyes, the blue in his eyes are swarmed with hazel.

The eyes of an Arvenaldi man.

Just like the eyes she knows in any life she could ever live.

I could not kill him if I tried.

Even if he is sided with the enemy, Laven would want to see his father again.

Venny is dropped and he grunts as he lands hard on his feet. He looks up at her from the ground and Ivella steps away.

"I want to go home just as much as you do. Now," he stands, and she sees all that her husband is in his father. "Do we have a deal?"

"You saw everything when you touched me," she says. "You lied."

"Because I would like to see my son again and keep my head."

Can someone once known for all his good be trusted after serving for the opponent?

For Ivella, there is only one way to know.

She must pick the lesser evil.

"And what exactly will this bargain consist of?"

Venny lazily smiles. "We must form a heist."

Ivella stares at his hand being held outward, but she has a request of her own.

"We will form your heist, but I want something in return as well." Venny waits for the High Queen to give her request. "When we succeed, and I go home, I plan to leave here with thousands of Warriors, not just my freedom. I need armies so visceral Old Voschantai would quake."

Venny holds his hand out farther, solidifying her request. Ivella takes it, sealing a deal much deeper than a bargain.

THE CITADELS
Vaigon Citadel and Quamfasi Citadel

VAIGON CITADEL
THE REALM OF THE WOLVES

TERSEIUS – NORTHERN COURT
of Vaigon Citadel

WANORA – SOUTHERN COURT
of Vaigon Citadel

PARTALOS – EASTERN COURT
of Vaigon Citadel

GORDANTA – WESTERN COURT
of Vaigon Citadel

QUAMFASI CITADEL
(Xenathi/New Quamfasi)
THE REALM OF THE WOLVES

ETHIVON – NORTHERN COURT
of Quamfasi Citadel

NADREXI – SOUTHERN COURT
(The Sunset Province)
of Quamfasi Citadel

THE HOUSES
House Arvenaldi, House Valendexi, House Provanseva

HOUSE ARVENALDI
Vaigon Citadel – Realm of the Wolves

LAVEN HEPHAESTUS ARVENALDI, II

High King of Vaigon, Head of House Arvenaldi, Head of The High Four,
First Rider of Dragons in the Realm of the Wolves

IVELLA ARVENALDI

Head of House Arvenaldi, Right Hand to the High Queen of Provas,
Awaited High Queen of Vaigon, Seventh Lead in House Valendexi,
Fifth Lead in House Provanseva,
First Rider of Dragons in the Realm of the Wolves

AMIAS HERACLES TORANDI

Right Hand to the High King of Vaigon, General of Vaigon Citadel,
Second of The High Four, Second Lead in House Arvenaldi

ROANER KORSANA

High King's Assassin, Third of The High Four,
Third Lead in House Arvenaldi

MORANO VIXELTA

High King's Emissary, Fourth of The High Four,
Fourth Lead in House Arvenaldi

LEVORA APOLLA ARVENALDI

High Princess of Vaigon, Fifth Lead in House Arvenaldi

HUA BERVENDA

General of Vaigon Citadel, Sixth Lead in House Arvenaldi

EZRA HARST
Roaner's Emissary, Lord of Vaigon, Messenger of Vaigon

PHYV ARVENALDI-ROVECH
Lord of Vaigon

GREYCE ROVECH
Lady of Vaigon and Ramana

HOUSE VALENDEXI
Quamfasi Citadel – Realm of the Wolves

VALLEHES PATROCLES VALENDEXI
Former High King of Old Quamfasi,
Current King of New Quamfasi, Head of House Valendexi

PENELOPE HEGGA VALENDEXI
Former High Queen of Old Quamfasi,
Current Queen of New Quamfasi, Head of House Valendexi

VORIAN PENEHES VALENDEXI
Former High Prince and Heir to Old Quamfasi,
Current Prince and Heir to New Quamfasi,
Emissary of New Quamfasi,
Second Lead in House Valendexi

ESME FONDALI
Right Hand to the Queen of Quamfasi,
Third Lead in House Valendexi

STELINA FONDALI
General of Quamfasi Citadel, Fourth Lead in House Valendexi

IRA FONDALI
Assassin of New Quamfasi, Fifth Lead in House Valendexi

NAIUS FONDALI
General of all Quamfasi Mandems, Sixth Lead in House Valendexi

IVELLA ARVENALDI

Head of House Arvenaldi, Right Hand to the High Queen of Provas,
Awaited High Queen of Vaigon, Seventh Lead in House Valendexi,
Fifth Lead in House Provanseva,
First Rider of Dragons in the Realm of the Wolves

ETHEL SHEREYN

Lady of New Quamfasi

KADEN SHEREYN

Lord of New Quamfasi

HOUSE PROVANSEVA
Provas Citadel – Realm of the Fae

STRAVAN PROVANSEVA

High King of Provas, Head of House Provanseva,
Former Ruler of The Realms, Rider of Dragons

DYENA PROVANSEVA

High Queen of Provas, Head of House Provanseva,
Rider of Dragons

SLOAN PROVANSEVA

High Prince of Provas, Second Lead in House Provanseva,
Rider of Dragons

SAVARINA PROVANSEVA

High Princess of Provas, Third Lead in House Provanseva,
Rider of Dragons

DAEVIEN JORDESQA

Duke of Jordesqa Court, Fourth Lead in House Provanseva,
Rider of Dragons

IVELLA ARVENALDI

Head of House Arvenaldi, Right Hand to the High Queen of Provas,
Awaited High Queen of Vaigon, Seventh Lead in House Valendexi,
Fifth Lead in House Provanseva,
First Rider of Dragons in the Realm of the Wolves

Made in the USA
Coppell, TX
08 October 2023

22599133R00404